ROMANCE MACABRE

Implores the willing slave never to be set free from Love's
Addiction . . . even as they draw their final breath.

First Published in Great Britain 2020 by Mirador Publishing

First edition: 2020

Romance Macabre

Ixidorr Hack

Contents

Introduction

I see you have come back for more.

I bring you a fresh set of dark, twisted tales of love. A bumper collection of tales that brings my little, romantic project to a close.

Romance Macabre is not so much a sequel to its sister book, *Cupid's Ruin*, as an *equal*, together completing my magnum opus on Love. This time, you will be delving into twenty-four short stories rather than the longer short fiction of the previous book, once again exploring unusual relationships and the dark vagaries of love. Twenty-four short stories to represent twenty-four roses. One rose to represent each hour in the day; I hope you will dream of me once every hour. A dozen roses asks you to 'be mine' whereas two dozen roses tell you 'I'm yours' . . . *whether you like it or not . .*

What makes both books two of a kind and utterly unique is that they reflect my married life, my evolution as a writer after getting wed. Marriage changes people, hopefully for the better, sometimes for the worse. It has certainly helped me inject some magic into my work, but I also make sure that the wild man, kept in check most days, is not too far away. Ready to be given full rein to unleash his own brand of madness and mayhem on the printed page.

I have brought back some old characters and created some new ones. The origins of some of these short stories are based on real, personal experiences, but I have taken a few liberties, fictionalized the events, of course, including another trilogy of Gallic wanderlust. Infatuations and infidelities, encounters unresolved and love unrequited. Deception and intrigue, a brief encounter or two and a home invasion, midlife crises and funerals, teas and fleas, alien beings and ancient gods — they're all present and correct. Even Jane Austen makes an appearance somewhere.

So let us, once again, celebrate and explore the marriage between Love and Horror.

Let me take you to places you've never been before and show you things you know shouldn't exist at all.

Here are my twenty-four *withered* roses. With hugs so tight they crack ribs and kisses so deep they steal your soul.

Care to dance?

Ixidorr
July 2020

Acknowledgements

The Cornish Patient is dedicated to Katie, whom my wife regarded as her best friend and who saw my wife through nursing school. My wife misses you dearly. RIP.

The Wake goes out to the loving memory of Patricia, my wife's erstwhile grandmother, who was the first person to welcome me into the family and whom I will always regard as one of the most interesting people I ever met. I shall miss our lovely literary debates. RIP.

A big thanks to Guy, who was gracious enough not to mind me muddying his name again for the sake of a story or two. After all, my good man, it's only fiction!

And another special mention to my wife, Hannah, whose remarkable artistic temperament and enduring love of horror continue to inspire me. I will always hold a torch for you. You were always quirky, a wild one!

List of Tales

I Love You More Than You Know: A stalker obsessed by an actor decides on more extreme measures to keep her man.

Every Dog Has Its Day: A fixation with her neighbour turns into something dangerous.

Ma Puce: During an extraordinarily hot summer, a couple is visited by a flea infestation that quickly spirals out of control.

Gods of Halitosis: Bad breath is not good for any relationship, particularly when there's no way of getting rid of it.

Moone & Starr: While clearing out the attic, a woman finds her erstwhile mother's old love letters and decides to follow in her mother's footsteps to a remote spot in the woods.

Predictable Joe: Fed up with her life, a farmer's wife murders her husband . . . only for him to come back and act like nothing happened.

Steeping Beauty: For those who love tea . . . and what happens when you drink a bad batch of it.

An Audience with Jane: A visit to the Jane Austen Museum reveals a fascinating glimpse into the past and a greater understanding of this renowned authoress.

Take Two: In an interracial tale, a hotel receptionist, romanced by a successful curry mogul, soon learns he might have other plans for her.

Aunts and Nephews: Guy Hastings relates his time at University and describes how he came to enter the adult film industry.

The Cornish Patient: Following the death of her best friend, a newly-qualified nurse decides to work as the 24-hour carer for a dying, old man, who begins to make a miraculous recovery as she experiences ever-more romantic dreams.

Blight One's Troth: Just married, a scion and his beautiful wife face a wedding night they will never forget, in the shape of a home invasion where all bets are off.

The Art of Mimicry: A wife decides to honeymoon her husband in a villa she stayed in as a teenager in the South of France but begins to suspect the owners of plotting their downfall.

Night of the Wild Boar: Celebrating their twenty-fifth wedding anniversary, an unhappily-married husband with huge gambling debts decides to kill his wife for the insurance money.

Temps Morts à Paris: Hoping to revive its failing fortunes, an English rock band decides to record its next album in Paris with dire consequences.

Blessings of Pan: Moving into their new home, a married couple discovers the local villagers are deeply immersed in the pagan worship of an age-old god.

American Suburbia: Living in a gated community, a lonely, washed-up writer in the grip of a midlife crisis regrets the love affairs that destroyed his marriage.

A Glass, Darklier: A vicar's daughter married to an army officer enters the world of espionage.

Checkout: A husband trying to understand his wife better following the breakup of their marriage chooses a course of action that he thinks is only too fitting.

Hastings In A Hole: After a disastrous film-shoot and engulfed in a tidal wave of guilt, Guy decides to check himself in for sex addiction therapy.

Chance Encounter at Rippendale's: Trapped in an elevator together, two people discover they have much more in common than they could ever possibly imagine.

The Octopus Pot: Holidaying in Loch Ness during Hogmanay, Dr. Marcus Havers helps a widow experiencing a bizarre reaction to her grief by using an equally bizarre, impromptu remedy.

The Wake: Observing a Catholic wake for their deceased grandmother on a cold January evening, the living family members learn that some secrets from the past have the power to impact on the present.

Rookery Nook: After nearly a decade apart, a successful photojournalist revisits an old lover, a has-been author, on the windswept Cumbrian moors and becomes embroiled in the supernatural goings-on in his dark house.

Creep
— Radiohead

I Love You More Than You Know

"Teach not thy lip such scorn, for it was made
For kissing, lady, not for such contempt."

Richard III, Act I Scene 2
William Shakespeare

I

I worry about you . . .

In the OL' JAVA BEAN café, Juno Hepper sat at the window-table, opposite her best friend, Rita Clemmons, gazing out on to the rainy street, toying with those words in her mind. *I worry about you.* How often had she used those words in relation to her boyfriend, Nathan Foy? Of course, she worried about him! She was his *girlfriend,* after all!

I worry about you . . .

The acting bug had come between them. Nathan had suddenly developed an itch to perform on stage, and so, because of his remarkable good looks and extremely expressive nature, his excellent ability to memorize his lines, the ease at which he could throw himself into character, he received a callback, audition after audition. He'd even auditioned as the new Milk Tray Man, but the director, being a very narrow-minded traditionalist, turned down Nathan's rather brilliant twist on the revived Milk Tray ad of the mysterious, James Bondesque figure leaving the box of chocolates in the sleeping lady's bedchamber and disappearing off into the night. But when the lady wakes up and opens the box, it is *empty! The Milk Tray Man has eaten them all.*

But the latest play, *Antony and Cleopatra*, due to show at CHERTSFORD VICTORIA THEATRE, would be his first romantic role and promised to give him his big break, a springboard from which he could further his acting career. The issue was the kissing scene between the two leads. This would be Nathan's first stage kiss, and Juno could not stand the idea of it. She loved this man to bits, with all her heart, but she felt her heart was going to stop every time she thought of him getting aroused while 'rehearsing' his love scene with the hot, new leading lady. He hadn't quite cheated on her, but it was almost as good as. "Our love is such Torture/Bliss," Juno told her redheaded friend, Rita, over a steaming mug of coffee. Next to her cup rested her half-read novel, *Three Act Tragedy* by Agatha Christie. The muted, spiky strains of *Black Hearted Love* by PJ Harvey & John Parish played on the coffee-shop speakers. "I help him read his lines. And *this* is how he repays me?"

"Is he going through with it?" Rita asked her.

Juno nodded, through her fringe of strawberry-blond curls. "He claims it's just acting, and I should get over it. He said I was being jealous."

"That's rather inconsiderate of him, and very convenient, too," Rita observed. She paused to quote good, old Iago: "*O, beware, my lord, of jealousy;/ It is the green-eyed monster, which doth mock/ The meat it feeds on.*"

"Do I have a right to be jealous?" Juno reasoned with herself. "I think I do . . . and it's *not* jealousy! If acting is his dream, who am I to get in the way? I don't want to hinder his career, stifle his creativity, restrict his repertoire, limit his roles, in case he resents me for cramping his style. But I will not share my boyfriend with another woman, real or pretend!"

Rita was on Juno's side. "So it's all right for him to practise making out with a stranger on the stage, but telling you it's 'just acting', and 'get over it', because you're the one he's coming home to at the end of the day, is a cop-out, an *insult* to your intelligence – total dog putty! You can't have your cake and eat it too! Even if he's not doing anything, he's still giving the impression he is. The love scene still involves real bodies, and his lips and body should not be at the disposal of his work colleagues. Acting is all about illusion, and for the illusion to work, he has to draw from his own real emotions to make, in this instance, the *kiss* work."

"*Thank you!*" Juno acknowledged, adding her own views. "I thought I was going crazy. I believe the bedroom should be a sacred place, and you belong to your boyfriend and he belongs to you. Nathan should respect the sanctity of our relationship and never cross its boundaries. Holding hands with someone, kissing someone, Frenchie or not, engaging in certain kinds of embraces and erotic touching, baring intimate aspects of your body, making love to someone, you're meant to share with your other half. And *them* only! Those moments should be something private and special, not for the world to ogle at."

"Acting is an industry to which certain people are drawn. Unfortunately, the bottom line is acting is a profession that makes the person unaccountable in whom they are portraying because it is just a 'love scene'. I think acting is a socially-sanctioned excuse for cheating on your significant other!"

Juno continued the exchange. "You're right! Having lived with this man, I've discovered how self-absorbed actors are. I really think actors have nothing useful to say. Vanity drives acting. Nathan pays no attention unless it's 'me, me, me!' Oh, the prima donnas! Because of this uncontrollable, deep-seated need for attention and adulation, I'm relegated to second place. Actors'll do anything to get the fame they desire even if it means hurting the one they allegedly love." Juno paused for thought. "Our relationship should never come second to his 'art', unless he's so self-centred he doesn't care. A kiss now, what next? Full frontal nudity? No, this will *not* do!"

Rita was speaking from the same hymn sheet. "I agree, acting is a dickhead's-and-cunt's profession, if you pardon my French! It's so much like prostitution, getting paid to kiss someone, touch someone, to feign love and attraction! Alfred Hitchcock and I speak from the same page when we say that actors should be herded and treated like cattle!"

Loss of inhibitions was a cause for concern and criticism. Juno disclosed to Rita of the time that Nathan told Juno of his fellow actress, Anita Stedman, in the changing room. Anita changed her costume in front of everyone, baring herself with no regard for her own dignity. Nathan was so shocked he had to turn away, embarrassed. This was the same girl he was due to kiss in the name of art. "I suppose the other halves of regular movie stars go through the same crises. I suppose those million-dollar fees these movie stars command must make it easier to ignore."

"I need to meet your new boyfriend."

"Come by tomorrow evening, and I'll introduce you to Nathan. I worry about him so, so much. The very idea of him kissing another woman is poison to my entire being, and I can feel it accumulating to toxic levels, sickening in its intensity."

Rita felt her friend's mental anguish. "You go confront him, girlfriend!" she advised with encouragement. "You need to tell Nathan exactly how you feel about it!"

"I will do my best to make sure he fully understands."

II

Nathan Foy strode down the street, deep in thought, hands in his pockets. The spring rain had let up for now. Nathan was mulling over a few things in his mind. He needed to get this latest performance just right so he could hopefully head off to the bright lights of the London West End. He was growing more and more confident in his own acting ability – he was turning into quite the thespian. He could boast some powerful acting chops. The real test of a good actor was whether they could improvise rather than reverting back to script – he could do just that. Opening night in a week's time would be crammed with a fine crop of theatre critics and journalists. But there was something else playing on his mind . . .

Nathan turned, confronted the woman who was following him. The woman stopped walking, caught red-handed. They looked at each other for a long moment. Neither spoke. Then, Nathan broke the silence. "I'm sorry . . . do I know you?"

The woman sported distinctive strawberry-blond locks, which covered half her face. "No," she replied. "I'm Juno."

Unusual name, thought Nathan. *Juno, as in the Roman goddess of Love and Marriage.* Nathan continued to probe, "I don't get it, Juno, but...are you...are you following me?"

Juno sounded surprised and amused at the same time as though it was the most hilarious thing she had ever heard. "Am I doing what?"

"Following me," Nathan reiterated. "Well, are you?"

"No, why do you ask?"

"Because I seem to see you everywhere I go!" Nathan observed, trying to make sense of it all. "I go to the restaurant and I see you, at the tennis club you're hovering by the entrance, in the theatre you're sat in the front row, in the lobby of my apartment building I find you talking to the concierge . . ."

"No need to exaggerate! I'm not following you – I promise you I'm not," Juno explained candidly. "I'm just admiring you from afar, *without* your knowledge. I'm going on a romantic walk with you *without* you knowing about it, that's all . . ."

Nathan was suddenly at a loss for words. When he spoke again, his voice was shaky. "What the hell is that supposed to mean? . . . Are you *stalking* me?"

"I'm not a stalker," Juno continued to reassure him, laughing. "I just like to watch you naked sometimes . . ."

Nathan could not believe his ears. This was going from bad to worse, creepier by the second. "Jeez . . . You watch me *naked!*" he exclaimed incredulously.

"Yes, in the shower," Juno responded, calmly, matter-of-factly "I live across the street from you. I can see directly into your apartment. Oh, and by the way, you're out of milk."

"You ARE stalking me!" concluded Nathan, beginning to panic.

"I'm not a stalker," Juno insisted. "It's just obsession. There's a world of difference. Even if my doctors may not agree with my school of thought. *You see I worry about you so.*"

"Doctors? What doctors?" But Nathan had a horrible suspicion that this woman might not be right in the head.

"No need to trouble your handsome little head. Everything will soon be all right once you accept me in your life. You see I'm just following my dream. And *you* are my dream . . ."

This was getting crazy, thought Nathan. He was dealing with an obsessive fan. He should have been flattered by her attention, but it was getting way over-the-top. Why she was fixated on him didn't make any sense, unlike if he had been a GP or psychiatrist or gynaecologist, who often suffered this kind of inappropriate regard and overfamiliarity from certain adoring patients. He had never been an object of obsession or one to have a secret admirer. He wasn't even famous, let alone a movie star or TV celebrity. This was a million miles away from being stalked by paparazzi on a Mediterranean yacht. He wondered if she was dangerous. "Okay, I see . . ."

"You are the dream I have been waiting for," Juno informed him, dreamily, melodramatically. "What's wrong with pursuing your dream?" She stared at him, giving him an odd yet loving look. The look of adoration wasn't reciprocated. *This is sooo Torture/Bliss!* "You look scared . . . Why should you look scared?"

"Scared?" Nathan replied, breaking into a cold sweat, his expression tinged with fear. "Why should I be scared?" *I've got some madwoman obsessing over me, watching my every movement, even when I'm in the bathroom. I need to put a stop to this* . . . "Excuse me, Juno, I really must go . . ."

"Take me with you . . ." requested Juno breathlessly.

Nathan looked at her one more time, then hurried away as further drops of rain fell.

Juno watched Nathan disappear down the street. Softly, she whispered: "I love you more than you will ever know . . ."

III

The love-of-her-life stirred, rising back up to wakefulness.

"Rise and shine, mister!" announced Juno.

Nathan discovered he was in his own apartment, lying stretched out on the bed, wrists and ankles strapped to all four bedposts with ribbon, in hung-drawn-and-quartered fashion. He was suddenly aware of his own nakedness, wearing nothing apart from his black silk boxers. He also realized he had a bleeding gash on the back of the skull and vaguely remembered being struck hard over the head. His head growled furiously with pain.

"What the hell's going on?" he demanded, half-furious, half-afraid. That woman, who had been following him, stood over him.

"Just keeping our romance alive," said Juno rather amorously. She remembered him beating a hasty retreat in the downpour, following him to his apartment building, knocking him over the head with a rolling pin. She had been surprised by her own strength. The area of skull where she had struck him was badly dented, creating a depression, a hollow, which Nathan seemed presently oblivious to. Nor did he appear concussed.

Nathan struggled against his bonds, but they were held fast. "What do you want with me?"

Juno produced a pair of sewing scissors from behind her back, opening and closing them with sinister intent. "You are the man I love, and you are the man who is going to betray me."

Nathan stared at the deadly scissors, moon-eyed, the sharp blades glinting luridly, threatening to inflict some serious damage. "Betray you, how? If I've done something to offend you, you need to tell me what it is so I can straighten it out once and for all."

"You know Robert De Niro perfected the role of the stalker: Travis Bickle, Rupert Pupkin, Gil Renard, Max Cady . . ."

"So you admit it?"

"Admit what?"

"That you've being stalking me." Nathan thought of this woman who had been stalking, lurking, watching from the shadows, spying and skulking, waiting, preparing to make her move. *These boots are made for* stalking! He wondered what she had in store for him, his eyes fixed on the scissors she continued to deliberately and ominously open and close. Should he *Play* Juno *for Me*? Or expect the full bunny-boiler treatment?

"Stalking is such an ugly term," declared Juno. "I prefer to call it 'looking out for you'. Do you think I'm the jilted lover, or someone with a self-perceived slight, whose goal it is to get back at you or frighten you? Or would you call me incompetent, someone who lacks the necessary social skills but still has a sense of entitlement over the person they're obsessing or fantasizing over?"

"Don't you see that what you're doing – this unwanted intrusion in my life, taking me hostage – is a crime?" Nathan reasoned with her, shaking his wrists, bound tight, in emphasis.

Juno struggled to dodge the question. "I'm not repeatedly ringing you, sending you gifts or stalking you on social media. I only wish to pursue a deep and intimate relationship with you, full of passion. Is that so wrong?"

"But I don't feel the same way about you," Nathan replied, then realized he'd put his foot in it.

Juno's expression darkened, shot thunderbolts. "You dare *spurn* me?"

Nathan listened, suddenly very scared. He couldn't believe that such crazy people walked the streets. This woman was certifiable, completely cuckoo! He tried to ground the conversation, defuse some of Juno's anger. "It's just a crush – it'll soon pass. Besides, I don't get why you should be fascinated by me. I don't deserve your scrutiny or any special treatment. It's not as if I'm listed on the Map to the Stars. More to the point, the last theatre critic's review of my performance advised 'no sane director should ever allow this ham near the stage again'. So you see I'm not worth it. I'm just a struggling actor, a *nobody*!"

"That's not true," Juno said, her voice and countenance softening, growing absurdly adoring again. "I've seen you perform, and you perform brilliantly! Big things await you. You're charming, captivating, magnetic, a handsome devil, able to hold the audience in the palm of your hands. *The fame of an actor is won in minutes and seconds, not in years,* as Bram Stoker intimated . . . I'm sure you know what you're worth, someone with an ego like yours."

"What is it I've done to make you sore?"

"*Acting is a marvellous profession . . . If you can spend enough time playing other people, you don't have to think too much about your own character and motivations.* Dean Koontz." Juno hesitated, let her words sink in. "You cheated on me."

"Cheated on you? How?"

"With that *bitch*, Anita Stedman!" Juno spat in contempt.

It clicked. "You mean the love scene, the *kiss*?"

"There!" Juno hissed, full of venom and vitriol. "Even you know! You admit it, do you?"

"But it's just work – just acting."

"She had her hands all over you, and don't you dare say it's *just acting!*" Juno nearly screamed. "I'm not going to let you go near that woman again! You cannot kiss anyone else but me! And certainly none of those spread-legged floozies on stage! You belong to *me!*"

Nathan realized he needed to do some serious negotiating with Juno, even if it meant using a little deception to get out of this tight spot. Such was the price of fame that, with celebrity worship, unhealthy obsession could easily spill over into frustration, anger and violence when the obsessed fan's advances were not being reciprocated. The stalker's response ranged from the simple, pestering nuisance to the downright malicious. Nathan realized he had to be resourceful. He thought he should use all that charm Juno had spoken about on her. "Of course, sweetheart, I won't ever betray you again. Anita is finished. I'll tell her that tonight. Then you and I can go on a glorious trip to Paris, the City of Lights, together where we can make love to each other all weekend. Darling, you can ride me right now . . . if you *just* let me go . . .?"

"Nice try, buster," said Juno darkly. "I know your game!"

Nathan was disappointed. No matter how deluded the woman was, she had easily seen through his charade. He was wondering what he should do next, when the doorbell rang. He prepared for the right moment.

Juno didn't seem worried. "Be quiet," she told him, and went off to answer the door.

Quiet was not what Nathan had in mind. The moment he heard the door open and the sound of muffled voices, he let out a thunderous roar. "HELP ME! I'M IN HERE! YOU GOTTA CALL THE POLICE! SOME CRAZY WOMAN IS HOLDING ME HOSTAGE!"

Juno and a red-haired woman emerged from the hallway. Juno rushed over and smashed a savage fist into his face, instantly silencing him. "*Shut up, you bastard!*" she sneered down at him. "You try that again and heaven help you!"

Nathan blinked, startled. Blood sluiced from his cut upper lip, and he could feel a couple of broken teeth. The excruciating pain in his jaw presently accompanied his existing headache. He looked at the other woman, imploringly. "You've got to release me . . ."

But the other woman was giving him the once-over, like a dirty, old man eyeing an attractive woman up and down. Then, she blurted out something he wasn't expecting. "*Niiice!*"

"I told you he's amazing, didn't I, Rita?" said Juno, excited.

"You sure did, girlfriend!" replied the newcomer called Rita.

"You know each other?" Nathan said in dismay.

"Of course, we do," answered Rita. "We're the greatest of friends. BFF in textspeak."

"Please help me . . ." he murmured to Rita, seeing all hope vanish in a flash.

"Not a jot, old chap. You've been very naughty, haven't you?" Rita turned to Juno. "I've got Hugh Grant coming into town tonight, so I'm going to be busy. I'll make sure I don't get stopped by the police again. What are you going to do with–" she glanced down at the bleeding, vulnerable, near-naked man strapped to the bed with undisguised disdain. "–*him*?"

"Rita, didn't you say that acting was a socially-sanctioned way of cheating on your significant other? This unfaithful little shit is about to learn that hell hath no fury, as the saying goes. . ." Juno's attention was drawn back to the scissors she was holding in front of her, as was Nathan's, causing him to further panic inside. "Stephen King said: *Monsters are real, and ghosts are real too. They live inside us, and sometimes, they win.*"

Nathan didn't much care for this woman's library of quotes from horror writers, nor for the writers themselves. Both women were quite, quite mad! Infatuation had turned into something psychopathic and dangerous. He had to get out of here, away from these professional stalkers, before they did something horrible to him. Except he didn't know how. He was helpless, totally at their mercy. And those scissors looked particularly menacing.

"I dreamt Stephen King owned an antique bookshop, where he stocked only his favourite books," Juno informed him with a touch of nostalgia.

"Look, I don't give a fuck about Stephen King!" Nathan screamed. "Just let me go, for chrissakes!"

"Mind your language!" warned Juno with the utmost seriousness. "Can't you see there are ladies present?" Nathan went quiet. "*Fiction is the truth inside the lie,*" Juno continued, quoting King again. "You're about to find out, Nathan Foy, that horror has never had it quite so *insane!*" Then, she advanced towards a trembling, sweaty Nathan with the scissors, each slow opening/closing motion of the blades producing a sickly, slicing sound, ready to do their final business, her friend Rita watching them with morbid fascination. His eyes bulging as though about to pop, his heart way up in his throat, Nathan was wrongly under the impression she was going to stab him with them [*God help me! Oh my God, please HELP me!*] or worse, lop off his penis.

[*Our love is such Torture/Bliss*]

[I worry about you]

Instead, with a whispered promise, "*I will make sure you do not kiss another woman!* Ready for your close-up?" Juno pressed a hand on his forehead to pin his head to the bed as she focused her efforts on his mouth, and the fleshy trophy she hoped to showcase like a butterfly on her mantelpiece in similar fashion to so many others in her possession, and began to calmly and methodically snip around his lips with the blades of the scissors . . .

March 2016

Every Dog Has Its Day

"For life nor nature cares if justice is ever done or not"

Patricia Highsmith

I: Isla

The day got off to a dreadful start.

First, the dog, a white, rambunctious Westie called Rowdy, had peed on the doormat and was desperately clawing at the front door to go outside. Isla Beresford let him out into the garden to do his business and mopped up his mess indoors, dropping the doormat in the washing machine. Secondly, the car, an old, blue Ford Fiesta, wouldn't start so Isla had to cancel her one-Saturday-a-month shift at the DNA lab, where she was employed as a Biochemist, rather than waste money on a taxi. To top it all off, her husband was so badly hungover, having been out the night before drinking with the lads from the munitions' factory, where he worked as a machinist, that Isla had to nurse him in bed, where he was laid out flat, damp flannel across his forehead, trying to stave off the bouts of diarrhoea and vomiting. He contemplated but chose against propping himself up, finding some sense of normality with the hair of the dog, a can of Holsten Pils by his bedside. Isla decided to refrain from nagging him, for doing this to himself every goddamned week, at least not until he was up and about and more lucid.

THE JUNIPERS, the old, Victorian cottage they had lived in for nearly ten years, was a single-storey bungalow with exposed brickwork and high ceilings, providing only nominal loft space, the latter also doubling as a small office for Isla. Today, Isla chose to work from home, writing up gene analysis reports on her computer while popping down and periodically checking in on her ailing husband and not before feeding the dog, with the intention of taking him out for a long walk later in the morning. There was another reason why Isla planted herself in the loft-cum-home office.

Despite its limited space, the loft housed a disproportionately large, circular window at its farthest, narrow alcove. Set at loft level and partially hidden by boxes of junk, this particular window looked down beyond the fence separating the neighbouring property from hers and directly into the neighbour's back extension. The view from the round window captured the patio decking at the back of her neighbour's property, another period cottage/bungalow, MILL HOUSE, and the steps that led up to the well-travelled towpath behind the small garden, overrun with brambles and vegetation and a brown, mouldering fall of autumn leaves. Isla often walked her dog along the very same canal behind the row of houses.

The previous owner of Mill House had pulled down the old conservatory and built a beautiful glass-and-oak extension, shaped like a barn with gable roof, combining an open-plan kitchen at the far end of the structure with a light and airy living space, before selling the house at a more equitable price, such is the custom of property developers. The house had lain vacant for some time before the new owner moved in only six months ago. It was a woman in her late twenties, somewhat younger than Isla, who had only introduced herself briefly to the Beresfords the day she moved in as Gisele Hidalgo. She did not organize any housewarming, either. She would be occasionally spotted at the EAT AND GO café down the road, always alone, and otherwise remained reclusive, keeping herself to her house. She must be a writer, reckoned Isla, since Gisele would be seen most days sitting on a bar stool at the kitchen island, beavering away on her laptop.

Isla watched Gisele every day. It was with rather more than an idle curiosity that Isla gazed down at her neighbour, bespeaking an intense fascination that stemmed from something deeper, almost primal. For Gisele was the full package, a slim, nice-looking woman, dark hair styled short in a pixie cut, manner exuding an independent and creative spirit, whereas Isla was slightly on the big size, whom Rory loved anyway, since her fuller frame gave her a certain youthful, baby-faced cuteness and her bowl cut the faint resemblance of a chubby Joan of Arc. Rory liked to refer to Isla affectionately as his 'pom-pom girl'. Even if Isla was a sucker for Harrison Ford, whom she sometimes jokingly described as her 'onscreen husband', and Colin Firth, whom she stated 'only truly smiled with his eyes', she had developed a strange preoccupation with her comely neighbour. Isla was prescribed antidepressants. A baby was not forthcoming, and she and her husband had financial worries. So Gisele became a thing of fascination for her. Isla even installed a camera up in the loft to watch what her neighbour got up to when she wasn't around. Nothing unusual. No men, no guests, no visiting family, not much in the way of entertainment for Gisele except her laptop or occasionally cruising the television channels. And, all the while, Gisele fiercely protected her privacy, apparently unaware of the silent observer.

As usual, Isla worked on her computer while snatching glances across the boundary at her neighbour in the extension. All at once, Isla stopped what she was doing and took a long, hard look. The angle was perfect. There could be no mistaking from her present vantage point.

Gisele was slumped across the island, an empty vial of pills and a nearly empty bottle of vodka by her side.

As Isla conceded, the day started atrociously.

2: Gisele

Isla promptly rang the Emergency Services. The police broke down the door to Mill House, and Isla watched from her secret window as the ambulance crew worked with a sense of urgency to rouse an unconscious Gisele. Isla was relieved when the paramedics managed to revive her. They carefully placed her on a stretcher and wheeled her away, out of sight, probably to undergo a thorough medical assessment and physical workup at the local hospital, where the staff would also decide whether to pump out her stomach.

In the days that followed, Isla took on the role of the dutiful neighbour and visited Gisele at FAIRVIEW GENERAL. Car repaired, Isla would use her generous lunchbreak at work to drive down to the hospital and spend a couple of hours there. Gisele always slept in the afternoons, and Isla would sit in a chair and watch her sleep. They did not speak and, unless the nurses informed Gisele, she may not have known she had a visitor every day. Isla could only speculate as to the reason behind the overdose. The woman had survived a major suicide attempt. Obviously, the motive had been to kill herself. Why would someone so smart and talented want to end it all?

Then, one afternoon, Gisele wasn't there, and Isla experienced the terribly upsetting thought that Gisele had died. Until the staff informed her that Gisele had been discharged home, having been declared medically fit. Sure enough, Gisele was visible in the extension when Isla next went to observe her from the loft window.

There, at the island counter, was Gisele, wearing her usual dark dress and stockings, working on her laptop as though the last few days had never happened.

Rory was out of action for a couple of days, and Isla tried not to be cross with him. She was only too glad when he returned to work since he was not eligible for sick pay.

As another week came to a close, a small envelope dropped through the letterbox. Hand-delivered, without any postage marks. When Isla pulled out the small decorative card from the envelope, it read: *Many thanks for keeping me alive. See you at mine at 1pm. Gisele.*

Isla accepted the little thank-you note, a token of Gisele's appreciation, and the invitation to meet up for lunch. Leaving Rory behind to tend to his hangover, after another Friday night of drinking with his buddies, Isla popped round her neighbour's house at the appointed time.

The early November sky murky and overcast, the air chilly, Isla tramped to the back of the house, where Gisele was expecting her in the new extension, once a source of interest from the other side of the fence. Isla did not know what to expect when she got there, butterflies fluttering in her stomach. "I wouldn't dream of imposing . . ." she said hesitantly when Gisele opened the door to the extension.

Gisele greeted Isla warmly. "Not at all. We're just two girls here." They went inside and sat at the island, where Gisele had fixed a bowl of Caesar salad. They ate heartily and healthily. They drank Sancerre and chatted like old friends. The radio played in the background, *Gone Daddy Gone* by Violent Femmes. Gisele had a varied taste in music, as much a rocker as a hepcat.

Their initial discourse was neutral and unremarkable, above-board. Isla spoke about her day job, a more interesting topic of conversation, working with fragments of human DNA, occasionally for forensic purposes and sometimes to determine parentage cases for the Child Support Agency. Gisele discussed her other neighbour, another reclusive woman, a retired accountant, living alone, with a terrible weakness for drink and stricken with alcohol-withdrawal seizures and particularly nasty falls. Best time to get her was first thing in the morning. Her friendly black tom often roamed the garden, making up part of his regular territory.

"I've seen you watching me from your window," Gisele said abruptly, pointing to the circular loft window, clearly visible from where they sat at the island counter.

Isla stopped eating and her face flushed. Gisele had known all along. Isla thought of her own pale, round face peering down at Gisele – what Gisele must have seen without giving any inkling that she knew she was being watched. Yet there was no real need for embarrassment since there was no accusation in Gisele's tone, just gentle acknowledgement. But did she know about the secret camera that Isla had put up there to spy on her neighbour, replaying the afternoon's footage when Isla returned from work? If Gisele did, she didn't let on. From here, the loft window itself was as impossible to miss as a vast, star-gazing porthole. "I just could do with some company sometimes."

It was the best explanation Isla could scramble together at such short notice, but it was enough to satisfy Gisele. Gisele did not press further as to why Isla seemed compelled to watch her. "You must have guessed from your observation deck that I'm a writer. I'm not particularly well-known, but I'm able to live within my means from my steady trickle of book sales."

"What do you write?"

"I'm an author of chick lit," Gisele informed her, "but not of the saccharine type the Bridget Jones generation is so familiar with. Sylvia Plath, among others, is my divine inspiration. Very few female writers come close to her suffering. Ted Hughes lacked any understanding or sympathy for her and proved to be nothing but a wife-beating brute. Like her, I consider myself 'a victim of introspection'." Gisele went on to quote: "*When you are insane, you are busy being insane — all the time.*" She gestured to the wooden plaque, next to a series of other plaques with famous sayings and expressions, on the extension wall, a direct quote from Plath:

Dying
Is an art, like everything else.
I do it exceptionally well.

I do it so it feels like hell.
I do it so it feels real.
I guess you could say I've a call.

Isla didn't know what to say. She decided honesty would be the best policy. "It's all very dark and morbid . . ."

"You're not alone in your opinion. It's the typical response of most people." Gisele pointed again to the wide oculus in Isla's loft. "As a writer, I can relate to you looking at me from your window over there. Life is extremely ordinary and finite and repetitive and meaningless, whether we actively busy ourselves doing nothing or we seek the grace of contemplation and appear to do so much more. As far as metaphors go, writing is about gazing through an internal window and scribbling down what can be observed, existing in a strange no-man's land between the everydayness of life and the wider perceptions of the mind, bridging the gap between reality and the imagination. Writing is an act as secret as dreaming, with the writer holding as unique a perspective as you discreetly looking out of your window without me knowing. But what happens when cracks appear and spread, and the window shatters and shards of broken glass begin to fly off? The window no longer affords any barrier or protection and you're *thrust*, fully exposed, into the world – and the *unknown*."

"Spoken like a true writer," Isla said, appreciating the evocative way Gisele identified with her. "You must be good at your craft."

"Oh, I get by," replied Gisele modestly.

Isla brought up something that had been playing on her mind. "Life is precious. Every living thing on this planet, no matter how small, values its own life. Even somebody in a coma, a neurovegetative state, clings on to dear life. So how could things have got so bad that an intelligent, articulate lady like yourself would want to take your own life?"

It was the inevitable question, Gisele supposed. She saw it coming. After all, it was that very event that had brought both women together. "It's a long story – or maybe not so long." She took another sip of Sancerre. "I was in a relationship with someone. Ever heard of Aubyn Blinkensopp?"

"You mean the MP?"

"Yes, the Right Honourable Aubyn Blinkensopp," Gisele began. "I met him at a writing junket. Don't get me wrong, I would normally spit in the face of the Establishment, but, on this occasion, he showed a romantic interest in me and I was instantly attracted to him. Me with my feminine wiles, him with his womanizing ways. I became his mistress. For a while everything was dandy – we'd meet three afternoons a week at his rented Chelsea apartment and indulge in a spot of fun: coke, champers and sex. We never discussed politics, even though I knew he was involved in selling arms to the Saudis or, as a Euroskeptic diehard, he was making pots of cash from the embarrassing shambles they call Brexit and siphoning off all his profits to the Cayman Islands to avoid paying taxes in the UK. Then he just *changed...*"

"Changed, how?"

Gisele's expression became morose, her voice now tinged with melancholia. "He lost interest in me, saw me less and less, shut me out. Apparently, he'd found his next girl, and he soon asked me to vacate his flat. I should have left sooner. He used to get drunk and hit me."

"Why did you stay with him?"

"He lavished me with gifts, love, money. He promised he would divorce his wife and make me a Lady." Gisele paused for a moment before continuing: "I don't know if it was learned helplessness or the second-best mentality of having been raised by narcissistic parents, but I had grown dependent on him. I told him if he left me, I would kill myself. In the end, he paid me off rather than face a scandal."

"I'm so sorry . . ."

Her eyes began to well up. "How could someone, who had put me so high up on a pedestal, treat me with such utter contempt? I was so heartbroken I went straight to a Soho prostitute!"

"He must have hurt you so bad, you just needed some love," Isla surmised, not finding the idea of Gisele sleeping with the same sex distasteful or surprising. "You've had such a terrible time of it."

"I moved here to get away from my grief. His hush money – a small windfall – helped me buy this house." Tears spilled over. Isla put an arm round her neighbour, offering a sympathetic shoulder to cry on. "On my own, trying to evaluate my relationship and my life, I grew more depressed, overwhelmed by a sense of emptiness, loneliness. I felt as though I was suffocating in a bell jar. I thought of slitting my own wrists in a warm bath, imagining myself lying in the tub, as my heroine Sylvia Plath must have once imagined doing, my blood pulsing out of my open arteries, flowering the bathwater like poppies, my life slowly, painlessly ebbing away . . . But when it came right down to it, I couldn't go through with it. I just wasn't made of harder stuff. Valium and alcohol seemed the next best solution."

Gisele clung on to Isla's comforting embrace for a moment or two. "Thank you for sharing," Isla murmured kindly. "I was so worried."

"I didn't mean to frighten you. I just wasn't myself. Suicide is such a selfish act. I'm eternally indebted to you for saving my life. You *are* absolutely right. We only have one shot at life. Best to make the most of it, never relinquish it unnecessarily and so cheaply. Aubyn Blinkensopp is not a man worth dying for – nor any other man."

"Maybe you're not as selfish as you think," Isla opined of her new friend, "considering you value your life now."

"I suppose some good has come out of this episode." Gisele looked Isla straight in the eye. There was kindness, gratitude, affection in that look. "If it hadn't been for that congenital hypocrite, Mr. Dickless himself, the Right Honourable *member,*" she pronounced 'member' with a twisted, hateful sneer of her lips, "then I wouldn't have met you."

Isla warmed to her final comment, an affirmation of their friendship, pleased that Gisele had trusted her enough to confide in her. Not easy being a depressed suicidal in any walk of life, disclosing the harrowing story of your life to someone you don't know, but to be able to acknowledge that a problem shared is a problem halved was the first step towards recovery. If Isla had been afraid she might be walking on eggshells when she first stepped into her neighbour's house, she was delighted to admit, up close and personal, Gisele had turned out to be an extremely hospitable lady, approachable and forthcoming. Isla was glad she knew something of substance about her neighbour. When Gisele leaned forward and kissed her on the lips, Isla did not resist. It felt completely natural.

3: Detective Finkel

The man who knocked on the door of Mill House looked like someone from a 1940s film noir. Except he didn't comport himself with the sinister, threatening manner of a shady crime character, by all appearances more Oliver Hardy than Orson Welles. He was extremely overweight, all triple chin and jowls and belly sagging flabbily over his belt, and dressed in a two-piece grey suit that had seen better days and a white shirt, tainted by food stains, top button opened and black tie loosened, the ensemble completed by a crumpled brown mac. He wore a tatty, grey trilby, which he removed from his head, out of politeness, when the door was opened. He had made a half-hearted effort to shave, apart from his bristly whiskers, and his thinning, grey-golden hair was swept across in a greasy combover. He was sweating profusely, adding to his unhealthy complexion, as though on the verge of a heart attack. He dabbed his damp forehead with a dirty handkerchief.

"Miss Gisele Hidalgo?" he asked tentatively. It was two days later, and the day was as dreary as ever, threatening rain. Gisele hazarded a nod, catching the scent of salami and cigars on his breath and the distinctive whiff of stale Scotch. "Is this a convenient time to talk?"

"What's this about?"

"Oh . . ." mumbled the visitor and fumbled in his jacket pocket. He extracted a business card which he promptly handed to Gisele.

She turned it over and read it: *SAUL FINKEL. Private Investigator. Finders Seekers Detective Agency. No case too small.* "Like I said, Mr. Finkel, what's this about?" Gisele asked coldly.

"Can we talk inside?" he asked. "I promise I won't be long."

Gisele relented. "Of course, where's my manners?"

She ushered him into the cottage, suspicion still in her eyes. She did not shake his small, chubby hands.

"Nice place . . ." he said, taking in the hallway, admiring the rustic décor, the old-world charm.

"Thanks," she said, touching upon the history of the place. "This house and the houses either side, together, used to be a gin mill in the Victorian era. Working conditions as terrible as a workhouse. I wonder how many children perished here so revellers could get drunk . . ."

It was a bleak, gloomy comment, one that Detective Finkel used to appraise the woman who had spoken it. Her dark skirt and blouse and short, dyed-black hair and lipstick, a dark shade of cherry, spoke volumes. There was often a sob story behind those who fervently dressed in black, a reflection of their lugubrious state of mind. There could be no misinterpreting the strong depressive, starkly pessimistic quality to her appearance and outlook. Here was a woman unhappy with her life, possibly her upbringing, moody, melancholic, *miserable*. Gisele Hidalgo existed in a dark place. He wondered if she'd ever attempted suicide. "Not haunted by the ghosts of these poor children, are you?"

His words were meant to be rhetorical, harmless, a weak attempt at a joke at best, but they produced a dour response from Gisele: "In all seriousness, I do not find your remark vaguely amusing!"

Not the reaction he hoped for, but Finkel was apologetic, nonetheless. "Sorry, I didn't mean to offend—"

They entered the timber-framed, light-drenched extension. He had to admit it was a work of art, the epitome of craftmanship. "I should get one of these for my own house—" He stopped in mid-flow when he saw the other woman sitting there behind the island counter. She was a big lady, her huge, pendulous breasts squeezed into her dress, somewhat dowdy, if not attractive in her own right. "I didn't know you had company . . ."

The woman got up from the stool, strode over and shook the visitor's hand. "I'm Isla. I live next door."

"Saul Finkel . . . pleased to meet you."

"Now that we've all been introduced," Gisele said directly, "what's your business here, Detective Finkel?"

Finkel paused, gesturing to the armchair nearest to him. "Do you mind?"

"Knock yourself out."

Finkel helped himself to the chair and waited for both women to seat themselves opposite on the leather couch, with its sheepskin throws. He got down to business, fishing out a small notepad and pencil from his pocket. "I'll cut to the chase. I'm here in an official capacity to look into the disappearance of one Aubyn Blinkensopp. Do you know him?"

"I know *of* him," said Gisele slowly. "He's that Member of Parliament, whose made the news recently for his sudden vanishing act."

"You didn't happen to know him, did you?"

"Why should I?" Gisele responded sharply. "I never personally met the man."

"Now that's not entirely true, is it, Miss Hidalgo?" Finkel said, quite unexpectedly. "You were in a relationship with him, were you not?" Gisele shifted uncomfortably in her seat. "Please cooperate. Lies can be so very messy."

Gisele took a short while to reply. "Alright," she admitted indignantly, "we had an affair. How could you possibly know that when he kept it secret from the rest of the world, for the sake of his reputation?"

"It's my business to know," said Detective Finkel.

"I told the police everything I knew."

"Scotland Yard have reached a dead end in their investigation. All evidence seems to point to him being somewhere abroad and the sneaking suspicion he doesn't want to be found. Meanwhile, his case will remain open until there is something more concrete." Finkel continued, getting to the crux of the matter: "Blinkensopp's wife knew all about his affairs, including his relationship with you. He had a habit of telling his wife who he was sleeping with. She's got her own thing going on. Don't ask me why — the loose morals of the obscenely rich, I guess. She instructed me to find him. I'm just following up on any leads." He produced a fat, ugly smile at Gisele. Darkly, confidently he added: "Please don't let my appearance fool you. I always get the job done."

If Gisele was rattled, she didn't show it. Her ongoing hostility towards him took care of that. "Why me?"

"We have a log of his mobile calls. You were the last person to speak to him."

Gisele stood up and walked round the back of the couch, positioning herself directly behind Isla. Finkel's eyes followed her and watched as she began to massage Isla's neck and shoulders. Isla must have surely approved, the manipulation of her muscles almost sensuous, for her eyes closed as the tension gradually drained away and her mind drifted to another place, a tranquil place. Surprised, Finkel watched Gisele work her magic and an instinctive thought crossed his mind. These two women were closer — *tighter* — than just neighbours, as thick as thieves, possibly even intimate. What did the other woman know?

"He dumped me over the phone," Gisele replied with a flash of anger. "The bloody coward! That was the general gist of our conversation. You can imagine how emotional it was for me."

"Did he mention where he was going?"

"No, I didn't ask. I doubt he's gone the same way as Lord Lucan. I'm sure he'll turn up."

"I hope so, too. Is there anything else you can tell me? Anything at all?"

"There's not much else to tell," Gisele said, trying to sound casual. "We had an affair nobody was meant to know about, he broke my heart and I left him. *End of.*"

"I see . . ." Finkel sighed wearily, sounding disappointed. "You know the more information you can give me, the better I'll be able to protect you."

"From whom do I need protection?"

"The papers, the nosy media."

"I think I'll take my chances."

"I get the feeling there's something you're not telling me . . ."

Gisele avoided answering the question and brought the interview abruptly to a close. "Detective Finkel, I think you've taken up enough of my time. Please make your own way out . . ."

Her request was blunt, explicit. Finkel had no choice but to comply. He hauled himself awkwardly up from the armchair and waddled sluggishly to the extension door. "Thank you for taking the time to speak to me. I'll be in touch. In the meantime, if you think of anything else, please do not hesitate to contact me." He dawdled by the door, spotting something on the wall. It was a plaque – the extension was full of plaques – with a darkly-comic breakdown of one particular word: PSYCHO THE RAPIST. "I'm guessing you took therapy sessions."

"A long time ago," admitted Gisele. "But I quit. I keep that as a reminder."

"Cute . . ." Detective Finkel commented. He noticed something else, this time on the narrow bookcase. "I see you like Patricia Highsmith."

"What's it any concern of yours?"

"I always had a soft spot for that talented sociopath, Tom Ripley. Don't you?"

What was he implying? Did he think he knew her? Gisele responded brusquely: "I thought you were leaving . . ."

Detective Finkel replaced the book on the shelf and, putting on his hat and uttering a customary '*Ladies . . .*' departed.

Gisele stopped rubbing Isla's shoulders. "*Bastard!*" she muttered under her breath.

Isla opened her eyes. She'd never seen Gisele so furious. "Just a fellow making inquiries. Surely, it shouldn't bother you if you've got nothing to hide."

"I don't take kindly to threats from a fat, bloated alcoholic, who thinks he's some kind of hard-boiled detective!"

Outside, Detective Finkel stepped into his car, deep in thought. That Hidalgo woman not only laboured under a depressive disposition, for which she had probably seen a shrink once, but she also held a serious grudge against the world. He knew one thing for sure. She wasn't telling him everything. She certainly knew more than she was letting on. She was holding out on him and he didn't like being stonewalled. If the politician had ended their affair, what did they say about spurned women? Hell hath no fury and all that? That dark place she occupied got a whole lot darker. A phrase floated into his mind: *femme fatale*. Call it a hunch. Suddenly, he felt very close to cracking the case. He saw his own celebrity in the papers. Maybe the way in was the neighbour, the same neighbour whom she was carrying on with. He planned to catch that Beresford woman alone. In the meantime, he would keep tabs on Miss Hidalgo's movements.

It was only when Rowdy dropped something he'd dug up at Rory's feet as Rory arrived home from work that the situation would come to a head.

That window, again. That imaginary window. The figurative glass broke, exploded, propelling its confusion of splinters outwards like tiny spears, stabbing everything in its path. As the glass screen to the outside world completely disintegrated, the frightening realm of the unreal bared itself, crept inexorably closer and reached in . . .

4: Rory

Back from work, Rory was taking off his boots on a footstool by the front door when Rowdy, who had a natural instinct to dig holes, dumped a small, gleaming object on the floor before him. Rowdy scurried off to the kitchen, waiting for his master to feed him. Rowdy was such a playful boy, who especially enjoyed playing with his raggy toys, teddies and kongs. He was also a little foodie, who loved treats, and enjoyed nothing more than to potter around, exploring the outdoors, digging up interesting things. He appreciated a gentle fuss and lying next to his owners when the day was done. Rory picked up the discarded object. He called over his wife: "Isla, look what Rowdy found!"

Isla, who was busy making dinner, came into the hallway and saw what Rory was examining with frowning concentration. He passed it over to her. It was a gold wedding band and, judging by the size, the groom's. *Whose?* The design of the ring was plain, with no other distinctive features except for a tiny engraving inside the ring: *To A.B. With Love.*

A crucial detail, Rory was quick off the mark, identifying the owner of the wedding ring. "I think it belongs to that MP who vanished, the one you said that Gisele woman was dating. What's his ring doing in–?" The puzzlement gave way to an expression of stark realization, as he put two and two together. "I don't want you talking to that woman again. I think we ought to call the police."

"Let me ring them," said Isla, feigning an air of composure while inwardly starting to panic. "You freshen up. Dinner will be ready in a couple of shakes." She dropped the ring in her pocket. "Let me keep a-hold of it until the police get here."

"Okay, I'll let you deal with it," said Rory, happy to relinquish responsibility to his more than capable wife. "I'll take a quick shower, then I'll be with you." He disappeared down the hallway, closing the bathroom door behind him.

Isla re-entered the kitchen, dialled her mobile and was on to Gisele like a light. She updated Gisele on Rowdy's discovery and how Rory wanted to take the matter to the police.

On the phone, Gisele sounded pissed off. She went into an unexpected barrage of quotes, intended partly for dramatic effect but also serving as a practicable means of calming herself down. "*My New Year's Eve Toast: to all the devils, lusts, passions, greeds, envies, loves, hates, strange desires, enemies ghostly and real, the army of memories, with which I do battle – may they never give me peace.*"

"Hey?"

"*In view of the fact that I surround myself with numbskulls now, I shall die among numbskulls, and on my deathbed shall be surrounded by numbskulls who will not understand what I am saying . . .*"

"What *are* you saying?"

"*My imagination functions much better when I don't have to speak to people.*"

"Won't you quit it with the quotes?" demanded Isla with skittish impatience. "I'm talking to you! What do we do?"

"Highsmith," Gisele explained, laughing slightly madly. "Always the mistress of ambiguity." She acknowledged the bind they were in. "What you do, my dear, is wait for me. No point in catastrophizing. I'll be there shortly."

When Rory stepped out of the shower and wandered into the kitchen, a towel still wrapped around his waist, Isla was sitting at the kitchen table, wringing her hands. The saucepan on the stove was bubbling, the strong, herby aroma of beef stew deliciously scenting the air. Rowdy was tucking into his food bowl on the far side of the kitchen. "How long will dinner be?"

Isla looked up. "Fifteen minutes."

"How long did the police say they'd be?"

"I never called them . . ."

He frowned. What Rowdy had discovered was a significant find, and Rory could not comprehend his wife's reluctance to inform the authorities. "I don't get it. Why didn't you? Don't you think it's an important piece of evidence in an ongoing police investigation?"

A voice spoke up from behind him: "She didn't because I told her not to."

Rory jumped, spun round. Gisele stood in the hallway. It was only the second time he'd ever met her – the first time when she had moved in next door – and she was still dressed in black, her maroon lipstick contrasting sharply with her pale face. At the time, he had described her as easy on the eye, fanciable. He did not change his opinion.

"Holy shit!" exclaimed Rory. "How the hell did you get in?"

"I let myself in . . ." Gisele walked past Rory with a deliberate aloofness and stood beside his seated wife. "I understand Rowdy's been very busy, digging in my garden. I should have patched up that gap in the fence long ago." Isla handed Gisele the ring. Gisele studied it. "Certainly a wedding ring – *Aubyn's* wedding ring. An oversight on my part."

"What did you do to him?" asked Rory.

"Before he was about to fly abroad, I invited him round to my house one last time," Gisele recounted. "Lured him back with the offer of sex. I requested he come alone. I slit his throat, stripped the flesh from his body, ground it down in a blender and scattered it in the woods for the crows to feed on. His bones I dissolved in concentrated hydrochloric acid and flushed down the toilet. I must have dropped his ring in the garden."

Neither of the Beresfords said anything for a moment, grappling with the information Gisele had stuffed down their throats. Their neighbour was a killer. She had brutally murdered her former lover and methodically and cleanly disposed of his mortal remains. Rory looked positively shocked, utterly speechless. Isla spoke first, remembering the visit from the private detective earlier. "Why didn't you tell me you murdered him?"

"Why should I?" Gisele said defensively, without any great show of sentiment or emotion. Without any trace of remorse, either. "Not the kind of thing anyone mentions in passing. I got up the gumption to give Aubyn the horrible death he deserved for the way he hurt me. He was doing illegal things so I decided to do something *very* illegal to him. He was nothing but a pathetic little prick with a delusional sense of superiority and entitlement, a millionaire not worth the price of salt!" Then, Gisele was all sweetness and honey. "Now your husband knows too much," she warned, addressing Isla. "We need to do something about him. He's putting our relationship at risk. I only wanted a fresh start with you, Isla. I want our love to blossom. We don't need any distractions. Everything else is noise, if you take my meaning."

Rory couldn't believe his ears. He looked to his wife to provide him with some kind of sensible explanation. Most of all, he needed her unfailing support. "Isla, what is she talking about? She just said there's something between you two! Tell me it's not true!"

"I'm sorry, Rory," Isla replied quietly, averting her gaze. "*We're in love.*"

Her answer only filled him with further incredulity – and the first stirrings of rage. He thought of strap-ons and scissor action and sixty-nine positions he and his mates sometimes joked about over a drink. He had never pegged his wife as queer. "Have you gone batshit crazy?"

Isla couldn't help but feel regret for her husband. He was a machinist and a very accomplished DIY man, who liked tinkering around the house. He also had exceptional green fingers. He had invested a lot of spare time doing up the house and garden and he was proud of the result. She recalled why he married her: *I did it for you. I'm not fussed whether or not we're married. I'll still love you either way.* Even if he was still a hunk, aside from that unfashionable stubbly growth he sported on his chin, she had fallen out of love with him. The money worries continued to pile up and sex had become a dull, insipid affair, a soulless Monday night routine, whereas Gisele had brought excitement into her depressed life – and something different in terms of a relationship. The woman had been more depressed than even Isla. Gisele had admitted to killing her despicable louche of a lover for many a justifiable reason, regardless of his prominent political standing, after which she had attempted to top herself when overcome by guilt and despair. Isla had dutifully rescued her from the grave for which Gisele was forever grateful. Happenstance had brought the two women together. Attraction and a certain wayward passion kept them together, interested in each other. Now Rory threatened the foundations of that very relationship . . . and jeopardized her newly-perceived sense of freedom. "Rory, I know it's not exactly the kind of thing you were expecting to hear, but I can't live with you anymore."

The bombshells came thick and fast. First, their neighbour's grisly confession to having butchered her ex-lover in cold blood, getting rid of the body in unspeakable fashion. Secondly, his wife's decision to part from him after ten years of marriage for this black-hearted murderess. "Why, Isla? Whatever I've done wrong, I'm sure we can work it out. I still love you, dammit!"

"What do you think we should do with him?" Gisele asked Isla with a look of wicked amusement. "He knows too much."

The ominous tone with which Gisele spoke to his wife did not sit well with Rory. He suddenly felt very exposed, wearing only a bathtowel. "Don't you come near me, either of you . . ."

"He's already dead," Isla told Gisele. "*He doesn't know I've been slowly poisoning him.*"

The revelation caused Rory's head to spin. His world came crashing down around him. It was bad enough his wife wanted to leave him but, worse still, the knowledge she had been feeding him poison for God knows how long sent deeper shockwaves through his system. And, all this time, he had put down his physical unwellness to a five-alarm hangover.

"Bravo, girl!" applauded Gisele. "I didn't know you had it in you! How long do you think he has left?"

"Not long . . ." said Isla. "I've been adding a small dose of thallium to his meals for several weeks now."

It suddenly explained why he'd felt so rotten for so long, why he endured a constant stomach ache, why his hair was falling out and why he was experiencing tingling and numbness in his hands and feet, why he'd suffered the worst hangovers in his life after only a few drinks with his workmates. As a Biochemist, his wife had access to nearly every poison. Lately, she had begun skipping meals whilst he ate, telling him she was dieting. All of a sudden, Rory felt extremely wobbly on his feet, his balance abruptly abandoning him, his vision swimming in an ocean of haze before him. Groggy, he grabbed the nearest corner of the kitchen table to steady himself. It was more the shock of the fateful news that his wife had delivered rather than the actual, accumulative effects of the poison. "How could you do this to me?"

Isla had never seen her husband so distraught, so understandably scared, that she was struck by a pang of remorse for her own wrongdoing. He could not cope with her horrendous betrayal and appalling unfaithfulness. Was she gradually losing sight of what's right and what's wrong? It was almost as if she was leading a double life, like she was a different person altogether. Yet, she reminded herself as firmly as possible that all that really mattered was her love for Gisele. "I don't expect you to forgive me. Don't worry, darling . . . it'll soon be over."

"Enough of the chit-chat . . ." Gisele declared and kicked the kitchen table against Rory, taking him by surprise. The table slammed into his hip, toppling him, sending him tumbling to the floor. Rowdy started barking loudly, sensing his master was in peril. Isla picked up her Highland terrier and, in the gentle, soothing tones of a consoling mother, opened the kitchen door and put him outside, shutting the door on him. He continued to make a racket, barking behind the closed door, trying frantically to get in.

Rory rolled around the kitchen floor, clutching his hip in wincing, excruciating pain, uttering a rapid, blasphemous stream of expletives. Gisele picked up a heavy canister of olive oil and whacked it over the head of the fallen man. Rory became still, runnels of blood trickled down from the gash in his temple.

For a moment neither woman spoke. Then Isla asked nervously: "Is he dead?"

"Not yet . . ." replied Gisele ruthlessly. Sure enough, his chest was still rising and falling. "Now that he's out like a light, it makes our job so much easier."

Both women stood over Rory, looking down on his body. "What are you going to do with him?"

"What are *we* going to do with him?" Gisele corrected her. "Remember, we're in this together."

But Isla was already having second thoughts. "I can't go through with this. He's my husband . . ."

"The same husband you were silently poisoning?" Gisele reminded her. "You are *not* going to chicken out on me, Mrs. Beresford!" She attempted to motivate Isla, to bring her out of her guilt-ridden lethargy. "Act now, grieve later!"

Isla's doubts persisted. Except she had very little say in these ghastly events. The consequences were otherwise too serious to contemplate. "What do you intend to do with him?"

"Exactly what I did with Aubyn's body," Gisele told her. It wasn't as though she hadn't been in this tricky situation before. "Make mincemeat of him and feed his remains to the wild animals . . ."

Isla shuddered. Was this to be the fate of her husband? It would be a horrible, undignified way to die, keeping in mind the gruesome manner in which Gisele planned to dispose of the body afterwards. Did Isla really want to see Rory end up as crow-feed? Gisele had got away with it once already when that politician had finished it off with her. Could she get away with it a second time? Isla felt herself only getting deeper and deeper into things that should never have concerned her in the first place. *That blasted window! If I hadn't been watching her, none of this would have ever happened!* Things wouldn't have gone this far. She would not have become a willing accomplice to murder. Isla understood why sometimes ignorance was a genuine preference. *But should I have let Gisele die from that cocktail of alcohol and drugs? And if I hadn't saved her from her misery, we would never have met . . .* fallen in love.

But was love worth murdering your husband over?

Admittedly, she had been poisoning him for quite some time, debating when to give him that final, fatal dose. Coming out of the closet was the best thing that ever happened to her. Maybe now was a blessing in disguise, the time for a fresh start. Isla resolved to go along with Gisele's plan, just to see closure to her old life with Rory. Gisele's plan sounded foolproof, having proved successful once already. Again, they nearly had it in the bag this time round. What could possibly go wrong?

5: Rowdy

Along the private lane, Detective Finkel sat in his battered, brown Renault, eating a Krispy Kreme while surreptitiously surveying both houses with his binoculars. He was on a stakeout, his shift due to finish in a couple of hours when a colleague from the detective agency would replace him for the night. His presence had so far gone completely undetected.

But he was about to discover that someone knew he was hiding out in his car.

A sudden, importune yapping suddenly jolted him from his contemplations. It was coming from outside the car. He opened the driver's door, compelled to investigate the disturbance. The commotion was coming from a wiry-haired, white terrier, a Westie, a curtain of fur over its dark eyes, and it was barking like crazy. It never ceased to amaze him how the smallest dogs always seemed to make the loudest noise. For a moment he got the idea that he'd been caught watching the house and the owners had decided to sic the dog on him in order to ward him off. But the excitable state of the dog and the shrill urgency of its barks suggested it was trying earnestly to convey a message of sorts, tell him something important.

"Hey there, who's this little handsome fella?" he said affably, putting away the box of doughnuts and stepping out of the car. A light spattering of November rain began to fall from the sullen, twilit sky. It was growing chilly again, his breath condensing into mist. The dog didn't attempt to bite him, just danced around his ankles. "What's up, old boy?" He patted its head, the dog responding by wagging its tail agreeably. It allowed him to read the name on its collar: ROWDY. Very fitting – Rowdy by name, rowdy by nature. The dog belonged to the people at The Junipers, one of the houses Finkel was surveilling. "Rowdy, is someone in danger?"

The dog suddenly scooted on ahead, stopping at a short distance to look back at him. Rowdy went on to lead the way with Finkel following on the heels. Rowdy paused every so often to make sure Finkel was still behind him. He trotted up the short path, guiding the big detective round the side of The Junipers to the kitchen door. Finkel tested the handle. The door was unlocked. Finkel entered. The dog followed suit.

The kitchen was deserted. At first glance, nothing out of the ordinary – food simmering on the stove, plates and cutlery laid out on the kitchen table – that is until his eyes happened to look downwards. He spotted a small, crimson pool on the kitchen floor, the first sign of trouble. He knelt down, inspected it. Unmistakable, *definitely* blood, already starting to go tacky. Something violent had occurred here, and he needed to explore further. He took a quick swig of Scotch from his hipflask, which he promptly replaced in the pocket of his mac, and, reaching inside his jacket, he unlatched his chest holster and plucked out a Beretta 950. As a detective, violence from those he investigated often proved to be an occupational hazard; hence, he was licensed to carry a small firearm in case the situation turned ugly.

The incoherent twitter of voices from somewhere in the house. He heard that Hidalgo woman's voice distinctly, above all others. He couldn't make out what she was saying. Cautiously, gun at the ready, Detective Finkel crept out of the kitchen and down the short hallway. Rowdy did not give the game away, either, moving stealthily beside him, not emitting so much as a peep, ears jacked up and alert. Finkel followed the sound into the bathroom. The bathroom door was ajar and Finkel peered in.

The bathroom was misty from the shower Rory had taken earlier, the windows and the bathroom mirror fogged over. Now, what Finkel witnessed was Rory laid out in the bathtub, naked and supine, being strangled by a length of cord. Isla tried to hold down his kicking legs while Gisele did the wetwork. Rory thrashed about helplessly, his hands coming up to his throat in a desperate attempt to remove the garrotting implement squeezing his airways shut. His eyes bugged furiously, he could not breathe and his face had turned deep purple. He didn't have long left. "*Die*, you dick swab!" Gisele screamed unmercifully, working strenuously, using all her strength to tighten the cord around his neck, maintain the pressure. In an accusatory tone to Isla, she said: "We should have used cheese wire, like I suggested, and let the blood drain down the plughole . . ."

Isla did not respond, agonizingly watching her husband get strangulated to death.

"Just racking up the corpses, are we?" Finkel intervened, handgun trained on Gisele. "Get away from him!"

Reluctantly, Gisele stopped choking Rory and took a step back. The enraged ferocity in her expression, the uncontainable, burning ire, told Finkel she did not appreciate the ill-timed interruption. The cord round his neck loosening, Rory gasped for air, breath quickly returning to his lungs. He went into a heavy paroxysm of spluttering coughs.

"You're going to be okay, buddy," Finkel reassured him, throwing him a bathrobe from the hook behind the door to hide his modesty. Rory nodded gratefully, still trying to take in lungfuls of air and bring his coughing under control.

Finkel turned his attention to Isla. Caught in the physical act of murdering her own husband, a look of deep shame painted her face. "I'm surprised at your complicity in all this. Anything to say for yourself?"

Again, Isla did not speak.

"Why don't we all be good people and take a nice, little trip down to the station?" Finkel remarked. Maintaining his gun on the more dangerous of the two ladies – Gisele – Finkel extracted his mobile from his inside pocket with his other hand and began dialling the number for the Emergency Services. "The police will be taking you both in for questioning and Mr. Beresford over there will probably need medical attention . . ."

His attention momentarily focused on his phone, the distraction provided ample opportunity for Gisele to react. Things happened very quickly. Before he could fire his weapon, Gisele charged, screaming, at him with lightning speed, a fruit knife emerging from the pocket of her cardigan. She leapt onto him and stuck the knife into his stomach, throwing him off-balance and sending both his gun and phone out of his grasp and clattering to the floor. Gisele proceeded to stab him repeatedly in his corpulent belly where he fell, in a mad, murderous frenzy of hate. Taken by the element of surprise, he did not know how many times she stabbed him – a dozen times, or more? – but he was partially aware his substantial folds of belly fat cushioned some of the potentially fatal blows. However, it wouldn't be long before the small blade eventually pierced his vital organs. Fighting against the rising, wracking pain, he rolled over to his side until he was on top of her, his Falstaffian frame knocking the wind out of her and pinning her to the floor. His wounds continued to gush, covering her in his blood.

Nearly recovered, Rory went to his aid, but Isla smashed him over the head with a bath jug, the porcelain shattering and bestrewing the floor. Rory went flying, thudding against the edge of the bathroom door, splitting his forehead, splashing the wall with blood. The impact left him unconscious, bleeding steadily across the tiled floor.

As Finkel continued to press his entire weight on her, Gisele struggling to free herself from beneath him, Isla picked up the Beretta and pointed it at him. "*Get off her!*"

Finkel glanced round from his prone position and realized his time was up. Isla had the upper hand. He pulled himself painfully off Gisele and lay resting on his side, squinting frustratedly up at Isla, waiting for her next move.

Catching her breath, Gisele rose wordlessly to her feet and kicked Finkel savagely in his tender belly. Finkel doubled over, clutching his stomach, wincing at the exquisite pain. More freshets of blood oozed out of his stab wounds, spreading across his shirt in a vivid, crimson bouquet until it was completely drenched. "Dick swab!" Gisele sneered. She looked over to Isla and, pointing at the detective, instructed her. "Shoot him!"

Finkel stared up expectantly at Isla as she directed the gun towards him, finger beginning to squeeze the trigger . . .

Rowdy, who had been silent throughout this sequence of events, sniffing and licking the bleeding wound on Rory's head, using his teeth to try and shake his master awake, suddenly entered the fray.

He began to stalk Gisele, circling her, snarling and growling, preparing to pounce.

"It appears the private dick's brought company," Gisele said, amused. "Ah, look who it is: Rowdy." Except her look of amusement faded fast when she realized, from his aggressive tone, the dog was primed. "Good doggie, nice doggie," she said, trying to mollify him. But Rowdy was having none of it. He delivered a series of sharp, staccato barks, the threat imminent. *Ruff-ruff-ruff.* "Isla, you'd better call off your dog!"

If Finkel thought Rowdy's bark was worse than his bite, he couldn't have been more wrong. The crescendo of barks ended with Rowdy springing into action, leaping up at Gisele. Gisele was ready with her knife, but Rowdy moved too quickly for her. Rowdy's teeth and claws sank deep into her leg, clenching her flesh with the redoubtable tenacity of a terrier. Gisele screamed at the ensuing pain, unable to shake off the dog mutilating her flesh, and brought down the fruit knife in an arc, the blade lacerating Rowdy's back leg, enough to cause him to let go and pitch his hurt in a distressing howl. He limped off, whimpering.

"*Not my dog!*" cried Isla, horrified. She did fire the gun. But, instead of the intended target, Finkel, she shot Gisele. Her reaction was automatic, pure instinct. The noise of the gunshot reverberated around the bathroom like an artillery blast.

A look of surprise crossed Gisele's forehead, her lips forming an O. Then, Gisele staggered backwards and collapsed gracelessly on the floor. Blood dribbled out from the centre of her chest. Isla dropped the gun in shock, Finkel swiftly gathering it up. He reached across and checked Gisele's carotid. She was dead.

He pulled the gun back on Isla. "You've got a lot of explaining to do, ma'am." *Oh, yes, she damned will . . . furnish us with the bigger picture.* "Boy, did you back the wrong horse! Gisele Hidalgo was a low-down, calculating bitch! She took you for a patsy, someone to take the fall. You never knew she planned to walk out on you, do a runner. She bought a one-way flight to Buenos Aires . . . *for one person.*"

Isla stood frozen for a moment, then she plumped herself down on the rim of the bathtub, lost to her own dark thoughts, whether or not she registered this new damning information about the woman she loved.

Feeling queasy and slightly dizzy from the blood loss, smarting from his injuries, Finkel half-crawled, half-shuffled across the blood-streaked floor to check on Rory. The shiny, white bathroom resembled a scene of carnage.

Rory was coming round. Maybe the gunshot had jolted him awake, maybe not, but he was conscious, gingerly touching his bloodied forehead. "What the hell was I drinking last night?" he murmured, slightly disorientated.

"You're going to be fine . . ." Finkel told him wearily. "The police are on their way." They surely would have heard everything that happened in the bathroom from his still-connected mobile.

"I promise never to get rat-faced again," Rory murmured. "I've eaten a shit sandwich today. I don't want to taste any more shit."

The dog sat next to Rory, nursing his wound. Detective Finkel could not have been more grateful to the dog for his timely intervention. The dog had saved his life. He supposed every dog will have its day. And, luckily for Rory, Rowdy had ably demonstrated that the duty of a dog was always to its master. Westies could be stubborn things, but they were also very active, highly intelligent and unreservedly independent creatures. They preferred digging, chasing and hunting to lounging around all day. Due to their energetic nature, it was the responsibility of their owners to supply them with exercise and endless activities to gain their obedience. Not that they were averse to being in the house alone when their owners were at work. No, they considered being inside the house alone during the daytime as work, an opportunity to protect the house from any intruders, taking the role of a fearless guard dog very seriously, jumping into action if required to defend their abode and their master. "Smart pooch you got there," Finkel told Rory, who merely absently nodded back his acknowledgement. "He's done you proud. You should reward him for his bravery." Rowdy assented to Finkel inspecting the gash on his hind leg, blood matting the white fur. Fortunately, it was superficial, a graze. "Just a flesh-wound, old buddy," Finkel said, beaming at the dog. "You'll soon be running around in no time." He stroked the dog, ruffling his hide. "Who's a good boy, then?"

Well-chuffed, Rowdy woofed back at him and wagged his tail. He liked being appreciated, already anticipating the delicious, doggie treat he surely deserved for his sterling efforts.

Ma Puce

Steven and Angela Hardistry never thought their cat, Blizzard, would come home from the Vets with fleas. After all, Blizzard was a housecat, wholly accustomed to the comforts of indoor living . . . I mean how could an indoor cat possibly get fleas? Steven asked Angela incredulously. They watched Blizzard suffer for nearly a month, washing himself excessively and scratching himself like crazy, pulling out big clumps of his beautiful silk, white fur before they cottoned on to the actual possibility that he might have acquired fleas from somewhere. The first tell-tale sign was the presence of 'flea dirt' upon combing him, tiny, dark specks of flea faecal matter distinctly contrasting against his beautiful white fur and composed predominantly of digested blood, which stained red if immersed in a drop of water. By that time, it was already too late because the flea infestation had spread to the rest of the house.

From where Blizzard contracted the fleas remained a matter of debate for a while until the owner of DOONE LODGE cattery, Lorna Deighton, into whose care the Hardistrys placed their trust when they went on a weekend break to Cornwall, came up with the answer. She told them Blizzard got it from the Vets. And the temporal relationship between Blizzard receiving his annual check-up/vaccination and the outbreak of fleas, manifested by their cat tearing his hair out at every opportunity, made complete sense and the debate an absolute certainty. From her long experience of looking after cats, Lorna suggested that PETS AT HOME, accommodating COMPANION CARE at the back of the store, operated a typical corporate model, focusing on maximizing the profit margin with as much cost-cutting as they could get away with, and people brought their cats and dogs into the shop – and, in turn, the surgery – with not a care in the world. Lorna doubted the Vets was as thorough as it should be after business hours in terms of domestic cleanliness, let alone sterilizing the place. She spoke of a cat she had looked after quite recently at Doone Lodge who had gone to the grooming salon next to the same Vets only to return home with fleas. She advised that cats and dogs should always be treated for fleas after they returned from any cattery or veterinary practice as a precaution.

Not that Steven and Angela were not guilty of making the situation considerably worse by not identifying the problem sooner. Keeping in mind their naivety on such matters and the substantial delay it took them to treat Blizzard's flea problem, they in fact kept pushing the poor little blighter into the second bedroom down the hallway, so as not to disturb their sleep any further, every time he kept meowing loudly – and rather greedily – for food in the middle of the night. It might have seemed cruel at the time, but, as far as they were concerned, they were only setting boundaries, even if there was an element of convenience attached to this course of action. Besides, both of them had to work in the morning, holding down extremely busy jobs, Steven an English Lit teacher in a Secondary School swamped under with student exam preparation and Angela a medical secretary with the overstretched local adult community mental health service at Oaks Fold. The importune meows would eventually abate, and they caught up with Blizzard in the morning, feeding him his breakfast while continuing to scratch their heads as to why their cat kept ripping his fur off and kept looking so distressed. It soon became apparent from the cattery owner's canny observations what the problem was. But the damage had already been done: the second bedroom, where they had kept dumping their cat in the small hours, was now a heaving hotbed of fleas and, as the main carrier, Blizzard transmitted his fleas to every room he investigated. That meant everywhere around the house – and comprehensively. For cats are renowned for their meticulous nature.

To know your enemy, you must think like them, reflected Steven.

Even if Steven had taught Science from the syllabus while covering absent or sick work colleagues, Science was never his strong suit. Steven could not imagine how a housecat could contract fleas. He had always considered fleas as something reserved for the pale, malnourished children of Dickensian workhouses. Or the grooming ritual of monkeys picking fleas off each other. His mind went as far back as the early seventeenth-century Italian poet and writer, Giambattista Basile, whose works were currently undergoing something of a renaissance, and who, in one of his fairytales, described a flea as big as a sheep. Steven could even relate to William Blake, who famously painted *The Ghost of a Flea*, an unsettling, darkly gothic work depicting a grotesquely-muscular, vampiric being drinking from a bowl of blood with a flick of its slithering tongue. But now Steven had to put on the scientist's thinking cap to address the plague visiting his house.

From what Steven learned online, fleas, external parasites to their warm-blooded hosts, could lie dormant for one hundred days, waiting for the right conditions to feed and breed. Female fleas needed to feed on their hosts before breeding and, if they could not bite into cats or dogs, then they would readily target humans with itch-inducing bites. A single female flea could consume up to fifteen times their bodyweight in blood and lay up to fifty eggs per day and this bloodlust could last for longer than three months, propagating two thousand young in a lifetime. Visible adult fleas formed less than five percent of the population, the rest just setting up camp in the pets' bedding or hiding under the furniture, avoiding sunlight, hanging out in the moist and shady spots around the house, lying in wait. Waiting for the night to come when they would emerge, seeking our warmth – and blood.

The itching, the need to scratch, was the worst part. For Steven, it brought flashbacks of the time he got scabies in junior school, the maddening itch, the horrible, excoriating rash across his body from repeated scratching, the risk of a secondary bacterial skin infection, the scabies mites burrowing into the webs between his fingers, just about visible under a magnifying glass. The Hardistrys would wake up in the morning with multiple flea-bites on their legs, concentrated around their ankles, the preferred feeding ground. Lately, however, some of the fleas displayed the audacity to attack them during broad daylight and anywhere on the body. It didn't help that the married couple was accustomed to sleeping in the buff at night. One weekend, as a heatwave struck the nation, Steven discovered a flea silently sitting on his shin in the study. In all his thirty years on this earth, Steven had, remarkably enough, never seen a live flea before. It was a tiny, reddish-brown thing, and even if the species was hated the world over, one could conversely argue that there was a terrible beauty to its evolutionary design. Its slick, laterally-compressed body allowed it to roam freely through fur and feathers and evade capture, its agile hindlegs adapted for jumping great distances, sometimes fifty times its body-length.

"What you doing there, *ma puce?*" Steven asked it casually. Funny how '*ma puce*' literally translated as 'my flea' in French, yet it was used as a term of endearment, meaning 'sweetheart'.

The flea continued to quietly feed on his blood, its saliva anaesthetizing the area it was feeding upon.

"Nobody likes someone interrupting their dinner, my little darling," Steven remarked and, with that, he grabbed the squirming creature with his thumb and index finger and attempted to squeeze it. It was an extraordinarily difficult task due to the flea's incredible slipperiness and thinness. But Steven managed to crush it between his fingertips, eventually. Its crushed body stained his fingertips with a tiny smear of blood. Steven's blood. Maybe his wife's blood, too.

He experienced an epiphany. He thought of John Donne's famously-erotic and somewhat metaphysical poem, *The Flea*, about a flea feasting upon the blood of a courting couple, the man's blood and the woman's blood mingling within the flea's blood, in many respects three lives circulating as one, a metaphor for intercourse and conception or, more precisely, the gentleman's strong desire to consummate his love for the young lady, viewing the act itself as innocent.

Steven wondered if the flea he had just killed had also fed on his wife. It wouldn't surprise him.

Yes, you must think like your enemy before you really know them.

The Hardistrys considered the treatment options before calling Pest Control.

First things first. Treat the source, contain the infection and gain some degree of resolution. In this case, Blizzard – the Typhoid Mary, so to speak – who had disseminated these despicable bloodsucking pests around the house. Flea-combing revealed numerous full-grown fleas, wriggling visibly in and out of the white fur of their host, biting him, causing him to frequently scratch himself. It made Steven think of the Black Death, spread by the fleas on the rats, decimating the population of Europe, and shuddered.

The Hardistrys didn't have children, but at least, for now, Blizzard made the perfect substitute, an important member of the family. They kept him as a house pet because Angela dreaded the prospect of him catching a disease, coming home injured or having some stranger knock on the door with the grave news that he had been run over by a car. He was a well-adjusted cat, sociable and energetic and playful, even if carrying the saggy tummy common to most housecats. A good boy, regardless of his nightly meowing or his periodic propensity to quietly vomit up a hairball somewhere, often in the familiar-smelling wicker basket of clothes underneath the bed. Most impressive and formidable of all, he was a killer of wasps and spiders.

Presently, Blizzard graced them with his sleeping presence, curled up on the loungeroom couch, either as a way of socializing in typical feline fashion, telling his 'parents' he felt safe, or maybe just sleeping off the wasp stings. He awoke blearily. Angela stroked him. He purred. Made a change. He hadn't been sleeping well of late. Understandably. Cats need a good, sound sixteen hours of sleep a day, otherwise they wake up cranky, unrefreshed. They had watched him fall asleep, only for him to wake up ten minutes later to scratch himself vigorously behind the ear and then force himself to sleep again, before waking up again, a pattern he was struggling to endure. Even if he was a young senior now, they affectionately viewed him as their 'middle-aged kitten', and they watched the suffering of their cat, helpless, with a sad heart. The poor thing must be exhausted, thought Angela.

The over-the-counter stuff, the *Bob Martin*, had been utterly useless, so they had paid the Vets a second visit. Blizzard had hissed and howled horrendously, highly aroused. It wasn't so much he was a housecat and he could smell other animals in the consulting room, sensing a threat, but being handled, even if gently, proved to be somewhat dangerous and he tried to bite the vet the moment the vet laid hands on him. The vet, however, managed to accomplish at least a partial examination. Blizzard's skin must hurt like hell from all the scratching, the vet informed them, since he discovered it to be red and raw in patches under the fur. He wrote them out a prescription for *Advocate*. The Hardistrys paid the itemized bill and departed the surgery with the medication.

"This will only take a moment . . ." Angela told her cat in gentle, reassuring tones, presently.

Then, Steven held down Blizzard in prone position and Angela applied the *Advocate* to the scruff of his neck, parting the hairs, directly on the skin. Blizzard struggled during this time, hissing and growling like a rabid animal, but the moment the treatment was done, he was freed, and all was quickly forgiven once he received a few catnip treats for his patience. Blizzard enjoyed being catnipped.

The active ingredient in *Advocate* is Permethrin, combined with other insecticides to make sure, and its mode of action, Steven read up, was to distribute itself into the layer of subcutaneous fat all over the body, poisoning any adult fleas or hatching larvae feeding off the cat's blood with the desired fatal consequences. The house spiders would do the rest and mop up the flea carcasses; Steven never thought he'd see the day when he'd be rooting for the spiders.

Fleas are tricky things to get rid of. There is no magic formula. Treatment of fleas involves an integrated approach. The primary carrier had been treated. Now it was a case of attending to the house. The Hardistrys didn't have a particularly big place, a rustic, two-bedroomed cottage/bungalow in Oaks Fold, so they didn't find sanitizing the place too strenuous or labour-intensive. They used *Indorex* spray on the house, recommended by the experts, finished off can after can. Angela vacuumed each room thoroughly, across the skirting board and wooden flooring and soft furnishings, every nook and cranny, since fleas liked keeping themselves to dark, humid places, and washed all the clothing and bedding on a high temperature before hanging it all out to dry in the intense summer heat. They worked industriously, diligently, each a *Clean Machine*, as the Seattle Rockers, The Presidents of the United States of America, might have described them. Steven himself found these essential, down-to-earth domestic duties somewhat rewarding, actually satisfying, glad in the knowledge that their house was a shrine to cleanliness.

Steven and Angela took days off work to fight the infestation. Fortunately, Steven was coming to the end of term and his students, none of whom required remedial lessons, were already sitting their GCSEs. Angela took a break from her secretarial duties at the community mental health service.

The spell of great weather continued. Even if the cat had stopped scratching, fully-treated, now napping undisturbed, finally at peace, the flea comb no longer picking up any new live ones, the Hardistrys could not seem to make a dent on the overall flea population. From all the countless flea-bites they had sustained, both looked like they had the bloody measles! They sprayed the whole house, hoovered like demons and washed the linen to get the house flea-free.

But the fleas would not go away.

Even if the cat was completely cured, the fleas were still there, clearly visible to the naked eye, intermittently crawling in and out of their dark hidey-holes, hopping and feeding on the humans. The flea numbers were still substantial, and Steven wondered if the damned things had developed some kind of resistance to the insecticide spray.

School was now in summer recess, and Angela took more annual leave, unsure when she would return to work. The couple continued their focus on eliminating the fleas from their beautiful home. Success eluded them. The heatwave visiting the country did not give any indication of letting up, one of the most prolonged periods of hot weather in living memory, and the weathercasters compared it to the Summer of 1976. Climate change was cited as the cause of the European-wide scorcher, despite the empty counterclaims of the climate-change deniers. Wildfires raged in Greece, some set deliberately so burglars could loot the evacuated homes. Temperatures in Spain and Portugal were expected to reach forty-eight degrees Celsius. However, the experts were soon warning the public to be on high alert for an imminent, perfect 'flea storm', as soon as the drought conditions were eased by rains, when millions of homes would suffer one of the biggest onslaughts by these despised household pests for years. As the thirty-degree temperatures dropped with the arrival of moist, cooler air, billions of dormant flea cocoons, the developing pupae waiting for a humid atmosphere to complete their life-cycle, would start breaking open to reveal tiny, bloodsucking horrors, invading homes and creating misery for pets and humans alike. Incidences of flea outbreaks had apparently increased in recent years due to milder winters and the installation of central heating in most homes.

With the summer flea season almost upon them, Steven and Angela, irritable from a lack of sleep, miserable from the constant assault by the fleas on their flesh and the indescribable itchiness of the resultant, widespread nuisance rash and tired from treating and re-treating their lovely home, resorted to the penultimate line of defence in a last-ditch attempt to decontaminate their house: the flea bomb. It had apparently worked for some people and, according to some online reviewers, was the most powerful and effective way to eradicate a home invasion of insect pests, as close to fumigation as any non-certified exterminator could come. The idea was to light the wick of the tiny, Permethrin-enhanced candle in a closed room and let the smoke spread and disperse into every tiny crack and crevice. After three hours, open the windows. The Hardistrys used a flea bomb on every room, one after another, in the hope their lingering and unendurable problem would be solved. Their plan had to be coordinated carefully since the only snag was that Permethrin was hazardous to cats. All this time, with the spot treatment and the insecticide spray and the flea bombs, they were conscious they might be poisoning their cat. Blizzard slept a lot but did not seem to suffer the effects of the flea bombs set off around the house – or maybe the excessive somnolence was a sign of subacute Permethrin poisoning. Fortunately, he did not go off his food.

Astonishingly but more troublingly, the flea bombs did not work, the fleas still in hungry, rampaging numbers. Perturbed that the fogger insecticide had proved completely ineffective, Steven even wondered if he had only purchased dud items. Time to call in the professionals, it seemed. At a loss and out of his depth, having exhausted all interventions, Steven called Pest Control, a company called CREEPY CRITTERS. Steven explained the situation, gave the lady at Customer Services a full run-down, from start to finish. He did not want to miss anything out. The lady at Customer Services was satisfied the couple had tried everything available and met the threshold for their service. She would assign their best man on the case. She asked him, Mr. Hardistry, to kindly hang on for forty-eight hours, since the company was currently fully booked-up, and their man would be with them soon enough.

Two days they would have to wait. It didn't seem soon enough. Steven wondered if they should check into a hotel in the meantime.

Angela, on the other hand, appeared more positive, more hopeful. "Why throw money away on a hotel room? We've borne this infestation for so long, I'm sure we can wait for a couple more days. I mean what could possibly happen in two days?"

A lot, it would turn out.

The waiting seemed to take an eternity. The Hardistrys, meanwhile, were seeing things that didn't make a whole lot of sense. The first of the two events that defied explanation was the actual evolution of the fleas. They appeared to have grown larger.

The Hardistrys were met by a myriad of flea cocoons attached to the bedroom ceiling, hanging down like small drops of hardened glue, distinctly ashen-grey and the shape of miniature light bulbs, accommodating the pupating larvae.

Every so often, the couple would witness a noisome pupal hatching event, and the adult fleas that emerged appeared larger than a housefly, bigger than even a bumblebee, and, flexing their new hindlegs, were capable of jumping to the other side of the room in one, single bound. They were ravenous, and if the Hardistrys were ever off-guard, they would feast on their blood, particularly at night, stealthily, without inflicting pain on the individual and with an intelligence that seemed strangely out of place. The look of widespread measles was soon replaced by hot, angry swellings, resembling boils, across the body, and these unsightly lumps itched horribly, post-feeding.

"Is this normal?" Steven asked his wife, alarmed by the inordinate physical size of the fleas. Insects shouldn't be this big since they breathed through spiracles, which technically restricted their physical dimensions, their overall size. Indeed, it was precisely because of this primitive respiratory apparatus that all insects were the size humans were familiar with.

"I don't know," replied Angela, getting a broom to crush an emergent adult flea from one such cocoon into a pink, gloopy pulp. "Maybe these are the super-fleas that the news reports keep talking about."

As explanations go, Steven was far from convinced. But if these really were the super-fleas of news reports, then the males were well-hung, their genitalia at least half the length of their body, prepared for accelerated breeding. The specialist from Pest Control might have his work cut out.

However, speaking of personal appendages, Steven had his own private thing to contend with. In eight years of marriage, they had enjoyed sleeping naked together as well as making love almost every night. They could not deny the recent drawback to sleeping in the nude. And Steven, always at war with his lower self, enjoyed ravishing his wife, who could have been a model in another life, but presently his male organ was not in the best of shape, having acquired a series of horrendous flea-bites down the length of his genitalia whilst he slept an uneasy sleep. The bell of his penis was inflamed and disfigured by a cluster of small, uneven swellings, maddeningly itchy, sensitive to touch.

"You should get that seen to," Angela had advised him, disappointed and frustrated by his sudden lack of commitment to one of the bedrocks of their marriage: their nightly passions.

Indeed, nerves were frayed. "I will . . . when we're home and dry," Steven promised irritably. "Stop ragging on me!"

Passing water was awkward, excruciating, and as they tried to get on with their lives, despite the exploding flea population in their midst, Steven was fully aware that the sorry condition of his penis had begun lately to seriously impact on their nocturnal lovemaking. He tried to grin and bear it, but it was becoming just too difficult to ignore.

The night before Pest Control would pay them a visit, they tried to revive their physical intimacy in the dim, romantic glow of the bedside lamp. Coitus now proving to be too painful for Steven, he stopped in mid-flow.

"What is it . . .?" asked Angela, eyes opening, stirring prematurely from her sexual reverie, unsatisfied and slightly puzzled by his reluctance to complete the act of love.

Once he withdrew, he experienced a curious tingling sensation down below, and both lovers watched, with high, avid horror, as the largest of the existing, dreadful-looking carbuncles on the tip of his penis suddenly popped open in an ooze of unhealthy, bloody semen and a glistening black bug dropped onto the bedclothes, a hundred tiny eggs tumbling after.

The specialist from Creepy Critters arrived at the Hardistrys' residence at close on five the following afternoon. Ulysses Kripke had given them a courtesy call thirty minutes earlier to confirm his arrival, but nobody had picked up the phone. Still, from what Customer Services had informed him from their recent conversation with Mr. Hardistry, the couple was overwhelmed by a raging, treatment-resistant infestation. Ideally, Kripke should have made a call-out a couple of days previously, except Creepy

Critters had been inundated by a deluge of anxious callers. Kripke was an extremely busy man, but this was his last act of duty for the day.

Presently, he stood on the doorstep with his flea-busting equipment strapped to his back. Another afternoon scorcher, but apparently cooler weather was on the way, perfect conditions for a full-blown flea epidemic. He pressed the doorbell again.

Nobody came to answer the door.

Just as he was considering whether he should ring them again or leave a note, he noticed the front door was unlocked. He pushed the door and it swung open. The hallway was Paris-rooftops grey, somewhat dark in the absence of sunlight. "Hello," he called out. "Anybody home?"

No sign of the owners.

He stepped into the house.

There was something strangely disquieting about the pervasive silence, suggesting lack of habitation . . . or something much worse. He thought of crypts and tombs and mausoleums . . . and shivered, in spite of the oppressive afternoon heat.

He checked the door to his right. It revealed a small, nondescript bathroom, white-tiled walls and wooden flooring, the shower, toilet and washbasin gleaming, immaculate. Nothing out of the ordinary. "Hello?" he called again.

He tested the next door on the right. He gained admittance into a modest, rustic-style kitchen, the sun streaming in gloriously, illuminating the dustmotes in the air. He might have considered it a beautiful kitchen, if it were not for the dirty dishes piled up in the deep enamel sink, gathering flies. It was only when his eyes surveyed the broken crockery strewn across the floor, some pieces splashed with what resembled congealed tomato ketchup, that he realized something was seriously amiss. He knew it was blood even before he knelt down to pick up a damaged mug and sniff the coppery scent of the scarlet smear across it. It was like there'd been a fight in here, some violent confrontation. Suddenly alarmed, and afraid, Kripke wondered if he should skedaddle out of here and call the police.

The sound of light scratching from the cupboard under the sink alerted him to an unknown presence, making him jump. He stared at the cupboard long and hard, deciding what to do next. The scratching sound came again. The house might be home to more than just a flea infestation. Surely, his work would become doubly difficult if he ended up dealing with rats as well. He grabbed the small doorknob of the sink cupboard and, plucking up enough courage, just for a quick peek, he pulled open the door, wary not to get bitten by any resident rat . . .

His eyes picked up movement in the dark of the cupboard, something larger than a rat, a white, furry thing, and for a moment, he panicked and nearly slammed the cupboard door shut. Then, understanding kicked in, and he realized he was looking at a cat amidst the array of household cleaning products.

The cat was cowering in the cupboard, its golden eyes wide with fear and alarm.

"Hi there, little fella," he said softly, beckoning to the cat. "What's got you so spooked?"

The cat came to him and he picked it up. The cat was trembling in his arms and he held it for a few moments, comforting it with gentle reassurances. Again, he wondered why it was hiding away, what had frightened it so.

Another sound, a different kind of noise, like a soft *bump*, attracted his attention. He froze instantly. *He was far from alone.* A second louder, pulpous thump brought him out of his paralysis. The sound had emanated from behind the closed door directly down the hallway. He placed the cat on the floor, and it retreated into the cupboard under the sink.

The sound came again, a squishy buffeting against the door, and Kripke had a sudden urge to run. Except he was here on a call-out and he had a job to do, and it would be greatly remiss of him if he didn't investigate. Kripke was an alcoholic and he took a nip of Scotch from his hipflask to gain some measure of Dutch courage against the dread stirring his guts, having promised himself to be Sober for October and that he would keep a moustache for Movember. Against his better judgement, he went to the end of the hallway and slowly, cautiously but dutifully, nudged open the last door.

The door opened up into the master bedroom, the light from one of the bedside lamps casting a low, eerie glow around the room, the corner shadows deep and forbidding. In his line of work, Kripke saw all kinds of things. He had not been prepared for the scale of the infestation. Mr. Hardistry had not been kidding when he had made that urgent phone call to Pest Control. For what Kripke saw on the threshold to the bedroom was a scene from some xenomorphic hell, and he could not blame the DTs on this count.

Husband and wife lay on the marriage bed in quiet repose as though sound asleep. Except Kripke knew the husband had died some while ago. His naked body looked grey and mottled, probably stiff with rigor mortis. Kripke realized the man's penis and scrotum were missing, and the body was raddled all over in ghastly lumps, some of which had erupted, leaving behind ragged craters, others that seemed to bulge and contort and undulate. From where he stood, Kripke saw one such tumour burst open and black, bean-sized bugs spill and crawl out in a pile of white, oval eggs. But it wasn't the man's corpse or the larval pupae, the impossible size of rats, glued to the ceiling and in the process of hatching, emerging from their cocoons as imagoes, that immediately grabbed his attention, but the woman on the bed, next to her husband's corpse, and what was happening to her. Kripke couldn't be sure if she was still alive or dead, but it was the giant thing on her bosom, feeding off her, that sent him to the edge of madness.

Before a cosmic, catastrophic extinction event would eventually kill them off, Kripke had read somewhere that the poor, old dinosaurs had also once been bedevilled by fleas, or more precisely 'mega-fleas', *Pseudopulex jurassicus* and *Pseudopulex magnus*, ancestors of the modern flea, their strong claws allowing them to successfully grasp the scales of the dinosaurs, stay latched on to their hosts and prevent them from being dislodged, while their extended mouthpieces pierced the soft underbellies and feasted upon the blood.

Kripke didn't know if what he was witnessing now was a throwback to those prehistoric times because he certainly wasn't dealing with *Ctenocephalides felis*, the simple cat flea, or those nasty jiggers one heard about from the African continent. Nor could he fathom how Mother Nature could have possibly allowed such an obscene transgression of her laws. It was with initial stark disbelief he beheld the disturbing sight in the bedroom, but he also knew his eyes and his mind were not deceiving him.

The giant flea sitting on the woman's chest made Kripke think of the incubus in Fuseli's nightmare vision. The creature was as enormous as an Alsatian, wingless and scaled all over in hard, reddish-brown plates, brimming with bristles, its body flattened sideways almost like that of a two-dimensional being. Its hindlegs were pure sinew and its legs ended in powerful claws that clenched the sides of its victim. But the greater horror was the long, curved proboscis that had impaled the woman's neck and was guzzling up her blood. Sucking up her blood in an upward, scarlet flow like a rubber tube siphoning up petrol from the tank of a car. It continued to glug up the woman's blood through its stylet to be deposited in its engorged, red belly . . . until it abruptly stopped feeding, its vibrating antennae stiffening to attention. The flea – or super-flea or mega-flea or *mutant* flea, whatever the hell it was – did not possess simple eyespots as it should have done, but red, mammalian eyes, and their slit-like irises suddenly detected another presence in the room and latched on to Kripke standing in the doorway. Eyes radiating a dark, unnatural intelligence. Eyes indicating hunger.

Kripke managed to survey the entire room, saw *everything*, in the briefest of moments, full of idiotic horror and incomprehension, and, when the giant flea saw him standing there and fixed on the intruder, his shock momentarily evaporated, self-preservation jolting him awake, and he instinctively reached for the jet on his backpack, turned it on and aimed the nozzle at the alien nightmare. Insecticide sprayed out, showering the colossal bug in vile-smelling liquid . . . but he might as well have been using a water pistol for all the good it did.

Instead, he only angered it.

The massive, blood-sucking creature on the marriage bed emitted a shrill, ululating whistle, sounding seriously pissed, signalling to its brood to attack, triggering a mass emergence. The huge cocoons on the ceiling began to simultaneously split open as their moulting larvae, now fully metamorphosed into adult fleas, emerged ravenous, sensing fresh meat. In that split-second when the monstrously-perverse haematophage prepared to pounce on him, Kripke decided enough was enough and closed the bedroom door, blocking out the unspeakable freak show in his midst, the wood shaking in its frame, sagging against the sheer number of bodies bouncing against it.

Professor Kripke, time to bring the curtain down on this flea circus . . .

I declare this house uninhabitable until further notice.

Only one thing for it . . . Only one, sure thing that can stop this insane level of unwelcome pest . . .

Dousing the bedroom door with cooking oil from the kitchen, he set the place on fire. The hallway went up in flames very quickly, trapping the repellent horrors in the bedroom. Grabbing the cat from its hiding place under the kitchen sink, Kripke fled, terrified by the knowledge of what he had just witnessed and survived, and the overarching realization that the country was on the brink of an unimaginable epidemic. In his arms, the cat howled in anguish – the poor thing had been through a lot. Kripke intended to burn the house down, incinerate the abhorrent monstrosities in their tracks. He did not hear the windows of the bedroom distend and crack and shatter from the intense heat . . . or see a frog-hopping abomination of fleas come swarming out.

Fleas, don't you just hate them?

September 2018-October 2018

Gods of Halitosis

"To expect to be kissed while having bad breath is the secret of a fool"

Dejan Stojanović
Serbian Poet

I: The Walking Smell

"Your breath smells rank." There, she said it.

Evan Corbluth stopped just short of kissing his girlfriend, Paréce Duchaine. It was the cool of the evening, and he had just come home late from a hard day at the financial consultancy firm where he worked, TOUCHSTONE PARTNERSHIP LIMITED. Paréce had long since packed up shop for the day at five, DELISH, the deli restaurant she owned. She was presently making dinner in the kitchen of their luxurious house in Oaks Fold. The small radio on the kitchen counter quietly played *Incense and Peppermints* by Strawberry Alarm Clock. "You saying I've got bad breath?"

"*Very* bad breath," Paréce replied, glancing up from the Veal Milanese she was slaving over. "Your morning breath smells likes farts! This is much worse. I can't describe how foul it is."

His breath smelled worse than flatulence? "Do you have to be so blunt?"

"Someone's got to tell you," said Paréce, matter-of-factly. "Best it comes from someone who loves and cares for you rather than one of your business colleagues, who are just putting up with it, too afraid to give you some honest feedback and save you the embarrassment."

But Evan looked embarrassed alright. Inside, he was also astonished his work colleagues hadn't mentioned anything to him, particularly with the sheer number of clients on his caseload and the busy schedule of meetings and conferences he attended. Surely, they must have noticed. "It's that bad?"

"It's not something a couple of Tic Tacs is going to cure. Goes way beyond any lingering garlic or onions on your breath from last night's dinner. Worse even than when you indulge in the occasional cigar with your buddies behind my back and deny you ever smoked. You know you can't fool me with your Sergio Leone's *A Lungful of Tar.*"

"I don't know what to say . . ."

It wasn't the first time they were having this conversation. Evan was such a heart-throb with his glamorous body and flawless looks, complete with piercing blue eyes and smouldering lips, not to mention a bank balance in keeping with a world that thrived on Capitalism, Trade and the Markets. No sign of body odour, either – he genuinely made a concerted effort to physically smell immaculate. Even his hair smelled incredible. But his breath was another story. When he'd originally fallen for her, she had been ecstatic. His breath hadn't been an issue at the time. The problem had a more recent onset; the unpleasantness of his breath had become hugely noticeable four months ago after they'd returned home from a romantic break in Naples, Italy. For a perfectionist like Paréce, who had nightmares if the material of her expensive dresses even so much as bobbled or if she did not top up the customer's latte with the right amount of foam, she could not find divinity in his breath. The terrible reek from his mouth grated on her, someone with an acute sense of smell like hers. She had such an obsession with her own pearly whites and oral hygiene that she despaired that his sense of smell was not so sensitive. Besides, her boyfriend believed that bad breath, knockout breath, honky breath, pongy breath, doggy breath – call it what you will, also known as 'halitosis' – was something that other people suffered from. Could it be he didn't know he was smelling his own breath when he complained about other people's breath? Surely, it went with him everywhere he went, but it wouldn't surprise her if he just ignored it. "Haven't you noticed I protect myself with my creams, body lotions and essential oils – I douse myself in the stuff? Like I said, your breath smells worse than your farts in the morning. How is that even vaguely possible?" She was an avid horror reader. "They could market you as H.P. Lovecraft's *The Walking Smell.*"

"Don't you think you're being a bit harsh?"

She registered his hurt expression. Except sometimes you had to be cruel to be kind, to speak some hard truths. She continued: "I remember my old boyfriend. I used to spend the evenings in anticipation of his arrival, even panicking when he arrived home late in the evening. But then he'd climb into bed with me and thought it fun to just let it rip and stink out the bedroom. Why, I mean, *why*?" She looked at Evan searchingly. "You know what happened? When he couldn't be bothered to change, I left him."

Her words sounded ominous. Was there just the hint of a threat? Surely, not. Evan tried to smile, lighten the mood. "Then I wouldn't have met you." He leaned forward with a silly smirk on his face and grabbed her shoulders. "Now I must kiss you . . . with my foul breath."

Paréce struggled in his arms as he forcefully planted a huge, wet smacker on her lips. She quickly detached herself from his embrace, grimacing at the overpowering flavour. "*Yuck!*" She couldn't believe he wasn't taking her concerns seriously. "Please don't do that again!"

"You're hurting my feelings. Can't a man kiss the woman he loves?"

"Not with *that* breath!" Paréce replied, getting exasperated by his still-complacent attitude. She had said it to him nicely. But he seemed to pay little attention to her. Stronger words were certainly called for. Of course, if they were ever going to be intimate, then he would brush his teeth right before their makeout session at her insistence, even if he gagged when he brushed his tongue, finishing off with a generous squirt of mouth freshener. Except, even then, while having sex, she hated kissing him which only made her feel like a prostitute. It was always amazing what you were willing to look past someone when you genuinely loved that person. But enough was enough. She did not want to continue to smell that revolting odour from his oral orifice that could kill a canary at ten yards. "You need to do something about it."

Evan appeared more thoughtful, more serious, if not slightly annoyed. "What exactly do you suggest?"

"From now on, the price of a kiss demands constantly fresh breath." She gave him a suggestion. "A visit to the dentist wouldn't go amiss. Nip the damned thing in the bud."

II: I Love the Smell of Sulphur in the Morning

Mr. Herbert Quinlan stared down at his patient in the dentist's chair. Mr. Quinlan was a grey-haired senior partner at HORIZON dental practice, close to retirement.

He had to admit that Evan's breath was particularly fragrant today. Heck, he was being too kind. Frankly, it was pungent, *repulsive*. A combination of rust and metal and tiny, crawling things at the bottom of a garbage can, feeding on last week's scraps. Even after donning his surgical mask, the stench was horrendous. It made him want to gag. He even had to excuse his dental assistant from the room since she had turned pale, on the verge of vomiting.

"I'll try and see if I can diagnose the problem," Mr. Quinlan was saying. It was odd, considering Evan had a pleasing smile.

Evan spoke quietly, conscious of opening his mouth. He could catch the faint look of revulsion on the dentist's face every time he did. "I don't understand why my breath is so bad."

"There's an entire evidence base behind halitosis, considering it affects two-thirds of the UK population." Mr. Quinlan hoped to enlighten his patient. The next patient had cancelled so the dentist had some time on his hands. "Let's go back to basics and go from there . . ."

"I'm all ears . . ."

"Scientifically-speaking, there are four hundred different types of naturally-occurring bacteria in the average mouth. Bacteria goes to town on any food particles trapped in the mouth, such as in damaged gums and tooth crevices as well as across the rough surface of the tongue, its smothering of food debris and dead cells an ideal habitat for the anaerobic flora, allowing them to flourish, overpopulate and further thicken the coating on the tongue. The smell is from substances called volatile sulphur compounds, caused by the breakdown of these proteins, essentially the smell of food going off in the mouth, of *decay*. These bacteria produce compounds such as cadaverine, putrescine, hydrogen sulphide and methyl mercaptan, releasing the unpleasant whiff of rotten eggs, spoiled cabbage, rancid cheese, off-milk, even excrement and – *no kidding* – the high, gassy foetor of a decomposing corpse!"

"That's gross!" exclaimed Evan. He didn't want his mouth to smell like a dead person, six feet under.

"Put simply, you're growing an entire ecosystem in your mouth. The most powerful mouth freshener will not save you if you've got food debris trapped between your teeth, decaying."

"Duly noted."

Mr. Quinlan continued his short lecture from behind his surgical facemask. "A dry mouth is the commonest, most obvious cause of halitosis. People often notice it when they wake up in the morning. The flow of saliva diminishes when we sleep so there is less 'flushing' of food, more noticeable in those who particularly sleep with their mouth constantly open, hence the morning breath. This means that those suffering from sleep apnoea, characterized by the sequence of snoring, gasping, choking, are worse off. Dehydrating after exercising may also cause bad breath. So too does alcohol. Anxious people may experience a dry mouth and bad breath. Certain medications, such as antihypertensives, antidepressants and beta blockers, dry out the mouth as a side-effect and result in bad breath. Everyone knows that the caffeine in coffee can dry your mouth out and – *hey presto!* – you've got latte breath! Smoking is another common culprit. Aside from its characteristic dragon's breath, tobacco also dries up the mouth and can lead to bad teeth and periodontal disease. Gum disease is the most common disease in humans. In the case of smoking, the stimulant properties of nicotine constrict and kill off the finer blood vessels of the gums, causing shrinkage of the gums and loosening of the teeth, the bane of most dentists, myself included, and many a housewife, if their husband smokes."

Evan could attest to the distinctive aroma of a fine cigar on his breath. Paréce knew he smoked even if she sometimes pretended he didn't. A 'fool's habit', she called it. Evan listened on to his dentist.

"That conveniently leads us to oral hygiene – or, dare I say, the lack of. Poor oral hygiene causes gingivitis and periodontitis, what I deal with most in my surgery every day. Tooth decay provides a mechanical haven for trapped food and bacteria alongside a lot of excruciating pain for the individual.

"Then you have the other causes of halitosis. Certain medical conditions, such as postnasal drip, where mucus hardens at the back of the throat, or in sinus infections and chronic bronchitis, where there is excessive mucus formation in the throat, only increases acidity against the alkaline properties of saliva, creating a field day for bacteria. By the same token, acid reflux is another time-worn classic. Cancers, and the chemotherapies used to treat them, too, dry out the mouth and we're back to bad breath.

"Which brings us nicely along to those distinctive odours that clinicians need to be wary of. Fishy breath suggests kidney failure, a mousy smell hepatic failure. The scent of rotting flesh is common in those who suffer tonsil stones since bacteria have a tendency to breed in the tonsil crypts. And the number of times I've been privy to the faint scent of faeces from infected gums due their production of foul-smelling toxins I cannot even begin to count!" Mr. Quinlan paused. "I want you to try something. If you want to smell your own breath, perform this simple test . . ."

Evan did as instructed. He licked the back of his wrist, let the saliva dry for a minute and sniffed the result.

"Your girlfriend isn't making a fuss over nothing, is she?" Mr. Quinlan confirmed.

"You probably know what sulphur smells like. There it is in all its glory!"

Indeed, his little experiment had proved successful, a little *too* successful for comfort. The dried saliva on the back of his wrist smelled hideous. *Like sewage. Or what Hell must smell like.* "You called them volatile sulphur compounds?"

"Home tests are now available that use a chemical reaction to test for the presence of polyamines and volatile sulphur compounds on the tongue." The dentist's eyes suddenly lit up with excitement. "But we now have a way of measuring bad breath. It's called a halimeter." He extracted a small box from one of the cupboards, ripped it out of its plastic covering. "It takes a sample of air and measures the amount of volatile sulphur compounds in parts per billion." He passed the gadget to Evan, who turned it over in his hands, inspecting it. It was just a straightforward device with a plastic tube, lacking the airbag of a police breathalyser kit. "Blow into it. It's very simple."

Evan exhaled through the plastic tube and handed it back. The dentist waited for the electronic display to give its reading. When it did, Mr. Quinlan let out an exclamatory whistle.

"A normal reading is less than 200 parts per billion," he explained. "Anything above 300 parts per billion is a problem." He hesitated before giving Evan the news. "And yours is 1000 parts per billion."

"How is that possible?" Evan said, startled by the result. More than three times the acceptable limit?

"I don't rightly know, if you say you're doing everything right," Mr. Quinlan said, confounded. "Something of a mystery. You seem to have a perfect set of gnashers, all in splendid shape. I'd even describe them as 'sparkling white'. No hidden cavities to speak of. Your X-rays are completely clear." He could not even come up with any lines for improvement regarding the man's teeth. However, he considered a suitable course of action for the severe halitosis. "What I suppose I can do is refer you to a dental microbiologist at the local hospital for investigations." He proceeded to take a swab of Evan's buccal mucosa and tongue which he placed into a tube and labelled, ready for dispatch. "In the meantime, I can only give you the advice any good dentist can. Maintain proper care of your teeth with good brushing habits and use oral mouthwash after you eat. Swill it around your mouth for at least a minute before you spit it out. Floss your teeth at least once a day in order to remove any food residue. Brush the back of your tongue, too, or our Reception staff will happily give you a tongue scraper, if you want, to remove any coating on the tongue. Drink plenty of water to keep your mouth moist. Equally, you can also chew sugar-free gum to stimulate saliva production to keep your mouth alkaline and pleasantly watery. There are plenty of foods that are good for breath. The polyphenols in apples and green tea break down odorous compounds. Vitamin C-rich fruits and vegetables like oranges, tomatoes and broccoli create an inhospitable environment for bad bacteria. Greens such as spinach, kale and lettuce normalize the alkaline levels in the mouth, preventing dry mouth. The strong oils of fresh herbs neutralize breath odour. Ginger and cinnamon and fennel have antibacterial properties and break down those odour-producing volatile sulphurous compounds. Aside from these tips, limit your sugar intake if you have a sweet tooth. Cut out dairy products from your diet, if you find pleasure in milk, cheese or yoghurt. And, need I say, please do your utmost to give up coffee, wine and cigarettes." He gave Evan the halimeter as a parting gift. "Until I get the results of your mouth swab back, please keep a record of your readings – morning, noon and night. I want to see if there is a pattern to the readings at our next appointment. I'm also guessing you may need to work closely with our dental hygienist."

With that, Mr. Quinlan shook his hand and hurried him out of his office, still wearing his mask, leaving Evan somewhat bemused by the lack of clarity to his problem, the absence of a clear solution. He never imagined things could get any worse.

III: The Gods of Halitosis

Evan did everything that was expected of him. He took great interest in his dental care. He brushed twice a day, gargled with mouthwash after meals and flossed regularly. He tried different combinations of mouth-freshening products, including dental probiotics, which his dentist neglected to mention. He chewed gum and popped sugar-free mints: peppermint, spearmint, double mint, menthol eucalyptus. He avoided tutti frutti or berry-flavoured sticks of gum since his breath would end up smelling like a field of strawberries sprayed with cow manure. He adjusted his diet, ate more fruits and greens, reduced his cheese and wine intake and quit coffee and smoking, pronto. Yet, despite his best efforts and having put all these measures in place, his breath remained atrocious. The gum was like a band-aid over his nasty, putrid breath and toothpaste a metaphorical bandage over the putrescence spilling out of his mouth.

Paréce experienced a pang of anxiety in her stomach each time she had to be in close proximity to her boyfriend, apprehensive at the level of stank his mouth might reek of that day. She resolved not to stand too close to him. Soon his malodorous presence became too much for her to bear and she refused even to share the same room as him, a difficult decision on her part. They began to eat at different sittings, sleep in separate bedrooms, an arrangement he was forced to accept. The fact that his halitosis was now harming their relationship affected his self-esteem and damaged his confidence, impacting on the quality of his existence. He took time off work when his boss took him aside and complained about how Evan seemed to stink out the conference room like an unwashed hobo; the firm would welcome him back once he'd addressed the problem. Evan began to suspect that his bad breath was a symptom of something far more serious. His concerns only grew more pronounced each time he checked his breath on the halimeter, thrice-daily as his dentist had advised. By the end of the week, the device detected a reading in excess of 3000 parts per billion.

The hygienist executed the perfect deep clean, but the figures in his breath diary did not drop. Herb Quinlan invited him back to his dental practice. When Evan went back, he stank out the entire waiting room with both the patients and Reception staff covering their mouths, protesting over his repellent breath. In the antiseptically-sterile atmosphere of the waiting room, even his own nostrils could not miss the pervasive, putrescent odour emanating from his mouth, of dead animals and clogged septic tanks, as though he were rotting from within.

"I've got both good news and bad news," Mr. Quinlan told him when he was safely in the consulting room.

Evan knew from the expression of eye-watering disgust on the dentist's face, surgical mask notwithstanding, that the problem was significantly worse than last time around. "Let's start with the good news."

"Okay, your microbiology results have come back, and they've managed to isolate the bacteria that is causing your bad breath."

Suddenly, Evan was hopeful. "Now we're getting somewhere. Tell me more."

"It seems to be an unknown strain of *Sulfolobus*."

The word 'unknown' did not sit well with him. "And?"

"*Sulfolobus* is a thermophilic bacterium."

"Which means?" Evan had a terrible feeling.

"I did a bit of research. *Sulfolobus* is normally attracted to heat and found in places rich in sulphur, like volcanoes."

Evan frowned. He had heard of bacteria that fed on metal. Somehow, he had contracted a bacterium that existed in lavamen. "I don't understand . . ."

"Neither do I," admitted Mr. Quinlan. "It doesn't make any sense. There's never been a case of it infecting a human."

Evan asked the crucial question. "How will you treat it?"

"I'm at a loss, I'm afraid. There's no definite treatment for it. That's the bad news."

Evan stared at Mr. Quinlan. He did not speak for a few moments. "So what do I do? The halimeter continues to register ever-increasing readings and I'm practically suffocating the people around me and you're telling me there's nothing you can do for me?"

Mr. Quinlan wasn't entirely bereft of options. "There is some hope. The military wing at CHERTSFORD MEMORIAL HOSPITAL has got wind of your unique predicament and thinks they might be able to help you. It's offered to investigate and treat you."

He let Evan chew on it. Evan was in two minds. On the one hand, he wanted his wholesome breath back so he could get on with his life, which up until recently had been the very picture of normalcy, while, on the other hand, he didn't fancy the idea of being a test subject for some secret military experiment, perhaps joining a bunch of other people with the same problem to create an unstoppable army of halitosis monsters. "I don't know."

"Think it over," Mr. Quinlan wrote down a name and telephone number on a slip of paper and handed it to Evan. Evan read the name: *Brigadier Letwin-Smith*. Then, Mr. Quinlan wished Evan farewell and good luck, completely washing his hands of him.

Evan's departure from the dental surgery caused the occupants of the waiting room to retch, a terribly disheartening sight. He wondered how he could have acquired the volcano-loving bug. The answer soon came to him: *the trip to Naples*. Paréce had been fortunate enough not to have caught the same disease he had caught while rambling across that particular remote tract of hillside, now an extinct volcano, because she had not sipped from the same spring he had knelt down to taste. Evan decided to give the army official a call as soon as he got home. God knows what the damned bug was doing to his body.

Walking down the high street to his car, he was appalled by the behaviour of the other pedestrians in his vicinity.

An old lady raised a handkerchief to her nose as he passed by.

"Mommy, I don't feel well . . ." a little girl out shopping with her mother complained queasily. The mother glanced down at her suffering daughter, concerned, before favouring Evan with a stern, almost vicious look and hissing at him, as though warding off demons: "Be gone with you!"

A group of teenage boys loitering outside the newsagents clambered off their bikes and, with collective moans of physical distress, spilled their guts out on the kerb.

"Man, it smells like your sister's minge when she's on her period!" one of the boys remarked, ribbing his friend. He got a slap on the back of his head by his mate for his efforts.

Further along, a middle-aged man in a business suit emerged from the post office to be struck by an invisible wall of miasma. The businessman gagged, doubled over and emptied the contents of his stomach several inches from Evan's shoes, splattering the pavement with a pool of his half-digested breakfast. He pinpointed the source of the stench. "Holy shit, that's *vile!*" he uttered in between dry heaves, pointing an accusing finger at Evan.

Evan hurried along, shaking in alarm, not comprehending how his problem breath could have become a rapidly-spreading plague.

Then, the truly unexpected happened.

Something fell to the ground from a great height. Evan realized the sky had dropped a dead pigeon at his feet, all blue-grey fur, eyes shut, wings folded, claws curled. Then, another came tumbling down. And another. More birds – pigeons and sparrows and the suchlike – rained down, people stopping in the street to take in this disturbing spectacle, unheard of except in Biblical stories or UFO lore.

Death breath, thought Evan, panicking. *I've finally got* death *breath! My breath is now so dangerous, it kills . . .*

The birds kept falling out of the sky, thudding on the pavement around him, lifeless as stone. Evan was only too relieved to get to his car. He climbed into the driver's seat and shut the door, taking a short breather. The birds continued to drop on the hood and roof of the BMW with a soft thump, and Evan was forced to put the key in the ignition and drive off. His breath immediately stank out his car, as foul as if he were hiding a rotting human corpse in the boot, so he pulled the windows down and drove on, leaving a trail of dead birds in his wake.

It now occurred to him why the military had suddenly taken a keen interest in him. Imagine them creating a weaponized germ or, more likely, using his actual, evil-smelling breath for the purposes of chemical warfare. Imagine them developing and manufacturing a concentrated, more potent version of his death breath for mass production, capable of poisoning the air over an enemy city and incapacitating its population.

He had to get home and make a couple of urgent phone calls.

He arrived at the house shortly after and stepped out of the car. Death quickly followed suit. Flocks of birds plummeted to the ground until his driveway was littered with their small, fresh corpses. The neighbour's black tom hurried away into the bushes, retching as though it was on the cusp of coughing up an enormous hairball.

Evan stumbled into the house. Fortunately, Paréce was not home but would be expected any time soon. The gods of halitosis were surely smiling up at him from whatever dark sewer they festered in. He had developed the Midas touch, so to speak, in an olfactory sense. Every living thing was at risk from him. He had to warn Paréce.

He rang his girlfriend's mobile. Paréce answered.

"What's up?" she asked casually.

"Don't come home!" he warned.

"Why not?" she said, suddenly alarmed.

"I'm *toxic*" he explained hastily. "Whatever's happening to me is accelerating at a ridiculous pace!"

"Do I need to call an ambulance?" she said, now very scared.

"No, you'll only be putting the ambulance crew in danger!"

"Then what should I do?"

"*Just stay away!*" he screamed at her and cut the call.

His putrid, noxious stench had already filled the entire house, like the awful, stomach-turning odour of multiple bodies under the floorboards – and much worse. He felt hot and sweaty, aware he was spiking a fever. In the kitchen, he poured cold water over his face. He realized the smell was no longer merely on his breath but also coming out of his pores, corrupting his sweat. He despaired.

Only one thing for it. He dialled the number written on the scrap of paper the dentist had given him.

The call was immediately answered by an army type. "Hello, who's this?"

"Evan–"

"Ah, Mr. Corbluth, thank you for ringing me on the emergency line," the man on the other end said in precise, clipped tones. "You're through to Brigadier Letwin-Smith. I've been expecting your call."

"I don't know what to do," Evan babbled. "I've acquired some kind of infection from a recent holiday in Naples. My body is exuding a fast-acting poison that contaminates the air and kills everything that comes near me . . ."

"You must be in the fulminant stage of the illness," explained Brigadier Letwin-Smith. "My advice is to stay put and I'll get a relief team across to you as soon as possible."

"Okay, I'll be waiting," Evan urged, emphasizing his moribund condition. "Please be quick. I don't know how long I have left." As the call ended, Evan made his way to the lounge and sat down in an armchair and waited. The vaseful of red roses on the mantelpiece suddenly wilted, withered and died.

IV: The Army Comes to the Rescue

The Military arrived half-an-hour later. They had been on standby. They cordoned off the house and initiated a quarantine protocol. They had been told to set up a zone of containment. They would not grant Paréce, who arrived on the scene following her wretched phone call from her boyfriend, access to her house. She could only weep behind the lines, distraught.

Army medics, dressed in Hazmat suits and carrying flamethrowers, entered the house. Their atmospheric recording equipment registered a reading that went off the scale. The gaseous spikes on the spectrometer were reminiscent of the acid skies of Venus. No living thing could possibly survive in this highly-noxious environment.

The three-man squad crept down the hallway slowly, cautiously, flamethrowers at the ready. They did not encounter any resistance.

The man they sought sat calmly on an armchair in the lounge. They knew from the moment they laid eyes on him he was dead. His skin was sickly-grey and mottled. His eyes were wide open, staring up unseeingly at the ceiling. His irises had cataracted over. Rigor mortis had set in, the muscles and joints of his body having stiffened up, locked tight. From their estimate, he had died quite some time ago which might not exactly make sense if he had spoken to the Brigadier less than an hour ago.

The dead man in the chair turned his head in their direction.

The suited medical team recoiled, took a step back, startled.

"What's . . . happening . . . to . . . me?" Evan croaked, his vocal cords frayed, speaking from beyond the grave. He got up, joints creaking audibly, opaque, sightless eyes focused on the three visitors, and began to lurch towards them. The medical unit continued to step backwards. Life had found a way to survive, unhindered by death, undeterred by an absence of any discerning signs of cognition, speech or otherwise, such was the progression of the disease. The brain stem and higher functions might be mostly gone, but Evan had retained his gross motor functions.

"We've got a live one!" the Lead Medic, Dr. Lieutenant-Corporal Sadler, radioed in to Command Central. The response came through immediately, and he passed on the orders to the other two medics in the room. "You know the drill, men . . ."

Orders were orders. As Evan approached them, moving with a clumsy, lumbering quality, arms jerking idiotically, they activated their flamethrowers. A precise, satellite-directed missile strike would have been the best option in dealing with this kind of biological threat, but unfortunately this was a built-up, residential area. His superiors could have blamed it on a terrorist explosion, but the public were less inclined these days to swallow the Military's lies. Instead, Dr. Sadler and his colleagues were forced to improvise. Evan instantly caught fire and the flames spread rapidly around the room, setting alight the curtains, carpet and wallpaper.

The Hazmat suits protected the medical unit from the intense heat and billowing smoke of the raging inferno in their midst.

But the man would not die. They continued to feed the fire, maintaining their live streams on the living corpse as he continued to shriek like a banshee, a fireball of incinerating flesh, turning round and round on himself, waving his flaming arms in a jittery, mindless death-dance.

Before the men were blinded by the thick, black smoke, Dr. Sadler pulled out his regulation revolver and fired it directly into the zombie's head, a flaming trajectory of brains spewing out from the back of the skull like oatmeal set on fire. Evan, or what had once been Evan, collapsed to the floor in a fiery heap, flesh peeling off layer by layer and cremating, until he was reduced to charred bones and ash.

"We've dispatched the shambler," Dr. Sadler affirmed into his com. "Threat eradicated." He ordered his colleagues out of the lounge, away from the blazing conflagration. They would let the fire burn itself out, contained in the one room, and if it continued to spread the arriving mop-up crew could extinguish it and clean up. "We'll bring his remains to the lab," he informed Headquarters. "Sorry we couldn't bring him in in one piece." Even if he didn't like the idea of reanimated cadavers roaming the countryside, Dr. Sadler did not intend to disappoint his superiors. "But we won't be coming back empty-handed. We may just have another shambler in the making . . ."

Outside, Dr. Sadler walked over to Paréce, whose face was awash with tears, watching the dense smoke pour out of her front door, rise up and disperse. No second guesses as to what had transpired inside the house. "*You murderers!*" she bawled at them shrilly, furiously, utterly helpless.

Her voice was nearly drowned out by the sound of rotating chopper blades. Overhead, black helicopters circled like vultures, preparing to land.

"Grab her!" Dr. Sadler commanded the nearest soldiers, who promptly seized her by the arms. They had already sent any fascinated onlookers scurrying back to their homes.

"What the hell are you doing?" screamed Paréce, struggling wildly against their rigid holds. "Let go of me! *Let me go!*"

Dr. Sadler raised his atmospheric recording device to her face. The device emitted a high-pitched, electronic squeal, the sound a Geiger counter might make in a field of high radiation. "Ma'am, you're coming with us! Unfortunately, you have little choice in the matter . . . if you want to live, that is! Didn't anyone ever tell you that you've got bad breath?"

March 2019-April 2019

Moone & Starr

"Where perception is, there also are pain and pleasure, and where these are, there, of necessity, is desire."

Aristotle

Haidee Moone discovered the letter and map when she was clearing out the attic. She had not been expecting to find anything so significant, so sentimental amongst the clutter and pieces of junk, so when she extracted the still cologne-scented letter from the envelope, she let out a start. Her mother's lover, Eldron Starr, had composed the letter to her mother some eighteen years ago, dated the same day her mother disappeared from her life.

Haidee's father, Ernest Moone, had claimed that Haidee's mother, Stella, had run off with Eldron, and Ernest had supported his only daughter during this period of loss. Ernest had divorced Stella *in absentia*, and father and daughter had quietly got on with their lives with not so much as a mention of the woman, who had betrayed her husband and abandoned her five-year-old child. Haidee had got used to having no maternal figure in her life, and growing up, her mother became a barely-remembered memory. Until presently, of course.

Haidee read the letter:

My darling Stella,

It has been nearly one year since we started seeing each other and I have treasured every moment of our time together. I do not want it to end, for my life would be incomplete without you. Words cannot describe how much you mean to me and how much I cherish every waking moment with you. I miss you horribly when I don't see you. *I crave your beautiful body when I am alone. I even dream about you when you're not around to share my bed. I know you have a young family, and it pains me greatly that we are doing this without their knowledge, tasting the forbidden fruit so to speak, but deceit becomes a necessary part of life when two people love each other, as deeply and profoundly as we do. Recently, I have been thinking long and hard about us and I think I should take our relationship to the next level. I hope you don't mind. After all, you will always be my Number One Star.*

I would like you to meet me tonight at midnight in a very special place. I've never taken you there before, but the enclosed map should guide you to me, as long as you follow its directions to the letter. There is a road, not on any normal map.

I look forward to seeing you again and showing you things you cannot possibly imagine...

Eternally Yours,
Eldron

PS: Did I ever tell you how much I love you?

Haidee went through the letter a second time, more thoroughly, and its cold, hard reality hit home. The letter was dated 23rd August 1999. The last time she saw her mother.

Old memories, long-since buried, were exhumed. A wave of emotion swept through her. She pushed back tears that threatened to spill over.

It was a lovely letter, very moving. A love letter that demonstrated the deep bond that her mother shared with this man. She had loved him enough to leave behind her young family and never to return. From the contents of the letter, the man who had stolen her mother away sounded as though he had been equally devoted to the woman he loved. Just two people madly in love. A love, unconditional, at the expense of everything else. *Good luck to them!*

Her mind dug up her mother's voice, a kind and nurturing voice, and the distant memory of her mother holding her hand at the school gates on her first day at nursery: *Don't be afraid, my little Haidee. You're my Number One Star. And, as my Number One Star, I know you'll shine. Show everyone how brightly you shine. Because you are amazing and I will always look out for you.* Haidee vaguely recalled her mother's long dark hair that day, the contrast of her freckles against her pale skin, her natural scent when her mother knelt down to kiss her daughter, along with the comforting smile affirming she'd be waiting by the school gates to gather her up in her arms at the end of the school day. The *absolute* reassurance that everything will be okay. Haidee's inaugural day at nursery had turned out fine. Yes, she had shone. Like the brightest star in the heavens, and all the other kids had looked up to her. Because her mother had inspired in her all the confidence she needed, elevating her, and promising to watch her back. *I will always look out for you. Cross my heart and hope to die.*

But this ancient history was now marred by the first stirrings of anger. It seemed her mother had borrowed from her lover in reference to her daughter *'my Number One Star'.* Its uniqueness belonged to Eldron, not her mother, and it made Haidee hate her mother even more.

I will always look out for you. Nothing more than empty words, Haidee thought dispassionately.

But humans are curious creatures, and it would have been unnatural if Haidee had not experienced an instinctive yearning to see the secret rendezvous that Eldron had spoken about in the letter. Haidee wanted to visit her mother's last known location, from where her mother had decided to desert her family. Haidee needed to know. For her own peace of mind.

Haidee unfolded the map. Eldron had plotted a route, indicated by a bold, red meandering squiggle following the geographical features of the map, ending in a decisive X-marks-the-spot. Haidee thought she knew the lay of the land and getting there looked straightforward enough.

Minutes later, she was downstairs and on her mobile, leaving a message for her father. "Dad, I found something important in the attic that I need to investigate. Back soon . . ."

She emerged from the house and got into her small, white Fiat. Dusk on a midsummer's eve. The full moon, bloodied and bloated and colossal, swallowed up most of the sky, redder than any strawberry or harvest moon, a rare, astronomical occurrence the scientists called a 'supermoon'. Far from being a perturbing sight, there was something magical and dreamlike about the phenomenon. She switched on the headlights, illuminating the woods across the lane.

Map spread open and resting on her lap, she set off.

To follow in her mother's footsteps eighteen years later.

Haidee never expected it to be easy. She thought she had achieved closure with her mother's abandonment of her family all those years ago – maybe she was too young to remember – but she realized a part of her hadn't. It was like an itch that needed to be scratched. All she knew about this man, Eldron Starr, was the occasional snippets her father had volunteered during times of quiet brooding, of moody introspection. Her father never cried which was odd. Although her father had raised her well, helped give her a well-adjusted childhood, despite a motherless upbringing, she knew he had never got over the loss of his wife. The burden of grief still sat heavy on him. Haidee remembered her father once telling her how happy he and her mother had been. He had adored his wife, loved her dearly. Even when he had discovered she had been cheating on him, it did not change the way he felt about her. It is not easy for any man to be cuckolded in such a manner, to learn that another man is sleeping with the woman you married, let alone accept the fact that the woman you love and adore has chosen to run off with her lover, leaving behind a young, vulnerable child, but he coped with the disappearance of his wife as calmly as he could. Some men turn the room of their loved one into a shrine, many turn to drink, others hang themselves. Ernest Moone put all his effort into providing for his daughter, attending to her needs without fail. Haidee was smart enough to get through University and attain a degree in Biology and obtain a subsequent teaching post in Sixth Form, but all this was accomplished with the knowledge that her father, *not* her mother, was watching her back. Sometimes he would stop and look at Haidee in a certain way, a quizzical look, almost reminiscent, and Haidee would wonder if Ernest could see his erstwhile wife in her. Like Haidee, closure eluded him, too, and the first step towards closure is forgiveness. Haidee got the sense that although her father had been quick to divorce her mother, he had forgiven Stella for what she had done to him and her daughter. The white elephant in the room was Eldron Starr.

Ernest worked as a Paralegal. According to him, Eldron had taken over the local Estate Agents in Friarsgate and Haidee's mother had gone to work for him. As the letter in Haidee's possession indicated, Eldron and Stella's affair had gone on for a good twelve months before Stella decided to dump her husband and forsake her daughter without so much as a by-your-leave. Haidee had only met the man once. She had been four years old, around about the same time her mother joined the firm. Eldron, sharp-suited and wearing sunglasses, had dropped her mother off at home around seven-ish in the evening. Both had been in good spirits, giggling and joking. On the doorstep, Eldron had introduced himself to Haidee's father, a civilized, congenial exchange. Looking back now, Haidee recalled how Ernest Moone had described his love rival's appearance: *the man's a looker.* But what Haidee remembered most was how this man, her mother's new boss, knelt down in front of Haidee and in the presence of her parents, handed her a rainbow-swirl lollipop, with the friendly words: *Mommy and Daddy tell me you've been a very good girl, and you should be rewarded. Instead of holding a party to celebrate your amazingness, I gift you with something yummy for your tummy.* Then whispering into her ear, loud enough to be overheard by her parents. *I shall wait for you . . .*

It wasn't so much what he said that she remembered but *how* he said it, with an emphasis on the word 'wait'. Like some mac-wearing pervert at the school gates. As though she had been *marked,* and the lollipop served as some dark baptismal rite. She never ate the lollipop, somehow afraid of this man, whom her mother worked for, and his words echoed down the years.

Eldron Starr sold up his business around the same time Haidee's mother disappeared. Neither was heard of again. All that remained were broken hearts and sad, disturbing memories. And, of course, a voice from the past speaking through the letter she had found in the attic, advising her to follow the map.

[*There is a road, not on any normal map.*]

Outside, it grew steadily darker, the headlights keeping track of the quiet road. The moon appeared even larger and redder, like dripping blood. *Hungrier,* almost vampiric. *Can you wish upon a supermoon?* her mind blurted out, and she considered the peculiarity of the thought.

Can you wish upon a Starr*?* This time, the weirdness latched on to a creepier notion.

[*I shall wait for you. I shall WAIT for you.*]

Even atheists believe in something, and Haidee was suddenly struck by the notion that Eldon Starr was a man who drew belief from others, convincingly, effortlessly.

He'd make a very charismatic cult leader, banging on about God and the love of Jesus.

Except God doesn't exist.

It depends on your definition of 'God'.

Haidee remembered a quote by Walt Whitman: *God is a mean-spirited, pugnacious bully bent on revenge against His children for failing to live up to His impossible standards.* Baudelaire took it one step further: *God is the only being who, in order to reign, doesn't even need to exist.*

Jesus was an alien. Indeed, the world had gone back full circle to those chariots in the sky. The meaning of existence had eluded the human race, who relied too much on the power of blind faith.

Haidee continued following the directions of the map. The farmsteads and country-dwellings dwindled away the further she went, and the landscape grew wilder and flatter, uncultivated, occasionally sprouting untamed woodland in the distance. Then, before she knew it, the single country lane disappeared completely from under her car, and she was driving over grassland, the suspension of the vehicle receiving a series of jolts from the rough terrain and potholes and increasing profusion and thickness of the strands of grass as they tried to wrap themselves around the wheel-axles. It soon felt as though Haidee was driving through dense brushland, and there was a sudden realization that she couldn't go on unless she wished to damage the car. She brought the Fiat to a halt and switched off the engine, shutting up the DJ on the radio who was speaking over the intro to *Desire Lines* by Deerhunter.

By the light of her torch, she checked the map. Yes, she was still heading in the right direction. She thought she knew this place like the back of the hand. *Why is it I've never been here before?* [*There is a road, not on any normal map.*] Perhaps, the map indicated an ancient road line. There were plenty of old, abandoned roads in these rural parts that had returned to the wilderness.

Under the watchful gaze of the enormous, blood-red moon, Haidee stepped out of the car.

I walk from here.

It wasn't long before Haidee found the journey eerie and ominous. Initially, the weeds and briers grew thicker and higher until it became heavy going. Before it had been undrivable, but now it was becoming unwalkable; she was almost wading through the vegetation as though it might be waist-high water.

But it was her long-lost mother that kept her going. Her parents had separated during early childhood when her mother had run off with another man. The map and mysterious letter, written the day her mother disappeared, presented an opportunity for the heartbroken daughter to reconnect with her estranged mother, presumed missing, on some deep, emotional level by following step-by-step directions to a former undisclosed location guided by her mother's lover. Somewhere, there was the hope of finding answers to her long-gestated questions, achieving some degree of closure. Maybe she hoped she would find out what happened to her mother, perhaps even be reunited with her one day.

However, her mind could not let go of the anger from that historic betrayal. *We are responsible for the decisions we make, the actions that shape our lives. Sometimes we succumb to our desires, dark and stupid and shameful though they might be, affecting not only ourselves but the ones around us. Mom could have made up some excuse when Eldron gave her his home phone number. She could have turned him down when he bought her the first drink. She could have declined his invitation to his house. She certainly could have refused to accept his first kiss or his goddamned tongue down her throat! Mom came home every evening to a family who knew nothing of what was going on behind their backs. Mom led a lie. I was always protected by Dad. Dad took it the hardest. Poor guy.*

Yes, this was genuine Poe territory, a fearsomely morbid place ruled by the memory of lost loved ones; that cryptic letter buried in the attic had sent Haidee on a frantic quest to find her absent mother.

Haidee was suddenly aware of the oppressiveness of her surroundings, of a stillness that seemed curiously unnatural and almost unreal. The gathering dusk had ceded to a deafeningly quiet evening. No buzz of insects or hooting of owls or the rustle of foraging creatures in the undergrowth. Midsummer's eve should be rife with wildlife, but the sprawling, desolate wilderness offered no sounds. Ahead, the woods she approached and cautiously entered, as instructed by the map, magnified the godless calm a thousandfold. Time seemed to slow down. Her torch guiding her along, Haidee noticed to her consternation that she could no longer recognize the species of the trees the deeper she walked through these woods. 'Haunted woods' was a notion that sprang to mind. The trees sloped at bizarre angles, as though consciously leaning down to look at the vulnerable woman in their midst. Their trunks took on grotesque, gnarled features, their branches twisting upwards to the heavens. Some of the trees were seriously stunted and this sickness spread, became more prevalent the further into the woods Haidee trekked. Her shoes tramped through the soft, dank moss and mulch. But it was the fallen fruit the beam of her torch singled out. Fallen fruit when it wasn't even harvest-time. Fruit that barely resembled any earthly variety. Haidee wasn't sure if these objects matting the woodland floor were apples or oranges, for they had grown to phenomenal proportions, beyond overripe. Even if they hadn't appeared grossly misshapen, rotting, bubbling horribly, oozing that miasmal mustiness of old mouldy cellars, Haidee knew that they wouldn't have been fit for human consumption, tasteless or bitter or so revolting as to instantly induce an uncontrollable fit of vomiting. But the blighted orchard was about to reveal something far worse.

Haidee's torch picked out animal life amidst the dead trunks. The vestiges of animal life. The remains were predominantly skeletal. The intact, hideously-calloused skeletons of former creatures, the size of large dogs, and a number of bones of smaller animals, all blasphemous-looking and nameless. Like with the fiendish trees and strange, decaying fruit, something had poisoned the soil, mutated and killed off the animals, something far more noxious than toxic agricultural run-offs. It was as if the air thrummed with an energy, the same vibrant energy that no life here could have withstood and survived. Spooked-out, Haidee worried for her own safety and well-being and wondered if she should turn back lest she should get a dose of something unnatural and lethal.

And all the while, between the high bare boughs of the trees clawing at the sky, the supermoon – this immense, celestial body coinciding with it being so close to the Earth, practically at its perigee, an occurrence that scientists had not predicted for this night – brooded ruddily, enhancing the eldritch atmosphere of the woodland nocturne. People had long associated the moon with lunacy and barking dogs and werewolves. True, the crime rate shot up and the A&Es were busier than normal. But what about a moon this size, at its closest to the Earth? What might people say about this supermoon? Scientists claimed it was the moon's gravitational effect on the water content of the brain, just as it affected the movements of the tides, that brought on a temporary state of madness. By the same token, this supermoon promised a madder experience, no longer the benign guardian she had initially imagined.

The latter, weird part of the journey had filled Haidee with a foreboding, a dread expectancy. The place was not good for the imagination, she thought. It was a wild, crazy place, a Lovecraftian setting. Her long, strenuous walk soon revealed a clearing, where all life perished. A blind spot where Haidee would discover an old, abandoned well, a peculiar and portentous landmark. An eye of the storm, clearly demarcated and resonating with energy, upon which the sanguine moon shone down, promising nothing less than insanity.

The map had brought her here.

'X' marks the spot.

Haidee was here. The last spot where her mother met Eldron Starr before she disappeared. Now that Haidee had found it, she did not know what to make of it. The well at the heart of this dark, secret place was bordered by dead things, crumbling, mouldering trunks and deformed animal skeletons. The air vibrated with an unquantifiable electrical charge, generating the smell of ozone. The moon, huge and heavy, threatened to fall out of the night sky under its own weight and bleed all over the earth. Even the peculiar pattern of night-stars would have mystified the more experienced stargazer.

Haidee was beginning to wonder what more she could do here, mission accomplished, when her presence activated something.

"You are ripe . . ." whispered a ghostly male voice from somewhere close-by, causing Haidee to jump and survey her surrounds for the sound.

A mist began to pour out over the rim of the well, like dry ice exposed to warm air. Within this mist existed a constellation of tiny lights, below incandescence, like a swarm of fireflies, the coordinated nature of its motion suggesting a sentience. The phosphorescence and heatless congregation of lights amassed in one spot, rose up tall, grew as bright as a five-hundred watt bulb and, following a blinding flash that caused Haidee to momentarily cover her eyes, it was dark again.

In its place was a man, dressed in a black suit and black shirt.

Haidee recognized him immediately. The same man who had taken her mother away from her and tore apart their happy family. The same man who had offered her the rainbow-swirl lolly.

He had not aged a day.

Haidee suddenly remembered how her father had described him: *The man's a looker.* No longer a child but a full-grown woman, Haidee had to agree with Ernest. Eldron Starr looked gorgeous, divine even, while others might have called him 'devilishly handsome'.

Eldron Starr ran his fingers through his dark hair. Dark eyes watched Haidee closely. He smiled. A dark smile. "Greetings."

"Hello?" Haidee said nervously.

"I knew I would see you again some day. I have waited so long for you. How you have grown . . ."

Haidee registered the amused, almost knowing way he uttered those words, as though giving her the once-over. Yes, she was a woman now, indeed well-endowed and old enough to think for herself, but no woman deserved such sexist comments. "After what you put my family through all those years ago, you're hitting on me?"

"You are *ripe*," he said boldly, lustfully, shamelessly, "*sooo* ripe . . ."

"*Stop saying that!*" Haidee reprimanded him, demanding: "Where's my mother?"

"I will tell you," promised Eldron, "but first a peace offering . . ." He brought out his hand from behind his back, and Haidee shone her torch upon what he was holding. It was a rose, a single red rose. He stepped forward and, in a single romantic flourish, handed it to her. She accepted it, marvelling at the lustrousness of the petals, the drops of glistening dew resting on them. "It's not just a rose . . ." Eldron added enigmatically.

"Not just a rose, you say?" murmured Haidee, subdued, suddenly overcome, enchanted by the sweet, tranquilizing scent of the flower. "You . . . might . . . be . . . right . . ." She closed her eyes as she entered a state of sensory narcosis, the languor of a lotus-eater.

"You'll feel love like you've never felt before . . ." he whispered into her ear.

Her passions were on fire. She felt hands caressing her, slowly and sensuously removing her clothes. She could not describe her extraordinary desire for this man. It was way beyond humanly possible.

"We will always be together . . ." Eldron pledged.

Haidee remained immersed in this intimate trance, enjoying both the apathy and her body being ravished, until another familiar male voice snapped her out of it. *"Leave my daughter alone, you sonofabitach!"*

Highly aroused, she opened her eyes, unexpectedly ripped from her reverie. She found herself laid out on a hollow log, dressed only in her underwear. The familiar figure of her father, hair thinning but curiously handsome after all these years, stood watching her with a mixture of anger and concern. Across from him, several yards away, stood Eldron Starr, sporting a wicked grin. Was this a ruse to give her hope so he could take it away again? Humiliated, Haidee quickly slipped her dress back over her shoulders and began buttoning it up, recovering her dignity. What had got into her?

The red rose wilted in her hand, drooped, withered. She dumped it on the ground, where it instantly decomposed, disintegrated, greyed, turned to ash, blew away. Haidee got up and ran into her father's arms, hugging him tightly, thanking him for coming to this terrible place with its prodigious blood moon and saving her from Eldron's powers of dark bewitchment and seduction, just in the nick of time.

"You took my wife," Ernest warned Eldron. "I won't let you take my daughter."

"I wouldn't have let him," Haidee intervened, detaching herself from her father. Except she knew it was a weak argument, recalling herself being sexually engulfed in her stagnation, at the carnal mercy of her father's nemesis, only moments earlier. Completely nonconsensual, of course, going against the grain of her favourite poem, *Madonna of the Evening Flowers.*

"Haidee, you don't know what this man – this *thing* – is capable of," Ernest warned his daughter.

"Ah, the Moone women," Eldron chuckled. "Ripe for the picking. I have become quite the family tradition!"

"No more!" shouted Ernest. "Damned if I let you!"

"You?" Eldron mocked. "How can an old fool like you possibly stop me?"

Ernest did not respond to Eldron's demeaning rhetoric. Instead, Haidee asked him: "How did you know where to find me, Dad?"

"You left a message on my mobile, remember?"

"But how did you know I'd be here?" It was at that moment that Haidee connected the dots. How could the letter have found its way into the attic? Surely her mother would have taken it with her nearly two decades ago in order to find this specific spot. *Her father.* That would explain why the letter had got to the attic, gathering dust. Her father had put it there. "You knew about the letter, the map?"

Ernest nodded.

"What happened to my mother?"

Ernest decided to disclose what he had been holding back for eighteen years. "I found out your mother was cheating on me. So I followed her to this place. She met Eldron here. I don't remember anything else. I must have passed out. I awoke to find the letter and the map on the ground, but there was no sign of your mother. I never saw her again. I kept the letter in the attic as a memento, of my last contact with her. I never thought you'd find it and come here."

Haidee confronted Eldron. "Well, mister, the question from the lady to the bastard still stands! Where the hell's my mother?"

"Do you know what it means to lose the moon while counting the stars?" Ernest Moone asked his wife, Stella. He was somehow young again and he could not believe he was back in the house the night she disappeared, as though eighteen years of his life had never happened. Maybe he had been granted a second chance to rectify matters, a miraculous opportunity to set things right.

"No," Stella responded gently. She looked beautiful as ever, adorable. Long dark hair cascaded down her neck and shoulders. Delicate pale features in contrast to her deep blue eyes. Ernest saw her in their daughter.

They were sat in the kitchen. It was approaching midnight. Haidee was long since in bed, sound asleep. He dimmed the lights until their reflections faded and the night sky became visible through the kitchen window. "What do you see up there?"

"The moon and stars," Stella observed.

"Exactly!" agreed Ernest emphatically and went on to explain. "The moon and stars symbolize two different kinds of people in your life. The moon represents the people who care about you, such as family and close friends, supporting you and helping you through tough times, through difficult crises, like the moon itself brightens up even the darkest night with moonlight. The stars are probably those people you want to be friends with, exciting but not particularly important, who look great from afar but don't truly care about you, only good enough to offer a short-term buzz, like the stars shining in the sky that cannot give you enough light in the dark. So, if you chase after people who don't value you, instead of cherishing the people who genuinely love you, then you will be left behind with nobody to care for you. *Because if you get busy counting the stars, you may get lost in the darkness without the moon.*"

"I see . . ." said Stella, averting her gaze for a moment. Then, looking back at her husband, she declared: "I do love you and Haidee . . ."

Ernest asked the obvious question, "Why'd you do it?"

"A lot of reasons," began Stella. "People cheat, not because it's about dishonouring their spouse, but because they've lost all respect for themselves. Or maybe it's just lust, plain and simple, hurrying us along the forbidden path, blinding us, making us ignorant to the future suffering of our loved ones."

"Someone said: *Trust takes years to build, seconds to break and forever to repair,*" Ernest stated, sorrowfully. "You know I never stopped trusting you even though I knew you were being unfaithful to me. You were under the influence." He thought back to recent events, his growing mistrust. It wasn't so much the changes in their intimacy and her work routine, but her suspicious phone habits that rang alarm bells and, of course, her taking to wearing a different perfume altogether, one Ernest never bought her. "True love doesn't lie, cheat, pretend, hurt or make the other person feel unwanted. It's supposed to be the cure for all ills and worries. Secrets and lies kill off relationships."

"I'm sorry . . ." Stella said quietly.

Ernest could feel his own swelling anger. "Sorry you didn't appreciate our life together? Or the fact you forgot your child?"

"Don't say that . . ." Stella said, sounding ashamed. "You know how much Haidee means to me."

"If you must choose between me and the other man, I suggest you choose the other man," Ernest told her honestly. He realized this chance at changing things, changing his own hurt, was not going well.

"You cannot imagine how much I still love you and Haidee," reiterated Stella with affection. "I want things to be the same again. Can you ever forgive me?"

Ernest was tongue-tied, unsure how he should respond.

"Forgiveness does not have to be earned," Stella said, hopeful. "There is always an element of faith involved." She moved closer to him. "I would be a fool not to learn from my mistake . . . *It will not happen again.*" And she went to kiss him on the lips.

Her promise was enough, convincing him she genuinely meant every word. It melted any animosity he might harbour towards her. She would be finishing the affair, no doubt. He returned her kiss, pressed his lips harder against hers, with all the love and desire he could muster.

"What are you doing . . .?" Stella suddenly pulled away and seemed to say. "Stop it!"

But Ernest was lost in the moment. "But you wanted us to make up," he murmured dreamily, softly kissing her neck.

"Stop it!" Stella demanded with more urgency. "Please stop it, *Dad!*"

Dad . . .? thought Ernest, puzzled and suddenly afraid, and he emerged from their passionate clinch, opened his eyes.

His worst suspicions were realized. He was not in the kitchen at home anymore (probably never was), starting to get hot and heavy with his nearest and dearest, but actually in the dark of the woods, by the mysterious well.

His grown-up daughter's expression was a mixture of fear and confusion. Their faces were inches apart. "What's got into you, Dad?"

Ernest backed off. "What happened?" he asked. Except he knew . . .

"You were talking to yourself," replied Haidee. "Then you tried to kiss me . . ."

The horror and disgust in her voice made Ernest momentarily want to kill himself for sharing an incestuous kiss with his only daughter. But his attention was drawn to Eldron Starr, who threw his head back and laughed a deep, mocking laugh. "You did this!" Ernest confronted the man.

"Of course!" admitted Eldron, wagging a finger at him. "The hilarity of the gag! Can't stay away from your own daughter! Naughty, naughty! You must be quite hard up!"

Ernest glanced back at Haidee, nodded a message of reassurance, promptly understood and readily accepted by her: *We shall speak no more of it.* Yes, he was here with the two of them and the spectres of his subconscious. Ernest understood that none of his time with his erstwhile wife had been real. The vision of Stella had been nothing more than a figment of his inner desires, designed to placate him, *torture* him. Somehow, Eldron Starr had the power to cast illusions, play with the mind, make people see things. But Ernest knew that Eldron was more than just a mere magician or illusionist. He didn't know what yet, and he suddenly didn't want to know. "Damn you!"

"No more games!" demanded Haidee. "Where's my mother? Where's Stella Moone?"

"Okay," acknowledged Eldron, "enough fooling around. I shall now reveal all." He grinned broadly at Haidee. "Your mother is right here."

"I said, *no more games!*" Haidee screamed at Eldron. Catching her breath, she added: "Stop toying with me! I'm not my own mother, stupid!"

"I didn't say you were," replied Eldron Starr, grinning obscenely. He unexpectedly pointed to Ernest Moone. "*He is.*"

The cosmic being, presently going by the name of Eldron Starr, hailed from the remotest fringes of the Universe, just within the absolute outer limits beyond which existed other realms of matter, force and energy. He crash-landed on Earth hundreds of millions of years ago, a vast, pivotal moment in the history of the planet, for it was the electrical storm of his ship's wake, as it plummeted through the atmosphere, that inadvertently generated the first amino acid and provided the necessary phosphorus, present in the cell membrane and the DNA of living organisms but rare in the Universe, soon to herald the advent of life that would eventually rise up from the primordial slime. At what point does matter become life and when does life revert back to matter? For between an atom and an amoeba lay something truly profound. His injuries were so extensive and life-threatening he was forced to hibernate in order to allow his complex biosystem to repair itself, to regenerate, slumbering through prehistory, missing the dawn of mankind and the rise and fall of ancient empires, passing through the epochs, until humans had settled in the area that would later become the village of Friarsgate. Once completely healed, he emerged from his hibernation to discover a world distinctly different and diverse from the one he had arrived on, surveying the life he had kicked-started into being and expedited into evolving into an intelligent species, albeit hugely primitive from his own kind.

A shapeshifter, Eldron Starr decided to blend in with the settlers, these lesser creatures, and it was not easy for him to take human form, comparable to a human trying to look like a cockroach. But he managed an interpretation of a human after numerous grotesque approximations, eventually perfecting the art of glamour and sustaining a more aesthetically-pleasing human appearance. His true, natural form was outside human comprehension, and for those few who unfortunately managed to gaze upon it, the closest conventional minds could get to approximating his actual shape within Earth's physical dimensions, the onlooker was driven to incurable insanity.

As a survival mechanism, Eldron Starr possessed immense psychic powers, terrorizing the human mind beyond all logic and reasoning, tampering with perception and interfering with memories, leaving a psychic imprint.

But, most of all, Eldron Starr, like every living thing, needed to feed. Walking the backroads of reality and casting his malevolence across the land with each passing generation, Eldron discovered an affinity for the fairer sex and set about seducing the women of the village. He did not feed on human flesh but devoured the sexual energy of women, particularly enjoying the delicacy of their infinitesimally small hormonal and neurochemical changes, their unique pheromones and heightened consciousness during sexual desire. He was attracted to women of reproductive age, what he called 'ripe', relishing their neural energy, their glow of sexual charge. He was able to tap into the human female at a DNA level, sending the victims into early menopause or reducing them to old hags, and in some cases completely draining them of their femininity and converting the XX chromosome to XY, the reverse of male frogs that change sex in order to reproduce during a female drought. This masculinization of women explained why there was a peculiar over-representation of men in Friarsgate and the surrounding villages.

Yet, regardless of being the catalyst to the origin of life on Earth and possessing the power of gods and drawing various mythical names through the ages – Eater of Lust, the Thief of Love and the Sex Dweller from Across the Aeons – this ancient transcendental evil, whispered in underground circles, realized upon waking he could not go back home. He was stranded on Earth, trapped within Friarsgate in fact, unable to venture outside of its boundaries. The well became his source of power and he set it up as a teleportation device to instantaneously transport objects across interstellar space to the other side of the Universe, at which point he discovered another purpose to his existence. Unable to use the transcosmic device on himself to get home, he shipped the most delicious women to his home world instead, whom his alien race kept on sex farms, bringing a whole new meaning to the term 'sex slave'. For centuries, Eldron Starr provided his fellow civilization beyond the stars and on the edge of all space and time with a plentiful and consumable supply of sexual energy. *Female energy.*

Sometimes Eldron Starr wished he could be made actual flesh, so he could walk the earth in the permanent physical form of a human being whilst maintaining a dual existence as a godlike being, because he knew there was an entire planet of women to explore. Instead, due to his 'pseudo-flesh', a projected simulacrum composed of living hard light, requiring him to be close to his power source for it to be sustained, Friarsgate became his exclusive domain, and himself a plague upon the people who lived there. His essence inhabited the well, like a genie in the lamp.

The wishing well.

Haidee Moone had made this journey with hope, even though it had occurred to her that her mother might be dead, that Eldron Starr might turn out to be an evil man, a killer . . . but she now knew he was something much, much worse. Even if the mystery of her mother's disappearance had now been solved, her fate had ultimately raised another greater, darker truth, not quite what she expected. Haidee was horrified by its implications. It was just too fucked-up to conceptualize, to comprehend.

Alarmed, shocked, 'Ernest' Moone was not thinking about the loss of his wife anymore but the loss of 'his' womanhood, 'his' transformation into a middle-aged, balding man, the transgender process occurring at the most fundamental, genetic level. Maybe Stella Moone – for that's who 'he' was – did not remember any of her life before her gender reassignment because she had her husband's memories supplanted in her head that overlaid her own, Eldron Starr personally hand-picking strands of consciousness and in the process altering her identity. But, now, it was not only her maternal estrangement from her daughter that caused the wrenching pain from deep within but the mental and physical estrangement from herself that cut her up badly and brought her to the edge of emotional collapse. Except it was the concurrent fury that kept her sanity afloat, kept her in the real world.

"Never wondered what was wrong with your old, shrunken todger, like it was cut at its root by garden shears?" Eldron Starr actively taunted, with a huge, vulgar grin. "I bet you're going to be the darling of the LGBT movement. Maybe you feel like throwing on a dress and reciting *The Vagina Monologues*? The man with the micro-penis . . . and pussy? Or should I refer to you as an 'it'? Why don't you just look down there and tell me whether you are *both* genders, like a hermaphrodite, or *asexual*, like a eunuch?"

Stella did not respond to his cruel mockery of her private parts, her sexual ambiguity, casting aspersions on what she might be categorized as, and just confronted her former lover and nemesis with the face of a man. How could she have forgotten she was once a woman? Her eyes reflected shame, except it was the underlying anger that Eldron Starr saw. He did not see any trace of fear in the woman's dark stare.

"I have offended you . . . I didn't mean to," he apologized, but one could tell by the tone of his voice he did not mean a single word. He was thoroughly enjoying himself. "Yes, let's be more transpositive instead of transphobic, shall we? Would you prefer 'gender fluid' or 'non-binary' or 'transperson'? Would you like others to use 'they' as your pronoun, like the French use the plural '*vous*' when addressing someone as a sign of respect? *Or should I stop acting like I actually give a fuck?*"

Stella could not hold herself back any longer. "Shut up, you pathetic, *pathetic* piece of shit!" she exploded.

"Touchy, touchy . . ." chuckled Eldron, greatly amused.

"You're the one stuck here, you pathetic *loser!*" Stella derided.

The humour was gone from Eldron's expression, replaced by a hateful malevolence. "Do not cross me . . ."

"There's nothing you can do to me," Stella continued to challenge him. "You've already done all you can. You are *spent!*"

"That's where you are wrong!" Eldron said darkly. "I can remove my glamour. And you can see me for what I really am."

The ominousness of the promise caused both women to shudder, but courage prevailed. Outwardly, Stella invited: "Do your worst . . ."

The boldness of her response, the sheer lack of fear, angered Eldron. He had never been talked to like this before. His countless victims had always been petrified of him, and a small number in awe. But not this. His skin glowed dimly in the moonlit night, his eyes burned like candleflames. "So be it! I shall give you exactly what you want!" Suddenly, his faint hue deepened, intensifying into a more distinct luminosity in the dark.

The illusion of human dissolved. Eldron Starr's appearance was a nightmare from Fuseli. A croggling, uncanny valley of metamorphosis culminated in his actual appearance. His true shape was terrifying. The two women beheld a huge spiderlike being, eight feet tall, as pink and hairless as a sphinx cat, a deadly claw at the end of each of its eight curved legs to strike down any prey, mouth filled with shark's teeth, multiple lantern eyes on its head. They blinked simultaneously, fully focused on mother and daughter, watchful, predatory, hungry, even though its enormous, engorged abdomen glowed weakly with a partially-digested fraction of Haidee's sexual energy, absorbed during the initial, prematurely-concluded sexual encounter between Eldron Starr and Haidee.

Madness threatened to take the two women.

Events took a rather unexpected turn. Before the abhorrent alien thing that had once assumed the shape of Eldron Starr could spring one of its muscular front legs with its lethal claw and stab the human flesh in easy reach, Stella pulled out her husband's gun from her tweed jacket pocket and discharged the entire chamber directly into the improbable creature. The gunshots sounded like naval blasts in the dead silence. Except none of the bullets struck its body, as the monster switched between corporeal and insubstantial, from the physical to the ghostly and back again, allowing each bullet to pass straight through it. The gun clicked empty. Stella gasped when she realized Eldron Starr — or the towering, noisome-pink spider-thing that he really was — remained untouched, unhurt, by her volley of rapid-fire.

But it was Haidee, who had also come armed who managed to defeat the Eater of Lust before them, using a completely different approach. The rainbow-swirl lollipop emerged from her pocket, the same rainbow-swirl lollipop that Eldron Starr had given to her on the doorstep eighteen years ago. She had kept it but never eaten it or brought it out of its shrink-wrap. And she had discovered to her astonishment that, unlike every sweet, this particular Rainbow Swirl did not liquify, turn sticky, gooey or mouldy throughout those years. Nothing short of a miracle. Except she knew it was a cursed thing. She remembered Eldron Starr's words as he knelt down on the doorstep to hand her the lollipop. *Mommy and Daddy tell me you've been a very good girl, and you should be rewarded . . . A yummy for your tummy . . .* Because, even back then, she had figured out [*I shall wait for you*] that the Rainbow Swirl represented something quite symbolic and scary: ownership. If Haidee had consumed the lolly, Eldron Starr would have owned her or at least until he was done with her. But Haidee was not going to let him claim owner's rights over her, enslave her. And in doing so, in refusing to eat the sweet treat but saving it for another day, a day that she may have unconsciously foreseen, a day like today, at this particular moment as unique as a once-in-a-lifetime event, like the perfect realignment of the planets or the singular eclipse of a supermoon or Halley's Comet flying visibly close to the Earth, she had gained some immunity from his horrible persuasiveness.

Throw it back at him, she thought, resolutely, hopefully. *Give him a taste of his own medicine!* Heart thumping madly against her ribs, her mind trying to understand the vision of the shifting, spidery abomination whilst still holding on to her sanity — the actual, physical form of Eldron Starr — she hurled the Rainbow Swirl into the Stygian mouth of the well. *How many wells do you see in a woodland without any signs of human habitation nearby, a cottage, say? This place is a teleportation point that streams your atoms and energies to another part of the Universe. The well is also the source of Eldron Starr's otherworldly power. A well into which you can drop a penny and make a wish. And the wish itself will* actually *come true!* "You have no power over us!" she invoked out aloud. "I bind you, Eldron Starr, to *nowhere!*"

The alien abomination — this insanity-inducing, monstrous bug — abruptly screeched wordlessly into the night, ear-splitting cries of fury. And, satisfyingly for Haidee, of agony. *Pain.* The unearthly stricken cacophony of sound began to gradually diminish, and the unspeakable creature began to shrink, like some fairytale ogre you can only defeat with a kiss or a spell or a *wish*, getting smaller, deflating further with each insult: six foot tall . . . five-foot-three . . . four-foot-two . . . three foot . . . one-foot-nine . . . one-foot-one . . . eight inches . . . five inches . . . two inches . . . Like Matheson's Shrinking Man but speeded-up.

Now Eldron Starr was nothing more than a tiny piece of phosphoresce, his other state, like slowly oxidized phosphorus, as his final sentience disappeared down the well.

Haidee took stock. The ritual had worked. She had outwitted Eldron Starr, the evil extraterrestrial entity, a superbeing whose spaceship had accidentally sparked off all creation on Earth by converting complex chemistry into something fundamentally alive and who managed to survive through the ages by parasitizing the neural energy of 'ripe' women during mating, sometimes changing them into men, a genderbending byproduct of the sexual feeding process. Restricted to Friarsgate, he transported the female of the human species back to his home planet as cattle. Haidee had wished him away, bound him to *Nowhere*, banished him to the dead space between universes. Haidee decided to come back to this life-stealing, reality-warping place in the daylight hours with a sledgehammer and smash up the wishing well, with its still-active transportation channel to another world, seal up its entrance for good. She hoped to make Eldron Starr's exile from the Universe a permanent thing.

Under the supermoon, filling the night sky and bleeding red, Haidee embraced her very manly-looking mother, whom she'd presumed all along to be her father. "I'm glad I found you, Mom."

"This is all new to me, too, my darling," Stella Moone replied, with a small, sad smile. "It's taken me so long to know who I really am." Memories breaking through: giving birth, holding her baby – Haidee – in her arms in the hospital bed. She knew more memories would gradually resurface as Eldron Starr's dominion over her psyche faded.

"Mom, I'll help you adjust," Haidee Moone promised her mother, whose physical permanence as a male she, too, as her daughter would need to adjust to. "Might take a while to pick up the pieces of our life together." Yes, mother and daughter would resume their life together [*There is a road, not on any normal map*] but with goalposts that had shifted considerably in their former relationship. It begged another, obvious question: if her father was in fact her mother, with her father's memories overwhelming her mother's own, her mother in a sense thinking like her father for nearly eighteen years, where was her *real* father? The thought suggested that although Haidee had got her mother back, it was her father, Ernest Moone, she should have been searching for all this time. Haidee needed to know where her father was, even if she anticipated the worst. So she could give him a decent burial.

Somewhere in the woods, not far from the two freshly-reacquainted ladies, the ground stirred and a long-decomposed hand reached up from the earth, more gleaming-white bone than grey, desiccated flesh, animated by the last residual traces of alien life, the spell broken. On the ring finger of the left hand, the decades-old corpse still wore a wedding band into which were carved the initials, *E.M.*

September 2017-October 2017

Predictable Joe

"Every parting gives a foretaste of death, every reunion a hint of the resurrection."

Arthur Schopenhauer

She christened him 'Predictable Joe'. She never said that directly to his face, mind, but only behind his back, as she did not wish to humiliate him. Joe Hickey was, after all, her husband of seven years' good standing, and Charlene wanted to avoid a bust-up. Yet she doubted Joe would be upset by the moniker she had given him, the prospect of an argument breaking out appearing highly unlikely. Nevertheless, Charlene kept his nickname to herself.

When she married Joe, fifteen years her senior, Charlene Hickey had held an idealized vision of a husband. A husband was meant to provide for his wife financially and serve as her household-running partner, be her lover and soulmate and best friend and always stay faithful to her, as well as act as her go-to-buddy, offering practical help, dispensing invaluable, if not infallible, advice and, most of all, functioning as a secure source of emotional support. Charlene had dreamed of a social life full of mutual friends and dinner parties and late-night dancing. Expectations, she soon discovered, were too great for some men to meet. True, HICKEY'S FARM had brought them financial stability, and she knew Joe would never cheat on her because of his commitment to his work schedule, but she was left greatly wanting in the department of go-to-guy since he seemed thoughtlessly unreceptive to her emotional needs, a life partner who never understood her feelings and barely fulfilled his duty in the marital bed, a perfunctory, self-gratifying pattern of 'two pumps and one squirt', let alone acknowledging her unequivocal importance in his life.

She did not sign up for this. She blamed Joe for their longstanding isolation. She sought variety from the tedium of her daily chores. She knew there was a whole world out there, beyond the boundaries of the farm.

Their opinions differed. Joe would tell her they had a wonderful marriage since he did not make many demands on his wife or expect much from her: he only relied on her to do the housework and put dinner on the table as well as provide a warm body to share his bed with, once he was done for the day working the fields. When they had first met, she had been instantly attracted to this husky, handsomely-chiselled, well-to-do gentleman farmer, and they had spoken about having children and seeing their grandchildren. But, after seven arduous [*pump-pump-squirt*] years, there were no children to raise. Charlene did not know if the absence of kids was a blessing or a curse. She tried to be positive, take it as a blessing, considering there were no little ones tying her down, keeping her here. Not even any pets. Affected by the death of their loyal sheepdog, Old Shep, lost to old age thirteen months ago, Joe had not had the heart to replace him.

Discontented with farm life, dissatisfied with her love life and disappointed he had not placed her at the centre of his social universe, Charlene yearned of selling up, moving out and living in the city – God knows they could afford it – but Joe refused to discuss the matter or even contemplate it each time she broached the idea to her husband. He reminded her of the proud ancestral tradition of passing the farm from one generation to the next. The eighty acres of land he owned, and which she was privileged to, had belonged to his family for many generations, along with the rest of his liquid estate, and willed to him by his father on the deathbed. It would be a cold day in hell before he would sell his farmland to some profiteering livestock company, who might exploit his acres for the inhumane and environmentally-destructive practice of factory farming.

Hell, no! Joe was averse to cruelty and treated his animals, even if some were eventually destined for the dinner table, with the respect they – and the preciousness of life – deserved. From four in the morning, he would get up and milk the cows, put the sheep to graze, feed the chickens and give the pigs their swill before spending the afternoon tilling the cornfields in spring, reaping them at the end of summer. He managed to carry out all his responsibilities to the farm, including gathering the harvest, all by his lonesome, like a workhorse, without the need to employ any farm hands. He got things done and hated 'slowpokes'. By the early evening he would walk into the house and sit down to dinner. Every day, the same routine, come snow, rain or shine. Hence, Charlene had named him Predictable Joe. Her own private joke.

Uncertainty can be anxiety-provoking, but too much predictability can lead to monotony, familiarity to contempt. There must be more to life than the everyday monotony of her existence, she assumed, and if he was not prepared to negotiate with her or listen to her suggestion, then she wanted out. But she knew no Court in the land would grant them a divorce. First, Joe Hickey would surely object. Secondly, she didn't have enough grounds to file for divorce. Even though Joe had no other interests except his farm, and he might choose his work over his wife most days, he never once quarrelled with her, got drunk or hit her. So, just because he had no time for her did not mean they qualified for divorce. With divorce no longer a feasible option, there was only one course of action that Charlene could think of.

That Sunday evening, at six-thirty-seven, as Joe stepped into the farmhouse and wiped his shoes on the doormat, strode over to the kitchen table and sat down, Charlene plunged a rusty, old hatchet into the back of his head.

The axe split his head open like a melon, spattering blood and exposing his squirming brain. Joe's body jigged like a puppet mindlessly in the chair for a few hideous seconds until its twitches and tremors subsided, and it went completely limp across the kitchen table, hatchet buried in the shattered skull.

A calmness descended over her, a weight lifted. Charlene suddenly felt strangely liberated. *Free.* Free to do whatever she wanted. Getting her bearings after a few minutes, she looked back at the inert figure of her husband, sprawled abysmally across the kitchen table, and wondered how she should dispose of the body. She realized she hadn't thought things through properly. Her murderous actions had not been part of some greater premeditated plan, but driven by impulse, on the spur.

The fruit cellar would have to do for now until she conceived of a more foolproof plan to get rid of him safely and devised a believable cover story to explain his absence and avoid arousing suspicion. *But, first, down to business . . .*

The gruesome, frightfully-sweaty task of removing Joe and cleaning up after him took almost two hours. Using all her strength, Charlene prised the hatchet out of his splintered head, and it came away with a sickly, bone-crunching squelch. She dragged his bleeding, lifeless corpse by the legs down the hallway until she reached the door of the fruit cellar. Turning on the single dusty lightbulb, she peered down into its dark, musty confines. With another monumental effort, she lugged her husband's dead body down the stairwell of the fruit cellar, his head bouncing off the stone steps in dreadful, wet thuds, leaving a trail of blood and gore in its wake. Suddenly, she was among the wicker baskets of potatoes and root vegetables and shelves stocked with sealed jars of fruit preserves and savoury chutneys and steel kegs of homemade beer alongside old, manual farming equipment. It is said that millions of spiders invade homes during the fall, mating season for the giant house spider, but their fat, swarming presence and the sticky abundance of cobwebs did not deter Charlene. But rats were a different matter; she knew if she caught sight of a single rat she would scream. Maintaining her composure, she dumped Joe's still-warm corpse unceremoniously on the cold stone floor and covered him up crudely in a large sheet of sack cloth. Then, she completed her back-breaking work by carefully scrubbing the blood off the floors and machine-washing her own blood-soaked clothes.

She showered, cleaned herself up and made supper. She would sleep on it. Hopefully, she would feel different in the morning, maybe conjure up a more workable plan of getting shot of her husband's body for good. And move on with her life.

Easier said than done.

That night, she dreamed.

Charlene is jolted awake by a loud commotion coming from downstairs. As she walks fearfully down the stairs to investigate, using a torch to guide her, she realizes the noise is coming from the main hallway. Somebody is banging repeatedly on the door of the root cellar.

"Let me out!" she hears Joe's highly-agitated voice from the other side of the door. "Let me out, for chrissakes! LET ME OUT!"

How can it be Joe? *she is thinking.* I killed him . . .

Joe has detected the torchlight from under the door. "Who's there? Is that you, Char?"

"It can't be you," Charlene utters, shaking her head. She's surprised he doesn't sound pissed after what she's done to him. Maybe he's got concussion or amnesia and it's just a matter of time before he dies. "Go away!"

"But it is me: Joe, your Joe!" his voice tells her through the door. "I'm lonely. It's so dark and cold down here, I could use your company."

Charlene is wondering if she should find the shotgun and finish him off. "Stay where you are. I'll be with you in a couple of seconds."

But he answers for her. Suddenly, there is menace in his voice. "I'm coming to get you, Charlene! You've been a very bad girl! Too sassy for my liking . . .!"

Charlene is suddenly scared, and she checks if the door of the fruit cellar is still locked and bolted. She realizes it is somehow neither and, before she has the chance to turn the key or push the bolt into place, the door swings open . . .

Terror seeps into Charlene's mind when she sees the dark figure step out into the hallway and her torch illuminates his face – and head, which seems to have been partially cleaved in two.

He lumbers towards her, a shambling thing, as she remains frozen, rooted to the spot. "You didn't need to do what you did, Char. We could have talked." Unblinded by the torchlight directed on his face, he moves closer, hands reaching out. A grin, grotesque and playful, crawls over his lips. "Feeling sassy, are you, Char? Feeling sassy?"–

–Charlene shrieked, suddenly awake. She was relieved to discover she was in the bedroom, alone. It was past midnight. Shafts of moonlight slanted into the room. *Just a dream. Just a dumb dream...*

She did not sleep for the rest of the night, not just afraid to dream again but thinking about what she'd done, the murder of her husband turning over in her mind like a motor. She wondered if she'd done wrong, could not quite come to accept she'd had any other choice. Joe had been a simple man with a big work ethic. A view he shared with Charlene was a man's pride was his land and his joy should be his wife. He often said that if one was prepared to work on the land, Nature gives – Nature was kind like that. Charlene had to admit he never treated her badly. Except he just didn't pay any meaningful attention to her. Her husband failed miserably on that front. She had thought about having an affair with Buck Cassidy, whom she was sweet on and whom she saw when she occasionally went into town to collect the groceries down at his FEED & SEED store, but opportunity to conduct an affair never arose without the prospect of Joe getting suspicious. Besides, everyone knew everyone in this small-town, hick community. Even the women in her quilting circle were blabbermouths, whose foolish tongues were quick to wag.

But now things were different with Joe gone. And Charlene considered widows more desirable and eligible than divorcées just because divorce was the product of the collective flaws of both parties whereas widowhood generally resulted through no fault of their own.

Who's going to know?

Bury him in one of the fields? Sink him in the brackish waters of the marshes? Dissolve his body in quicklime? Dismember him, bundle his parts into bin bags and drive his remains to some secluded spot faraway? Blame it on the gangsters who supposedly inhabited some of the farmsteads in the boondocks? She remembered one particular nasty-looking hoodlum paying them a visit almost a year ago, requesting protection money. Joe had stood his ground and the mobster had threatened to come back with his goons. The man had not returned; Joe telling the Sheriff might have had something to do with it. But perhaps now, with Joe no longer in the equation, she could approach the Mob and maybe they could take the farm off her hands quickly and easily and for a good price. It was freehold, after all.

Then, maybe stop spending time mooning over Buck. She could start afresh elsewhere, close this chapter in her life and turn the page.

In the meantime, disposal of the body took high priority as did the bare-bones' running of the farm. Even if he was a reclusive man, Joe's presence would be missed by the townsfolk. She needed to concoct an explanation for his disappearance and deal with any complications that might arise.

Before attending to only the essential duties of the farm that morning, beginning with the cows that needed a good milking, Charlene checked on the corpse in the root cellar. She thought of her dream, but, this time, in the reassuring light of day, there was no fear or squeamishness. Joe was still where she'd left him, untouched. Under the sack cloth, his body was pale and mottled and already beginning to stiffen up with rigor mortis. She decided she would get rid of the body tomorrow. To the bottom of the marshes it would go.

Having completed the crucial tasks of the day, between phone calls to realtors and livestock companies, inquiring about the potential sale of the farm, she took herself indoors and ran a long, hot bath. She had got undressed and just stepped into the water, preparing for some seriously relaxing '*me*' time, when a grinding noise somewhere outside distracted her.

Somebody was running the tractor.

Then, as if by magic, the chugging stopped.

Puzzled, and a little afraid, Charlene got up from the bath, dripping wet, and, wiping the condensation from the bathroom window, peered out into the prevailing dusk.

The red tractor stood eerily silent in a nearby field and not in the barn where she'd last seen it. Panic and a terrible dread engulfed her, an overpowering sense that she was about to witness something unexpected, something utterly inconceivable and highly disturbing. She tried to fight this ghastly foreboding, failed hopelessly.

She threw on her bathrobe and walked cautiously downstairs, barefoot, when the front door opened, and Joe Hickey entered the farmhouse and sat down to dinner.

She knew she wasn't dreaming this time.

Yet Joe sat there at the kitchen table, as large as life. Like yesterday never happened. She could not explain it.

"Where's my dinner?" Joe asked, none too pleased at the empty table.

The seconds spun out. Charlene could not speak.

"Well . . .?" Joe demanded to know.

Once the shock slowly abated and Charlene got her tongue back, she seemed more able to reply. "It'll . . . It'll be with you in two shakes of a lamb's tail."

"I always have dinner waiting on the table after a hard day's toil," Joe reminded her. "I don't ask much from you . . ."

The man sitting at the kitchen table smelled strongly of sweat and grass and fertilizer. How often had Charlene demanded he shower before sitting down to dinner? But her request always fell on deaf ears. But these were smells she was familiar with, and the man possessed the same striking physical characteristics as her dead husband, even down to the old scar on his chin. Yes, it was Joe all right. Not some undisclosed identical twin or evil double or ghost.

And therein lies the problem. Hadn't she killed him yesterday, jammed an axe into his skull?

"What's for dinner?" Joe inquired innocently.

"I'm going to rustle up some big, juicy steaks . . ." Charlene replied, going to work on two slabs of meat with a tenderizer. "You deserve a reward for all the hard work you put into the farm and for keeping me in the life I am accustomed to." *And for coming back from the dead . . . Not a lot of people can claim to do that. Joe, you'd win that award with flying colours!*

"Thank you kindly . . ."

Charlene popped the two ribeyes on the skillet and the meat began to cook and sizzle. *Surely, I didn't imagine the events of yesterday. So how can this man be sitting here, living and smelling and breathing and talking like Joe?* The whole situation was spooking her out. It was just too weird, *crazymaking.* Only one thing for it, she decided. She grabbed the meat cleaver, walked over to Joe and, in one quick, determined effort, brutally slashed his throat.

His hands came up briefly to remove the meat cleaver wedged in his throat, but it was already too late. He did not have the strength to grip the handle. His hands dropped to his sides and he fell forward onto the table in a profuse spray of carotid blood as the meat cleaver nearly decapitated him, his head lolling to one side.

Charlene watched him die. There was no sympathy or remorse on her face. She watched her husband die with an implacable, stone-cold expression. She watched the blood pool vividly across the kitchen table, drip down its sides, before she leapt into action.

The evening was a re-creation of yesterday's awful scene, a case of déjà vu.

Charlene carried out the grim, unpleasant task of dragging Joe's freshly-murdered corpse and dumping it in the root cellar, followed by cleaning up the blood in the kitchen and the hallway. Three hours it took, and by the time Charlene had finished covering up the crime, she was exhausted. She retired to bed and slept.

All done! she thought, as she thankfully drifted off into a dreamless sleep. *Joe's death this evening must be final,* absolutely *final.* Hopefully.

But it was never final. At six-thirty-seven p.m. the next day, Joe Hickey walked into the farmstead, and after the initial shock had passed, Charlene was forced to kill him again, slitting his throat, this time with a kitchen knife. She cleared up after herself.

The following day, afraid that the pattern would repeat itself, she sat at the dining table with a shotgun pointed at the front door. Sure enough, the moment Joe Hickey entered the house, she fired, blowing him away with one shot to the stomach. She got rid of his body, too.

Every evening at precisely six-thirty-seven, he would step into the farmhouse, alive and well and with no memory of the previous evening, and she would confront him and kill him off swiftly — stabbing him through the heart, smashing his skull in, putting a bullet through the forehead, even poisoning him — but the stubborn fool kept reappearing at the exact same time of six-thirty-seven.

Worse still, each violent demise took something out of her, out of her conscience, her sanity. She could not make head nor tail of what was happening to her. Was her guilt playing up, and it was all happening in her head? Or was there something truly supernatural at play?

A great silence hangs over the earth, in that hiatus of entombment, between death and resurrection, she remembered the pastor preach in Bible school when she was growing up in a house of unhappy parents, the same pastor who had repeatedly thumped home: *This life is passing, provisional, a probationary period for the next.* But what of the Resurrection? Jesus had risen from the dead and ascended to Heaven. Way before the Passion, Jesus had performed countless miracles such as raising the dead, including prompting Lazarus to rise up from the grave. *Lazarus, come forth!*

Were Joe's many deaths and subsequent resurrections a sign from God? Had God singled out her husband for hallowed greatness? Was his recurrent haunting of her a test of her faith? A punishment for her sins? *Testament of her damnation?*

For she realized now Joe would never stop, *never* die. He would always come back. She could kill him again and again and again, but he would live forever.

Even in death the man was predictable. *Good Ole Predictable Joe.*

Charlene grew more isolated, breaking contact with the outside world. Her daily input into the administration of the farm became less and less with each passing day, forgetting Joe's oft-spoken wisdom: *The farm won't look after itself.* Without feed, the animals began to starve and die. The fields were left to overrun. The farm machinery began to rust. Charlene could not sleep, could not rest . . . knowing that Joe would walk through the front door at the designated hour. She did little else, except focus her entire efforts on waiting for her husband to come home so she could slaughter him mercilessly by one means or another.

In the end it was a single, distressing long-distance phone call to her only brother, Sherman Wells, the paranoid, nonsensical jabberings of a madwoman, that alerted the authorities to her plight.

Sheriff Hildritch knocked on the door of the farmhouse. He got no response. "Mrs. Hickey, this is Sheriff Hildritch. Are you in there?"

Still no response.

He tested the door. It was unlocked.

He turned to his three deputies gathered on the steps behind him, issued instructions, a need to exercise due diligence and assess the lay of the land. "Holsters at the ready."

The men nodded, heeded his warning.

Fingers poised on his own unlatched holster, Sheriff Hildritch pushed the front door. It creaked open . . .

Encountering no resistance, he rushed in. His deputies swarmed in after him.

Their eyes grew accustomed to the brooding, midmorning light of the hallway and picked out the lone figure sitting at the dining table in the adjoining kitchen, facing them. It was Charlene Hickey and she clutched a shotgun in her hands, aimed directly at the front door, at the police officers. Music from the record player emanated at low volume in the background, *Hell Cat* by the Bellamy Brothers.

Fenton Hildritch would have reminded anyone who met him of some sheriff from a rootin'-tootin' Western. He was a tall, heavy-set man with a ten-gallon hat above his shock of grey hair, matching the colour of his bushy eyebrows and handlebar moustache. He was also a seasoned, no-nonsense law enforcement officer, earning the confidence and respect of his men. Already he knew, upon setting eyes on Charlene and the twelve-gauge, double-barrel shotgun in her grasp, that a crime had been committed, and a serious one at that. Sheriff Hildritch kept his revolver in its holster, and with a nod signalled to his men, one or two trigger-happy, to stand down. He did not wish to rock the boat, preferring to negotiate with the woman first. "Mrs. Hickey, do you know why we're here?"

Charlene glanced at him with a vacant, distant look in her eyes until she registered his question and life returned to her features. "I know . . ." she murmured.

The song reached its climax and a fraught silence descended, broken only by the faintly audible hiss of the record player.

"We're here on behalf of your brother, Sherman," Sheriff Hildritch explained. "He's been worried sick about you after you made that phone call to him last night. We thought we'd check in on you and see if we can help in some way." He took off his hat and nodded to the shotgun she was carrying. "But it's gonna be mighty difficult to talk to you with that thing pointed at us."

Charlene lowered the shotgun. "You can talk . . ."

Some of the tension eased from the room. But the police officers remained wary of any sign of danger. "Thanks for being civil with us, Mrs. Hickey," Sheriff Hildritch said, relieved the situation was de-escalating, in hand. He still needed to disarm the woman which he would do in due course, once he made her comfortable, once he gained her trust. For now, however, it might be a case of walking on eggshells as he continued to assess the situation. Negotiation was key. "Looks like you've been under a lot of strain lately. How you been holding up?"

"I can't do this anymore . . ."

It was the comment of a woman who sounded defeated, exhausted, *broken.* "Do *what* anymore, dare I ask?"

"Joe . . . he's so damned *predictable!*"

Good, he was getting to the nub. "What's Joe done?"

"All I ever wanted was to run a gift shop — selling doilies and china pigs and the suchlike — in the big city with the sale of our farm, and he wouldn't even sit down and talk it through. Refused to give it any consideration."

"A mighty fine idea you got there, if you ask me. Maybe we could convince him to see it your way."

Charlene saw right through his suggestion. "Don't humour me . . ." she said bluntly but without any express hostility.

"My apologies for not being totally upfront with you," Sheriff said, wholeheartedly, and proceeded with the utmost honesty. "It's just that it's mighty peculiar nobody's heard hide nor hair of Joe in over a month. Mind if I ask where he's been hiding? I don't want to get a warrant to search the premises. I was hoping you might be gracious enough to tell us."

Charlene did not evade the question, did not lie. "Downstairs. Root cellar . . . You

~ 104 ~

ain't gonna get much out him right now. But he'll be up for talkin' later."

Sheriff Hildritch was glad to be making headway with the woman, but there was something deeply ominous and curiously disconcerting about her last remark. The woman looked in bad shape. *Haunted* would be a better descriptive. *Tortured* even more accurate. Dark circles under her eyes betraying weeks of sleeplessness. She had also lost considerable weight since he'd last seen her almost a year ago regarding that whole Mob business; her body seemed to have wasted away through stress and worry and a lack of eating, giving her an almost emaciated frame, exacerbating her cheekbones and giving her skin a dry, sickly pallor. But it was the madness in her expression, the dull, glazed vacancy in her eyes that bespoke an emotional numbness, the product of something terrible she had either seen . . . or *done*. Call it years of police experience, but Sheriff Hildritch was convinced she had killed her husband and gone gaga in the process. Not to mention the general neglect of the farm, the sorry state of the dead, fly-infested animals on the land when driving up to the house. "Thank you, Mrs. Hickey, for cooperating with us. This won't take a moment."

He nodded to Deputy Marvin Elkins, who immediately understood the instruction. The eyes of the remaining police officers followed him down the dark shadows of the hallway, his cautious progress accompanied by the squeaking of his police-issue boots, until his silhouette and the penetrating beam from his torch disappeared down the root cellar. Eyes tracked back to Charlene Hickey, who appeared lost in her own certifiable preoccupations. A critical moment. Vigilance was called for.

It didn't take long for Deputy Elkins to get back up. As a matter of fact, he returned in a terrible hurry. "Mr. Hickey, anyone down there?" his colleagues heard him call down into the cellar. Then, with a sudden, mortified expletive, he bounded back up the cellar steps. His face was as white as a sheet and wore a wide-eyed, creeped-out look of alarm. Beads of perspiration pricked his forehead. He was quivering all over.

"What did you find, Marv?" Sheriff Hildritch addressed him directly, prepared for the worst.

It took a few moments for Deputy Elkins to regain some measure of composure, gather his thoughts and stutter out a response. "I-I s-s-seen nothing like it . . ."

"What's down there?"

Deputy Elkins told them. If Sheriff Hildritch had already thought the worst, he had not thought of the *absolute* worst, the mind-spinning worst. What came spilling out of Deputy Elkins' lips sounded garbled, irrational, unimaginable, as crazy as the confusion gripping Charlene Hickey. According to Deputy Elkins, there were rats down there gnawing on dead meat. Not just rats but spiders – lots of spiders, *huge* spiders – inviting him into their parlour. The cellar had contained baskets of mouldy produce, festooned with a dense, sticky network of cobwebs. The gagging stench had been godawful, and Deputy Elkins had just stopped short of upchucking. But his freakiest, grisliest, most unspeakable discovery was of the many bodies down there in different stages of decomposition. All with one thing in common. They were of the *same* person: *Joe Hickey*. If what Deputy Elkins said was true, it seemed Charlene Hickey had not been idle. She must have really hated her husband to kill him over and over again . . .

Before Sheriff Hildritch or the rest of his lawmen could wrap their heads around the revelation their colleague had imparted, Charlene spoke up with a voice soaked with despair, a voice reflecting her hellish experiences. "You saw it, too. I was praying it was all in my head. I can't climb out of the pit I dug anymore. He will always keep finding me . . ." She did what any desperate woman would do in these circumstances, forced to relive an ugly, monstrous action, a self-condemned pariah whose fate hung delicately in the balance, dangling at the end of her tether, a fraying thread that would inevitably snap. She followed in the footsteps of Poe's conscience-stricken characters. Without warning, she held up the loaded shotgun, put both barrels to her chin and pulled the trigger. The deafening explosion shook the foundations of the house.

The police officers watched, shocked and dismayed, unable to act, as her head was blown clean off, splattering the room in blood and bone and bits of brain and a generous smattering of shattered teeth. Her lifeless body tumbled to the floor in an undignified heap, her head a mangled, unrecognizable shell. Set loose from her grasp, the shotgun rattled to the floor beside her.

It took a brief, equally-deafening silent eternity for the police officers to take stock of the situation.

When their paralysis finally broke and reason and discipline flooded back into their minds, Sheriff Hildritch gathered his men. He glanced down at the dead body of their only homicide suspect, who had as much as confessed to killing her husband. "Shame we couldn't stop her. The woman gave us no opportunity." Back to the men, he spoke briskly, business-like, thinking back to Deputy Elkins' wild description of the multiple, mouldering corpses in the root cellar. "We've got a major crime scene on our hands. A crime scene that makes no goddamned sense at all! I need to see it to believe it! Call Dispatch and fetch Forensics down here, pronto!"

What happened next freaked out the police officers, including the normally level-headed Sheriff, and sent Deputy Elkins, already traumatized by the unnatural, corpse-laden sight of the root cellar, straight into a long period of sick leave.

Behind them the front door abruptly swung open and Charlene Hickey wandered in, oblivious to the gory presence of her own gunshot suicide on the kitchen floor and full of life and good health and physically identical in every way, right down to the tiniest freckle . . .

Joe Hickey had always wondered why one of his fields never fallowed. He could not explain why one particular field of corn, in the furthest acre of his farmland, stayed forever fertile, even during the winter months. Mystified, he walked around that specific plot, looking for a clue to its extraordinary, unlimited abundance of ripe, lush cornstalks. Like it was nurtured by some secret miracle feed, he had thought at the time. *My land must surely be blessed.* He never uncovered the source of the mystery.

However, unbeknownst to him, his very presence in the field had set off something. *Something not of this planet.*

The alien artefact had lain in the soil since it fell from the sky during a meteor shower, untold centuries ago. The remnant of an extinct, space-faring species. An ancient piece of nanotechnology that still functioned to this day. In the centuries gone by, before the first white man ever set foot on this continent, the Native Americans had looked to the night skies for answers and, in particular, the constellation of Pleiades. The native people identified this starry cluster as the abode of their ancestors as well as the home of the Star People, or *Chuhukon*, whom they believed benevolently watched over the earth and continued their visitations in human form. The tribal chiefs were immensely thankful to the Star People for each bountiful harvest and attempted to communicate with them during the sacred, peyote ceremonies. The legends of celestial beings travelling in luminous disks would form a staple of the culture and heritage of the North American people.

The highly-sophisticated, extraterrestrial hardware in the cornfield operated as a cloning device, generating living copies of any organism in physical contact with it, the creation of new life consistent only with the machine's existing DNA library. Joe Hickey had touched it without knowing it, and, with each death, the lack of a signal, caused by the absolute cessation of consciousness, had triggered off the cloning mechanism, the nanites within the artificial DNA sequencer engineering a perfectly-identical replacement, complete with the memories and complexities of his previous existence before the break in transmission. Perfectly healthy, too, not some cheap, inferior cloned copy. Charlene had probably done likewise, some while back without realizing, got her imprint on it, her genetic code stored for ectogenesis at a suitable juncture, coming into effect if the frequency of her consciousness ever flatlined. Thus, this psychically-linked failsafe protected against mass production of genetic clones. One could try and alter or scramble the prerecording as much as one liked, but the copy would only reassemble itself in exactly the same manner as the original.

If you can keep your head while everyone around you is losing theirs . . .

Whereas the world squabbled over the confounding, unearthly discovery in the cellar of the farmhouse, none the wiser, the Hickeys got on with their lives, wondering what all the fuss was about. For their innocence held a cosmic, Tree-of-Knowledge wisdom only the Dead-in-Resurrection could possibly know. Joe and Charlene Hickey would, with time and a few violent hiccups along the way, make up for their differences, revive their love for one another and live happily ever after.

Ad infinitum.

January 2018

Steeping Beauty

"Under certain circumstances there are few hours in life more agreeable than the hour dedicated to the ceremony known as afternoon tea."

The Portrait of a Lady (1880)
Henry James

Ambrose Hetherington was just stepping out of his car, having returned from a week-long business trip, when he was greeted by a hullaboo. Elspeth, his wife's best friend, ran out of the house, screaming, and hurried down the driveway towards him. She looked pale and shaken and *afraid.*

Ambrose stopped her. "Elsie, what's happened?"

"Ambrose, I'm so glad you're back . . ." she said, obviously in shock. "It's Connie."

"Connie?" Ambrose replied, catching her fear, suddenly alarmed at the mention of his wife's name. "What's happened to Connie?"

Her expression took on a distant, puzzled look. "I don't know. She's not been quite herself lately. But *today* . . ." Elspeth did not finish the sentence, losing the thread.

Ambrose became even more concerned. "Is she unwell? Do we need to call a doctor?"

"I don't think any doctor would be able to help her . . ."

"Good God, woman, what are you saying?"

"I've not seen her like this before! *I've never seen anything like this!*"

It was mid-afternoon, the sun smiling down over the upmarket town of Upper Nasebury.

"Stop speaking in riddles!" Ambrose demanded to know. "What's *wrong* with my wife? Tell me, for goodness sake!"

Elspeth stared at Ambrose, with a vague and faraway look in her eyes, trying to keep recent memories at bay. She did not wish to relive what she had witnessed. But her face slowly filled up with a courage Ambrose never thought she had. Steeling herself, determined not to break down again and give in to the madness rapping at the door of her mind, because Connie's husband was depending on her and needed to know the truth about his dear, sweet wife, Elspeth recounted her many social visits to Connie over the last few days. And what had occurred . . . all because of that *accursed* tea!

Constance Hetherington was a tea drinker — an *avid* tea drinker — and, by all accounts, quite the authority on the subject. She enjoyed talking about tea to her guests during high tea or afternoon tea. Elspeth was her most popular guest and longest and dearest friend, so the two of them would often partake of a variety of teas whilst Constance regaled her with the interesting history and bountiful health benefits of tea with amazing gusto. Constance had got into the tea habit when she was only four years old and she had never looked back. She thought she had explored every facet about tea throughout her lifetime and was only too eager to impart her remarkable knowledge of this delicious and wonderfully-refreshing drink, the most widely-consumed beverage in the world, second only to water. Over the last week, Constance had been far from disappointed that Elspeth had been her only company, whilst her husband had been away on business. She valued Elspeth's daily companionship and relished educating her over a nice, steaming cuppa. Likewise, Elspeth greatly appreciated her time with Constance, despite Constance's rather haughty manner, and, instead of being bored, sat marvelling at her friend's extraordinary know-how, riveted, spellbound. Constance had once proudly stated that if she were to ever appear on *Mastermind,* 'Tea' would be her specialist subject.

The tale of tea was as fascinating as its therapeutic effects. According to Constance, the consumption of tea spanned at least five thousand years, long even before the Ancient Egyptians built the first pyramid. Its earliest recorded history, however, dated back to the fifth century BC when some of the earliest Chinese dynasties advocated green tea for its medicinal properties. Portuguese merchants travelling back from the Orient introduced tea to Europe in the sixteenth century. Drinking tea in Britain became a novelty in the seventeenth century with even the diarist of the times, Samuel Pepys chronicling it in his journal. The British East India

Company established tea plantations in India in order to break the Chinese monopoly on tea. The popularity of tea began to grow and, towards the eighteenth century, it was a major trading commodity.

Initially promoted as an all-purpose medicinal drink and tonic, which only the elite could afford, tea grew increasingly fashionable and was soon sold as a recreational drink in the coffee houses and the first tea shops of London. As its price continued to fall and its availability soared, tea became the British national drink by the 1750s. Britons were not just drinking tea, but drinking *sweet* tea, and they increased their import of cane sugar from the West Indies. As the tea markets flourished, Britain began exporting opium from north-west British India (where modern-day Afghanistan lies), trading it for tea. By the 1840s, China suffered a spiralling drug epidemic, already experienced by the Victorians, and its government took special measures to ban opium, disastrous news for the British Empire, for whom tea now provided an important source of tax revenue. The escalating British trade deficit led to the Opium Wars.

With the Tea Act of 1773 prompting colonists to throw their tea into the Boston Harbour and culminating in a legendary British defeat in the American Revolution, and the opinion that waging another war, this time with China, might also prove costly, it was the Englishman's thirst for Chinese tea that allowed the British to come up with a cunning plan. Britain stepped up cultivation, production and commercialization of tea in India in areas such as Darjeeling, Assam and Ceylon. As Indian tea arrived at the European shores in ever-greater quantities, its price dropped even further and, by the late nineteenth century, tea had become an everyday beverage for all levels of society. Tea production contributed in part to Britain's dominant position in the world by the end of the nineteenth century.

Constance brought her teaching session up-to-date, throwing in some statistics for good measure. "Nowadays, the tea industry annually harvests over six billion pounds of tea, with there being over fifteen hundred varieties of tea — excluding herbal teas — to suit every palate. Remarkable, when one considers that all tea comes from the same plant, *Camellia sinensis*. Particularly relevant to our times is an emerging market of estate teas. These gourmet, loose-leaf teas are comparable to fine wines in many respects since they are picked from a single tea garden and, like every good wine, each harvest will vary from year to year, depending on climate, rainfall and other seasonal conditions."

When one tried to define 'Britishness', one might think of the Royal Family or Wimbledon or cricket on the village green or a game of footie or fish 'n' chips or Stonehenge or good, old British weather. But it was afternoon tea, using the finest porcelain, which the rest of the world commonly considered quintessentially English. And it was at the ROSE BLOSSOM TEA GARDEN where Ambrose originally romanced Constance some thirty years ago. This quaint, little tea-room was tucked within an elegant, eighteenth-century townhouse in Bridlington, offering traditional home comforts and a cosy atmosphere and wood-panelled walls, decorated with contemporary paintings, and serving classic cream teas consisting of scones and clotted cream and jam and a more-than-generous pot of gold leaf. She remembered discussing the ongoing conflict between the Devonshire method (cream first, jam on top) and the Cornish way (jam first, followed by cream), preferring the former. *Afternoon Tea* by the Kinks, Constance reminisced, had been playing in the background during that very first date, adding to the air of intimacy. This establishment would soon become their favourite haunt. He had been so handsome and dashing, and she had been a real head-turner, the belle of the ball. She had really got him, a well-respected gentleman, all day and all of the night. They had fallen in love with one another that day. They courted some more and married shortly after. Ambrose enjoyed his brew but didn't drink tea to the same degree as his nearest and dearest, preferring a glass of VSOP on occasion. He often referred to his tea-loving wife as his 'Steeping Beauty'. She called him 'Pumpy'. They lived for tea – and each other.

Constance had stored a library of quotes in her head; rattling them out at the most unexpected of moments always impressed Elspeth. Constance told Elspeth one from C.S. Lewis: *The return from the walk, and the arrival of tea, should be exactly coincidental, and not later than a quarter past four.* P.G. Wodehouse concurred: *The cup of tea on arrival at a country house is a thing which, as a rule, I particularly enjoy. I like the crackling logs, the shaded lights, the scent of buttered toast, the general atmosphere of leisured cosiness.* Saki pointed out the social aspect of drinking tea: *Find yourself a cup; the teapot is behind you. Now tell me about hundreds of things.* Henry Fielding agreed with this means to an end: *Love and scandal are the best sweeteners of tea.* And how did Ralph Waldo Emerson, as an American man of letters, describe the virtues and positive qualities of tea? *So of all the particulars of health and exercise, and fit nutriment, and tonics, some people will tell you there is a great deal of poetry and fine sentiment in a chest of tea.*

Both Ambrose and Constance adored the murder-mystery, their favourite authoress, Agatha Christie, a great British institution in herself as well as her famous creation, Jane Marple, the senior, nosy spinster and ultimate armchair detective, who possessed a canny knack for solving every murder by doing little else except simply gossiping to the suspects over tea. *Yes, Keep Calm and Make a Nice Cup of Tea. Indeed, Everything Stops for Tea.*

George Orwell published an article in the *London Evening Standard* in 1946, describing eleven golden rules for preparing the perfect cuppa. His essay was titled, *A Nice Cup of Tea*, the first of its kind on the subject.

"You mean the same chap who wrote about Big Brother and totalitarian animals?" Elspeth asked, surprised.

"The same fellow, indeed!" Constance replied, thrilled. "Whether he was occupied in creating the Orwellian nightmare, Mr. Orwell was also interested in the social mores of post-war Britain, barely able to govern his anger at the inequalities of the class system. Another great piece of literature he wrote was *Books vs Cigarettes* in which he expressed his shock at the idea that the average working man would rather buy cigarettes than books, when it costs less per annum to build a small library than smoke heavily. My Ambrose packed his cigarettes straight away, striving to be healthy of body and mind, and began collecting books, hence his pride and joy." Constance indicated to the tall bookcase of leatherbound hardbacks against one wall of the drawing room. Portraits of nobility as well as foxhunts hung around the red-and-white, stripey walls. A few silver ornaments and gilded photos of Ambrose and Constance in their younger days rested on the mantelpiece. Cast-iron pokers protruded from a wicker basket by the unlit hearth. The furniture around the drawing room was antique Victorian and the two ladies sat across from each other in brown, leather Chesterfield armchairs, gazing out at the view from the French doors, of the manicured gardens and the rambling woods beyond. It was late afternoon on a sunny Tuesday and time for tea. Highly-decorative porcelain cups and saucers and a steaming teapot rested on a silver tray on a low, walnut coffee table between the two women. Constance played mother.

"Eleven rules, you say?" Elspeth asked.

"Eleven '*outstanding*' rules!"

"How do they fare in your opinion?"

"Exceedingly well, Elsie. I'll tell you . . ." said Constance eagerly and jumped straight in. "Let's begin from the top. First off, Orwell claimed that Indian or Ceylonese tea was more stimulating than and superior to Chinese tea. Such a sweeping statement for starters – how's that for controversial? Yes, the tea from the last days of the Viceroy might have been more expensive than the 'economical' tea from war-ravaged China, but Orwell speaks only from personal preference, nothing more, rather than appreciating the joys all teas offer, a blend for every occasion."

"That's very savvy of you, Connie," said Elspeth, suitably impressed.

"Secondly," Constance observed, "Orwell advises that tea should be made in a teapot, particularly one made of china, although ceramic or pewter will do just as well. Silver or enamel is a big no-no. I think he's right on that count. Can you imagine how appalled he'd be if he were around today to discover that most of the population boils water in *plastic* kettles?"

"I'm sure he would be spinning in his grave."

"His third piece of advice was that the teapot should be warmed beforehand by placing it on the hob, ensuring an even warmth inside and outside. I believe he borrowed this from the ceremonial way the Vietnamese prepare their tea. Why not just simply warm the pot by swirling a small amount of boiled water in it, I say?"

"Makes sense."

"Quite . . . Fourthly, Orwell advised tea should be strong, approximately six teaspoons to a quart teapot, and a little stronger with each passing year. I would be apt to agree, provided the tea is of superior quality, otherwise it would just be bitter and undrinkable."

Elspeth nodded slowly in understanding.

"Fifth, Orwell states that one should refrain from using any muslin teabags or strainers-in-pot to 'imprison' the tea. There are merits to his claims, but I must also disagree to some degree since, for me, it deserves a wider discussion. I think it depends on the type of tea and the 'flush'. Unless you have a device that removes the tea leaves, you will certainly end up stewing your tea. One should also note that Tetley began producing their first teabags in 1940, an idea borrowed from the Americans, greatly unpopular with the general British populace, but it was only at the end of the war that the government began doling out tea rations, with teabags coming fully into mass production in 1953 as a more convenient way of making tea. As far as I'm concerned, there are many problems with teabags. A lot of commercial teabags contain tea dust called 'fannings', a byproduct of the manufacturing process and the lowest grade of tea, nothing more than tea-leaf waste and prone to going stale and mouldy very quickly. As for the paper used for making teabags? You know paper should turn to mush when placed in boiling water? Teabag paper doesn't because it's treated with epoxy resins so as to increase its resistance to soaking, or bleached with chlorine, releasing dioxins, also harmful to humans. Even the molecules of nylon teabags will begin to break down when submerged in hot water, leaching dangerous toxins, too. And in today's day-and-age of cheap tea brands, pesticides are often sprayed onto tea leaves, released when brewed, in the long term causing irreversible liver damage and infertility problems and seriously damaging your immune system, thereby promoting the growth of cancers. But all of this is purely academic, and I do not wish to rip apart teabags or cause a public panic over the nation's favourite cuppa. I strongly advise buying only organic, responsibly-farmed loose-leaf tea, free of pesticides, toxic chemicals, artificial flavourings and 'evil' GMOs. Even if you're using innovative and health conscious methods to bag tea, teabags still compress tea, and Orwell emphasized that tea leaves should be allowed to flow freely within the brewing vessel. I admit there is a certain beauty to watching the loose leaves expand, unfurl and swell as they steep in a teapot. The same rules apply to tea balls and fancy tea infusers: if the tea cannot flow freely in the steeping vessel, you are not enjoying the tea at its full potential, not extracting its full flavour. But, as I mentioned earlier, you still need something to remove the tea leaves once the tea has been steeped enough."

"Fascinating . . ." Elspeth murmured, looking fascinated.

"In his sixth point, he advises you use water that is still boiling, achieved by taking the pot to the kettle at the same time maintaining the kettle on the flame whilst you pour. To be honest, that's neither here nor there. Orwell also mentions boiling water only once, which I thoroughly agree with. Always use freshly-drawn cold water in the kettle, as the abundance of oxygen in it helps bring out the flavour of the tea. Remember, water gradually loses its oxygen with each re-boiling."

"Noted . . ."

"His seventh rule states that one should stir or shake the pot once the tea is made, allowing the leaves to settle. Self-explanatory, I think."

"Indeed."

"Eighthly, Orwell advocated the use of a breakfast cup, such as a mug, instead of flattish, dainty china teacups since, I suspect, china loses heat quickly and therefore cools faster. He must have liked his tea hot, but I think it's really down to personal taste. I use the finest bone china." Constance poured Darjeeling into both their porcelain teacups. "Ninth in his rulebook, Orwell suggested pouring the cream off the milk before pouring the milk into the tea. I may have to agree with him, as I don't particularly like the idea of tiny blobs of cream floating about in my tea."

"Yes, a quite distasteful sight."

"His tenth is probably the most controversial of all. Orwell was a tea-in-first person as it allowed one to control the amount of milk one put in rather than if one poured the milk in first, where one might not be able to exactly measure the quantity. Milk is thought to neutralize the tannins and regulate the acidity of the tea. The Tibetans and Himalayan people even drink butter tea, made with yak butter and salt. But that is beside the point. Who needs milk anyway? If Orwell knew what we know today, he would have been amazed to learn that tea, like coffee, loses all its antioxidant properties the moment you put a drop of milk into it."

"Is that so?" Elspeth asked, astounded.

"Absolutely!" affirmed Constance before moving on. ""Last of all, Orwell points out that one must not destroy the flavour of the tea by adding sugar. Otherwise, one might as well use salt and pepper. I agree. Tea should be bitter and an expression of its natural flavour."

"Gosh, that's quite the eye-opener," commended Elspeth when her friend had finished.

"Glad to have been of service," said Constance, pleased. "Personally, I only use freshly-boiled water for black tea and let it steep for less than five minutes, as opposed to green tea where, as a rule, I use water at a slightly lower temperature and a shorter steeping period." She hesitated for a moment, taking a sip from her teacup. "I suppose Orwell's essay is a reflection of his times, but I have endeavoured to do my best to update his arguments for the twenty-first century. I see eye-to-eye with him on most counts. Still, the debate rages on. But all agree that tea is the symbol and talisman of civilized man whilst conversely and equally being the respite and antidote to the ho-hum of civilization, and it should be treated with reverence and respectfully prepared. No doubt, if Mr. Orwell were alive today, I would certainly have the courage – and the audacity – to invite him round for tea and a chit-chat!"

Prime Minister William Gladstone once described tea as a 'drink-for-all-seasons': *If you are cold, tea will warm you; if you are too heated, it will cool you; if you are depressed, it will cheer you; if you are excited, it will calm you.*

"What's not to love about tea?" said Constance brightly. "The taste, the aroma, the blends, the well-documented, health-giving benefits. The tradition of drinking tea goes as far back as the early Buddhist texts and Chinese manuals on healing herbs which consistently described the tea plant as being a potent medicine for cleansing the body and purifying the spirit, promoting good health and longevity of life."

It was Wednesday and, at the designated hour, Constance had set the coffee table in the drawing room in preparation of her cherished ritual of tea for two. Elspeth, as usual, was in attendance and captivated by her hostess's inexhaustible knowledge of tea. According to Constance, the art of conversation alongside an ardent appreciation of tea separated the nobility from the lower orders.

"Picking tea leaves releases an enzyme that oxidizes the plant and makes it go darker in colour," Constance explained, once again in her element. "Heating will denature this enzyme and allow the tea leaves to keep their lighter, vital colour. Thus, what determines whether the tea will be classified as a Black, Oolong, Green or White Tea will be down to the amount they are oxidized and their heat treatment. You can therefore infer that the white and green teas are the least oxidized unlike the oolong and black teas that have ever-greater levels of oxidization. Because all varieties of tea come from the same plant, *Camellia sinensis,* they therefore have the same health benefits but in varying proportions."

Constance shifted slightly in her seat as she gestured to the tea they were drinking on this glorious, sunny afternoon. "White tea is the world's rarest tea and can only be picked for a few weeks in any given year. Authentic white tea is only grown in the Fujian province in China and tends to have the most delicate and sweetest of flavours, its subtle nuances evoking bamboo or almonds or floral bouquets. Due to its higher proportion of young bud leaves, white tea is usually very low in caffeine, making it a good choice for people who are watching their caffeine intake. Because the leaves of white tea are picked when the plant is young and they go through very little processing than green tea, white tea contains more catechins, a certain type of flavonoid, itself a polyphenol, and natural antioxidant, than green tea. Catechins give white tea and, to a lesser degree, green tea its astringent, slightly bitter taste and are also found in wine. They hinder free radicals in the body. Simply-speaking, free radicals are unstable molecules missing an electron in their outer shell so they damage living tissue by stealing an electron from healthy cells. The antioxidant properties of white tea are one hundred times more potent than even that powerhouse, Vitamins C. So one can imagine white tea improves the workings of the immune system and prevents the onset of cancer, particularly lung, colon, pancreatic, prostate, breast and skin cancers, with scientists even claiming tea can de-activate the carcinogenic constituents of cigarettes. These antioxidants preserve the skin's natural elastin and collagen, slowing down the aging process, and limit further brain cell deterioration and even rejuvenate already-damaged brain cells, reducing the risk of dementia. White tea has antiviral and antibacterial effects, shortening the duration of or altogether preventing infections. White tea lowers the likelihood of heart disease. The calcium and fluoride content of white tea helps maintain healthy teeth, gums and bones. White tea also speeds up the body's metabolic rate, aiding weight loss, and offsetting the levels and spikes of the stress hormone, cortisol, thus blocking the formation of new fat cells and minimizing the accumulation of abdominal fat."

Constance allowed Elspeth to absorb the numerous facts. When Elspeth didn't raise any questions, she continued: "Green tea has gained a lot of popularity in recent years, with many people referring to it as a 'wonder herb' and adding it to their diet.

Traditionally-steamed, fresh green tea leaf, such as sencha, once steeped, yields a yellow liquor. The Japanese generally whisk an expensive, finely-powdered, ceremonial-grade tea, called matcha, in hot water to create a frothy, bright-green beverage. Like white tea, the potent antioxidants in green tea help suppress dangerous free radicals and stop tumour formation as well as actually *kill* cancer cells. Green tea reduces cholesterol and triglyceride levels. Green tea improves blood flow around the body, by widening key arteries and lowering blood pressure and reducing the risk of clots, thereby promoting a healthy heart. Green tea regulates blood sugar and reduces the risk of developing diabetes and even slows down the progression of the disease, boosts metabolism and helps burn body fat, cleanses the body and detoxifies harmful chemicals, prevents and fights tooth decay and halitosis, combats the joint inflammation of arthritis and inhibits different viruses from causing illnesses. It has also been claimed that green tea can protect against Alzheimer's and slow down the natural age-related decline in cognitive function. The amount of caffeine in green tea is higher than white tea, and caffeine is well-known for relieving tiredness and increasing wakefulness. Theanine, an amino acid found in high grades of tea, not only increases memory, focus and concentration, it acts as a mild relaxant and mood enhancer, helping counteract the nervousness and jitteriness seen with caffeine-only drinks. Thus, people who drink tea will describe a 'calm alertness'."

Again, Constance waited for Elspeth to digest the information and allowed a moment's pause for questions. None were forthcoming, Elspeth seemingly satisfied with all she had heard so far. So Constance resumed, "Oolong, meaning 'Black Dragon', is a semi-oxidized, semi-fermented tea from China and Taiwan, a hybrid of green and black teas. Examples of the finest oolongs include Formosa Oolong and the Iron Goddess of Mercy. As oolong teas have higher oxidation levels than green tea, they also have lower catechin levels. However, although catechins decrease with oxidation, theaflavin and thearubigin levels increase. Some scientists state that oolongs have the best of both worlds, studies suggesting that whereas catechins (antioxidants found in green tea) are especially suited for cancer prevention, immune system function and slowing down the aging process, theaflavins and thearubigins (antioxidants found in black tea) may prevent heart disease and have other positive effects on the cardiovascular system. So these polyphenols in oolongs help defend the body against stroke, dementia, heart disease and cancer. They reduce clot formation and cut down on bad LDL cholesterol. More than just a fat burner, oolongs contain niacin which detoxifies the body. With higher fluoride levels than green tea, oolongs prevent dental cavities from forming. The theophylline contained within tea, absent in coffee, improves respiratory function and is even synthesized by pharmaceutical companies as oral capsules to treat severe cases of asthma. Oolong teas are also famous for aiding digestion and maintaining gastrointestinal health."

Constance paused again. But Elspeth looked content. "Most people are familiar with the celebrated Indian black teas, Assam or Ceylon," Constance enlightened her, "or Darjeeling, the latter sometimes referred to as the 'champagne of teas', each known for its signature flavour. However, there is a long tradition for tea companies to rely on the skills of tea blenders to create new blends, like types of strong breakfast teas or more delicate afternoon teas, imbuing the tea with a certain characteristic. The tea leaves of Lapsang souchang, for example, are actually smoked over burning pinewood to infuse the tea with a deep, dark, smoky character. Although Indian Masala Chai is spiced whilst Earl Grey contains bergamot oil, both utilize a black tea as a base. Black tea leaves are fully oxidized. For those looking for a real caffeine fix and an efficient energy boost, black tea is an excellent choice. Black tea does, however, contain low levels of catechins, but simultaneously has the highest levels of the flavonoids, theaflavins and thearubigins. Research shows these compounds are just as effective as the catechins in green tea at lowering cholesterol and protecting blood vessels from inflammation and operating as a blood thinner like aspirin, thereby preventing heart disease and strokes, as well as scavenging free radicals to reduce oxidative stress and cellular damage and cancers and the formation of wrinkles and the physical signs of aging."

Constance raced down the final straight, with the last of the traditional teas. "Pu'erh teas produce a dark, hearty brew that tastes earthy and mellow but lack much of the astringency of other types of teas. It is said that the pu'erh teas improve with age. There are many famous vintages, but the true pu'erhs from the mountainous tea farms in the Yunnan province are considered the most prized. Japanese houjicha is another, popular choice. Pu-erh teas are naturally low in caffeine but contain high amounts of flavonoids, lowering cholesterol and blood pressure. A useful probiotic and able to aid the digestion process by inhibiting the absorption of cholesterol from the gut, it is best to drink pu'erh tea after a particularly heavy or greasy meal. Because pu'erh tea literally shrinks fat cells and lowers triglycerides in the blood, causing weight loss, it is now included in many slimming tea formulas because of its effect on body metabolism." Constance summed things up. "So that's tea for you. Variations on a theme, subtleties of its subtypes and health-promoting effects. I hope I have shone a positive light on this ancient brew. Any wiser?"

"I certainly am, Connie," Elspeth replied, happy with the day's learning. "Most educational and entertaining. Who would have thought tea is capable of so much? All those antioxidants . . . Connie, you must be the healthiest person in the world! The *antioxidized* lady!"

"Tea means everything to me," Constance emphasized. "I drink it religiously. For me, there is no cheaper or simpler pleasure than tea. It is the elixir of wakeful tranquility, of clarity of thought, a liquid wisdom that stimulates heart-to-heart conviviality. Its benign, consciousness-altering nature has even aided meditating Tibetan monks in their quest for nirvana."

"*Great love affairs start with champagne and end with tisane,*" Constance reminded Elspeth of Honoré de Balzac's immortal words. It was late Thursday afternoon and amidst another round of tea and crumpets and stimulating conversations about tea, the two of them sat together conservatively in a rich man's paradise. "Herbal teas take their name from all manner of well-steeped infusions of leaves, roots, flowers, fruits, seeds or bark derived from a plant other than the traditional tea plant. The French use the term 'tisane' to prevent any confusion with true tea. They may not have the superpowers of the *Camellia sinensis* plant, but herbal teas offer their own coloured liquors and enticing flavours and subtle aromas and, since ancient times, they have been revered for their extraordinary therapeutic properties or, as some call, 'healing powers'. Most herbalists will tell you one is likely to get more all-round benefits from an organic herbal tea than from any vitamin pill. Hydration for a start, and the fact they are rich in vitamins and minerals, and for being one-hundred-percent caffeine-free, of course. So if you drink herbal tea every day, you should experience significant improvements in your mood, your skin and your overall sense of well-being. And, a word of advice: always steep the herbal tea in a covered vessel to contain their health-giving essential oils. Each of these botanical herbs has a virtue of its own which I will now spell out as succinctly as possible. Yes, and please keep up if you can. You'll need a brew by the time I finish telling you all this!"

Seated in their usual spot, Constance made herself comfortable and cleared her throat before once again demonstrating her ongoing obsession with tea. "The bergamot in Earl Grey tea is by itself well-known for lowering cholesterol, almost as effectively as statins, as well as supposedly improving the thickness of one's hair – Captain Jean-Luc Picard of the Starship Enterprise swears by it!" Constance chuckled at her own witticism, a stab at a joke – humour was always a good way to liven up any presentation, she thought – shame she didn't have an overhead projector and slides – with Elspeth joining in her laughter, before resuming: "Almost unique to the Cederberg Mountains, just north of Cape Town in South Africa, the rooibos shrub makes a most refreshing tea called 'Redbush'. High in antioxidants, a steep of rooibos strengthens the body's immune system and stunts the growth of cancer cells, lessens the risk of heart disease and wards off any signs of aging. In fact, it has the most anti-aging properties of any plant on earth and can even reduce sun damage to the skin and treat allergic skin reactions, such as rashes and eczema. With no caffeine to boot, it removes anxiety and stress and affords a peaceful night's sleep. Equally, a strong infusion of chamomile flowers calms the troubled mind and helps the person relax, combating insomnia, and, when taken after a meal, soothes the stomach, making it an excellent digestive aid. Not only improving skin quality with its cleansing and moisturizing properties, regularly drinking chamomile tea has now also been scientifically proven to reduce insulin resistance and can even keep existing diabetes in check. In the days of old, it used to be referred to as the 'plant doctor' because of its multiple curative properties. Lavender tea has been used for generations as a natural remedy to promote relaxation and induce sleep and soothe the digestive system and any respiratory difficulties. Verveine tea, another French favourite, is a mood enhancer and stress reliever, a digestive tonic and an anti-inflammatory as well as an alternative remedy for painful menstrual periods and herbal agent for stimulating lactation in breast-feeding mothers. Valerian, apart from its notorious cat's-pee scent, relaxes mind and body so effectively it is a common ingredient of most sleepy teas, alongside chamomile, lavender and verveine. Rosehips is the fruit of the rose plant and its tea provides an excellent source of Vitamin C, important for the immune system in fighting and preventing respiratory infections as well as its role in maintaining good adrenal health, regulating the stress hormones. Dried hibiscus flowers can be made into a tea that can lower blood pressure, reduce high cholesterol levels and strengthen the immune system by providing a healthy dose of Vitamin C and its other antioxidant properties. Nettle tea, despite being made from the leaves of the stinging nettle, offers a homely remedy for an assortment of ailments such as anaemia, reducing rheumatism, managing coughs and colds and congestion and treating urinary tract infections. When consumed, a tea of dandelion and milk thistle is a detoxifier of the liver, almost as powerful as lemon. Ginger tea's immune-boosting properties make it an effective weapon against almost every type of bacterial infection, and by adding honey and lemon, one has the ultimate germ-fighting cocktail, capable of warding off every chill; ginger can also relieve an upset stomach and its anti-inflammatory properties have been proven to benefit arthritis sufferers. Peppermint tea relaxes the muscles of the intestinal tract, relieving the spasms of an irritable bowel, thereby reducing abdominal gas and bloating and colic, and the indigestion and heartburn of gallstones, although one should be aware that it can also reduce the libido if drunk in large quantities – not a bad thing sometimes!" Constance hesitated, averting her gaze for a moment. Elspeth didn't ask. "Cardamom tea helps relieve nausea, treats indigestion and reduces flatulence as well as proving to be an excellent expectorant for colds and a stabilizer of mood swings in premenstrual tension. A cup of ginseng, like the jasmine flower, is an aphrodisiac, increasing fertility, and an energizer, rapidly easing tiredness and perking you right up; ginseng is reported to give the regular drinker a 'glow'."

"Oh, my giddy aunt!" responded Elspeth breathlessly, the perfect audience. "You learn something new every day!" Constance had confidently stamped her seal of approval on the tisanes. "That's quite the list! You are a regular encyclopaedia!"

"Oh, I try . . ." Constance joked, feigning modesty at the compliment. "Everything you wanted to know about tea . . . and more."

"So many teas to choose from."

"Decisions . . . decisions . . ."

"Beneficial in so many different ways."

"Remarkable, isn't it, what they can do?"

"You should have opened a tea shop," Elspeth suggested.

"Yes, I've wondered about that, too," Constance said, mystified. "Why I never wrote a book about tea, either, I'll never know!" Then, more proudly: "They used to say I threw tea parties worthy of the Mad Hatter himself. Gallons of tea and endlessly long."

The two ladies laughed.

"Yes, once upon a time . . ." Constance reminisced, a little sad, "before I withdrew from social circles and community events. Sometimes I grow restless, yearning for the old days."

"You can always resurrect those classic tea parties of yours, I suppose."

"Maybe I can. Food for thought." Constance shifted to a slightly more serious note. "There's one more herbal tea that I think you should be privy to. A package arrived today by international airmail from Argentina. Ambrose kindly bought me a surprise gift from where he would be on business this week."

"How thoughtful and *romantic* of him!"

"I suspect it is yerba maté." Pronounced *erba mah-teh*. "All the way from the rainforests of South America."

"Quite extraordinary! Yerba maté? Never heard of it, I'm afraid."

"No worry. That's why you have the luxury of sitting with me. I can always fill you in. Betterment, I call it," Constance explained, illuminating her friend. "As for maté, it is a traditional brew of the dried leaves of the evergreen holly, *Ilex paraguariensis*. The custom of the indigenous population is to drink it through a straw called a bombilla in a hollowed-out gourd filled with maté leaves, steeped in hot water, and shared between a circle of people, passed around from person to person, like the ayahuasca brews are shared amongst shamans. Maté is actually more popular than coffee in South America, outnumbering it by ten-to-one. Not surprising since, remarkably for a herbal tea, maté has a higher antioxidant content than tea, more energy-boosting ability than coffee and a greater, 'feel-good' euphoric effect than chocolate. Although maté contains a stimulant similar to caffeine, conveniently called 'mateine', it has a natural ability to energize whilst bypassing those jitters associated with coffee."

"What's it like?"

"They say it has a strong, earthy flavour."

"You haven't tried it yet?"

"Afraid not," Constance said, and a moment's sadness tinged her expression. She told Elspeth, rather confidentially, that despite her decades-long experience of tea and vast expertise on the subject, strange though it might sound, she'd never tried yerba maté. "Don't let it get around." She suddenly brightened up. "But I plan to do so on the morrow as a pick-me-up. Care to join me?"

Elspeth sounded dubious. "If you don't mind, Connie, I think I'll give it a miss for now, thanks."

"Of course not, Elsie. I can completely understand your reluctance, trying something so exotic, so *foreign*."

"Please let me know how it goes."

"Indeed, I shall . . . in case you change your mind and wish to be a little adventurous. You know the South Americans call it the 'Drink of the Gods'," Constance added proudly and somewhat dramatically.

But, little did they know, the exact plantation in South America where this particular crop of tea had been harvested had been the site of a meteorite crash only six months earlier.

"It was that accursed tea!" Elspeth repeated in the driveway, adamantly. "A bad batch of tea. I know it was!"

"How so?" responded Ambrose, trying to remain calm.

"That Friday afternoon when I went round to partake of our usual custom," Elspeth recalled, "I could tell things weren't quite right with her. Connie was more animated than usual, talking a hundred words a minute, the effect you get if you drink too many cups of coffee in a short space. She admitted she'd drunk the new brew you'd ordered from South America and described elation. It made me think she might have taken something more than just the maté plant, that maybe one of those drug cartels we always hear about had put something else in. And the way she was drinking the tea, not sipping it elegantly like she normally does, savouring the flavour, but drinking it with thick, ugly slurping noises, without any social etiquette, as though she were using her tongue to stir and suck up soup. That wasn't all. There was something wrong with her skin, too. *Her complexion.*"

Ambrose was getting the creeps. "What do you mean?"

"Tea has done wonders for her skin and her general well-being, kept her looking ten years younger. No silicon or botox or nips and tucks like old wine-swilling and chain-smoking Maude Fenwick down the road. But, on Friday, Connie's skin was darker, drier, *rougher*, like she'd just returned from holidaying in the sun with a desert tan and not taken any moisturizer with her. Her lips, too, were chapped, dry, untended-to, and it worried me she had barely taken notice of her physical appearance when she has always been such an elegant and fastidious lady, full of poise, dignity and grace. Statuesque in her beauty. But that wasn't the worst part…

"If I thought her agitation, loquaciousness, manic mood, dark, coarse skin and godawful, greedy sucking noises were bad enough, she would not show me her arm, her *left* arm. The right hand she would use to deliver the tea to her lips, but she kept her left arm hidden beneath her shawl. It was during the course of the afternoon that she inadvertently and forgetfully *snaked* out her arm from underneath the shawl — or something *like* an arm. Except what emerged didn't look much like an arm, and at the end of it wasn't a hand at all! The flesh was brown and irregular and grainy, and the hand was curled into a claw, with just too many fingers that *weren't* fingers, things that would not look out of place on a scarecrow. Then, Connie must have realized what she'd done and hid her arm again, playing it down, acting as if nothing happened, acting as though I hadn't seen anything out of the ordinary. But I wasn't listening. I was panicking. I quickly gave my apologies and left." Elpseth's distress was alarmingly evident, but she persevered as best she could to complete her retelling. "I avoided her on Saturday. She kept ringing me. She just poured verbal diarrhoea down the phone, as though she were high on maté laced with Bolivian marching powder. Her conversation did not make a shred of sense, like the talk of basket-weavers in an asylum. I stopped picking up the phone after a while, dreading each time it rang. I didn't know what to do!

"But today, I felt terrible. I think *guilty*. For not being there for my friend. Abandoning her when she needed me most. So I decided to pluck up some courage and pop round, see how she is, see if she needed anything." Elspeth's voice was rising again, growing high and hysterical. "People don't want to believe in the strange things that happen in this life. There're things in the darkest corners of the world that would drive a man insane. What I saw in those two seconds when I entered the house will last me a lifetime . . ." Elspeth's eyes were as huge as saucers, as she tried desperately to bring her panic under control, avoid reliving whatever horror she had just witnessed. "And poor old Mildred Moss, your housekeeper," she murmured. "I hadn't seen her since Friday . . . It was the tea, you see, the damned tea!"

"How can you be sure? My wife has a remarkable reputation for eccentricity."

But Ambrose knew from Elspeth's detailed and increasingly disturbing narrative that his own argument sounded flimsy without checking in to see how his wife was doing. Elspeth did not respond. She did not wish to talk any further, and Ambrose respected her wishes. She needed a breather, a chance to recover her faculties. "You wait here," he said, poised to go in. "If I'm not back in ten minutes, call the police."

But Elspeth grabbed him, held him back, implored him: "Don't go in there if you know what's good for you! *Please!*"

"I have to! If my wife's hurt, I have to help her!" He pulled away from Elspeth and her warning and headed towards the open front door of his house, not knowing what to expect.

It was that time of day again. Just in time for afternoon tea on the lawn. Perfect conditions on a bright, glorious Sunday afternoon. The sun beat down from a blue, cloudless sky, but the country house looked curiously shadowy and forbidding as though shunning the fine weather in its midst, refusing to admit the warm rays of sunshine through its dark, seemingly-impenetrable windows. Ambrose Hetherington was acutely aware of his own footsteps as he approached the front door and got the unsettling sense he was walking into a haunted house.

Regardless of the deepest apprehension and dread stirring his guts, warning him that he might be a walking into danger, his mind was focused on getting to his beloved wife. *Stiff upper lip, old chap. Let's see what shape my Connie's in . . .*

Making it through the oak doors, Ambrose's nostrils picked up a dry, subtle fragrance that lingered in the air, of dead flowers compressed in a photo album. Underlying this pleasant scent was the faint smell of something having crawled under the floorboards and died.

Ambrose moved slowly, cautiously, growing more conscious of the clack of his shoes on the parquet floor. The house radiated an unnatural chill, inconsistent with the summer weather. *So far nothing odd to report, Colonel, all quiet on the Western Front.* Past the lobby Ambrose negotiated the main hallway, from where he took the first door on the right.

Initially, he took a step backwards. His expression became strained with a sudden, dawning realization accompanied by a dumb, unbelieving terror. His throat tightened, his heart constricted. Elspeth had said it was the tea. In that moment, Ambrose vaguely recalled reading a crazy newspaper article, months back, about the impact a meteor shower had made on a specific, now-suddenly familiar region of Argentina. It was wildly rumoured that every living thing in the meteorite crash-site had suffered, the vegetation growing obscenely large and tasting revolting, the cattle on the pampas deformed into grotesque shapes and driven mad, the peasants cultivating the tea plantation developing abnormal growths and way-too-many appendages, changing somehow, producing stillbirths with bizarre congenital defects. Ambrose hadn't thought any more of it until now. For confronting him was the first-hand evidence.

Worse than just a bad crop, the tea had probably been contaminated by an interstellar mutagen that had transformed his wife into an abomination that moved and respired and lived. From Elspeth's account, the disease had possessed a short incubation period, and Connie's cells had divided at an accelerated, exponential rate, creating a lifeform barely resembling anything human. Connie had become a thing of horror, a meteorite-infected human plant, growing like poison ivy, rapidly spreading across most of the walls and the ceiling of the drawing room, a monstrous alien thing with a multitude of slithering, crawling limbs, composed of gnarled bark, branching out in a fractal-growth pattern and sprouting leaves and shoots and buds and runners, boughs that poked out of the windows and phototropically reached for the bright sunlight beyond the French doors. Yet, she was a prisoner in her own hybridized flesh. Ambrose could still see Connie in all of this. Somewhere in there was his wife.

"Connie, dearest, it's Pumpy," he announced gently, keeping his voice in check.

Her face, more bark than skin, knotted atop the main trunk and barely-recognizable torso, turned to look down from the corner of the ceiling, pinpoint the source of sound. The rest of her metamorphosed body, comprising green foliage with its leafy tributary of veins, overran the drawing room. Eyes rolled about in their sockets until they came to rest on him, peering down at him from the very rim of the Universe, green-irised, glittering like emeralds and brimming with an upperworldly intelligence, probably the most alien feature of all.

"Pumpy, is that you?" Her voice wasn't human at all. It was low and raspy, like two sticks of dried wood rubbed together.

Ambrose was beside himself. "Connie, what's happened to you?"

"Nothing I didn't wish for."

It wasn't the response Ambrose expected. He prodded her further. "How are you holding up, dearest?"

"Getting the hang of my new figure," the enormous crawling, spreading plant-like organism whispered, like dry kindling.

Her viridescent eyes shifted to the bookcase – Ambrose's small library – and, for the first time, he discovered what had become of their visiting housekeeper. It was also where the uglier, ranker odour in the house originated from, polluting the pervading gentler, sweeter floral scent.

Mildred Moss, in their service for twelve years, was cocooned in a web-like trellis of stem-like appendages, her body all swollen up and ghastly pale, one particular sucker shoved into her mouth and down her throat, feeding off her, pumping nutrients into the mother plant. Her eyes opened briefly and unseeingly, causing Ambrose to start. Then, Mildred's eyes closed again, as though she were merely in the midst of a troubled dream. Ambrose could not believe she was not dead but forced to endure this unspeakable torture, as his wife consumed their housekeeper's body from within. He had to rip his eyes away from the moribund form of Mildred ensnarled within a crisscrossing entanglement of squirming, rustling branches, a tendril invading her mouth and slowly sucking the life out of her, reducing her to living decay. He pleaded with the absurd plant-thing that was once his wife. "Why. . .?"

"*Soooo hungry* . . ." she whispered, as though this was justification enough. Then, almost unexpectedly, as though registering the sickened tone of his voice, she asked with emotion: "Don't you love me anymore?"

The apprehension within this searching question, communicating a genuine fear of loss and a confirmation of unaltered affections, humanlike, *wife-like*, stumbled him. Should he be disgusted by her? It wasn't her fault she was what she was. Wiser still was the decision not to seek medical attention. What on earth could the doctors do for her? *If you think I deliberately ordered the maté from South America to get rid of my wife, then you're gravely mistaken. I love my wife. I cannot afford to lose her.* Even if she had turned into something from a Lovecraftian or Quatermass nightmare, she was still the same adorable woman he married, *his* Connie, his Steeping Beauty. *Mad about tea.* She had become the thing she had loved most, fittingly enough mutating into a human tea-plant. Ambrose decided he should let her bloom and bourgeon, *evolve*, even if it meant her terraforming the entire planet, because his life and Mother Earth belonged to her now. Ambrose knew it wasn't rational, but he utterly adored her, fondly remembering all those romantic trysts to all those tea-rooms in the country over all those decades, every single visit logged in his mind and vividly recalled, but never once neglecting their favourite, most sacred place of all, not far from here, the Rose Blossom Tea Garden — their first date.

A single tear trickled down his cheek. A peculiar sort of compassionate smile touched his lips. He hoped it would not leave an intensely bitter taste in his mouth. He plucked a few tea leaves from the tip of one of the roving branches and asked his dearest wife: "Care for a spot of tea?"

August 2017–September 2017

An Audience with Jane

"Think only of the past as its remembrance gives you pleasure."

Pride and Prejudice (1813)

Jane Austen

I

The bronze memorial plaque mounted at the front door read: JANE AUSTEN LIVED HERE FROM 1809-1817 AND HENCE ALL HER WORKS WERE SENT INTO THE WORLD. HER ADMIRERS IN THIS COUNTRY AND IN AMERICA HAVE UNITED TO ERECT THIS TABLET. SUCH ART AS HERS CAN NEVER GROW OLD.

Emily Hesketh and her boyfriend, Tobias Hardwick, lingered silently and [one half] respectfully on the threshold of JANE AUSTEN'S HOUSE MUSEUM, preparing to enter the residence where the fabled authoress had lived out the last eight years of her life. The air was warm and filled with a soft breeze and the twittering of birdsong, a fine day in early April. Across the street was the sixteenth-century THE GREYFRIAR pub, serving real ales, a doorstep away from some nice, old-fashioned tea-rooms.

It never ceased to amaze Emily how Jane Austen had earned less than eight hundred pounds for all her works combined during her lifetime, not exactly a fortune in those days, but all six novels had been in continuous print since October 1833. It was only after her death that her efforts would be truly vindicated. Jane Austen would join the pantheon of great literary figures, her books gaining historical significance among scholars and critics alike, rife for academic study and now taught in classrooms the world over. Her extraordinary insights into the social customs and mores of the landed gentry during the Georgian Regency turned her into a force to be reckoned with, told with powerful realism, genuine wit and bitter irony, and much imitated by generations of writers since. And her words were laid down with the polished English of a different era; they didn't even have typewriters in those days, just printing presses.

Indeed, Emily was, like so many others, an absolute admirer of Jane Austen and even held a weekly book club in her Upper Nasebury apartment over cheese and wine, relishing the opportunity to be lost in Austen, so to speak, with like minds. Austen was, to so many people, the perfect antidote to the hustle-and-bustle of modern living. Austen had gained popularity – and *respect* – as a feminist writer of subversive fiction, disguised as romance, in a male-dominated society, a period when women held a subservient role to their male counterparts, wholly dependent on marriage to secure social standing and financial security, many choosing to marry for money rather than marrying for love, and many historians cite the origins of the struggle for the equality and the independence of women began with this remarkable woman, this spokesperson and figurehead, bringing the plight of impoverished and disenfranchised women to the public conscience.

Whereas Emily was a true, dedicated Janeite, practising the act of Austenolatry, Tobias was . . . not so much. Jane Austen was not one of Tobias's favourite people. He had no sympathy for the woman. Her comedy of manners – and errors – did not appeal to him. She was, in his uncharitable opinion, the first chick-lit writer; look no further than the insufferable Bridget Jones, who obviously took a cue from Austen, including creating her own Darcy, and one could not understate the well-written bilge Austen had inflicted on the world. Whereas Emily had declared *Pride and Prejudice* a great read, her preference was *Emma*. Tobias, by comparison, preferred the dark, gothic beauty of the Brontë sisters: the crimes of the heart, the tyranny and betrayals and scheming, the moral ambiguity of the characters, the danger, mystery and intrigue, the madness and the supernatural visitations. He could vaguely accept *Northanger Abbey*, Austen's attempt at the Gothic novel, including Cathy Morland's horrid imaginings mistaking life as the same as fiction, even if it shamelessly doubled as satire. *Northanger Abbey* was apparently the first book Austen wrote and the last that got published shortly after her death. Even her unfinished work, *Sanditon*, completed by a continuation writer and published posthumously, was considered a classic, according to Emily. Tobias, however, totally agreed with Mark Twain's sentiment; Twain had hated Austen's work with a passion, claiming that an ideal library was one that didn't contain a single volume of Jane Austen. Even if it contained no other books!

"I'm bumnumbingly bored," Tobias grumbled, presently, disinterested as ever.

"Already?" Emily chided gently. "Don't be such a grumpy boots, Toby! We haven't even been in yet!"

"Do we have to?"

"Give it a chance, *please*," Emily replied, half-exasperated, half-imploring. "Go out on a limb for a change." She went on to remind him, "Besides, you need to finish off that screenplay you started. This place should inspire you. It might even be an experience you may never forget!"

She opened the door and entered, and Tobias followed her into the building, rather reluctantly.

True, Tobias was a respected scriptwriter for television and radio, but recently he'd been lumbered with writing a screenplay for a costume drama. He was no Andrew Davies. Instead of doing a serious piece of writing, which would have warranted a lot of research, Tobias had decided to play it safe and just parody Jane Austen's *Persuasion*, set in the decadent trappings of early nineteenth-century Bath society, a suggestion that went down well with the television producers. He had got as far as completing the courting scene between the two leads, where the female character in the play delivers a bombshell to the rake-of-a-gentleman . . .

II

(Excerpt from *Merrist Grange*, a screenplay by Tobias Hardwick)

SCENE 5

JANEY: I was told always to be fastidious in my choice of men. So, *no*, I don't think I can see you!

CAPTAIN BAGSHOTT: I believe I am the perfect choice for a 'fastidious' woman.

JANEY: I see you suffer no lack of confidence.

CAPTAIN BAGSHOTT: I am a naval officer, after all, [*smiles*] and a distinguished one at that!

[*He points to the Medals of Valour pinned to his uniform.*]

JANEY: But you have a reputation, a *nefarious* reputation . . . A reputation as a gambler and a philanderer.

CAPTAIN BAGSHOTT [*wincing*]: My so-called nefariousness should not be a matter of concern. You must not surrender to such rumour.

JANEY: I hear you expect ladies to hurl themselves at your feet.

CAPTAIN BAGSHOTT: Not so, fair lady. I have the utmost respect for the fairer sex.

JANEY [*confused*]: How can that be?

CAPTAIN BAGSHOTT [*with as much charm as he can muster*]: My philandering days were over when you graced me with your innocence! [*beat*] May I ask what you think might happen if you were to come out with me?

JANEY [*uncertain*]: I don't know . . . I am not *experienced* . . . in that way . . .

CAPTAIN BAGSHOTT: May I ask in what way you mean?

[*The man smiles wickedly, enjoying her difficulty.*]

JANEY: The way I think . . . you are referring to.

CAPTAIN BAGSHOTT: And that is?

JANEY [*flushed*]: The two of us *alone* together! . . . That is what you mean, isn't it?

CAPTAIN BAGSHOTT [*laughing*]: Not even for tea?

JANEY: No, I couldn't . . .

CAPTAIN BAGSHOTT: I know a lovely place just near here. I would love to take you there and get to know you better. [*Beat*] No? [*smiling again*] The cake is on me!

JANEY: Well, I shouldn't . . . I have to see my aunt in an hour. She does not take kindly to tardiness.

CAPTAIN BAGSHOTT [*triumphant*]: Excellent, it is settled then! We have a full hour! Come on, I want to know everything about you!

JANEY [*appalled*]: Everything? No woman should divulge everything!

SCENE 6 [*Exiting the tea-room*]

CAPTAIN BAGSHOTT: Well, that wasn't so terrible, was it?

JANEY [*flustered*]: You should not have made me stay so late. I fear now I'm in trouble with my aunt.

CAPTAIN BAGHOTT: I'm sure she will understand. Simply tell her you had tea with an exceedingly handsome stranger!

JANEY: You know I am not sure this confidence of yours is necessarily appealing.

CAPTAIN BAGSHOTT: You'll get used to it.

JANEY: Will I? How forward and presumptuous you are!

CAPTAIN BAGSHOTT: Would you like to meet me again? For dinner? I am on shore leave till the Thirteenth.

JANEY: Well I . . . I'm not sure . . . I suppose it depends what your intentions are . . .

CAPTAIN BAGSHOTT [*with a dastardly grin*]: My intentions are entirely honourable.

[*They stop walking and face each other.*]

JANEY: Curious . . . Your words say one thing, but your eyes say another. You wish me to be your next conquest?

CAPTAIN BAGSHOTT [*surprised*]: You can see through me?

JANEY [*fixing him with a stare*]: Like a veil. [*sighs*] If you must know, I am acquainted with your wife. And we are very much madly in love . . .

III

The village of Chawton, Hampshire, could date its history as far back as the Domesday Book, in which it received a brief but noteworthy mention. Jane Austen's brother, Edward, had been raised by his childless fourth cousin, Thomas Knight, and upon his adoptive father's death in 1812, he inherited the estate in Chawton among others and the heir formally changed his surname to Knight. Edward Austen Knight already owned half of Chawton, including his own stately residence, Chawton House, nowadays serving as the CENTRE FOR THE STUDY OF EARLY ENGLISH WOMEN'S WRITING. Edward would kindly offer his mother, two sisters and family friend, Martha Lloyd, the use of Chawton Cottage to occupy rent-free for the rest of their lives. Following the mischief and misery of Bath and Southampton, Jane was pleased they were returning to the security and country living of rural Hampshire, greatly missed since her childhood at Steventon Rectory, and the four ladies moved into 'the Cottage' in July 1809. The Jane Austen Society converted the cottage into a museum, preserving the feel of the home their idol had shared with her mother, sister and that same family friend, and the establishment was first opened to the public in 1947.

Emily never tired of the experience, having visited the museum umpteen times, but she knew it would be an education for Tobias. She was keen to be his tour guide, pointing out all the essential aspects of the cottage juxtaposed to Jane Austen's time.

The old granary now served as the museum entrance and gift shop, next to the Learning Centre, where a film of Jane Austen's life played on an endless loop. And, beyond, the house was a true, unforgettable museum of Austen's life, filled with priceless relics and giving the lasting impression one had been transported two hundred years backwards in time.

The Drawing Room was a bright and airy place, its elegant window overlooking the garden. It housed a Clementi square piano where Jane Austen gave her fortepiano recitals. The Dining Parlour contained the finest Wedgewood china. Breakfast was the only meal prepared in the dining parlour, with all other meals cooked in the kitchen. The writing table upon which Austen penned her immortal masterpieces was a dodecagon of walnut, resting on a single tripod, and so incredibly tiny as to be mistaken for a lampstand. The creak of the door, which had since been left undisturbed, would alert Austen to the approach of someone, whereupon, as rumour had it, she would quickly hide her manuscript and quill. In the Vestibule hung the portrait of Jane's wealthy brother, Edward, above the fireplace. The display case contained letters, sheet music and other family memorabilia. The Reading Room was filled with reference books and other research and, in particular, one of the biggest collections of foreign language editions of Jane Austen's works in the world. Upstairs, Chawton Cottage had boasted six bedchambers. However, Jane and her sister, Cassandra, had shared one bedroom. Jane had slept on a tent bed. The closet in the corner of the bedroom still contained a chamber pot and a wash bowl. The Austen Family Room contained a lock of Jane's hair woven into a brooch as remembrance, the original auburn hair faded with the passage of time. Martha Lloyd's Recipe Book consisted of handwritten recipes, household advice and medicinal remedies for the family. A mannequin in narrow satin stood by the window. The display cases in the Dressing Room contained a tableau of satin slippers, fans, shawls, intricately-designed handkerchiefs, a needle case and a snuff box. The patchwork quilt was particularly stunning, composed of sixty-four different fabrics, the three thousand diamonds with floral motif hand-stitched together by all the Austen women. Jane in her lifetime had proved an excellent seamstress, a shockingly proficient dancer, fluent in French and a dab hand at the pianoforte, alongside her acclaimed literary skills. Jane had been largely home-schooled since her short stint in boarding school, and her father had nurtured a creative, intellectual atmosphere growing up. Jane had often read her writings out aloud to her family and at social functions. There was even an Admirals Room in the museum presently, dedicated to Jane's sailor brothers. Francis Austen became Admiral of the Fleet and had been knighted, Charles Austen rising to the rank of Rear Admiral. Charles had captured a French ship and been rewarded with prize money, with which he bought his sisters' jewellery, including topaz crosses and gold-and-turquoise rings.

The Kitchen was attached to the main house and one entered via a separate door outside. It possessed a range and a bowl of dried lavender, which the visitors at the

House Museum could place into the small bags provided and take home as mementos. Aside from the art of baking, the Bakehouse was used for washing clothes and fraying off the skin of slaughtered pigs. Outside was a well which provided the water for domestic use. The cellar below stored salted foods. The Garden was rife with flowering plants including peonies, mignonettes, columbines, sweet william and rose madder. There was a shrubbery walk with laburnum bushes and trimmed hedgerows. The Austens had practised self-sufficiency in those days: fruit picked from the orchard, honey harvested from bees, and chickens and turkeys kept in pens. The cottage garden also contained a small bed of edible medicinal plants, including meadowsweet as an astringent, pot marigold used to heal stings, bites and burns, garlic for expelling worms, peppermint as a digestive, hawthorn as a relaxant, rosemary as a tonic and St John's Wort for the treatment of melancholy.

Emily and Tobias wandered back into the house. "Have you seen enough?" Emily asked her boyfriend.

"Enough to want to go home?" Tobias said, bored out of his brains.

"Not inspired then?" Emily asked.

He grinned. "Should I be?"

Emily walked back through the house, followed by Tobias, and returned to the writing desk, that famous and impossibly-small writing desk, upon which Jane Austen penned her novels. At Chawton, Austen would be granted the freedom to write and rewrite, tinkering, tweaking and perfecting her work. Her Chawton home would prove to be the most productive period of her literary career, with Austen thoroughly revising her manuscripts to her own satisfaction, of which four of her novels would be successfully published, receiving favourable reviews from the critics. Even the Prince Regent would express his admiration for her work.

They were alone in the room now, with no sign of any other visitors. Emily stood by the desk, her hands gliding across the polished walnut, meticulously searching underneath the rim of the tabletop.

"What are you doing?" Tobias asked, puzzled.

"Looking for something," replied Emily as her fingers skated across the underside of the table, her efforts becoming more frantic, as though hunting for a button or trip-switch. "There, it's done!" she exclaimed triumphantly.

"I don't get you," Tobias said uncomprehendingly. "Done *what?*" He suddenly felt chilly as though the old red brickwork of the house was drawing heat from his body. Curious, since it still looked quite warm and sunny outside. "I don't know what you're up to, but I'm starving. How about going across the road to the pub for some old-fashioned grub?"

But Emily was looking at something somewhere over his shoulder. She winked at him, indicating he should follow her gaze.

Puzzled by her strange behaviour, Tobias turned his head round and froze.

Two women, dressed in early nineteenth-century fashions and chattering amongst themselves, entered the room, unclasped the straps of their bonnets and hung their hats on the hat-stand.

Both couples seemed as startled to see the other. That is, until Emily spoke, addressing the slimmer lady on the left. "I did not mean to startle you, Miss Austen."

After a brief moment of cogitation, recognition registered on the genuinely-attractive, late-thirtysomething lady's face. The other woman just looked at her companion blankly. "Ah, Miss Hesketh of Upper Nasebury, you grace me with your gentle presence again. It has been far too long since we last saw each other. How have you been, my dear?"

"How do you do?" Emily responded, and curtsied.

Tobias had been watching this innocent exchange with a bewildered expression and deeply-troubled thoughts when the words Emily had used began to sink in. "You mean this is Jane?" he exploded in stark disbelief, "*Jane Austen?*"

IV

"Indeed, sir, I am she," Jane Austen replied by way of introduction. "And this is my sister, Cassie." Cassandra Austen nodded, also curtsied. "And who might you be?"

The uncertainty and confusion did not completely clear from Tobias's mind. He tried to speak, his eyes locked on the two so-called Austen women, but no sound emerged from his dry throat.

Instead, Emily came to his rescue. "This, dear Jane and Cassie, is my gentleman-friend, Mr. Tobias Hardwick."

"Pleased to make your acquaintance, sir," Jane responded, amiably enough, offering her hand in greeting. "Tobias is a strong Christian name."

Tobias took it, shook it, almost automatically, his mind in a half-daze, his heart way up in his throat. When he spoke, his voice was hoarse, cracked. "I doff my hat off at you, Miss Austen . . . if only I had a hat . . ."

His comment, somehow ad-libbed in the heat of the moment, produced a much-needed chuckle from all the ladies present, softening the tension.

"I see, Mr. Hardwick, you have an admirable sense of humour," said Jane warmly.

"He tries . . ." Emily answered for him. "Call him Toby."

Jane looked slightly uncomfortable with the idea of communicating on a first-name basis with this unknown-quantity of a gentleman. "If you wish, Emily. What does the gentleman think? How should we address you?"

"Just call me Toby," Tobias mumbled, still reeling from the unreality of the situation.

"We do not like putting on airs," Emily added.

"A commendable attitude," said Jane, smiling. "I do so much dislike standing on ceremony. I know friends who have been expelled from polite society for refusing to observe social etiquette. As long as we are in agreement, it is settled then – Emily and Toby, it is."

"Neither Toby nor I should protest to this arrangement," assured Emily.

Jane decided to administer her duties as hostess. "Shall we retire to the drawing room? Some tea, perhaps?"

Emily accepted the invitation. "That would be lovely. I sooo longed to escape . . ."

And, so, Jane led them to the drawing room, Cassie and their guests following on the heels.

Along the way, Tobias tugged the sleeve of Emily's jacket urgently. He was thrown for a loop by Emily's familiarity with the two ladies and how easily she had fitted into the language of the time as snugly as if it were a glove. *Like she'd met them before . . .* "What *is* this?" he whispered. "What's going on?"

"Just follow my lead," Emily advised quietly. "Please be civil and dignified. Not a simpering simpleton."

This is a joke, right? disputed Tobias, still struggling inside. *This* must *be a joke! They're playing me for an April fool! Either that or you've just seen your first ghost!* The notion nearly brought on a dead faint . . . until it occurred to him. The Curator of the Jane Austen Society had probably set this whole thing up, using a couple of actresses to pose as Jane and Cassandra Austen as part of the Jane Austen Experience. A spot of interactive drama for the paying guests, no less. Tobias wondered if Emily had arranged all this purely for his personal benefit.

Except that seemingly rational explanation he had conjured up evaporated in a breath when they entered the drawing room. The fortepiano was still there, but the information signs and display cases were gone. The resident eighteenth-century furniture and sumptuous couches gave the room a lived-in look, all very neat and cosy. The museum had done a damn fine job in recreating the interior design of the old cottage, but how could they have moved the furniture around so quickly? And to what end?

He stood in the doorway, surveying the room, slack-jawed, gawping.

"The look of guppy fish at feeding time," Emily mused, amused, when she noticed Tobias standing there paralyzed by the door.

"Do not fear, Toby," Jane reassured him, "tea is on its way. It should revive your senses."

Moving quite stiffly, Tobias joined the others in taking a seat. He remained watchful, alert. Emily had once informed him Jane Austen used to write behind a door that creaked in warning when visitors approached, and by the noise Jane would avail herself to hide her manuscript before they entered. Tobias remembered Emily fiddling with that same writing table, groping underneath for something. The term he had summoned up was 'trip-switch'. What if Emily had accessed a trip-switch that had stopped time from flowing forwards and had sent them back through a time slip? *What if they had time-travelled two centuries into the past?*

That's ludicrous! he screamed inside, yearning sane reasoning. *That's utter lunacy! I'm riding a unicorn down Crazy Street!*

A green muslin gown Jane Austen wore with all the trimmings, ankle-length and high-waisted, from which her columnar torso rose up to a swanlike neck, topped off by a brown shawl; Cassandra in similar dress, albeit sunflower-yellow and complete with a lace collar, slightly bigger in build and purportedly three years older in age than her sister, in whom Tobias could see the family resemblance, his own black leather jacket and modern clothes so ridiculously out of place here. Pugs, foxhunting, cricket on the village green, and, like now, tea and scones in the afternoon. Tobias thought of that comment Emily had made [*I sooo longed to escape*] and he finally overcame his dubiousness. He made a conscious decision to dispel his doubts, go out on the same limb Emily had spoken about earlier. He pinched himself to see if he was dreaming and realized he wasn't. Even though he had been mentally ready for flight moments ago, where would he run to? Time had stopped here. Sweet reason took charge. *No, you're not crazy! Just bowled over! And justifiably so!*

Heart no longer stuttering, Tobias relaxed for the first time since arriving here. Could he be actually living the warm, gentle life Jane Austen suffused in her novels? He hoped so.

Tea and refreshments arrived, presently, courtesy of one of the servants, whom Jane thanked graciously. Emily went for cream tea, but Tobias opted for the wine. "Have some Madeira, Toby, and go with the flow," Jane invited him.

"Indeed, I must imbibe to be inspired," replied Tobias congenially. He swore to himself – and Emily – he would make a decent effort. *Get into the spirit of the thing.*

When in Rome, as they say . . . He raised his glass of wine as a toast and, with a hearty "Chugalug!", began to drink.

"Quite . . ." responded Jane.

"Go easy on the wine," Emily warned her boyfriend.

Tobias smiled a mischievous smile. After everything he'd seen so far, he certainly didn't want to be sober.

"Aside from the scones," Jane announced, "there is a slice of game pie for the gentleman and Duke of Marlborough crackers with Somerset cheddar for everyone. Plum cake, if you prefer something sweet. The spiced figs should tickle your taste buds."

"The apothecary cannot understate the delightful potency of figs," Emily informed Tobias knowingly, causing him to visibly start. He then reminded himself that he was in the presence of three fine ladies, who were more than just a little versed on the whole subject of romance.

"More so than Spanish fly . . ." Cassie added matter-of-factly.

Jane merely smiled at Tobias, as though enjoying his awkwardness.

I think this promises to be a very memorable afternoon, Tobias thought to himself, trying not to betray his discomfort. *Very memorable, indeed . . .*

V

The atmosphere was convivial, and the afternoon flew by swiftly. The ladies conversed like old friends. Jane lavished most of her attention on Emily; it was like they had never been apart. Tobias still could not believe how Emily could be in Jane's intimate circle, let alone how he had got here.

[*I sooo longed to escape*]

There is nothing like staying at home for real comfort, Jane reminded everyone.

Tobias just sat and drank and watched them chatting away. Jane updated Emily about the outcome of the Napoleonic wars, how England and its allies had finally triumphed at the Battle of Waterloo in 1815. From a safe distance, Jane had followed the progress of the French Revolution and learned the sad news of the guillotining of her cousin Eliza's husband. Then, Jane regaled them about her and her sister's adventures in Winchester. Mother was still in Winchester, visiting their favourite brother, Henry. They planned to move down there to be close to Henry, who had recently followed in the footsteps of his father and taken up the cloth after his bank had failed catastrophically, depriving him of all his assets, leaving him deeply in debt. Henry and Frank could no longer support their mother and sisters so the ladies could not afford the upkeep of the cottage. Jane and her sister received Emily's sympathy. Jane still enjoyed riding the donkey carriage, but it was never any protection against the weather. Tobias learned that all traffic for Winchester and Alton passed through Chawton, the sixteenth-century pub across the road operating as something of a rest-stop and coach house. Jane mourned her own dwindling youth and ill-health; her lethargy and tiredness upon simple exertion had worsened. She hadn't felt this unwell since attending boarding school at the age of eight, when she contracted Typhus and nearly died. Emily and Tobias both knew something Jane didn't: the nature of her existing illness that had plagued her for many years. Alas, she would die within one year and be buried in Winchester Cathedral. Curious how this same month should mark the two-hundredth anniversary of the death of the Bard. Tobias was not a medical man, but he had read somewhere that for a long time Addison's disease had been cited by modern scientists as the cause of death of Jane Austen, but the new thinking now was one of bovine tuberculosis, otherwise known as Consumption, from drinking unpasteurized milk. Should they tell her? Would it make any difference?

Emily remained tight-lipped, kept this vital piece of information to herself probably because medical science was still in its infancy – there was no hope – but more so because 'the Past was the Past', as she had once told Tobias. Those words now took on a whole new meaning. *The Lord giveth and the Lord taketh away.* Nevertheless, it was Jane who counselled that nobody should leave this life without a sense of completion.

But it was when the conversation turned to affairs of the heart that Jane grew animated and suddenly seemed to forget all about her health problems. For the benefit of her gentlemanly guest, Tobias, she revisited the time she fell head over heels in love with Tom Lefroy at the age of twenty. "It was more than just a mere passing fancy," she said, looking back. "Unfortunately, marriage would have been impractical. Tom did not possess the financial means to provide for me, and his uncle found me unsuitable and suggested he should marry into a family with more money." Following the aborted romance with Tom Lefroy, Jane had received a marriage proposal from a long-time and well-to-do friend, Harris Bigg-Wither, and although she accepted the offer at first, she reconsidered over a sleepless night and retracted her acceptance the following morning.

Tobias pondered over Jane's recollections, her love affairs with Lefroy and Bigg-Wither. *Ironic how one of the greatest writers of romantic fiction never married. She must have kissed, but I wonder if she ever made love? Experienced the closeness of two bodies?*

"Do you have any regrets?" Emily asked Jane gently, sensitively.

"I should damn the Fates," said Jane, eyes slightly moist with sorrow. "*The more I know of the world, the more I am convinced that I shall never see a man whom I can really love.* It grieves me that nothing more became of our declaration of love. 'Maiden aunt' my wonderful niece, Fanny, calls me. I do think about that chapter in my life sometimes. *It is always incomprehensible to a man that a woman should ever refuse an offer of marriage.* But I also know from personal experience that broken hearts can be mended by Time." She told Emily of Dr. Haden, the family physician in Winchester, a man nearly half her age, whose handsomeness could make any woman's heart flutter like the wings of a tiger moth. "Oddly enough, I do not dream of being a doctor's wife. He is but a distraction. Nothing can become of my physical attraction for him." She paused, added: "Passion fades with time. Friendship remains and the affection of others, a fondness not even my quill can express or give justice to." She focused on Emily, her conversation taking on a livelier note. "There's me wittering again! My dearest friend, tell me about your fine gentlemanly friend . . . if he does not mind us discussing him!"

Tobias was smiling again, partly inebriated. "Don't let me stop you, ladies."

He glanced at Cassandra, who had been curiously reserved but quietly listening throughout and did not look as though she'd be speaking any time soon. She and Jane had been inseparable since childhood and, like Jane, had never married, spinsters to the end. Could the literary world ever forgive her for burning all the lifetime of letters she had received from Jane upon the death of her sister? Had this deliberate bonfire of correspondence been anger at her loss or a coming-to-terms with her grief?

"We have been acquainted almost eleven months," Emily informed her.

"It must be a long courtship."

"He is a writer of stage."

"You mean like Shakespeare, writing plays for theatre?"

"You could say that . . ."

To Tobias's sheer astonishment – and utter shock – Jane lifted a pile of papers from the corner of the couch, a manuscript scribbled by quill and tied together by a piece of red string. "I see, Mr. Hardwick, you wrote this particularly engaging piece: *Merrist Grange . . .*"

VI

For a moment, Tobias could not speak. How could this woman know of his latest work, let alone have a copy of his manuscript two hundred years in the past, handwritten when he had in fact typed it? How could it be scribbled in long hand, *in his handwriting*, even though he didn't remember doing it? More to the point, how could it be in Jane Austen's possession?

Then, even more enigmatically, Jane said: "*Merrist Grange* is the reason among others why you were brought to me, Mr. Hardwick."

"How-how did you manage to get a copy?"

"Do not be alarmed," Jane reassured him. "It was delivered to me by the mercy of the stars. Just as you both were delivered to my doorstep."

Emily added: "A truly magical day you weren't quite expecting, Toby."

Tobias tried to comprehend the extraordinariness of the situation, considering everything that had gone before, whilst struggling to maintain some modicum of composure. "I don't get it. How–?"

"Wouldn't you like Miss Jane Austen's take on your manuscript? Her *critique?*"

Forget the mechanics – the *hows* – of it all, Tobias told himself, calming down. The *why?* was suddenly glaringly obvious. Tobias discovered he was in a unique position. Here, right before him, was the dangling carrot, the inducement. Jane Austen was willing to give his work some input, a chance to review the tale he had struggled with for several weeks. "Pardon my consternation. It would be a great honour to hear your thoughts on my work. I would greatly value your opinion, Miss Austen, and, dare I say, *criticism*. The sharper the better."

"It is a very interesting premise," Jane began thoughtfully. "Wethinks your Captain Bagshott is a gentleman lacking integrity."

"A knave!" burst out Emily.

"A rake!" seconded Jane

"A roué!" Emily added another barb, grinning.

Jane: "A brigand and a mountebank!"

Emily: "A cad and a bounder!"

"An *ass!*" exclaimed the two ladies in perfect unison and instantly burst into gales of laughter, leaving Tobias dumbfounded. Baffled, he wondered if the joke was on him.

Once Jane had composed herself, she resumed: "Quite the man of disrepute, your

Captain Bagshott, despicable even." She produced a sad smile. "I speak to you with complete discretion. Such are the cruel, rigid customs of the socialites of our era and the dreadful anxieties of our fashionable homemakers." She hesitated before continuing scathingly. There was frustration, and irritability, in her voice. "Unless you are born into money and privilege, or marry into it, you do not stand a chance. The secret to happiness, they say, should be a man with an enormous income and a large family estate. It is also common knowledge that there is a scarcity of good men. A man blessed with scruples can be a man without a guinea to his name. High Society is filled with insufferable men, horrid, ill-mannered gentlemen, whose idleness has become an occupation, living a mindless life of intemperance and dissipation, of gluttony and carnal knowledge, motivated by greed and a hunger for power, scrounging on their family name and frittering away the family fortune, beating down on those disadvantaged in breeding. The illusion of gentlemanly conduct and chivalry and that ridiculous notion that honour can only be satisfied by a duel at dawn – bah! Men are proud, ignorant and prejudiced. Men just want to be obeyed."

Tobias further wondered if this, aside from being a magical day, allegedly, was a day for man-bashing. Jane Austen was no shrinking violet. "And what of the ladies of your polite society?"

"For those who claim my work is sentimental, they have not been reading closely enough. Sentimentality does not enter into my writings. You will always find the outspoken, headstrong heroine somewhere amongst either the scatterbrained but virtuous girls or the conniving, scheming ladies in my books. Oh, the tedium of polite society! The overbearing expectation to comport oneself like a lady even when one does not want to or the vexatious assumption that women must pursue natural womanly pursuits! All those accursed books on etiquette that are supposed to teach conduct and social norms, a must-read for a lady, when one would rather be engaged in a work of gothic fiction, which in spite of being all the rave these days, the educators of our age consider dangerous, worrying unnecessarily that these lurid writings will corrupt young, growing minds."

Tobias experienced a stranger thought. Considering everything he had seen so far, what if they were to meet Jane Austen, not at Chawton, but at Northanger Abbey? Now wouldn't that be an exciting, utterly mindwarping experience? Metafictional even? He decided not to share it with the others.

"I shall endeavour, dear Jane, to maintain the boundaries of propriety," Emily said primly.

"Your company is most refreshing, Emily," Jane acknowledged, her waspishness gone. "You are a lady through and through." She turned her attention to Tobias.

"And you, good sir, have conducted yourself with great decorum, despite today's events tending to the peculiar." She redoubled her efforts on his script. "To continue, your Janey is of a higher moral standing than your Captain Bagshott, of stronger character. Some might describe her love of Mrs. Bagshott as improper, going against convention, conduct unbecoming of a lady, deviant – a *sin* – but I believe Love takes many forms, and some say that the love between two women can be deeper than the love between a man and a woman." She smiled at Cassie who smiled back, nothing less than the companionship and wholesome love of two sisters keeping them together. "Between you and me, Mr. Hardwick, I like it! Your play works because, in my own promethean way, it would prove unpalatable to the Establishment. The originality of the idea would sell. Here, however, an obscenity trial would sink it, as our bigoted legal system would deem its contents indecent. Society, unfortunately, is not broadminded enough or ready to receive such a diversity of love yet."

Tobias buckled. He was sold. He surrendered to Jane Austen's validation of his work. *For the first time today, and for the first time in my life, I actually appreciate Jane Austen*, he thought, overawed. *She's a regular stand-up girl!* In his opinion, Jane had proved herself a remarkable woman, and he wondered why he hadn't seen it before or why he had considered his own costume drama a chore. Women were second place in her society, lived in an age of female repression, which explained why Jane had published her own novels anonymously, not so dissimilar to the Brontës and George Eliot, who had written under the guise of a male pseudonym, capturing the penury of women and the mendacity of men, constantly challenging the class structure and secretly pioneering the empowerment of women. And Austen had justifiably in the centuries that followed become part of England's fine literary heritage. He had to admit that modern English was a bastardized version of the gentrified language spoken in the Austenesque world; the English language of modern times had gradually degenerated, regressed, guttersnipe had crept in, whereas one could not deny the polished and poetic discourse of Austen's time, the beautiful prose, elegant and articulate, *erudite*, all grammatically correct and untouched by colloquialisms, and commanding a graceful and witty turn of phrase. "I am grateful for your insights."

"It is always a great pleasure getting the male perspective when discussing literature with a fellow writer, and one so impressive, capable of breaking down our complicated social mores. *Let other pens dwell on guilt and misery.*" She turned to Emily. "Such a fine lady as yourself, of child-bearing age, should tie the knot, settle down and raise a family."

"I ask your permission, Miss Austen," Emily said, somewhat coquettishly. "What thinks you of my Toby?"

"You have chosen well. I find him considerate, attentive, respectable, even if he did look positively mortified when he first arrived here. Handsome, not at all a coarse or objectionable fellow. Assuredly, more agreeable than the other prospective suitors you've brought here."

"I thought he wouldn't last five minutes here, but he has proved himself most capable."

"There is something of the Fitzwilliam Darcy in him," Jane said to Emily. "I rank Fitzwilliam Darcy up there with Hamlet and Heathcliff, the strong, silent type, awkward in company, stoical on the surface but a passionate lover inside, the antihero, perhaps. And you have previously told me he earns more than ten thousand pounds a year, more than Darcy's income!"

Toby couldn't believe it. More kudos from Jane, and of the highest order at that! He thought of his generation's version of Mr. Darcy, emerging from the river following his swim, his dripping white shirt clinging provocatively to his manly chest, not the way Austen had envisaged it. Or maybe she *had* but was too polite not to describe it in all its ravishing glory. "Thank you, Miss Austen. My humility knows no bounds."

"You approve?" Emily said, eyes widening, overcome by joy.

"A most excellent match, Miss Hesketh!" Jane said, speaking from authority. "Fortune smiles upon you. I admire the courage of your convictions, your choice of gentleman. I shall pray at St. Nicholas's Church for your love to flourish."

Tobias suddenly said, "*A lady's imagination is very rapid; it jumps from admiration to love, from love to matrimony in a moment.*"

Emily gasped, taken aback by the quote. "How do you know? That's one of Jane's eternal truths."

It was also Jane's turn to be surprised. "It seems you have been holding back from us."

"I may be a man, but I'm not all that ignorant," Tobias said with a knowing grin. "I read a little. I did my own research, of course, before I came here. Did you not say, Miss Austen: *It is a truth universally acknowledged, that a single man in possession of a good fortune, must be in want of a wife?* And did you not add: *Single women have a dreadful propensity for being poor, which is one very strong argument in favour of matrimony?* But: *Happiness in marriage is entirely a matter of chance?*"

"I am most impressed! You are indeed a man of many talents and much refinement! Miss Hesketh, you cannot let this gentleman slip though your fingers! Remember, somewhere between Love's Grace and Love's Folly lies the gateway to True Love."

"I fully share my sister's pleasure at the news," Cassie congratulated the couple, agreeing wholeheartedly.

Emily couldn't have looked more pleased, as satisfied as a cat that had caught the canary. Tobias had gained Jane's acceptance as a writer, and Emily had received Jane's blessing to consummate her feelings for Tobias.

VII

"Stay for dinner," Jane asked expectantly. "We are making calves' brains."

"Most kind of you, Jane," said Emily, "but I think we'll give it a miss on this occasion. We ought to head back. I'm indisposed tonight, entertaining guests."

"Shame you cannot stay," said Jane, sounding disappointed. "I hope I have not been negligent as a host."

"On the contrary, we can only thank you most humbly for your kind hospitality. If you must know, I'm hosting my book club, dedicated to you, in fact!"

"An honour most sublime," Jane said, growing wistful. "I envy the world you are going back to, where women are equal to men."

"No, again, the pleasure was all mine," Emily answered, equally envious. "I wish I could live in your world, so charming and timeless and innocent."

"Until next time, my dearest friend?"

"Until next time, Jane. I shall return. Promise."

"I shall always be here if you long to escape."

They hugged like the old friends they were, soon to be separated by an ocean of time. It brought a tear to the eye. Cassie was similarly emotional.

"It was a pleasure to meet you, Miss Austen," said Tobias in a dignified manner, affecting a polite, gentlemanly bow.

"Likewise, Mr. Hardwick," Jane replied, beaming. "Please take good care of Emily, and I wish you every success with your play. . ." She paused and, with a twinkle in her eyes, said: "And please call me Jane . . ."

Then, Emily took Tobias into the next room and began playing with the magical writing table located in Jane's sanctum sanctorum, opening up the door between the past and the future, jumping forwards in time. If Tobias thought he was going to be stuck in 1817, he was greatly mistaken. They returned to the early twenty-first century, the reality he knew. The enchanted cottage, where Jane had lived during the last leg of her life and had spent polishing her work to literary perfection and achieved successful publication, had been converted into a museum once again. A mother and her five-year-old daughter watched them appear from nowhere, stunned speechless by the sudden materialization of these two people in the room.

"Just a time trip," Emily told the mother mysteriously. "Let me know if you're interested . . ." Tobias just smiled at them naively, as if nothing untoward had occurred. Without so much as a by-your-leave, Emily and Tobias departed, leaving the mother to contemplate the staggering sight she and her child had seen.

"How was that?" Emily asked Tobias as they stepped out of the building. They blinked to the late afternoon sunshine. The swallows dipped and soared. The air was fragrant with late spring flowers.

Tobias realized they had spent four hours in Austenland. "I'm almost at a loss for words."

"I'm deeply impressed by you, too. You've read Austen. I never knew."

"Back to the real world, I guess. *Life seems but a quick succession of busy nothings.*"

"Okay, okay, enough of the showing-off."

"I haven't even got started yet! Some of Life's great mysteries: How could Elizabeth Bennett's sparring dislike of Darcy develop into consuming love for him? Of the two — Anne Elliot or Captain Wentworth — whom does the reader blame for their eight-year estrangement? Does the reader think Henry Tilney has the capacity to love Cathy Morland? Why is Fanny Price's character so dichotomous, both unlikeable and yet endearing? How could anybody have the gall to marry someone they had cradled as a baby as Mr. Knightly did Emma? And, in the separate romantic entanglements of the Dashwood sisters, does sense triumph over sensibility in the end?"

"You're so full of surprises! You told me you only read a little?"

"I read a *lot!*" corrected Tobias, grinning. "Now aren't you the surprising one with friends in high places?"

Emily smiled and kissed him on the cheek. "Maybe Jane can answer some of those elusive questions, next time."

Tobias picked up on something Emily had discussed with Jane earlier. "Other suitors?" he recalled.

Emily responded, not entirely embarrassed. "I took my suitors to meet Jane. I ran them past Jane so she could vet them. I suppose my search is now over, my most beloved." Emily was gazing at Tobias with something akin to adoration. "One day, I very well may go down on one knee and propose to you."

"Why not now?" asked Tobias playfully. "You know I very well may say *yes.*"

"It wouldn't be romantic if you knew. No, I want it to be a surprise, an occasion to remember for years to come."

"Like the day you've just shown me?"

"Yes, I told you it would be worth it."

"Like a profound religious experience," Tobias confessed, "life-changing, unforgettable . . ."

They clambered into their white Fiat Abarth, and Tobias started the engine. The radio sprang to life, spinning out *The Way I Feel* by the Lemon Trees. During their eccentric adventures in Jane Austen's world, he had gathered enough material to authenticate his screenplay. The woman deserved his respect. This great writer of English fiction, whose accomplishments had the literary elite fawning over her, had turned him into an ardent fan. Austen may never have married or born any children, but she was gifted with a woman's intuition and fertile imagination. Her powers of observation and discrimination were second to none, true to life. It had been a thoroughly worthwhile learning experience. For the truly initiated, Chawton Cottage awaited those who wished to communicate with the past and their idol on some spiritual level – indeed, it could be perceived as a place of pilgrimage.

"Why don't you just set your story in Chawton?"

"You know, I think I just might . . ."

March 2016-April 2016

Take Two

"There is only one real sin and that is to persuade oneself that the second-best is anything but the second-best."

Doris Lessing

I

Postlands

When the newcomer approached the reception desk of the POSTLANDS HOTEL, Bethany thought he looked like an Egyptian doctor.

It was nearly midnight and Bethany, whose duty tonight was to man the front desk, was intrigued by this fellow, a needful distraction from the less-than-engrossing article she had been reading on the current trend of young men growing beards to ridiculously unfashionable proportions and dyeing their hair to a 'silver fox'-look in a bid to appear older and distinguished. *So much for the latest goss, thank you very much!* The night shift, along with brain activity, had already slowed down to a soporific crawl. The man before her was tailored in a blue business suit and carrying a man-bag, out of which protruded a rolled-up copy of the evening edition of the *Chertsford Echo*. He seemed curiously foreign, perhaps Middle-Eastern, from his sandy complexion and dark hair, but his handsomeness could not be understated nor his level of sophistication by the perfect, polished English when he spoke, without a hint of an exotic accent. "I made a reservation…"

"Under what name?" Bethany began to busy herself.

"Haroon Bashir,"

Bethany checked the computer and discovered the man's booking was registered on the system. The name was possibly from the Indian subcontinent or maybe Arabic? In the UK he hailed from Rochdale, Lancashire.

She gave him a hard copy of the booking confirmation and he provided her with a signature. "What is the purpose of your stay, Mr. Bashir? Business or pleasure?"

His response was a given. "I'm here for a conference."

"Business it is," she informed him as she handed him the swipe-card. "Your room is 402."

"Thank you . . ." he said, but he paused just as he was about to go. "I don't want to sound forward, and I don't wish you to think less of me, but would you mind if I ask you out to dinner, that's if you're not already seeing anyone?"

Bethany was taken aback by the unexpectedness of the invitation. For a moment she did not speak. Then, slowly, she emerged from her shock, her voice slightly faint, squeaky. She realized that she should take the offer of a date from this man – this Muslim businessman, who bespoke culture and couture and confidence – as a compliment. She was immensely flattered. And, no, she wasn't seeing anyone. "The hotel manager has stipulated that the employees should hold a professional attitude in his employment and should not be seen fraternizing with the guests. But since I don't like the hotel manager, I accept . . ."

Haroon's eyes lit up. "I am most delighted – and deeply humbled – by your willingness to go out with a strange man you have only just met,"–he read her name-badge pinned to the lapel of her purple uniform–"*Bethany Holcombe . . .*"

"I'm a big girl now," Bethany said, feigning confidence herself. "I choose whom I date and whom I don't."

"I hope you like Indian food."

"Love it."

"Seven p.m. tomorrow, at The Mogul restaurant in Chertsford?"

Bethany knew of THE MOGUL in the centre of town, walking distance from the hotel. Newly opened, apparently. "Sounds smashing. I'm only working half-day tomorrow."

"It's a deal then. I shall see you there!"

He was about to head off, but he hesitated again. He turned, a grimace of guilt on his face. "I have a confession to make. I don't have a conference . . .What I mean is I *did* have a conference, but I attended it earlier today . . . it's finished, done and dusted. I came here tonight to the Postlands Hotel because I've seen you work here before and I really wanted to ask you out." He rushed and stumbled over his words and seemed to blush with the embarrassment of a shy teenager. "I hope you don't think I'm some kind of creep . . ."

The ball was in Bethany's court. "The thought had crossed my mind, but don't worry, I'll be there tomorrow." She smiled suddenly. "And only time will tell if you really are a creep . . ."

2

The Mogul

It was a short drive from her apartment in Chertsford, in a rundown street where the residences diminished rather dramatically in property value, to THE MOGUL in the town centre. She parked in a multi-storey car park. The walk to the restaurant was brief and uneventful. Bethany arrived dot on seven. She noticed that some racist graffiti artist had spray-painted over the first word of the slogan, CURRY IN A HURRY, to create SLURRY IN A HURRY.

Haroon was already there. Dressed in an open-collar white shirt and navy-blue trousers, he was sat quietly in one of the farther booths, sipping lemonade. When he saw Bethany arrive, he got up and greeted her.

"You look nice," he complimented her.

Indeed, she did. She was wearing a short, pink flowery dress, in keeping with the summer weather, showing off her gorgeous legs, partially tanned from repeatedly sitting on the balcony of her apartment to soak up the sun when not working and by far her best asset. "Thanks. Always great to get out of my work clothes."

"What would you like to drink?" he asked.

"Just a soda-water-and-lime, please . . ."

Haroon called over the waiter and ordered her drink as well as another tall lemonade for himself. The waiter handed them the menus in the process.

"How do you like the place?" Haroon asked her.

Bethany glanced around the restaurant. It was relatively posh, the dark sandalwood furniture complementing the Indian décor, and the walls hung with paintings depicting the time of the Raj. An old-fashioned raag spilled out from the overhead speakers. Added to this, the beautiful aroma of traditional spices wafted up from the open-plan kitchen area, making sure the customers could see the Chef cook their meals from scratch, using fresh ingredients, Bethany could not fault the place for striving for authenticity. "Nice."

"Do you like Indian food?"

"I prefer Italian, but I won't say no to an Indian once in a while."

"Italian's good," Haroon contemplated. "A lot of carbohydrate from the pasta and dough, but at least they have the expertise to use chilli peppers in their meals, which separates them from the French. Although having said that, I love French cuisine, too, and its extraordinary diversity of dishes. Did you know that with an authentic Italian pizza, the toppings are already prepared beforehand and the dough is stretched so thin that it should take only one minute in a wood-fired oven, preheated to four hundred degrees, to fully cook?"

It was news to Bethany. "Did not know that. I should try out the real deal some time." And so began some light, pleasant banter about cooking. Bethany reminded Haroon about how our food was now designed by a pesticide company . . . or even the likes of Heston Blumenthal. "Probably the most overrated chef in history. I mean he could market shit as food and demand an astronomical fee from the morons who think he's a culinary genius when he's just plain shit! Bacon ice-cream, I ask you? I heard insects are his latest food product. Who in their right mind would want to pay so much dosh for famine food?" Haroon agreed with her observations – and the angry rant.

"I guess Blumenthal's not your favourite person," he said, pausing before adding: "Mine, neither."

Of the Celebrity Chefs, they both equally agreed that Gordon Ramsay was too short-fused and vulgar, and Jamie Oliver too chavvy but traitorous enough to have sold out to the Establishment. They agreed that only the Hairy Bikers, true champions of Real Grub, and Hugh Fearnley-Whittingstall, of *River Cottage* fame, had anything useful to say about food. Not that Bethany claimed to be a foodie, but she got a sense that Haroon could pull it off as one.

The starters arrived. Bethany had gone for a portion of fish tikka while Haroon plumped for lamb seekh kebabs, genuinely spicy and not smothered in that 'cheap, awful red stuff', the colouring Bethany described used by a lot of less impressive Indian restaurants in preparing their kebabs and tandoori chickens. The main course consisted of *saag-aloo-gobi* with naan for Bethany, who informed Haroon that she was going through a 'teetotal-and-vegetarian' phase at the moment, and a hearty king prawn biryani for Haroon, the traditional version, he explained, alternate layers of rice and sauce.

They discussed movies and their favourite film stars. Few actresses spoke to Bethany like Claire Danes. She was surprised that Haroon had actually heard of her.

She had appreciated Claire Danes since first watching her in that contemporary version of *Romeo + Juliet* designed for a newer, younger generation. Although the idea of the characters spouting classic Shakespearean dialogue during high-speed car chases, with helicopters hovering overhead, was insane to say the least and must have caused the Bard to roll in his grave, Bethany had been gripped by Danes's performance, and her subsequent film roles became essential viewing for her. *Shopgirl* was a particularly sweet, satisfying and albeit sad story, even though it was nothing short of an ego trip for Steve Martin, who wrote the original bestselling novella. What was left out of the film, but was wholly relevant to the plot, was the ending from the book, the motivation driving the two characters' ongoing relationship, post-breakup.

The discussion moved on to Bollywood without stereotyping Haroon's film interests. Did she know any Indian actors? No, she didn't. Update: yes, she did, Art Malik, who appeared in both *The Jewel in the Crown* and one of the best Bond films ever, *The Living Daylights*, alongside probably her favourite Bond, Timothy Dalton. The people of the Indian subcontinent, Haroon explained, excelled in cricket, hockey and squash, but it was Bollywood where they found their escape. Yet, regardless of their puritanical values, Bollywood was as corrupt as Hollywood. He told her that geography played a huge part in selecting the Bollywood actors and actresses. "The men of northern India are tall and handsome and fair . . . much like myself," Haroon said, tipping a wink at Bethany, who smiled at his mock-immodesty, "so they cut more dashing heroic figures than the men of the South, who generally get smaller, darker and rounder the further south you go. However, the women of south India are treasured for their youthfulness and voluptuousness." Haroon told her that he had fancied Urmila Matondkar since watching her in *Rangeela*. A versatile actress, Matondkar's acting career included a later role in one of India's first horror films, *Bhoot*, translated as 'Ghost', a spinetingler to match even the best of Hollywood's modern horror classics. All very interesting, Bethany supposed. Haroon related the three must-see films for all those uninitiated to Bollywood: the original 1930s version of *Devdas*, starring probably Indian cinema's first real superstar, K.L. Saigal, a man who was well ahead of his time, a powerful singer, much imitated, but also a notorious drinker, who had died way too young; *Baiju Bawra*, a historic piece about the eponymous musician's romance with his muse during the Mughal emperor Akbar's medieval reign; and then there was *Sholay*, the first curry western, which most people had heard of and which ultimately catapulted Amitabh Bachchan's career to superstardom.

Soon, conversation grew decidedly more personal. They were keen to know a little more about their date.

Bethany spoke about the difficulty she experienced in sharing her feelings, not that she was an unsociable individual. Despite being a wallflower, she was used to getting chatted up by men, Haroon being one such example. Not that she paid much mind to these men. "A wallflower I may be, but I don't suffer fools gladly," she informed him. She had survived a pile of near-misses in her twenty-three years on this planet. She always seemed the second-choice girlfriend for most men. Older men approached her often while in the midst of a midlife crisis, searching for a bit on the side, an object of desire that could make them feel young again. Younger men, whose primitive adolescent hormones surged through their system, rather immaturely perceived her to be 'easy' and were often surprised when she gave them the cold shoulder. She somehow never made the grade for the sensible men of the late twenties and early thirties, whose priority had become to find a suitable wife, and she was constantly disappointed with the lack of attention she received from these genuinely eligible bachelors. Haroon was sympathetic towards her. He went on to ask what she wanted to do with her life. Bethany informed him she had worked as an au pair girl when she left college, but the husbands had always hit on her and the wives had accused her of stealing their husbands. Sometimes they refused to pay her because of this misunderstanding. So she had entered the hospitality industry. She got a job at Postlands Hotel so she could pay her way through University, studying Health and Social Care. She wished to be carefree and happy, but life generally sucked. She had no boyfriend, lived in a rough part of town and had already acquired a student debt of twenty thousand pounds.

"Thank you for sharing," said Haroon in between spoonfuls of his rice. "I guess it's my turn." He paused as though wondering where to begin. "My family hails from the Punjab region . . . Lahore, to be precise. If you know anything about Punjabis, you'll know that they are the smartest, most educated and progressive people in the Indian subcontinent, some might call us the 'intelligentsia', no disrespect to the rest of them, even if Punjabi itself is regarded as a 'common' language compared to the more poetic Urdu. The further north and south of the Punjab you go, the more backward the people get, even if Kashmiris, up north, are regarded by many as the most beautiful people in the world. The British Empire had a tendency to exploit the precious resources of other countries, and the British occupation of India was no exception. I mean the largest diamond in the world, the Koh-i-Noor, is now part of the Queen's Crown Jewels. Although the British improved the quality of life of the Indian population, including providing education, their departure led to the Partition of 1947, ripping the country in two. Muslims, Hindus and Sikhs, who had once got along as closely as brothers, were at each other's throats in acts of rioting, rape and bloodshed. Jinnah is revered by Muslims as the founder of Pakistan during this time of war and independence. He is practically worshipped by most Pakistanis, idolized as their national hero. But what most Pakistanis won't accept, or simply turn a blind eye to, is the knowledge that being University-educated and very Westernized, frequently visiting Britain, Jinnah used to drink alcohol and eat pork. Overshadowed by his colleagues in the All-India Home Rule League, including Gandhi and Nehru, led to jealousy, with Jinnah demanding his own Muslim homeland no matter what the consequences.

"You see Pakistan is a crooked country, Afghanistan even more so. Pakistani politics have been corrupt since the country's inception, and you will discover that Pakistani presidents have a much shorter shelf-life than their counterparts in India, removed from office by assassination, execution or corruption charges. Even today, there are more Muslims in India than there are in Pakistan." Bethany was surprised by Haroon's open criticism of the political system in Pakistan. There was something refreshing about it, *honest*. She believed Britain's politicians fared no better. "The East India Company having plundered India's natural wealth and turned man against man in a bloody civil war, dividing the nation in half, why shouldn't Indian immigrants flood the UK and enjoy the amenities of the West, get back what they are owed? Some might call it payback!"

It was after the *rasmalai* dessert and during the after-dinner coffees that Haroon spoke about his family. "Hameed, my grandfather, was a first-generation Asian. His fellow countrymen followed suit. He went into the curry business, initially working as a dishwasher. I encountered fewer of the challenges my forefathers faced. Racism was still rife even in my day – I was referred to as a 'Pakman' which later became 'Paki'. They say that the term made its way to the Pacman of Atari 2600 fame, but I suppose that may be just a myth. '*Fuck off back to Paki-land*' was another common derogation inflicted upon us by the punks, skinheads and far-right thugs as well as certain bigots in the police force. What the idiots didn't realize was that 'Paki' actually means 'pure' in our language, but that's purely academic.

"My father, Hakeem, with enough money accumulated from the toils of his father, built a curry house, in Littleborough in 1974: THE TAJ MAHAL. I used to work in the restaurant after school. I soon left education without any qualifications, but I worked full-time in our family-run business, twenty-five hours a day, eight days a week, it seemed, until I inherited the restaurant from him."

"It must have been a hard life," acknowledged Bethany.

"It was – but worth it."

"What about girls? There must have been some girls who took your fancy."

Deep in reminiscence, Haroon smiled. "Yes, there was one such girl. The whole Bhangra scene kicked off in the 1990s. It was a time of cassette tapes, corner shops and those glittery musical heroes of Asian kool, of teenagers bunking off school to attend secret daytime gigs. The Asian girls would arrive at these dos wearing their traditional *salwar kameez* and carrying a plastic bag of clothes and they'd go straight into the toilets and re-emerge having changed into jeans and leather jackets, looking like Olivia Newton-John. The headache we caused our parents, the generational culture clash. Still, great stuff! I remember the first Bhangra gig I went to at the HAMMERSMITH PALAIS. The Pardesi Music Machine were playing, and in a cloud of dry ice, they kicked off the show with their rock number, *Balbeero Bhabi*. The girl I danced with that night I instantly fell in love with. Her name was Kuldeep Kaur, a Sikh girl. She appeared before me like a vision, all long black hair and big, round eyes and a smile so enchanting a man would have done anything for her. She was possessed of the beauty of a Mughal princess and her voice was as sweet as a nightingale's song. I had always been a bit of a Romeo in my younger days and I couldn't resist. She was different. She was special. One in a million. Our love was written in the stars. Use whatever tired cliché you like.

"We started seeing each other. Her father soon found out about us and was on the warpath. There was talk of Honour Killings. My own father was none-too-pleased, either, stating I'd brought shame on the family. Indian families still have a Victorian mentality around arranged marriages and marrying into their own kind. My father insisted I marry a well-educated, down-to-earth girl from an Indian madrasa. My father once told me about the hell my aunt suffered when she was my age and eloped with a local boy down to the Sindh. Even when the confrontation between our respective fathers nearly broke into fisticuffs, I stayed with Kuldeep, and we got married. I converted her to Islam, and she quietly followed my religion. But I never had the heart to ask her to change her name.

"We had many years of happiness together. A comfortable life. But a child did not grace our life, and Kuldeep was soon past reproductive age. It did not matter — we had each other." The nostalgia was now gone from his voice. "*Then she turned senile.* The doctors diagnosed her with presenile dementia. There were increasing periods of confusion alternating with shortening spells of lucidity until she could no longer look after herself and she stopped talking altogether. In the end she couldn't recognize me, couldn't even recognize her own reflection." Haroon stopped for a moment, his voice choked, on the edge of grief, and Bethany did not push him any further. "I think of her, now and again, how she used to be, so full of life, of zest. *Balbeero Bhabi* will always be our song."

Bethany listened patiently, sympathetically, letting him spill out his life story, the tale of his first true love, for defying his parents in the name of that love, her woeful degeneration to an unrecognizable stranger. "I'm sorry," she said, grasping his hand on the table with hers. He appreciated the gesture.

"Thank you for listening."

All of which meant Haroon must be in his late forties/early fifties. Widowed, it seemed, no children.

"*Balbeero Bhabi* is the song of your country?" Bethany joked, lightening the mood.

Haroon smiled. "As far as I'm concerned, my national anthem."

The waiter came over. He did not present the bill. "Is there anything else I can do for you, boss?"

"Boss?" uttered Bethany with a start. Then it clicked. "You own this restaurant?"

"Yes, and the original in Littleborough, although my cousin runs that one." He instructed the waiter. "No special favours, Farhan. Treat me like any paying customer."

Haroon paid the bill and handed the waiter a generous tip. He turned to Bethany "They divvy up the tips, adds a lot to their basic salary. Though I do pay my staff well. Keeps them happy, gives them more motivation to work, brings in the punters." He paused. "I really was at a curry conference, you know, if you can believe such a thing exists. Even we have to learn new recipes and approaches to cooking curries."

So it seemed he had two houses in the UK, up north in Lancashire and one she discovered in nearby Outer Bridge, and another family home in Lahore, not to mention his two thriving restaurants and manufacturing his own line in curry sauces. He might not be a style guru or trendsetter, but it seemed Haroon, as a successful businessman, was widely respected in the Indian community. Bethany asked something that had been pressing on her since the offset. "Why me?"

"I know my priorities," Haroon told her gently, "the value of something, a thing's worth." He looked deep into her eyes. "And I can say for sure you are worth it."

3

Night of the Second Date

The evening at The Mogul had been a pleasant, enjoyable experience. For once Bethany had willingly given out her phone number and, without any hesitation,

Haroon had accepted it. Another date was soon to follow. He invited her to spend an evening at his house in Outer Bridge, and she, too, without harbouring any doubts, accepted the invitation. The evening offered the promise of romance.

Although Outer Bridge had something of a negative, 'louts-and-layabouts' reputation, Haroon's property was a large five-bedroomed house in the nicer part of the district, detached and secluded. When Bethany got to the house, Haroon was already standing at the front door, anticipating her arrival. They exchanged greetings and Haroon took her coat, which he hung up on the coat-stand in the hallway. The house was built during the Edwardian era, large, commodious, but curiously uncluttered and sparsely furnished. The reception rooms looked spacious, made more so by the white shag carpets and white wallpaper, with the minimal presence of pictures or ornaments on display. The leather sofas, too, were white and deep, giving the rooms the appearance of a Winter Wonderland, if it were not for the fading summer light outside. Haroon had opened the French windows in the dining room, looking on to a patio and an unremarkable lawn, bordered by shrubbery. But it was the welcome aroma of cooking radiating from the kitchen, exciting Bethany's tastebuds, that truly defined Haroon, his house and his occupation.

Before long, they were chatting away like old friends whilst he cooked with the focus and expertise of a good chef.

"Yes, I still find the long fasts of Ramadan difficult," he was telling her. "But the feasts that break the fasts are what most Muslims look forward to the most. Now that Ramadan is over, we can enjoy our food again. You may not know, but there is a provision in our religion that allows someone who is unable to fast, say if they are taking medication or unwell, to pay a small donation to another person to fast for them. Of course, this practice is abused by certain rich businessmen, who gorge themselves all day long while some poor soul fasts for them. My father's been watching the Football World Cup since 1970. I started watching the World Cup from Spain 1982, in my opinion arguably the best World Cup in living memory. It was Ramadan, and both the Algerian and Kuwaiti teams played their matches while fasting; fortunately, theirs weren't the slow games you'd have expected. It was the tournament that sported the best Brazilian side never to have won the World Cup."

Bethany admitted she wasn't a great football fan ever since learning her father had been a Millwall supporter, in other words a notorious hooligan, back in his heyday, the only time ever Millwall entered Europe.

Haroon continued to cook dinner while Bethany continued to help out, like a nurse who assists a surgeon in theatre. The delicious sizzle of spiced meats in the frying pan mixed with the aroma of the skewered meats roasting in the authentic *tandoor* present in his kitchen caused her mouth to salivate, nearly dribble. In fact the kitchen had been modified, industrialized, to such an extent, equipped with shiny, metal surfaces for food preparation, a tall floor-to-ceiling fridge/freezer and all manner of pots and pans and essential cooking utensils hanging by hooks along the canopy of the central fluorescent-lighting, that Haroon could have opened an Indian takeaway right from his doorstep.

"So . . . what is the secret to a good curry?"

"The base, always the base – and *time*. The base can be altered slightly to create a completely different dish, and you do not rush it. You must spend enough time over it, perfecting it. Names like 'Vindaloo' and 'Korma' are a modern Western creation, nothing more than a marketing gimmick. In India or Pakistan, it's just 'curry' as an umbrella term, but the base can vary from region to region. The base makes the sauce makes the curry. I think friends should be tried and trusted. Even so, one of my best friends stole my secret recipe for his sauce and opened his own restaurant up north. One lesson I learned: there are no friends in business." He switched subjects. "Do you like Michael Caine?"

"Neither one way nor the other," Bethany responded. "I'm indifferent, I suppose."

"Michael Caine isn't one of my favourite actors, either. Always plays the same role. But he, like Christopher Lee, has undergone something of a renaissance." Haroon tried to remember the name of a film he watched recently. "Have you ever seen *Mr. Morgan's Last Love?*"

"Yes, it was a lovely film. So sad yet so hopeful. A man in mourning and a girl looking of love. I felt for the friendship forged between the two protagonists."

"I agree it was a decent watch," Haroon said, and went on to explain how afterwards he had decided to read up on Michael Caine, idly so, learn a little about him. But he was flabbergasted to discover the man was in his eighties and he somehow looked at least twenty years younger. Then, he realized why. "Do you know what his secret is?"

Bethany was intrigued. "No, what?"

"Turmeric. Aside from being married to a beautiful Indian model, the man's been taking turmeric capsules for decades. It's the staple of Indian curries and its active ingredient, curcumin, has antioxidant properties proven to reduce disease and increase longevity. Not only does it slow down the aging process, it reduces the build-up of plaques in the brain in dementia, aids the digestive process, protects against bowel cancer, and decreases the risk of heart attacks and strokes. Michael Caine's a living example of its benefits. Unless you've got diabetes from consuming too many sugary foods or heart disease from using ghee, which is just as unhealthy as lard, those reasonably-off and well-educated in the Indian subcontinent suffer less diseases and live longer. All because of turmeric, the key ingredient of most curries."

Bethany chuckled. "Well, you learn something new every day! Well done to Michael Caine for keeping the secret to his long life quiet!"

Then, there was a brief discussion about all the other health benefits curries had to offer. Whereas parsley, sumac and harissa defined Middle-Eastern cooking, traditional Indian curries relied on certain tried-and-tested ingredients: garlic (lowers cholesterol, regulates stomach acidity), ginger (anti-arthritic, cold remedy), cinnamon, (blood cleanser), cumin (works with vitamins to function as an anti-cancer agent in prostate cancer), capsicum (anti-inflammatory properties, reduces the risk of macular degeneration), cardamom (antiseptic); together the spices of the curry, or the actual specific spicy mix, garam masala, had antimicrobial properties, preserving the life of cooked or uncooked meat. The good, old chilli essentially gave the curry the kick it needed. The active ingredient of chillies, capsaicin, was responsible for the 'hotness' of a curry, post-ingestion. Chillies, scientists discovered, had the health-giving benefits of improving your circulation (by immediately raising the heart rate and blood pressure), reducing cholesterol (thereby offsetting the overall risk of cardiovascular disease), decreasing insulin requirements (so preventing diabetes), aiding digestion (and, of course, bowel transit), the antioxidant properties boosting the immune system and killing off stomach and pancreatic cancer cells (which is why those who ate a spicy diet tended to have lower rates of certain cancers than those eating a bland Western diet), reducing nasal congestion (breaking down phlegm in colds and 'flus, clearing the airways), increasing the basal metabolic rate (so allowing you to lose weight) and releasing endorphins in the brain (therefore reducing stress levels so it left you feeling happy, satisfied and relaxed). So maybe the spice traders of old, some of whom died in their far-reaching quest to procure these exotic condiments, knew something back then that scientists had only just proven recently.

Haroon laid the dining table with a veritable feast of Indian foods: samosas, kebabs and three separate curry dishes, one consisting of aubergines and okra, another of chickpeas, and the third tilapia fish, alongside an accompaniment of rice, rotis, poppadoms and chutneys. And garden variety salad, except Bethany had never seen red carrots; in fact, orange carrots did not exist in India, Haroon informed her. They ate heartily. Bethany enjoyed the variety of flavours, the unique blend of spices, the heat. She had read somewhere the reason curries had overtaken fish and chips as the national dish – why curries were deemed so addictive – was because the flavourful mix of spices and chillies caused an explosion of taste in the mouth, each mouthful driving the tastebuds wild, and confusing and tantalizing the senses in equal measure, hitting the same sites in the brain as music and drugs. Indeed, tonight's culinary experience was a masterclass in Punjabi cuisine, a well-conducted symphony for the palate. Already, she seemed to be sweating curry sauce through the skin pores, and maybe why flies found Indians so attractive was because of curry-flavoured chemicals they released in their sweat. However, Haroon made sure in this instance that he used the right amount of heat, that the meal wasn't too hot for her. As he informed her, *If it burns going in, it'll burn coming out.* Yes, Bethany didn't want her bum to be on fire!

Haroon didn't care much for food critics. These people, who claimed to be educated epicures, were only interested in stuffing their fat faces and being pampered in the process while belittling the efforts the restaurant staff put in. Most critics were good for nothing in the kitchen themselves, ridiculously inept at coming up with their own dish, and seemed only capable of trashing someone else's hard work. Maybe they were jealous of other people's creativity or just took their own Z-list celebrity status far too seriously, undermining those who really did know something about cooking. Too much weight was put on their opinion, making or breaking a restaurant's reputation. "I take no interest in these useless, self-important pricks! Fortunately, I've been lucky enough not to have had a run-in with these people or to have suffered their bullshit. Because I would tell them precisely what I thought of them and where to go!"

Once the food was hungrily devoured, a homemade evening meal that alone put a lot of Indian restaurants to shame, and would have made Madhur Jaffrey proud, after the plates and pans had been washed and dried, Haroon and his special guest sat next to each other on the white sofa in the main reception room, eating pistachio *kulfi* and sipping Darjeeling, and nattered away whilst they streamed the Oscar-winning *The Theory of Everything* on the TV.

"Wouldn't it be nice to have an equation that elegantly unifies and explains everything, from the quantum level to the wider cosmos, an equation that God uses? An equation that might even explain Love itself?"

It was a hopeful comment, and Bethany could see that Haroon was a man well-versed in a lot more besides cooking classic Indian dishes and making money from it. "When did you last go out with an Englishwoman?" she asked him.

"A long time ago," Haroon recalled. "Before Kuldeep."

"And what did you think of them?"

"I think white women are more tolerant, open to new experiences. You have no idea how white skin is treasured in Asian and African societies. Anthropologists say it's something to do with the concept that blemishes and diseases can be picked up on light skin which would otherwise remain hidden by darker skin. So when our ancestors were selecting a mate, they would go for lighter-skinned women, who were also younger, fertile, of child-bearing age."

"You're a genuine walking library!"

"Not really. I'm just curious. I just like to know things."

"Curiosity killed the cat, you know."

"But satisfaction brought it back," he reminded her with a Cheshire grin. She got up to leave. "Don't go, beautiful." He pulled her gently onto his lap, and he looked deep and amorously into her eyes. They kissed.

"*I desire you!*" he said, doing a comical impression of Bernard Bresslaw's Arab sheikh when ogling Angela Douglas's vulnerable heroine in that classic *Carry On* film. Neither would Bethany have minded an impression of Sid James's *Corrrrr!*

He took her upstairs then, and amidst an atmosphere of scented candles and music, they made out, filled with animal desires. Bethany gave herself willingly to him, this man who constantly strove to determine the right proportion of spices in order to create the perfect curry, just like Stephen Hawking searched for the ultimate equation. She would never call herself a gold-digger. Greed was never a motive, only the promise of love and a comfortable life.

She took off her blouse and skirt, revealing her best underwear above her slim, desirable legs. He enjoyed her body, from the elegant contours of her neck, past the pertness of her modest but determined breasts, to the tips of her luscious toes. She readied her legs for him, and they made passionate love, eventually basking in the afterglow of their first loving session. They slept together that night, contented in the knowledge that they had found someone to love.

Bethany appreciated his honesty and his feelings for her, and she granted him full access to her heart. *You will find no borders here,* she whispered softly into his ear as he drifted off to sleep.

4

Second Best

They continued to see one another, relishing the other's company and the lovemaking each encounter entailed. Haroon paid off her student loan, much to her joy, and bought her small gifts, initially taking her to Selfridges, then Harrods next time, until he proposed to her at his house two months after they first met, popping the question during a leisurely walk at the local pond. As the midday sun dappled the shimmering mirror of water, upon which glided files of swans and cygnets, which Bethany fed scraps of crusty bread, she accepted the marriage proposal, and preparations began for their forthcoming wedding. Just as Pardesi's *Balbeero Bhabi* had reminded Haroon of his first wife, *Namumkin* by Pakistan's premier rock band, Vital Signs, would become his personal song for Bethany. *Namumkin*, roughly translated, meant 'impossible' in the Indian language. *Impossible.*

Two days before departing for Lahore, Bethany caught up with her father to tell him the good news. Brian Holcombe lived in the Council estate of Netherton, within one of the flats at the Seven Sisters. He was none-too-impressed by Bethany's announcement.

"You are *not* marrying a Paki!" he told her, expressing his long-established racist views, reflective of the yob that he had once been. Despite his chronic bronchitis and breathing difficulties, brought on by decades of chain-smoking, he was still a formidable character among the UKIP faithful. "You should have seduced and married one of the rich blokes, whose kids you used to care for! What's wrong with marrying your own kind, an Englishman, a salt-of-the-earth true Brit?".

Bethany could sense the old man's disappointment, manifesting as open criticism of her choice of husband. "Please, Dad, if you hadn't noticed, we live in a cosmopolitan society! You should be happy for me!"

"Not a chance, girl!" he wheezed, opening another can of Carlsberg. "You've darkened my doorstep with your visit, choosing to cavort with the enemy! I will have nothing more to do with you!"

Bethany did not cry at his stark rejection of her or need to remind her own father he had disappointed her all her life and sent her mother into an early grave, which is why Bethany had emancipated herself from his care once she'd turned eighteen. But at least she had done her duty as a daughter in informing her only kin of her imminent wedding, whether he liked it or not. She left then, but not in a flood of tears. She could hold her head up high and be proud of her decision to marry Haroon, even if she had not obtained her father's blessing for the impending nuptials.

Her only real friend, Leanna Cormack, who worked at RIPPENDALE'S Department Store, was more receptive and congratulatory. "You finally did it, Beth, and I hope it goes without a hitch!" The two of them went on the town, taking in a show at CHERTSFORD VICTORIA THEATRE, doubling as a modest hen party. No male strippers, no drunkenness, no ladette behaviour. Just an impressive stage version of *Shakespeare Wallah*, based on the original Merchant-Ivory film, unique in many ways for introducing the interracial onscreen romance between Shashi Kapoor and Felicity Kendall while behind the scenes occurred the real-life romance between

Kapoor and Felicity's sister, Jennifer.

As a Muslim and averse to alcohol, Haroon never entertained a stag party, and he and his bride-to-be soon set off to Pakistan.

For nearly the course of a millennium, Lahore served as regional capital of the Punjab during the successive Hindu Shahi, Mughal and Sikh empires as well as under British Raj before Indian independence. Bethany understood Lahore's special place in Indian history. Whereas Karachi was now the economic hub of the country and Islamabad the government administrative capital, Lahore could be described as its cultural heart, hosting the arts and music festivals and being the home of Pakistan's film industry (Lollywood). Lahore bespoke the romance Indian poets had with the city, and it was also the birthplace of the Sufi-driven Qawwali musicians, singing their highest praises to Allah. Lahore was the perfect fusion of traditional and modern. Progressive, forward-thinking, as Haroon had previously described, which Bethany could now see for herself.

Located within the beautiful walled city of Lahore, also known as the Old City, stood the BADSHAHI MOSQUE, built by the Mughal emperor Aurangzeb in 1676 to house a strand of the Holy Prophet's hair. The sandstone walls of the Lahore Fort were built over a century earlier than the grand masjid. Inside the Badshahi Mosque intricate carvings adorned the walls and ceilings. This iconic landmark of sandstone minarets on all four corners and great marble domes was able to accommodate nearly one hundred thousand people, making it the seventh largest mosque in the world. Haroon and Bethany wed in the Badshahi, where they completed the *Nikkah*, the official signing of the marriage contract between the couple. Haroon was dressed like a maharaja, complete with *sherwani* and turban. Bethany wore a native, heavily-embroidered dress in rich red, made from the finest silks, her skin prepared the night before in patterns of henna during the Mehndi ceremony. In front of the imam and an intimate gathering of Haroon's family and friends, Bethany was instructed, along with Haroon, to repeat a few lines of the Quran to sanctify their union in the old Islamic custom. Both Bride and Groom sealed the marriage ceremony with their signatures and a solemn '*Qubool hain*', a vow of 'I accept'.

The wedding reception, or *Walima*, followed in Haroon's family home, a white colonial mansion of Indo-Saracenic style with Victorian gothic flourishes. It was a lively, extravagant affair, complete with bridesmaids and flower girls, a dancefloor and DJ, classy centrepieces and elegant Persian carpets and graceful ornate drapings, creating an atmosphere as lively and colourful as a Mela. Credit to the wedding coordinator for executing the wedding smoothly and flawlessly. The Reception was attended by close relatives, extended family and friends; there were no slumdogs to speak of. The gentlemen were dressed in suits and the ladies wore *salwar chemise* tricked out in embroidered fabrics of bright pastel colours. Bethany discovered that Muslim weddings focused on feeding the guests whereas Sikh weddings, as Haroon informed her, involved a lot of Bhangra, Bicardi and Brawling, which often involved police intervention, as had been the case with his token Sikh reception, at the insistence of his [then] in-laws, following his Islamic union with Kuldeep all those years ago back in the UK. Bethany met Haroon's entire clan, who welcomed her as one of their own, showing off the new Bride to everyone without objectifying her. Haroon's sister, Halima, was already talking about children which Bethany responded to in noncommittal fashion. Haroon's outspoken uncle, Riaz, a doctor in Rawalpindi, was quick to remind everyone of how Imran Khan was a crooked politician and a hypocrite to boot for deflowering Sir Goldsmith's eighteen-year-old daughter, Jemima, but insisting his own sisters marry the Islamic way. *Such double standards. The man should have stuck to cricket!*

The feast was a banquet fit for a king or, in the case of Haroon Bashir, a curry mogul. Every type of Punjabi food was catered for in staggering quantities. There was singing and dancing. *Mitai*, a form of Asian sweets, was offered to the Bride to close the *Shaadi* (Wedding), and flower garlands and rose petals were thrown at the Happy Couple, like confetti, ahead of the Honeymoon.

However, Haroon and Bethany decided to spend some time in Lahore before embarking on their honeymoon; it gave Bethany a chance to explore the city's mosques, markets and monuments. She frequented the bazaars, rode rickshaws through the streets and partook of the local cuisine, the constant smell of spices tickling the senses awake. The famous places of Lahore, as with the Badshahi Mosque, were a tourist's delight. The breathtaking splendour of the SHALIMAR GARDENS, laid out during the reign of Shah Jahan, was designed to mimic the Islamic paradise of the Afterlife described in the Quran. The JAHANGIR MAUSOLEUM, a place of peace and solitude in an otherwise busy city, marked the resting place of the eponymous Mughal emperor, who is once quoted to have said: *The most welcome and painful moments of life are within marriage.* Lahore's world-renowned universities, built during Victorian rule, included the GOVERNMENT COLLEGE UNIVERSITY and the KING EDWARD MEDICAL SCHOOL; the LAHORE COLLEGE FOR WOMEN, founded in the 1920s further demonstrated the Punjab's progressive nature. The wedding and Bethany's short sojourn in Lahore proved a memorable experience, magical even. She felt privileged to experience her husband's culture, to be walking the land of his ancestors.

Its palm-shaped islands with their sky-high towers overlooking the Persian Gulf,

Dubai, on the other hand, was a fast-paced cosmopolitan city, a land of glamour and glitz, seamlessly weaving exotic Arabian traditions with the richest luxuries of the West. The honeymooners checked into the BURJ AL ARAB, standing on an artificial island just off JUMEIRAH BEACH, at one thousand feet the third tallest building in the world and its shape designed to mimic the sail of a ship, so convincingly one might have been forgiven for thinking the entire structure would sail away. Not far was the BURJ KHALIFA, a super-skyscraper, which being nearly three times taller than the Burj al Arab was classified as the tallest building in the world. The newlyweds enjoyed basking in the sun during the day, perhaps riding the camels on the desert sands inland certain afternoons, and dining in the outstanding gourmet restaurants in the evenings, and at night either joining the bonfire parties on the beach or making slow, sweet, sensuous love to each other.

They returned back to the UK after a fortnight's Arabian honeymoon, both heavily tanned and recharged and refreshed to start their new life together.

Although Bethany considered changing her name by deed poll, not that Haroon requested her to, she decided not to after he took her to his house in Rochdale to check in on his other curry house, in Littleborough. Bethany had grown accustomed to wearing traditional Indian dress, her new norm both out of respect for her husband and because the baggy-fitting silk clothes were extremely comfortable and colourful. He had been commended by his family and friends for marrying a white, non-Muslim girl – a *gori*, in Punjabi – but he did not ask her to cover her face in a hijab-and-burqa or expect her to change her religion, which she had been prepared to do.

His residence in Spotland was a large, white, pebble-dashed house, and walking through the door, Bethany suddenly had a bad feeling.

The house was roomy and sparsely-decorated, but there was an unwholesome smell, the faint scent of stale urine, that lingered unpleasantly in the air, the odour growing stronger, the source of which would become apparent, the further up the two flights of stairs Haroon guided her. Haroon took her up to the attic. Haroon had mentioned a surprise.

When Bethany saw what the surprise was, she stopped dead in her tracks. She was too horrified by the sight before her and her husband's dreadful betrayal.

In the attic sat an Indian woman, roughly in her fifties judging by the greys in her long, plaited hair, huddled on the bed, hugging her knees. Mute and catatonic, she sat staring ahead into space, unresponsive to any conversation. The other woman who sat nursing her, Bethany recognized from her Lahori wedding as Haroon's only sister, Halima. They shared an awkward silence. There were no second guesses as to who the woman sitting motionlessly on the bed, looking blankly ahead, was.

"This is Kuldeep," Haroon announced, wiping drool from the corner of the bedridden woman's mouth. "I thought you should both meet."

Bethany stared at the woman, Kuldeep, Haroon's demented wife, his first love, a terrible secret he had kept as close to his chest as had the fictional Mr. Rochester.

Haroon and Bethany had their first argument that day, also their last. It was a lot to expect, asking your latest wife to look after your previous wife, who had completely lost her marbles and seemed no longer capable of caring for herself or communicating her needs. A loved one who was now mentally infirm, totally incapacitated, wasting away to sagging skin and mere bones. Why didn't he just hire a nurse? And why had Haroon tricked Bethany into marrying him? Bethany had felt enough love to marry him in the way he had desired the most. Had he done this to other unsuspecting girls? Did he have a harem full of women hidden somewhere and Bethany constituted just another trophy wife? Worse, what if he was a Bluebeard, a Monsieur Verdoux, whereby she might have to save herself from being executed by pleading and negotiating with him or, perhaps, using a mode of distraction, resorting to the resourceful manner in which Scheherazade managed to finally convince the Sultan to spare her life? She didn't wish to find out one way or the other. Maybe he didn't love her at all and only needed her services as a carer. Maybe his first wife was where his love really lay.

All the good men are taken, and you're left with the nutters! Shame! This was not how Bethany envisaged married life to be. Haroon had turned out to be a creepy sort of guy, after all.

Bethany had wanted to be special in his life, second to none, not second best.

5

Take Two

"So how did you get out of it?" Leanna asked her.

"It wasn't particularly difficult," Bethany responded. "Once I'd calmed down after throwing a few F-bombs at him, I told him I was going to report him to the police for bigamy unless he cut me loose."

"And he let you go?"

"Yes, on the proviso I never see him again."

"He might do this to another girl."

"Possibly, but I think the outcome will be same – the marriage will not be deemed valid in the UK – and I think in the end he will get caught, arrested, particularly if the next girl is not so innocent and forgiving."

The two friends were sat in OL' JAVA BEAN café, enjoying iced tea on a sunshiny afternoon.

"I can't believe he was expecting you to care for his senile wife . . ."

Bethany remembered that day in the attic, post-honeymoon, and the crazy wife, reduced to an unspeaking, drooling statue. The stink of urine, like that in a nursing home. Haroon had certainly been expecting too much of Bethany, expectations that were too absurdly selfish and could not possibly be met by anyone sane. "But at least he loved his first wife enough to remarry and have his new bride look after her."

"So conceited of him," said Leanna, disgusted. "And he really thought he could get away with it?"

"Love is not hearts and flowers and gifts. It's not! It's tough, messy, painful." Bethany considered Haroon's deception, and maybe he never considered it a deception but was only following guidelines set down in his religion. "I did a bit of research after my experience," she began thoughtfully. "Islam is beset with problems and contradictions, none as ludicrous as the whole practice of polygamous relationships. The Mormons were taken to Court for this evil practice, but at least they had the common sense to back down and outlaw it from their religion.

"I can understand where polygamy came from in Islam. Polygamy supposedly arose because too many men were killed in battle, fifteen hundred years ago, when Islam was establishing a firm root in society, leaving a surplus of women and orphans on the sideline." Bethany recited a verse from the Quran for Leanna's benefit: *And if you fear you cannot act equitably towards orphans, then marry such women as seem good to you, two and three and four; but if you fear that you will not do justice (between them), then marry only one or what your right hands possess; this is more proper, that you may not deviate from the right course.* Quran 4:3. "Muslim apologists attempt to justify polygamous behaviour by claiming Muslim men in those days married many wives due to them being war widows, who were left with nothing and with nobody to care for them or their offspring. Also, polygamy was designed to curb adultery, improve the overall quality of family life and support the equal rights of women. Seems sensible on the surface and well-thought-out, doesn't it? But, of course, this is total hogwash!

"In a religion that actively preaches that women are lesser creatures, who should be submissive, faithful and obedient to their husbands, gender equality immediately goes out the window." Bethany added that Muslim countries fared the worst in terms of female oppression or observing the family code, with Saudi Arabia having the second highest divorce rate in the world and polygamy being held responsible for nearly two-thirds of divorces, the loss of trust, sincerity and compassion in the polygamous marriage mostly to blame, the wives relegated to subservient creatures. "God only knows why polygamy is still practised in the twenty-first century. Not forgetting that when a man dies, he potentially leaves behinds four widows. Defeats the argument against those in favour of polygamy immediately.

"The man has absolute power in Islamic teachings. The husband is not obliged to seek his first wife's permission if he so wishes to marry another woman, with no similar provision available for the woman. Even if the term 'harem' is meant to be a place that is protected and forbidden, except to the Master of the Harem, it is mostly used as a sex palace or sexual playground. Not to mention the Quran gives license to capture women and use them as sex slaves just in case four wives wasn't enough! So where's the justice in that? Debasing women from the sacred position of wife to the lowest station as concubine just to sate the Muslim male's sexual appetite!"

"Sounds like Islam is still stuck in the Dark Ages," Leanna commented.

Bethany focused on the crux of the matter. "The inherent problem lies with Muhammad. By the fifth century, the Roman Empire was wholeheartedly embracing Christianity. And Muhammad was an opportunist seeking to rewrite the Bible while it was riding on a wave of popularity. He saw the chance to create his own religion by whatever means possible. There was a lot wrong with him. You can either look at him as a demagogue, a master of bullshit, an egotist and misogynist, a violent warlord openly preaching religious intolerance or, if you choose the deferential line, a reformist at best. If Muslim men can take up to four wives, Allah made their prophet a rare exception. Everyone knows Muhammad was a serial polygamist. Besides the numerous concubines he kept, he married a lot of women – *Nine? Eleven? Fifteen? The number is disputed but I don't really care!* – and consummated his marriages with most of them. It is recorded he achieved this rare feat because Allah apparently bestowed him the strength of thirty men in the bedchamber!" Bethany explained that many of his marriages were clearly based on lust, not compassion, and Muhammad ultimately divorced six of his wives, for unfair and uncharitable reasons such as if they suffered from leprosy or even because one of them he considered was too old for him, this despite him wedding a six-year-old! "The hypocrite would not even let the husband of his daughter, Fatima, take a second wife. Makes Imran Khan look like a saint! The jealousy of his existing wives allegedly angered Allah who advised Muhammad to divorce them all unless they allowed him complete sexual freedom. Allah – the Islamic interpretation of God – took a keen interest in Muhammad's needs, empowering him to do whatever was convenient, like allowing him to take as many wives as he chose. No surprise Muhammad founded a religion that gives high regard to men's baser sexual desires, sanctioning other women into the marriage bed just to satisfy the man's lust. In other words, if I were to take an educated guess, Muhammad did whatever he liked, citing Allah as his advocate, when Allah really had nothing to do with it! You know Freud claimed that the holy prophets were psychotic and their followers neurotic.

"The real telling thing is the Quran itself, supposedly the Last Word of God. Outside scholars will claim that the original Arabic version is in fact a coarse and crude piece of writing, but its many translations, such as in Farsi and Urdu, even English, have endeavoured to poeticize the work. What is particularly mentionworthy is the word '*nikkah*', passed down from ancient Arabic kufic script. If Muhammad wanted to have sexual relations with a woman he coveted, Allah would allegedly grant him permission, under the rubric of *nikkah*. Nikkah translates as 'to marry' in other languages, but in purest Arabic, in its absolute literal sense, it actually means 'fuck'!"

June 2016-September 2016

Aunts and Nephews

"If only we could all escape from the house of incest, where we only love ourselves in the other, if only I could save you all from yourselves."

House of Incest (1936)
Anais Nin

I started out in Fine Art. Nude Art was my fascination: Manet, Degas, Titian, Rubens, Rembrandt, Botticelli and his Venuses, and all that. I was fascinated by the beauty of the female form and how it always brought desire into the eyes of men, leading inevitably to the oldest act known to Man. *Sex and beauty are inseparable, like life and consciousness,* as D.H. Lawrence so neatly put it. *The greatest living experience for every man is his adventure into the woman.* I progressed from Art class to the world of Pornography in a single leap whilst at Chertsford University. Might not be as respected as working as a legitimate artist, Porn, but it pays so much more unless you make it big in the Art world, achieve legendary status. Porn has a tendency to polarize the public, but I consider it to be as good as any Turner prize crap, like painting with shit or turning the light on and off in a large, airy, empty loft installation and calling it 'Art'. I recently read about a controversial performance artist called Günter Brus, who covered himself in his own excrement, drank his own urine which he immediately vomited up, and after a public display of masturbation, was promptly arrested by the police and hauled away to the clink. Credit to him for his bravery in doing what he believed in, but if *that* bullshit is Art, then so must be the erotic medium I work in.

I suppose my interest in the aesthetically-pleasing shape of women – *The human soul needs actual beauty more than bread,* my literary idol, D.H. Lawrence, again –

stretches even further back, well before most teenage boys were inspecting the ladies' underwear section of the *Great Universal* catalogue for a glimpse of nipple through the fabric. You see my mother was a not a pleasant woman, cold, austere, a shrew. She could have drawn blood from a stone. I'm amazed my parents stayed together as long as they did. I guess the lack of intimacy she showed my father meant he drank. When it came to his drinking there were no limits, and she ragged on him day and night, but I guess the alcohol kept him in a good mood, made her easier to ignore. That probably explained why he relied on a lot of pornographic magazines. I discovered them when I was six. It was my adventitious introduction into the World of Porn. I guess it was because of my mother's disinterest in me, the general lack of maternal affection, I took up Porn in the end. She's a woman who certainly needed a good shagging. Apparently, I was conceived when my parents were drunk on their wedding night. And she vowed never to drink again, a promise she kept. As well as never to give my father sex again, because of that same fear of losing control.

My father's jazz mags were an education, and a godsend, as I grew up, playing with myself in my spare time, trying to make sense of my hard-on, until I had my first wet dream at twelve years of age when it all became clear to me. True, spanking the monkey became an easier pastime thereafter. Without my mother's knowledge, my father took me to a brothel the day I turned thirteen as a Birthday present – or perhaps as a rite of passage. I suppose my father was a major-league drunk, who didn't sober up until his sixties by which time he had developed cirrhosis of the liver. His oesophageal varices were so bad, causing him to profusely vomit blood and preventing him from eating through his mouth ever again, he was requesting a vodka bolus through a PEG tube from his hospital bed in Olde London Towne. More power to you, man! I never told him about the porno mags I found in his dressing-table drawer because I did not want to embarrass him, particularly on his deathbed, even if he was always a bit crazy.

My teenage years were one, long wank! I think most boys should have a girlfriend at that age, discover love and sex in a mutually-consenting capacity, but I think masturbation is something we Gents do out of sexual frustration and desperation throughout our lives when the other half is not giving or forthcoming. Everybody knows ninety-nine percent of men wank and the remaining one percent lie! The Victorians applied spikes around the penises of maturing boys to prevent them from developing an erection at night. The Catholic Church forever demonized the whole idea of flogging the bishop, even after sweeping those priests with their proclivity for altar boys under the carpet. Organized religion used to say that masturbation causes brain damage and blindness or leads to a life of crime and rape, or the penis will just shrivel up from overuse and fall off, but in today's more liberal and well-informed society, everyone accepts that masturbation is an enjoyable and infection-free form of sexual activity in the privacy of your own bedroom. I was supremely self-taught on the subject. A regular Sir Wanksalot!

You might judge me harshly by how I broke into the arena of professional pornography. You may already know me, Guy Hastings, if you know good porn! My big break into the porn world involved my friendship with a medical student, going by the name of Ethan Sett. And what he was doing after hours provided me with the inspiration, planting the seed of a plan as twisted as a contortionist performing auto-fellatio. Ethan was doing something I wouldn't even have dreamed of in those drug-addled days.

He was fucking his aunt.

Yep, it was Chertsford University. First Semester, Freshers' Week. Summer had come and gone, marked by the World Cup. I was glad the overhyped England team had got knocked out of the competition relatively early so thankfully the people could now concentrate on some real football. The presenter asks his panel: *What do you think went wrong for England?* The pundit's imaginary response: *I think, mainly, it's the fact they're shit!* Wise words.

So this story I bring to you is an autumnal tale when the wind is whistling and the leaves are swirling past windows. Yes, we were larging it up, student-style. Extraordinary how the politicians hadn't yet figured out that free beer for all students would be a sure-fire Election winner instead of knocking up tuition fees and student loans and leaving the average graduate twenty grand in debt before they'd even stepped out into the big, bad world.

I made three new friends down at THE GRINDER, the Student Union bar: Waldemar Spake, Ethan Sett and Charles Stroud. Yeah, that's right! Spake and Sett, whose surnames sounded like they belonged to a couple of gravediggers. Or perhaps even bodysnatchers. Charles Stroud just sounded like a toff.

We wandered back, staggering, down the crowded, lively avenue of other shit-faced Freshmen on that cold September evening after closing time to our student residence, WENTWORTH HALL. University was a time of leaving your formative years behind and striding into adulthood with your head held high, smarter and more independent, enlightened and cultured, than those who entered the job market at sixteen.

Waldemar's dorm room (like ours) was nothing unusual, four walls cramped with self-assembled, chipboard furniture.

"A-ha!" I exclaimed in my best Alan Partridge impression, pulling forward the wardrobe. Lo and behold, behind the wardrobe were some porno mags.

"How did you know?" Waldemar asked, not the slightest trace of embarrassment in his voice. Like me, Waldemar was 'self-taught'.

"That's precisely where I'd hide them!" I told him. "Certainly not under the mattress which is the norm. Way too obvious."

"My mom says she keeps my bedroom as it was, back home . . . she doesn't like to throw anything away, including what's under the mattress . . ."

"Wise woman."

"Just goes to show, Growcock, you're one helluva 'stand-up' guy!" Charles Stroud added.

"Hey, cool T-shirt," Waldemar pointed out in admiration, as I took off my leather jacket for the first time this evening.

I glanced down at the black WOMEN'S LUBRICATION FRONT slogan on my white T-shirt as contentious as the legend, FBI: FEMALE BODY INSPECTOR, on my old sweatshirt. I was amazed campus security hadn't stopped me from wearing it, or my normally-observant Art teacher, Mr. Tipperton. Or 'Mr. Titspervert' due to his leery interest in his female students. Or maybe he *did* notice and didn't object to it, thought it cool. "Thanks, man." I repaid the compliment. "Nice hair."

"Do you know how long it takes me to create this mussed-up look?" Waldemar decided not to tell me since he was now rolling up a doobie. I was a weed lightweight. And I knew I would be in for a serious mash-up tonight, having already consumed seven pints. "There is a reason for everything in this world," Waldemar, a pseudo-intellectual studying Biotechnology, philosophized. "There is even a reason for God. Drugs allow you to see behind the façade of reality. People say reality hides the penultimate – and *ultimate* – truth."

I was nonplussed by some of the shit he came out with. "Who *are* these people who say these things?"

"Professor Leary and PKD – you know who?"

I didn't know much about them, but once we'd sparked up, it didn't matter anymore. We four sat there in the dorm-room like half-statues, off our heads, quietly giggling at nothing in particular.

Then we were talking again whilst Charles Stroud, the first of us to be completely monged, succumbed to a drug-induced coma, crashing out on the floor. It was talk of girlfriends, or the general lack of. But University was the place to discover the opposite, fairer sex – and quim. I didn't know about Charles, but myself and

Waldemar were girlfriend-less. However, Ethan indicated he was seeing someone, and we latched on to him quickly like the couple of skeevy old men we were.

"Way to go, me old stud!" I celebrated. "Haven't been here one week, and you're already hooked-up!"

"Who is it?" Waldemar followed up, with bloodshot eyes and a wide, inane grin. "Anyone we know?"

But Ethan was reserved, almost bashful. "I don't think it's worth it . . ." He turned to me, attempting to deflect the conversation away from himself. "What about you? Any ladies in your life?"

"Don't be coy! Let us in on your little secret! *Details, please!*" I egged, excitedly, reining in his evasiveness. "When one of the lads gets some action, we band of brothers are united behind a common cause! Only we can provide you with the moral support you so rightfully deserve!"

I think Ethan must have known we wouldn't rest until we got all the sordid details out of him, which is why I suppose he spilled the beans. Or perhaps because he was stoned to the gills and more able to leave his guard down. "If you must know, it's an older woman."

"You mean *Harold and Maude* older woman?" inquired Waldemar.

Ethan looked at Waldemar blankly, not getting the film reference. I preferred the idea of a seductive, experienced, sex-starved Mrs. Robinson-type. "No, she's a relative of mine."

"You mean like Jerry Lee Lewis/Myra Gale Brown kind of relative . . ." Waldemar tried to clarify, "but much older?"

"No, my *aunt* . . .!" Ethan snapped in the peeved-off tone of someone who just wants to be left alone. "*There*, I said it!"

By putting him under pressure, we had got the necessary information out of him. *Straight from the horse's mouth!* It took us a little while to process the news such was the enormity of it. "When you say 'aunt', you mean by marriage?"

"By blood. My mum's *youngest* sister."

Waldemar was appalled. "Oooh, isn't that incest or something?"

Ethan didn't say anything, taken aback.

"I mean I've seen your mother," Waldemar continued. "Please don't tell me your aunt looks like your mother?"

"What's wrong with my mum?"

Waldemar told him.

"My mum *doesn't* have a beard!"

"That's a matter of opinion."

I steered the conversation away from the mother-insults. Besides, his mother suffered from Cushing's disease. "Out of all the beautiful women someone as handsome as you could have dated, how come you ended up with your aunt?"

"Sonja's a beautiful woman. Total Marisa Tomei-lookalike. Growing up, I always had a crush on her."

"That has to be one seriously sheltered upbringing," Waldemar opined, "when the only girls you can choose from are your mother, sister or aunt!"

"Man, that's fucking hardcore!" I said, expressing my opinion. But Marisa Tomei was good. I could see the attraction. I could live with Marisa Tomei. "I aspire to be a gentleman pornographer. Sleeping with my aunt is something that I might do – I never thought it would be you!"

Ethan was turning bright red, likely out of embarrassment and shame. "I should never have opened my mouth . . .!"

"No, man, it's cool!" I reassured him. "At least one of us is getting their end away!"

Charles said likewise, opening his eyes for a moment, "Yeah, giving some proper, serious wood!"

Waldemar sounded uncharacteristically judgemental, "Whatever floats your boat..." He paused before adding: "It would certainly explain why you keep a tattoo of your mother over your heart. I wonder what old Sigmund would say about all this. He'd probably have a field day!"

"At least I don't wank in my socks!" stormed Ethan.

"I enjoy having a good wank in a sock," Waldemar replied, unfazed by the leaking of his own secret. No pun intended. "Contains the mess." He put his hand on his own crotch and tugged, with an offer no-one could possibly resist: "Care to use the other sock? One for the road?"

"Why not use our favourite pastime to get a steady income from the Wank Bank," I suggested to the others, "to supplement our Student Loans? Though I do suspect Waldemar would make more money than the rest of us combined!"

Waldemar grinned back at me, taking my comment as a compliment.

Here we were at Uni, living a world of sex and drugs. Life was good.

"Are you going to introduce us to the pretty lady?" Waldemar went on to ask.

"Your aunt's not available, is she?" I followed on.

"What exactly do you mean by that?" Ethan was getting more and more hacked-off.

I continued the wordplay, euphemizing suggestively, "Do you think she might be *accommodating?*"

It was Waldemar's turn to do an impression. "*Doh!*" he uttered, Homer Simpson-style. *Family Guy* would have been more apt.

And we cracked up laughing as if it were the funniest thing we'd ever heard.

Then, when the buffoonery was over, Waldemar yawned so deeply, he risked his soul escaping; but, then again, he'd probably tell anyone he didn't have a soul.

"I feel completely arseholed," I said, rising to my feet, swaying. "Shall we just take our clothes off, scooch down and shit on the floor?"

"You mean 'sleep' on the floor," Waldemar corrected me, "like old Charles there?" Who, at this moment, was fast asleep and snoring loudly in the corner of the room.

"No, I meant 'shit'!"

"I'd show you a lot more respect if you crapped on the stage in front of everyone at the Grinder than in my room," said Waldemar before deciding to call it a night around midnight.

"I hate you, guys," Ethan said, half-pissed and half-pissed-off. "You're such wankers!"

"Sorry to hear that," I said with genuine remorse. We left the room then, including old, sleepy Charles.

I stumbled down the hallway to my own room, my mind ripped on alcohol and weed, and I slept off the cocktail rather soundly. I hoped to pistol-whip my arse back into shape on the morrow, once the drugs had worn off, and planned to *actually* attend some lectures. However, Ethan's unexpected disclosure, the fact he was playing it loose with his aunt, stayed with me, invading my dreams and sowing the seed of an unspeakable idea in my head, that sprouted, grew and took shape, until the leaf-blower man did his damnedest to piss me off first thing in the morning.

"How long has it been going on for?"

Just as I've tried to be representative of our repartee the night before, I will do likewise with my conversation with Ethan the following evening. I did not want to force the issue upon him, but I knew Ethan would tell me in his own time. I didn't realize it would be so soon. That light-bulb moment still illuminating the athenaeum of my mind, and with Waldemar checking out the University Film Club and Charles the budding political scientist putting himself forward for the Debating Society, I had taken Ethan aside that evening, and we were presently chatting over a couple of bevvies in one of the quieter corners of the Grinder. On the bar's speaker system was Tommy James and the Shondells singing *I Think We're Alone Now*.

I think today he was more responsive to a cross-examination, more persuadable to lightening his load.

"She's only seven years older than me, my mum's sister," Ethan explained, sipping his pint of beer. "I suppose the first time was when I was sixteen and we were fooling around in the bedroom one afternoon. She came to wake me up from my afternoon nap. We got into this tickling contest. We lay on opposite ends of the bed, tickling each other's feet under the covers, and that was when I really appreciated her beauty, and her *feet* – all dressed up with black nail polish and anklets and toe-rings."

"Feet are good," I agreed, maintaining the flow of conversation.

"I tickled her feet to death that afternoon, but I was rock hard when I left that bed, driven wild by the shapeliness and exquisite scent of her feet: the tangy essence of sweat mingled with a light earthiness of dirt. I find bare feet on straw, like in barns and stables, particularly arousing. And I think she must have noticed my bulge because she pulled me over by the hand and stroked it. There was no anger or shame. She didn't do any more that day, but something out of the ordinary had occurred, an unbreakable barrier that would normally exist in a familial relationship had been pulled down like the Berlin Wall. I was aching so much I jizzed my jeans in front of her."

"Always the done deal! Happens to the best of us!"

"And the kicker is, she watched me explode into my pants and appeared highly amused."

"Maybe she enjoys a good tease."

"My mum was in the next room, enjoying her own siesta. I was sure I was going to get found out."

"But I can only assume, by you sitting right here in front of me, you got away with it?"

Ethan nodded. "My mum's too old-fashioned. She believes I'm too young to have a girlfriend."

"Aren't we all?"

"Then, Sonja started visiting me more often, on some lame pretence or other – her house was just down the road from ours. I knew it was to see me. She asked my mum if I could spend more time with her because I was her favourite nephew and she was lonely. She wanted me to teach her the unique language of science, headed as I was to medical school."

And Ethan told me how it happened. Sonja got him drunk on red wine, high on weed, one evening, and one thing led to another. She told him he'd kept her waiting for far too long. When they first kissed, it *wasn't* like kissing his mother, as he had initially feared. The aunt made sure of it.

When asked if he liked it, Ethan stated she took his virginity on his seventeenth Birthday – a skanky, Albanian whore took mine when I turned thirteen, if you recall, so maybe myself and Ethan weren't all that different – and it felt 'damned good'. According to Ethan, Sonja was so damned experienced that she could still turn him on three or four times a night and get him to perform sexual miracles, when he didn't know he had it in him. For those hours, the whole idea of aunt and nephew was forgotten. He took to wearing polo-necks for days afterwards in order to hide his multiple love-bites since his mother did not believe he was old enough to have a girlfriend . . . let alone contemplate a forbidden, intimate relationship between her own son and her sister. "Sonja showed me the love of an older woman."

I was moved by the sentiment even though I thought that family should be an asset in one's life, not a liability just as it was in both our cases. "You know they say men feel the horniest in their late teens while women reach their sexual peak in their early thirties before the libido wanes." I wondered out aloud why she couldn't have picked someone more age-appropriate rather than seducing her own nephew. The woman must have serious issues.

True, she'd gone out with guys, but they didn't stay very long once they realized she was something of a gypsy, working as a Tarot Reader. Like going out with a lady embalmer, whose occupation involves cosmetically enhancing the appearance of a corpse to make it look more lifelike and presentable for family viewing. Get a proper job, woman! I wondered how often Sonja had dealt the DEATH card from her tarot deck and freaked out her customers. Her reputation as a fortune-teller went far and wide, it seemed, and, these days, men just didn't want anything to do with her, calling her the 'Voodoo Lady of the Black Roses'. So I suppose Sonja must have been lonely, too. And I guess when your nephew falls for you in a big way or is doing you a big, big favour, you make the most of it.

Funnier still, it turned out she was also paying Ethan for those nightly loving sessions. It was her idea to pay him, part-fund his University course. But the idea of turning your own medical student of a nephew into a toy-boy – or rent-boy – I did find somewhat appalling. He was up to his eyeballs. Ethan was such a nice lad, a good mate, and so handsome he could have copped any girl. But somehow he'd got himself mixed up with his aunt – a mother-figure, in many respects. It was *so* D.H. Lawrence!

Incest had been practised as far back as the pharaohs of Ancient Egypt. The insane Roman Emperor Caligula was rumoured to have had his wicked way with all his sisters. Then, there were the Japanese dynasties and the South Pacific islanders who indulged in a little intrafamilial sex. These days, Muslims married their first cousins while some Jews still married their aunts. Some African and South American tribes still married close family members. In Western culture, the incidence of incest was predominantly confined to the stepfather/stepdaughter relationship or between stepsiblings. Not only did it not bode well for any offspring, concentrating the gene pool and magnifying any congenital defects, as Ethan explained, but it was a major social taboo. And a religious taboo, even if Waldemar might have proclaimed that there was no God, so don't worry!

That old perv, Henry Miller, looked at the concept of taboos in a completely different light: *Whenever a taboo is broken, something good happens, something vitalizing. Taboos after all are only hangovers, the product of diseased minds, you might say, of fearsome people who hadn't the courage to live and who under the guise of morality and religion have imposed these things upon us.*

But in this instance, was it a good thing that Sonja Turkel had broken a taboo and taken advantage of her own nephew?

The logistics of this affair were equally interesting. Ethan had this routine going. He would skive lectures during the day (attending only the seminars because all seminars required the students to be signed in), study the contents of the lectures in his bedroom (while the other students were sitting through these very lectures, bored shitless), and be ready to take it easy in the evening, doss and chill (the other students in the meantime now finally sitting down to do some actual studying, maybe studying for twelve hours until they'd gone blind or mad). He'd spend a good few hours with his mates down the Grinder before finally taking the train from Chertsford to Outer Bridge to resume his affair, under the sexual tutelage of his aunt, Sonja paying for the return taxi to his University digs in the morning. *That* was his daily routine. So, despite banging his aunt every night, Ethan was a very disciplined scholar. He was somehow able to separate his sex life from his studies. "Nothing wrong with making mistakes as long as you learn from them and don't make the same mistake twice. I always tell myself each time that the next time will be the last time . . ."

It occurred to me. If Sonja wanted a regular fuckbuddy, why not me? It had to be less obscene. "The question still stands: would your aunt be accommodating?" I asked, diving straight in. "Because, dig this, I could take her off your hands, if you want."

But Ethan was having none of it. "No, you *dig*! She's my aunt! I'm crazy about her!"

"Even if she's getting a bit more demanding, more possessive of you, lately?" I said, shooting straight from the hip and proving myself to be right on the money. Ethan went quiet. "Not a lot of young men get nookie off their aunt. You're one in a million, sport! I understand your loyalty to her, but I can bet, after eighteen months of the same old jazz, you're not as crazy about her as you once were. Care to wager, if the shit hits the fan, you're going to have to face the music, too? Don't forget it takes two to tango."

Ethan was visibly rattled. "I'm old enough. I'm free to do what I want. You can't take away my freedom."

I spoke my mind and told him bluntly – a little too bluntly, "I think you forfeited that luxury when you fucked your aunt!"

"Fuck you sideways with a cactus, man!" exclaimed Ethan, empurpled to the point of apoplectic. "If you're going to diss me, I won't discuss it anymore!"

"Someone as bright and intelligent as you, so full of promise, setting foot in University to read Medicine, destined to becoming a doctor, probably one of the most noble and enviable professions in the world, your whole life ahead of you – I don't want to see you throw it all away." I genuinely meant what I said. I was only trying to get through to him, sincerely hoped he would see some sense, think with that remarkable brain God had gifted him with, not with what was dangling between his legs.

"I'm going now . . . If you ever mention this subject again, I will piss in a pot and throw it in your face!"

"But of course. We will speak no more of it." And we never discussed it between us again. Even when Waldemar and Charles pestered Ethan silly, his lips as well as mine remained sealed. He'd study the day away at home, gulp down a few snakebites and smoke some joints with us in the evening, then disappear for the rest of the night. Only I knew where he went and I didn't share his whereabouts with the others, even if they suspected. Because that initial speck of an idea had matured into a precious pearl of a plan. I couldn't shake off my conversation with Ethan from the previous evening, when he disclosed the confidential details of his affair, or my dream from the night before that, after he first made a mention of his relationship. Some people say that family and friends come first. Others claim it's a dog-eat-dog world and it should be every man for himself. I suppose I plumped for the latter.

I wanted to make a film. It would be my ticket out of University and into a whole new career as a film director. I should have done Film and Drama studies instead of Fine Art, but I didn't think I would have lasted the distance. Unfortunately, I didn't have the academic discipline to apply myself consistently. I knew I wouldn't have made the final cut, dropping out sooner or later. At least, presently, I saw an opportunity. An opportunity to make it big, to do something novel. A golden opportunity had presented itself right on my doorstep.

You're going to say I fucked his aunt and filmed the whole thing, and you'd be very much mistaken. No, I followed Ethan one night without him ever suspecting he was being followed, taking the short train ride to Outer Bridge and trailing him, undetected, from a reasonable distance. Outer Bridge wasn't the greatest neighbourhood on this planet, but nor did Ethan travel down a street that represented the worst place to live, either, the night mellowed at intervals by lamplight. In fact, before I knew it, he had opened a wrought-iron gate and was toddling up a path to the doorstep of a white bungalow — detached and secluded — on the junction of the street and surrounded by a wooden fence, spray-canned on its outer aspect with the graffiti legend: LOBO SOLITARIO, which translates as 'Lone Wolf'. I waited for the woman to let him in before creeping up the path myself, making damned sure no-one saw me enter the grounds. There were no flowers on the patch of lawn on either side of the slab-stoned path, just high, unkempt grass, and I snuck round the side and looked in through the lounge-room window.

The lounge, although relatively tidy, was filled with things belonging to a typical Tarot Reader: a grinning human skull, photo-stills of movie zombies, dolls that might have easily doubled as poppets. There were shelves of definitive volumes on Major Arcana and their historic value: from a translation of the Book of Thoth to their use for occult, Kabbalistic and divinatory purposes, also looking at their New Age applications, as well as making further, more outrageous claims that, together, Major Arcana served as a universal source of medical knowledge, from which one might generate Eternal Life, or provided the only absolute authority on God, All Creation and the Hereafter. Also present amongst the collection I spotted a book by Sallie Nichols, exploring the archetypal significance of the Tarot trumps within the framework of Jungian individuation. A vaseful of black roses rested on the coffee table — I'd never seen black roses before, knowing how rare they were, expensive to buy. Maybe she grew them.

I hadn't seen his aunt before — Ethan hadn't volunteered any photos — and I was curious. *Very* curious.

When my eyes clapped on Sonja, I realized that Ethan had not been exaggerating. She was indeed a beautiful woman, sexily clad in a black dress, the upper clasps of which she had deliberately unbuttoned to show off the top of her cleavage. Black hair and black nail varnish. *Voodoo Lady of the Black Roses.* I now, also, understood the facial comparison with that Brooklyn-accented actress, Marisa Tomei. The likeness was uncanny. *My Cousin Vinny* sprang to mind.

Like a private dick on a stakeout, I watched them from the window as they lit up a juicy, fat one, drank and laughed, kissed a little. *It's nothing like kissing my mum,* Ethan had told me only just yesterday. The black, tapered candles flickered, the incense burned, smoked fragrantly. Then, around midnight, Sonja and Ethan retired to the bedroom and undressed, the curtains remaining undrawn. My luck held. I was just glad the bedroom wasn't on the first floor, and I didn't have to climb a tree and balance myself precariously on a branch in order to film the show. Lurking in the shadows, I pulled out the small camcorder, which I hoped would make me famous — or notorious. My hands now trembling, I raised the mini-cam and focused, zoomed in, sharpened the lens, set it on REC. I didn't want to miss a thing.

There she blows . . .

I did not notice the cold air around me, the mist on my breath, as I watched them, like the peeping tom I had become, make the beast with two backs, their flesh half-exposed under the covers, the aunt riding her nephew in a spellbinding performance. She had a gorgeous body, milk-white and lissom, with a nice rack and rump and a perfectly-trimmed snatch to match. *Picture that, baby! Aunt and nephew fucking like there's no tomorrow!*

Sooo DH Lawrence!

Some people like to watch. In the beginning I was one of them.

I must have been there for about forty-five minutes, mesmerized by the live sex show, filming them under the cover of night, before the pace between the two lovers quickened to the point when Sonja arched her back and uttered a cry of ecstasy, Ethan completing the act of passion with a whooshing climax of his own, and myself conscious of my own raging cockstand and a desperate need to beat my meat.

And when their sex session was temporarily over, I relaxed for a moment, stretching my camera-holding arm . . . which just happened to accidentally strike a metal watering-can on the outside sill, knocking it over to go clattering to the ground with a very audible clanking noise, loud enough to wake up the neighbourhood and suggest the presence of a burglar.

The unexpected commotion caused the two lovers to turn towards the bedroom window, and I'm sure Sonja saw me — I had a horrible sense that she had been fully aware of my presence all along, and maybe my boner — and, with a mental *Thank you for your hospitality, your time and, most of all, for your company,* I vaulted over the fence.

Yes, I was home-free, got away with it scot-free.

I took the last train back to Chertsford, reliving the entire lurid event in my head, and I was so pumped up, so damned hard from what I'd witnessed, I had to finish myself off in the communal bathroom back at Wentworth Hall.

There's a word, some of you might use, for what I had just done or when referring to my character: floccinaucinihilipilification.

I didn't waste any time delivering my tawdry film to a 'reputable' purveyor of filth the next day. They accepted it without question and paid me handsomely for it. What made my directorial debut unique and extremely marketable was there was no acting involved since it was an actual slice of reality – the porn company liked the incestuous and twisted nature of it, the fact that no permission had been given for the lovers to be filmed – which should satisfy a very particular clientele. A perfect fetish piece. I maintained my anonymity at the time for obvious reasons. They even packaged it with the title I suggested: *A Cunticle: How to Cock-up at University.*

But what about Ethan?

He didn't confront me the next day. Initially, I could only assume either he genuinely didn't know I'd filmed him having sex with his aunt or his aunt didn't tell him. Did she want to be filmed?

To be honest, Ethan wasn't all there when I saw him that following evening. He looked physically shattered, mentally drained. No, he was too far gone, rambling incoherently about 'watchers', which he wasn't able to elaborate on. He just sounded paranoid, on the edge of a nervous breakdown. Perhaps, he did know, but he didn't know it was me who'd done the dirty on him. Imagine being sure but not knowing who it was or what's become of it – it would be absolute murder on the nerves. His internal disintegration, that not-quite-there look in his eyes, caused us great concern, but, then again, I suppose there is no shame in being unwell. Then, like a phantom, he vanished for a whole fortnight until we heard the news.

The newspapers spoke of a mugging in Netherton. A medical student had been tragically stabbed to death outside the Seven Sisters high-rise flats. What he was doing in Netherton was anybody's business. The muggers, a group of shell-suited, little shits, who must not have been older than fourteen, were wired on Crack and would probably have sold their grandmothers for pennies as long as they managed to score some more. The killers were rounded up and brought to justice. They claimed, instead of handing over the wallet like a good boy, their victim had refused, spouting some crap about 'porn' and 'watchers', doing exactly what they didn't expect their victim to do. They said he sounded and looked 'crazy'. He kept goading them, calling them names, until his killers had no choice but to act. Three fatal stab wounds to the abdomen, according to the Coroner, rupturing the spleen, ripping through the guts and leaving the victim choking on his own blood, death far from instantaneous. They got ten years apiece.

I think, by that fateful night, Ethan must have known it was me. I think he welcomed his own death. I don't think he could live with the guilt. I think Susan Sontag captured it beautifully: *Tamed as it may be, sexuality remains one of the demonic forces in human consciousness – pushing us at intervals close to taboo and dangerous desires, which range from the impulse to commit sudden arbitrary violence upon another person to the voluptuous yearning for the extinction of one's consciousness, for death itself.*

But on the police report his death would always be recorded as a mugging and stabbing.

It's hard enough being a teenager – that awkward stage in one's life we've all been through – when one is at the mercy of one's hormones and one is only just discovering one's own sexuality, trying to determine how it fits into the rest of one's life in a healthy manner while navigating a society rife with stigma and taboo. And in a situation when your own aunt has stolen your innocence and got her hooks in you and acts as though she owns you, those problems multiple a thousandfold.

I neither heard hide nor hair of his aunt again. She just disappeared off the map. In fact, when I went to give Sonja my condolences, to tell her how highly Ethan spoke of her, the house had been vacated, and there was a FOR SALE sign up by the gate.

The grapevine suggested she had been found out because Ethan's dad turned out to be a bit of a dirty wanker himself and had discovered the porn film of his son fucking his sister-in-law by chance. It is further rumoured Sonja skipped the country.

That was my breakthrough into Porn, as a Uni dropout. Yes, I was Born for Porn. That crazy world of Porn. Real big business. Internet pornography gets more hits than Amazon or Facebook combined. Even Microsoft has done its bit in sponsoring porn stations but, for some strange reason, always neglects to mention it.

God may have rested on the Seventh Day. But my cock didn't! I singlehandedly pioneered *The Cum Show* on the Adult Channel. John Holmes I may not be, but my penis was still the envy of a lot of men, its helmet's head colossal enough to make a porn starlet feel like a virgin again. My dick pics are auction material unlike most men's, which get shot down in flames. I have my own Wonderland, a chalet in swanky Upper Nasebury, complete with its own swimming pool. I live the life of Bacchus or Dionysus, and read and re-read my favourite author, D.H. Lawrence. To quote D.H Lawrence: *How beautiful maleness is, if it finds its right expression.*

It's not as if simple beauty doesn't turn me on anymore. It's not as if my idea of romance is lifting the bedsheets and waving my semi-erect baton at the woman sharing my bed. A glimpse of Susanna Reid's legs during *Breakfast News* still leaves me Horny in the Morning. *For those early risers.* As I mentioned earlier, my ambition was to be a gentleman pornographer, but I suppose that ship sailed a long time ago. Yet, I do not jerk off to fucked-up shit anymore. As long as the girl's hot and reached legal age, I'm right in there like a shot! Girls dreaming of being a centrefold and hungry for cock! *My* cock, to be precise! And old Harry Monk, the money shot, if you get my drift! These women have taken their clothes off, and you think they're still minging? Not a jot. They may be a 'six', but they're still very doable, still worth a good munch of their pussy and a decent play with their clit. I'm quite the accomplished MILF man, if needs must. And creampies pay the most! I've fucked the booty off a black bitch called 'Jacinta', interracial-style, while listening to Rap Crap. I've eaten out and subsequently hammered pussy in many unhygienic ways. I even cured a pair of lezzies by dressing up like a tranny and fucking them three ways from Sunday. I've done bondage shoots: blindfolds and whips and chains. I've proven time and again that the donkey punch is not a myth. And, to all those discerning voyeurs out there, you might remember me doing a Crowley, shouting out chess moves while having sex in the other room – and I still *won*! But I can assure you I have become more restrained with age, less warped.

I wouldn't call my former trouble-and-strife 'disfigured', but there was something about her that didn't quite fit right. She really liked to test the limits. And Krista Avery was always my favourite girl. A girl who has French-kissed and Deep-throated her way to stardom. Krista, who did twenty men in one single ninety-minute sitting once in front of the cameras, I think deserves a round of applause. I thought I'd do my part and once fucked the entire working talent of a strip club in one night, recording the whole event for the benefit of the discerning viewer. I suppose Krista was so dedicated to her art that she didn't mind gobbling up spunk even if it had the smell and consistency of chunks of cheese. Her work was so filthy, watching one of her films on a computer could give you an STD! What would her father say, I wonder? She formed a cult after she claimed she slayed the Sexed One – or the *Oversexed* One – blowing his dumb ancient brains out and destroying an alien planet. Who'd believe her? Sadly, these days, it's a long-time, no-see situation.

As Alfred Kinsey outlined: *The only unnatural sex act is that which you cannot perform.* Before his research on the sexual practices of Western society, his English counterpart, Havelock Ellis, had already stated: *It is only the great men who are truly obscene. If they had not dared to be obscene, they could never have dared to be great.*

And Sex really is Big Business. *Sex really sells.* Maybe it talks to the mating instinct in all of us.

The whole world got an erection on Viagra, an erection that lasted all day long. I cannot imagine how many medical and pharmaceutical conventions must have been fuelled by party drugs and Viagra when it first got FDA approval. God gave us Parkinson Disease so we could give ourselves a good hand-job!

Yessiree-Bob, if sex is fun, what's wrong with getting paid a lot of money to fuck the most beautiful women in the world? Even couples use pornography as a sex aid, particularly when their relationship is on its last legs. Men and women have been fucking each other since the beginning, and they'll keep fucking till the end of the world, so I ask you again, why not make a little money out of it, turn it into cock-gripping entertainment?

Things are looking up. I hope to break America some day, soon. How hard can it be? A nation trying to get over its own arseholery. Nothing says America quite like voting in an Idiot of a President. *Twice*. Even if he did rig the elections and got egged on the way to his inauguration. Someone who can't string a single sentence together, a thicko, good for nothing. I've never seen anyone stick their head so far down a toilet and still miss! Speak the shittest lot of shit ever! Too much money, too little brains or talent. Compared to that half-wit, I'm a fucking genius! Well, I'm a fucker these days and he's still a wanker! You've never been fucked until you've been fucked by me! But I bet I can still beat him in a Wank Contest. Who can wank the longest and hardest, quickest and farthest? Always sucking up to the NRA, who themselves are compensating for their own sexual inadequacies. *I mean, shoot them with a dildo gun!* Americans celebrate a lot. Any American kid who learns to potty train has a Graduation ceremony. Get mediocre grades in High School for lack of effort and you get a Graduation ceremony. Fuck the Prom Queen and you get a Graduation ceremony. I look forward to fucking one of those FOX & FUCKING FRIENDS bitches, who don't quite have buck teeth but a mouth she cannot close. A constant open mouth with those Botox, BJ lips that can suck dick as good as any Porn star. Yes, one of those prim, proper, conservative, hypocritical, sanctimonious, *self-righteous* bitches, whose pussy looks like a limpet and is in dire need of rejuvenation surgery due to all the extramarital affairs she can never tell her husband about. *A pussy that has been used to advance a career, pussy that is fingerlickin' good!* To quote D.H. Lawrence: *If a woman hasn't got a tiny streak of harlot in her, she's a dry stick as a rule. I encourage, nurture the harlot.* And I certainly aim to please in the same vein as Lady Chatterley's diamond-in-the-rough. These Republicunts' God-fearing, Grand Old Pricks, who purport to be their husbands are probably just as bad – these old danglers think they're closer to God than anyone else, but in fact they're so full of sin – yet have the Goddamn nerve to preach family values to the rest of the world! *Oh, the sanctimonious, Teabagging politicians and their impersonal glory holes!* People in glass houses shouldn't throw stones, as the saying goes. I'm sure the hooker leaving the hotel suite in the morning is thinking: *Hope he doesn't have a wife. The things he makes me do, I'd feel sorry for her!* Never speak ill of the dead, as they say, but don't you just want to sprinkle some marijuana seeds on Nixon's grave and manufacture some weed? While in the UK, the High Street Wanks continue to fuck over the Taxpayer, since these Wanker Bankers have no qualms about letting another man fuck their girlfriends nor any reservations about whoring away their own mothers as long as they can make a few bob from it. The world we live in, hey?

It's amazing how the media is obsessed with rich people and celebrity. People famous for NOTHING. Paris Hilton, the entire living Kardashian clan, all the housemates of Biggest Bullshit Brother, etc., etc., etc., clinging on to their meagre relevance in society — and life.

Even Hollywood is not immune. Enrique Iglesias is apparently the Toupée Man. And *The World is Full of Poufs*, the latest action blockbuster. There're rumours that Clooney and Jackman are secretly gay, devotees of botty love, and their ladykilling image is only what they want their fans to see, a carefully-maintained illusion, and certainly not their boyfriends, who are allegedly kept hush-hush. Not your archetypal homos, mind. That shallow Hollywood culture, chockful of sycophants and prima donnas, most of whom probably still believe the movies began with Scorsese or Tarantino. You're still a celebrity when you flash your tits for money or get your crack banged on film.

I'm beginning to sound like that writer, Hank Schofield, who runs *Sayles Says* on his Twatter account. *Rant of the Day.* I suppose I should talk!

What became of my other Uni mates? Waldemar remained a weed smoker to his dying day. His persistent sore throat was initially misdiagnosed as GERD until the doctors later confirmed it was throat cancer. Five thousand people get throat cancer in the UK each year. That, unfortunately, was his luck of the draw, his losing lottery. A drug abuser till the end, he was rolling up his Fentanyl patches and chasing the dragon, breathing in the fumes, relishing that intense, instant hit. I remember him telling me as he lay there in a hospital bed, all wasted-away, riddled with secondaries, in chronic pain, a skeleton of a late-thirtysomething, attached to a syringe-driver, and yet somehow in good spirits: "This is as good as it's ever gonna get. I'm at peace because it'll soon be over. I will just disappear, become nothing. Believe in Life before Death, always. Religion is all about the Fear of Death. If there is an Old Fucker Upstairs and I'm judged by Him for not believing in Him, I will interrogate Him and demand to know why He didn't reveal Himself to us or give us a sign, why He's remained absent for so long. Why should His creations rely on blind faith when He supposedly gave us intellect, a brain, so we could think for ourselves? Do you think He cares? God's either a Narcissist, because He expects us to bow down to Him, or an Atheist, which is why He abandoned ship ages ago. People say if there were no God, there would be no atheists. Paradox. Depends how you take that. Anyway, everybody knows the Devil appeals to the boastful pride of man, the lustful, vainglorious part of him, and the Devil created Money so he could own the earth. But the Devil must know he's going to lose in the end. His argument, his reign on earth, is therefore redundant, and he's an even bigger mug for trying, for even thinking that he will triumph – completely *stupid*! No, I think I will take Hamlet's final words any day: *I die, Horatio. The potent poison o'ercrows my spirit . . . and the rest is silence . . .*" Waldemar coughed violently, and I thought I could almost hear his tumour. Then, after saying his piece, his body, ravaged by cancer and slowly withering away, drew its last breath, Waldemar's grievance with God now over. Or maybe it had just begun.

Charles became a Conservative politician. Yes, a politician, surprise, surprise! *Same shit, different piles.* How can anybody say so much to mean so little? These days we get confused, contradictory messages from politicians, and subsequently the media, so nobody knows what's true and what's not. This current approach to information-sharing is as common as the majority of twenty-pound notes we have in circulation reported to have traces of coke on them. Every time you see a politician on TV, doesn't it make you want to slap their cheeks – *face or butt, state your preference* – repeatedly with your bell-end and insist they put their head back up their arse where it belongs? *Our Prime Minister put his dick in a dead pig's arse as part of his initiation at University,* I remind Charles. *How dare you malign him like that?* Charles responds with mock-outrage and disgust. *Forgive me, it was a dead pig's* mouth, I correct myself, as if that makes it better. *Thank you!* Charles replies, satisfied. Charles told me he took up politics because power was an aphrodisiac, and he could violate all the PAs his tongue could cope with. And as a respected, every-scandal-hidden-under-the-rug Tory MP, he really let himself go. His washboard stomach disappeared with the times and, before he knew it, he was a fat bastard! *I used to have a six-pack, now I have a barrel,* he often quips, patting his enormous belly.

And me? Fit as a fiddle. I just returned from holidaying in Saravejo where the bullet holes in the buildings are preserved as a reminder of its bloody past. I don't want to be considered the moustache-twirling, eyebrow-arching, devilishly-chuckling villain of the piece, winking lecherously at the girls of St. Trinians, but I sit here all by my lonesome, in my chalet and my mind is Far, Far Away Elsewhere, dropping in on my brief stint at University. These days, I wear a beard, like I'm in some kind of hibernation mode, in between relationships. Sometimes, I embrace my 'nekkidness' for days on end, engage in a little Tantric sex; at least I've never been caught smoking dope and playing the bongos. Finding my Zen place is often very important to me as is practising Feng Chui in my spare time.

My career is vindicated by my fame. I have made money from the oldest, most pleasurable act known to man. I gained the necessary exposure and notoriety I needed to propel my career forward and make myself a household name by ditching Fine Art for the Hard Stuff, from those early films I produced, in front of and behind the camera.

Yet I cannot silence those demons inside my head, maybe only my guilt manifested as a family of voices, led by *her*, Sonja Turkel, Ethan's aunt. I do not trust that woman – that Voodoo Lady of the Black Roses – who scarpered off when the cat was out of the bag. I almost get a deep foreboding she is waiting to get even with me, plotting, scheming, the dark magical lore of her cartomantic tarot skills completely in her possession and a potential source of mystical power. It would be truly amazing, though, if she felt I did her and her nephew a huge favour by releasing that film. Until that woman resurfaces, my first work, at that time an innovative piece of filmmaking that sparked a trend, I shall not put my name to – its director will remain anonymous. I think of that haunted expression Ethan wore, empty of life, when I last clapped eyes on him all those years ago, and I sometimes wonder if his aunt's juju had a part to play in his death. Maybe we'll never know, but I do not wish to risk her hoodoo, jadoo or juju fucking up my mojo and I will therefore play it safe.

I am just trying to come clean with this confession, find closure, attain a measure of catharsis. Can I justify my actions, my treatment of Ethan, what some might see as a callous and calculated betrayal of our short friendship? I think, Gentlemen of the Jury, I shall let you decide. If you ever have the pleasure of watching that film, you'll understand that what I did, I did more for Art than Career. I may be many things, but I am not a traitor.

Pornography is the attempt to insult sex, to do dirt on it, D.H. Lawrence once suggested. That is where we differ. On this count, Mr. Lawrence and I will agree to disagree.

People condemn Porn as the orchestrated degradation of women, in the form of choreographed prostitution, rape, incest and assault, dehumanizing the female body to a worthless object and promoting an increasingly sadistic, misogynistic attitude in the viewer. I still firmly believe anal is about degrading the girl and just goes to show the porn stud is a closet pouf. Six months is the average shelf-life of a girl introduced to Porn, and she will never get her old life back once she leaves the business, forever an outcast of family and society. But who doesn't like watching a good frig or a bit of Sapphic love? The same people also complain about the effects of Porn on the brain, how it's wrecking relationships: how it activates the reward centres each time you tune in, releasing dopamine, making it as addictive as any drug, leaving you craving more and with a lesser density of grey matter, long-term, than those people who do not wank every ten seconds; how the brain becomes re-conditioned, associating arousal only with the sexually-explicit material on display rather than with an actual person, or leaving you with no libido when it comes to making love to your partner, or giving you the false impression that regular intercourse is boring and too much hard work, or killing the romance in your relationship by leaving you disinterested in wooing the person first or in sharing any acts of tenderness, focused as you are only with your own immediate, selfish gratification, your staying power greatly diminished when it comes to making out with the real thing.

But I turned out just fine!

April 2015-May 2015

The Cornish Patient

"I suppose sooner or later in the life of everyone comes a moment of trial. We all of us have our particular devil who rides and torments us, and we must give battle in the end."

Rebecca (1938)
Daphne du Maurier

Prologue

Névé Walmsley supposed she studied Nursing because her mother always claimed that there was no more a caring profession in the world than a Nurse. It certainly wasn't the Doctor who would only dip in and out of the wards, leaving instructions for the nursing team regarding the management of a patient. Medicine is only about healing the sick. Nursing is about caring for the sick, looking after someone through their illness, nursing them back to good health.

Admittedly, training as a nurse had been a hard slog – it was like learning a whole new language, the universal language of science – but it had all been worthwhile in the end. Graduating from Nursing School, as in any given profession, is always a joyous occasion, the culmination of all the years of poring over those ridiculously-chunky textbooks and cramming solidly for the exams, reaching a stage where the academic knowledge learned as an undergraduate could be effectively applied to the professional, clinical setting. A case of putting theory into practice and earning a humble few bob in the process while effortlessly striding into adulthood and gaining one's social independence. One of the unspoken final tests of one's competency as a nursing student is whether one could run a shift, delegating responsibilities to the various members of the nursing team, directing them to their general – and specific – duties. Névé passed with flying colours.

She recalled the final Graduation Ceremony, every graduate wearing their black ceremonial robe and mortarboard hat, in a building Florence Nightingale herself selflessly bequeathed to the ever-expanding Nursing School at Chertsford University. The Nursing School was also approaching the two-hundredth anniversary of her birth in a couple of years and planned to commemorate Florence Nightingale with a special service. Called the 'Lady with the Lamp', she famously organized the nursing of sick and wounded soldiers during the Crimean War, her far-sighted ideas and reforms influencing the very nature of modern healthcare. She had also once famously said: *Remember my name – you'll be screaming it later!* Névé's occasional boyfriend, Hartwin Purcell, a Senior House Officer in Cardiology, attended the graduation ceremony, giving her some moral support. The guest speaker and patron, the Right Honourable Charles Stroud MP, was bringing the proceedings to a close with one final anecdote: "You should all be proud of yourselves, each and every one of you. You are the future of our great nation, the backbone of the National Health Service with so many sick people who will depend on you throughout your lifetimes.

"It's amazing how the French can eat so much cheese and drink bottle-upon-bottle of wine and chain-smoke cigarette-after-cigarette and still have a low incidence of coronary heart disease. The Germans eat mountains of sausagemeat and drink gallons of beer and still boast low rates of coronary heart disease, obesity and liver disease. The Italians eat lots of wine and eat highly-calorific carbohydrate foods, such as pasta and pizza, while also claiming a low epidemic of heart attacks and cirrhosis. The Turkish people smoke packets of Turkish cigarettes, drink strong Turkish coffee and eat classic doner kebabs, dripping with fat, and also have a low prevalence of obesity and heart disease. But the British smoke, drink and eat in much the same manner as the French, German, Italians and Turks and have the highest incidence of obesity, heart disease, cancers and liver failure in Europe. And you might ask why? Is it the Mediterranean climate – and the accepted diet of olive oil, vegetables and fish, common to these other nations – that keeps them healthier than us? What makes us a sick nation? No, I say, is it hereditary, being born British? No, the moral of the story? Don't speak English!"

The laughter and applause from the audience summed up the events of the evening and the anecdote that Charles Stroud MP had regaled them with, as he advised the fresh batch of alumni be 'driven to excel rather than excess'. "Go forth and celebrate!" he said, his final words to the new nursing graduates. "Then, if you have time, help heal the English!"

It was a messy night, all round. It began in Névé's dorm room with a dozen or so nurses binging on vodka before going out on the town and crawling the drinking establishments of Chertsford in their blue nursing scrubs, allowing her boyfriend, Hartwin Purcell, with whom she shared a casual relationship, to tag along and finish early before going back on shift in the morning. The graduates celebrated all night with lashings of wine and beer and shots and risked adding to the statistics of the ailing English. Névé vaguely remembered waking up the following morning to find herself on the dorm-room floor of her dearest friend, Catie Millbank, with a banging hangover. Never again, she thought, never again.

Now a newly-qualified nurse, Névé took a job at the Medical Assessment Unit in Chertsford Memorial Hospital. For those who don't know, and as Névé was soon to discover, half of the stuff that comes through Accident and Emergency is crap, and the remaining fifty percent needs genuine urgent medical attention. Most of these cases end up on either the Medical Assessment Unit or the Surgical Assessment Unit, so one can imagine that some of the most serious, complex cases are on these wards before they either go back into the community or progress to the general wards. The acuity and turnover of patients was so high on the MAU, compounded by staff shortages, that the nurses frequently suffered stress and burnout. The knock-on effect was such that, during her shifts, Névé ended up looking after up to a dozen acute, seriously complex and demanding patients at a stretch, and her colleagues would be cynical, ungrateful and bitchy towards her and downright rude, sarcastic and unprofessional towards their patients, the bitchiest of them being the gay Charge Nurse, Patrick Benton, who thought he was some kind of Justin Timberlake and posted a bloody awful video of himself singing on YouTube, thinking he would make it big. The Practice Educator, Nicky Bale, wasn't a nice person, either, acting as though she owned the place and believed she had the power to fail new staff members during induction training if she didn't like their faces. Medication errors were commonplace, and physical observations were not always completed. If these things were properly investigated in the spirit of Safeguarding, if there was time, then a lot of nurses might have lost their PINs, but the NHS was keen for this not to happen. For Névé, working on the MAU was not everything it was cracked up to be, like being chucked into the deep end, a place of unprofessional attitudes and unsafe practices, but she survived, and, hey, work was work, and all experience was good experience. Névé learned a great deal in her first year as a Preceptor. Being graduated, you are in an entirely different ballgame; you are a nurse. Panic will not do. You must learn to control your anxieties, curb your irrational fears. Even Florence Nightingale herself said that very little could be done in the spirit of fear. Otherwise, you're bound to scare your patients. You must instil confidence and hope in the sick and those who need it most. Or all your kind words will feel artificial, *fake*.

The government had streamlined the NHS, shrunk and demoralized the nursing ranks with staff cuts and pay freezes and had unwisely done away with bursaries and now was unscrupulously going after the doctors, exploiting them as much as their nursing colleagues, so that the Health Secretary could finally justify privatizing the NHS whilst the CEOs, Managers and Agency staff continued to financially suck the NHS dry. Unfortunately, most of the emerging world leaders nowadays were invested in their own greedy, narcissistic interests than looking out for the people they were supposed to represent.

The cancer wards were a significantly more rewarding experience. In fact, her seniors were much nicer and the archetype of all nurses and the epitome of the most caring profession in the world. Névé supposed they had to be if they were constantly dealing with End-of-Life care. She could feel the compassion and humanity, sadly absent from the MAU. Becoming a Cancer Nurse Specialist, or perhaps working as a Macmillan Nurse, seemed like a good idea. The illness — and subsequent passing — of her closest friend at University, Catie Millbank, from bowel cancer pushed Névé to work in that field. Catie had been a mature student, five years older, and had been the first friend Névé had attached to in Nursing School. Catie was such a gentle, soulful creature, a totally tolerant human being and completely non-judgemental. Her headful of long red curls had brought her the nickname of 'Sideshow Bob'. When she first informed Névé that she had just been diagnosed with Stage 4 bowel cancer, Névé knew it was a death sentence and wept. The insidious-onset abdominal bloating, pelvic pain, rapid weight loss, rectal bleeding and anaemia had turned out to be something sinister, something truly frightening and untreatable. Névé thought of the cancer eating away her friend's body from the inside out. Such was the aggressiveness of the tumour, Catie's transformation from a bright, bubbly, lively, trim redhead to a tired, drawn-out individual, wig-wearing and all skin-and-bone, had been incredibly rapid. The bowel surgery did nothing and, once the two courses of chemotherapy had also proven unsuccessful, Catie checked into a hospice and passed away in the small hours. She must have given up in the end, had enough, did not wish to prolong her suffering. The body is designed to cling on to life even in the most extreme circumstances, such as a neurovegetative state, a coma, but once the will to live goes, the already-compromised physiological systems completely pack in. Catie's illness and subsequent passing couldn't have been sadder, a terrible tragedy. You plan your whole life ahead of you and then you get a terminal diagnosis, driven by your faulty genes, and suddenly everything changes for the worst. So horribly sad.

Névé was by her friend's bedside when she died. So too was Catie's husband, Tom, and their two children, Izzy and Lillie, aged five and three, respectively. God, or Fate, or Nature, had a lot to answer for. It was cruel enough taking the life of an honest, hardworking woman in her prime, but to take away the life of a young mother, leaving behind a husband and two young children was unconscionable. The death of a loved one psychologists always rated high on the Life Events scale. The grief was enormous and the panacea slow-coming for her family. The girls were still young to fully understand what had happened to their mother and why she would not be coming home, but Tom was inconsolable. Névé checked her own feelings for Tom, driven by her sympathy and pity for the man and his family. Widowers were so much more tragic and trustworthy and even *sexier* than divorcés because they didn't fuck up their marriage. Instead, it was taken from them.

Catie did receive a good send-off. Half the graduating year had turned up to pay their last respects. It was a beautiful funeral service: the vicar delivered a touching eulogy and Tom gave a fitting tribute to his wife and, to mark the solemn occasion, Névé said a few kind words about her dearest friend. After the burial, Névé participated in the wake, an emotional event for all concerned. Névé would continue to check in on Catie's family, see how they were holding up and if they needed anything, maintaining periodic telephone contact.

The tragedy of her friend's death might have propelled Névé into Palliative Care, but most of all she felt she needed to get away for a while – perhaps take a six-month sabbatical. Some people called Palliative Care a 'dead-end job', unkindly describing cancer victims as 'half-dead, green people'. Névé remembered the Consultant entourage. Often in the pocket of the chemotherapy companies, the Consultant would insist you needed chemotherapy to prolong your life by three months. Except he wouldn't tell you that you would spend that time constantly vomiting and shitting. The cure was sometimes worse than the disease. Hartwin did not have the same luxury, workwise, but he accepted her decision to put some distance between them. He could always phone her whenever he wanted and maybe pay her a visit if he had some time off. As a nurse, and perhaps in the wider job market, her skills would be required everywhere, whatever nursing work she chose to undertake – any experience is good experience, as the legend went – even in France if she could speak French. After putting an ad in *The Lady*, advertising her RGN Services, Névé received a phone call from a nursing agency, who suggested possible work and a live-in position in

Cornwall, in Boscastle to be precise, delivering twenty-four-hour nursing care to a dying, elderly man in his home.

Without any hesitation, Névé accepted the post.

I:

I Will Possess Your Heart
    – Death Cab for Cutie

I

Névé accepted the post because she thought it would make a pleasant change from what she was used to. It also paid significantly more than her salary in the NHS, even without London weighting. Agency posts always offered more pay, but the pay-packet from this particular post surpassed even the best of them. It would be a month-long stint, two fortnightly shifts with a weekend's break in between, and the opportunity to extend her post if she and her employers were satisfied by her performance. Névé looked forward to her new position: straight one-to-one nursing instead of working on a ridiculously busy ward with dangerously low staffing levels. Occupational Health endeavoured to maintain wellness in the workforce and promote the peak of productivity even when facing six-figure salaries for the NHS bosses in scandalized, unsafe hospitals while frontline nurses were run ragged on understaffed wards on a mere pittance of a wage. Névé didn't want to betray the NHS and go agency. Except what choice did she have? Her best friend had died, and Névé needed a break. And working in Cornwall offered a change of scene. One might have described it as 'a busman's holiday', and one wouldn't be far wrong.

She was met by a sudden crawl of traffic on the approach to Stonehenge, popular with druids, hippies, party-goers and nature-lovers who were due to converge there to celebrate the Summer Solstice, and came across numerous signs for Wookey Hole during the straight, five-hour drive across Southern England.

A famous vicar going by the name of Reverend Sabine Baring-Gould once wrote: *Cornwall, peopled mainly by Celts, but with an infusion of English blood, stands and always has stood apart from the rest of England, much, but to a lesser degree, as has*

Wales.

Jutting outwards from the southwest of England, Cornwall pointed towards the Atlantic Ocean, where countless generations of souls had lost their lives to the fickle sea. Shipwrecks and smugglers, rocky crags and bottomless bogs, thick mists rolling into port and hiding secret coves, and tales of mermaids, who would lose their tails once they fell in love with a human. As dusk would fall, the Cornish folk, after a day's worth of fishing or mining tin or catering for the out-of-towners, would gather around their hearths and tell each other their oldest tales of legend, horror and mystery by firelight. Indeed, this was supposed to be the land of Bucca, of piskies, identical little people, and knockers, elfin dwellers of underground mines, of giants throwing rocks from the summits of Cornish hills, resulting in tors, and giant-killing characters named Jack. Of changelings, ugly babies of pixies swapped cuckoo-style with human babies, and of young, married couples getting lost on their wedding night. The Cornish people still firmly held on to their strange beliefs that young women with red hair cannot make good butter, or that a white hare possesses the soul of a girl who died from grief after being deserted by her lover, or that ants are basically druids, condemned to insect life for refusing to accept Christianity, on the last leg of their earthly existence. Cornwall was also supposedly the seat of power from where King Arthur once reigned over the land, where a large black dog roamed the moors and where the ghosts of the tortured lovers, Tristam and Iseult, met at midnight, and where the Devil lurked.

Névé thought of all those famous writers who had originated from or stayed in Cornwall. Cornwall was, of course, Daphne du Maurier country, author of *Rebecca* and *My Cousin Rachel*, who lived and set many of her stories here. Winston Graham's series of *Poldark* books, for instance, delivered a historic romance at a time when Cornwall sought independence from the rest of the UK. The late Poet Laureate, Sir John Betjeman, was particularly fond of Cornwall, which featured prominently in his poetry. William Golding, author of *Lord of the Flies*, lived and died in Cornwall. D.H. Lawrence often visited Cornwall, considered it his favourite writing retreat. Richard Wagner's opera, *Tristan und Isolde*, takes place in Cornwall, as does Gilbert and Sullivan's operetta, *The Pirates of Penzance*. Spy Master, John le Carré, and the prolific non-fiction author, Colin Wilson, both still live in Cornwall.

Fourteen miles south of Bude and five miles from Tintagel lies the North Cornish village of Boscastle. Névé arrived at *Kastel Boterel*, Cornish for Boscastle, well ahead of schedule. She decided to take a bit of a gander before she went to her official destination. The steep hills of stone cottages and medieval longhouses led down a path to the headland and, of course, between looming cliffs of slate and shale, the small

Elizabethan harbour. Although the harbour hosted a number of small trawlers and little fishing boats at anchor in the cove, its tortuous entrance was difficult to gain access to due to the big swells that threatened to drive the vessels against the walls of the channel. Boscastle's blowhole beneath Penally Point, on the northern side of the harbour, was called the Devil's Bellows, thumping and snorting a vertical waterspout every hour at low tide. Out to sea, one might see if one were lucky, Atlantic grey seals and bottle-nosed dolphins and basking sharks, highlighting the unspoilt nature of this medieval harbour village. Not far from Boscastle, Crackington Haven boasted a mighty bulwark of cliff, called High Cliff, rising up to seven-hundred-and-thirty-five feet, the highest in Cornwall. Boscastle had a wide choice of traditional pubs, tearooms, farm shops and cafés, many 'award-winning', all serving locally-sourced produce and freshly-caught shellfish. Crab sandwiches were on the menu as was Stargazy pie, with its baked fish-heads, as well as the famous Cornish pasty, 'patented' by the Cornish people and not to be mistaken for any inferior copies elsewhere. There were plenty of interesting shops and art galleries, selling everything from leather goods, rock crystals and gems, original paintings and pottery. Aside from the boat trips out of the harbour and the official National Trust visitor centre housed in an old blacksmith's forge, the MUSEUM OF WITCHCRAFT AND MAGIC was high on the list of attractions, and Néve made a mental note to visit the place more formally in a fortnight's time during her weekend relief. Curiously enough, she had heard the museum was the only building to survive the devastating flash flood of August 2004.

This must be the place, Néve thought in her head, coming to the house at 47, Vapery Lane. Up on Furze Hill and down a meandering, narrow cobblestone street, a short walk from the priory ruins, PENNRYCK was a narrow, terraced Georgian house with granite walls and a shingled roof.

Néve emerged from her green Mini Cooper, which she parked on the kerb directly outside the front door of this fine, old building, and, carrying her two pieces of luggage, she stepped up between the neoclassical columns at the oaken door and rang the doorbell.

Nobody came to meet her.

She tried again, pressing the bell.

Nobody responded.

Banging the brass knocker on the door a couple of times and waiting, she turned the doorknob and discovered the front door to be open.

She stepped inside.

Néve found herself in a hallway. Dark, marble flooring and stark, grey walls with crumbling plaster, barren of any pictures, but full of dense, dusty cobwebs in the corners. Fortunately, Névé wasn't afraid of spiders.

"Hello, anybody there?" she called down the hallway.

Moments later, somebody's face appeared round the corner. It was a pleasant, friendly African face. "Goodness me," the black nurse said, eyes lighting up, coming down the hallway to greet the visitor. "Hi, I'm Rhonda . . . Rhonda Apenteng." She wore a navy-blue matron's uniform. "I hope you weren't waiting outside too long. The bell doesn't work."

"I'm Névé . . . pleased to meet you," she replied, shaking the other woman's hand. "I hope you don't mind. The door was open."

"Not at all," said Rhonda. "I've been expecting you. You came in good time. I'm glad you got here in one piece. Must have been a long trip from Chertsford."

"It was a long drive," Névé said brightly, "but I'm raring to go!"

"You really do have a positive attitude . . ." Rhonda acknowledged. "I'll give you a handover." Taking Névé's arm, Rhonda led the newcomer down the hallway into a sitting room doubling as a makeshift hospital room, with a hospital bed, a leather armchair and life-saving, monitoring equipment already set up, and through into the door at the far end of the room. Névé barely got a glimpse of her patient as Rhonda hastily pulled Névé into the adjoining private bedroom. This was where Névé would be sleeping. A fresh matron's uniform lay on the bed. Rhonda's bags were already packed. She was in a hurry to leave.

Having shown Névé her sleeping quarters and the en-suite bathroom in which Névé noted a sink, toilet and shower/bath combo, Rhonda brought her back out into the sitting room. Névé was able to study the old man for the first time. Head above the bedcovers, he was more than old – he looked ancient. Leathery wrinkles, pronounced cheekbones, eyelids closed in deep, hollowed sockets, thin, downturned lips and a balding, wispy, white-haired skull. An arm had fallen down the side of the bed, sporting paper-thin skin, mottled by liverspots, and a gnarled hand curled into jagged fingers. Névé placed the fallen arm back under the covers. "How's our patient?"

"I've only been here for the weekend, but he's hanging in there . . ." Rhonda replied. "You know he's well over one hundred years old?"

"Wow!" exclaimed Névé, looking back at the ancient-looking, unconscious figure in the bed. "He's done well for himself!"

"Strange fella . . ." Rhonda added. "It's rumoured he's spooked out many a nurse..."

"Really?" Névé said, suddenly intrigued.

"Some of the nurses booked by the agency have left very afraid. One went mad."

"You mean he scared them off?" Névé said, surprised. Then, she remembered how the nursing agency had been somewhat furtive and economical in giving out details about this man in case she didn't go through with the gig. "How? He's just a harmless, old man at death's door."

"That's what I thought!" Rhonda agreed. "But he does have a mighty strange presence, even if he is dead to the world . . . like he casts a spell. I don't know if it's the loneliness of the job or whether it's something else, but you sometimes feel and hear and see strange things." Her expression grew slightly perplexed, as though she remembered something peculiar, then it was back to a gentle smile.

"I should be fine," Névé reassured Rhonda – and herself. "These two weeks are going to fly by, I'm sure."

Rhonda grabbed her bags and hurried to the door, pointing to a final room furthest down the hallway. "Kitchen." She added: "And stick to the ground floor. All the doors on the first floor are locked and strictly off-limits." At the front door, she paused. "Did the agency explain he's a DNR?"

"Not for resuscitation?" Névé said. "Yes, they mentioned, but I suspect the nursing agency will provide us with their tacit approval and cover our backs if we decided on the contrary. Anyway, nobody's going to die on my watch!"

"Spoken like a true optimist!" Rhonda said, genuinely impressed by her colleague's confidence. "My boyfriend's waiting in the car," she stated to explain her haste. "I'll be back to relieve you in a couple of weeks. In the meantime, good luck – and *respect!*"

When Rhonda was gone, Névé changed into her nursing uniform and sat down in the leather armchair. *Providing round-the-clock care to a dying man shouldn't prove too challenging – or de-skilling, as some might suspect,* thought Névé, confident. *Working with all these monitors should pump prime my nursing knowledge. Like working in ICU.*

2

Névé decided she would keep it simple. Her primary and absolute focus would be her centenarian patient, to whom she would be a live-in carer. *You cannot stop the flow of time. Even if you're having the shift from hell, rest assured in the knowledge your shift will eventually end.* She would get her respite in due course. In the meantime, the next fortnight would be an opportunity for her to do her job properly.

Conscientiously. *Efficiently.*

She expected the fortnight to pass by relatively quickly. When not immediately attending to the needs of her patient, she hoped she would find ways of availing her time. Her own needs would be well-catered for, she knew, the downstairs quarters more than adequate, far from belonging to a slumlord, and sufficiently stocked-up of provisions and entertainment material. Such was the way with time, the first few days would go painstakingly slowly, but as the days merged into one, the days would fly by, and before she knew it, her first fortnight would be up. Those were her expectations.

Already dressed in her matron's outfit, Névé busied herself with the monitoring equipment, getting to know her patient. Yes, Kestran Tregaskin was reportedly one-hundred-and-four years old, a ripe old age, and, indeed, he looked it. He was a bony, gaunt, wrinkled husk of a man. He slept like he was dead, arm outstretched over the side of the bed, like something out of a Victorian momento mori. *You're ancient, man,* Névé concluded without humour or mockery. *Really old. You are . . . the* Fogeyman.

Shouldn't he be in a nursing home or hospice?

No, he's entitled to decide where he wants to spend his final days . . . He's come home to die.

Doesn't he have family who could care for him?

Probably not – why else would he be here?

Névé wondered what he might be like if awake and talking. Perhaps his communication might be marked by senility, or a dementing process, leaving him with things he couldn't remember. Or couldn't remember the things he couldn't remember. He might be a stranger to himself, cognitively incapable of knowing who he was.

Surprisingly, no underlying medical illnesses were recorded in his casenotes, except the cruel ravages of old age. Organs that would obviously some day just wave a white flag and give up the ghost. Totally 'natural causes', as would be recorded on the death certificate.

There was no hint of a stubble on his chin; it appeared Rhonda and the succession of nurses had been shaving him. Névé also noticed the vaseful of red roses on the bedside cabinet, recently changed since their petals were velvety and lustrous. He must be a romantic fellow, Névé concluded. Kestran continued to require infrequent and very small feeds through his nasogastric tube to maintain some degree of sustenance, even if his bowel motility had slowed right down, his stomach close to quiescent. There was an incontinence sheet laid out beneath him, nevertheless, to collect any motions. He continued to receive intravenous fluids, and Névé continued to record his fluid input and output on a chart. Urine collected in a catheter bag, a healthy, straw colour, with no suggestion of chronic kidney failure. Névé planned to continue administering daily, subcutaneous heparin injections to prevent blood clots from forming in his calves and to keep turning the patient frequently to prevent bedsores, the bane of nursing practice.

The constant monitors showed him to be haemodynamically stable. Blood pressure was steady, partly due to the volume provided by the IV fluids. He had a strong, regular pulse, inconsistent with someone so frail, so fragile. His three-lead ECG did not show any deficits in his heart rhythm. Oxygen saturation hovered around the ninety-seven-percent mark, demonstrating uncompromised lung function, with no need for a ventilator or assisted respiration. He was apyrexial in his body temperature, with no clinical signs of any chest infection or pneumonia.

So far, all in reasonable working order. The man was holding on in there. Good for him!

Névé gave Hartwin, her on-off boyfriend, a call.

He wasn't on shift and he picked up the phone on the third ring. "Geddon me, bewty!" he burst out.

"Pardon?"

"You know me – been learning a little Cornish in my spare time, as should you!" he replied, pleased to hear her voice. "Means 'Greetings, friend'."

"Oh . . ."

"I thought you would have forgotten all about us mortals back in Chertsford," he said.

"Not at all," responded Névé.

"How goes Cornwall?"

"Not seen much of it yet, but the drive down was delightful."

"And your patient?"

"An old man. Aged over a hundred."

"Over a hundred?" Hartwin exclaimed. "Bleddy hell! He's done remarkably well for himself! What's his secret?"

"I'll be damned if I know," responded Névé, with a note of sadness in her voice. "He's lived such a long life, it's a shame he has to spend the rest of his golden years restricted to a bed. He has his own hospital room in his house. Except he's very much unconscious. Quietly living out the last few days or weeks of his life in a deep sleep before Death comes looking for him."

"I suppose we will never be able to change the nature of human existence."

"We mustn't give up trying . . ."

"I hope you won't be too bored, providing one-to-one, full-time nursing care."

"Don't worry, I'm rarely, if ever bored," Névé told him. "I've got things to keep me occupied. Besides, it makes a pleasant change to look after only one patient for once, deliver a truly personalized, patient-centred form of care."

"Good to hear," Hartwin said amiably. "You truly are 'some maid'."

"Come again?"

"'Some maid' is an accolade of respect in Cornish slang."

"You really have picked up some Cornish, without even visiting the place!"

"Try and make the most of your time. I'm glad things are copasetic." *Copasetic* was his latest buzz word. Not Cornish.

They talked about other things. "A birdy told me you're planning to cycle from London to Brighton for charity this year."

Hartwin was completely amazed. "That's news to me! Not quite sure how you saw me as a potential cyclist . . . I'm barely a potential pedestrian! My penchant for fast food after a particularly gruelling shift coupled with a studious avoidance of exercise have honed a near-legendary lack of endurance and stamina that has made me the paragon among the rabble they call ward staff! I shall support whoever's brave and fit enough to go the distance for a good cause enthusiastically from the comfort of my local kebab shop!"

Névé smiled, amused. *Typical!* Why wasn't she surprised? Hartwin spent his workdays standing outside the hospital grounds with the other usual suspects, including the health unit coordinator, that ragtag of shivering smokers, getting a nicotine fix. Still, she appreciated his sense of humour: *When I was young, I wanted to be a comedian . . . Nobody's laughing now!* Oh, the irony of it! But, most of all, she appreciated his charitable nature. "I know you're generous with your sponsorship money."

Hartwin was immodest in his reply: "That's me: good heart, generous spirit!"

"When do you think you'll visit me, experience a little Cornish atmosphere?"

He considered before providing a jokish response: "Dreckly!"

"Whatever does that mean?"

"Oh, it's a timeframe alright, somewhat vague, if you will."

"I'm guessing it might be some time before you pay me a visit?"

"Zackly!" *Couldn't agree more.*

"You're quite the comedian!"

"Born in a barn, were 'ee?"

Névé tittered and took a stab at the Cornish accent herself. "'Ave you got barnacles on the brain?"

Hartwin was impressed. "Not bad. Not bad at all."

They chatted for a few more minutes, on other, lighter matters, before Névé brought the call to an end. She promised to keep in touch, which Hartwin welcomed. "Ibeleebn," he told her. *Time for me to go.* He wished her the very best.

When Névé had hung up, she got up from the armchair and checked on her patient again, who hadn't moved or opened his eyes. She glanced at the monitor screens measuring his vital signs. He looked comfortable. She changed the empty IV bag with a fresh one, running the intravenous fluids through very slowly, drip by drip, so as not to overload his already aged systems. She fed him small amounts in the NG tube, syringing the device with water afterwards to keep it patent. The truly peculiar thing she found, for someone so old and bedridden, was Kestran Tregaskin was not on any prescription medication whatsoever – no anti-arrhythmic medication for a dicky ticker or strong non-steroidal analgesics for age-related arthritis or alpha blockers for a leaky, enlarged prostate – which was an achievement in itself and which otherwise she would have had to administer via the NG tube. It bespoke volumes as to his longevity.

Yes, she would get through this. Her professionalism and painterly love of quiet and Nature would see her through. She thought she should be able to keep him alive. Except he seemed to be doing well on his own.

She wondered what kind of life he had led. What was his story?

Névé made a quick supper and prepared to turn in for the night. She thought she would sit by the bedside of her patient for a little while, keep a vigil, before she retired to her own bed. Still sat in the armchair, she put her head back and, to the soft, rhythmic ping of his heartbeat on the cardiac monitor, she closed her eyes . . . and nodded off.

3

Névé finds herself sat on a fallen log in a stretch of countryside during the last traces of sunset. The summer air is warm, and she is wearing a short, provocative tartan dress as though modelling for Victoria's Secret, her feet bare as though she is about to take a tumble in the hayloft.

"You look beautiful," says a male voice, and a figure dressed in a white, loose-fitting poet's shirt, complete with frills and full bishop sleeves, on top of dark, tight leather trousers and jackboots, sits down beside her. "Sometimes you're gorgeous, but

most of the time you're just lovely."

Névé acknowledges the compliment, "Thank you." She asks a more pertinent question, taking in the enchantment around her: "It's so calm and peaceful and relaxing here. Where am I?"

"You're somewhere few people have the privilege of beholding," the man informs her. "This is the land of knights and kings, where chivalry and romance are still alive and well. It's called The Westlands, but I prefer to call it 'The Heartlands'."

"Rather befitting the place," replies Névé. She looks around her. Across the way, birch, oak and hazel fill the valley along with hawthorn and blackthorn. Moneywort, lizard clover and butcher's broom accompany the meadow-grass on the heathland. The lapwings and common snipe prepare to roost for the coming evening as do the spotted woodpeckers and grey wagtails. Golden plover and curlew prefer the grazed grassland, and skylarks flit among the grassy tussocks. Red-billed choughs and jackdaws add their own numbers to the diverse avian life. The babbling brook attracts sand martins and kingfishers and its crystal-clear waters are home to flounders and gurnards, sand eels and seahorses and otters. Horseshoe bats come out after sunset. Orchids grow by her feet and, from a nearby Davey elm, Névé hears the hoot of a snowy owl.

The dragons and giants seem curiously absent from this medieval kingdom.

The sepia tones of the sun have disappeared on the horizon, and the full moon resides in an aspect of the twilit sky. She spots a waterfall in the distance, its silvery waters cascading down into a small lake, the origin of the running brook.

"Am I dreaming?" asks Névé, feeling the light, warm breeze on her face, a breeze that feels as real and fresh as the floral fragrance in the air.

"You could say that . . ."

"And who might you be, if you are part of my dream?" she asks the newcomer.

"I am a Moonreacher . . ."

His cryptic response makes her think of her surrounds bathed in the soft, powdery glow of the moon. She studies the figure sitting next to her. The blond hair and chiselled face. Handsome would be an understatement. She wonders where her mind has dreamed him up from. "What, no name? Just a title?"

"You know my name already."

She suddenly stops. If one is to radically age his face, make his hair significantly greyer and give him lots of wrinkles . . . goodness me! At that moment, it clicks that he is the same person as her patient, except a younger incarnation of him. The similarity is unmistakable. "You're Kestran Tregaskin?"

"And you're the nurse who's been tasked with looking after me," the man acknowledges. "Such a noble profession. You must be a very caring, skilled and resilient individual, maybe even able to accept your own mortality. You have my complete admiration and respect."

"Hi, I'm Névé." She offers him her hand and he readily takes it and, with a small bow, gently grasping her fingers, kisses her on her knuckles. Névé feels honoured by his gentlemanliness.

"Névé . . . such a strong Christian name," he observes.

She looks into his washed-grey eyes, their unusual, smouldering quality, and feels the flutter of butterflies in her stomach. "How is it possible that you're the same chap I'm nursing? You look so much younger and fitter and healthier."

"I think you already know."

Perhaps it is the loneliness of her shift, working with a mute, unconscious, bedbound patient, that her mind has conjured up an image of what he might have looked like in his younger days to provide her with a bit of company, someone with whom she can have a natter. It is a saucy interpretation because he is devilishly handsome – and gallant. "What does your title denote?"

"I help women like you find love," he says simply.

"How do you achieve that, may I ask?" Névé wonders if he is some kind of medieval match-maker.

"Oh, I have my ways . . ." he replies enigmatically.

"For what purpose?"

"So they can be loved and adored."

"What if they're not interested in love?"

"Everyone wants to be loved," the handsome stranger tells her. "I can make it happen."

"You got some kind of love potion or something?"

"I do not like divulging my secrets at this early stage," Dream Kestran states, shutting down this line of inquiry. "Do you like the Heartlands?"

"I think it's – timeless." The wooded valley, the meadow flowers, the glorious birdlife, the pale moonlight, the lovely waterfall. She spots a deer – a young buck – in the distance.

"The Heartlands can be our place, our rendezvous," he promises. "You will always find me here. This unique place grants various points of access: the earth, the pit, the heavens, the cosmos."

Again, Névé contemplates why her head would make up such a place and such a handsome fellow. Could it be that she's already starting to feel lonely, homesick, lovesick?

"Time has not been kind to me," Dream Kestran continues slightly sorrowfully. *"Recently, I have grown tired. I've been waiting for someone like you for a very long time. You cannot imagine how grateful I am to have such a charming companion in you. Tonight is the beginning of always and* forever.*"*

II:

The Nurse Who Loved Me
— Failure

I

The urgent beeping was almost as loud as an emergency klaxon going off. It ripped Névé out of her nap and she immediately leaped into action. She quickly realized what had set off the alarm. The oxygen saturation screen was recording nothing. Yet when Névé checked on her patient, he was still pink and well-perfused, not in the least bit blue or cyanosed or suffering any respiratory distress but rather breathing normally. Then, it occurred to her that the sats probe had inadvertently slipped off his finger when he had shifted slightly in his sleep, making his oxygen saturation unreadable and raising the alarm. Névé refitted the sats probe on the tip of his index finger and saw the oxygen saturation creep back up to ninety-seven percent on the monitor screen. The rest of the physical parameters, one of the cornerstones of nursing, were still within normal limits. Extraordinary that this gentleman was waiting to die yet his vital signs told a different story. She was relieved — all was well with the world again. Crisis averted.

Once again, she dwelled on the concept of human mortality and her role as a nurse. *A nurse is the one who opens the eyes of a newborn baby and gently closes the eyes of a dying man.* It was indeed a true blessing, in her experience, to be the first and last to witness the beginning and end of life itself. She would care for this man as best she could, tirelessly, selflessly, keep him alive as long as nature intended. That would be her nurse's duty at Pennryck. The constant care from a nurse, she supposed, was as important as any complex operation performed by a surgeon.

Névé got on with her day, tending to her patient, keeping him alive and comfortable, and did not dwell on her dream from the night before. With not much else happening, she kept herself sufficiently occupied during the long days. She skipped Baz Luhrmann, who had included a modern dance/hip hop soundtrack to a movie adaptation of *The Great Gatsby*. He had already royally screwed up Shakespeare and now seemed intent on doing the same with F. Scott Fitzgerald, who must surely be spinning in his grave. With a lack of authenticity and credibility, Luhrmann's ignorance merely insulted the viewer's intelligence and his work should only be seen as an insignificant footnote in Hollywood.

No, Névé put on the Detective Channel in the background. Hartwin, who considered himself an armchair detective, had once told her his perfect viewing pleasure on a Sunday would be Poirot, Jonathan Creek, Sherlock Holmes and Columbo, and not necessarily in that order. Columbo was presently on, shaking down his latest suspect. A true-crime documentary would follow about the horrible tragedy of the Oaks Fold couple who did not accept that family comes before profit.

There was also her smart phone, which could be a potential source of information and entertainment. Névé had read somewhere that, apparently, nearly three-quarters of the modern generation had a mobile, spending on average three hours of screen time each day. She didn't know if that was a good thing or a bad thing.

Still, there was also quiz night on television to look forward to. *You don't need to be clever,* thought Névé. *You just need to know the answers!*

Reading a good book was another option. She had brought *Rebecca* along with her, one of her favourite, all-time reads. *Last night I dreamt I went to the Heartlands again,* she thought, semi-quoting the opening line of the book.

With an interest in art, she could also pass her spare time sketching and doodling.

Or maybe, as an absolute last resort, playing solitaire by herself.

Indeed, there was plenty to do, enough to stave off the bouts of boredom.

She enjoyed her work. She thought there were two types of nurses. The first type of nurse was proud, compassionate, dedicated, wasn't quick to call the doctor. The second type, like Mrs. Gamp from *Martin Chuzzlewit,* was not interested in caring for others, hated her job and overestimated her own self-importance, inflicting misery on the doctor and her patients. Névé hoped she could identify herself with the first group.

The old man slept on, always positioning his head towards the nearest light source, overhead or desklight, as though drawn to its radiance. Névé remembered a quote by Florence Nightingale: *It is a curious thing to observe how almost all patients lie with their faces turned to the light, exactly as plants.*

It wouldn't be long before Névé visited the Heartlands again. She began to look forward to the end of the day. Reward for her day's labours. Retiring to bed, falling asleep and waking up in the Heartlands. It would become part of her sleeping life. *Sleep soundly and deeply and don't forget to dream*, she reminded herself. It was always the same setting, the receding sunset and the approach of dusk—

—*"Sit with me a while,"* says her male companion, who is dressed like a poet or a painter or a Rock star. *"How's our patient?"*

"You mean you?" She sits down right beside him on the fallen log. She doesn't know if her patient in the makeshift hospital room, lying there old and dying, is entering her head, exploring her dreams, creating some kind of internal landscape . . . or vice versa, she is inhabiting some elaborate dream-state or engaging in some form of astral projection. Whether or not the Heartlands is a real place, it certainly looks real. Feels real, smells real. But she cannot be sure. Or could it be their individual dreams have somehow merged and they are dreaming the same dream, as one? *"We both have a mutual interest in his well-being. He's doing well. Still unconscious but stable."*

"I'm sure you're doing your best."

"Strange, I'm dreaming about you when I sleep and I'm tending to a much older version of you when I'm awake."

"I must save you," he says abruptly.

"Why do I need rescuing?"

"On that hospital bed, I am a constant reminder to you that we all walk in the Shadow of Death. If you take your life too seriously, you're never going to get out alive, in a manner of speaking. You can spend your life living or constantly afraid of dying."

"But I'm the eternal optimist!"

"Maybe the optimist in you can see us getting closer . . ."

"You act like you're trying to serenade me!" And what a place to serenade someone. The darkening twilight. Starlight and the rising, summer moon. The ancient forest, the lush valley. The warm, evening breeze. The fragrant, floral bouquets. The lively, chattering strains of wildlife. Black coots gliding on the cool, clear waters of the brook. The misty waterfall. Quoting Daphne du Maurier: A dreamer, I walked enchanted, and nothing held me back.

"They don't call it the 'wooing place' for nothing."

"That's rather presumptuous of you." Except Névé knows she is growing more and more enamoured by him with each visit to this stunning, scenic spot, their secret location.

Dream Kestran turns to face Névé, clutches the sides of her face, looks directly into her dark eyes with his enchanting, faded-grey eyes, and kisses her passionately on the lips. In a long clinch, he blows a fine dust into her face, unbeknownst to her, emerging from his mouth and nostrils.

When he withdraws his face from hers, Névé is still lost in the moment, eyes closed. She continues to taste his kiss on her lips. She feels a brief, soaring euphoria, an experience that disappears as quickly as it has enveloped her. "What was that for?"

"I could not help it. You are keeping me alive in that room. You deserve my sincerest gratitude." He adds: "And, as a Moonreacher, my purpose is to bring love to women like you."

"It sounds like I'm not the first woman who's received your affections . . ."

Dream Kestran responds with a whimsical flourish: "But you won't be the last . . ."

Névé punches him playfully in the arm, mock-offended. His reply is meant to be a stab at humour, judging by the light-hearted manner in which he has delivered it, but Névé wonders if there's any underlying truth to his comment. No, she trusts him—

—It was halfway through her fortnightly shift that Névé noticed something very peculiar about her patient.

Is it just my imagination or is he getting younger?

Kestran's face was still as wrinkled as a prune, but now on par with the prematurely-aged skin of a woman in her forties who has spent too many years in the sun. That is, Kestran now had noticeably fewer wrinkles. His hair seemed thicker, too, and Névé could see the first strands of blond.

He's progressing . . .

What does that even mean?

The body has a way of repairing itself, even in old age.

Is there such a thing as reverse aging?

Can the day get any more rewarding? Maybe I'm doing something right, optimizing the care he is receiving. Life finds a way, like a flower sprouting out of a scorched desert.

The days passed. She nearly lost track of time. Soon, her two weeks were up.

When Rhonda came round, on schedule, to relieve her colleague for the weekend, Névé asked her to make a critical observation about their patient: "Do you notice anything different about him?"

Rhonda studied the old man permanently sleeping in the hospital bed. "What am I supposed to be looking for?"

Névé blurted it out when Rhonda couldn't come up with the answer. "He's grown younger!"

"Girl, you're such an optimist!" exclaimed Rhonda. Then she continued more thoughtfully. "But you know what you're saying is impossible."

"Don't you see it?" Névé insisted earnestly.

"He's just an old man on his deathbed, trying to cling on to life. Whether he's lost some years or not, he still looks like he's over a hundred. Unfortunately, his systems are destined to pack in, and he will perish one day soon. It's inevitable." She grasped Névé by the shoulders, looked straight into her eyes and gave her direct, friendly advice. "I think you've been by yourself too long. Go out and enjoy the summer. Come back refreshed."

Disappointed by Rhonda's reply, Névé picked up her car keys. Admittedly, she was cream-crackered but not sleep-deprived. "See you in a couple of days."

2

Finding the sharp tang of the local salt air refreshing, reviving her senses, Névé kicked off the weekend with a visit to the MUSEUM OF WITCHCRAFT AND MAGIC, a whitewashed, slightly sinister-looking building on the outside, crooked and lopsided. Inside, it explored magical lore, making comparisons with other belief systems, from ancient times to the present. Each section was devoted to a particular aspect of witchcraft from the persecution of witches in the Middle Ages to modern Wiccan practice. There were collections of charms and curses and healing herbs. Magical tools such as glass knitting needles, objects that were used for scrying such as black mirrors, crystals and crystal balls and protective talismen made by soldiers in the trenches of World War One. The Museum also had an extensive library with over seven thousand books and an archive of documents. There was even a Wise Woman's Cottage inhouse. Névé took her time whether looking into all the display cases and drawers, contemplating the images and items she was seeing, poppets and amulets and some relating to certain pre-Christian deities of nature, such as Pan, or staring into the face of a preserved human skull. The exhibits on the first floor, too, covered a lot of ground, exploring the likes of Crowley and the Golden Dawn and taking the magical arts to the present day. But it was the powerful painting of Baphomet that captivated Névé as she stumbled across it in the section on Satanism. It was a picture of a horned, cloven-hoofed god standing behind a luscious, stark-naked maiden, his clawed hand coming round to grasp her left breast.

Névé stared at it, fascinated. It spoke to her. It somehow made her think of Tregaskin and her dreams.

"Beautiful, isn't it?" came a voice from behind her.

So absorbed had she been by the painting, Névé nearly jumped at the interruption. She swung round. Behind her stood a rather obese lady, dressed in a white gown and brown sandals. Her grey hair was weaved into a single plait and she wore a ridiculous amount of jewellery, mainly cheap baubles: necklaces and hand bracelets composed of various, colourful gemstones.

"Yes, it is . . ." Névé replied. "Beautiful, that is . . . and intriguing."

"Remind you of anyone you know . . .?" The other lady offered her hand. "I'm Gertrude Asher . . . and you're Névé—"

Névé was more than just surprised; she was almost shocked. *Remind you of anyone you know?* "How could you possibly k–?"

"Boscastle is a small community," explained Gertrude. "Word gets around." She paused before continuing: "You're the nurse who's been called in to watch over Kestran Tregaskin."

"That is correct."

"We are grateful you are here to look after him in his hour of need," Gertrude said. "He's an important part of Boscastle. Some say his ancestry dates back to the de Botreaux family, who settled here in the twelfth century . . . just as I'm descended from the first Boscastle witches. White Wiccan."

"That's quite the heritage." Névé should have guessed Kestran possessed a nobiliary background.

"The shallow pursuits of the rich. Like a sylph, he will returneth unto us. Ours is not to reason why."

It was a curious thing to say, and it made Névé look back at the painting of the Horned God cupping, squeezing the fair maiden's voluptuous breast. *Remind you of anyone you know? He will returneth unto us . . .* Névé shivered. She had to get out of here; Gertrude Asher was doing a good job of creeping her out. *What do you expect? She's a witch!* But Névé seemed more than able to call upon her sound, usually reliable logic. *We rationalists, scientists, clinicians believe a curse is driven by hypnotic suggestion and is the only reason certain potions work as herbal remedies. You should give them as much credence as Dianetics or homeopathy.* "I have to go . . . it has been an interesting tour of your museum."

Gertrude smiled a gentle smile. "You know, Névé, I like the cut of your jib. It was a pleasure to meet you . . ." Before Névé took her leave, rather hurriedly, Gertrude added as a parting shot: "Hang in there and you might see a miracle! Unless it is already unfolding!"

There was something Gertrude was insinuating that Névé could not quite immediately put her finger on. She left the Museum of Witchcraft and Magic somewhat perturbed. She had other things to contend with.

Did the weekend give Névé enough time to explore the rest of Cornwall?

Perhaps a fleeting visit to Tintagel, that Arthurian-themed village, with Merlin's Cave, where the grand wizard supposedly concocted his magic potions, and its thirteenth-century castle, which is thought to be where King Arthur was conceived and born. The shops on the high street sell various Arthurian memorabilia, and the numerous galleries showcase arts and crafts devoted to the Arthurian legend. Camelford, near Slaughterbridge, would contest the site of Camelot; maybe there is some truth to its claims since Camelford does sound curiously similar to Camelot.

Why not take in Launceston Castle, former Norman stronghold and once the capital of Cornwall, another heritage site snapped up by the National Trust? The motte-and-bailey structure still survives today alongside the stone keep and ruined gatehouse. And, since we're in Launceston, why not take a ride on the steam train to Newmills and discover a proper railway cat and a deserted ghost station halfway through the twenty-minute journey?

What about a ferry ride or a glass-bottom boating trip from Bodinnick to Lostwithiel or Looe or Fowey?

Whether it's 'rumbletums' or you're just plain peckish, why not enjoy a nice, traditional Cornish pasty at AUNT AVICES on St. Kew Highway, washed down with real apple juice from Cornish Orchards whilst the biker kids consume Scrumpy Jack?

Travel to Padstow with the shifting sands of its Doom Bar at the estuary and its very hungry and aggressive seagulls intent on devouring your fish and chips.

Then there's Port Isaac with its picturesque harbour, maze of pretty cottages and constant reminders of *Doc Martin*. Névé had actually met Martin Clunes. He had sat down next to her on the platform-bench at Clapham Junction. She hadn't been able to hold her tongue too long, with his presence attracting the attention of all the other passengers, and had to ask: *I've done my utmost to remain as cool as possible but when does the next series of* Doc Martin *come out?* He had replied: *January.* He had boarded the train to Exeter St. Davids. Névé had considered him an absolute gentleman, not 'Badly Behaved' at all.

Cornwall was the land of waterfalls. Somewhere between Tintagel and Port Isaac was the village of Tregardock, nestled between two of North Cornwall's most visited locations, complete with a spectacular waterfall that cascaded over the mouth of a shallow cave and under which people were known to strip off and shower on a hot, sticky day. Then there was Culm Coast with its own inviting waterfall, its other landmark, Hawker's Hut at Morwenstow, once the refuge of the poet, Reverend Robert Hawker, who was also the vicar between 1835 and 1874 and who wrote the Cornish anthem, *Trelawney*.

Bisected by the A30, Bodmin Moor was the perfect place for a ramble. You might find free-roaming sheep on either side of the road. Black clouds over the moors. A single laburnum tree stood alone on the misty heathland. Here you could find the Tors, granite weathered into precarious towers of rock, and the stone circle of the Hurlers and adjacent standing stones. Dozmary Pool bubbled with the enduring myth of Jan Tregeagle – a composite character made up of several generations of the Tregeagles, who were powerful lawyers and magistrates between the sixteenth and eighteenth centuries and notorious for their callous brutality and underhanded deeds whilst allegedly making a pact with 'Old Artful' (the Devil), bargaining their soul for power, fame and fortune. As penance for his wicked, earthly crimes, including sleeping with his sister and murdering his wife as well as cheating an orphan out of their inheritance, Jan Tregeagle would be condemned by Old Artful for an eternity baling out Dozmary Pool with a leaking limpet shell, and it is thought that his ghostly wailing can be heard on certain dark, stormy nights. Somewhere on the moor, also, strides the mythical Beast of Bodmin, perhaps an escaped black panther . . .

While you're still around Bodmin, JAMAICA INN, with its cobbled courtyard, beamed ceiling and real ale, invites you to experience the novel made famous by Daphne du Maurier in tableaux, light and sound at the smugglers' museum. An eerie tale about the lamps of old wreckers luring ships to their destruction. Take a photo-opportunity with the heroine of the book, Mary Yelland, or if you're feeling courageous enough, Francis 'Demon' Davey, the albino Vicar of Altarnun and archvillain of the piece. Enter the memorial room to the writer, including her Sheraton writing desk on top of which rests a packet of cigarettes and a dish of her favourite Glacier mints. Stay the night in one of the sixteen en-suite guest bedrooms – where you can sing sea shanties about drunken sailors or maybe discover a ghost or two.

Why not take a tour of Davidstow Creamery and taste some of the finest vintage English Cheddar?

Walk the linked alleyways and passageways of Polperro – the so-called 'shining jewel of the Cornish coast' – with streets so narrow that no cars can pass through. Visit the Heritage Museum of smuggling and fishing. Sit overlooking the quay, its rock pools exposed at low tide. Then there's that mysterious brownstone house at the top of the hill. Perhaps haunted.

The biodermed, 'global garden' of the Eden Project, near St. Austell. The Lost Gardens of Heligan. Pencarrow House. Penjerrick Garden.

Take a boat trip to St. Michael's Mount, an island fortress and place of holy pilgrimage. Take in the splendour of the Minack, an open-air theatre and concert venue, in Penzance. See the Cornish lookouts at Land's End.

Fly by helicopter to the Isles of Scilly, full of seascapes and golden beaches and where Névé's brother and sister-in-law once honeymooned.

But it was St. Ives Névé wanted to revisit. Revisit because she had last been here as a thirteen-year-old with her family, catching up with her retired uncle, who had been a stamp collector with Sotheby's. Even if her uncle had long since passed on, Névé wanted to see if anything had changed since she'd last visited over a decade ago. In many respects, St. Ives was the archetypal Cornish fishing port while also comfortably relying on the tourist industry. Névé remembered how quiet the streets had been, but now the upmarket seafront was too busy and overcrowded, packed with pedestrians, the general street congestion making walking difficult. Aside from the numerous arts-and-crafts' shops and galleries Névé remembered, St. Ives still had the waterfront bistros and magnificent beaches, with friendly donkeys offering children rides on the silken sands, and, like Newquay and Bude, made the place lively and popular with the surfing crowd. The local cinema was apparently playing a double feature: *Bait* followed by *The Lighthouse*.

Indeed, it was the artistic inheritance of St. Ives Névé was most interested in. In fact, the unique quality of light, a sea-mirrored, enchanting quality, had captured the imagination of many an artist, and St. Ives became a centre for the Arts in the 1920s, with the leading artists of the St. Ives school including the likes of Patrick Heron and Terry Frost, Bernard Leach working with pottery and Barbara Hepworth creating modernist sculptures. The art scene continued to flourish with a branch of the Tate Gallery, the TATE ST. IVES opening its doors in 1993, standing imposingly above Porthmeor Beach, celebrating the rich artistic heritage and modern culture within the seaside town.

Névé had a passion for art, whether it be Pollack's fractals or the dark personality of Giger or the broad sense of humour of Arcimboldo or the way Picasso painted his subject's eyes, one higher than the other on the same side of the face — so trippy! A bright, airy, modern building, the Tate did not disappoint, housing a respectable collection of artwork, including a landscape Turner painted here and a couple of paintings by Sickert and Whistler and a bronze sculpture by Henry Moore, another one of his permutations of the human form, alongside the works of more home-grown artists.

No trip to Tate St. Ives would ever be complete without casting an eye on its permanent exhibition, the BARBARA HEPWORTH MUSEUM AND SCULPTURE GARDEN. Barbara Hepworth escaped to St. Ives following the outbreak of the Second World War and purchased Trewyn Studio circa 1950, living there until her death in 1975, aged seventy-two. The studio would be damaged in the fire that would cause her death, and an effort was made to reconstruct Trewyn Studio exactly as it once was when she was living and working there. The downstairs room, entered directly from the street, now housed a special display with images of Hepworth, a sculptress of great renown, at various stages in her career, a timeline of her life story. Up the stairs was her studio, reconstructed in loving detail. The studio displayed wood and stone carvings, covering every period of her career. Névé had to admit they were all good to look at, but, most of all, she liked *Fallen Images*, a more complex marble carving befittingly placed in the centre of the room, completed only a few months before her death. The studio led into the garden, Hepworth's own creation and private space, filled with sculptures made from metal and bronze. Névé was overawed by two enormous and rather impressive pieces of work, *Two forms (Divided circle)* and *Four-square (Walk through)*, full of abstract beauty but with nothing romantic in their conception, rather giving prominence to man's relationship with the natural landscape. An internationally-acclaimed pioneer in the field of sculpture, Hepworth is regarded as one of the greatest sculptors of the twentieth century.

On the way back to Boscastle, Névé enjoyed a Sunday roast at the Quarryman Inn, Wadebridge.

All in all, it had been an exhilarating experience, if not an exhausting weekend. Yet the shadow of Tregaskin had haunted her throughout. She couldn't stop thinking of him. Watching over her like a guardian – or a lover. Now that she was back at Pennryck, it was with some trepidation – and yet with an equal sense of longing – that she went back to attending to her special Cornish patient.

Time to do what she came here to do and look after a dying man and, if she could, keep him alive. She remembered the White Witch's words: *Hang in there and you might see a miracle. Unless it is already unfolding . . .*

Making sure she'd made all the safety checks on her patient, turned him over to avoid bedsores, fed him small amounts in his NG tube, changed his incontinence pad and catheter bag, all vital signs within acceptable limits, Névé readied herself to sleep by his bedside. To the sight of the slow drip of the intravenous fluids, she fell asleep—

—*She is back in the Heartlands, at the wooing place, the lover's tryst. It is just after sunset and the grey, ashen hues of twilight shape the coming evening. The full moon, surrounded by moving, silver-edged clouds, casts its brilliant white light across the landscape. The air is warm, the valley rife with animals foraging in the undergrowth and birds nesting in the trees.*

"*Did you miss me?*" *asks Dream Kestran perched next to her on the fallen log.*

Once again, Névé wonders if her real-life patient exudes some kind of mental sphere of influence from his hospital bed, using her dreams to communicate with her…or it's all in her head. Has he dreamed up this whole alternate version of himself, in a perfect world he's made up? "*I don't know what you've done to me, but I couldn't stop thinking about you.*"

"*Do you crave me when I'm not there?*"

"*In a sense, yes.*" *Almost as if he were a walking, talking drug . . .*

"*Do I make you happy?*"

"*You know you do!*"

"*Never be afraid to express your emotions.*" *He looks meaningfully into her eyes, and she cannot help but feel weak at the knees. She loves his eyes, their pale-grey colour, the intensity of his stare, perfectly matching his blond curtains and perfectly-sculpted facial features. She thinks he looks like a Greek god or the powerful offspring of a god and a human. What species of human is a Moonreacher? No, she also loves the rest of him, all of him.* "*I have the power to make things beautiful when they're not. All I have to do is reach into your heart and touch the core of your being.*"

"*You have my permission.*"

"*The French poet, Musset, once said:* Life is a long sleep and love is its dream," *Dream Kestran recites competently.* "*To quote another Frenchman, Anouilh:* There is love, of course. And then there's life, it's enemy.*"

"*That's so beautiful,*" *acknowledges Névé, feeling all these different emojis.* "*You're so beautiful . . .*"

"*Then, let love be our life and our life be our love,*" *declares Dream Kestran.*

"I second that," yearns Névé. "Let our love develop, grow, evolve, never expire."

"I can make it happen," Dream Kestran reminds her. "To love, you must allow yourself to be totally vulnerable, give yourself completely to me."

"How? With a kiss—?"

Getting to his feet, Dream Kestran reaches down and pulls Névé tightly towards him, her body slight and vulnerable in his arms. He kisses her softly, but she returns the kiss harder, more hungrily.

When his lips detach themselves from hers, she draws in a quick breath, then sighs with passion. Her senses reel, her mind swirls. Every part of her body is tingling, engulfed in an exquisite bliss. Enraptured, she slides her right hand beneath her dress, beneath her panties, reaches the dark curls of her pubic hair and dips her fingers into the wet cleft between her thighs, touching the dampness down there. "I don't want you to stop . . ." she gasps, highly aroused.

"When it is time . . ." Dream Kestran replies, chuckling as Névé removes her hand from her groin and brings her carnal feelings under control. "But before then . . ."

He pulls out a white handkerchief from his pocket and unfolds it to reveal a small, shiny object. It is a gold ring, Celtic in design, studded with diamonds. He goes down on one knee. "Will you marry me?"

Névé cannot believe her ears. This is all so incredible! Her new friend, her pure hunk-of-a-friend, whom she cannot get enough of and who has acted the perfect gentleman with a romantic twist, is proposing to her. It is music to her ears. A heavenly choir. The singing of the spheres. She doesn't refuse. "Of course, I will marry you . . ."

"With this ring I bind you to me . . ." Dream Kestran mutters as he slides the ring on the fourth finger of her right hand. "I grant you the gift of love."

Névé tests the fit by waggling her fingers. The diamonds twinkle in the moonlight. The warm breath of wind brushes her cheeks. "It's perfect. Does that mean I'm yours now?"

"We have become two bodies in one soul."

She has never been engaged before and she is utterly thrilled. She remembers something her brother once told her when he got engaged: You don't marry someone you can live with — you marry the person you cannot live without. But doubt is never far away. If fortune favours the brave, why do fools rush in where angels fear to tread? And does it have any true relevance or real meaning if she got engaged in her dreams? She asks the man who is now affianced to her. "How many times have you been in love?"

Dream Kestran doesn't reply—

—When Névé awoke the following morning, she saw she still wore the engagement ring. It seemed getting engaged in the dream world had somehow translated into real life.

III:

If Love Is The Drug Then I Want to OD
                    — Brian Jonestown Massacre

I

Névé couldn't believe she had just got engaged to the dream incarnation of her patient. He was such a charmer, so seductive and persuasive. But what mystified her was how it was possible to bring that ring out of her dream and into reality. *Yes, please explain, how any of it is possible?*

Névé changed from her blue scrubs back into her matron's uniform and started the day.

She was engaged! How could she still be wearing the ring in the real world? And her patient didn't look much like a senior citizen anymore. He continued to get younger, as though he had discovered the Fountain of Youth. Kestran Tregaskin's wrinkles had nearly practically all but disappeared, his skin was firmer, and his grey hair had taken on a blondish hue. If he were able to cast off a few more decades, the bedridden Kestran would almost be on a level with the Kestran of her dreams. At the Museum of Witchcraft and Magic, Gertrude the White Witch had spoken of miracles.

The day passed by pleasantly enough, and Névé got on caring for her rejuvenated patient. But her mind stayed on the ring she wore. It was such a fine-looking engagement ring she didn't want to remove it. But she did try to get it off her finger. She used oil and butter and soap and still it would not budge. It was almost as if it was glued to her finger.

She was engaged.

What did it mean? Would marriage follow? Physical intimacy? With her elixir-drinking patient?

No, she had to stop herself from being rash and impulsive again in her decision-making.

But he's so gorgeous! He makes me desire him . . . constantly. Makes me yearn him when he's not there. No man has ever had that kind of effect on me before.

Having completed her physical health checks, she put on the TV as another summer's day came to a close, largely to distract herself from her thoughts, and discovered the movie adaptation of a Richard Matheson fantasy novel: *What Dreams May Come*. It was a love story across Heaven and Hell, starring the ever-reliable Robin Williams. A fine comedian who kept the world in stitches. A mensch driven by mad energy. One in a billion. On this occasion, however, there was very little humour, as he took on a serious, romantic role, trying to rescue his suicidal wife from her own personal hell in the Afterlife.

Soon it was getting late. Dare she sleep?

Midnight. When reality is thin. When the other dimension spills in. Or the mind transmits into another realm, a realm of dreams. Perhaps a dream form of astral projection. Transportation to a very special place. Back to the wooing place. To meet her friend – her *fiancé* – at the lovers' tryst in her dreams–

–And as I live and breathe, the Devil shall appear, she recounts an old saying. She must have fallen asleep in the armchair again, at the patient's bedside.

She sits barefoot and pretty on the same fallen log, surveying the wooded valley and fields and meadows, full of wild animals, preparing for another night of rest. The sky points towards duskfall and the departure of sunset. The full moon is slowly ascending.

"How's my bride-to-be?" Dream Kestran inquires, appearing from down the lane and sitting down beside her.

His sudden appearance causes her to start. "What does it all mean?" she manages to compose herself and ask him.

"It means we are one, destined to put our love into practice and share our life together."

"I don't know if I want that . . ."

"Are you having second thoughts?" Dream Kestran asks, concerned.

Should she be worried? He's so dreamy and damned sexy, and it would be a shame to turn him down, back out of it. It's like he's put a spell on me. Like he's exuding some form of perfume, pheromone, or *love dust,* each time he kisses me, breathing it into my face, filling me with a euphoria. Clouding my judgement, manipulating my thought processes, pushing away the sensible side of me. *"Yes, I am. I don't know if getting engaged is the kind of thing I would do."*

"*Your doubts are understandable. But, rest assured, our love for each other will save us, allow us to forge a beautiful life together. Don't you want that?*"

"*I do . . . but . . .*" But she is torn.

"*You're doing a splendid job getting me well, for which I am eternally grateful. You are truly invaluable to me, both as a nurse and as my intended. I cannot lose you. Once I am well enough to walk and talk in that hospital room, all your doubts will melt away. You'll see—*"

–It was in the small hours that Névé awoke. Another vivid, haunting dream, food for thought. She checked on her patient, who was getting better by the day. Impossibly so. She noticed the IV line had stopped working. Back turned to the bed, she put a syringeful of heparin in it to unblock it, and seeing the line resume its drip-drip-drip, she felt someone pinch her bottom.

Startled, she jumped upright and noticed that Kestran Tregaskin, despite still being unconscious and unresponsive, wore a small, mischievous smile.

2

The doubts lingered. A part of her didn't mind being engaged to this Cornish aristocratic fellow, but her other self got an intuitive sense that not everything was as it seemed and that she was not yet seeing the whole picture. To her, Kestran's motives were not entirely clear. Did he really love her or was it something else he was after? She struggled to handle her incertitude. She loved this man, practically *craved* him, except she supposed it felt like an artificial love or a love that had been instilled – *supplanted* – in her.

Sleep reopened the door to the Heartlands. When she went to the wooing place next, there was initially no sign of Dream Kestran.

But the place was populated by dimly-perceived ghosts—

–*Mist obscures the eerie twilight. Névé can make out blurry, spectral shapes in the fog and shudders inwardly. The fog begins to clear, and the moving figures take on more distinctive forms. Strange sounds emerge from the gloom, accompanying the visitation. Moans, wailings, shrieks, a chorus of lament.*

Partially materialized and semi-transparent until the vaporous spirits take on a fuller, solid form.

There are lots of women, of varying senior ages, ridiculously underdressed in skimpy clothes and drawn to her presence.

They all look distressed, sad and forlorn, strangely lost. *They come over to her, gather round her where she sits on the familiar log waiting for her betrothed, and one of their number takes on the role of spokesperson, a mouthpiece for the rest of them.*

Névé is gobsmacked by the sheer number of these elderly ladies, who have somehow stepped into this romantic, summer dreamscape from some other nightmare, and how they've taken a sudden interest in her. Their despair is almost palpable.

The spokeswoman for these disconsolate ladies speaks up, introduces herself: "I'm Bryluen. And you are his latest recruit?"

The term puzzles Névé. "Recruit?"

"I'm being polite," *says Bryluen, all old and wrinkled, long, white hair flowing down her back, and wearing a white nightdress, varicose veins tracing a roadmap across her sparse, slack legs and her bare feet bulging with bunions.* "I mean slave."

It is such a strong word that its sinister nature causes Névé to shudder. "Who are you all?"

"We are all the women that Kestran has trapped here over the ages."

Névé surveys the maudlin congregation of ladies, some middle-aged, most significantly older, who have come together on common ground. "That's crazy! Surely this is a make-believe place belonging only to me and Kestran! So where did you all come from?"

"We have always been here. Except Kestran keeps us hidden from view, from you. This is not your dream; Kestran's imagination built the Heartlands. His mind sustains it. He can project his will into this world whenever he sleeps."

For the first time in her visit to this twilit, moon-filled place, Névé is in direct communication with somebody other than Kestran, a different person who is keen to give her some of the answers that have previously eluded her. "And what exactly does he want with me?"

"We have watched your courtship with Kestran from an invisible, mute position. But you're in grave danger. Whatever you do now, we beg of you, do not marry him."

"Why ever not?"

"Because you too will become lost, ultimately joining our pathetic ranks. We are his brides." *Bryluen pauses to let the words sink in before continuing:* "I was twenty when I came to the Heartlands. I'm now eight-five. The other ladies here can recount similar stories, lost lives. He will promise you the heavens, but he will take away your dignity and your youth. He will reduce you to a slave. So many ladies have died in the Heartlands from old age. Some have died from too much love, driven to the fatal heights of ecstasy by his powerful essence. I myself felt so high with passion when I first met him that I thought my heart was going to explode. Remember, he is a Moonreacher, an ancient tribe of creatures that preys on the vital energy of humankind."

This is all beginning to make sense now, no matter how far-fetched the explanation is. My life is wrong, thinks Névé. I can see that now. She suddenly feels pity for all these unfortunate ladies, these poor, desolate souls, who have been used and abused by someone they thought loved them. Left to rot and fester in this accursed place. Grow old and die.

Another lady, somewhat portly and well past her prime, called Endelyn, steps forward to tell her tale: seduced and snatched up in the 1960s, she has spent the rest of her miserable life here, not quite living and not quite dead. A third lady by the name of Mabyn, slimmer and possibly the youngest of the group, now in her forties, recounts her own tale of woe: she was nineteen when she foolishly got engaged to Kestran. He entranced his victims into becoming his slaves – or a food source. Chewed them up and spat them out, in a figurative sense. "He still indulges in a literal love feast with us whenever he feels like it, sometimes with all of us at once. He doesn't do sex in the traditional way, just fills us up with love and absorbs our emotional energy. His 'love' seized up my heart. I died in his bed." All the other ladies, too, have a tale to tell, but Névé doesn't have time to listen to all of them. Disappointed, most moan their all-consuming grief, some stifle their wrenching sobs, others silently weep.

Névé is grateful to them, particularly Bryluen, whose name is Cornish for 'rose', for enlightening her on her fiancé and the fact she has learned early on that she is being led like a sheep to the slaughter, so she can do something about it. These ladies have already been through it. Névé is also sympathetic to their dreadful circumstances. Whether they are spirits or still in their bodily forms she cannot be sure. To reference Daphne Du Maurier, It doesn't make for sanity, does it, living with the devil? They have endured hell and damnation and agony for their love for Kestran. Névé does not wish to suffer the same fate. She, too, feels used, betrayed and humiliated, her trust taken advantage of, seduced by this monstrous, centuries-old polygamist, making her feel very special before feeding off her unique energy of love. It disgusts her, enrages her. "I'm not going to let him get away with it . . ."

"We can never escape because we are all addicted to him, as he feasts on our vitality. But you're young and fresh, you're new, you can get away . . ."

"Hell hath no fury, right?" Névé reminds the others. Even if these ladies have sent her little affair into the brine, she is grateful to them for opening her eyes to her true, perilous situation.

"Open the gates," requests Bryluen. "Free us from this age-old prison, our oblivion. Afford us the gift of death."

"I'll see what I can do—" Névé promises them, staring down at her engagement ring.

The air is suddenly filled with the sounds of unseen feral creatures. Vicious snarls, nasty hissing, restless shrilling and screeching and caterwauling, growls and barks and squeals and shrieks, animals howling in the distance. Getting louder, closer. Menacing, baying for blood, threatening to maul. Suggesting a massacre might be in the making.

Then follows an unearthly mewling, like some wroth beast dragging its claws down a sheet of metal.

The women bewail their fear. Women kept on a figurative leash by wild animals which, too, are subservient to their master.

The animal sounds recede. The fog lifts. The moon comes out.

Névé cannot continue her conversation with these women because Dream Kestran comes wandering down the path from the forest glade and sits down next to her. When Névé looks around, all his old brides have vanished. Sometimes though, a moment is just too long or, perhaps, long gone. And Névé decides it prudent to wake up, angrily and wordlessly leaving a newly-arrived Dream Kestran in the lurch and utterly bemused—

—When Névé awoke the next morning, sun blazing in, she realized her patient had completely rejuvenated to be as young as his dream version. Blond, muscular and handsome. And, oh, so dreamy! Except he remained in a deep coma. Not long now. Her experience last night, visited by Kestran's catalogue of romantic conquests in the Heartlands, had been an eye-opener, a vital piece of information about her 'beloved', *their* beloved. *Just goes to show how reputations are hard-earned and easily lost.* These ladies, now old and forlorn and trapped in that place, had already gone through what she was about to go through. Their warning couldn't have come at a more opportune moment.

She rang Hartwin. She felt she needed to tell someone she knew of her strange experiences who might also be able to help her get out of her current pickle, dignity intact.

Hartwin answered. He was pleased to hear from her but could only talk for a short while as he was getting ready for work. So Névé gave him a quick summary of her dreamlike experiences with her patient, her astral travels into the Heartlands, getting engaged to him and encountering his wretched, incarcerated brides. The situation certainly wasn't copesetic, using his descriptive. When she was finished, she asked his opinion: "What do you think?"

"I should say congratulations on your engagement, but instead I'm going to say — *what the hell?*" Hartwin exclaimed. "I think you've got too much time on your hands! What you're saying is crazy! I don't know if you've been alone too long and you're suffering cabin fever or something, but have you completely lost your mind?"

It wasn't quite the reaction she was expecting. She knew it was a lot to take on board, but she had expected him to be slightly more supportive. Névé was adamant. "Ghosts, demons, vampires, the Devil. I only believe in what I can see or hear."

"And what is that exactly?" Hartwin challenged her. "An old man getting younger, *stronger?*"

"I know it's crazy, without reason, but I'm dealing with something profound, *supernatural.*"

"And you're engaged to him? I thought he was unconscious!"

"He is."

"So how the hell can you be engaged to him?"

Névé was getting frustrated. "You're not listening to me . . ."

"Of course, I'm listening!" countered Hartwin. "You're saying you've got engaged to your patient, a comatose man, an old man who refuses to die but instead has dramatically and completely de-aged in the time you've been there. A man who desires to trap you in a place his imagination created and live off your remaining years of life."

Névé had never heard Hartwin sound so incredulous, so judgemental. She'd mistakenly assumed he would understand. "I shouldn't have called you . . ."

"No, you did the right thing calling me," replied Hartwin, slightly more helpfully. "I think I need to see you. Let me get my shift over and done with. Then I'll drive straight down to Boscastle."

3

Hartwin Purcell sped up the A-road, keen to get to Boscastle as soon as possible. Four hours he had been driving, and the satnav informed him he should be arriving there around midnight. He'd got through his shift without fuss, but his mind had been elsewhere, replaying the telephone conversation with Névé in his head. Skepticism aside, from what she had imparted to him, he was worried for her, worried that the lonely, lengthy shifts might have taken a toll on her mind. She had apparently got engaged to Kestran in some fairy world, and the next step from fantasy was madness. He had foregone the idea of asking the police to do a welfare check on Névé since he suspected they might not appreciate his reason or have enough grounds; anyhow, the police did not have a legal duty to protect you.

Hartwin had sorted out the suspension of his Ligier 50 Sports only yesterday, and what was once a bumpy ride had now become bouncy. He had grown frustrated at Stonehenge, trailing a line of slow cars, their drivers gaping at the silhouette of the prehistoric monument at dusk. Flintstone cars, like they were using their feet instead of an engine. He impatiently overtook them all, receiving angry honks from the drivers, even though he wasn't doing anything remotely dangerous.

Now an hour to go before his final destination, he drew in a deep breath. *Holy mother of fuck!*

Instead of reminding him TIREDNESS KILLS, the message on each successive road sign read: DIE.

Was it just his imagination playing tricks on him? Yet, when he slowed down and looked at the next sign, it too told him to DIE.

I must be really tired to have actually started hallucinating, he considered, thinking back to the long shift he had completed at the hospital followed by the long drive whilst worrying himself silly about the mental well-being of his valued friend far away.

But *was* he tired? *Was* he hallucinating? *Depersonalizing?*

He had pumped himself full of caffeine before he'd set off, and he felt wide awake and alert and ready for anything. He thought of the loneliness Névé had endured in the last couple of weeks, slowly going crazy, losing touch with reality and dreaming up a fantastic account of her experiences with the comatose patient, whom she had ultimately got engaged to. What of the freaky road signs he was seeing, presently? What if there was truth to her narrative?

Hartwin sensed a mental force pushing him back. And he soon realized it was fear. It was being projected from somewhere far away . . . as far away as Névé, perhaps? Someone – or something – did not want him to reach Névé.

Using his cool, collected clinician's reasoning to dispel the fear as simply irrational and unjustified, Hartwin kept on driving. After all, he was just an ordinary man driving to get to his precious girlfriend, even if the road signs were issuing the edict he DIE, instead of reminding him to DRIVE CAREFULLY or SLOW DOWN.

Die? thought Hartwin. *That's awfully final . . .*

The dread and sense of derealization did not leave him but steadily grew stronger. He used all his internal resources not to give in to it.

Lightning split the night. The world was ashen in that second. Thunder rumbled in its wake.

Taken by surprise, Hartwin didn't know where the storm came from when the weather forecasters had predicted a dry, warm summer's evening. Rain lashed the windscreen, Hartwin forced to turn on the wipers. He continued to chase his headlights in the wind and the wet and the dark. The storm howled, the gale tossing broken tree branches and other loose debris into the road.

Lightning forked to earth, striking the lower trunk of a tall pine on the side of the road in an explosion of electrical sparks. The whole world suddenly seemed to run in slow motion, time drawing out, as the trunk detached itself from its shattered, charred roots with a loud *Crack!* and toppled over, gravity sending it plummeting down in an ominous, perfectly-descending arc . . . and just as Hartwin instinctively floored the accelerator.

In a hideous, heart-stopping moment, the pine tree clattered across the entire width of the road, just avoiding smashing the roof of the Ligier and fatally crushing its occupant by a whisker.

Hartwin kept his foot on the gas, visibly shaken but also relieved he hadn't taken the full, prodigious weight of the falling tree, the steep trajectory of which he'd only just managed to speed past and survive by the skim of his teeth. He presently left the dangerous obstruction far behind him,

Fuck, that was a close call, a near-miss! This is not how I want to be remembered on my tombstone!

Except Hartwin got no respite to reflect on his narrow escape, his brush with death.

An old woman, barefoot and dressed in a rain-soaked white nightdress, appeared from out of nowhere in the middle of the road, directly ahead of him.

Hartwin did not have time to consider how one moment the road could be clear, the next she could be standing there, and had less than a second to slam on the brakes. Too late to swerve the car, either, and, in that blink of an eye, he struck the woman full-on, flinging her across his windscreen.

Yet the devastating force of his car connecting with the lone woman did not produce a meaty thud or, in any way, crack the glass of his windscreen. There was no physical impact.

Hartwin brought the car to a screeching halt. He turned the engine off. The headlights continued to illuminate the forbidding, storm-tossed night. Shaking terribly, it took him a few moments to compose him. He got out of the car, into the thunderstorm, and went round the back, expecting the worst, a dead woman in the road, limbs completely smashed and pointing at unnatural angles, bleeding from a broken skull, blood washed away by the rainwater.

Except there was nobody there.

He shielded his eyes from the wind and the pelting rain, surveyed his surrounds in a complete three-hundred-and-sixty-degree turn, including the ditch, but still could see nothing unusual, nothing to indicate he had ever been involved in a road traffic accident.

How was that possible?

Unless he had hit an apparition in the middle of the road, an *illusion*, seeping in from another reality. He thought hard, trying to make sense of his confusion. The woman's name came to him: *Bryluen*. Névé had mentioned it when she had related her mad experiences to him on the phone.

At a loss, now completely drenched by the thundery downpour and slightly dazed, he walked over to his car and sat back down in the driver's seat. He was quaking inside. He brought his panic back under a modicum of control, staring out of the windscreen, listening to the sound of rain drumming the roof, the engine silent, the headlights bringing an element of sanity to the squally, almost unreal countryside ahead and the darkly-veiled woods on either side.

Somebody really doesn't want me to go to Boscastle.

"May I have a word?" rose a voice from the back seat.

Hartwin craned his neck round, slowly, and his eyes widened in stark terror. All courage shrivelled up inside him. He wanted to scream, but all he could do was stare, wearing a petrified expression, his mind unable to comprehend the chilling presence in his car. It was Bryluen, the same old woman he'd just run over. Alive and well and unhurt. Except not quite there, as though composed of semi-translucent glass, pellucid, like an illusion – or a *ghost.*

"Go to your girl," the phantom in the back seat instructed urgently, lips moving out of sync with her words, her voice presently coming from somewhere faraway. Relaying a message . . . a warning. "Get her out of Pennryck before it's too late . . ."

His paralysis releasing him, thinking his heart was going to seize up, Hartwin finally unloosed the godawful scream that had been threatening to break free but had been suppressed earlier, a hideous stridency of sound suggesting a mind that seriously risked unravelling.

When Névé next glanced down at her patient from the armchair, she noticed his eyes were wide open. Faded-denim, grey eyes looking at her, studying her.

It was the witching hour, and her patient was awake.

It did not startle her.

He spoke to her. "Aren't we all better now?"

She did not reply. The man lived two lives. One life born of his imagination, the other of a dimension of flesh. She had dreamed of a young man, who turned out to be an old man in real life. Yet the old man had youthened into that same young man, bone, muscle, sinew regenerated. Almost comparable to resurrection itself. The wondrous miracle, as foretold by Gertrude the White Witch, was complete.

Névé found it difficult to adjust to the sight before her. A part of Névé couldn't believe such mad, impossible things could be happening so close to home. But it did not quite faze her.

"I recognize the care and dedication you showed in looking after me," Kestran acknowledged. "I would be doing you a great discourtesy if I didn't express my appreciation for helping the medicine go down and bringing me back to the land of the living. You truly are a miracle worker, a lifesaver, a *saint*!"

Still she did not speak.

"What's going on with you?" Kestran said, getting slightly impatient. "I get a sense you're unhappy with me."

She came out with it. "I know about the other women you keep as slaves."

"I gathered as much . . ." Kestran said, irritated by her rebuke. "You met the others, even though I kept you apart?"

"They have saved me from a life as your slave."

"Rehoboam had eighteen wives and sixty concubines," Kestran reminded her. "His father, Solomon, supposedly had seven hundred wives and three hundred concubines. And, when you talk about slaves, the twentieth century boasted the highest number of slaves in the world, an estimated forty million slaves, which is six times more than those exploited by the transatlantic slave trade, those Africans imported to the New World."

Névé remembered from Sunday School how King David, beloved hero of the Old Testament, raped Bathsheba. In those days it was meant to be an honour, completely normal, if the king raped young women, a mark of sovereign status and virility. But, since then, times had changed. *Radically.* Imagine what people would say nowadays if Prince Andrew put his hand down someone's dress. But it wasn't Methuselah or the Bible Néve was thinking about. She was thinking about Scheherazade, from *1001 Arabian Nights.* Yes, Scheherazade, who was spinning out stories all night for her new husband, the paranoid, despotic king, who had got into the habit of marrying a new bride every day and beheading her in the morning so that she would not get the opportunity to be unfaithful to him. Scheherazade was telling tales, keeping him entertained, to stay alive. "My life is so wrong. My job has become a poisoned chalice. I thought it was a nurse's calling. But now I know the truth. I am a rock, and you keep chipping away at it, reducing me until there's nothing left."

"*To undergo such maiden pilgrimage;/But earthlier happy is the rose distill'd,/Than that which withering on the virgin thorn./Grows, lives and dies in single blessedness.*"

It was a quote from *A Midsummer Night's Dream.* He was using his wiles to seduce her again, get her back on his side. But Néve stood her ground, even if she was caught between dread and desire. "What is this love that you speak of? Your fine words butter no parsnips. Your easy words are without true feeling and no longer have any effect on me. All I hear is your deception and *lies!*"

"I'm in the happiness business, remember?" replied Kestran, somewhat surprised at Néve's change of heart. "Many's the time I dreamed of you and I'm sure you of me. Why deny yourself something that you want?"

"That's the thing, I don't want you in my life anymore . . ."

"Don't you understand I live to love?" he said, getting desperate, realizing he might actually be losing his prize.

"In order to drain your lover – or should I say, *victim* – dry? No thanks!" Néve spoke emphatically, almost triumphantly. There was derision in her voice. "Kestran Tregaskin, you will never have me!"

"You listen to me," Kestran demanded, growing louder. Anger bubbled up from just beneath the surface. Néve was now seeing a different side to him, a side he had kept hidden from her all along. "All I expect from my women is devotion, *absolute* devotion! No more deferments. Kiss me and my nepenthe will help you forget your troubles."

"You've got a nerve!" exclaimed Néve. Her mind had been on the fritz. This Papa Lazarou had robbed her of her reason. Except her current predicament wasn't remotely funny. She wondered what the #MeToo movement would say about Kestran's harem. "The hell I will! I never took kindly to being pressured for sex! I may not know what you are – what Moonreachers are – but you can no longer sway me! I will never be yours!"

"Just as vampires need living blood to survive," Kestran explained proudly, "Moonreachers live off the human emotion called Love. Some of us are as old as Ancient Egypt. We adapted to the human world and travelled down the centuries, growing stronger with each woman that fell in a breathless swoon at our feet. We once threw Etruscan fertility idols into the lake, we later fed off the Court of the Borgias, and we subsequently revelled in the decadence of the Weimar. We are evolved from human beings, elevated to the next level, superior in every aspect, the pinnacle of human existence. We are, of course, immortal and make even the gods tremble. Lesser humans are afraid of us . . . as they should be."

"Immortal or not, as an energy vampire you are nothing more than a parasite draining the energy of the living. Without Love I'm guessing your energy gets depleted."

Fixing her with a malevolent stare and using a darker tone of voice, Kestran warned: "I just want you to start appreciating what's been handed down to you . . . or pray to God the night goes swiftly!"

It was a threat, and there was a finality to it. Kestran was referring to the engagement ring, of course. But as his brides had indicated: the ring signified ownership, *not* love. "I'm leaving you. I made arrangements, but I'll be damned if I remember what they are."

"You *cannot* leave me!"

"I was blind, but now I see . . ." It was the presence of mind that protected her. To his horror, she ripped off the engagement ring from her finger and discarded it in the yellow sharps' bin. This time, it slid off easily, probably because she supposed she didn't love him anymore.

"*Nooooo . . .!*" Kestran screamed, thrashing about on the bed. Behind him on the bedside cabinet, the ornamental vase was now filled with dead, sagging roses.

An invisible hand scooped up the stethoscope from around her neck and flung it across the room. Those same ghost hands seized her hair and attempted to lift her up. Her scalp exploding with pain, Névé waved her arms above her head to shake off the hands grabbing a fistful of her hair but only snatched air. From somewhere nearby, some sadistic bastard was playing the violin crazily. Her ears were bombarded by a frenzied, riotous, shrieking swirl of sound, drunken, dissonant, distressing, disorientating.

Kestran Tregaskin turned this way and that on the hospital bed, writhing in utter agony, wild, furious animal sounds crawling up from his throat, hissing snarls and nasty growls. The IV stand tipped over and clattered to the floor.

Suddenly, Kestran stopped thrashing and, back arching into an excruciating, opisthotonic lock, spine curved bell-shaped, only the top of his head and back of his heels touching the mattress, a sinister gasp hissed up from the back of his throat, like steam escaping a boiling kettle. The exhaled puff of air became a low, whispering breeze. The gathering breeze in the room began to fill up with a dark, vaporous haze. The nebulous, black mist curled, billowed, swirled in the room, weaving and pulsating, coalesced into a fuller presence, forming and reforming, morphing into a fiendish face. In the centre of the room was now the enormous, smoky-tendrilled face of a demon with a jutting brow, downslanting, jet-black eyes, a long, prominent snout for a nose, a wide, crescent-shaped mouth that seemed to be filled with pointed teeth and to drip like melted wax.

Trying her utmost to ignore the cacophonous screech of violins splitting her ears and the horrible pain racking her scalp from her hair being yanked and stretched at the roots, Névé thought she could guess what this thing confronting her must surely be. From the innermost depths of Kestran's being, an unspeakable manifestation of his blackened soul. To make matters worse, the accompanying smell was foul and astringent, making Névé want to gag. The grotesquerie grinned and drooled and gloated, eyes gleaming like polished, black pearls.

[Upstairs, the doors unlocked, swung open. His mind was a doorway to other jarring worlds penetrating into our reality, other heartlands where he dwelled all at once.]

A monstrous growl rose up from deep within the frightening, fluctuating entity, the sound of a large, wild beast that is seriously pissed, and the demonic face retreated a tad, as though preparing to lunge. Obsidian eyes narrowed, mouth gaped wider, fully revealing its set of sharp, deadly teeth. Névé covered her own eyes but could not help but peek between her fingers, thinking that this might be it, that she might have enraged Kestran a little too far, that she might actually be goner. She prepared to die, for Kestran to suck the last traces of life out of her . . .

His huge, nightmarish face jumped at her as if to gobble her up, to sink his pointy teeth into her, the guttural, growling noise exploding into a reverberant, deafening boom, like a cannon being fired.

But Névé did not die. Instead, inches from her face, Kestran's power waned, dissipated, as he expended all his energy in one thunderous burst. The hellish, waking vision dissolved, soon without shape or substance, ribbons of dark mist breaking up, tattered remnants that disappeared altogether.

[The doors upstairs closed, shutting off the mental manifestation of other realms, other kingdoms Kestran inhabited simultaneously.]

Machinations comprehensively thwarted, Kestran had been summarily banished back to the Heartlands, only one of several dream-worlds he occupied.

Suddenly, the grip on Névé's hair loosened and the mad, discordant melée of the violin lowered to a decrescendo and ceased. It was quiet again. In the aftermath, Névé heard the words, *You are my ruin!* somewhere in her head, and when she looked again, Kestran Tregaskin had aged considerably. He was old again — as old and frail and comatose as when she had first arrived to care for him. Over a century old. She wondered if she should use a pillow and smother him where he slept, get it over and done with, make it look like the old man had croaked, that his crooked, longevous body had finally given in. But she knew he wouldn't die. Because he was ageless. Probably too old to die.

At that moment, Hartwin Purcell burst unexpectedly into the room, immediately embracing her, putting paid to her morbid train of thought and her self-reproach and disgust for even considering such a thing as a nurse. He was soaked to the skin. "That was some hairy, scary drive . . ."

"You're a sight for sore eyes!" Névé was so pleased to see her part-time boyfriend she kissed him hard on the lips. "You managed to make it!"

Hartwin stopped hugging her and stared at the vulnerable, dying man tucked up under the covers in the hospital bed. "Just about . . . it's funny, that. I got past all the roadblocks that man put up." He glanced at the sleeping form of Kestran and gave Névé a quizzical look. "That's the old man you were talking about? He doesn't look particularly young, fit or healthy to me."

She was about to explain to him that her patient had severely aged again after she'd discarded the engagement ring, her rejection of him expediting the aging process, but she didn't have the energy. "Never mind." She added: "My life makes sense again."

"Glad," Hartwin replied, relieved. It had been one hell of a journey down; he'd seen some seriously crazy stuff of his own, and he would never again doubt her account of events. He grasped her right hand and noticed her ring finger was bare. "I guess you're no longer engaged." Névé nodded, to which Hartwin requested, "I guess now that everything's copasetic, let's get as far away from this place as possible."

"Not just yet . . ." Névé reminded Hartwin about her duty of care, that she did not intend to abandon her patient in the middle of the night. He understood. Calling the nursing agency, she told them she had to get back to Chertsford rather urgently, citing a family emergency. Could they provide an agency nurse to immediately take over the shift? She would stay put in the meantime until the replacement nurse got here.

The agency accepted her explanation and was quick to respond. The nurse, who arrived less than an hour later, was none other than Rhonda Apenteng. "Going so soon?"

Névé was economical with the truth. "I have to get back."

"He got to you, too, didn't he?" Rhonda said, knowingly, causing Névé's brow to furrow.

"If you know so much about him, why do you do it?" Névé asked her colleague. Inside, Névé was thinking of the poor, imperilled wretches whom she had encountered in the Heartlands, trapped in the astral plane, pleading to break loose from their captivity, their intractable circumstances. Their captor, Kestran Tregaskin, had plundered their lifeforce like some kind of emotional vampire, specifically their intense love for him, heightened by his egotism, gaining power from it, reducing them to mere hags. Maybe it was something of a blessing their presence would fade with time, become too weak to sustain their tortured existence any further. Get the release they so desperately sought from their limbo. Névé was thankful she had escaped the same terrible fate, unscathed. "Why nurse him?"

"I put him in the coma," Rhonda disclosed enigmatically. "He cannot hurt me." She said no more and wished Névé the absolute best in all future endeavours.

Névé stopped in the hallway, an open palm gesturing to the front door. "Shall we, Dr. Purcell?"

"Why not, Nurse Walmsley?" Hartwin said, equally amused.

Névé sighed, satisfied her short stint as a twenty-four-hour, live-in nurse and carer for a dying, elderly man had come to an end, even if somewhat prematurely. As they said, all experience was good experience. "Lead on, good sir."

Without changing out of her uniform, Névé followed Hartwin, who carried her luggage, out of the house. Outside, the ill-lit street sounded hollow, amplifying the smallest of sounds. A low mist drifted in from the sea, making its spectral way along the channels.

"Let's go home, by jingo," Hartwin said, "and live a long and happy life!"

Epilogue

In 2004, a flash flood devastated a North Cornwall coastal village. A quarter-of-a-century later, at precisely two-twenty-one in the morning, as the people slept, another storm came to Boscastle. The heavens would open up and release a deluge of near-Biblical proportions on the village. Gale-force winds battered the village. There would be no time to deliver a flood warning. The giant flood threatened to wipe out the village after the area's average monthly rainfall fell in just two hours. Whatever dark force was at work at Pennryck also held court in the wider village, descending upon its inhabitants like the darkness after dusk.

Piddledowndidda? *Was the rain torrential?* Or to take it one step further, Pizendawn. *Expect some serious torrential rain.*

Like a monsoon, the water gushed down the streets, tearing down everything that stood in its way, poured down the steep, hilly incline, submerging the village, and made its way to the harbour. The torrential downpour caused extensive flooding.

There were no bells in the tower of Forrabury Church, but people could have sworn they heard the ghostly peal of bells as the storm swept the village. Elsewhere, as the unprecedented rain lashed down, the wind rose to a hideous wailing, like the ghost of Jan Tregeagle. Grief flowed with the brown water, rising, twisting, raw power without mercy or conscience. Soon the streets lay below turbid water that would become an insurance nightmare by the morning, leaving a trail of dirt and debris in its wake. Some people called it the 'End of the World'. Others believed they had been visited by the 'wrath of God' for their wrongdoings. But Gertrude Asher, the curator of the Museum of Witchcraft and Magic, which had mysteriously survived the last flood and would again survive another flood due to the protection spells she had cast to fortify the building, knew it was Kestran Tregaskin who had set the flood in motion, unleashing his full wrath on the people. Névé must have wounded him and got away, and he must surely be as mad as hell.

Névé and Hartwin were not around to experience this terrible flood. They had already left Boscastle an hour earlier. They read about it in the newspaper and were thankful they hadn't got caught up in it. Névé came to the same conclusion as Gertrude Asher about the origin of the flood: Kestran Tregaskin was surely furious.

In the following weeks, Névé put her peculiar experiences at Pennryck far behind her and got on with her life, emerging stronger from her ordeal of fire. Hartwin felt their short time in Boscastle had made their relationship equally stronger and realized he loved her, so decided to propose to her. Névé accepted his proposal, and they prepared to wed in the coming year and start a new life together.

But, before the big event and close to the two-hundredth anniversary of Florence Nightingale's birth, Névé would return to the NHS and face a newer, greater challenge: this time, a threat of global, catastrophic proportions. Whether engineered by the US military and deliberately taken to the Wuhan province by American agents with the hope of infecting the Chinese population in order to give the US the edge in its trade war against China by destabilizing the Chinese economy, except the plan backfired, or perhaps having leaked out of a Wuhan virology lab, or, as the scientific community speculated, it was something that had got passed on to humans by a bat that had bitten a pangolin that had crapped on the floor of a Chinese wet market, Névé would begin work in NHS Nightingale to fight Covid-19.

February 2020–April 2020

Blight One's Troth

"In a moment it had come, the first serious dispute of their wedded life. It had come as all such calamities come, from nothing, and it was on them in full disaster ere they knew."

Their Wedding Journey (1872)
William Dean Howells
American Novelist

I

A woman posted a letter addressed to the CEO of HORNBACHER FINANCE:

7th February 20–

Dear Sir,

I'm going to be open and frank with what I'm about to request. I am seeking a rich husband. I wish to marry a guy with an annual salary of one million pounds or above. Some might say that I'm being greedy, but what does a girl have to do to achieve her ambition in life? I don't think I'm asking too much. Age is no impediment. I have always found the wives of the rich to be only average-looking and uninteresting in person, whereas the mistresses and girlfriends of these rich men tend to be airhead bimbos with no redeeming features when it comes to personality. I, on the other hand, am an extremely attractive woman, have a great deal of style and very good taste. And, to top it off, without blowing my own trumpet, I'm going to be 25 this year so you can see I have lots of reproductive potential as well as plenty of time with which to become your perfect, lifelong companion.

If, however, you think my requirements are too high, I humbly ask you to kindly list the names and addresses of the bars, restaurants, gyms and other hangouts that most of the rich, eligible bachelors frequent.

Yours Faithfully,
Miss Trudie Dunham

The written reply on company headed notepaper from the CEO of Hornbacher Finance read:

10/02/20–

Dear Miss Dunham,

I admit I was greatly intrigued by your letter and your forthrightness. Let me get this straight: you are looking to marry a millionaire banker and willing to trade your beauty for money? I don't fault the ambitious tone of your letter, but I suppose there are many girls in the world in exactly the same position as you, dreaming of marrying a rich man.

Indeed, my annual income easily exceeds well over a million sterling, since I am not only the CEO and chief stockholder but also the only son and heir to the firm, which therefore should comfortably meet your requirements.

However, please allow me to analyze your situation from my perspective as a professional investor. From a business sense, it would be a bad decision to marry you exactly because you are exchanging Beauty for Money. Even if I pay for your beauty, fair and square, your beauty will fade with time while my money will only accumulate. In other words, my income will continue to increase with each passing year, but you will not continue to remain beautiful forever. Hence, from an economics' standpoint, my wealth can be classified as an appreciation asset while the asset of beauty you're offering me will depreciate, possibly exponentially, and will have greatly devalued twenty years from now. It is an inevitable fact of life.

Explaining it purely from a 'trading position', if the trade value of a commodity dropped, we would sell it, and it would be a terrible idea to keep hold of it, long-term. The same, I suppose, applies to the price of your beauty and with the marriage itself. I don't wish to be cruel, but any assets with significant depreciation value are generally sold or sometimes 'leased' — but, of course, no man in their right mind should ever lease their wife. It also occurs to me that if, by chance, you are looking for a quick marriage and hoping to divorce me soon after to secure half my assets, in the form of alimony and including part of my estate, I'm nobody's fool, either.

At this stage, I am prepared to date you but not marry you. Unless, of course, there is something else you can offer me. Why not do the resourceful thing instead and explore some other means to make yourself rich, rather than simply searching for a rich fellow?

I hope this has been helpful.

With Kindest Regards,
Channing Hornbacher, CEO
Hornbacher Finance Company

2

The disseminated wedding invitation read:

Mr. Channing Hornbacher
Son to the late Conrad and Thérèse Hornbacher

&

Miss Trudie Dunham
Daughter to the late William and late Tess Dunham

request the pleasure of your company

at their forthcoming marriage on

Saturday 14ᵗʰ February 20–
@ 12pm

at the Excelsior Hotel & Spa, Chertsford
(address and map enclosed)

Followed by the Wedding Reception
A right, royal roister you shall ne'er forget!

3

Dearly beloved, we are gathered here to celebrate the union of this fine, young couple...

Channing had booked the wedding venue for the day, one hundred guests in attendance. The EXCELSIOR was an exclusive five-star hotel and spa resort on the outskirts of Chertsford that had once hosted the aristocracy and where those vacationing could enjoy its Michelin-starred dining experience or take advantage of the relaxing spa treatments in complete luxury and opulence. Jags, Mercs, BMWs, Porsches and Maseratis were parked in the ample car park. The executive suites were not inexpensive, nor the chalet-style cabins on the grounds. The hotel was surrounded by plenty of green, rolling countryside for leisurely strolls. A golf club and tennis club were in walking distance. It was unseasonably warm weather, no sign of rain, not a cloud in the sky, for a Valentine's Day wedding.

Valentine's Day was a great festival, whether you were in a relationship or utterly alone and incapable of being loved in the middle of winter. Possibly still paying off the Christmas you had with somebody who subsequently ditched you. Or, perhaps, Valentine's Day represented a time when you were starting out on a new stage in your love life . . .

To a violin-swirling *Wedding March* from the violin quartet hired by Channing,

Joseph Dunham gave away his niece, Trudie, who walked down the aisle to gasps of awe and admiration from the guest. She wore an unconventionally-simple, mermaid wedding dress, veil-less and sleeveless, showcasing her perfectly-chignoned, blond balayage, sparkling blue eyes, graceful neck and collarbone, and crafted in sunflower-hued, silk taffeta, designed by the renowned dressmaker, Vivienne Westwood, and custom-made for the occasion.

Tailored in a swanky, grey top hat and tail, Channing Hornbacher, along with the seated guests, watched his bride-to-be walk down the aisle, followed by the bouquet-carrying, child bridesmaids, each wearing a light pink dress.

In front of the vicar, Reverend Bronwen Wittendoon, they spoke their self-written vows to one another, Trudie beginning first: "I will try in every way to be worthy of your love. I will always be honest with you, kind, caring, patient and forgiving. I promise with my whole heart to have, hold and honour you from this day forward, in tears and in laughter, in sickness and in health, through sorrow and success. I promise above all else to live in truth with you. For the rest of my life. In this world and the next. Because one lifetime with you could never be enough. There is still a part of me today that cannot believe that I'm the one who gets to marry you. For that, I'm eternally grateful. I will make certain you do not regret your decision. I love you."

Then it was Channing's turn to reciprocate, uttering the vow he had personally crafted: "I see these vows not as promises but as privileges. I am privileged to know you, for allowing me to cherish and adore you. I promise faithfulness and devotion, respect and attentiveness. With my hand on my heart, I give you a sanctuary of warmth and peace. My promise that I will walk with you, hand in hand, wherever our journey leads us. I shall be your comrade in adventure, your accomplice in mischief. I vow to have the patience that love demands, to speak when words are needed and to share in the silence when they are not. This is my sacred oath to you, my equal in all things. Thereto I plight thee my troth."

These were the marriage vows they made at the heart of their wedding day, words of commitment to a shared life, penning their own promises to truly personalize their wedding, spoken in some other variation by millions of couples over the centuries. Declarations of Love spoken before God and in front of family and friends. The lifetime commitment of these promises and statements was represented when they gave the rings to each other, as a symbol of unending love.

His Best Man, Fergus Quayle, dressed in an identical outfit to the groom, stepped forward and temporarily fumbled the rings but managed to complete the important task bestowed upon him.

"This completes the marriage," Reverend Wittendoon declared after the exchange of rings. "According to God's Holy Ordnance, I now pronounce you man and wife. You may kiss the bride."

Turning to his bride, Channing hooked an arm round her waist, leaned her back and like some Golden-Age-of-Hollywood, movie-matinée hero, delivered a powerful kiss on her mouth. For a moment Trudie was overcome, blinking rapidly, but she eventually managed to regain her senses.

"I think congratulations are in order," Reverend Wittendoon announced. "You are now free to sign the Register, as a legal record of the occasion."

Whether the guests giggled or grabbed for the Kleenex during the marriage ceremony, they were soon gathered round the wedded couple, clapping and cheering and offering their heartiest congratulations.

After the photo opportunities, the wedding party retreated indoors and enjoyed a veritable banquet, dining on spit-roasted suckling pig, the highlight of the feast. To mark the occasion, the elegant seven-tiered, tres-leches wedding cake was layered in whipped-cream icing and studded with delicate, sugar-paste flowers. The newlyweds' initials *C & T* were stenciled into the cake's bottom layer and an edible representation of the happy couple stood embracing one another on top. Trudie cut the cake with unerring precision and distributed it to the guests, piece by piece.

The violin quartet joined them indoors and played on in the background, providing its interpretation of such timeless classics as *Air on the G String*, *Palladio 1st Movement*, *Perfect Day*, *Nights in White Satin*, the list went on.

Then, it was drinks at the open bar, champagne and mimosas, followed by, of course, the speeches.

The Best Man, Fergus Quayle, stood up first, tinkling his champagne flute for attention. The guests silenced. "I've known Channing since we were children, and he is one of the few people in this world I have constantly looked up to. We have a bromance, so to speak." He received a few good-humoured laughs. "As you can see, he is quite the handsome fellow but not obsessed with his image. He's ridiculously wealthy, one of the finest arbitrage traders I know, but one who does not rely on his ego or net worth and who is certainly not one to put on airs, a truly upfront, straight-as-a-ruler kind of guy. He's a fiercely intelligent, incredibly articulate and well-cultured individual, who doesn't have a bad bone in his body and can do no ill will. In fact, he is known in society circles as a philanthropist, whose generous donations at fund-raising events have often helped those less fortunate than him; he contributes regularly to various nascent inner-city projects. Foremost, he is a humble man, who struggles with the praise lavished upon him. He was never one for romancing and, although he was something of a fish-out-of-water with the fairer sex, I am pleased our

Veddy Briddish Charmer took the plunge and found someone of a like mind to spend the rest of his days with, settle down and become a family man. Mazel tov, my good man!" Smiling, he now directly addressed the bride and groom together. He raised his glass in a toast. "It has been an absolute honour and a privilege to be part of this happy event. I wish you both health and happiness always!"

Applause and cheers from the guests.

Channing's mother, Thérèse, raised herself up, slightly inebriated. She was a slim, naturally elegant woman, silver hair fashioned into a bob, attractive for her age. She spoke with a faint French-Canadian accent. "Thank you all for coming to this wonderful occasion, making it a special day for all of us." She paused, thoughtful, before continuing: "Channing was never a problem, growing up. Polite, well-behaved, he was always respectful to his elders. It is with great sadness his father cannot be here today to witness our only child wed. It must be an equally terrible shame that neither of Trudie's parents can be with us today, either, but the hope is that the loved ones whom we've lost are perhaps here in spirit to celebrate this matrimony. I am grateful to our extended family and our friends for their kind support over the years, for making it happen. From a mother to her son: you have done me proud and I wish you and your good wife a long and prosperous life together. I will always be there for you both. Trudie, I am not losing a son but gaining a truly amazing daughter. Please take good care of him. He means the world to me. And, it just goes for me to say, I welcome you into our family . . ."

Trudie appreciated the sentiment, nodding towards her new mother-in-law. It brought a tear to her eye. Thérèse Hornbacher received a round of applause from the guests.

When the commotion had died down, Channing rose to his feet. "Thank you, Mother, and thank you, Fergie, for your kind words. You know I love you both. Fergie, you have stood by me all these years as the brother I never had, and Mother, you have raised me to be the man that I am today. I will never disappoint the memory of my father." He turned to face Trudie, who smiled back. "And to my beautiful bride, my love for you has been instant. You have won my heart in a single heartbeat. I will take my responsibility as your husband very seriously, and I promise to keep you happy for as long as it takes. I cannot go wrong now with such a fine woman as you by my side. I shall love you uxoriously and I like being demonstrative towards you. I would move heaven and earth for you. Because you deserve it." Some merry murmurs from the guests, to whom he turned to again. "As singletons, we have each other . . . and we have *all* of you, family, friends, colleagues, who have come out to celebrate with us. It means the world to us that you're here. We couldn't have done it without you. Thank you for keeping us company today."

Maintaining some form of tradition, the happy couple slow-danced, cheek to cheek, on this occasion to the original version of *Nights in White Satin* on the dancefloor, where others would soon join them to the subsequent disco music that would play on into the evening.

Then, before the newlyweds departed, a good number of the guests lit Chinese lanterns in the prevailing dusk and sent them floating up into the air, to wish the married couple luck on their nuptials.

4

Channing thought it strange, this crazy, little thing called Love. According to one William Shakespeare: *Love looks not with the eyes, but with the mind,/And therefore is winged Cupid painted blind.* But, sooner or later, everybody began to understand that Love was more than just verses on a Valentine's card or the romantic goings-on in a romcom. Everyone eventually realized that Love was real and *true,* one of the most powerful of emotions and perhaps for some the most important thing in their lives. For Love was the creator of one's favourite memories and the very foundation of one's fondest dreams. Love was a promise that was always kept, a fortune that could never be spent and a seed that could flourish even in the unlikeliest of places. And this radiance that never faded, this mysterious and magical joy, was the greatest treasure of all – one known only by those who love. And didn't everyone of us want to fall in love? Because it was an experience that made us feel most alive, *completely* alive, a unique experience where every sense was heightened, every emotion magnified, when our everyday reality shifted, allowing us to figuratively soar towards the heavens. For some it might only last a moment, less than a night, an afternoon, an hour. But that did not diminish its value, because one was left with memories that one treasured for the rest of one's life. Love lived in the Present, hoped for the Future and tried not to brood on the Past. In the long run, Love even made allowances for one's partner's imperfections, their human weaknesses. Love could survive a steady chronicle of irritations, conflicts, compromises and disappointments. Altogether, *that* was the power of love.

And what of marriage, not a marriage of convenience but a marriage founded on Love? At the beginning of a marriage, everything felt new and exciting. One had romantic date nights planned weeks in advance, and what may become future annoyances were just endearing, little quirks that made one love one's spouse even more. But, unfortunately, if one was looking for a Cinderella Happily-Ever-After storybook marriage, one was apt to be seriously disappointed because that honeymoon stage couldn't last forever. Eventually, things were sure to simmer down, and one might find oneself feeling, well, *bored*. However, finding ways to surprise one's spouse, whether with a gift or a thoughtful act, or enjoying new experiences and setting new goals, had a way of reinventing the relationship and keeping one's marriage feeling fresh, *alive*. There were five languages of love: words of affirmation, acts of service, receiving gifts, quality time and physical touch. It was easy to get stuck in a rut, become lazy and complacent, afraid to step outside of one's comfort zone, and just too easy to take the relationship for granted. Marriage demanded love and honesty, tolerance and good communication, needed to be constantly nurtured and viewed with realistic expectations and enlivened with a sense of humour to be wholly successful. And *spontaneity* was key. It was advice Channing had been brought up with from an early age, the message hammered home by his parents over the passing years. Moonstruck partners pledging eternal love today, Channing wondered how the starry-eyed picture of him and Trudie would fare down the coming years together.

Whilst the guests continued their festivities back at the Excelsior Hotel, the newlyweds headed back home to change out of their bridal clothes and pick up their luggage before they set off on their honeymoon in Palm Beach, Florida. The family chauffeur, Jack Atherton, drove them in the black Bentley. They sat in the back seat. They were presently driving through Upper Nasebury. Honey-hued, thatch-roofed stone cottages lined the quaint streets. They passed an ancient pub and a medieval church.

Channing had been surprised to see his mother's sister, Aunt Jeannie, looking all dolled-up and weird at the wedding. She had pumped herself full of Botox – into the forehead, under her eyes, around the nasolabial folds – giving her face a permanently stiff, inflated look. Still, at least, the lines of communication were open again between his mother and his aunt.

"I want to hear it . . ." Trudie was presently requesting.

"Sonnet 116 is the one for you," replied Channing.

But Trudie had a different idea in mind. "Why not Sonnet 18? I want to hear Sonnet 18. Pretty please!"

"Okay, okay . . ." Channing conceded, appreciating her excitement. "*Shall I compare thee to a summer's day?/Thou art more lovely and more temperate:/ Rough winds do shake the darling buds of May,/And summer's lease hath all too short a date:/Sometime too hot the eye of heaven shines,/And often is his gold* complexion dimm'd;/And every fair from fair sometime declines,/By chance or nature's changing course untrimm'd;/But thy eternal summer shall not fade/Nor lose possession of that fair thou ow'st;/Nor shall Death brag thou wander'st in his shade,/When in eternal lines to time thou grow'st;/So long as men can breathe or eyes can see,/So long lives this, and this gives life to thee."

"So beautiful . . ." said Trudie dreamily. "I could listen to it – to *you* – all day. I do like it when you speak it to me."

"I'd still go for Sonnet 116," Channing advocated. "*Let me not to the marriage of true minds/Admit impediments. Love is not love/Which alters when it alteration finds,/Or bends with the remover to remove:/O no! it is an ever-fixed mark/That looks on tempests and is never shaken;/It is the star to every wand'ring bark,/Whose worth's unknown, although his height be taken./Love's not Time's fool, though rosy lips and cheeks/Within his bending sickle's compass come:/Love alters not with his brief hours and weeks,/But bears it out even to the edge of doom./If this be error and upon me prov'd,/I never writ, nor no man ever lov'd.*"

"Poetry, Shakespeare?" Trudie said, with unmistakable awe in her voice. "You're so cultured."

Channing returned the compliment. "You're not bad yourself."

"Not as enlightened as you, though . . ."

"I went to a prestigious college," he told her, adding, "where I learned pig Latin!"

Past the open, rolling countryside, normally rife with wildflowers in the summer, now somewhat barren apart from long grass and weeds, they came to a long stretch of road from where the Hornbacher residence branched off.

Channing continued his talk of love. "Plato once said: *Love is the joy of the good, the wonder of the wise, the amazement of the gods.*"

"*You know you're in love when you can't fall asleep because reality is finally better than your dreams.*" She added: "Dr. Seuss."

"Cute," Channing replied. "I guess you can't go wrong with Dr. Seuss."

Trudie snuggled up against her husband's shoulder. "There was a famous German philosopher called Goethe. He said: *Love comforts like sunshine after the shower, the great beautifier.*"

Channing sounded a little cautious. "I know Goethe. He also said: *Love is an ideal thing, marriage a real thing; a confusion of the real with the ideal never goes unpunished.*"

Trudie looked up at Channing with a small, puzzled frown in contrast to Atherton in the front who glanced at his rear-view mirror with mild amusement in his eyes. James Blunt sang *Wisemen* on the car stereo, the volume turned down low. "I hope we can take the real as close to the ideal as possible."

"All we can do is try our best," Channing reassured her and decided to enlighten her further. "You know many modern-day marriage traditions get their origins from ancient times. As we embark on our own honeymoon, newlyweds used to aid fertility by drinking a brew made from honey during certain lunar phases, and it is from this tradition we derive the origin of the word 'honeymoon'."

"You learn something new every day!" said Trudie, positively impressed. "You are such a wealth of knowledge!" Then, a moment's silence fell between them before Trudie asked: "What if we fall out of love?"

The question came so unexpectedly, it caused Channing to glance curiously at Trudie. It was an odd thing to ask on one's wedding day. He saw the troubled look in her blue eyes, the uncertainty on her pretty face.

He kissed her nose softly and sat back in his seat. He didn't want to doom their marriage before it had even started. He was only being his usual realistic, pragmatic self. He responded with an old Arabian parable. "A wise physician once said, 'The best medicine for humans is love.' His patient then asks: 'What if it doesn't work?' The physician smiles and answers, 'Increase the dose.'"

"You mean there is no remedy for love that wanes with time but to love more?"

5

Through the electronic gates and the long, elm-lined drive, they soon arrived at HORNBACHER MANOR, a prestigious, executive mansion which had accommodated generations of Hornbachers over the decades. Channing came from Old Money, and built in the 1930s, his family home was a place of gracious living and contemporary grandeur. Set over four floors, the house boasted a cinema room, a billiard room, a gym, an indoor swimming pool and a wine cellar. It was perfectly air-conditioned throughout. The family employed a landscape gardener who tended to the spectacular private gardens with their raised flower beds and a feature pond. The Hornbacher estate occupied eight acres of land, mostly wooded, ideal for pheasant-shoots and containing numerous rabbit warrens. One might even see the occasional deer nibbling on wet grass in the glades. The house enjoyed outstanding southerly views. Somewhere beyond the forest was Oaks Fold.

Channing led his new wife through the front door, turning on the lights and inputting the security code into the digital keypad, deactivating the system. He reset the alarm once inside, from force of habit. He shivered slightly. Outside, it had turned chilly, now a typical February day, and the sky had already darkened.

The lobby was an expanse of marble flooring, with an oak staircase leading up to the ten, double-sized bedrooms.

Trudie had once commented that some might describe the all-white décor of the residence as 'a cardinal, interior-design sin'. *Where's the contrast?*

I like it, Channing had told her. *Bright and immaculate . . . it reminds me of Heaven.*

Inside the lobby, Channing hugged and kissed Trudie passionately on the lips. "We made it in one piece. Time to get ready for our honeymoon when I can have you all to myself." His voice echoed dimly in the otherwise emptiness of the lobby.

Trudie appeared delighted. She waggled the veritable rock on her ring finger. "I can't believe I'm married!"

"You are, indeed, Mrs. Hornbacher," Channing replied, amused. "How does it feel?"

Her eyes sparkled liked the diamonds on her ring. "Good!"

"Let's change and get our things. Atherton will drive us to the airport. We have to be there by seven-thirty, latest." Holding her hand, Channing took her upstairs to their triple-aspect bedroom, complete with four-poster bed. Slipping out of their wedding clothes, they threw on some designer casuals – Trudie in a fetching red dress and black stockings, black shirt and jeans for Channing – and engaged in some pleasant chatter before picking up the three suitcases they would be taking with them. They quickly made their way downstairs, back to the lobby, where Channing dumped the cases and excused himself to momentarily go into the kitchen to get a drink of pressed orange juice. Trudie did not partake, just waited by the bags. The kitchen possessed bespoke oak units and a walk-in pantry.

When Channing returned to the lobby, Trudie appeared slightly anxious. "What's the matter, darling?" he asked her.

"There's something going on outside . . ."

"Outside?"

"Yes, but I don't know what it is. I thought I heard a cry."

"Are you sure?"

"Yes . . ."

"There's only Atherton outside in the car, waiting to take us to the airport." Channing listened but heard nothing. Just silence. But sometimes silence hid things that should be left alone. "I'll go and investigate . . ."

Channing headed for the front door, but Trudie pulled him back. "No, don't," she fretted. "It might be dangerous."

Channing stared hard at his wife. Her eyes were big and round. Something had clearly spooked her. "Okay . . ." he considered. He took a different approach. "Stay here," he told his wife and, with a sense of urgency, hurried into the drawing room, leaving her to mind the bags in the hall.

The drawing room housed an inglenook fireplace and a floor-to-ceiling bookcase on which rested a library of dusty first editions. Family portraits hung on the walls alongside some original works by Basquiat, Channing's favourite, bohemian painter, as well as Auerbach, another of the great Neo-expressionists. Without turning on the light, leaving the room immersed in the late-afternoon darkfall, Channing strode up to the window, pulling aside the curtain veil.

Despite the descending night outside, the window gave a clear view of the front of the house, including the courtyard and the tree-lined driveway that disappeared into the distance. The Bentley sat in the forecourt, front doors wide open, silent. No sign of the chauffeur.

Except, as Channing's eyes adjusted to the gloom outside, he saw the outline of a partial left hand, dangling limply from the passenger seat. The rest of the body was not visible from the open passenger door, suggesting it was surely slumped on its side across the front seats. *Oh, shit!* thought Channing, the icy finger of fear reaching into his heart, concerned for the condition of his chauffeur, trying to make sense of what might be coming. *We're not alone . . .* Sure enough, his eyes picked up two dark, shadowy figures moving stealthily towards the house. They both wore masks.

Channing quickly turned and made his way back into the lobby. "There's somebody out there . . ." he uttered and stopped suddenly in mid-step, frozen.

Trudie was still standing by the luggage, and behind her stood a third masked figure, who had somehow already managed to gain entrance to the house. Channing saw the stark, trembling expression on her terror-stricken face, her chin tilted upwards by the stranger's hand, and the deadly blade of a hunting knife pressed against her exposed throat.

6

For a moment, nobody spoke. The seconds spun out into a brief eternity, as Channing stared, horror-struck, at the intruder holding the knife to his wife's delicate neck.

Then, as his mind steadied itself, his paralysis left him, and the words came thick and heavy. "What do you want?" he demanded to know, afraid that if he made any sudden movements, his wife would be a goner.

The front door opened and two more masked figures, the same figures he had seen coming towards the house, entered. One was shorter and stockier than the other, both still shorter than the stranger who'd taken Channing's wife hostage, but all were dressed in black and donned surgical latex gloves, their faces covered by identical masks, the horned, gnarled red masks of the Devil, giving them a threatening air of menace, enough to instil fear in anyone. Each, like their leader, brandished a similar hunting knife. Now Channing had three intruders to deal with whilst worrying about the safety of his wife and the unconscious state of his chauffeur, who could possibly be dead.

When the main intruder spoke, he spoke with a deep, booming voice, mechanical in its delivery. He was using a voice frequency modulator to disguise his actual voice. "Money!"

Channing enjoyed boardroom confrontations, but this was a confrontation he could have done without. He was dealing with a different kettle of fish. "If it's money you want, I can give whatever you need. Please don't hurt my wife. Be gentle with her – she wouldn't hurt a fly. We just got married."

Presently, the foremost intruder let go of Trudie and pushed her towards her husband.

Channing put his arms round Trudie and held on to her tightly. They were both shaking. "Are you okay, my darling? Did he hurt you?"

Trudie didn't reply, merely shook her head against his chest.

"Money is the currency of the Devil on this earth," boomed the leader of the trio. "We thought of holding banking institutions to ransom. Getting paid in Bitcoins or deleting entire bank records. But this plan is simpler, *easier*." He paused before adding: "Time, Mr. Hornbacher, to share the wealth! You will, indeed, give us what we came here for . . . *or else* . . .!"

Channing couldn't underestimate the threat in those words. He had to comply or he and his wife might not come out of this situation alive. "I've got some money in my safe – a few thousand – and some bonds. I hope that will be enough." He glanced anxiously at the Devil-masked strangers, hoping for a quick resolution.

"We were hoping for something slightly more," replied the Head Devil in those dark, electronic tones, "but we can start with your safe . . . and go from there."

"Okay," conceded Channing. He looked down at his wife. "Are you going to be okay, darling?" She nodded, but at least she had stopped shaking. He detached himself from her embrace. Turning to the masked intruders, he said, more boldly, "Let's get this over and done with!"

"Phone, please," the Head Devil demanded impatiently.

Channing had no choice but to hand over his mobile, which the Head Devil promptly dropped to the floor and stamped on, crushing it under his heel. "Remember, no funny business," he warned.

Still holding Trudie's hand, Channing quietly led the group into the drawing room, with its paintings and books, and made his way towards the door at the end. He opened the door, switching on the light, and suddenly they were all gathered in the study. The mahogany writing desk was bare, but a PC rested in the corner of the room. A connecting door led to the billiard room. More artwork adorned the walls, including an oil seascape by Turner, reproduction or otherwise, on the farthest wall. Channing lifted the painting off the hook and placed it carefully on the floor, revealing a safe, made of reinforced steel, built into the wall.

"Open it!" demanded the Head Devil. "You can leave with your life so it should be a win-win situation all round!"

After a moment's hesitation, realizing he had no choice but to proceed, Channing began revolving the small, lock-control cylinder back and forth, dialling in the code, the necessary sequence of numbers for the door release. He heard a sharp click as the safe unlocked. The Devil-faced intruders watched him with growing anticipation as he twisted the handle to open the cabinet.

Inside lay a rolled-up wad of notes and some investment bonds. The Head Devil immediately caught sight of the old Luger resting atop of the pile which Channing's great-grandfather had once prised from the cold, dead hands of a Nazi officer during the Normandy landings. Before Channing could do anything, the Head Devil reached in and grabbed the lot, including the gun. "I'll take that, thank you!" He kept the Luger, which he promptly checked and discovered was fully loaded with an eight-round magazine, and passed the money and the bonds to his fellow intruders, who whooped in delight. They shoved the cash and documents into a shoulder bag.

"You don't need to count them," Channing told them. "There's about ten thousand pounds in total, including the bonds." Whilst the masked intruders seemed to revel in their new-found wealth, Channing asked them tentatively: "Can we go now?"

The Head Devil stopped celebrating and dashed all hope. "You can go when we say you can go!" The voice-modulating device gave his anger a dark, demonic tone.

"I thought—"

"You thought, what?" the Head Devil bellowed. "You think ten thousand pounds in cash is enough to keep us happy? It's nothing but small change!"

Channing saw his wife cower at the dread power of the voice. Channing put his arms round her, feeling her tremble. "Please . . . you're frightening my wife."

"We will let you go once our mission is accomplished," the Head Devil informed him.

Channing wasn't sure if Atherton was alive or dead, whether these bastards had slit his throat. "Like you let my chauffeur go?"

"Your chauffeur will be fine," the Head Devil explained. "Just a knock on the head. But he'll wake up with one hell of a headache."

Relief washed over Channing. Atherton would be okay, thank God. He spoke directly to the Head Devil. "What else do you need?"

"We want you to make a bank transfer."

"How much?"

"Fifty million pounds wired into an offshore account of our choosing."

"That'll ruin me!" Channing exclaimed, outraged. "I don't have that kind of money! That's pension funds, financial holdings, shareholder assets—"

"Your insurance will cover it!" the Head Devil declared, growing impatient, pointing Channing's gun back at him. "*Don't test me!*"

Channing took stock of the situation. Here he was in the midst of a home invasion on his wedding night, his poor wife already threatened once with a knife to her throat, and now these sonofabitches demanded he bankrupt his company's account. "Everything will be okay," he whispered into Trudie's ear, and, in one quick move, driven by impulse and anger, he lunged unexpectedly at the Head Devil, rugby-tackling him to the ground. The Head Devil toppled backwards, banging his head on the marble floor, splitting open the skin, the gun falling from his grasp. Channing scrambled for the gun. Seconds later, the two Devil-masked comrades pulled Channing off their leader before Channing could reach the gun, each grabbing one of his arms, and dumped him unceremoniously on the floor, their knives pointed at his face.

The Head Devil took a short while to recover his senses. He got up, touching the skin breakage – the gash – at the back of his head, now starting to bleed. He reclaimed the gun from the floor, trained it back on Channing. "*You shouldn't have done that!*" he roared and smashed Channing viciously in the face with the butt of the Luger, cutting his lip and causing his left cheek to swell up. Channing reeled for a moment from the savage blow, as good as any sucker punch, but once the fireworks dissipated from his vision, he saw the Head Devil grab his struggling, screaming wife by her beautiful hair and half-carry, half-drag her through the connecting door.

"Where the hell are you taking her?" Channing yelled, suddenly terrified for her safety. He tried to get up, to follow her, to help her, but the two goons held him down by the shoulders.

"That was very stupid of you!" bellowed the Head Devil, enraged. "And, for the price of your stupidity, I will get the pussy juices flowing!"

Code for sex. Already Channing knew what the Head Devil planned to do to his wife.

"Let me teach you a lesson you will never forget!" he heard the Head Devil chuckle gleefully, the hideous laughter amplified and increasingly distorted by the voice modulator. Trudie continued to scream and kick against his hold. She and her captive disappeared into the billiard room. "Consider this a transaction, a down payment, not a trade-off!"

Channing listened in dismay to the sound of his wife being flung across the billiard table in the next room.

"You don't have to do this . . . please, *no!*" he heard his wife plead. Then, the awful, heart-stopping ripping of her dress followed by the inevitable hoggish grunting against her wild, agonized moans, her pitiful protests muffled by a hand placed firmly across her mouth.

7

Channing stayed put, did not speak. He did not make any attempt to try and rescue his wife. The two Satan-masked accomplices stood guard over him, prepared to stab him if he tried anything funny. Helpless to act, Channing squeezed his eyes shut, clenched his teeth, held his tongue as he heard the Head Devil rape his wife, each savage thrust poison to his mind. When he had imagined his marriage would be tested, he had not expected it to be tested so soon. And certainly not in this evil, unspeakable manner. These men were monsters.

The noises from the billiard room abruptly stopped, the despicable deed completed, and the Head Devil presently stood in the doorway, carrying a limp Trudie in his arms, having had his wicked way with her. Still somehow holding the gun with one hand, he strode forward and dumped her unconscious body next to Channing. "Now you can see we mean business!" came the harsh, electronic voice.

Channing held his wife, once pure as the virgin snow, now violated and only semi-conscious, her blond hair now pulled open and entangled, numerous ladders running up her black tights, her red dress torn and tattered and unsalvageable, ripped straight down the middle, revealing her black underwear. She was in shock. She tried to speak, eyes half-closed, but she could only produce some low, incoherent groans. Using his silk handkerchief, he lightly dabbed the blood dribbling from the corner of her mouth. He wondered how long it would take her to get over her horrible ordeal, perhaps never. Channing held on to her for a whole minute, her head resting on his shoulder, gently rocking her back and forth to comfort her, console her, pull her out of her confusion. "I got you . . . I got you now . . . It's going to be okay . . . it's going to be okay. . ." he whispered into her ear.

The Head Devil reached down and slapped him across the face. "Wake up, buster, get it together!"

Channing had been utterly humiliated, and his new bride had suffered the brunt of his defiance. Hate, anger, vengeance, *murder* filled his mind. He wanted to murder these men, murder them one by one, torture them first, of course, slowly, horribly, with cold-blooded precision, before letting them watch him rip their hearts out, as payment for the unendurable pain he and particularly his wife had suffered at their hands. He looked up at the Head Devil and calmly replied: "I'll give you your money, but you have to let my wife go. She needs medical assistance, an ambulance."

"Are we negotiating now?" the Head Devil deliberated, chuckling into his mask and voice transmogrifier. More seriously, he said: "Sorry, no ambulance! It's not up for discussion!" He looked at his two silent partners-in-crime, gestured to Trudie. "Put her in the chair and tie her up." His mute accomplices did as instructed, pulling Trudie from Channing's arms and dumping her in the black, executive swivel chair behind the mahogany desk. Soon her wrists were tied together behind the chair and her mouth gagged with Scotch tape. She did not struggle, just sat slumped in the chair, drifting in and out of consciousness.

"Anything else happens to her and you die first! Tell your men to back off! Let her be. . .!"

"You are in no position to threaten us!" the Head Devil warned Channing, continuing to point the gun at him. "Do not dare disobey me again! Be smart! Don't try anything funny!"

Channing didn't reply. He got up wearily and moved to the PC, sitting silent, on the L-shaped computer desk in the far, window-facing corner of the study. He seated himself down in the second leather-backed swivel chair.

The three masked hostage-takers gathered round him. The handgun was still trained on him. Channing turned on the hard drive and monitor and began typing into his desktop. He logged into his bank details, his online financial statement and recent transactions. "Into which account should I make the transfer?"

The Head Devil rummaged into his trouser pockets and extracted a piece of paper. Uncrumpling it, he handed it over to Channing. "Fifty million pounds. No messing, no silly ideas."

Channing read the numbers scrawled on the paper. He began typing into the keyboard. "You won't get away with this."

"You'll never know . . ."

Channing stopped typing. He jabbed the keyboard, and the screen went blank. He looked up at the Head Devil with a fierce, comprehending stare. The situation had taken on a further, dark turn. "You never had any intention of letting us go, did you?"

Devil Mask was suddenly on the back foot. He'd been rumbled. "You were never meant to know. What we do with you once your job is done is our business. It's certainly more frightening when the future is uncertain."

"Only cowards hide behind masks!" Channing challenged the intruders. "Who are you really behind those masks? Somebody I know, perhaps?"

"Get on with it!" demanded the Lead Devil. "We don't want any more delays!"

"No, I won't!" Channing said, defiantly. "If you think you're going to get another penny out of me, you're just pissing in the wind! Because, at this moment in time, you can't do shit to me! You need me alive!"

The Head Devil countered with a threat, "But I can do some real hurt to someone else, somebody you *love* . . ."

And the Head Devil took a step back to allow Channing a glimpse of what he meant. Channing caught a view of the figure behind the writing desk, head slumped forward, gagged and unconscious.

If he'd thought Trudie had experienced the worst already, he was gravely mistaken. "Don't you think she's been through enough?"

"Only if you *don't* comply with my demands!"

And, past the image of his poor, desecrated wife, Channing saw a tall silhouette suddenly appear, framed by the doorway to the drawing room.

The three intruders followed the direction of his startled gaze.

Still dressed in his black chauffeur's uniform, Jack Atherton staggered, stumbled into the room, multiple runnels of blood trickling down from the gash on his forehead. "Th-Thank God I f-f-found you. I-I don't know what h-h-happened . . ." he murmured, probably concussed.

Incensed by the continued interruptions, the Head Devil didn't waste any more time. His first reaction was to turn the Luger in the direction of the wounded man and fire, point-blank. The aim was clean, impossible to miss. With the reverberating sound of thunder, the bullet smashed into the chauffeur's face, incinerating his left eye and exiting the back of his head, splattering the white wall behind with a dripping, scarlet abstract of blood, fragments of skull and brain, the consistency of oatmeal.

8

Atherton created enough of a distraction for Channing to leap into action. Before the chauffeur's body had even hit the floor, Channing took his chance, pushed past his fear. He propelled himself out of swivel chair, deliberately ricocheting off the Head Devil, who unbalanced and fell backwards, startled by the unexpectedness of Channing's physical response, the gun dropping from his grasp. Channing did not attempt to pick it up this time but instead barged into both the masked accomplices, toppling them over like bowling pins, and jumped past the fallen, dead body of his unfortunate chauffeur before sprinting out of the study. He glanced back at his listless, semi-conscious wife behind the writing desk – she wasn't going anywhere – and decided against taking her with him since she would only slow him down. He would come back for her later. A decent tennis player, fit and athletic, he raced like a rocket through the drawing room until he made it to the lobby. *Escape, flee, pursuit,* he thought, envisioning a desperate outcome. Indeed, the temptation was to run out into the night, except he knew the killers would end up in pursuit, and he'd probably never make it to the gates if the man was a good shot; the killer would probably shoot him dead at ten yards. Neither did he wish to risk making his getaway in the Bentley, since it might be disabled. This was a well-planned operation he was dealing with. No, he wanted to keep the home advantage and knew of a much safer place.

He ran up the grand staircase, taking two steps at a time. He could now hear his kidnappers, having regrouped, descend on the lobby. "Stop!" And a shot was fired, grazing the banister in close proximity to Channing just as he made it to the first-floor landing. He did not stop or look back. *You'll make it as long as you strive and persist,* he told himself.

There were plenty of rooms in the house and plenty of hiding places, but his mind was determined to get to the safest place of all.

Down the hallway, guided by the night-lights overhead, he took the stairs to the second floor, then down the second-floor hallway, to another set of stairs. Then, down another hallway and more stairs. He climbed the final stairs and raced down the fourth-floor hallway to arrive at his destination. He could hear footsteps in pursuit. At the end of the fourth and final hallway was a steel door with a security camera monitoring the hallway. He punched in the code on the electronic keypad. The red light blinked green, and suddenly he was inside the room, locking the door behind him. Motion sensors automatically turned on the lights of the chamber.

Channing found himself in the panic room of the house, on the fourth floor and built like a fortress. It had never been used in his lifetime – in anyone's lifetime – but this was exactly the kind of dire situation it was designed for. He never thought he would be using it. The room always made him think of an air-raid shelter or a nuclear bunker. Rather than something hi-tech, it was rather basic, never having been upgraded. Nevertheless, it was soundproof and fireproof, and Channing could safely hide out in here in peace while calling the authorities and waiting for rescue to arrive.

A man's home was his castle, he thought, and nobody had a right to enter his home without his permission. Here, in the panic room, he would be very, very secure.

A single emergency light provided the illumination, giving off a dim, rufescent glow across the minimalistic furniture and steel walls. The panic room smelled of dust and must, but the electronics were working fine, once he'd rebooted them. The surveillance monitor came online, revealing the fourth-floor hallway outside the panic room. The three masked intruders were already gathered by the door.

"*Open the fucking door!*" Channing heard the Head Devil bellow, enraged, through the intercom.

"I now have the upper hand, you murderous bastards!" Channing responded, activating the two-way communicator. "You can keep on knocking, but you can't get in!"

"We're giving you one last chance!" the Head Devil warned. "Open the door, or your death will make the papers for a long time to come!"

Grinning triumphantly, smelling the sweet smell of success, Channing reached for the red telephone. Putting the handset to his ear, he was about to dial the number for the Emergency Services, when, in that instant, the door suddenly bolted open and the three Satan-masked intruders entered.

Channing's smile turned to dismay as shock caused him to drop to his knees. He'd had no time and nothing at all to barricade the door with. He was at a loss. The Head Devil retrieved the telephone receiver from Channing's grasp and carefully replaced it on the switch-hook. The Luger was aimed back at him, and Channing did not wish to test the man's resolve again, particularly not after witnessing the violent, bloody demise of his chauffeur.

"Who's pissing in the wind now?" the Head Devil mocked, threw it back at him, jubilant. "Still think you've got the upper hand?"

Realization struck. What had been bothering him all along, he hadn't been able to quite place . . . until now. They had managed to get through the electronic gates without raising the alarm. Then into the house, and they had presently managed to find a way into the stronghold of the panic room. It should have been impossible. It occurred to Channing that they already knew the damned code. The only way they could possibly know was if his wife told them.

9

This was all too much for Channing. Trapped in his own panic room, at the top of the house, and surrounded by a gang of nameless, masked intruders, his new bride apparently raped on their wedding night. Far from the happy ending he envisaged, this was not how he intended to spend his wedding night – or Valentine's Day, for that matter. Except they had been ably assisted by his wife. She had been in on it all along. Her crime stood out in sharp relief.

"I want him within my sights from here on out!" the Head Devil told his men. He re-focused his attention on his captive. "Well, well, my Veddy Briddish Charmer . . ."

Channing remembered that expression from the wedding and even before that, from the office. Its familiarity jolted him to full realization. The man had slipped up. "Fergie, is that you?"

"Fergie? Fergie who?"

"It *is* you, isn't it?"

"Boss, he's got you," his short, squatter masked accomplice, who until now had maintained his silence, said.

"Shut up, Esteban!" the Head Devil bellowed at his accomplice, then realizing his own mistake, "for fuck's sake!" The Head Devil paused for a moment, deliberating, before finally removing his mask. The face of Fergus Quayle shone bright and clear. "No point in keeping up this masquerade – he knows who we are now!"

His two goons followed suit, identities unmasked. The low, red lighting gave their faces the illusion they were covered in blood.

"*What the actual fuck is going on, Fergus?*" Channing said in stark astonishment. "Esteban? And Georgie, too?"

Esteban Alvarez's mother was the housekeeper for the Hornbachers. "Hello,

Chan…" he greeted, no longer speaking in those sinister electronic tones built into the Satan mask. There was some embarrassment in his voice.

George Sloane was Aunt Jeannie's lanky son, Channing's first cousin. Except his expression showed no fear or shame.

"How could you do this to me, guys?" Channing berated despairingly, unable to bring his incredulity to bay. "I've always been good to you! Unlike my father to his friends. I've been there for you, given you whatever you needed, never deprived you of anything!"

"Slavery just became indentured servitude," stated George, fixing Channing with a cool, steely stare.

Channing couldn't believe Fergie managed to reel in his cousin. What were the odds? He should have known this was an inside job. Even if Georgie had led a life of privilege, like Channing, he was greedy, lazy as hell, the type of kid who would rather lounge around and spend his mother's fortune, scratching his arse all day, than work. And if he was ever forced to work, he preferred other people to do the work for him. "I thought family sticks together."

"Blood may be thicker than water," said George, "but not when money is at stake."

"I guess money really is the Devil's currency," admitted Channing sadly. "Do your parents know what you've been up to?"

"Not a clue," George replied.

"Why should you have everything?" Fergus said, rounding on Channing, clearly furious. "You've led such a charmed life. Born with the silver spoon and everything laid out on a silver platter!"

"You're meant to be the Best Man!" Channing said in dismay. "I treated you like a brother! Why would you do this to me?"

"Bite the hand that feeds me? Rip it off and shit it out?" Fergus deliberated again. Channing needed to know, he supposed, what all of this was really about. "I have no compunctions when it comes to finishing you off, no loyalty towards you, never did. I am the product of your father's affair with my dancer mother from decades ago. Their *love child*. The illegitimate son."

"You mean we're brothers? Half-brothers?"

"You're not far wrong. Same father."

"That's crazy!" Yet, Channing had never considered the family resemblance. Fergus's red hair notwithstanding, as opposed to Channing's dark curtains, he possessed the same shape of the nose, the same jawline. Even the eyes were the same clear blue.

"No, it's not untrue."

Channing had always known his father, Conrad Hornbacher, to be a notorious womanizer. His mother, Thérèse, had put up with a lot when the man had been alive, sticking with her husband for the sake of her marriage and her only son. Was this current situation Channing was embroiled in payback for his father's years of skirt-chasing? There was a certain poetic justice to all this, an inevitability even. "You didn't have to do this. You could have told me."

The revelations were coming thick and fast. "No, I kept it my little secret. I was from a broken home, my mother visited by all kinds of mean-tempered lowlifes. As a young child, I could hear her plying her trade at night in the bedroom next to mine. Your father paid off my mother when she confronted him and threatened to tell the world. And, then, my mother just gave me up, calling me a burden. That's what adopted children are. *Discards*."

"That's unkind."

"I discovered during my childhood who my father was, the man who had abandoned his own son. I hated him, *loathed* him. I was determined to get my own back on him and promised to make something of my life. He would never find out who I was . . . or, if he did know, he kept quiet about it, kept his distance. Me and you would become friends from an early age – you'd remain completely oblivious of our kinship. I got into your trust, worked my way up your company, became your business associate." He forced a hard, determined smile. "Now the bastard son will take back the company and the inheritance that is owed him!"

"So you hatched this plot?"

"Not by myself."

"If only you'd told me, I could have given you whatever you wanted."

"It's so easy for you!" blazed Fergus. "You waltz into the office and boss your staff around! You don't know how hard it is for me! Expectations so low, yet I somehow manage to limbo under! But *you* – you are fucking, stinking rich!"

"You're not badly off yourself."

"You are one of the so-called beautiful people who will make beautiful babies."

"Not with Trudie, it seems. And raping her was one big charade?"

"No, I fucked your bride in the billiard room, good and proper! With her consent, of course. Made it look real so you would have no further doubts that we meant serious business. She's always been a filthy bitch, even before I can remember. You see, we've been lovers for a long time, Trudie and I. We planned this whole caper together."

Channing felt a mixture of confusion, anger and loss at what to make of his wife's betrayal. All of it had been an act on her part. He'd been royally duped. His mind staggered under the weight of the information. He said nothing.

"You're such a dolt with women," Fergus continued. "I'm amazed you fell for her charms and actually *married* her! I was hoping you might marry her."

"Nobody deserves that kind of punishment."

"I guess you're a glutton for punishment."

"The oldest reason to marry, hey: money?" Channing said, resigned to the fact he was being held captive by his former friends, who had privately conspired, together in collusion with his own wife, to relieve him of his fortune. She had been a key player in the conspiracy, perhaps the architect. "Who would have thought it?"

"Slightly different take, mind you. Hard luck, old buddy. Don't take it personally."

"It sure as hell feels like it," Channing replied, sounding embittered. Then, the all-important question. "What are you going to do with me now?"

"There is still the small matter of the fifty million pounds," Fergus reminded him. "We want what we came here for."

Channing remained calm, assured even. He held his ground, defiant to the last. "I'm not going to help you get your greasy fingers on it. Not even my wife knows the code to my bank account."

Fergus nodded "It's like that, is it?"

"It's like that, I'm afraid."

"Then we go with Plan B."

"Which is?"

"When we kill you, she will get your entire fortune as the grieving widow."

But the deadly threat did not have the impact Fergus was expecting. He found Channing's recovered confidence somewhat baffling. "You forget one thing. I haven't slept with her, not even when we were dating for the short time we were going out together. You've both been extremely short-sighted. You should have done your dirty business *after* the honeymoon. Now you and Trudie won't see a single penny. Our marriage will be annulled."

10

Sex was one of the greatest gifts in marriage. It was meant for physical pleasure, emotional connection and procreation during the course of a lifetime. Even if it wasn't meant to be the foundation of a marriage, it was certainly a level of intimacy that was established by God for husbands and wives, allowing them to show their spouse continued affection, gentleness and tenderness, willingly giving them their body for as long as they were both living. This did not give a husband or a wife license to misuse their spouse, nor cheat on them by taking in another lover. But, sometimes, they had no choice. In marriage, a bad, one-sided sex life was something a wife could not live with forever, and if the husband was unwilling to resolve the issue, then the wife was entitled to find someone else who might satisfy her sexual needs. There was a case for premarital sex. It gave the couple a chance to see whether they were compatible for one another in all aspects of their relationship. Unless mutually agreed upon by both parties, sex should never be taken off the table. Also, to demand sexual performances from their husband or wife was considered nonconsensual, a form of rape, a sin of equal footing as adultery in the eyes of God. Rather than giving their body, unnecessarily punishing their spouse by withholding sex was considered an inappropriate use of a sacred gift, too. But why would Channing decide not to freely give his body to his wife?

"Hello, darling." Channing had been escorted from the panic room on the fourth floor back down to the drawing room. His wife stood there, no longer the abused, befuddled woman but alert and perceptive. Her dress was still torn, her long hair severely matted and her cheeks dripped with eyeliner, yet it turned out she had agreed to have sex with her lover while giving the impression of being raped. Channing still couldn't entirely believe her deception and betrayal, the manner in which she had seduced him in order to gain access to his estate, rob him of his riches. He had meant every word in his marriage vows at the wedding ceremony. Now she had broken his heart.

"What happened?" she duly asked, seeing her accomplices' exposed faces, no longer wearing their Devil masks.

"He knows," Fergus told her.

"The pretence is over," Channing added.

"You got sloppy!" Trudie rounded on Fergus. But she could forsee a silver lining. "I suppose that makes it easier for us to deal with him . . ."

"How does it make it easier?" burst out Fergus, gesturing to Channing with an accusatory finger. "He's been holding out on you!"

Trudie didn't comprehend. "I don't get you . . ."

"Why didn't you *fuck* him? That was all you needed to do!"

"He always declined," Trudie replied, not quite understanding the line of questioning. "Always used the honeymoon as an excuse. Why is so relevant?"

"I will be seeking an annulment," Channing said flatly. "You get nothing."

It clicked. But she had an answer. "I could always lie. Who's going to know?"

"The police will investigate my death," Channing explained. "You, my dear, will be the prime suspect – the spouse always is. They will see your log of communications to Fergie, the calls and texts between you two, what you were planning, your infidelity and complicity in this crime. They will know where you've been, of any secret meetings you had between you . . . from those pesky cell tower pings. Even if you stick by your story of a break-in and get away with it, which I doubt, the Coroner will discover we never consummated our marriage. You think they won't do a thorough autopsy on me? Maybe a forensic examination on you?"

Trudie turned to Fergus. "What do you suggest? I do an erotic lapdance, peel off my clothes layer by layer, make him horny, make him *cum*? Collect his spunk in a turkey baster and insert it into myself?"

"That would be awesome!" commented George with a grin. "A little S&M wouldn't go amiss right about now, either!"

"Georgie Porgie, kissed the girls, made them cry!" Trudie derided, then gave him a verbal slap in the face: "*Shut it!*"

"Yeah, shut your goddamned face!" Fergus seconded.

George went quiet, his cheeks blooming roses with embarrassment. About time, too.

"Why didn't you fuck me when we were going out?" Trudie asked her husband. There was feeling in her voice, fake, of course.

"Probably an image thing," George interjected, unkindly. "Just clench your buttocks when he tells you he's gay!" It brought a chuckle from Esteban, not Fergus who maintained a stern expression.

"You mean sleep with you?" Channing corrected his wife. "Make love to you?"

"What are you – a prude?" Trudie mocked.

"I'm a conventional man," Channing replied. "I believe in tradition. You joined a very conservative family."

"Why *did* you marry me?"

"Marriage isn't always about Love – or fucking. In many respects, marriage is a way of making a strategic alliance between families, expanding the family and protecting bloodlines. I did a background check on you. Your parents are *not* dead, as you claimed. You are one of the estranged daughters of Piers Heymans – from his first marriage. He later fled to the Bahamas during the global financial crisis, having stolen millions in funds. His company still exists. My ulterior motive? I wanted to meet Piers Heymans in Palm Beach, where he is currently vacationing. A part of me married you — and married you so fast — to obtain a merger, make a move on his former company. It was all about mergers and acquisitions."

"We're all about murders and executions!" George quipped, half-serious. The others ignored him.

"Clever," said Trudie, her husband's secret plan for her father sinking in. "There's me planning to claim your estate when all along you wanted to swallow up my father's company. You're quite the slippery customer." She echoed the crux of the matter. "You should have fucked me!"

"You don't think I have fire in my loins? You're an incredibly beautiful woman! I wanted to lose myself in you on our honeymoon." Channing went on, his voice growing harder: "Except you're nothing but an opportunist, who makes Mick Jagger's gold-digging reject seem like a novice!"

Trudie slapped him. Channing instantly slapped her back with the back of his hand before his captors grabbed both his arms. Trudie touched her cheek, which stung. "You've complicated matters."

Channing realized he'd been right all along. Trudie had been in charge of this whole operation. She'd likely dreamed up this entire heinous plan. She'd probably even suggested his best buddy rape her whilst her husband watched. "Today's events have been a blessing in disguise! At least now I know what you're really like! I only wish I could have found out sooner!"

"It hasn't been a picnic for us, either!" said Trudie irritably.

"All the gang's here," said Channing, grinning, "just like old times. Where do we go from here?"

"You give us what we came here for," Trudie reminded him.

"I'd rather pull out my fingernails with some pliers," remarked Channing.

"That can be arranged," Fergus muttered.

"I look forward to it."

"Your stubbornness is not going to get you anywhere," Fergus informed him.

"On the contrary, I will take great pleasure in breaking your balls. Poor little Fergus: hellbent on seeking revenge on his absent father!"

Arms held firmly by George and Esteban, Channing received a vicious uppercut to the jaw from Fergus. He could feel a broken tooth. His chin was beginning to swell up, accompanying his already badly bruised cheek. Fergus warned: "There's more where that came from."

"What the hell are we going to do with him if he's not cooperating?" George asked.

"Oh, he'll cooperate . . ." said Trudie ominously, a dark smile forming on her lips.

"Let's do as he suggested. We torture him until he gives us what we need."

"I didn't know you were such a talented girl," remarked Channing. "Is torture one of your specialties too?"

"We can improvise . . ."

Channing grinned back at her. He was past caring. "If I must die, I might as well die in good shape."

II

"You will cooperate with us!" Fergus warned, getting frustrated.

"Or you'll kill me?" Channing said, the smile refusing to fade from his face. "So be it!"

"We could do this another way," Fergus told him.

"We chop off his fingers, one by one, until he cooperates?" George suggested, waving his hunting knife threateningly at Channing. "Show me those jazz hands! The things we could do with a little precision cutting!"

"Think, you dolt!" Fergus raged back at him. "How's he going to use the computer keyboard?" Slightly calmer, he turned darkly to Channing. "No, I have a different plan in mind." He gestured to the holdall, which Esteban handed to him. "I came prepared for this very eventuality." Fergus rummaged through the bag and pulled out a syringe, filled with a white liquid. "Know what this is?"

"What?" Channing said, now sounding concerned.

His fear suited Fergus just fine. "Glad you asked." He ordered his two goons. "Put him in the chair and hold him down!"

Suddenly, Channing found himself grabbed and dragged to the sofa, struggling, unable to break free. Esteban and George sat either side of him, holding his arms tightly.

"If he's not going to cooperate, then we make him!" Fergus told his team.

Trudie interjected, stealing her lover's thunder. "That there syringe contains truth serum. Sodium thiopental or, to give its other name, Pentothal. Not easy to come by, but we have our sources. We should be able to extract the necessary information from you. Passcodes, passwords, the lot!"

"You don't think the Coroner will be able to do a toxicology screen?"

"We will be long gone by then . . ." Fergus replied.

Channing tried to wrestle his fear back under control. "Here comes the Bride, the

Devil by her side!"

Fergus laughed. "Handsome devil, please . . ."

"*The Fucker and the Whore*!"

Fergus's smile vanished. "You will soon be eating those words, my friend!" He uncapped the syringe.

George offered another proposal. "You could fry his brain, disable him for the rest of his life. Turn him into a vegetable. The least he deserves."

Trudie added her own thoughts. "I could fuck him when he's dosed up and nicely woozy, consummate our marriage, so long as the limp fuck can get it up! He won't know what he's doing once that stuff is inside him, like some date-rape drug."

"All excellent ideas," Fergus said, warming to the suggestions. He handed the gun to Trudie, who felt its shape and weight in her hand. He moved towards the sofa and ripped open Channing's black shirt, exposing the chest, the buttons flying off in all directions.

Channing stared aghast at the hypodermic needle, glinting luridly in the light. "I'm certainly not fucking a cunt that's had another man's dick in it less than five seconds ago!"

"Shut that prick up!" screamed Trudie at the put-down. "You will do exactly as we tell you . . .!"

"Long have I awaited this moment," Fergus said, triumphantly. "On par with Cain killing Abel." He brought the tip of the needle towards Channing's chest and, for a moment, Channing thought that Fergus was going to inject the damn thing directly into his heart. But Fergus moved the needle downwards and brought it in front of the navel. Already, just the idea of being injected into the umbilicus Channing found wincing, nauseating. Channing tried to resist the armholds, but George and Esteban tightened their grip. "This is going to hurt . . ." As he was about to pierce the navel with the tip of the needle, prepared to press the plunger, Fergus declared: "You will tell us everything we need to know . . ."

"What's going on?"

Fergus spun round and discovered Thérèse Hornbacher standing there in the middle of the room, a look of stark horror on her face. He slipped the cap back on the syringe. "Not another fucking interruption!" he cried, highly irritated.

"Georgie? Fergie? Trudie?" Thérèse asked, shocked. She had left the party early in order to come back home and lie down and rest. Instead, she was confronting a scene she could never have expected in her wildest dreams. She repeated her question: "What's going on?"

But she must surely have figured out what was happening by now. She was surveying a scene where her own son was being held down by her nephew and the housekeeper's son, the Best Man standing over him with a particularly nasty-looking needle and her new daughter-in-law waving a gun around. No second guesses. Everything seemed to fall into place in an instant. A shrewd woman, Thérèse Hornbacher had always known her dead husband's infidelities would come back to haunt the family. Bite them in the ass. Yet she had never let on to her son. She had wanted to protect him from the truth.

"Now *she* knows!" George shouted. "So much for your fucking plan! Can this get any more fucked-up?"

Trudie addressed Fergus. "Maybe you should fuck her, too!"

Thérèse looked startled, appalled. She couldn't believe she had heard something so vile spoken by the woman she'd welcomed into the family just hours before.

"She's not your enemy here," Channing implored, horrified by the obscene suggestion. "Let her go."

"How can you be a part of this, Georgie?" Thérèse asked him, appealing to his conscience. "I wet-nursed you as a baby when your mother was seriously ill in hospital. I watched you grow up. I attended your high-school graduation. Is this the thanks I get?"

Her pleas brought a flush of embarrassment to George's cheeks. He didn't like being told off.

"Shall I shoot the bitch?" was Trudie's acid-tongued response, usurping her previous suggestion with a greater threat.

"No, we've got ourselves a little family get-together," Fergus replied, assessing the situation. "The more the merrier." He checked the grandfather clock. It was already approaching nine. "I think we might just have got ourselves some leverage now. Channing will have no choice but to comply with our demands." To his two accomplices, he ordered: "Grab her!"

As instructed, both George and Esteban released Channing and leapt up from the sofa. They quickly overpowered Thérèse, seizing an arm each.

Trudie strode up to Thérèse and slammed her in the side of the head with the butt of the gun. Thérèse lost her balance and dropped to the floor, stunned.

Trudie turned back to Fergus. "Where's he gone?"

The sofa was empty. Channing was nowhere in sight.

12

"Through the door, into the study," Fergus said, sounding exasperated.

"So much for you paying attention!" Trudie screamed. "What do I pay you for?"

"This is getting way out of hand," said George. "I'm done!"

"You're done when I say you're done!" Trudie blasted him.

Fergus sent in Esteban first with the hunting knife, motioned to George to follow, providing him with the Luger, which Trudie was initially reluctant to relinquish.

"Why me?" Esteban protested.

"So that we're all absolutely clear, we need his *fucking money*!" Trudie screamed back at him. "So grow a pair!"

"Fall in line!" Fergus ordered Esteban in full support of Trudie. "We will keep an eye on Thérèse. It doesn't look like she's going anywhere anytime soon." Thérèse lay sprawled on the floor, out cold. "Can you *please* bring Channing to heel?"

Esteban went into the study cautiously, serrated blade at the ready. Channing wasn't hiding anywhere. He was met only by the stiff corpse of the chauffeur. It occurred to him that Channing must be in the billiard room. He crept closer to the door and stepped into the room.

Channing came out from nowhere. He had nothing left to bargain with, and the bastards had threatened to rape, then shoot his mother. Housed in a glass cabinet, he had never kept the twelve-gauges he used for shooting pheasants loaded with cartridges. But he kept a spare set of golfclubs in the billiard room, behind the door. He swung the 9-iron into Esteban's face, immediately demolishing his left eye. The hunting knife fell from the man's grasp.

Channing proceeded to kick him in the balls – *Fuck the Queensberry Rules!* – and kneed him in the jaw as he doubled over, severing the tongue, blood filling the mouth of the victim, overflowing. Bringing Esteban to the floor, who was by now choking on his own blood, Channing stamped on his face several times, hearing the wet, sickening crunch of bone like a sledgehammer beating a ripe pumpkin, stopping only when Esteban was left with only half of his head intact.

Then, George entered and instantly froze at the gruesome sight of his dead accomplice, who seemed to have only half a face. Emerging again from behind the door, Channing knocked the Luger out of his grasp and pulled George towards him like a mugger might pull an unsuspecting victim into the dark of an alley. The momentum momentarily unbalanced George, who tumbled to the floor.

Caught in an emotional storm, running on adrenaline – and his own bitter wrath – Channing comfortably picked up the Luger and pumped bullet after bullet into George. The gunshots were loud, making the confines of the billiard room reverberate like an echo chamber. He fired the first shot into George's left arm, then the second shot into his right arm. George began screaming like a baby. Strategically selecting his next spot, Channing shot him in each leg, completely incapacitating him. Finally, instead of killing him outright, Channing delivered the next bullet into his crooked cousin's stomach, silencing his screams and leaving him to slowly – and quietly – bleed to death. George began gasping for air, his breathing growing rapid and shallower, gradually losing consciousness.

Satisfied, Channing calculated the number of spent bullets. Did he have enough bullets left? He thought he did. Two bullets, one each for Fergus and Trudie.

"I didn't know you had it in you, my Veddy Briddish Charmer," came a male voice from behind him. "Are you sure you're not like us?"

Channing did a hundred-and-eighty-degree turn, a split-second short of firing the weapon again.

Fergus stood in the doorway, staring in fascination at Channing's handiwork, the messed-up fate of his two accomplices; one side of Esteban's head had been completed pulverized, a sliver of tongue by its side, and then there was the bloody, bullet-ridden body of George. Next to Fergus stood Trudie, and Channing got an overwhelming sense of déjà vu. Except, this time, Trudie held a hunting knife to her groggy mother-in-law's throat.

George and Esteban were both gone now, thought Fergus. "If you want a thing done properly, sack everyone else and do it yourself!"

Channing stared back with the look of a cornered wild animal. His heart thumped unhealthily in his chest, his mind a whirl of confusion. He couldn't shoot Trudie without being absolutely sure he wouldn't hit his mother, who had a knife to her throat, requiring only one deadly slip of the wrist. He spoke directly to Trudie: "The tally of the dead is rising. Want to join it?"

"Want to see which one of us bites the dust next?" said Trudie.

"You will not see another sunrise, dear."

"No matter how famous you are, you will always end up on the slab," said Fergus with a philosophical tone. "Life's a one-way trip. Destination is the grave, sometimes sooner than later. Want me to give you a helping hand? Shall I be your *facilitator?*"

"I have two bullets with your names on it," warned Channing.

"Hand it over," Fergus said calmly, "or we slit your mother's throat."

Channing deliberated, eventually decided with a heavy heart to give over the gun.

He surrendered.

"This has turned into quite an evening," Fergus said, but it was Trudie who unexpectedly stepped forward, half-holding her mother-in-law upright, and snatched the gun from her husband. She released Thérèse, who collapsed gracelessly to the floor. Thérèse stirred, murmuring incoherently, still reeling from the blow to her head.

"Trudie, give me the gun," Fergus demanded, beckoning for the shooter with his fingers.

But Trudie had other ideas. Or perhaps she had lost the plot. Instead of handing it over to him, she pointed the gun at him and pulled the trigger . . .

13

The gun-blast was as loud as an artillery shell fired from a cannon. Fergus gave Trudie a look of wide-eyed astonishment before he realized what had happened. Then, he collapsed, spilling out on the floor, dead.

As Channing reached for her, Trudie turned the gun on him. One bullet left in the clip, if he remembered correctly.

"You didn't have to do that."

"I have my reasons," she said. By way of explanation, she added: "He was no longer any use to me." She saw Channing shuffle towards her again. "Back off or I swear I'll shoot!"

Channing stopped where he was, three metres separating the two of them. What a day he'd had to endure! A day that had once seemed ripe with the promise of love, after a perfect Valentine's Day wedding, had descended into a nightmare of momumental proportions. Masked intruders crashing the wedding night. Friends turned enemies. The ensuing bloodbath. Channing had always thought of Trudie as a sugar-and-spice-and-all-things-nice kind of girl. He'd never pegged her for a seductress . . . or a stone-cold killer.

"The plan's changed," Trudie told him, maintaining the gun in his direction. Her eyes flashed with a mixture of vitriol and triumph. "You don't think I can play the poor widow, who survived this ghastly ordeal?" And she meant every word. Maybe she *had* lost her mind, oblivious to the obvious flaws in her plan. "This is where I leave you and collect my reward."

Someone tugged at her ankle. She looked down and discovered Thérèse, who by now was slightly more awake and pulling at her ankle. Trudie kicked away the hand.

Channing seized the opportunity. It proved sufficient a distraction for Channing to lunge forward and grapple the gun from her grasp. He pushed Trudie away from him.

"I'm so sorry to do this," Channing said with a sad smile, and there followed a deafening explosion of sound as he emptied the clip, "but it's always personal."

Trudie dropped to the floor, lay there, clinging on to dear life. She was bleeding out of her stomach, the blood pooling on the floor around her waist.

Channing knelt down next to her. He stared into those beautiful blue eyes he had once fallen in love with. There was still a part of him that loved her, had been proud to marry her, would have moved heaven and earth for her, that presently imagined that, perhaps, he had somehow dreamed up this entire, terrible evening. He should give her a fitting end. "Maybe I should have read Sonnet 147: *My love is as a fever, longing still/For that which longer nurseth the disease,/Feeding on that which doth preserve the ill,/Th' uncertain sickly appetite to please./My reason, the physician to my love,/Angry that his prescriptions are not kept,/Hath left me, and I desperate now approve/Desire is death, which physic did except,/Past cure I am, now reason is past care,/And frantic-mad with evermore unrest;/My thoughts and my discourse as madmen's are,/At random from the truth vainly expressed:/For I have sworn thee fair, and thought thee bright,/Who art as black as hell, as dark as night.*" He paused, regarding her face closely. Despite her fatal wound, the look of excruciating agony on her face, he noticed she was still listening to him. Yet, even if he still had feelings for her, he could not ignore her wickedness, how she had callously and unscrupulously plotted his downfall. "Or maybe I should be reading from *MacBeth*." He held her hand, stroked it. "Your beauty is no longer the valuable commodity you can barter with but an uneconomical liability, I'm afraid."

"I did love you . . ." Trudie managed to muster through her pain, her life slowly ebbing away.

Was she lying again? Asking for forgiveness? "You promised to marry me," Channing told her, "but your troth . . . it's *blighted.*"

"Are you just going to let me die?"

"I'm giving you the same courtesy you were going to give me. This is where we part, my dear."

"Until Death do us part?"

Channing reached down and kissed her gently on the forehead. "Until Death do us part . . ." As he watched her relinquish her struggles and die, he thought with a pang of sadness and regret: *The people we no longer are exist in a life not lived . . .*

14

When the police arrived shortly after, they discovered Channing kneeling beside his dead wife. It had been an unprecedented, particularly nasty evening. He was fully prepared to give his statement to the police.

His mother would be fine, just a knock on the head. The paramedics would take her to hospital, check her over.

The members of the local community would be in shock over the horrific massacre at Hornbacher Manor, the scale of the conspiracy against their favourite son. The newspapers and media stations would go crazy over the unspeakable scandal.

In the days that followed, as he tried to put the traumatic events of his wedding night behind him and tried to get on with his life, Channing would sometimes think of his wife. Her death would be a stain on his conscience, but it would not leave him the broken man he expected to become. He would be reminded of a quote from the legendary playwright, Tom Stoppard: *Every exit is an entry somewhere else.*

And, when the dust had cleared, Channing would travel up to Chertsford and meet up with his long-term mistress in her luxury, penthouse apartment.

May 2020-July 2020

The Art of Mimicry

I

"Oh my God!" exclaimed Janey, not believing her eyes. "Our flight's been cancelled!"

Peter tried to make sense of what Janey had discovered online when she had routinely logged in on her laptop to wirelessly print out the boarding passes. He maintained his calm even if it was the worst possible way to kick off any holiday, let alone a honeymoon. "Did they give any excuse?"

"Something about the Air Traffic Controllers in Marseille being on strike!"

"France is a socialist country. Unlike conservative Britain, the Trade Unions are big over there. Always striking for some reason or another. Something of a French tradition." He searched for a sensible solution. "Any other flight companies operating?"

Given direction, Janey explored a couple of choice websites for any scheduled flights out of Heathrow. They were in luck. "Air France are still flying." Her panic subsided, visibly so. "Phew!"

"Problem solved," said Peter, with cool satisfaction. "Let's book it, even if it's at short notice and slightly dearer."

Janey kissed him, filled with sheer relief. She paid for the earliest flight, accessed the boarding passes and they prepared to set off for their flight, which was scheduled for the following morning. She also promised never to travel with any budget airlines ever again. "It will be nice to see what it's like to fly on a French airliner."

It was indeed nice. Nice to travel in style. Better seats, more leg-room, no screaming babies. The French language spoken around them was music to their ears. Without sounding like a snob, Janey had to admit there was a classier breed of clientele onboard. The air stewardesses handed out free goat's-cheese-and-walnut sandwiches to the passengers, if they didn't like anything with smoked salmon, alongside the unlimited hot and cold drinks.

It wasn't a direct flight to Marseille. They had to catch a connecting flight at Amsterdam with the same airline company. Peter understood why people said that there was often a lot of waiting around at the airport. Still, it didn't give him any time to go outside the airport and pop into one of the hash boxes that might be walking distance or a short taxi-ride away. Their luggage was automatically transferred onto the next flight, and they touched-down safely at MARSEILLE-PROVENCE mid-afternoon.

They arrived in Marseille to a near-deserted airport. Its air of emptiness was somewhat disorientating. They passed through Passport Control and picked up their luggage at Baggage Reclaim, dispelling Janey's momentary dread they wouldn't find it there, but that it would still be going round and round the conveyor belt in Amsterdam. Soon they were heading out of the main terminal. The weather was hotter than the unexpected heatwave engulfing England, and the light brighter and different and getting some used to. Looking at things from another angle, it was interesting how they had gone from the cannabis capital of Europe to one of the major historic heroin capitals in the space of an hour. And if that French political drama was anything to go by, you'd find three-bottles-of-wine-a-day Gerald Depardieu as the fictional mayor of Marseille, snorting coke and suffering a heart attack.

They hired a grey Twingo from a car rental store and drove out of the airport, Janey in the driving seat. Hiring a car instead of doing a ferry-crossing and driving down the entire length of France meant they wouldn't be able to bring much stuff back with them to England. They didn't mind.

They got to their holiday villa in the hills of Claviers, Var, within two hours after much anxious ado around the head-spinning bends. Each of the houses possessed a garage from which a steep driveway opened up onto a narrow, winding lane, and VILLA CHARMILLES was no exception.

Yes, Peter and Jane Hepworth were on their honeymoon, and Janey was going back to the same place she had stayed in, with her parents and then-boyfriend, Clark Lambert, twenty years ago, when she had been a vivacious seventeen-year-old. This time, with her husband in tow.

Do you always take your boyfriends here? Peter had joked harmlessly.

Only if they're worth it, she responded, equally lightly. *Believe me, you're only the second.*

I'm honoured...

She had chosen this timeless, wild spot among others to revisit the house where she had enjoyed her most memorable holiday, from another age, but an inquisitive part of her wanted to see what had become of her former boyfriend, her first love.

Because Clark Lambert owned the villa.

2

Countryside and tranquillity, music and relaxation, a life of simplicity and *art de vivre* – that's what they'd come here for. Ancient ruins dotted the land, some bespeaking Roman influence; Provence took its name from having once served as a 'province' of Rome. It was also a place steeped in medieval history and the tales of kings and queens. It inspired the Stella Artois ad, even though it was a Belgian beer. While the French were creating Kronenberg 1664, England was by contrast suffering the Great Plague soon to be followed by the Great Fire.

Set under the azure sky, the village of Claviers was nestled amidst the wooded hills of oaks and firs and olive groves, offering a rare glimpse of a peregrine falcon or a wild boar. A river flowed through a valley shaped like a natural amphitheatre. In the glades and fragrant meadows, wildflowers blossomed in glorious abundance, lavender and primrose and poppies and garlic flower, filling the air with the vibrant breath of summer, a generous, solar bouquet that sent an intoxicating quiver to the heart. Such places often hold great enchantment for those venturing souls – and sometimes dark *secrets*, like carving your initials on some remote tree in a quiet woodland that you may never find again.

In Peter's opinion, the geographical layout of the property vaguely reminded him of something out of *The Pink Panther*, the film classic starring Peter Sellers and David Niven. The villa was three-tiered and terracotta-floored throughout with the occasional Persian rug thrown in for good measure. From the front door, a bedroom and en-suite bathroom were situated to the left. Elevated, south-facing, the balcony window commanded a spectacular view of Claviers in the distance. On the right, a staircase with an iron balustrade led down to a large central sitting area with leather couches facing one another across a low, mango-wood coffee table. Adjacent to it, a further sizeable alcove-like space provided further couches in the entertainment area with its large plasma TV and home cinema system. The record collection consisted mostly of *Yé-yé* music, worth exploring, and *Bonnie and Clyde*, performed by Serge Gainsbourg and Brigitte Bardot, proved to be a song worth listening to. On the other side of the centrally-situated couches was located the second family bedroom with plenty of wall-fitted, wardrobe space and another en suite. A short set of stairs descended to the dining area, with its long dining table, seating eight people. Here, food could be served from an open-plan kitchen, a whisker away, the door to the utility room by the refrigerator. Accommodating essential housekeeping equipment, the utility room itself contained another door, only shoulder-high and locked, probably the cleaning closet. Around the villa, cornflower-blue shutters opened up outside the bay windows to keep the intense afternoon sun in check.

Framed prints of famously-sublime visions of Cézanne, Dufy and Picasso occupied the walls, establishing a Provençal feel to the house. However, it was the painting by an unknown artist that grabbed Peter's attention. Two figures, a man and a woman, dressed in hat and raincoat and carrying a single open umbrella between them against the first drops of rain, stood on a Parisian street corner, backs turned to an open café window where, closest to the observer, rested a pair of wine glasses on a round table, their rouge contents untouched. To a Sunday painter like Peter, there was something beautiful about the scene. Maybe it was the realism of the painting, the presence of the couple as witnessed from the perspective of the café window with its unconsumed wine glasses, the suggestion of romance between the twosome sharing an umbrella against the grey lowering sky, the 1920s period detail of the street . . .

Except for these pictures on the walls, Janey was surprised the house had not changed one bit since she first visited it almost two decades ago. Too many dull browns, not the colours of Provence, and the place certainly needed remodelling, renovating. It could have been sheer laziness on the part of the owner, but its décor raised a creepier thought, as though it had been deliberately preserved this way, like a shrine to her maiden visit.

Still, the perfect place to shag, as far as Peter was concerned. Time to get their groove on. *Boom-boom,* as Janey called it. She liked bouncing up and down on him, as though riding a horse. *Those feet,* Peter reminded her, overwhelmed with desire, *and those toes I have sucked I do not know how oft!*

The first thing the newly-married couple did was complete their conjugal duties across the dining table, desperately craving each other's sexually-charged bodies, their synchronized orgasms like electroshock. Naked and sweaty and spent from their physical exertions, they lay together for a short while on the dining table before they decided to put their clothes back on and check out the outside of the villa.

The grounds weren't particularly large but inviting, nevertheless. The family bedroom opened on to a small seating area, complete with garden furniture, and from here stone steps drifted down to the well-tended swimming pool across from which, tucked away in one corner, was a fully-operational, open-spit barbecue, sheltered from the sun and beneath which rested a pail of charcoal. The vegetation around the garden included rhododendron bushes and the flowering shrubs of rose, lilac and hibiscus as well as a fair share of olive trees, their fruit yet to ripen. A huge, marrow-shaped conifer, possibly a juniper, sprouted up from a rockery. Yellow broom filled the air with the sweet fragrance of honeysuckle.

As the afternoon deepened, Peter and Janey lay on the sun-loungers by the swimming pool, gazing at a procession of clouds in the burnished sky, soaking up the energy-sapping rays of the sun. They felt a light breeze on their faces, providing some relief from the scorching heat of the day. Janey periodically took a dip in the swimming pool to cool off.

Janey had fallen in love with sloths since watching a recent Attenborough documentary — 'slow and cuddly', as she described them, far from the creatures that might bore you to death, and presently she took interest in the wildlife around her. A gourmet scent of honeyed floral notes attracted the foraging bees. The ants looked big and mean and dangerous but turned out to be gentle creatures, fleeing in panic if she prodded them. The flies, on the other hand, seemed a little too friendly. Janey rescued a couple of maybugs from the swimming pool which were able to revive themselves and fly off. However, she was completely unprepared for the mosquitoes coming out at dusk and feeding on them like vampires.

At the approach of evening, Janey watched a spider's web next to her snag a bee. The bee managed to break free, only to be caught again. The spider emerged and started wrapping the bee until the bee was completely cocooned. Janey suspected the spider of biting the bee and watched as the spider undid the packaging, poisoned its prey and carried it away for dinner. The whole act took less than fifteen minutes. Nature could be so cruel sometimes. Yet there was a sense of foreboding about the sight she had witnessed, as if the horrible death of the bee at the hands of the merciless spider was some kind of omen. A thought popped into her head: *Come into my parlour.* Janey shuddered.

Finding a bite to eat was not a problem for the visitors. The owner had left a welcoming hamper for his guests, with plenty of goodies, including baguettes and paté and camembert and a chilled bottle of rosé. Even the mushroom-flavoured crisps had a certain magic to them. The lavender ice-cream was particularly appetizing. Janey wasn't particularly hungry, her appetite diminished by the memory of the spider gobbling up the poor old bee.

After a light supper, Peter and Janey went back outside, sat by the swimming pool. They switched on the external lighting. In the distance, the earthlights of Claviers twinkled back from the other side of the gorge. Moonlight reflected off the rippling waters of the swimming pool. Peter slowly sipped his wine and watched his wife with quiet admiration as she engaged in a bit of night-swimming. His 'Golden Girl' on account of her blond hair, Janey was not averse to a midnight swim. Meanwhile, Janey's mind dwelled on the owner, whom she last saw twenty years ago. She wondered if he still had a thing for her.

3

The following morning, Peter was up and ready and raring to go. He and his wife decided to visit the *Carrefour* supermarket in Draguignan to stock up on groceries. Despite taking the scenic route, Janey developed an irrational fear of hills, suddenly afraid of driving off the edge or rolling back down the steep inclines, losing faith in the Twingo to manage the roads. She asked Peter to drive them back. He tackled the hairpin bends and winding, twisting roads more confidently, but he blew her faith in his driving skills when he asked her to warn him if he was driving too close to the edge. After much fluster and panic, they managed to make it back to the villa safely, and Janey decided neither of them would do any more driving for now, preferring to make it a relaxing holiday instead of an active one.

"You prude!" he had called her during the stressful journey back, not allowing his frustration to compromise his control of the steering wheel.

"You prune!" she replied, holding on to her passenger seat for dear life, as they argued.

All was forgiven by the time they arrived at the villa, and they leapt into the routine of more sunbathing and swimming under the blazing sun.

The rest of the morning passed by uneventfully. At midday, they came back into the house to prepare lunch. It was cooler indoors.

Famished, they ate their croque-monsieurs at the dining table and made passionate love in the family bedroom. Attuned to the rhythm of each other's bodies, they climaxed as one, a sweet, poignant moment, an athletic reflection of the hot-blooded affections they shared and an important reminder of their marriage vows. The only sensible way to love, Peter informed his wife, taking a page from Françoise Sagan, was to love to the point of madness. Could it be achieved? They would try their damnedest. They were banking on great sex and lots of babies in their marital union.

"What do you want to do now?" Janey asked her husband, catching her breath.

"More of the same?" Peter replied, next to her on the bed.

"Why not?"

They went back out and sunned themselves for the majority of the afternoon, hoping to repeat the cycle of sunbathing and lovemaking, until, that is, the sky darkened and they heard the distant rumble of thunder. A thunderstorm was predicted.

They returned indoors as the first drops of rain fell from the heavens, a fine, misty rain. The thunder sounded louder now, more formidable, and the sky outside appeared unusually grey and overcast.

Still dressed in swimwear, beach towel wrapped around their waists, flip-flops on their feet, they were about to grab some chilled Perrier from the fridge to quench their thirst when a strange noise caught Peter's ears. He froze. Janey stopped behind him, taking his cue. They listened.

It was a dull skittering.

Janey heard it, too, and a frown formed on her forehead. Peter was now sure he had not imagined the sound. Both sets of eyes travelled in the direction of the noise. It was coming from behind the door to the utility room.

Peter was the first to move. He pushed open the utility-room door. He cautiously wandered in. Janey was slow to follow, more hesitant, slightly afraid.

There was nothing peculiar in the utility room, nothing to indicate the source of the noise. The washing machine stood silent, the ironing board untouched, the empty washing baskets stacked up neatly alongside the redundant, folded deckchairs and the shelves of cleaning products.

The noise came again, curiously muffled, and this time Peter was able to pinpoint the direction of the sound. It was emanating from behind the cleaning closet.

Could it be categorized as a skittering or a scuttling or a soft scraping sound? He could not be sure.

The first thing that sprang to Peter's mind was mice, or worse still, *rats.*

Peter glanced at Janey, whose imagination seemed to be operating on the same wavelength as his. Her eyes were wide with fear. They stared at each other, then their eyes moved back to the cleaning closet. The mysterious scraping noise grew steadily louder as though whatever was creating the sound was drawing nearer. All of a sudden, the noise ceased. The silence beyond the closet-room door sounded loud and ominous and aggravating. Peter grabbed the broom by the handle, turning it upside down so that the brush was head-height. There followed the jingle of metal and the clink of metal upon metal, the sound of a key turning within the lock, and the housekeeper's closet door creaked open, outwardly. Clasping the handle firmly, Peter was preparing to swing the broom at any intruder when a man's head popped out of the door, a huge grin on his face. "Tally ho!" the man chirped in greeting and emerged from the low doorway, rising up to full height. He was accompanied by a second figure, this time a woman, initially crouched low, half-crawling, but eventually standing up straight once she'd cleared the doorway.

They appraised the modestly-clad couple, who stared at them with gaping expressions. The man wore a beige linen suit, the woman a white, sleeveless vest with a summery-blue halter skirt and brown sandals.

"Sorry to have scared you . . ." the newcomer said, wiping dust and cobwebs from his shoulders. "I'm Clark Lambert and this pretty lady is my wife, Elise."

The newlyweds recognized the names of the couple before them. At last, they were face-to-face with the owners.

"Some people use the front door . . ." Peter commented, slightly irritably.

"Forgive the dramatic entrance . . . I like to surprise my guests."

"Consider us surprised!" remarked Peter. "Where did you come from?"

"From next door," Clark explained. "This tunnel connects the villa to the basement of our chalet, one house along."

Peter peered into the doorway of what he had presumed was the cleaning closet and discovered a musty passage cut into the rock of the hillside that disappeared into darkness. He noticed the battery-powered torch in Clark's left hand. Clark reached out his other hand. Peter shook it. He did likewise with Elise. "How do you do?"

When it came to Janey's turn, she was unexpectedly slow to take the hands of the visitors. She had remained oddly silent throughout the verbal exchange between Peter and Clark. After a perfunctory handshake with Elise, a woman apparently of few words, Janey stared intently into Clark's handsome face. There was no sign of recognition in his blue eyes. She prodded his memory. "I'm Janey. Don't you remember me?"

Clark frowned as he rooted through his mind for their last encounter. Finally, he said with an apologetic expression. "Should I?"

"Never mind . . ." murmured Janey when nothing was forthcoming.

Let off the hook, Clark got down to business. "Well, Peter and Jane, we're hosting a dinner tonight and you will be our guests of honour. It'll be just the four of us."

"That's very kind of you," responded Peter. "We wouldn't miss it for the world."

"Splendid! How does eight o'clock sound?"

"Eight it is."

Shaking their hands again, Clark went to go, Elise following suit. "See you soon."

Peter walked them to the front door, watched them depart. When he turned to Janey, she appeared strangely preoccupied. "What is it, darling?"

She spoke her mind. "He doesn't remember. How can he not remember who I am?"

He sensed her annoyance. He also detected disappointment. "Maybe he's forgotten."

What if Peter was right? She herself had barely recognized Clark. He looked so different, so much more mature, from the gangling seventeen-year-old boy she had once dated. *Except–* "He *should* remember. I'm a memorable person! I mean he was my first love – and vice versa! I heard his family supposedly bought the villa shortly after we broke up upon returning to England."

"Twenty years is a long time . . ." Peter said, reassuringly. "Why not ask him when you see him at dinner?"

Janey did not share with him the sentiment that something didn't fit quite right. Her mind went back to the unfortunate, captive bee, drugged and dragged away by the spider . . . to be subsequently *dined* upon.

4

Sure enough, next door, a less-than-half-minute walk up the hill, was the chalet, LES QUATRE VENTS. It was a lovely edifice, more wood than stone, not unlike the kind of residence one might find on the Alpine slopes. A BMW roadster was parked in the driveway. Yonder, upwards, was the FORÊT COMMUNALE DE CLAVIERS with its hiking trail up to LA CHAPELLE SAINTE-ANNE perched on the western summit of the hills.

It was always fun going out, getting dressed up. Casual smart was the dress code for the evening. Having changed into more suitable attire, Peter in a white, short-sleeved shirt and burgundy chinos and Janey in a short, sunflower dress, they paused at the front door, distracted by the sound of barking behind an iron gate to the side of the house, a patch of garden accommodating a number of dogs: two grey whippets, possibly mother and daughter, sleek, beautiful creatures, and a brown, big-boned Great Dane, elderly and somewhat doddery and slobbering excessively. The couple communicated with the dogs through the side-gate; each animal seemed pleased to see them. Excited by the visitors, they made their acquaintance by sniffing their hands through the bars. That was when the couple noticed a cat amongst the canine troupe, its tortoiseshell fur going grey and its left eye suffering the milky opacity of a cataract.

Suddenly, the front door opened and out stepped Clark, dressed in a grey shirt and blue chinos. "I see you've met the rest of our family . . ."

The dogs began to instantly snarl and growl at the figure in the doorway and made themselves scarce, leaving the cat to linger alone behind the gate.

Janey, who was already sweet on them and a little saddened by the cat with the cataract, spoke first. "They don't seem too thrilled by your presence."

"They're just having an off-day or probably mooching for more food," Clark said by way of explanation, but it was an explanation Janey did not find particularly convincing. It was the behaviour of animals sensing a threat, animals that seemed positively spooked.

"Who's that lovely thing?" Jane inquired, gesturing to the moggie.

"Bernice," Clark replied. "She's the grande-dame of all cats. Not as active as she once was. Approaching twenty years, you see, but still going strong."

"She's utterly adorable, as are the rest of your pets."

"She'll appreciate your attention, like a faded film star." Clark turned to go back into the house. "Mustn't keep my guests waiting. Come inside, please."

Janey crossed the threshold after a quick "See you later, sweetums!" to the cat. Peter followed her in. They surveyed the interior design of the chalet.

Unlike the villa they were currently renting, the décor of the chalet was more in keeping with the rustic hues of Provence, lots of gorgeous golds and oranges and subtle blues and greens to compliment the timber framework. The chalet was much smaller than the villa but decidedly cosier, and the bohemian soul of the place could not be understated. The lobby opened up to a dining room, the table already set. "Nice place you got," Peter told his host.

"Thank you," replied Clark humbly. He checked his watch. "Your timing could not be more perfect. Eight on the dot."

At the request of their host, the visitors took their places at the dining table capable of seating six. Elise emerged from the small kitchen, wearing an exotic dress and carrying a tray of small dishes laden with duck liver parfait with truffle butter, red onion marmalade and toasted brioches, their starters. "*Bonjour, Monsieur et Madame.* Dinner is served. *Bon appetit!*"

"America points too much towards the automobile culture of the Drive-thru," Clark was saying, immediately tucking into his appetizers, washed down with a glass of Kronenberg Gold Bier. "The ready-to-eat packaged food of the supermarket aisles. We have none of that here. Here, the French enjoy a refined, varied cuisine, where the ingredients — perforce seasonal and local — dictate the dish. They despise factory farming and GMO. Their market-fresh, quality produce combines the concept of conscience and their way of life. Food inspires the way people live; for example, they take their time over lunch, let it digest during the afternoon siesta. Isn't that right, Elise?"

Elise nodded.

"We've seen French cooking make a major comeback," observed Peter.

"French cooking never needed to make a comeback," countered Clark. "It never left."

"Contrary to popular belief, I think the French are a very friendly and understanding people," Janey said truthfully.

"You are too kind," Elise said, with that delightful French accent. "Tell me about yourselves." She glanced at Janey's wedding ring. "How long have you been married?"

Janey grinned. "Two days. We're on our honeymoon."

"Honeymooners?" exclaimed Clark, surprised. "We had no idea! Ah, *la lune de miel!* The lunar month which follows a wedding, when the newlyweds are crazy in love, as sweet as honey. Your presence here is all the more special. We're honoured that you have chosen to conduct your honeymoon with us and turned our little villa into a fine honeymoon suite."

"You are most welcome!" added Elise.

"It's certainly worth it, speaking as lifelong city people," said Janey, beaming.

Elise suddenly became thoughtful. "Sorry, I do not wish to pry, but how old are you? You seem a little too mature to get married. Most people have divorced three or four times by now."

"Elise, please!" Clark interjected, half-amused, half-annoyed. "What kind of question is that to ask our guests?"

"No, it's quite all right," said Janey. She turned to Elise. "How old? That's one question, as I'm sure you know, a woman never answers. Suffice it to say, we're not young. We both married late. We were too career-focused."

"Where did you meet?" Elise followed on.

"Peter and I have known each other for years," Janey replied, holding her husband's hand. "We were good friends for a long time before we decided to step our relationship up to the next level. We work together as co-directors at a small, independent creative design agency back home in Chertsford: *Graphic Flourishes*. We have a number of important clients, including several theme parks. But we're thinking of packing it all in, selling off the firm, and starting afresh elsewhere. Maybe retire, settle down. Paint. Or write a book together."

"How much is your firm's net worth?"

"Three-quarters-of-a-million, give or take," Peter replied. "There are certainly enough prospective buyers, interested parties."

"Wowser!" Clark whistled. "Those retirement plans must look awfully inviting!"

"And yourself?" Janey asked him. "What do you do for a living?"

Clark cleared his throat before jumping into his life story. "Before we met, we used to be actors on stage. We did a few TV commercials, nothing fancy. But we never became household names, alas, no recognition at Cannes, so to speak. and I'm sure you've never heard of us before."

"No shame in toiling in obscurity," said Peter helpfully.

"I blame the critics – nothing but gas pipers, full of hot air – who thought we were no good. The work eventually dried up, so we just went into property development. We discovered Claviers and we stayed." Clark paused for thought. "I mean what's not to like? Clean, country air, sparkling, crystal waters, a simple way of life, back to nature. Business has never been better. Meeting new guests, week upon week, many like yourselves who come here from far and wide."

But Janey picked up on something. Clark had used the word 'discovered'. Her face formed a puzzled expression. She tried to jog his memory. "You really don't remember me?"

"You asked me that before," said Clark, with a furrowed brow.

"We were something of an item, back in the day. You came here with me and my parents a long time ago."

Clark frown deepened. "I may have. I really can't remember. Maybe you've mistaken me for someone else . . ."

His reply was enough to shut up Janey, her persistence vanquished. Janey couldn't understand why the man could not remember dating her in his younger days. Whatever the reason, it grated on her, but she wisely decided not to pester him about it further, at least not this evening. It wouldn't be civil.

Elise disappeared into the kitchen to get the main course. Clark conveniently changed the subject. Beers dispensed with, he opened a bottle of red wine. "There was a time, as late as the 1970s, when the wines of Provence were seen to be distinctly inferior than those of the rest of Europe. Now they flood the world market, reflecting a rise in standard and expertise. I'm something of an amateur sommelier. I can tell you how to drink wine. You follow the five 's's: sight, swirl, sniff, sip, savour." He demonstrated the technique in front of his guests. Indeed, Peter managed to capture the silky harmony of texture and the smooth, succulent notes of lavender, brambly fruit and blackberries on the palate. The wine went down a treat.

Another romantic ideal of this country, supposed Peter. Vineyards and olive gardens, brushed by the Mistral and nurtured by the Mediterranean sun and coastal rain. "I could never imagine the weather here getting cold," he ventured.

"You'd be surprised," said Clark. "Rule of thumb, if it snows in the Alps, it'll snow in Claviers. It snowed last winter."

"You're kidding!" was all Peter could say before Elise returned with a red Crueset pot. The main course consisted of *civet de lievre*, translated as 'jugged hare', with lardons-and-onion potato sauté. The stew provided a new, exquisite experience: a sun-warmed earthiness with wisps of wild woody herb, baking spices and a shake of the pepper pot.

The rest of the evening passed by pleasantly enough. Conversation was both personal and cultured in the broadest sense. They discussed a range of topics, hot off the press. Prince Harry's wedding to Meghan Markle was a point of conversation. "I have no loyalty to the Royal Family," Clark was explaining, getting nods of agreement from his guests. "That's why I live in France, where they did away with the Royal family centuries ago. But I suppose it's good to see the Windsors branching out, exploring different heritages. Must be a kick in the teeth to Prince Philip – let's see him open his mouth! It would come as no surprise to me if Meghan was already pregnant, ergo the shotgun wedding. The court of public opinion in those more discerning have viewed the older generation of Royals as always lacking substance, emotion and relatability. The Queen was nominated for the Nobel Prize for her life's work. What the hell for? *What* life's work? Princess Diana should have been nominated for her humanitarian causes, but instead she got bumped off by MI6 at the behest of the Royal Family for the purposes of damage control, all because she outsmarted and outshone them at every turn and made them look bad – no doubt about it! That is what the Queen on her high horse will be remembered for. I mean, has everybody forgotten about the Paradise Papers? They're good boys, Diana's children. As far as Royal-sanctioned homicides go, shame they never questioned the death of their own mother as anything other than accidental."

"The Royal family is not even educated," Janey said with disdain. "They just know how to speak properly."

Peter grinned. "Janey believes she belongs in high-society circles."

Janey returned the smile, her expression growing wistful. "Unfortunately, I'm not much of a social climber."

"Would you ever move back to England?" Peter asked Clark.

Clark gave a slow shake of his head. "Do you think I would go back with the state British politics is in at the moment? Not mentioning the Russian-funded, electoral fraud perpetrated by the Brexiteers, selling snake oil and lies. The Labour Party's having to deal with antisemitism in its ranks while the Tories are in hot water over Islamophobia. I'd rather stay put, thank you!"

Peter spoke about the 'Spiderman' hailed as a hero for scaling some building in Paris to save a child dangling from a balcony. "Heroism at its finest." Something suddenly occurred to him. "Speaking of Paris, when is art not art?"

Clark shook his head again.

"When it's a Bansky . . . did you hear about it?"

Nobody but Peter had a clue. Peter elaborated. "Six paintings appeared overnight mysteriously in Paris, making stark political and social statements. Banksy strikes again!"

The four people at the dinner table debated whether Banksy's street art of monumental portraits carved into crumbling walls, illuminating urban vistas, could be classified as art or was nothing more than glorified graffiti, creative vandalism. You certainly couldn't collect a Banksy in its original form, only prints. The answer in the end eluded them as did the identity of this vigilante artist. They concluded whoever this artist was he was indeed talented — and rightly pissed off with the world they presently lived in.

Peter agreed with Clark. "Yes, it is a crazy, inverted world we live in, where black people strive to be lighter-skinned and white people try to be dark."

The conversation drifted on to Hollywood. Johnny Depp became the subject of discussion. Once a versatile and quirky and extremely-bankable actor and considered by some as something of a popinjay, Depp had somehow managed to fritter away almost all of his six-hundred-and-fifty-million-dollar fortune on sprawling mansions, islands in the Bahamas, private jets, luxury cars, Andy Warhol artworks, old guitars and vintage wine.

"I very much doubt he is a true wine connoisseur, drinking vodka for breakfast and indulging in a spiralling drug habit," Clark observed. "Now, after an expensive and acrimonious divorce from Amber Heard, who alleged he used to beat her, he's in a major court battle with his own financial management team. Good luck to him!"

"I feel sorry for him," sympathized Janey. "He cuts a sad and tragic figure."

"It's like he's become a caricature of his hero, Hunter S. Thompson, whose ashes he blasted into space for a few million bucks," Peter reminded them. "How crazy is that?"

"To me, his circumstances remind me of Elvis when he was on his last legs," Clark said ominously. "I hope he can pull himself together before it's too late . . ."

On this dramatic note, a silence descended, as though in reflection on how the lives of the Rich and Famous could change so drastically, in a desperate and dreadful reversal of fortune. How the mighty fall . . .

"Glad we're not actors anymore," Clark added. "From one former actor to another, we like our life, don't we, Elise?"

Elise nodded, smiling lovingly back at her husband.

"Did you recently read the papers about that pair of international criminals, who impersonated a rich, elderly couple in Monaco, stripped them of their jewels and are currently on the run, wanted by the police and Interpol?" Janey blurted out blithely and out of the blue as they finished up on the artisanal cheeses and coffee and a glass of Cognac.

Clark looked askance at his wife, shifting uncomfortably in his seat. "I'm impressed by your knowledge of the local news. Always good to keep up with the day's events. Janey, you're right as ever! These ruthless professional criminals, known as the Loriens, also struck St. Tropez recently and are thought either to have gone into hiding somewhere in Provence, waiting for the dust to clear — a truly troubling thought, believe me! — or are suspected to have skipped over the Alps into Italy."

"Let's hope they've fled to Italy," said Peter, yawning. "I wouldn't want to bump into them."

His yawn was contagious, Clark following suit. "I sincerely hope the authorities get them. It's no fun knowing they're still at large and might even be hiding out somewhere nearby." He checked his watch. It was nearly eleven. "It's getting late . . ."

"Thank you for inviting us," Peter told his hosts and, in particular, complimented Elise's cooking. "And a particular thanks to you, my dear, for preparing this fine feast. It was sumptuous."

Elise accepted the compliment with a small curtesy. "*Merci* . . ."

"No, the pleasure was all mine," reciprocated Clark. "Good food, good wine and, most important of all, good company — what more can a man ask for? You make a lovely couple and me and Elise both look forward to catching up with you both again, hopefully very soon."

"*À bientôt*," Peter told them at the front door.

"*D'accord...*" Elise said in approval.

"Toodle-oo!" Clark said to Peter. "Let us know if there's anything you need to make your honeymoon special. Remember, a honeymoon is a once-in-a-lifetime experience – or it's supposed to be!"

"Will do."

After the exchange of farewells, Peter escorted Janey back to the villa. "You're awfully quiet all of a sudden. Don't tell you're stewing over the fact Clark doesn't recognize you?"

"I don't trust them," Janey remarked unexpectedly. "Call it a woman's intuition."

"Really? Next you'll be telling me they're the master-criminals everyone's been reading about. Because that *would* be crazy!"

"I don't know. But it would damn well explain why he doesn't remember me from before."

"You know there's other rational explanations. Perhaps, he didn't want to let on he knew you from before in front of his wife. Or ever considered he might still have feelings for you and he's too embarrassed to admit it?"

"You think so?" Janey piped, appearing slightly relieved, pleased even.

"Should I be jealous?" Peter asked casually.

"No competition. I married you, remember?" Janey kissed him.

They made love before preparing to sleep, the French doors thrust open upon their sweet, naked unity. Peter slept soundly. Janey could not sleep, lying wide awake, listening to the hooting of a Scops owl outside, the thin, reedy drone of a mosquito in the room intent on sucking her blood. She thought about the news topic she had inadvertently raised at the dinner table, of those international jewel thieves sought after by the authorities. What bugged her the most was not the mosquito buzzing around her head or the news of the criminals who had managed to evade the net of the police, but the mystery of why Clark wouldn't admit to remembering her. It might turn out to be an innocent enough explanation, as Peter had suggested, but something told her – that woman's intuition, as she called it – that something was very wrong. She thought she would speak to Clark privately and ask him, in case there was something he was dying to tell her.

It would be another two days before she got the opportunity, and the answer, when it came, left her hysterical and half-mad. Also, by then, it was already too late.

5

Janey kept her ears to the ground, monitoring the comings and goings of the chalet. But she was liable to be greatly disappointed. The mysterious goings-on she anticipated from next door never materialized. There were no strange noises in the middle of the night. She caught no compromising sight of their neighbours, let alone odd, disturbing behaviour. In fact, there was no sign of them or their car. If their neighbours were nowhere in sight, she wondered, who might be feeding Bernice and the dogs?

But just because there was nothing peculiar going on next door did not preclude strange and inexplicable events happening elsewhere.

The Hepworths did not drive and maintained much of the same daily routine, Peter working on his tan, Janey periodically peering next door in search of suspicious activity. Nothing to write home about, and the nightly lovemaking of honeymooners wouldn't be suitable material to write about, anyway. Except that queer sensation of something amiss did not leave her.

Other times, they would wander into town for a change of scene or to pick up something from the *Proxi* grocery store, and it was during one of these casual walks that they shared an event too weird to explain in the sane, rational sense.

Where the road into *Centre-Ville* took a sharp, right bend was situated a bar, a café and a restaurant, together with a bank and the tourist information office. Nothing unusual, just everyday scenes of people going about their business or enjoying a beer in the sun. The road then journeyed straight on before turning on itself downhill and officially leaving Claviers. A row of cars was parked on one side of this direct stretch of road, makeshift steps leading up to a small cemetery. On the other side of the road was a boules' strip and a war memorial and park benches under the trees where one could sit and gaze across the valley at the villas on the hillside. From the park benches in the village centre, Janey managed to identify their holiday villa amidst this vista of other villas by the architecture of the place and the conical-shaped evergreen proximal to the swimming pool. Peter had to agree with her. She had an eye for detail as acute as his, if not better. She took a photo on her phone for posterity's sake.

They trekked back up to their villa, carrying their groceries, consisting predominantly of bottled mineral water. It was a sauna out there and they relished the exercise. Soon they were back at their digs and preparing to lie on their loungers. Except, when Janey looked back at the centre of Claviers from beside the swimming pool, she realized two people identical to themselves presently sat on the very same bench where they had sat only half-an-hour earlier, from where they had spotted their villa, photographing it in the process. Identical in every way, right down to the baggy clothes and sunglasses they had worn when they had gone into town. It was a jarring experience, and it took Janey nearly a whole minute to inform Peter, who removed his sunglasses, for a clearer inspection, following the direction of her tremulous, pointing finger. She wasn't imagining it. Sure enough, he and Janey sat on the bench under the shade of a plane tree, close to the war memorial and parched boules' lawn. Tiny figures they might appear from this distance, but they bore enough detail even from afar not to obscure their unmistakable resemblance.

"Take a picture!" Peter suggested, shaking himself. *Is that us? Watching ourselves at the house while watching ourselves in the village centre?*

Janey clicked her mobile camera. Down in the centre of town, the other Janey seemed to raise her own phone as if to take a picture of the villa as Janey had done previously. Up at the villa, Peter and Janey watched their doubles get up from the bench and start making tracks with their bagful of groceries and mineral water prior to disappearing behind a building and completely from view.

Peter and Janey looked at one another and realized instantly they were thinking the same thing. The lookalikes they had spied on the park bench were heading home. Villa Charmilles. They would be here in ten minutes.

Neither Peter nor Janey spoke. Presently, they returned into the house and, from the lower dining area, stood staring intently up at the front door, with round-eyed expectancy and fear, waiting with bated breath, not knowing how they would react to the sight of themselves walking into the house.

Except no other version of themselves came in through the front door. They waited and waited and when sufficient time had lapsed, Peter loosed a long, enormous sigh through clenched teeth, the anticipation easing off. "You know what this means, don't you?" he said.

"What?" Janey responded, jumping at the sound of his voice.

Excitement was evident in his voice. "Show me the pictures."

Janey accessed the two photos. Nobody could question the content of the picture she'd just snapped from the swimming pool, of Claviers, moments earlier. No flights of the imagination since Janey and Peter were clearly right there on the park bench next to the war memorial in the image. In the preceding photo, taken from the village centre when they had singled out the villa, they had missed an important detail. Two human-shaped specks by the guiding evergreen in the proximity of the swimming pool had gone unnoticed, suggesting Peter and Janey were at the house at the same time they were in the village centre. It was nigh impossible getting their heads round the two photographs. No debating their presence in both images though, taken thirty minutes apart.

However, Peter made a commendable effort to get a handle on the situation, break through the profundity of what they had just witnessed. "People talk about doppelgängers or evil doubles. I, on the other hand, am more inclined to explore scientific explanations. Maybe those characters are us from a parallel universe. However, might we be encountering a temporal anomaly in a universe of infinite possibilities? Could it be that our versions on the park bench managed to glimpse our future selves in the villa while our future selves, who are in fact our conscious present selves, managed to capture a vision of our past selves on the park bench? Both versions are still us, just at different points on the timestream — or maybe for a moment trapped in a partial time loop that eventually smooths itself out. Time catching up with itself? How does that sound?"

Janey wasn't a science-fiction buff like her husband, and she struggled to follow the rationale of his explanation. "Bonkers!"

"True, it's not the kind of thing you see every day, but it's the best I've got, I'm afraid," Peter said apologetically. "Gives me hope that the Universe can play tricks on us and sometimes such inexplicable occurrences are not always the invention of the mind."

They heard the distant hourly chimes of the church bell and went back to lounging in the sun. They did not discuss the strangeness of the afternoon any further but decided to broach the subject with their respective friends and families once back home, get a wider take on it. Janey's hair had turned blonder in the sun whilst her husband's hair had become thicker and greyer. And only one more night of mosquito bites to endure. *What if we're living in* The Twilight Zone? Peter joked in a deliberately spooky voice. *What if we're never allowed to leave these hills, doomed to be eaten alive by the mosquitoes?*

6

"They cancelled our flight *again!*" Janey exclaimed at her laptop that evening, her voice full of incredulity and disgust.

"You're kidding!" said Peter, astonished.

But Janey was already making arrangements to book themselves on an Air France flight, which she managed to achieve in impressive timing. Air France was so much more reliable. "Our holiday was ruined when easyJet cancelled the original flight..."

"Why not take back the positives of this holiday?" Peter suggested.

"Positives?"

"Being with my beautiful and utterly adorable wife on our honeymoon."

"At least I got a nice tan," said Janey.

"That too."

"Such a waste of money," Janey observed, obviously frustrated and annoyed at the repeated failures of the budget airlines.

"The travel insurance company should refund the difference and for the added distress and inconvenience caused," advised Peter. True, they had a genuine case rather than buying into the rampant compensation culture abroad, Brits being the worst offenders. Neither was he prepared to accept any insincere sob story from the airline company.

"I really want to say goodbye to our neighbours," admitted Janey. Outside, it was already sundown and the approaching night promised to be hot and sultry.

"We can check if they're home," said Peter.

Janey thought about their first encounter with their hosts, the extraordinary manner in which Clark and Elise had introduced themselves, making a stage-worthy entrance from the cleaning closet. "Let's surprise them."

"Let's—" concurred Peter, grinning. "Should be fun."

Janey tested the handle of the cleaning-closet door in the laundry room. Their luck was in. Clark had forgotten to lock the door.

The passageway that connected the two houses was dark and dank, the couple having to stoop to avoid banging their heads against the low ceiling, their shoes scrunching debris. Like night cloaking a backstreet in a dusky, crime-novel half-light, there was a certain thrill to descending into the bowels of the earth. A small flashlight put them in good stead, its beam bouncing off the walls of the tunnel reminding Peter of cutthroat smugglers or the monstrous events in the Rue Morgue. They could always creep back to the villa under the cover of darkness if there was nothing significant to behold. Nobody would ever know.

Peter was the first to spot the door at the other end of the tunnel and, finding it unlocked, he crawled out of the hole, Janey sneaking out after him. The light from their torch flashed across the stone walls, and they found themselves in a medieval wine cellar. Peter strode over to the light switch and turned it on. The single, dusty bulb hanging from the ceiling cast a dull but adequate light across the cave, enough for the Hepworths to survey their surroundings. Nothing out of the ordinary, it seemed. Hiding in the dark, dusty unlabelled wine bottles were trellised, row upon row, across one wall, several closed oak barrels placed against another wall. Stone steps led up to a door. The place smelled of must and age. But discerned within the smell of old damp, Peter's nostrils picked up a low, pervasive and unpleasant odour, of leaky, long-defunct septic tanks, of old corruption. The low-grade, gaseous quality of the smell suggested something as simple as a small rodent had curled up in the corner of the cave and died. "What are we doing here?" Peter asked nervously. His initial excitement had succumbed to reservation. "You know we're technically trespassing."

But Janey's enthusiasm could not be dampened. "We're here to surprise our hosts. Just like they surprised us the other day." Past the inordinate rack of wine, she appeared distracted by the lid of one of the barrels, unnailed and slightly askew. House wine, home-made beer? She moved the lid aside to look inside . . . and instantly recoiled, her face blanching, her mouth dropping open in a silent scream. The lid clattered to the floor, echoing thunderously in the confines of the cellar.

Peter stared at Janey, took in the shock and terror in her frozen, ashen expression. "What is it?"

His wife's attention was fixed on the contents of the barrel and Peter had no choice but to cross the flagstone floor and look. He realized what she had seen.

There was no delicious alcoholic beverage in the cask. Instead, crammed in there, immersed in formaldehyde, head floating above the liquid, eyes open and lifeless, was a man. The prevailing odour of stale decomposition in the air was almost masked by the eye-watering acridity of concentrated embalming chemicals. It took Peter a few moments to gather his thoughts and figure out who the dead man was. It must have been horrible enough for Janey to accidentally discover a corpse pickled in a barrel, but, judging how the man possessed more than a passing resemblance to Clark Lambert, Peter knew that Janey was also mourning the loss of an old friend and the chance she never got to reacquaint herself with him. For the hapless man in the barrel was the *real* Clark Lambert.

The wine cellar had suddenly taken on the ambience of a dark, dank dungeon. Or a crypt. Already starting to piece things together, Peter moved quickly and prised open the second barrel with a crowbar. Sure enough, a second corpse floated in there, female this time, undoubtedly the real Elise. *Which could only mean . . .* "We need to get help . . ." he murmured, half-dazed but urgency in his voice.

Except the worst was yet to come. The door at the top of the stairs suddenly burst open, pulling the couple away from the preserved, dead bodies of the real owners, and a man wandered casually down the steps.

Janey glanced at the man who had entered the fray and back at her husband, startled. Presently, there was *two* Peter Hepworths in the cellar, almost indistinguishable from one another. Standing beside her, Peter stared at the physical image of himself, identical in every way even in the dim lighting, right down to the same clothes. The gun the other Peter carried, trained on them, gave him away.

The second Peter, alias Clark Lambert, spoke in the style of Peter. "Not so fast!" Switching to a mock-villainous voice, straight out of *Scooby-Doo*, he said: "If it wasn't for you pesky kids, we'd have got away with it!" He grinned, now cruelty in his expression. "No, we *will* get away with it! Don't say a word! No sudden movements! Or I kill you!"

Janey's Peter dropped the crowbar which clattered on the flagstones in a deafening rattle of sound.

As her paralysis broke, Janey freaked out at the sight of her two identical husbands, believing she had gone completely mad, and she let out the scream that had been straining to break loose since she'd happened across the unfortunate corpse of her former first love in the barrel. Her scream shook the foundations of the cellar, the long, protracted shriek of a madwoman, and when she could scream no more, she passed out.

7

When Janey awoke from her faint, she found herself in the unlikeliest of places. It took several moments for her vision to clear and for her senses to return. She tried to move but couldn't. She saw she was strapped to the driving seat of her Twingo, her hands tied to the steering wheel, itself locked in place. She turned her head and discovered her husband in the passenger seat, next to her, also trussed up like a turkey, head thrown forward, unconscious, a hideous, bleeding gash on his forehead. Memories of the gruesome discovery in the cellar and, of course, the two Peters almost caused her to shriek again. But she held put and tried to rouse him. "Peter, wake up, please, wake up!"

Her pleas fell on deaf ears. Peter did not stir, out for the count. The injury he had sustained across the forehead told her he had been hit hard. He'd probably be out of it for some time.

Although it was full dark outside, probably close to midnight, the headlights of the

Twingo were turned on, illuminating the narrow country lane and the two figures who stood directly in the beam.

Unlike the low lighting of the cellar, there was no mistaking their presence this time. Peter and Janey – or their doubles – stood ahead, talking between them. It was a surreal moment for Janey, watching herself and her husband standing there in front of them in the full beam of the car's headlights whilst she and her husband were sitting, tied up, in the car. Doppelgängers came to mind, again. Evil twins. Or maybe alien replicants, Pod people, say. But Janey was soon to discover a truth far closer to earth than conjured up by her overtaxed imagination.

Her own double was the first to spot that Janey was awake. Peter's double walked over to her side of the car and looked in through the driver's window. He did not speak in Peter's voice or Clark Lambert's voice but in his own natural voice. He spoke in the clear, enunciating tones of a Shakespearean actor. "You're awake."

"What do you want with us?" she demanded, anger creeping into her voice. "What have you done to Peter?" Janey wrestled with her bonds, but they were fastened tight. "Cut me loose!"

"I'm afraid I can't do that," the man – posing as Peter, real name Alfred Lorien, Alfie for short – replied. He looked the part, an illusion achieved by contact lenses and make-up and a false hairpiece. "Otherwise you're liable to escape, cause a scene. And we wouldn't want that, would we?"

"What's going on?"

"I think you know."

Janey's mind had already begun to fit the pieces of the jigsaw together. Everything made sense now. The reason why 'Clark Lambert' couldn't remember who she was. The frightened and wary response of Bernice the cat and her canine companions towards their owners – who were not really their owners, after all. The strange events in the village centre, the sight of their doubles across the valley, nothing supernatural about the whole thing, certainly not the Past trying to catch up with the Present, as Peter had postulated. As far as explanations went, these were the same notorious criminals, who had so far evaded the police, a husband-and-wife pair, daring actors, lovers of the high life, taking the identities of the people of whose riches they relieved. Yes, Janey knew all and she nodded in acknowledgement.

"Quite the *faux pas* on my part," Alfie elaborated. "How was I to know you shared a history with the real Clark Lambert some twenty years back? You see we were completely unprepared for this scenario. Believe me, you took us totally off-guard. We'd raised your suspicions and we knew it would only be a matter of time before you cottoned on to what was actually going on, before you saw right through our charade and exposed us. You snooping around our house told us your suspicions would not be satisfied until you knew. So we had to get our new plan into action. We assumed your identities in the village centre, tested the fit, a dress rehearsal for the main event."

"So you killed Clark?" Janey stated, feeling the loss and the hurt.

"We had no choice. We needed to disguise ourselves. Besides, we like dressing up. It's the bread-and-butter of an actor."

Her grief and rage spilled over. "You're nothing but crooks, murderers! *Failed actors!*"

Janey struck a nerve. Alfie's expression darkened, inflamed by her disparaging remark belittling his acting abilities. His tone grew steely, sharper, threatening. "I would advise you keep your opinions to yourself, if you know what's good for you! We've played so many different people, we've almost forgotten who we once were. Now we have a new role. *You two.* By watching you with hidden cameras in the villa, we have perfected your attributes, your mannerisms. Now don't you think we deserve to win the Oscars that actors lesser than us attain?"

The news that they had been secretly filming the honeymooning couple for the purposes of studying their personalities, even during intimate times, sickened her, made her feel horribly violated. She remembered the blessings Alfie had bestowed on them [*turned our little villa into a fine honeymoon suite*] at dinner. A wave of nausea filled her, a genuine desire to vomit and her head swam. She steadied herself. "You will never get away with it!" It was truly uncanny how Alfie was the spitting image of Peter, right down to the smallest detail. His likeness was so eerily close to the genuine article that one might have easily mistaken him to have been moulded into shape, causing Janey once again to entertain notions of the supernatural. A perfect impersonation. *Except . . .* "Peter's at least two inches taller than you."

"Don't worry, we'll pull it off!" Alfie said confidently, smugly. "George Burns once said: *the secret to acting is honesty. If you can fake that, you've got it made.* And Orson Welles claimed: *Fake is as old as the Eden tree.*" He paused, looking at her hard. "Know of the wisdom of cuckoos?"

Janey did not reply.

"I think Will Shakespeare was right on the money. Take *Love's Labour's Lost. The cuckoo then on every tree,/Mocks married men; for thus sings he,/Cuckoo!/Cuckoo! Cuckoo! O word of fear,/Unpleasing to a married ear.* From my *King Lear. The hedge-sparrow fed the cuckoo so long,/ That it had it head bit off by it young./So out went the candle and we left darkling.*"

"You like the sound of your own voice, don't you?" Janey said, deliberately antagonizing him.

Alfie ignored the remark. "Cuckoos aside, you should look towards the natural world to know looks can be deceiving. There are creatures that have chosen deception, treachery and downright fraud to either resemble dangerous animals for protection, such as in the case of the hoverfly and the bee, a concept called defensive mimicry, while aggressive mimicry defines those animals that pass themselves off as a wolf in sheep's clothing to get within easy striking distance of their prey; the ant-mimicking spider is one such case in point of this evolutionary copycatting. As actors we follow the laws of nature. We are masters of mimicry!"

"You are *so* full of yourself and so full of *it!*"

Alfie did not appreciate her *bon mot*, manifesting a look of annoyance. "What's so difficult to understand? To quote Oscar Wilde: *Most people are other people. Their thoughts are someone else's opinions, their lives a mimicry, their passions a quotation.*" He moved to the heart of the matter. He altered his voice, this time doing a perfect Peter soundalike, eerily so. "You must know there's a lot at stake. We have a business to sell. For three-quarters-of-a-million quid!"

So that was their game! "*You bastards!*" Janey muttered furiously, comprehending the outrageousness and unscrupulousness of their motives, the bigger, deplorable picture. "You will *never* fool our friends!"

"We've survived a lot more trickier situations," Alfie told her, gloating. "I'd be more worried about what we're going to do to you."

"What *are* you going to do with us?" She asked again, brutally afraid.

Alfie was once again imitating the original Peter's way of speaking. The man had captured her husband's mannerisms down to an absolute tee. "As I mentioned, we've been watching you closely. We know everything about you. We also know you have recently acquired a dislike of driving these hills."

A stomach-turning dread filled her. Janey knew where this was leading to. "No, please, no, don't do it!"

"Hope you enjoyed your last supper . . ." Alfie continued to torment her and reached into the driver's window and released the handbrake. In that moment, Janey took her opportunity. Rage flashed through her and, like a feral animal, she plunged her teeth into his right ear, biting down violently, ripping it clean off. Half-chewed like gristle, she spat out the severed ear into her lap. Alfie screamed and pulled himself out of the car, clutching the side of his head in monumental agony where his ear had once been. Blood poured out from the wound, dripping on the ground. He realized to his horror it was too late for him to retrieve his ear since the car had already begun to roll down the hill.

In the car, Janey drew a deep, steadying breath, bracing herself. She watched the figure of Alfie retreat, and Lea Lorien, who had achieved a remarkable imitation of Janey, run towards her partner-in-crime in concern. There was something deeply satisfying about her savagery, tearing off the bastard's ear. Janey had got the last laugh.

As the car continued to roll backwards, heading towards the edge and the long plunge down the precipice, the high panic did not materialize, and a calm sense of inevitability set in. Sitting in the rolling car, Janey had a few seconds to reflect on her honeymoon. It had been an eventful honeymoon and, in some respects, a nostalgia trip. She thought of the depiction of the umbrella-sharing couple in that painting that had so fascinated Peter, the metaphor of the undrunk wine. She thought about the two photos she had snapped that toyed with a paranormal explanation. She recalled the spectacle of the spider killing the poor bee, like a harbinger to the events that would unfold during the course of the honeymoon. She remembered the grisly find she had stumbled upon in the wine cellar, the murdered bodies of her former boyfriend and his wife stored obscenely in barrels, and felt no fear, only a sadness and a sense of closure. She glanced at her unresponsive husband beside her and realized she loved him more than he could possibly imagine, more than she had once loved from a more innocent time, back in the day. Maybe some day, in another life, Peter might appreciate the intense, burning passion she felt for him. Not today, however, since he was still out cold. She also hoped to get her own back at the murderous criminals, who had got into their confidence and ruthlessly plotted to steal their identities and take over their lives and whose ambitions stretched to unlawfully selling off their hard-earned business and pocketing the considerable proceeds. Her last thought, as the car tipped over the edge of the hillside, was how she would not let them succeed in their machinations, their designs on her life's work.

The Twingo plummeted down the hillside, jolting this way and that, banging against the trees, flipping over several times, gravity pulling it down like a boulder in a hideous, screeching melee of twisted metal and pulverized glass. The smashed car came to rest in an unreachable part of the hillside.

The petrol tank did not explode.

8

The Hepworths arrived back in England to a welcoming celebration of their homecoming, set up by their dearest friends. Not the real honeymooning couple, mind, but impostors disguised as the Hepworths. 'Peter' explained away his missing ear by stating he had lost it in a boating accident. Wildfires spread across the Var province in their wake, and the French authorities suspected foul play rather than blaming the prevailing heatwave.

While maintaining a low profile, shying away from the limelight in case they got caught out, the bogus honeymooners, relishing their current personas, went about the business of putting the creative design firm that Peter and Janey had built from the ground upwards on the market. However, the night before they would meet in the boardroom and sign all the deeds over to the potential buyers, they encountered an eventuality they never expected.

The real Hepworths came home . . .

June 2018-August 2018

Night of the Wild Boar

"From the moment I liberated Brigitte, the moment I showed her how to be truly herself, our marriage was all downhill."

Roger Vadim

"How does the South of France sound, my darling," Ray Hudson asked his wife, crushing his mobile phone against his ear, hoping it would minimize the noise around him, "you know, for our annual summer holiday?"

"Sounds lovely," he heard Valerie's agreeable response. "We should plan it."

"Will do, my darling, when I next see you."

"How goes the last day of the convention?" Valerie asked her husband.

Ray glanced around his surroundings, absorbed the hubbub of CASINO HESPERIA, before replying: "Such a bore. You know how it is . . ."

"Oh dear," said Valerie, concerned.

"But, as always, I am only too glad in the knowledge that I shall be seeing my beautiful wife again, very soon."

"When should I expect to see you?" Valerie inquired, hopeful.

Ray considered a suitable response. It was already ten in the evening. "Probably in the morning. Not looking forward to that three-hour drive."

"Don't worry, Ray," Valerie reassured him. "Take your time. Drive safely."

"Will do. Will turn in soon."

"Okay, I'll let you go, let you rest."

"I shall therefore bid you goodnight, Val, my darling. Love you . . ."

"Love you, too, Rayby-Baby," replied Valerie sweetly. "Nighty-night." And, with that affectionate exchange, she hung up.

Ray breathed a long sigh of relief. That was a close shave. He almost got caught out. Never get caught where you cannot be found. Yes, he was in a London casino when he had claimed he was at a corporate conference in Winchester. And, yes, Val's only real advice to him was, almost like a watchword: *I shall not be wasteful.* But Ray did not dare believe he had a gambling habit, even if he had run up hundreds of thousands in debt. Ray knew one day Sheldon, the mob boss who owned this particular casino, would call in what was owed to him, and Ray would get it in a horrible way if he didn't pay up. Ray had worked out how to source the money outside of his six-figure salary working for a major insurance brokerage firm. It was the excitement of the roulette wheels and the blackjack tables and the one-armed bandits, with their usual pool of lurkers, that kept him alive. And it all boiled down to the element of risk. Ray liked taking risks. He hadn't, however, expected to get so deeply immersed in the game. Ray did not accept that gambling was for 'losers', as most people claimed, the odds always stacked up in favour of the establishment. 'Gambler's Ruin' was a term most statisticians used: it's a proven fact that you're destined to lose more than you win, and every bog-standard casino capitalizes on this mathematical principle no end. Better to throw your money in the fire than make the croupiers, cardsharps and gamesters fatter. *The Cincinnati Kid* was probably the gold standard for gambling addiction and financial ruin. *The fool and his money soon parted,* as the saying goes. Even the Lottery was meant to be a mug's game.

Shifty Eyes has cleaned you out with a straight flush, crushed you under his heels like a bug. He's grinning at you like a Reno pimp. Do you give up the ghost? Of course not. You're lured back like a fly to a spider's lair. Except, this time, you put your house up as collateral. Not if the bank gets it first. And if you don't pay up, you're blacklisted forever and the crime syndicates, who own half the casinos in this godforsaken city, will single you out as the latest undesirable and pay you a visit, forcibly dunking your head in the nearest shit-streaked john or giving your arms a few extra joints where there were none . . .

Neither did Ray care about the concept of variable ratio reinforcement, a term psychologists used, to explain what kept the gambling bug alive and the gambler coming back for more. Ray had had his share of spectacular wins, infrequently though they were, and maybe tonight he might win big again, he hoped, he *prayed*, knock on wood. Lady Luck be favourable tonight. Always looking for the dead cert, rarely finding it. Sheldon's casino management staff had ripped a page out of Las Vegas and implemented ways in keeping their punters happy and gambling until they were cleaned out. Apparently, despite the higher concentration of oxygen that was being pumped in through the vents to keep the mind alert and focused, dispelling any shreds of tiredness, it was the only place one could smoke indoors. There were no clocks on the walls and the gambling activities were confined to the brightly-lit basement so one could not experience the passage of time, of day or night. There were even nappies available for the more hardened gamblers so they did not need to take any trips to the toilet. The periodic clink of falling money, either on the overhead speakers or actually in the slot machines – one couldn't be sure – gave additional motivation – and *incentive* – for the punters to keep going.

And then there was the gaggle of gorgeous-looking girls Sheldon supplied his clientele with. Escorts to stroke the male ego. As Ray stood in a darkened corner of the casino, partially hidden from the shopfloor, the same spot where he'd taken the phone call from his wife, the girl who had been fellating him came up for air, rising from her crouched position, wiping cum from her mouth. "How was it?" she asked him.

"An expertly-delivered dick-suck," he replied, relishing the warm glow of post-ejaculation. He still didn't know her name. He didn't care. "No teeth-marks this time."

"You need me for anything else?" the young, nameless brunette inquired.

"Nope, your job is done," he said, and watched her nod her head and wander off into the thick of it. Ray hurriedly pulled up his trousers. Sod gambling tonight! Time to get some kip before driving home tomorrow morning, keeping it all innocent and above-board when he eventually saw Val. He had to be careful regarding his extramarital activities; he remembered how he had been afraid of being found-out when the Ashley Madison website, an exclusive dating service that encouraged infidelity, had been hacked. Dishonesty and discretion were sometimes a necessary part of life. Of relationships. Of *marriage.*

I shall not be wasteful, Val had once advised him to repeat like a mantra.

Little did she know what he had planned for her . . .

They were celebrating their twenty-fifth anniversary, and both Ray and Valerie felt going back to the South of France might capture some of the old magic between them. Quoting Mark Twain: *Love seems the swiftest, but it is the slowest of growths. No man or woman really knows what perfect love is until they have been married a quarter of a century.* Claviers was where they had honeymooned all those decades ago. *Have we been together that long?* Valerie often asked. *Seems like only yesterday when we first met. How time flies...*

At least one of us can still look upon our relationship in a positive light, thought Ray within, not sharing her sentiment. *Our relationship fizzled out a long time ago. I'm the only one holding up our house-of-cards marriage. One has to marvel at my patience. Unfortunately, I cannot keep the pretence up forever.*

It was a couple of old flicks from the 1960s which initially gave him the idea: the extracurricular training Walter Matthau receives from his friend on how to cheat on his wife successfully in *A Guide for the Married Man*, followed by the sinister plan that the accidentally-married bachelor, Jack Lemmon, concocts in *How to Murder Your Wife*. Lemmon and Matthau, probably the greatest comedy duo since Laurel and Hardy. Of course, these films were a perfect reflection of the society at the time, a Battle of the Sexes, but after inadvertently coming across them on the cable channel one night he could not sleep sparked something inside him, got him thinking.

The recent extensive and expensive work they'd done on the house had made matters worse. Financially, at least, with Ray being economical with the truth. Valerie didn't know how broke they were. One would think that their grand old mansion in Chertsford might be an amazing home, but in all honesty, the house had no character or redeeming features whatsoever, except, perhaps, space. From its exterior it resembled a small school or a set of apartments. Modern design. High gloss. But so sterile and boring inside. The 1970s, when the house was built, died ages ago and would never return because that decade was so damned unmemorable. Valerie had originally chosen the house when they'd been dating, when he had actually loved her, and he had accepted her decision. But Ray fancied something rustic because country properties never faded or fell out of fashion.

His gambling debts piling up, with the threat of violence from the Mafia if he didn't pay up, and renovating a home he loathed, with money he didn't have, meant the banks were close to foreclosing on his property. The banks had already sent their final demands, which Ray had kept hidden from his wife. She didn't know how bad it was. She didn't have a clue.

A lot of men have committed suicide under such circumstances, stressed and depressed, unable to see any future, any way out of the hole they have dug. Others have committed crimes.

Ray had plumped for the latter. He was an insurance man after all in the corporate hierarchy. Years ago, he had taken out three insurance policies on his wife, who had done likewise on him, a sum amounting to seven figures. Now would be a reasonable time for the insurance companies to make good on their promise.

Ray had a plan, a very workable plan, some might even say *infallible*, and he knew that if he made a success of it, he could pack up his bags in England and, with the sale of his house and the insurance money, pay off all his outstanding debts and, at an appropriate juncture, comfortably move down to Monaco, a veritable tax haven, and try out his luck on the roulette wheels of Monte Carlo.

All he had to do was execute the plan with expert precision, collect the insurance and – *hey*, voila! – he would be a rich man.

Not to mince words, yes, it meant killing his wife. But at least it should pay dividends and secure his future happiness.

It was after watching Jack Lemmon and Walter Matthau on the cable channel when Ray began planning his wife's 'accident', hoping for a massive payout in the event of her death.

Ray decided to set the plan in motion.

The French do not impose road tax on the motorist. Instead, unlike the British government who taxes anyone who owns a car, the French recoup the money with toll charges, so the more you use the toll roads, the more you pay, probably a more fair and equitable solution. These autoroutes are therefore quieter and less congested. Taking turns to drive, the Hudsons managed their journey from the ferry port of Calais, up in the north, to the southern tip of France, the Provence-Alps-Côte d'Azur region, in approximately eleven hours, spending just over one-hundred euros in toll costs. Exhausting though the drive down was, it was pleasant nonetheless, with the Hudsons stopping off at the rest-stops along the way, set at convenient regular intervals, these recreation areas a damn sight more picturesque than the busy British service stations and doubling as picnic spots. Very considerate. Ray had to admit the French really took care of their motorists.

It got palpably hotter the further south on the autoroutes they travelled. It was slow-going in the initial stages of the journey before the hours began to whizz by due to the monotony of the straight drive down to Lyon; beyond Lyon, once again time was perceived to pass more slowly as they repeatedly checked the clock, counting down the minutes, anticipating arrival.

As night fell and a huge red moon filled the evening sky, they passed the only place of slow crawl of traffic at Lyon, the centre of everything, including providing passage to Switzerland, Luxembourg and Germany. Ray let Valerie take over the steering wheel as he struggled to stay awake or keep in his designated lane, close to hallucinating from driver's fatigue, infringing on the next lane, risking an accident. Fortunately, however, they made it to their holiday destination in one piece.

The trickiest part of the drive was negotiating the narrow lanes up the hillside in the dark, the circuitous route forcing them to drop to a crawl and at times turn one-hundred-and-eighty degrees, making Ray remember former long drives across the Italian Alps, until their satnav located *Ancien Chemin de Piedmont*, where their holiday villa, VILLA AQUITAINE, was situated. These particular roads would be integral to his final plan . . .

They were greeted by birdsong on arrival, the chattering of birds in the evening not an uncommon occurrence.

Locating the key for the front door, as per their landlord's written instructions, Ray and Valerie crashed on their beds that night, sleeping soundly, until the dawn chorus awoke them.

They breakfasted on croissants, coffee and orange juice, left for them in the fridge, and they basked in the morning heat on the veranda. It was a different shade of sunlight here, a lurid brightness one did not experience in England.

Their property was as they remembered it all those years ago, with whitewashed walls and a terracotta roof, not unlike the other properties in the Var province, with ivy crawling around the windows. Beautifully carved doors with ornate iron handles. Baby-blue shutters for the windows to keep out the glare of the sun during the hottest part of the day. Ray and Valerie lounged on deck chairs outdoors, next to the swimming pool, in glorious, chrome sunlight, with Ray appreciating his surroundings: an estate of cypresses and pines, and real fig and olive trees and artichoke bushes not yet ready for harvest. There were even enormous aloe vera plants, easily mistaken for cacti, on the grounds of the property. It was, indeed, a fascinating setting. From the villa they occupied, built on a great height, Ray surveyed the ancient, wooded hillside across the way, descending into a deep gorge, and glimpsed the occasional glint of distant traffic. Shaped like an amphitheatre, the steep, densely-forested valley was cut through by the River Rion and concealed the village of Bargemon on the other side, where, according to Valerie, the Beckhams owned a magnificent, nineteenth-century mansion. Ray was equally very quick to point out that, despite his lack of any discernible personality and a penchant for tattoos, including a barcode on his neck in case he forgot who he was, David Beckham played a decent game of football and used to practise shooting free-kicks in the evenings. His wife, on the other hand, was a talentless *noise*, only good for miming, and not posh or classy in the slightest. Call up the paparazzi at the drop of a hat, like media whores, or sell their own line of perfume, as if anyone with any actual talent would do anything so chavvy. And, together, what on earth did they know about French culture? *Money does not buy you class or talent! I'm sure the villagers will be glad to see the back of these English hooligans!*

Claviers had a population of seven hundred at the last census. It was set at a height of six hundred metres, the hilly terrain mostly terraced with supporting walls called '*restanques*' planted with pines, olive trees and green oaks. When entering Claviers, one was met by the gutted shell of the ruined old mill. The route to Grasse had once yielded amphorae, coins, weapons and sarcophagi, showing activity here during the Gallo-Roman era. The Saracens were repulsed by the Romans in 972AD. The Spanish Arabs laid waste to Toulon in 1178. The constant danger of attack explained Claviers' strategic fortified hilltop position. The Provost of Frejus demanded taxes until 1289. The Church St. Sylvestre was sold at the time of the French Revolution in 1794 but eventually and rightfully returned to the commune as a place of worship. The monument to the Resistance in the centre of town was sculpted by M. Pernus, a legend in these parts, highlighting how Claviers had once been a particularly active centre for the Resistance during the Second World War. The original vast gate of the town was situated to the right of the *Office de Tourisme*.

Indeed, it was a beautiful part of the world, almost untouched by the passing centuries, capturing the cosiness of these hill-towns, this unspoilt Provençal village perched in the luxuriant valley, sparkling with its fast-flowing river and crystalline rock pools. One could safely drink crystal-clear water from the street fountains. Marseille took the full force of the Mistral as it breathed down the River Rhône, but Claviers received only its tail end. Tourists often indulged themselves in the vineyard circuit or learned about the many cosmetic and therapeutic uses of the wild lavender that grew in great abundance.

And in this ever-rolling ocean of green, impenetrable mingling of evergreens, cork, deciduous oaks, pine trees and a hundred species of ferns and shrubs, amidst the smell of lavender and honey, the clouds of butterflies, stray foxes, dormice, lizards and scorpions, lived another creature, almost unique to these parts.

This was boar country. This was a land where the wild boar roamed.

Sometimes, as darkness fell, the reflection of a car's headlights would be caught in its eyes. Once native to the oak forests and the spread of ancient woodland, wild boars, or *sangliers* as the French called them, had encroached on areas inhabited by humans. These tusked animals were spotted in town streets, rooting through garbage bins. Their foraging for worms, mushrooms and plant-life had gradually been surpassed by their love of maize and ripe grapes, laying waste to cornfields and vineyards. Since the boar hunts had greatly disbanded in recent decades, and boars had the ability to reproduce prodigiously, their population was wildly out of control. And they possessed a reputation for ferocity. The wild boars ran amok, tearing up lawns if one accidentally left the garden gate open ...

For a moment Ray thought he saw an obscure face peering down from one of the bedroom windows, but when he blinked it was gone. Nobody in the house but themselves, he knew, putting the illusion down to a trick of the light. Or a trick of his mind. Was his conscience telling him something? A sign of something terrible to come? A sinister *foreboding*?

"That's enough sunning ourselves," chirped Valerie. "Time to do what we came here to do. Let's explore . . ."

Claviers was one hour from everywhere. Valerie always observed their itinerary religiously, completing something akin to a travelogue. She was keen to explore the Côte d'Azur over the next few days in her usual disciplined fashion and jot down her experiences. Their adventure kicked off in Grasse.

Grasse, in the Alps-Maritimes region, was an old-fashioned place, seeming to be forever stuck in the sixteenth century, with winding streets and flights of ancient steps in the *vielle ville* ('old town'). The Belle Époque esplanade was complete with a white casino and grand bandstand at the central plaza, sheltering an antique globe and offering a panoramic view of the city. They visited the MUSÉE FRAGONARD, one of the star touristy attractions, and bought an Aladdin's den of expensive fragrances. Ray felt that if he didn't leave Grasse, the perfume capital of the world, smelling like a *parfumeur*, there was no hope for him. He successfully achieved his ambition, fully met Valerie's approval, as a true Lord of the [Nice] Smells.

Mougins proved to be the Montmartre of the South of France, a mix of art galleries and restaurants, set on a hill, so damned steep in places, Ray was afraid their car would roll back down. Mougins was where Pablo Picasso lived out the last twelve years of his life. He died there. The MUSÉE D'ART CLASSIQUE DE MOUGINS displayed a private collection of antiquities, beginning with Egyptian relics in the basement and going up through the ages with each floor, capturing the history and culture of the Ancient Greeks, Romans, Celts and Gauls in chronological order. Ray was greatly amused by a humongous marble phallus on display in a corner showcase but refrained from making any juvenile comments about it. Alongside the armour, weapons, coins, statues and open, standing mummy-laden sarcophagi, numerous sketches and paintings, contemporary and old, reflected the classical nature of the exhibits. *Dying Minotaur in the Arena* and *Bearded Man Crowned with Vine Leaves* by Picasso himself. *Bacchanale* by Chagall. Warhol's *Birth of Venus* in the company of Dali's utterly-surreal *Venus as a Giraffe*. Even Damien Hirst's peculiar *Happy Head* cropped up, a plastic skull splattered with a multi-colouring of gloss paints. Mougins was also an epicentre of epicurean dining, but Ray and Valerie had come too early to celebrate the annual *Festival Gastronomique. Maybe some other time,* thought Valerie out aloud. *Still won't be as intriguing as that rocking* Clockwork-Orange *cock!* Ray kept to himself.

Their artistic journey continued to the Côte d'Azur proper, and, in particular, Antibes, or as the Massilian Greeks called it, Antipolis. Across the bay, in the distance, stood the Garoupe Lighthouse, built in the mid-nineteenth century on the now-exclusive *Le Cap d'Antibes,* famous for its luxurious residences and grand villas. But Antibes was also home of the MUSÉE PICASSO, confined within the walls of the Château Grimaldi. Picasso – yes, that man again – stayed in Antibes in 1946, a prolific period in his life, and he donated many of his enduring works to the museum. The museum boasted a collection of nearly two-hundred-and-fifty pieces – sketches, paintings, etches, ceramics, sculptures and tapestries – but Valerie was disappointed by how one floor was dedicated solely to photographs of the man, going about his daily business, either socializing or spending time with his young wife, Françoise, and his children, Claude and Paloma, when these family photos could have been better presented in a book about his life. His most celebrated work, emblematic of his stay in Antibes, was *La Joie de Vive,* also allegedly a parody of one of Matisse's classics. His drawings *Satyre, Faune et Centaure au Trident* and *Faune Blanc Jouant de la Diaule* and *Le Chèvre* epitomized the pipe-playing fauns and mythical woodland creatures that permeated his work as he strove to re-imagine the Arcadian idyll. But it wasn't Picasso's works which Ray would figuratively take back with him. A contemporary artist in homage to Picasso had created a stack of smashed acoustic guitars shaped like a tree while another had taken a sledgehammer to the giant bust of a titan, giving it the impression of being split by a bolt of lightning, the two halves of the shattered face laid out over a pile of rocks. Ray also learned that it was Cézanne who bridged the gap between Paris and the South of France, the transition between the nineteenth- and twentieth- centuries, the man's remarkable artistic endeavours evolving through Impressionism into Post-Impressionism and setting the stage as a forerunner to Cubism. An unexpected discovery in the old town was the MUSÉE DE L'ABSINTHE. Whereas on street level it was a store selling olive oil, sirops and all manner of brands of absinthe, downstairs was a single-room bar hollowed out from the ancient Roman foundations, replete with old posters and memorabilia and antique equipment fundamental to the absinthe-drinking ritual, including a rare collection of fountain dispensers. They partook of some absinthe in the downstairs bar and Valerie admitted she did curiously feel like that Van Gogh poster, the Old Master holding up a bottle of Absente 55 as evidence, his face blurred into three different directions as he tries to shake off his hallucinations.

The Côte d'Azur was the playground of Europe, a beautiful stretch of coastline, set against the backdrop of the jagged peaks of the Alps, boasting superbly-maintained top-class resorts renowned the world over, magnificent promenades and gardens, amidst a plethora of historic villages and fabulous countryside, glimmering bays interspersed with rugged, rocky peninsulas and dramatic cliffs falling straight into the sea. Here, in the French Riviera, tourists rubbed shoulders with the rich and famous. It had attracted artists, actors and aristocrats for the past one-hundred-and-fifty years, the *Who's Who?* of History.

Cannes played host to its international film festival where Hollywood A-Listers descended en masse on the palm-lined BOULEVARD DE LA CROISETTE in May each year, staying in the iconic seaside hotels or the palatial homes they owned, throwing decadent, over-the-top parties. Cannes was a marvellous resort, superbly-located, but in contrast to the glamour of the star-studded Croisette was *Le Suquet,* the old quarter, its medieval buildings and cobbled streets leading up to the fortified chateau on the hill, originally built by monks and now a museum and once used by Alfred Hitchcock when he directed Cary Grant and Grace Kelly in *To Catch A Thief,* the sum total reflecting the suaveness and elegance of the French Riviera. The twelfth-century tower was supposedly haunted by the Man in the Iron Mask. The old quarter offered a fabulous panorama of the bay and the old port and offshore islands, the jetty moored by hundreds of yachts. Ray and Valerie camped out at the PLAGE DE LA CROISETTE, where they soaked up the sun and admired the huge sand Buddha someone had created on the beach. There were lots of babies in prams, wheeled around by young ladies, and Ray suspected that many foreign girls worked here as nannies for the well-to-do types. Dior, Gucci and Chanel had major stores here, but Valerie was very skeptical of their value. *I guess when they were young and their line of fashion first came out,* Valerie opined, *they probably produced amazing dresses, truly imaginative and innovative and honest works, but now their luxury goods are nothing special, just going through the motions, really milking it, relying on their designer name to sell something mundane and uninspired.* In the restaurant, Ray was amused by how the stupid, rich, loud-mouthed American tourists tried to boss around the French waiters, unaware that the locals were practically insulting them to their faces in the trustingly poetic tones of the native language.

Slightly farther afield, past Antibes, Nice was the biggest city in Provence, second only to Marseille, and the gateway to Monaco and the Italian Alps. Founded by the Greeks in 350BC and once a holiday destination for the Victorian aristocracy, who wanted to get away from the deep English winters, the famous PROMENADE DES ANGLAIS curved around the entire length of the Bay of Angels, itself captured beautifully by Raoul Dufy in his paintings, while old Nice consisted of a labyrinth of narrow streets and stairways, vestiges of its medieval past. The ruins of the old castle, destroyed by Louis XIV in 1706, was now the most famous public park in Nice, Castle Hill offering an inland coastal panorama of the Harbour at sunrise, the Promenade des Anglais at sundown. The boom of the noonday gun could be heard far and wide, a custom since 1860. The hot day was rife with palms and pergolas, amblers from every nation and senior ladies walking small dogs. The Hudsons explored the variety of shops and restaurants in their cultural pursuit of Nicois life. They experienced a little Jazz in the bars. They visited the MUSÉE MATISSE and MUSÉE MARC CHAGALL, synonymous with this city, their prominent, career-spanning collection of works for all to see. Of all the sheltered coves, rocky islets and long sandy bays Nice had to offer, the Hudsons plumped for the ritzy COCO BEACH. They even tried some delicious Pissaladière. When in Rome, as Ray suggested, or Nice for that matter. He reminded Valerie of a famous André Malraux quote: *There's always a need for intoxication: China has opium, Islam has hashish and the West has women*, as they could see laid out on the beach. Valerie had to agree with Charlotte Rampling's observations that French women had been made beautiful by French society: *French women are aware of their bodies, the way they move and speak, and so very confident of their sexuality. Righty ho, yah!* Ray casually agreed with her, keeping any smutty comments to himself, knowing that some day the world would be his oyster!

Saint-Tropez was on the other side of Cannes and promised another day of rest and recreation in the sweltering heat. Legend had it that St. Tropez had got its name after the martyr St. Torpes, who had been unjustly beheaded at Pisa by the Emperor Nero in 65AD and his headless body placed in a boat and cast adrift before getting washed ashore on the future site of the town. Once a fishing town, St. Tropez now berthed more luxury yachts than fishing boats at the old port, also referred to as the 'Billionaires' Harbour'. It was a chic resort favoured by celebrities and the super-rich, its bohemian side dating back to the 1950s. The international jetsetters, the pioneers of French New Wave Cinema and the *Yé-yé* movement had put it firmly on the map. It was now the land of playboys and heiresses, a backdrop to the world's most glamorous beach-party scene. The preserved old town still retained its charm, amidst the parade of glossy boutique shops and trendy bars. It proved to be another afternoon of sunning on the single-most important crown jewel of St. Tropez's beaches, PAMPELONNE PLAGE, which ran along the main peninsular. No seaside promenade, no snack stands, no souvenir stalls. Just fine, white sand separating the Mediterranean coastline from acres of scrub-covered dunes. Beach towels furled over their shoulders, the Hudsons rented out a cabana and a couple of sun-loungers and parasols and picked a spot on the white sands. Valerie found it extraordinary and liberating that nobody batted an eyelid when she took off her bikini top. Ray didn't complain. The ethics of 'free love' and 'clothing, optional' permeated the summers here. Valerie supposed the naturists had won the argument on topless sunbathing, despite the harsh condemnation about this 'indecent' practice from the Church and French officials in the days gone by. They were probably the same people who in Lyon, in 584AD, voted on whether or not women should be classified as 'human'. Of the forty-three Catholic priests and twenty feudal lords who voted after a lengthy debate, the results were 32 yeas, 31 nays. That is, women were declared human by *one* vote! Ray and Valerie marvelled at the naked flesh on display under the blazing, Mediterranean sun, ranging from the trim and beautifully bronzed to the bloated and criminally pasty. It was lovely out here, picture-book, the deep, turquoise ocean full of swimmers and canoes and pedaloes and wind-surfers. Ferry rides to St. Raphael and St. Maxime. By the end of the day, they were ready to return to their villa in Claviers. *You look very tanned these days, my love. Why is that?* Ray observed, in rhetorical amusement. Valerie simply smiled back at him while admiring her own gorgeously-golden flesh. *Ad usque fidelis*, Ray said, quoting the old town motto, which roughly translated as 'Faithful to the end'. Ray bought some Bandol he knew only *he* would be drinking. It was best to avoid peak times as one could easily get caught in the bottleneck of the single, popular coastal road going in and out of St. Tropez, the traffic practically grinding to a standstill.

Ray thought back to the famous 'Corniche' road between Nice and Monaco and how he would be taking it one day. *Soon.* Monaco oozed wealth. He longed to see its very attractive *Jardin Exotique,* the Grand Prix in May, the Casino at Monte Carlo. He wished to live there like the super-rich and experience the French high life. A true bon vivant, drinking the finest Chardonnay, Sancerre, Montrachet, Cristal or Cheval blanc 1947. For Monaco, however, he knew he would have to go it alone.

Once he murdered his wife.

Located in Saint-Paul-de-Vence in the Provençal hills, one might find the hotel/restaurant, LA COLOMBE D'OR. Built on a rocky outcrop and surrounded by its medieval ramparts, Saint-Paul-de-Vence was one of the oldest and most beautiful villages in the South of France. Once ruled by the Counts of Provence, the fairytale charm of the village was enhanced by its maze of cobbled streets, houses of ancient stone and wisteria, little shaded squares and fountains, gateways and porches and an outstanding Baroque church. The narrow high street brimmed with upmarket art galleries and boutiques. The cemetery to the south of the village contained the resting place of Marc Chagall. The city walls provided wonderful views over the surrounding hills and hinterlands, the vineyards of the Loup Valley and the coastline of the French Riviera.

The FONDATION MAEGHT was a world-class museum of modern art, showcasing nearly twelve thousand remarkable pieces. The building had been designed by a Catalan architect who had somehow reconciled the conservative with the contemporary as well as allowing some of these artworks to be integrated into the building itself – or *in-situ* art: the Giacometti Courtyard which displayed the Walking Man alongside numerous matchstick figures and the curiously super-skinny dog, the Miro Labyrinth which collected a variety of alien shapes, tridents and eggs, the tiny chapel which boasted a Romanesque statue and a Braque stained-glass window, the mural mosaics of Chagall, the sculpture garden and Pol Bury fountain.

But it was La Colombe d'Or, a few minutes' walk from the imposing north gate of the village, Ray and Valerie were most interested in, particularly Valerie. She wanted to dine in the same restaurant her heart-throb, Nigel Havers, claimed was his favourite eatery. She had loved Nigel Havers since his various memorable turns in *The Charmer* and *Manchild* and *Don't Wait Up* and had even watched him on stage, originally in the relationship comedy, *Basket Case*, in 2011, in which his character and the character of his ex-wife are thrown together after the death of their old, faithful family pet, setting up a series of home truths and hilarious happenings. More recently, Valerie had watched him in a revival of *Art*, a tale of three friends arguing over the merits of a ridiculously-expensive blank, white canvas by some fashionable artist one of their number has spent a small fortune buying for which he is derided, testing old friendships. For a man in his 60s, Nigel Havers looked bloody good and could still play the dashing bounder with an eye for the ladies. Valerie often dreamed of Nigel Havers whisking her away one evening to this particular restaurant and whispering his love to her over a romantic, candlelit dinner. Yes, she liked a bit of Nigel! Ray Hudson, she joked, would have to do for now!

The 1920s saw an influx of artists to this village, including pioneers like Picasso and Matisse, attracted by the exceptional light and the promise of board and lodgings in exchange for some of their paintings, which the local hotel entrepreneur, Paul Roux, put up on the walls of his hotel and which still remained to this day. On the wall was a plaque: *Ici on loge a cheval, a pied ou en peinture.* (Roughly translated: *Here we lodge those on foot, on horseback or with paintings.*) La Colombe d'Or was the place to meet during the war, and the post-war era brought the international glitterati and a fresh generation of artists, like Braque, Chagall and Miro. Yves Montand married Simone Signoret in Saint-Paul-de-Vence in 1951. The French poet, Jacques Prévert, visited Saint-Paul-de-Vence and never left. Bill Wyman had a home here. Donald Pleasance died here. Other famous celebrities associated with the village included Kylie Minogue, Elton John and Rod Stewart.

La Colombe d'Or was a contradiction in terms, a typical *maison paysanne* which also somehow boasted the artistic splendours of the 1920s and 1930s and the Bon Vivance of the 1950s and 1960s, a timeless merging between Life and Art. Curiously reminiscent of an old Parisian restaurant and soon to celebrate its centenary, La Colombe d'Or possessed a nice interior, with traditional décor. The fireplace bore the handprints of the people, who helped build it, and upon the walls hung a priceless collection of paintings bearing the signatures of Picasso, Braque and Miro, whilst its Michelin-starred restaurant could seat nearly two hundred customers across its main dining hall and garden terrace. The cuisine consisted of traditional Provençale fare, haute cuisine, consumed in the typical laid-back Provençal atmosphere. The friendly service of this family-run business, still carried on by the Roux family, made the experience even more worthwhile. M. Renard, the Maître D', seated Ray, in burgundy chino shorts, white shirt and sunglasses, and Valerie, dressed in a white floaty dress and blue espadrilles, in the large outdoor terrace, as daylight faded. Valerie's hors d'oeuvre consisted of salmon carpaccio with smashed avocado while Ray went for crab and lobster with mango vinaigrette. In terms of the main course, Valerie chose pan-fried turbot with shellfish emulsion and salsify-tossed salad, and Ray thyme-roasted rack of rabbit served with salted artichokes and a galette of potatoes. Dessert consisted of mandarin sorbet garnished with exotic fruit for Valerie, a platter of fine artisanal cheeses for Ray. *Bonne dégustations!* They welcomed the carafe of rosé with their three-course meal. The restaurant continued to fill up as they sat and night fell, until they were dining by candlelight under a sky full of stars and a romantic strawberry moon. The only thing missing was Nigel Havers.

M. Renard continued to cordially chat to the couple. He spoke about how the wild boars were getting bolder, causing a lot of havoc, only yesterday having ripped up the golf course. They needed culling. A sow could produce a litter of nine piglets, but the new generation of villagers was no longer interested in hunting them, putting too much emphasis on animal rights. If only we hunted them again, restaurants would be packed, the Maître D' advised. *Have you ever tasted wild boar? The succulent flesh, the strong gamey flavour, the rich juices? Slow-roasted wild boar with spiced Granny Smith apple jelly would be a sure-fire hit!*

As Ray and Valerie finished their meals and moved on to the espressos, the Maître

D' emerged from the back with a large bouquet of red roses, a bottle of Bollinger in a bucket of ice and a couple of gooey chocolate cakes, each with a tiny burning candle in the middle. Ray presented Valerie with the roses. "Happy Anniversary, darling!" he announced. The other patrons seated in the terrace shared in the celebrations with a warm round of applause and the heartiest of congratulations. Handshakes with strangers were in order.

"Oh, thank you, dearie!" said Valerie, her eyes lighting up, accepting the bouquet.

Ray explained he had set this up, rung ahead of their reservation and arranged for these flowers, the bottle of champagne and the small presentation cakes. "Twenty-seven red roses," elaborated Ray, "because I love you, my dearest wife . . ."

"They're lovely!"

"As are you . . ."

"Even if I develop bingo wings in my dotage?" Valerie said cutely.

"*C'est pas une probleme, ma cheriée,*" he lied and kissed her. "You will always be beautiful to me." *Enjoy the moment whilst it lasts,* he thought inside, darkly. *Shame you'll be dead tomorrow.*

Their Silver Anniversary spilled over into the following day. They spent much of the following morning in bed, making love, and drinking from a personalized luxury bottle of champagne – with their name on it. To celebrate this landmark, Valerie had gifted Ray with a Swarovski crystal clock, engraved with the legend: MR. AND MRS. HUDSON EST. 14/06/1992. Ray presented her with an exquisitely-framed, seven-inch silver disc, similar to those seen on the walls of record producers, but bearing the sentiment: VAL, MY BEAUTIFUL WIFE, DO YOU REMEMBER OUR FIRST DANCE? XX Val was deeply moved, and she redoubled her efforts in bed. It felt good making love to Val, with Ray wondering whether he would chicken out of killing her, just like the reason employers gave you a three-month notice period if you chose to resign was so that you could conveniently change your mind about leaving. Court-directed, two-year trial separations between couples operated under the same premise – and same *hope.* No, by the time the morning gave way to the afternoon and they emerged from their love-shack, Ray was still intent on wishing her dead. He didn't care if he was going through some kind of midlife crisis. A quarter of a century with the same woman was enough to want to kill her. The death of his wife would allow him to close this particular chapter in his life and turn the page, venture into newer, greener pastures. To quote Simone Signoret: *Nostalgia is not what it used to be.*

What they had been told was a classical music concert in the village square, where men often played pétanque or boules, turned out to be a local French classic rock cover band who churned out songs by Pink Floyd, Tina Turner, the Beach Boys and the Turtles. They proved to be better musicians than singers of English lyrics but were pleased the entire town had turned out to watch them perform. Ray enjoyed four hours drinking beer in the square, nodding his head to the tunes breaking out on stage, whilst Val drank cup after cup of relaxing chamomile tea.

Then, as evening approached and the music finished and the crowd dispersed, they walked back to their villa. Thoughts were already turning to the drive back to England. Ray expected he would in all likelihood be driving home all by his lonesome because Valerie would be going home in a coffin.

That early evening, they enjoyed lazing poolside. The lowering sun glared down at them, the blistering heat of the day showing no sign of letting up. The place crawled with a diversity of insect-life. Friendly houseflies and dragonflies and maybugs. Not just daddy longlegs but *French* daddy longlegs: *Bonjour!* Huge ants that ran off, panicking, if Ray prodded them, instead of biting him or spraying him with formic acid.

Valerie took a dip in the pool, and the temptation had always been to push her in and keep her head under, watch her flop around in the water until she drowned. *Only problem is she's a bloody good swimmer!*

She was not loth to remind Ray about how sport scientists rated various physical activities in three domains – Strength, Stamina and Suppleness – and how Swimming topped all sports. Squash came a close second, but the third highest-rated sport was where Ray had set his eyes on.

Valerie loved to cycle. She had brought her folding bicycle on this holiday and had been cycling every evening for about an hour.

"Too many cyclists coming out these days," she noted.

"You suggesting all cyclists are 'gay'?" Ray joked.

"No, silly!" Valerie changed from her swimwear into a sunflower dress. "It's just that the Var province has a popular cycling route in the summer." She checked her condition. "Only had one glass all day. Not in the least bit squiffy. Except drunk on my love for you…"

"I hope you're not the kind of cyclist who thinks they own the road, holding up traffic."

"No chance of that happening here."

"Of course not . . ."

As far as murder plots go, an ocean cruise might have been a better bet.

Apparently, two hundred people went missing every year from cruise-liners, never to be seen again. Their disappearance was attributed to accidentally tripping over the railing and falling into the cruel sea rather than even considering their nearest and dearest had deliberately pushed them over the side. *Yes, a perfect murder, I wager.* But Ray knew the authorities were getting wise.

Instead, he thought a cycling accident would be as good as any. It was bad enough steering a car around the hillside bends, afraid of what might be coming the other way. *But something as vulnerable as a bicycle. Struck by a car. A hit-and-run. Mown down, killed instantly or left for dead. The car quietly drives off, the crime unwitnessed by anyone. Simple, efficient, foolproof. Sure-fire!*

Ray had planned it for this very evening. *Tonight's the night, baby!*

Happy ridings! Ray had said, kissing her. He had followed her into the villa.

Valerie had returned the kiss, apparently none the wiser. *Thanks. See you soon.*

Not if I can help it, he thought. Instead, he maintained his smile. A reassuring smile. With a *cheerio!* and a wave, Valerie disappeared out the front door, unaware that tonight she may not be coming back.

Ray watched her go, feeling a momentary sense of sadness about his wife's impending doom. Their marriage hadn't been all bad, at least for the first decade, but Ray could no longer accept anybody cramping his style. Twenty-five years together and it had come to this. But the rewards that awaited him hardened his resolve and he breathed out a whistling sigh of relief, accepting the inevitability of his decision.

Does that mean I get your life insurance? he reminded himself, rubbing his hands with black humour. Full of glee, he popped open another bottle of champagne and poured himself a flute. To celebrate. Yes, make it look all innocent and legitimate, as if he were celebrating a very important anniversary, which in many ways wasn't so far removed from the truth. He put on some music, the Turtles who had inspired him, before he'd even set off down this particular gruesome road.

He imagined how oblivious his wife would be as she merrily cycled along the winding road down the hill. Maybe she would gasp at the car that would come perilously round the bend, too slow to see her, hitting her head-on. Or there might be a car hovering dangerously close behind her, as she cycled on, intimidating her, until the driver chose the right moment to speed into her and zoom off. And, of course, no witnesses to the murder of his wife. She didn't stand an outside chance. Ray might have cooked up the idea, but he would leave it to Hilaire Aguillon to work out the logistics. Ray had paid him well.

The impact would be fatal, the scene of the accident terribly ugly. A passing car would find her bleeding, broken body beside the twisted wreckage of her bike and call the Emergency Services. Maybe Ray should call the police because his wife had not returned from her bike ride and he was worried that something had happened to her. Or, perhaps, the police would visit him relatively pronto and break the bad news and, like the grieving husband, he would present as distraught, mourning the senseless loss of a wife he had loved and cherished unconditionally. I mean they'd only just come here to celebrate their twenty-fifth anniversary, of all things! At some point, in the coming days, he'd have to tell their son, Joel, his mom was dead. Joel was studying at Oxford, his University course paid for, like with most rich kids, by the Bank of Dad, because he was so utterly thick and useless. And when the Inquest was over, Ray could comfortably claim the insurance and live a new life. Pay off his debts, sell their house and live out the rest of his days in Monaco. Whatever the laws of chance dictated, he'd be ready.

"You started celebrating without me . . ." a familiar female voice spoke up from behind him.

Ray stopped dancing – he hadn't realized he was dancing – and spun round. He dropped his champagne flute; it smashed on the floor with a soft, tinkling explosion. Valerie was standing there as large as life, wearing her sunflower dress, her dark hair tied back into a ponytail. She looked flustered, sweaty, her cheeks possessed of a rosy glow. He tried to make sense of the unfathomable sight before him. "You're back!" was all he could muster on the spur.

"Of course I am," she responded, sounding surprised. "Why shouldn't I be?" She peered into his face, his half-drunk, dumbfounded expression. "You look like you've seen a ghost."

The Turtles continued to play on the hi-fi in the lounge, their brand of music cheerful and lively and summery.

Then, Valerie went out on a limb. "You weren't expecting me to come back, were you?"

Aside from the initial shock, the guilt written all over Ray's face was the most telling thing of all. "What makes you say that?" he ventured, but his voice was weak and unconvincing, the terrified squeak of a five-year-old who has been caught red-handed stealing candy.

"You see, dearest Ray, I *know* . . ." Valerie began, uncharacteristic hostility in her voice. "I've known for quite some time that you planned to get me run over. Make it look like an accident. You paid our landlord to carry it out."

The game was up, Ray realized. But his puzzlement persisted. "How could you possibly know?"

"Because Hilaire told me everything before we even embarked on our holiday," Valerie informed him. She paused for a moment before asking: "I thought you loved me."

"My wife is only worth loving in the dark or when I'm drunk!" Ray said cruelly.

It was an unkind remark, but at least Valerie knew now. "All men are pigs . . ."

"You think I'm a swine, a dirty rotten scoundrel?"

Valerie corrected herself, thinking of Plutarch's *Gryllus* in which the witch Circe has transformed Odysseus's companions into animals, and when Odysseus demands she turn them back to men, she grants one of the enchanted pigs the power of speech and it proceeds to convince Odysseus why pigs are more intelligent and virtuous than any human. "No, let me scrub that. Pigs are smart, sensitive and, most of all, *loyal*."

"If I'm so bad, if our marital bliss is just a sham, why did you stay with me?"

"They say three-quarters of all marriages are unhappy. I thought we were just another married couple having problems and we might work things out."

"More to the point, why would Hilaire tell you, betray me?"

Valerie came out with it. "You see, Rayby-Baby, I've been having an on-off affair with Hilaire!"

Her words slowly sank in. Ray stared at her, agape.

Valerie continued, more hurtfully now. "I had sex with him twenty-five years ago on our honeymoon, when we last stayed here. It was only meant to be a fling. To get it out of my system before I set off on the road to matrimony. That is, until I thought Hilaire and I could relive old times again. Where do you think I've been for the last couple of hours?"

Ray couldn't believe his ears. This was getting beyond crazy. He studied her. Valerie did look hot and bothered, but it was the distinct musky smell emanating from her which gave her away. She smelled strongly of sex. "I didn't know you were like that," he murmured shakily, utterly shocked.

Valerie was on a roll. "Everything happens for a reason. You're a loser! That's why the odds will always be stacked up against you. Living a lie is like playing a game of cards, playing each hand while trying to control which cards are dealt. But that's beside the point. You haven't been paying much attention to me for quite some time now. Even our anniversary was a sham. I know about your girls, your gambling, your debts. You're in quite a tricky situation with Mr. Sheldon, aren't you, up to your neck, in fact? I even know about the letter from the bank threatening to foreclose on our house." Valerie hesitated, positively relishing his discomfort. "You wouldn't have got anything, anyway, because I decided to raise the stakes and cover all bets. Didn't you ever learn the game is rigged and the house always wins? I changed the beneficiary to Joel in the event of my death. And myself and Hilaire were thinking: wouldn't it be a lot more convenient for everyone if the insurance company paid out to *me* instead?" She laughed. "Poor stupid Ray – not a clue . . ."

Her series of sickening revelations, culminating in that brazen, contemptuous laugh, was enough to set him off. Ray could no longer contain his fury. As she stood mocking him, a deep growl emerged from the back of his throat, and his right fist swung out and struck her hard in the face. The force of the blow caused Valerie to sway backwards and tumble to the floor, stunned. Her vision swam for a few seconds, but when it cleared, her hand went up to the left side of her face, registering the pain. The left eye and cheek were smarting and already starting to swell up. She wondered if he had fractured her cheekbone. Ray reached down and grabbed her hair and, straightening up, began to drag her by her ponytail across the terracotta floor, moving towards the front door with purposeful strides. "*You BITCH! You FUCKING bitch! You'll be laughing on the other side of your cocksucking face once I'm done with you!*"

Valerie screamed, reeling from the concatenation of pain arising from her scalp, her hair being tugged from its roots. But, even in this awkward position, being hauled like a doll, adrenaline allowed her to endure the agony and gave her clarity of thought; she managed to reach under her dress and retrieve the Swiss pocket army knife she had been concealing in her underwear. Unsheathing the small blade, she thrust it into Ray's left calf.

Ray yowled, dropped his weight, released his grip on her ponytail.

Valerie moved quickly. She knew their relationship had reached the point of no return. Regaining a modicum of composure, she scrambled over to where Ray sat howling on the floor, nursing his leg with both hands, and ripped the knife straight out of the calf muscle, in a freshet of scarlet, and plunged the blade directly into his throat, goring his voice-box and windpipe and scraping against his spine.

She scrabbled backwards and watched her husband in his death-throes. He automatically, mindlessly and frenziedly clutched his neck with a round-eyed, idiotic expression, producing bubbling, agonal sounds, the blade piercing the delicate structures of his throat, spraying the air in profuse, spasmodic jets of blood. Soon, he could hold himself up no longer and, as he choked on his own blood and his brain was starved of oxygen, he collapsed to the floor, inert, *dead.* The dark pool of blood framing his head continued to spread outwards.

Valerie sat quietly for a few moments, consolidating her thoughts, regrouping, staring at the limp, unmoving body of her husband, whom she had just been forced to kill, overwhelmed by the nauseating odour of blood and sweat. It was simple. He had been plotting to bump her off and when she had learned of his evil plan and confronted him with it, he had decided to carry out the deed anyway. She had killed him in an act of self-defence during the ensuing scuffle. The nasty bruise on her face would be evidence enough of the violent intentions her husband harboured. Any court in the land would let her off. Who could overlook the trauma she had experienced? Ray had been a poor excuse for a husband, a liar, a cheater and a womanizer, not only a wasteful man who had blown away all their life-savings on his gambling addiction, but a man who had also conspired to kill his own wife for the insurance money. She remembered his dishonest response to her at St. Tropez: *Faithful to the end.* The sick mendacity of the man. He had deserved what he got.

Valerie got up and staggered to the front door, her yellow dress blood-soaked and sticky. She emerged out in the open, ready to play the shocked, beaten widow with gusto, whose very own husband had tried to kill her. Outside, it was dusk, the still air promising a sultry night. She would call her lover after she'd rung the police.

The call would never be made, but the police would arrest the landlord, Hilaire Aguillon, who would be very forthcoming, disclosing the entirety of the murder plot and the extent of his relationship with the Hudsons, accomplice to both, duplicitous in the planned killing of one or the other, providing evidence of the money wired into his account by the husband and secret videotapes of his sordid affair with the wife with the view to blackmailing her. The case would take the term '*ménage à trois*' to a whole new level, according to the French press. Their neighbours across the Channel continued to be a source of mystery and vilification for the public, their sympathies resting somewhat with their fellow countryman, who had been unnecessarily sucked into the Hudsons' perverse business, the outrage of it being committed on French soil, and who, in the end, had proven to be the smartest. *Zut alors!* sounded the *cri de coeur* of the Gallic nation. *These English – what can you do? C'est la vie!*

As Valerie exited the house and emerged into the prevailing gloom outside, the low, animal grunt to her left abruptly stopped her in her tracks, constricted her heart. She looked down and learned to her horror she must have left the garden gate open. For into the grounds had wandered a particularly mean-looking brute native to these parts. It was a wild boar, and although it looked as formidable as the Erymanthian Boar of Hercules' Third Labour, it was frozen by her presence, ears pointed, the coarse brown bristles of its coat standing erect, canines protruding from its stubby snout upturned into vicious tusks. It watched her with deep, feral eyes that were now beginning to glow in the fading light, nervously waiting for her to react. The sight of it in such close proximity caused Valerie to freak out, loose an instinctive, piercing scream. Her mad shriek caused the boar to panic, more frightened of her than she was afraid of it, forced into combat mode, and in a high-pitched whine, it charged at her, curved, razor-sharp tusks pointed in her direction. Valerie did not have the luxury to protect herself as two hundred pounds of rippling muscles and sinews, concentrated more in its humped shoulders and neck than its hindquarters, ploughed into her legs, unbalancing her. As though realizing it might have done something wrong or as if conscience-stricken and ashamed over its assault of a defenceless woman, the wild boar fled the scene. It bolted out of the gate in a confusion of beating hooves and terrified squeals, trampling underbrush, desperately seeking cover, to finally disappear into the dark of the woods.

Valerie fell, the world whirling around her. A young Odysseus killed a boar to save his elders, but not before the boar wounded him on his leg, leaving a permanent scar. Valerie was not so lucky and went the same way as Adonis. What killed her was not the penetrating wound to her upper thigh, namely the severed artery, but banging her head on an unmercifully-pointed rock, hearing her own skull crack and splinter, cave in. She died instantly.

And the boar, whose fortuitous appearance had completed this drama, was nowhere to be seen. The French aptly called the whole sorry affair: *La Nuit du Sanglier* (or The Night of the Wild Boar).

Nobody could have imagined their holiday, celebrating their twenty-five-year anniversary, would end in this bitter, absurdly tragic way. *Everything happens for a reason*, as Valerie had ironically told her husband. While Ray lay sprawled on the floor with a blade imbedded deep in his neck, bleeding out, juxtaposed with Valerie's freshly-bleeding body stretched outdoors, gored in the thigh, her neck bent to one side almost questioningly, her shattered head resting against the offending rock, its tapered edge buried in her brain, both sets of human eyes open and glassy and unseeing, *Happy Together* by the Turtles peaked, filling the house with the sound of love and harmony.

Their first dance.

And last.

June 2017-July 2017

Temps Morts à Paris

"The first time I died I didn't like it, so I came back."

Johnny Hallyday (1943-2017)

What if there were no tomorrow?

Temptation beckoned. Damnation awaited. Inspired by a Frances McDormand-Sam Rockwell movie vehicle, campaigners demanding justice for the Grenfell Tower fire hired three vans, each plastered with a billboard to drive through the streets of London and cumulatively reading: 71 DEAD. AND STILL NO ARRESTS? HOW COME? After openly refusing to acknowledge the devastating winter bed crisis, Theresa May contemplated selling off the NHS to Donald Trump. Meanwhile, another couple decided to prolong their poor baby's suffering by dragging his doctors' decision to rightfully turn off his life-support machine through the Courts, at the Taxpayers' expense, for their own publicity and media attention. In the Middle East, Benjamin Netanyahu, the man who originally lobbied the Bush administration to unlawfully invade Iraq, faced serious bribery, fraud and political corruption charges. America once again descended into a familiar pattern of feigned shock, empty prayers and condolences, insincere Right-wing news blather and diabolical inaction against the financially-motivated gun culture, following yet-another tragic high-school massacre, scapegoating mental illness for mass violence. The Dow Jones slipped six-hundred-and-sixty-six points. Paris received a deep fall of six inches of snow and the temperature crept as low as minus-six degrees. And, in Montmartre, the English Rock band, the Mind Rippers, recorded their last studio album.

Deep in the Marais, the five-star address of east Paris, with its art galleries, designer boutiques and classy bistros, the swanky NARCISSE HOTEL AND SPA accommodated one Heath Axton, the lead singer of the Mind Rippers in the penthouse suite, a 'pied-a-terre' rooftop cabin, complete with private pool and sauna. If one was ever in the mood for love, one could canoodle in the monastic bedroom, where God was curiously absent. If one wanted to smash a few guitars, throw a TV or two out of the window or get a delightful glimpse of naked groupies leaving the hotel suite in the middle of the night, one knew the hotel proprietors would maintain discretion and look the other way. For Heath, it was strange coming from a Catholic household, where God was worshipped day and night, to enter the life of a Rock star, whereupon all faith was abandoned and God became nothing more than an expletive or cuss-word. The hotel was close to the Picasso Museum, where *Nude in a Black Armchair* might catch one's fancy, Picasso at the height of his creative powers. A painting for the true voyeur in which the model was not so much sleeping as *orgasming.*

But it was at the RUE DES MARTYRS, a twenty-minute ramble from the Marais district, where the Mind Rippers would do their work. Rue des Martyrs, a narrow stretch of road that sloped to the foot of Montmartre on the way to the Sacré-Coeur, combined heritage and prestige with the avant-garde. Tradition had it that Saint Denis, the Patron Saint of Paris, was beheaded here in the third century and subsequently martyred, from which the street derived its name. Montmartre had once been situated outside the city limits, where there was no tax on alcohol, which is probably why it originally attracted the creative and drinking types. People still claimed to see the ghost of Degas, who once painted acrobats at the local circus on the corner. Gustave Flaubert mentioned Rue des Martyrs in *L'Éducation sentimentale,* reputed to be one of the greatest French novels to emerge from the nineteenth century, and the street also caught the attention of his protégé, Guy de Maupassant for his novel, *Bel Ami.* It was here where Émile Zola set a fictional lesbian dinner club and François Truffaut filmed scenes for *Les Quatre Cent Coups.* An octogenarian entrepreneur had been running a transvestite cabaret, *Madame Arthur,* on this very street for more than half a century. There were fashionable cafés and epicurean stores and one-hundred-year-old bookshops. A five-room – not five-bedroom but *five-room* – apartment could easily set you back 1.2 million euros.

Rue des Martyrs hid a music studio, BOOMBASS, behind an old wooden door painted black. Nondescript and rather unimpressive on the outside, extravagant and plush inside. There was a certain deceptive, mirage-like quality to this perfect hideaway, built over three floors. Steps led up from the unattended lobby to a bunch of vacant offices. Down the hall was a kitchen and dining area. Further along, the ground floor was equipped with a small cinema and projection room for the arthouse cineaste, an architectural design partly borrowed from the Max Linden Panorama. Downstairs, a long corridor stretched along the basement to the soundproofed, state-of-the-art recording studio. The décor was distinctly Art Deco throughout with numerous vintage references. Velvet chairs and brass lights provided a retro-glamour. A signed portrait of the erstwhile Johnny Hallyday from his days of Heavy Rock hung on one of the walls, complete with his motto: TO EXIST IS TO INSIST! His eyes stared back with a predatory, almost catlike expression.

The Mind Rippers had booked the music studio, busy with producing their final album before they split up and went their separate ways. As was the case with Rock bands these days, it wasn't outside remote possibility they might decide to reform ten years down the line to pay off divorce alimonies and drug debts, but they would cross that bridge when they got to it. They were pretty boys who had originally burst onto the scene in 2002 as a reaction to the endless parade of boy bands whose aural sewage had destroyed the music business. Originally an unknown, Heath Axton had once been in the audience of a gig, where it is alleged he famously said: *The only way I'm going to stay at this concert is if I'm allowed to go up on stage and knock out a few tunes. Nick Cave had better let me on.* Nick Cave obliged, and Heath Axton's far-from-amateurish performance on stage kicked off his career. *Pure Experiences* was a cracking first album. But, like so many Rock bands before them, the Mind Rippers advocated the use of drugs in their music (hence the band's name), and their perpetual preaching of how drugs were cool culminated in a drug-fuelled riot, the sky-high crowd weaponized against the riot police, along with the deaths of six students at one of their concerts in 2006, leading to a decline in record sales and talk of them disbanding. Dreams of glory lost – nearly. They never did break up and they turned from glorifying drugs to producing lame riffs on love and loss, which did not do them any credit. That tragic, fateful gig was probably the reason why they never broke America or achieved worldwide fame. A couple of albums followed, met with lukewarm reviews. *The Moors* album was set on the Yorkshire Moors with Heath Axton managing to do a respectable cover of Kate Bush's *Wuthering Heights*. *Eldritch Tunes* was their experimental take on Lovecraftian lore, paying musical homage to Brian Lumley, Ramsay Campbell, Neil Gaiman, Robert Bloch, Clark Ashton Smith and H.P. Lovecraft himself. They rounded off that particular album with an interpretation of the *King in Yellow*, but the standout track in the collection was *Crouch End*, a musical adaptation of a short story by Stephen King which Heath Axton considered King's finest. Heath had once claimed he had read *Salem's Lot*, his favourite King novel, in one sitting, starting at dusk and eventually completing it at dawn.

Unfortunately, the critics did not view these last two albums as anywhere near a comeback and the albums died with a whimper. Their music was like a Land Rover stuck in a field: the wheels are spinning, mud is flying everywhere, but there seems no possibility of moving forward. Ennui set in.

Until the band turned their focus on Paris, that is. Yes, Paris, instead of London. London, as far as Heath was concerned, was a dirty, noisy, busy city, congested, expensive and swimming in Russian mob money. *Overrated.* Anyone with half-a-brain, in his opinion, would find Paris the superior city. The soul of the nation was expressed in the shape of Marianne, the Goddess of Liberty, and Paris wielded its global influence by upholding the French Republic's humanistic values of openness, freedom, equality, fraternity and solidarity. Lovers of culture, fashion and music would be drawn to the City of Lights, of Love, of Art and Creation, and a sojourn here would be an enlightening, romantic and life-changing experience for anyone who cared to visit. One could easily walk the grand boulevards and the winding medieval streets and negotiate the hidden passages of Paris, marvel at the astounding architecture of the towering buildings and magnificent cathedrals, explore the galleries and theatres and cafés and soak up the contented mood of the people and relaxed atmosphere of a city unto itself. As opposed to the regression of Brexit, the future of Britain lost on the playing fields of Eton, with the Leave campaign championed by social failures and funded by the Russians, there was a progressive evolution of civilization in Paris long since before the healthy disintegration of international borders. Victor Hugo once pronounced: *He who contemplates the depths of Paris is seized by vertigo. Nothing is more fantastic. Nothing is more tragic. Nothing is more sublime.* Just as Serge Gainsbourg had derived inspiration from '60s London for some of his classic songs, the Mind Rippers planned to contrariwise record some Continental Art Rock in Paris itself, with a slight nod to the recently-deceased Johnny Hallyday, hoping their final product would send the indie clubs rocking into the night and allow themselves, as a Rock group, to go out with a bang.

They were a three-piece outfit, like their heroes, the Canadian supergroup, Rush, who in their early days sounded very much like a bunch of kids jamming in the garage, having a whale of a time. Rush were pioneers of the experimental, hard and progressive rock scene of the 1970s, evolving their music in keeping with the times, eventually achieving admission to the Rock & Roll Hall of Fame late in their career. Heath had hardly been impressed with their later unmelodious, uninspired productivity, reflecting a band on its last legs, despite all the talent and creativity on display, until the group decided to disband and retire after more than forty years in the business.

Heath Axton was the frontman and lyricist of his own trio, yet whose 1980s voice had enough versatility to growl and snarl, if required. He was also the bassist, and a decent one at that, even if in the beginning he was so terrible a bass player that his bass guitar was never plugged into the amp on stage and he gave the illusion of strumming to a pre-recording of the notes and chords that he was meant to be playing live. He had something of Jekyll-and-Hyde reputation, just as intelligent and knowledgeable as wild and downright crazy, and he was the one who received the most condemnation from the Press following that concert disaster that resulted in the tragic overdose of those six students. Randy Fogle was the electric, acoustic and rhythm guitarist, a skate rat before he'd joined the band, complete with ponytail and hipster beard, and a man who had already fathered eight love children by that time, with three more to follow once the band had achieved a modicum of success. His Child Support contributions were phenomenal. Despite being the drummer and percussionist and the loudest of them all in the studio, Bald Burton 'Burt' Mountjoy appeared the most reserved of the three who valued his privacy and was silent partner to his wife, Dorsey or 'Birdy', of five years' good standing. Together, Burt and Birdy could easily have been the names of *Sesame Street* characters. The band did use sessional instrumentalists sometimes, particularly for synth work, if the band ever dabbled in a bit of electronica, but not often. They were also a band who lacked a road manager at present after the last one, Steve Blackmore, accidentally hung himself during an act of autoerotic asphyxiation, emulating Michael Hutchence's dying moments.

Their producer, Philip Prentiss, had once overseen two relatively successful bands in his prime, the all-girl Menstrual Jam and those goth boys, Buggered Rectums, whom he had primed and pitted against each other for the purposes of publicity and record sales. Both bands had eventually disbanded, but it was on the heels of the unexplained disappearance of Hendon Flack, lead singer of Buggered Rectums, that he had formed the Mind Rippers. Phil had always been the driving force behind the band. Paris was his idea, even if it might now be a case of Producer and Rock group winding down, if not going out in style.

The vocalist and instrumentalists occupied the live room, with isolation booths available, if necessary, but it was the 'control' room where the professional editing, sampling and mixing took place to optimize the depth of the bass, the crispness of the highs and the sonics of electropop, fine-tune the sound, make it mellifluous. In charge of the digital workstation and all the recording studio software for mixing the mic and instrumental signals was the studio owner and audio engineer, Christian Fleury, who had previously worked with the local bands, Air and Phoenix. The multitrack recording still required polishing, sound engineer and record producer working in tandem.

The console room had two other persons present, watching Heath croon and Randy and Burt jam. Birdy, raven-haired and beautiful, had joined her husband here. She was a Vegan and a teetotaller and had forcibly converted Burt into both. He still secretly drank and ate burgers, facilitated by Heath, when Birdy wasn't around to keep an eye on him. She was also a New Ager, which Heath didn't think much of. New Age practitioners tried to be progressive and liberal, but in truth their spiritual beliefs were lazy and stupid, not particularly well-thought-out, utter nonsense, a direct throwback to intelligent thinking, pseudoscience of the worst kind. Not that Heath would tell her that nor Burt – poor guy had been roped into copulating across ley lines to improve fertility, into believing he could cure cancer with crystals and into finding his Zen to strengthen his Mind, Body and Spirit.

Beside Birdy stood Harmony Stone, silently watching the action from the control room window. Harmony was Heath's old flame, whose relationship with him from early on could be best-described as 'on-off'. She admitted her parents had been hippies to have given their children names like Heaven and Hope, or Charity and Chastity. Or Harmony, for that matter. Heath considered Harmony an extraordinary woman. As far as he was concerned, she was not your average groupie. A real wild child, she was a person accustomed to breaking taboos from an early age. She knew how to court publicity – and controversy. She came to the public conscience after allegedly being the first girl to auction off her virginity on the Internet at the age of sixteen. She was a notorious boob-flasher and a prick-teaser. She was always up for it and many a night of wild, torrid sex had been had with this little, brunette minx, who possessed more than just a passing resemblance to a young Grace Slick. And Harmony certainly slicked gracefully. She was also a wealth of Rock'n'Roll knowledge. She spoke about the conspiracy against the Sex Pistols by the Establishment to actively ban their anti-anthem, *God Save the Queen*, from the radio waves during the Queen's Silver Jubilee. Harmony also stood by the very plausible notion that Jim Morrison, seriously overweight, did not die the romanticized death in the bath the world is so familiar with, his heart finally packing in after years of drug and alcohol binges, but instead died a lonely, embarrassing junkie's death in a seedy Parisian nightclub bathroom stall, after using a powerful brand of heroin, and his corpse was transported by a couple of henchmen to the bathtub in his hotel to be conveniently found by his girlfriend, Pamela Courson, thus avoiding the club getting raided by the police and losing its licence. Harmony was convinced she knew this, just *knew*, almost as though she had lived through it, which seemed a crazy notion in itself. But it was during that massive five-year hiatus, when the band was considering splitting up following those nightmare tragedies at the concert, that Harmony came to his rescue, when Heath had been guilt-ridden, drink-sozzled and terminally depressed in that hotel room in Oxford. Perhaps there was a certain truth to the expression: *The Devil finds work for idle hands.* How often does one hear of Rock stars who kill themselves, either intentionally or unintentionally, because they're just too burnt-out, the years of chemical abuse finally taking their toll, or since they've done everything one expects from a Rocker, tested the limits, they continue to seek bigger, more dangerous and potentially fatal kicks? Heath had, in his despair, streamlined in order to end it all, injecting into his groin like any hardened heroin addict, and it was during those ambiguous moments between life and death that Harmony was supposed to have knocked on for him, found him unconscious and called the Emergency Services, even if Phil later took credit for saving Heath's life. Harmony had saved him from near-death and Heath had checked himself into Rehab. It had been an uphill struggle getting clean and tougher still staying clean. So deep ran his addiction that coming off heroin made him feel like a child snatched from its mother's arms or like someone suddenly parted from the one they love. After visiting him a couple of times in hospital, Harmony had left and vanished from the Rock scene, altogether. And then, after so many years apart, he had spotted her, quite unexpectedly, on BOULEVARD HAUSSMANN. Whereas he sported Ray-Bans and a designer stubble and a quiff, hidden by a *Crocodile Dundee* hat with a raven's feather tucked into the band, wrapped up warm in leather, unrecognized by the French public, Harmony looked like a proper French girl, wearing a stripy Breton top and a black beret. Except it was only two degrees out, and with the wind blowing from the north, it felt colder. Around him, Heath admired the Parisian women who were, as usual, oh so elegantly dressed. Harmony claimed she had needed a break for a little while, distressed by his overdose, but she was back and excited when she'd heard rumours that the Mind Rippers were in Paris to record another album. So glad Heath had been to see her, he had taken her on a jaunty shopping spree at the GALERIES LAFAYETTE, with its bazaar of designer shops laid out all under one iconic dome, and, with his wherewithal, he bought her *Dior* perfume, a *Louis Vuitton* handbag, a *Gucci* dress, *Miu Miu* shoes and *Christofle* cutlery. *To err is human, to loaf is Parisian,* as that man again, Victor Hugo, once claimed. Then, after a quick bite, they came back to the music studio on Rue des Martyrs to complete the final session of recording that afternoon.

Wouldn't the boys be surprised to see her? *Harmony who?* they would quip, pretending not to notice her. *I thought you were single.* And the lads did just the same again this time round, pretended to ignore her, when he re-introduced her to them. A running gag, Heath considered, just their way of teasing him.

"That's a wrap!" Phil announced through the two-way communication.

"I should bloody well hope so!" replied Heath through the live feed. His voice was dry and croaky from his intense singing, from the multiple takes. It had been a gruelling session, but, at least, the week's work was done and dusted. The band had powered through the recording session like true professionals. Time now for the sound wizards to do their thang. The Mind Rippers put down their guitars and drumsticks and departed the red-padded live room, taking the door directly into the control room. Burt went straight for his wife, Birdy, who hugged him and kissed him on the cheek. Heath walked over to Harmony, who looked more like Grace Slick than ever, and slipped his fingers into hers. He supposed Parisians were more likely to listen to Starship than Jefferson Airplane, but there was always hope to the contrary.

"You were brill!" Harmony complimented her Rock-star boyfriend.

"A fantastic team effort, gentlemen!" Phil told them, equally pleased. A few murmurs of approval and handshakes between the men. *Good to work with you!*

"How has it turned out?" Randy asked the sound engineer.

"*Très bon!*" Christian informed him. And, indeed, from first indications, preliminary playback of the raw material sounded the biz. Just a case now of tweaking and making a few minor adjustments to the sound.

"Our love letter to Paris might even turn out to be our magnum opus!" added Phil confidently.

Heath, too, knew they'd done a good job. He hoped their record producer was right. The song selection had captured the sublimely wonderful things about this fine city, each track dedicated to a specific facet of Paris, through its history, culture and people.

Between the ten songs on the tracklisting, they had covered a lot of ground. Out of the first track, *Madame Guillotine*, about the coming of the peasant revolt, emerged the second, *Hail to the Chef*, the gourmandizing of food after the French Revolution. There were many reasons Paris was considered the culinary capital of the world. Following the Revolution, the chefs who once cooked for the nobility, now finding themselves out of work, instead turned their dab hand to catering for the masses which soon gave birth to the restaurant. Gourmet cooking was available to everyone. The Mind Rippers were even able to throw in a reference to Marie-Antoine Carême, probably the first celebrity chef and the man who invented '*haute cuisine*' and the five-course meal. Foodies would tell everybody that the ingredients, cooking techniques and presentation were of a much higher calibre in Paris. Think AOC. The staples of life in Paris were plentiful, including cheap baguettes (the lack of baguettes once one of the causes of the French Revolution) and croissants (crescent-shaped to symbolize the victory over the Ottoman Muslims) and various delicious patisserie desserts, cheese, wine, fruit and meat, all better quality, farm-grown and containing less chemicals or preservatives. It came some way to explaining why the majority of Parisians were slim, even if they smoked and drank a lot. Parisians ate small portions and did not snack between meals and certainly never overate, maintaining a steady weight. They walked everywhere and took the Metro stairs daily (greeted by accordion players busking on the trains) and kept regular appointments with their pharmacists (who had suddenly taken on a whole, new health-affirming status). The French were the first nation to market their refreshing and health-giving mineral water. Their café culture was one of the truly great pleasures of being in Paris. There was something relaxing about sitting back, enjoying a café au lait and watching the world go by. Losing one's sense of urgency. This *laissez-faire* approach to life was conducive to health and longevity.

The Duranduranesque *Vogue Redux* was both a fashion statement and a salute to the Champs-Élysées. The French were recently voted the most fashionable people in the world. Running concurrently with their cuisine, Paris was deemed the fashion capital of the world, overtaking Milan, with Champs-Élysées being the epicentre of fashion. Champs-Élysées itself was regarded by some as the most prestigious thoroughfare in the world, as renowned as New York's Fifth Avenue for its shopping, sophistication and refinement. Its famous designers forged some of the funkiest and super-stylish costumes of high fashion, using the finest, seductive materials and creating endlessly attractive designs to build an enduring wardrobe of tailored masculine cool and unique feminine chic, sealed with a kiss. Where else, but in Paris, would one see a Chanel store on every street corner? Champs-Élysées was regarded by some as the most expensive real estate in the world and one paid for the privilege of parking one's *derrière* there with a ten-euro Coke.

The Artist Awakened by Absinthe was a quirky Rock number about wormwood, the precious constituent of absinthe, which was a popular drink among the artsy crowd of the Belle Époque era. Thought to spark the imagination of the artist – and Paris was an important centre of the Art world – absinthe was soon condemned for its sedative and devastating 'mind-rotting' effects, leading to its infamous ban in the early part of the twentieth century until restored to public access at the start of the twenty-first century.

Only French Women Know How was an *Yé-yé*-flavoured ode to the glorious, much-desired women of France, of Paris. Harmony notwithstanding, Heath loved these French birds with their stylish dress and the naturally olive tones of their skin. The French New Wave had introduced such women to the world as Brigitte Bardot and Jeanne Moreau. Even today, unlike Hollywood, such iconic actresses as Catherine Deneuve, Isabelle Huppert and Charlotte Rampling were treated like royalty and still commanded strong film roles, never relegated to bit parts.

Rock the DJ, borrowing the BPMs of French House music, explored the local Jazz scene which first emerged after the G.I.s from Harlem stationed in Paris introduced Jazz to the Parisians shortly after the First World War. Yes, these Frenchies knew how to boogie. The Nazi occupation during the Second World War meant the music scene went underground, which led the Parisians to invent the '*discothèque*', and the DJ was born.

Les Enfants Terribles paid tribute to Serge and Johnny. Particularly Johnny. Johnny, whose body of work the rest of the world would posthumously discover, unlike Serge Gainsbourg who was already world-renowned. Johnny Hallyday broke the classic '*chanson*' tradition in the 1950s by singing Rock'n'Roll and quickly became known as the 'French Elvis'. His five marriages and his drinking and partying and drug use maintained his 'bad boy' image until his recent death from lung cancer at the age of seventy-four. He sold more than one-hundred-and-ten million records and was reportedly seen live by an estimated twenty-eight million people during a career that spanned more than half a century. His recordings went gold forty times and platinum twenty-two times in France but barely sold a copy abroad. Hundreds of thousands of fans lined the streets of Paris for his funeral, where President Macron described him as a 'national hero'. Johnny Hallyday left everything to his forty-one-year-old fourth wife, and one can only guess his older biological children must have been seriously pissed. The Mind Rippers, with Randy on a rare, seven-string electric, gave Hallyday a Classic Rock-tinged eulogy not far removed from *Allumer le feu*. RIP.

The slightly lower-key tracks, *Silent Inhabitants of Père Lachaise* and *Love on the Seine*, segued into the final track, simply titled *Macron*. Whilst back in Britain the economy would continue to worsen, wages would remain stagnant, homelessness would rise, prisons would stay dangerously overcrowded, the transport system would crumble, the NHS would desperately gasp for more cash in the government's 'Survival of the Fittest' approach to healthcare, and the DUP would continue to milk it, full of their own self-importance, as it took the Tories to ransom, and the British politicians continued to lie, almost all of them, almost all the time, the Mind Rippers congratulated the French on refusing to be swayed by the flotsam known as the Far Right and electing a remarkable, centrist unknown as President, who was young, sexy and dynamic and, mommy issues aside, married to his former, much-older Lit teacher. The Mind Rippers imagined what it must have been like to be Emmanuel Macron walking the private gardens in the Champs-Élysées in contemplative solitude on Election night . . .

Philip Prentiss considered various names for their yet-untitled album, *Rock Stars in Paris*, perhaps, but the firm favourite so far, as suggested by the studio owner, was *Temps a bascule à Paris. Rocking Times in Paris.*

"I would suggest a farewell concert at Place Vendôme," Christian advised the band.

"The swansong," Phil agreed.

"I suppose it would be a nice way to go out," replied Heath. "We'll check our calendars." He looked at the others, thinking about the here and now. "Gentlemen . . . and ladies," he announced, bowing to the two women in the room, "*Maxim's* for dinner and party back at the penthouse suite." *And private jet from Paris le Bourget to London City Airport tomorrow evening once we've recovered from our hangovers!*

"Yes, let's paint the town red," seconded Randy with unrestrained enthusiasm, "and get some chicks who want to spend the night with a Rock star."

He received a silent look of disapproval from Birdy.

Suddenly, an unfamiliar man, with short, bleach-blond hair and tattooed all over and carrying a tan briefcase, entered the control room. "*Bonsoir tout le monde!*"

"Right on cue!" declared Christian. "Good timing!" he told the strange man. To the others, he introduced the man. "But first, meet Patrice Vassely, our local drug dealer."

"*Fuck!*" was Randy's reaction.

"Indeed . . ." said Heath, while the others nodded at the newcomer.

"Not for us, thank you," Birdy immediately declined, speaking on behalf of her Burt, too.

"Good, more for us!" noted Randy.

"I thought I should treat you, gentlemen," explained Phil, "in the good, ole Rock'n'Roll tradition. To celebrate your final accomplishment together. One last tango. Christian, here, knows the contacts."

"*Mon plaisir . . .*" stated Patrice amicably.

"Let's not keep the man waiting . . ." remarked Randy, already looking forward to a night of serious binging. Like the drug dealer, these were his peak hours. "Rock'*n*'Roll. Rock *and* Roll!"

"Innit?" Heath winked at Phil. "You're quite the enabler of your cash cows. Keep the talent happy!"

Phil returned the wink. "Absolutely! Gotta keep that money machine rolling . . ."

"Never too late to celebrate *liberté, egalité* and *fraternité*," Christian concurred with encouragement.

The group of people moved proceedings to the comfort of the large live room, amidst the silent instruments, and brought down chairs and a couple of tables. Its crimson, cushiony walls made Heath think of a human heart.

Patrice had everything for a night of partying in his briefcase: amyl nitrate, marijuana, cocaine, speed, acid, ecstasy, with lashings of wine and champagne and whisky and absinthe. Or maybe *not* everything. He could only produce tablets of DFI18 instead of heroin.

"What happened to the brown sugar?" asked Heath, sounding a little disappointed.

"There's currently a supply shortage in Paris," Patrice informed him. "There's a large shipment of heroin coming in from Morocco in the next few days. I'm afraid you'll have to do with what I have for now."

"Don't worry, Heath," Harmony interjected. She pulled out a small, clear polythene bag from her jacket pocket, filled with a dirty-brown powder, taking Heath completely by surprise. "*Fait accompli.* I came prepared."

"Jesus H. Christ, Harmony," exclaimed Heath, "you're an absolute star!" *My heroine offering heroin! You can't make this up!* He took the little brown bag and the necessary paraphernalia from Harmony, who never seemed in short supply, and slipped them into his pocket. He planned to use it very soon. "You should charge corkage," he suggested to the studio boss, Christian, who just smiled at the quip.

Cigars were smoked and champagne drunk – *Only the good stuff,* in Randy's opinion – before the band members proceeded to the harder stuff. In the meantime, there was *citron pressé* for Burt and Birdy.

The place was already beginning to get rowdy and everybody knew it was going to get messy. Important issues, however, needed to be discussed. Under the influence, of course. Aside from the final concert Christian had spoken about, whether or not it took place, the members of the Mind Rippers were soon either to start solo careers or pack it in altogether. Already tipsy, sipping from his whisky glass, Heath approached Burt and Birdy. "Valentine's Day is nearly upon us. What are your plans for the season of romance?"

Birdy answered for him. "We always watch *1984* on Valentine's Day. You know, Richard Burton and John Hurt."

"Yes, I'm familiar with it. Weird choice. You must be the horniest couple never to have sex!"

Birdy wasn't impressed by his remark. "If you must know, Burt's thinking of giving it all up and adopting a Chinese baby . . . aren't you, dear?"

Burt remained mute, averting his gaze, and looked a little morose.

"And before you bust Burt's balls," Birdy told Heath, "always remember drink provokes the desire but takes away the performance. *MacBeth*."

"Consider me reminded," Heath replied. "I think it when I'm drunk – or *high* – and write it when I'm sober, if you must know . . . But I guess you're right. Time for the wild man to settle down like a responsible adult and mourn the end of the party."

"You speak for yourself!" Randy joined in, grinning broadly. One hand carried a tumbler of absinthe, the other a joint. "For me, the party will go on forever . . .!"

"Rock on!" exclaimed Heath.

"Don't encourage him," advised Birdy coldly. "He's got a lot of children's mouths to feed. Otherwise, all the mothers of his children will sic their lawyers on him!"

"Don't I fricken' know it!" Randy groaned, suddenly brought down to earth. "Why you crowding my headspace?" He turned to Burt. "Tell your woman to stop giving me jip!"

Burt did not speak, just smiled sheepishly.

"Because you're on *Candid Camera!*" chirped Birdy. *Bright as a thrush,* thought Heath. *Just like the itching kind, down below . . .*

"I'll give you *Candid Camera!*" Randy remarked, tipping her a sordid wink. "Like photography, do you, Mrs. *Mount-joy,* nudge-nudge-wink-wink?"

Birdy did not care for the *Monty Python* reference nor the deliberate syllable-separation on her surname and the emphatic double entendre contained within. "Don't even think about it, buster!" she warned Randy.

Burt said nothing.

"As requested by Randy over there, we've booked some ladies for later, back at the hotel," Phil announced. "They'll be waiting in the wings until you fellas are done here. We can always take the party back there."

"New cities, new ladies, never gets tiring," Randy said gratefully. "I always look forward to these sexual free-for-alls!"

However, Heath decided to tease Randy, ignite some paranoia. He deliberately stared at that scab on his lips. "Sorry to make you self-conscious," which was Heath's intention all along, "but it looks like that cold sore's about to erupt all over your face. I bet you're wishing Burqas were in fashion."

"What the hell is this?" Randy demanded with frank suspicion, suddenly confrontational. "Do you want me to start? I've a right mind to pick up my valise and get the fuck out of here!"

Heath enjoyed pushing him. Randy wasn't a violent man. "No groupies for you tonight. Keeping away from you. You're diseased, man! Blood bogies up your nose, now a cold sore on your lips! Who's going to want to kiss you with that thing on your face?"

But it seemed Randy was not going to fall for the bait that easily. Somehow, he managed to take a step back and simmer down. Probably on account of the weed. "All health awareness goes out the window once the girls learn I'm in a Rock band. You'll be amazed how many girls let me eat them out with that thing on my face!"

"Always nice to get down and dirty sometimes!" Heath replied, looking at Birdy, who frowned and ignored the comment.

"A little hornswoggling never hurt anyone!" Randy recounted an old anecdote. "You know I once had sex with this girl for an entire afternoon, and her husband was sat in the car, waiting outside the whole time! Besides, I love getting those girls absolutely *fucked*, beyond salvageable, never to remember my face!"

Birdy turned away in disgust. Harmony just smiled politely. "Hey, a little decorum, please," Heath chastised Randy. "There are ladies present . . ."

Randy grinned. "Just spreading the love!"

"Man, you make Harvey Weinstein sound like a saint!"

"I guess Harvey Weinstein's wife left him when she discovered she was the only woman he hadn't tried it on with!" Randy joked, mocking the man once deified, now utterly vilified for his decades of repeated, horribly-abusive exploitation of power, movie starlets his victims. But then a frown crossed his forehead. "Nature calls." Clutching his backside, he stumbled out of the room. "Back in a tick."

Christian and Philip continued chatting over champagne. Burt and Birdy silently sipped their sugary lemon water. Having unloaded a good proportion of his wares, Patrice decided to do the moonlight flit. Giving the group his best wishes and a very friendly *adieu*, he was gone. And Harmony stroked Heath's quiff and lovingly smooched his cheek. She whispered into his ear. "What if there were no tomorrow?"

Heath looked at his muse with a puzzled expression, the woman whose presence his friends refused to acknowledge for their own amusement. "What do you mean?"

"Napoleon once told a young soldier in his ranks, a new kid on the block: *Tomorrow, you will know fear . . .*"

But Heath's attention was abruptly drawn away, distracted.

Randy came back, much worse for wear and reeking of shit. "Crapped my pants! But I cleaned myself up enough. Took too much acid. I saw the evidence in the toilet."

Heath played along, not missing the terrible odour lingering in the room, the others beginning to notice it, too. "You *think* you see the evidence in the toilet. You're suggestible."

"Is that why I'm seeing tentacles in the toilet?"

"A tentacled thing trying to crawl out of the bowl?"

Randy rambled on, not abandoning his non-sequiturs. "Two gay men. One wanted to die and offered to be eaten by his cannibal lover. Chopped off his own penis, which the other man fried in garlic oil before consuming it. True story, man, could only happen in Germany!"

"*Sacré bleu!*" said Christian, reeling more at the stink than the story. "Not cool!"

But Randy had gone off on one of his blinding rants, random as can be. "We're getting way too Frenchified! You'd better watch out for those fucking Huguenots, coming over to England from medieval France, religious heretics, doubting transubstantiation, questioning the symbolism of the Eucharist . . ."

"What is the *imbécile* talking about?" Christian exclaimed, mildly offended by Randy's drug-addled, racist nonsense.

Randy's erratic, unpredictable behaviour always had a familiar root cause. "The man's trashed!" Heath reassured the studio owner with a smirk. "He'll get a grip . . . *eventually*. Or lose it altogether!"

At that moment Randy threw up, a jet of projectile vomit splattering the padded wall.

"Aren't I glad Burt decided to leave this racket?" Birdy stated, utterly revolted. Her husband's maudlin expression suggested he didn't quite share her sentiment.

As Napoleon told one of his lowly, inexperienced soldiers: *Tomorrow you will know fear . . .*

Seating himself comfortably behind the drum-kit, knowing that Burt wouldn't mind one bit if he borrowed his throne, surveying the array of percussion instruments and the chamber beyond like a king, Heath dug out the small polythene bag from his trouser pocket and brought it up to the light. He grinned wickedly. The bag contained a dark brown powder, enough, he calculated, for one session.

Stages, he thought. *It's all a matter of 'stages'.*

The rest of the paraphernalia he plucked from the same pocket. He emptied the entire contents of the bag onto a fresh spoon, squeezed out a few drops of alcohol from a small pipette, then applied the flame of his Zippo from underneath. The heat dissolved the brown powder, quickly turning the mixture into a boiling, bubbling oil.

Most people simply go for champagne and a cigar; I prefer to celebrate with a different kind of fix. When it comes to getting high, it's always about stages. A few joints for starters, followed by a bottle of one of the finer single malts, rounded off with a fragrant sample of heaven direct from the poppy fields of the Khyber Pass. My take on a three-course meal. My girl by my side. What more can a man wish for?

Heath tied a short length of rubber tubing tightly around his arm, watching his veins bulge outwards. "Aren't you going to join me?" he asked Harmony, who was looking on expectantly, almost avidly.

"I like to watch," Harmony told him, this coming from the exhibitionist. "Don't fight it. Just let it happen."

"Randy's all about the effects. I'm all about the experience, as any half-decent Explorer of the Golden Brown will attest to."

Permission granted, he threw caution to the wind. *One last tango, one last spin of the dice. For old times' sake.* Using a fine-bore insulin syringe, he drew up the dark oil and, bracing himself, pushed the plunger, injected himself. *Allumer le feu*, came Johnny Hallyday's commandment. *Yes, crank up the dial to eleven.* The effect was almost instantaneous. Heath felt the needle pierce his vein, felt the stuff enter his bloodstream to go rushing onwards like a speeding train to Brain Central.

A wave of euphoria engulfed him, exploded through his body and blossomed outwards like a summer flower. His heart slowed, his respiration slackened, his senses dulled, his mind clouded over.

Been a while . . . he considered, filled with an impossible sense of well-being. *God, it feels good! Sure hits the spot!* Nothing else, in his opinion, compared to the exhilaration of a good hit. He always appreciated the love delivered from the spike of Morpheus. *This has got to be better than sex, present company accepted.*

Escapism was his life. It explained why he dabbled in drugs, even if he had to convey a certain image as a Rock star. Drugs took you places without you having to so much as move a muscle. No hard work required of you, no worries to bring you down; just sit back and enjoy the ride. Heath was an expert in the art of escapism. He liked escaping. He liked it just fine. Heath sat, sprawled, in his chair, feeling the heroin work his system, feeling himself float and drift, his eyes glazed, a big inane grin plastered all over his face. He giggled at nothing in particular. The room dissolved. He was lost in another world, a haze of narcotic bliss far removed from the rigours of reality, from the constraints of time, from the sight of his muse and his record producer and the mad vision of Randy flying high on a different kind of drug, tripping his head off, trying to paint the wall with his own puke. Heath hardly noticed, enjoying his present state of apathy. *Sometimes you just can't beat good old-fashioned sloth, dope-induced and guilt-free. Would you call it rapturous joy or joyous rapture or both?*

Float and drift, float and drift . . .

He did not know how long he had been in his zombified state.

Time sure does fly when you're having fun, baby, he concluded, yawning loudly. All of a sudden, he felt tired, extremely tired . . . tired enough to want to close his eyes. *Too much excitement for one day,* he supposed, finding himself unable to stay awake. *Need to close my eyes. Just need to close my eyes for one moment . . .*

So Heath did exactly that. All blissed out, he slumped forward across the drums, buried his face in his arms and shut his eyes. He nodded off. He napped, and soon his nap resolved into a deep sleep, but not before Harmony's words floated round in his mind: *What if there were no tomorrow?*

"I hate to break up a party . . ." Heath heard someone say. He thought the voice sounded like his record producer, Philip Prentiss. But he couldn't be sure.

Heath didn't know how long he'd been out, but it was six in the morning by his watch. Awaking from his dreamless sleep, he realized he was sprawled across the drums, the ceiling spotlights still on and shining in his direction, causing him to squint his eyes. He groaned. His body ached all over. His neck was as stiff as a board and his head throbbed dully. He had nodded off alright and, judging by the aches and pains, probably assumed the same posture for hours. But presently it was cold. Very cold. *Unnaturally* cold. So cold in fact that his breath condensed into mist immediately on contact with the surrounding air. Had the heating system packed in or something? Otherwise, where did this perishing cold come from? Getting rid of his hangover, however, remained his primary concern. True, he had fallen off the wagon last night, but, as was always the case, he was convinced he could jump back on. Shivering, he rooted through his pockets and produced a small vial, the same vial the drug dealer had given him the night before. He extracted two tablets of DFII8 and dry-swallowed them. They would begin to work as soon as they reached his stomach. As for his general aches, nothing that a hot shower couldn't cure. A fresh change of clothes – black for black, like for like – and he'd soon be feeling like his old self again, ready for his scintillating flight back to London and any other little challenges the day might bring.

Presently, he was alone in a room full of dormant guitars and amps and drums and mikes and feed wires. Nobody else about. Nobody at all.

Probably took the party back to the penthouse suite at the Narcisse Hotel, assumed Heath. *Left me here in peace, all on my lonesome. Thank you very much!*

There was a crazy attempt to daub an abstract on one of the padded walls, Randy having had one of his insane, hallucinogenic experiences, the vomitus now dried-on and hard. At least, he hadn't used his own excrement in this instance. Still, it would take some serious cleaning-up.

"Better start making tracks," Heath said out aloud. He got up from behind the drums and almost collapsed to the floor. His smile faded. He grabbed the nearest drum for support, barely in time. His legs were numb from the waist down (exactly what he didn't need right now), having fallen asleep. Annoyed by the inconvenience, Heath went about the earnest business of massaging his legs, trying to get the blood circulating again. *It's just one thing after another! First the deep chill in this room, then the absence of my band members, now this! Won't someone please give me a break?*

Sensation slowly returned to his legs. Soon they were crawling with pins and needles. Heath gritted his teeth, enduring the agony. He stayed put until his legs could bear his weight adequately. Grateful that he could finally walk again, he made for the door. His hangover, too, had abated.

The console room was empty, the hi-tech recording and mixing deck sitting silent. Outside, in the basement corridor, the lights were on. Nobody about. No sign of activity whatsoever. The hush, when he listened to it, had never seemed so loud. His nervous apprehension grew more acute as he wandered down the corridor and came to the stairs, where he hesitated a moment. He bounded up the staircase and arrived at the lobby, which was also deserted. He tried to decide which way to go. The cinema room on the ground floor or upstairs where the offices were located.

He headed for the main entrance.

He pulled open the front door and wandered outside . . .

He was suddenly stricken with shock.

Rue des Martyrs was completely deserted. *Forsaken* would be a better descriptive. Even at six in the morning, there should have been signs of life. Except there was nothing. No people, no presence of cars, no birdsong – an impossibility in itself. Just the empty, lifeless shells of apartments and shops and the last residue of snow and ice on the ground, all bathed in a dull, grey preternatural light.

Nothing but bleak, unbroken silence.

Like someone had asked the genie-of-the-lamp for Peace on Earth and the genie had granted the wish as literally as he could.

As if all the population of Paris had been whisked up to the Mother Ship.

Like Reality itself is winding down . . .

Clueless, confused, speculating absurdities, Heath returned to the safety of the Boombass music studio and the cold, tomb-like oppressiveness of the silence contained within its confines. He took the staircase upwards, full of single-minded determination, yet knowing full well he would not find anything there, either. He was not going to be disappointed. His quick dekko yielded nothing. Completing a thorough clean sweep of the long-vacated offices, he took a detour to the equally-deserted cinema downstairs and wandered back along the ground floor of the building, where the coldness grew definitely more severe and the silence gigantic and menacing, the quietness of a monster that is looking at you but unseeable itself, biding its time, purposely waiting for the right moment when you least expect it, when it will make its presence known and send you shrieking to the very brink of madness. The inexorable silence harrowed his soul, its keen watchfulness like that of some unseen predator into whose lair beings of flesh-and-blood ought not to tread.

"Where the hell *is* everybody?" The sixty-four-thousand-dollar question.

Heath made his way back to the lobby at a complete loss. The rest of his crew had vamoosed, his muse had abandoned him and all the inhabitants of Paris had mysteriously vanished, for some inexplicable reason leaving him to this interminable, accursed silence. The general coldness, stillness and emptiness were so intense and his sense of isolation so immense, Heath was struck by an overwhelming sense of dislocation. He could not have felt more alone in his life. Instinct told him that something strange and unforeseen had happened during the night. *But what?* Heath fought against uncertain fears, though sure that the nearness of another person would have been a godsend. Except there was nobody else here but him. Nobody at all. The silence spun out limitlessly, refusing the slightest break in its continuity, the tiniest crack. It marked the apparent suspension of all life and all movement, so much so that Heath felt like the last known survivor of some post-apocalyptic future. The enveloping cold could have been the resultant chill of a dark, nuclear winter.

What if there were no tomorrow? The words of his muse, Harmony Stone, echoed inside the mausoleum of his mind, and he wondered if in some odd, subconscious way they held some kind of earth-shattering significance. Shivering, Heath paused by the basement stairs, mentally drawing up a workable plan of action. Unable to.

"One hell of a comedown . . ." sprang a vaguely-familiar voice from behind him, causing Heath to start.

He spun round, startled, and uttered a profanity in French. "*Baise moi!*"

The hallway was full of ghosts. Not just ghosts, but faces he recollected from his childhood and his father's record collection. Faces belonging to Rock idols he had admired in his formative years, his interest stemming back to the tale in which Robert Johnson met the Devil at the crossroads and he returned incredibly transformed from a novice guitarist to the greatest guitarist in the world, a virtuoso. *I'm not fucking worthy!* John Lennon confronted Heath, bespectacled and strikingly handsome. Jimi Hendrix was also there, flamboyantly dressed and wearing a red bandana, full of casual nobility. Marc Bolan, glammed-up and looking curiously androgynous, not unlike Bowie. Kurt Cobain, all spots and grease and smelling like Grunge spirit. Johnny Cash had grown young, long before he would sing that emotional, heartbreaking cover of the Nine Inch Nails. Johnny Hallyday, too, looked extraordinarily young and hale, hitherto untouched by the spectre of cancer. But it was that leather-clad demon, Jim Morrison, whose shaggy-haired, imposing presence, raunchy voice and smouldering good looks had wooed the world and sent his female fans into sexual frenzy, who presently approached Heath Axton. "One hell of comedown, hey?" he said again, coolly.

Heath stared at him, at the other Rock legends, with inexpressible awe. Like the others, Morrison appeared in the spirit of good health, certainly far removed from the man who would eventually, unavoidably and tragically succumb to obesity and multiple organ failure, whose professional career had been quickly cut short by his inordinate hard drinking and massive drug cocktails.

"What's happening to me?" Heath asked the Lizard King.

"I think you know . . ."

"The hell I do," Heath replied, none the wiser. "All I know is that I've had the weirdest morning of my life."

Morrison managed a sad, understanding smile. "Go downstairs and see for yourself, Chief. The truth shall be revealed." He added as an afterthought: "And watch out for that woman. She's a li'l devil . . ."

"Excuse me?" Heath wondered whom he was referring to.

"Lured some of us to our fate," Marc Bolan, softly-spoken, elaborated.

"She came between me and June," Johnny Cash said, somewhat sorrowfully, "but I managed to resist her."

"The Nature of the Beast," Morrison explained. "Fire and snakes . . ."

"Hey, dude, we hate it to happen to you," Kurt Cobain warned Heath.

The Man in Black addressed Heath with the deep, solemn voice of authority: "May He in Whom we live, move and have our being bless you."

Johnny Hallyday, France's *Rockeur National*, stepped forward. "You must let go," he informed Heath, complete with French inflection. "We will all be waiting for you when you get back." He added, appreciatively: "And *merci beaucoup* for bringing me to a wider audience. *Tout va bien, je suis en pleine forme, mort aux idiots.*" *All is well, I'm in good shape, dead to the idiots.*

"Just don't be long," said Lennon in his characteristically-friendly Liverpudlian accent.

Heath glanced down the stairs, then looked back in panicky uncertainty at Morrison. "Down there?" he asked uneasily.

Morrison nodded gently. Heath could tell from their collective sympathetic expressions that whatever lay downstairs wouldn't be good news. The dead were speaking to him, communications from the other side. Something was gravely awry.

Heath left the league of Rock legends lingering in the lobby and took the stairs with slow, heavy reluctance.

He made his way down the basement corridor. He could hear more voices now and saw vaguely human shapes, walking directly ahead of him. He kept his distance from them.

He noticed these human figures were losing the power of invisibility. They had begun to take on their natural form. Ever so slightly at first, but the process was quickly gathering momentum. As they reached the live room, they became transparent, through which light refracted, almost as though their bodies were made from liquid glass. Their phantom shapes bled colour, pastel shades that soon deepened to the rich hues of reality, making them substantial, tangible. Heath watched this new development with quiet awe and went on to wonder whether the dimension he had strayed into was at last converging with the actual, physical world.

Phil led Christian down the passage. At least now Heath could see them, of which he was outwardly glad. His relief was short-lived, however, as he frowned at the scene unfolding before him. The record producer and the studio boss joined his other band members and the two ladies crowded around the arrangement of drums. Their backs were turned. The spotlights illuminated the drum-laden platform and the unseen star attraction.

"There you are," Heath said aloud. "I've been looking all over for you. Where have you all been?"

None of them heard him.

A rheumy-eyed Birdy handed a steaming cup of coffee to Burt, who humbly thanked her.

Randy looked distinctly worse-for-wear from his drink-and-drugs binge the night before, and he looked ready to burst into tears.

Only Harmony looked on, strangely fascinated.

What were they doing gathered here like this? Heath thought, perplexed. *What's going on?*

Then Burt spoke after taking a sip of his coffee. "I don't think he suffered . . ."

Christian said severely, "I should have known something like this would happen. I sensed a foreboding. This has never happened on my watch."

"You hear about it all the time," Birdy declared. "You never expect it to happen to someone you know."

"I think we need to call a doctor," Phil advised regretfully, grim memories of former bands he'd worked with resurfacing. From his crazy days as a record company executive to him now working independently as a music producer, he'd been a long time in the business and seen a hell of a lot. "I do confess I'm at a loss as to whether an autopsy should be performed. I suppose we must, at least to verify the cause."

Randy sniffed unhappily, holding back tears, and murmured: "That could have been *me!*"

"I'm here!" beat out Heath loudly, intelligibly, urgently. "*I'm right HERE!* Please give me a sign you're hearing me!"

Apparently not. He stood waiting for a few moments, but none of them acknowledged his presence. No gasps of overwhelming surprise. They all seemed consciously oblivious to him.

Except Harmony. Whilst everybody looked as despondent as mourners at a wake, Harmony pulled her eyes away. Her head creaked slowly in the direction of Heath and her gaze caught him directly in the eye. It was a chilling moment. Harmony detached herself from the group and walked over to him. None of the others noticed her leave.

Soon she was standing beside him.

"I don't understand what's happening . . ." he said, seeking the comfort of his muse and the hope for an explanation spelling out why he should be crazy enough to be imagining ghosts.

But a part of him already knew. The reason only *he*, as opposed to the others, could see her was because she was *not really there*. [*Harmony who? I thought you were single, Heath.*] And there was him thinking his mates were just fooling around.

"You've guessed it, Heath," Harmony stated, reading his mind. "No great stretch of the imagination."

"You are my Addiction?"

She nodded.

It explained her vicarious excitement, why Harmony Stone only reappeared when he started using drugs again. She had been there all along, accompanying him whenever the intensity of his drug use increased to a new dangerous level. A figment of his imagination, a manifestation of temptation in its most sublime, seductive form. *The heroine offers heroin. She is such a li'l devil!*

"Your new producers are waiting for you," she went on.

Too much information, too much to absorb. Heath suddenly saw the price of being a Rock star, the hollowness of fame. Drugs accessed regions of the brain that improved creativity, disinhibited emotions and increased lateral thinking. You could create wild things in that altered state, then put it all together once sober. *But never forever.* After a while the creative juices dried up and your talents withered away, and you were left with one major-league hangover, the drugs you once took to expand your mind destroying your finances, putting your sanity in peril and sometimes costing you your life.

The penny dropped. The full brunt of the situation struck him. Any residual sangfroid dissolved. "I have to know," he murmured, dread creeping through him. "I have to see for myself."

As understanding dawned, Heath edged closer, trying to see beyond the wall of huddled figures. He had a horrible feeling, but he knew he had to look if only to confirm his worst fears. Terror stole over him as a gap was freely volunteered. Now, for the first time, he suddenly understood the events of the morning: the stark coldness, the awful silence, the empty city. Heath couldn't believe he was one of the limbo people, between realities. Cocooned from the real world, existing in some sort of purgatorial state, a chrysalid waiting to be reborn. The Rock gods in the lobby must have simply come to ease him through the transition from Life to Death, help him cross over to the ethereal plane. No doubt a séance might be in order. Death was supposed to be a doorway to a better place. *Or maybe not.* Maybe Death sometimes opened a completely different door . . . the door to Damnation. Perhaps Rock'n'Roll *was* 'the Devil's music', after all. Heath understood why Harmony Stone had been nothing more than his mental interpretation of Grace Slick, and as Great Society's ancient track, *Darkly Smiling*, somehow echoed in his mind, he came to appreciate how we were all Masters of Our Own Fate and how he had become just another stupid, reckless victim of that oft-told tale of Sex, Drugs and Rock'n'Roll. *The Nature of the Beast.* Another one bites the dust, joins that exclusive '27 Club'. Harmony Stone had claimed another victim, adding his scalp to her private collection. Maybe the title of their final album together should be called *Dead Times in Paris*.

What if there were no tomorrow?

With an aura of inevitability, Heath saw through the gap. He saw a figure dressed in black behind the set of drums, slumped in the chair, head thrown back, a spike sticking out of his vein. He recognized him with the same monumental horror that always arises from making any such unspeakable discovery. For Heath Axton was staring disbelievingly into the pale, peaceful, very real and *very dead* face of himself.

February 2018–March 2018

Blessings of Pan

"So that was what she was teaching them. Something so beautiful and strange and, aye, damnable, that it had lingered on and on all these years in her memory. And the vicar shouted aloud: 'The accursed blessing of Pan!'"

The Blessing of Pan (1921)
Lord Dunsany

It had come to this.

They were all gathered here in attendance. Them, the villagers. The family doctor and the midwife stood on either side of the bed, ready with the warm water and flannels.

Virginia Hunton – or Ginny, for short – gave them the fearful look of a trapped animal, made worse by the twisting spasms of agony as the contractions started to increase. She did not want this to happen. But did she have a choice? Her waters had broken, and her confinement was coming to an end. Her time was imminent. The baby was coming out, one way or the other.

For a short moment, between the contractions, she tried to push aside her troubled thoughts and dwelled on the events that had led to this exact moment in her life.

Who, from the outside world, would believe her?

They had moved into their new house in Little Plumstead, somewhere between Church Falls and Becton-upon-Sea. Her husband, Finnick – or Finn, as he preferred to be called – had wanted a change of scene. He had used hidden roads, roads not charted on any map, to get here, like jumping between worlds. For Little Plumstead turned out to be a mysterious village that harboured a strange secret.

On the surface, it was a rustic, quaint village, its residences ranging from the humblest of homes to much sought-after real estate. One might have called it a place for cloud-watching, cobblestone-skipping and wood-chopping. Little Plumstead was also a private nature reserve, complete with grebes, redshanks, peacocks and nesting storks, boasting the first wild pair to breed on English soil since the fifteenth century. The woodland and animal sanctuary supposedly opened up to the public six times a year, only on bank holidays, when people from the surrounding communities flocked into the village. Ginny remembered the crane they had passed when driving through the dirt road that led to their house. A beautiful creature with lovely, brightly-coloured plumage. Except it kept twisting its neck round to peck at a large, pink tumour on its right shoulder. Poor thing. It made Ginny want to cry.

ARDENBROOK was a cottage of exposed stonework and beamed ceilings, as rustic as the houses they had passed. Inside, the décor consisted of lighter pastel shades offset by deeper hues. Paper in the grate as kindling, wicker baskets under the bed, ale-making equipment in the shed. Puffed-up, bolshie pigeons landed on the tended lawn in their droves. A mask of the Green Man adorned the apple tree, fallen apples scattered beneath, their delicious crunch tartness perfect for that special, home-baked apple pie. Ginny counted a dozen varieties of roses with hues ranging from pale yellow to blood red. The garden path led her to a moss-covered, bronze statue of the Greek God Pan. The figure was two-foot high, the upper half that of a horned, bearded man but with the hindquarters of a goat. He was blowing into a reed pipe and, for a moment, Ginny thought she heard the faint strains of pipe music from somewhere nearby. Then, the sound faded away, and Ginny thought she might have just imagined it.

The Huntons enjoyed the conservatory, which Finn described as sitting outside without going outside or sitting in the rain without getting wet. "That's why we've come here: to be out of the city and to see the stars," he told her. "Don't you think it's a magical place?"

Ginny laughed. "As magical as when you claimed to have kissed my verruca away? You do know I cured it with anti-verruca cream."

"I kinda figured . . ."

She thought about her new home, the garden, the surrounds. "Yes, it really is lovely here. Like being transported back to the Stone Age. Let's get out our hammer and chisel!"

Finn looked at her slightly perplexed. Sometimes he couldn't tell if she was joshing or just being cynical. "We need to prioritize reviewing our savings against any work the house might need. I think we should fully commit to following that budgetary plan, as consistently as we can, till the end of the year when we can see where we stand financially."

Ginny loved her little summer house, which she hoped to convert to an art studio. She was a teaching artist rather than an art teacher. Finn adored his wife, the cowlick, the button nose, the radiance in her smile. Equally, Ginny appreciated his foibles and peculiarities.

Finn lived for work, worked to live. He was a computer tech. She was reminded of his tenth-year work anniversary.

"I'm so glad to be celebrating my ten years with this firm," Finn informed his colleagues during his speech over cake and tea. "I can't believe I've been here ten years. How time has flown. It feels like I only started yesterday. Here's to the next ten years!"

He received a round of congratulatory applause.

His new boss, a man of humour, stepped up and said, "That's odd. I only started working here yesterday, and I feel like I've been here ten years!"

More laughs, more applause.

Except Finn never intended to keep on working there. That week, he resigned, much to the bewilderment of his boss and colleagues. He had never liked mixing with other people. At work, he could never be found, as though he spent the day hiding out in the store cupboard. He always seemed to put on his cloak of invisibility and disappear dead on quarter-to-five. Not that Ginny considered him unsociable in his home life. After a decade at the firm, Finn told his colleagues he was starting afresh, relocating, being one with Nature. His boss didn't think his reason qualified enough as an explanation. Neither did Ginny take her husband's resignation seriously, initially. "You want to become a hippie?"

"Not exactly," Finn had replied, trying to justify his decision. "We need a new start."

Ginny never thought Finn, a self-confessed indoorsman, would rhapsodize about the Beauty of Nature. But what was there to lose? She worked from home most days, anyway. His steady income at the computer firm would be sorely missed, but they had sufficient savings and he promised to find work elsewhere, maybe a different line of work. He said he'd never liked his job. Ginny was amazed how Finn could have endured a decade with computers when he didn't like working with computers.

So they'd moved to Little Plumstead, identified by Finn. "Why not give it a shot? If you don't like it, we can always move back, and I can go back to my old job."

The bohemian in Ginny could not decline his suggestion and decided to go along with his plan.

Already, she knew it was a rural idyll, not far removed from certain sleepy villages in Somerset and Dorset. A timelessness filled the air alongside a far-reaching floral fragrance.

The neighbours, too, were nice, very welcoming. Carl and Lois Turnpenny were around at Ginny's that very first day, bringing along their two children, Bennie and Bertie. The boys looked similar, almost like twins, except they were different heights and different ages, nine and six years, respectively. Ginny was instantly taken to these curly-haired, wide-eyed wonder kids.

"Ever had any children?" Lois asked Ginny while Carl showed Finn the house and garden. TUMBLEWOOD was as much a character property as Ardenbrook. A similar bronze figure of Pan occupied the garden in one quiet corner.

The Turnpennys had invited them round to theirs. Wine, cocktails, relaxation, smiling faces, good times – happy hour at the Turnpennys.

"We've never had children, not for the lack of trying," said Ginny regretfully.

"Shame," said Lois, watching Ginny fuss over the children, pouring them each a glass of lemonade. For the adults she presently poured a Martini each with an olive garnish. "Having children is a wonderful experience. Becoming parents gave us a greater sense of purpose and brought focus to our relationship. I bet you're good with kids. My two boys certainly seem to like you."

"Oh, how I wish . . ." Ginny said, leaving the thought to finish itself, taking a sip from her martini glass. "Finn is hoping the clean air and the bucolic lifestyle of this place will do the trick. Well, that's the hope . . ."

"What's the problem, might I ask?"

Ginny told her new neighbour her woes. She was plagued with a woman's problem, predominantly Endometriosis, the most common, benign, untreatable condition in the book. She suffered intense abdominal pain and heavy bleeding during her periods, pain on intercourse other times. She had gone through countless operations over the years, the surgeons always laparoscopically shaving the endometrial deposits followed by a few months of Zoladex injections to shrink any residual deposits. It was a nightmare of an operation, trying to find every last endometrial deposit, an almost impossible task. Sometimes the roots remained and the condition reccurred. But at least those endometrial seeds hadn't penetrated the thickness of the bowel wall nor had the repeated surgeries led to pelvic adhesions. After she experienced a series of spontaneous abortions without knowing it at the time, the doctors explained, much to her dismay, her uterine lining was almost incapable of holding a foetus. Of course, all of this meant she was subfertile, hampered further by a low ovarian reserve due to a shorter menstrual cycle. After the course of Zoladex injections, she was meant to be at her most fertile. "I remember falling asleep at the hands of the Anaesthetist only to wake up a split second later in the Recovery Room, groggy from the anaesthetic. I sometimes imagine partially waking up during surgery just to find them fiddling with my bits . . ."

Lois saw Ginny shudder and decided to put a consoling arm round her. "I'm really sorry to hear about what you've been through and how it's affected your chances to conceive." Lois paused before saying something Ginny wasn't expecting to hear, her voice suddenly taking on an optimistic tone. "But I have a good feeling about this. You just might get lucky!"

It was at the tail end of an Indian summer that the Huntons moved down to Little Plumstead and it wasn't long after when the miracle happened.

Finn had got to working with the commercial gardener, Bill Sedgley, learning a new trade and a refreshing change from his last occupation. As a paid apprentice, he did more than enough to earn his keep, working with his hands rather than with computer software. He and Ginny got to know some of the other people in the village. There was the elderly lady, Geraldine Margolin, the retired or maybe not-so-retired nurse and midwife. Mrs. Lavinia Foxley was the village draper, selling textiles and mending clothes. Ginny also became close friends with Flora Bayliss, who together with her two teenage daughters, Polly and Nancy, ran the florist's. Although agriculture and the arts and crafts formed the mainstay of occupations in Little Plumstead, the postman still went on his rounds, one could still purchase a newspaper down the newsagents, the mechanic still fixed cars and the local school still ran lessons. In fact, Blancherosa, one of the younger schoolteachers, struck up a friendship with Ginny, disclosing a little of the history of the village and described a culture that was largely pagan in nature, such as celebrating not Halloween but its roots, Samhain. But, overall, the Huntons spent most of their time with the Turnpennys.

Ginny continued to disclose to Lois her desperate desire for a child, and Lois would almost promise success by way of reassurance. *You and Finn keep trying with one-hundred-percent commitment and it should happen sooner or later*, Lois would encourage her.

Finn had spent much of that cold November day burning leaves, watching them curl and crisp and char in the incinerator. He came into the house, just as Ginny set down a delicious mushroom omelette on the dining table, consisting of the wild mushrooms Finn had picked a couple of days previously.

I'll be ovulating soon, Ginny had disclosed, to which Finn responded, rather jokily: *I look forward to your ovulations!* That had been two days ago. And, presently, Finn knew she was ovulating. His wife appeared all dolled-up and smiley.

"You look ravishing tonight," he acknowledged, feeling a stirring below.

"Sexy time in the dark?" she asked, borrowing his oft-spoken expression.

"I shall concentrate on fertilizing your egg tonight. . ." he said desirously.

"Must you be so clinical?"

He took his wife by the hand and led her to the bedroom, kissing her on the way. They tumbled onto the bed. Eagerly removing each other's clothes, they set about doing what couples do when their passions are aflame as well as, in this instance, working on creating new life. "Don't rush it," Finn told her breathlessly during the act. "I want you to *believe* we can have a baby."

"You sound like Lois," she replied, receiving her husband with a moan of heightened arousal. Yes, Lois, who assured them the guarantee of a child as just a matter of time.

Then, slick with sweat, spent from his efforts, Finn whispered his love into Ginny's ear, who responded in kind, and he physically detached himself from her and rolled over onto his side of the bed. When Ginny tried to talk to him, he was already asleep.

She decided she, too, should try and get some kip. She closed her eyes and drifted off. And dreamed. Dreamed of the Goatman–

–Ginny finds herself walking in the dark of the woods. She can see the wandering stars through the branches accompanied by the ascent of the full moon, which provides a fair deal of ivory-white illumination for her journey. Here, the November night is unseasonably warm. But it is the flute-like music that catches her ears – and her breath. It seems to be calling to her. And Ginny sees she is not alone. The strange tune has summoned the village girls. She follows the procession of girls as they skip and dance and traipse barefoot along the path, avoiding briar and gorse and thorn, in the direction of the curious pipe-music from a time long ago. The manner in which these fair maidens have stolen away into the woods reminds Ginny of how the Pied Piper cast his spell on the children of Hamelin.

Beyond the old, gnarled yew trees, Ginny and the company of young women arrive at a clearing. She sees a ring of standing stones, thirteen, tall stones, their smooth, weathered surface lit up by moonlight. Ginny concludes this must be a sacred site of pagan worship, the Old Stones of Plumstead the villagers often speak of. A great, roaring fire burns within the circle of ancient stones, further making the stones glow and lighting up the centre of the circle, where rests a flat stone, on which burnt offerings were once given to heathen gods but upon which now sits a figure from the Age of Antiquity. Olive-brown skin, shape that of an anthropomorphic beast. Whereas his upper half is distinctly human and muscular and rather hirsute, he possesses the hindquarters of a goat, with cloven hooves, and a pair of horns poke up from his headful of curly hair.

There is no fear at the sight of this mythological being, but Ginny does wonder if there was magic in the mushroom omelette she cooked earlier this evening. But there is certainly magic in the air. Pan is playing a reed pipe and its enchanting melody floats in the air and travels far to occupy every deepest hollow in the woods. Romance rises up from the smoke of the campfire while a sense of passion is delivered by the pipes, thrilling its listeners, filling them with longing and wild abandon. The magical power of the music lifts feet, hearts and minds. The young women strip off their dresses the moment they gaze upon Pan, as though gripped by some kind of mass hysteria, and they dance and whoop and stomp their feet, some weaving in and out of the Old Stones until they've gone round all thirteen. Blancherosa is amongst these young women, primordial firelight bouncing off her bare breasts, but she does not recognize Ginny, her mind lost to the lulling rhythm of the music.

Mistress Moon watches down from the night sky. Moonrise has its own unique place in certain ancient, pagan rituals, Ginny supposes, and is well-known to influence madness. The group of naked revellers within the magical circle of glowing stones resemble Dionysian maenads during a drunken orgy. For they are in the realm of a rutting god, whose pungent, musky odour excites them into a frenzy of unspeakable lust. The pipe-player holds them in thrall, like a snake-charmer hypnotizing a cobra, as they continue to dance with orgasmic abandonment.

In this magical lure of the woods, amongst the Old Stones, Pan delivers a dance of his own, the clop of his hooves beating upon the hard ground. It is his huge woody erection that the flock of enchanted women are now most focused on, as they worship his loins and taste of his intoxicating phallus.

Ginny is nudged, jostled, handled, pushed forward by her fellow women into the immediate presence of the great party animal and original horny devil, Pan, and she surrenders to his powerful magnetic pull. And, in this place of phantasy and phantasmagoria, where she cannot tell if she is awake or dreaming, she allows the flesh petals of her rosebud to open up to receive him, as swollen waves of orgasm completely consume her . . .

When all passions are exhausted, a voice, perhaps that of Pan, speaks to her directly into her mind: If you want to know what disappointed means, sleep with your husband–

–The rooster crowed at dawn.

"I did not wish to disturb the beauty sleep of my sleeping beauty," Finn whispered as Ginny stirred beside him.

"I had a funny dream. . ." Ginny told him.

"Funny ha-ha or funny strange?"

Ginny recalled her dream, the young women dancing naked and barefoot under the gaze of the full moon and her giving herself up to the melodious, musky pipe-player and enchanter from the woods. "I don't know . . . It was such a vivid dream . . . Like I was really there . . . But something feels different . . ."

"How do you mean?"

It was not long after that night that she fell pregnant.

The breadwinner was home, and the homemaker was pregnant.

Finn's gardening skills were coming along nicely; he was developing some outstanding green thumbs. Necessity was, after all, the mother of invention, as he reminded her. And Ginny continued to paint in the summer-house-cum-art-studio, two months into her pregnancy, something that seemed utterly impossible in the not-so-distant past.

"Get dressed," Finn told his wife. "We've been invited to dinner at Wildfoot Manor at eight."

"You mean Professor Daysheart's house?"

"The one and the same."

Finn showered and dressed himself in smart casual, topped off by a Barbour jacket to stave off the January chill. Ginny changed into a warm and comfy, Maison Kitsuné dress, black leggings and long boots and a vintage sheepskin jacket.

WILDFOOT MANOR was a modest country house on the edge of the village. Like the other properties in the village, it was made of stone and rustic in design. It belonged to one Augustus Daysheart, Classical Historian and the absolute authority on Pan. Professor Daysheart's doctorate, dissertation and subsequent published books exalted the God of the Woods, his views rarely challenged by his contemporaries.

He opened the heavy, oak front door to let his visitors in who had braved the howling winter's night. The snow was still a week away. The Huntons had never formally met the Professor but knew of him, and already they could tell he was an eccentric, pipe-and-smoking-jacket kind of fellow. "Welcome," he greeted them, sweeping a hand through his long grey hair. "Thank you for coming."

"These must be the new additions to the village," said the middle-aged woman behind him, wearing a fetching flowerprint dress and sandals, hair tied into a bun and whose pouty, trouty lips made her look as though she loved herself. "I'm Sylvia Daysheart, the old ball-and-chain!"

"Pleased to meet you both," acknowledged Finn, shaking hands with his hosts. "Thank you for inviting us."

"Pleasure is all ours," said Sylvia, whose shrewd eyes caught on Ginny. She took Ginny aside. "You're positively glowing. You must have an addition of your own."

"You're very observant," Ginny said, pleased. "Never thought it would happen."

"As I'm sure you've already discovered, this is a place where miracles happen."

Augutus Daysheart led them into the house. The interior possessed an old-fashioned charm with sconced lighting, wood-panelled walls and mythological creatures cast in oil-on-canvas, the atmosphere warm and homely, a world apart from the frigid, shrieking gale outside.

They soon found themselves in an oak-framed conservatory, the tall windows providing a sweeping vista of the frosty, wind-scoured landscape, glistening like icing sugar. The starry heavens were visible through the reinforced glass of the roof of the conservatory, the Evening star a noticeable, twinkling feature.

A fire burned merrily in the hearth, and a candlebrum with lighted candles sat on each end of the dining table. There were other guests present, enjoying various aperitifs, preparing to sit down to dinner.

Sylvia announced the new guests, who received heartfelt greetings. Mr. Clive Cherwell was there, the solicitor who had sold them their house. Lois and Carl Turnpenny had already been invited and were always pleased to see their neighbours. Polly Bayliss was childminding their two rowdy boys for the evening. Lois was glad to have a break from her screaming kids for the evening. *Shoot me now or pass me a bottle of wine!* she often quipped, coping with the demands of her children by drinking.

"Dinner is served," Sylvia informed her guests, bringing out the food. "Take your places." She lifted the lid of the silver serving tray. "*Voilà!* Lord of the Marsh!" Indeed, Augustus Daysheart carved up the six-kilogram goose, accompanied by seasonal vegetables and roast potatoes. It would be Bergamot lemon tart for dessert, later.

"Wine?" Sylvia was already pouring a nice, vintage red into everyone's wine glasses. Except– "Not for this one, mind," she said, getting round to Ginny, to whom she offered a non-alcoholic spritzer. "She's expecting."

"I think congratulations are in order!" declared Dr. Quintus Latimer, the senior village GP. "You need to come round to my Surgery so I can give you a check-up. I have a special interest in Obs & Gyn."

"And don't we need your birthing knowhow around here, indeed!" laughed Lois, already tipsy. "Babies everywhere!"

"I had Endometriosis," Ginny told the doctor, "that played havoc with any chance of conceiving. Until I came here and became pregnant."

"I guess the fresh air and the getting-back-to-Nature did you both a world of good!" Lois interjected.

"Endometriosis or otherwise, your womb will provide the optimal environment for the growing embryo," Dr. Latimer advised, tucking into his goose leg. "We have no naysayers here, but our only moratorium is that you don't smoke or drink or do anything that may harm your baby, including strenuous exercise."

Reverend Bramwell Whitworth, somewhat Pickwickian in appearance, joined in the discussion. "Exultations! Blessed be the fruit! Endometriosis is no obstacle to Pan. He likes his women. You and Finn will make such beautiful babies. You have been touched by Pan – therefore you are truly *blessed!*"

Ginny gave the vicar a peculiar look. Yes, she got it that Pan was big here. But for a man of the cloth to be exalting a pagan god? She wondered what the Anglican Church would say if it knew. She half-expected the good vicar to start spouting off some nonsense about protection spells and fertility rites. People speak of certain causes that bring people together in a cult run by some charismatic leader, who has even developed his own church. Maybe Little Plumstead wasn't so much a village as a commune for like minds. Not that she ever considered herself a religious person to criticize another's spiritual beliefs. "Thank you," she replied diplomatically. "You are most kind . . ."

The ate under the firmament of winter starlight, separated from them by the glass roof of the conservatory, and when they had finished their meals, they moved their dinner party to the comfort of the drawing room/library, with its Chesterfields and mahogany writing desk and floor-to-ceiling bookcase, and were soon on to the postprandial whisky and cigars. Professor Daysheart, who was right at home with his pipe and smoking jacket, turned on the radio to provide some musical accompaniment to the festivities and enhance the prevailing atmosphere. *Spiritualized* by Finley Quaye played, partway through.

Referring to the speakers, Professor Daysheart noted: "There's some crackling."

"Don't mind if I do," joked Reverend Whitworth in food-related terms.

Ginny watched the guests quaffing champagne and sipping whisky and smoking cigars and ye old toke. She saw Carl Turnpenny roll up a joint, seeds and stems and all, fire it up and pass it around, pink-eyed. Ginny stuck with her non-alcoholic fizz.

Relatively high, the eccentric professor went back to his favourite subject. "For the benefit of the new additions to our village," Augustus Daysheart said, speaking of the Huntons, "I think we should enlighten them on the lore of the village. They came here as husband and wife and they will settle down as mother and father. A miracle of creation, the propagation of life."

Finn and Ginny received a hearty cheer and a good, old round of applause from the other guests and felt a genuine sense of inclusion.

"Here, in Little Plumstead, the ancient past lives on," began the Professor. "People talk of religious synchronicities, and, yes, it is an old story. A story as old as Time itself. The Christian Church talks of religious liberty, but everyone knows this is an oxymoron. Christians are bound by the doctrines of their religion so there is no freedom." Reverend Whitworth nodded his head in agreement. Professor Daysheart continued: "There are religions older than Christianity. The pagan gods are just as important, more so even, than any of the newer, lesser Abrahamic gods. Why? Because there's no evidence Jesus even existed, his historical record nothing more than a myth. Outside the accounts of the Gospels, there is no mention of his name by any of the social commentators of the time. Yet, cutting through the bullshit, Paganism and the Church are inextricably linked.

"Pan, the Greek god of forests – and the figurehead of the original mystery cult – has long represented the pagan gods in general. With the advent of the Christian Church, communication with the pagan gods ceased, heavily suppressed by priests, who had a vested interest in eliminating religious competition by any means possible, including but not limited to lying, stealing, cheating, murder, genocide, extortion, torture and blackmail. As a result, public attention to the pagan gods disappeared about two thousand years ago. The new god displaced the old, banishing the goat-footed god back to the mythological realms."

"*O goat-foot god of Arcady*," recalled Dr. Latimer. "Oscar Wilde."

"Quite," continued Augustus Daysheart. "Certain deaths gods cannot come back from. But Pan means 'all'. Pan is an all-deity, older, primal, more universal. A god of Nature, *all* of Nature. Out here, you're closer to Nature – *all* living Nature. You don't get that in the city when you are out here with so much land. Whether it's the trees, plants or weeds or every thought, emotion, feeling, anxiety, *all* of it is Pan.

"The pagan gods may have given the impression they had disappeared for good, but it couldn't be further from the truth. The news of Pan's death has been greatly exaggerated. Pan is far from dead, only harder to recognize in the madness of the modern world. Thousands of years ago, the Roman philosopher, Seneca, once said:

not needing wealth is more valuable than wealth itself. Indeed, throughout the ages, money has been the root of all evil. These days, property developers destroy the spirit of a house by turning it into a set of apartments for more money. They say if you pay peanuts, you get monkeys. Even Glastonbury has sold out: why should people pay three pounds to relieve their bladder, the same price as a pint of beer there. Fear of Hell is exploited by the politicians and financial institutions through the global religious organisations to pacify the masses, keep them compliant, in line. The modern world is dirty and grey and *unjust*, where the bad people take great pleasure in screwing up the good people, and so we rarely trade with the outside world. Money is not important here which is why you got your house for a song."

Finn glanced at Mr. Cherwell, who gave a small nod of acknowledgement.

"Pan resides in this village," Reverend Whitworth took over. "We are all Pan's people, even the lawmakers of Westminster or the Pope himself, even if they don't know it!" He brought up his own views on the Christian faith. "I don't agree with the Pope when he says you should reserve your affection for children and don't waste your love and energy on pets. Not everyone can pop out a baby. I mean *he* can talk, leading a cowardly life of celibacy, a failure as a man! But the Church has always been an intolerant, corrupt institution throughout the ages with its followers committing heinous crimes in the name of God. You hear the recent story of a woman in a long-term coma who suddenly became pregnant? It turns out she was being raped by a male nurse, who also happened to be a devout Christian. Did you forget about the fertility doctor, supposedly also a religious man, who fathered two hundred children by using his own sperm rather than that of donors, because he wanted to play God? Do you not recount the sexual slavery of those nuns? A scandal involving cases where nuns were forced to abort the product of their union with priests – abortion is something Catholicism strictly forbids, except when it suits it?"

Once again, Ginny glanced curiously at the vicar. Even if the man was of the opposite persuasion, having defected from the Church, who was she to question the practice of a priest?

Finn, who had said very little so far, stepped in. "Are there many places like Little Plumstead?"

"There are only a handful like ours that have reverted back to the Wild and the Old Ways," Reverend Whitworth went on. "Wolding, for instance, Belhaven, for another. Waghorn and West Hayslip are similar settlements not far from here. The roots of the tale lie with my predecessor, Reverend Tuckerton. It was Reverend Tuckerton who broke away from the Church to bring our generation to the worship of Pan, showed us that the pagan gods are still active, living beings, immortal and powerful and more *real* than the Christian god."

"Oh, I remember Reverend Tuckerton," Sylvia mentioned fondly. "Such a lovely man. He showed us a new spiritual path."

"It is a path as sacred as any other," Reverend Whitworth added. "Except we do not need to fear our god. He is a caring, loving god, never demanding, always receptive to the needs of his flock, not the spiteful, punitive god of the Old Testament."

Dr. Latimer puffed on his cigar, chuckling. "Understood, old bean, understood."

Finn nodded his own understanding.

The Professor smiled. "If any of the ancient gods ever made it to the twenty-first century, what would they be doing now? Where or how might we contact them? If Pan is really here, which of us mortals could not use the helping hand of a friendly god once in a while?"

A silence descended and Ginny contemplated. As Minnie Riperton now sang *Les Fleur* on the radio, Ginny surveyed the people in her midst, these guests of the Dayshearts. They were the equivalent of Rotarians, except in the service of Pan. From the moment Ginny had stepped into the village, his influence had been all around her. The statue of Pan in every garden, a sentinel watching over them and protecting the house in the same way a crucifix might do. Little Plumstead was a village that belonged to Pan, where the people, even the priest, had abandoned Christianity for the tenets and customs of pagan worship. The arts and crafts and agricultural, outdoors' way of life in the village brought a renewed sense of freedom, a connection to the past, reaping bountiful harvests. The people appreciated the value of Nature, living off a land of plenty, and the natural resources never ran out. Farmers, growers and gardeners grew a wide variety of organic produce. People relied on solar power for their homes and still drank from firkins in the local inn. The village elders deliberated as to whether the community should develop its own currency. Ginny thought of the kids in school learning Greek . . . and a language older than even Ancient Greek. The language of the gods, the *original* language. The village had its own theatre. Blancherosa had invited Ginny to the latest play. The Amateur Dramatic Society had performed *Equus*. It was only when she saw it in Little Plumstead that the play finally made sense to her. The disturbed teenager existed on the forensic end of the Autistic Spectrum, harbouring a literal understanding of the gods. His sexual awakening, from visiting an adult theatre to his first intimate encounter with a girl, disrobing on stage, prompted him to blind the horses so they could not see him have sex. Excited, sexually aroused riding a horse, he certainly needed something between his legs! Lois joked rather crudely. But, most of all, Ginny thought of her erotic dream before she would conceive, remembering herself bending to the will of the pipe-playing Pan. He had since blessed her.

Yes, counterculture aside, Little Plumstead was a village unlike any other, a unique place, accommodating the disciples of a heathen god.

"What about those on their deathbed?" Finn asked. "I expect they regret their life of pagan worship, afraid they're destined for Hell."

"The Devil was based on Pan, one of the conceits of the Church," Reverend Whitworth responded. "Hell is a hackneyed concept, and it is wholly unfair to point the finger at our non-conformist faith. No, death brings out the best in our people here. A man about to die is at his most honest."

Finn and Ginny left the party around midnightish significantly enlightened.

March the Twentieth marks the wonder of the Vernal Equinox. The sun passes the celestial equator going north and from now on the northern hemisphere tilts towards the sun. A person at the North Pole would see the sun skimming across the horizon, beginning six months of uninterrupted daylight. A person on the Equator would see the sun passing directly overhead. So begins a time of spring lambs and birds feeding their hatchlings.

The gardening service, dormant over winter, was starting up shop again, its landscaping and decking business the most popular. In the furrowed fields of farmland, seeds became saplings. Everywhere, everyone woke up to the sound of chirping birds.

"Your baby's health is as good as yours," Dr. Latimer was telling Ginny at the Antenatal Clinic he ran. The baby, indeed, looked in good shape on the sonogram. "You're eating for two now. No drinking, of course."

"I've done my due diligence," verified Ginny. "No drinking."

"You certainly have a rosy glow about you. You should be at your healthiest. As I once mentioned, the body always provides the perfect environment for any developing foetus."

Ginny felt her baby kick for the first time that day at the GP Surgery, as though it was revelling in the attention it was receiving. "That's incredible!" she said, overjoyed. "I can *feel* my baby!"

"All humans have their own 'firsts'," Dr. Latimer explained when Ginny informed him of this miraculous event. "At conception, human life begins. The baby's first kick. Their actual birth. Thereafter, life occurs in a linear fashion. Babies achieve important developmental milestones. Toddlers learn. Children grow and achieve. Gangly teenagers transform into educated adults. Seeking a partner leads to romance and love

– physical love. And the cycle starts over again. One day, your children will have children of their own and their children another generation of children."

"And Little Plumstead will remain the same, unchanged by the passage of time," murmured Ginny, struck by a thought. "The descendants of Little Plumstead will pass on its legend to their children . . ."

"Always has been, always will be," he confirmed.

She decided not to tell Dr. Latimer of the dream that haunted her when she slept at night. A recurring dream of her running through the woods. *Brambles and nettles and thorns try to hinder her progress. The trees rapidly moult their leaves around her. She clambers over the deadfalls, the gnarled trunks of storm-ravaged trees, their twisted branches reaching out for her like the limbs of a kraken. She can feel the Universe staring at her with the eyes of Pan, seeing her without barrier. And when she looks at her god near the Old Stones, he comes forward with those curiously bent legs and animalistic grace, radiating a potent musk that she cannot resist. He continues to play a tune on his pipe as he approaches her, a tune not ancient and exotic but more modern and one she is able to recognize:* Lord of the Dance. *She can hum the tune:* Dance, then, wherever you may be,/I am the Lord of the Dance, said he,/And I'll lead you all, wherever you may be,/And I'll lead you all to the Dance, said he.

He has her in his sway. Under a spell.

It is only when he stops playing his pipe and traces his hand, with its long, curved nails, across her bulge that she thinks she knows what he wants. A sacrifice. *Pan wants to sacrifice her baby!*

Amidst the overpowering scent of his musk, pulling away from the hand stroking her belly, she tells the ancient god straight: "No, you can't have him! Never! God help me!"

Pan's expression darkens, twists, sharpens. He is furious, for he is not used to being defied. Without warning, his claws puncture and tear into her belly and, in a splash of blood and gore, he rips the growing baby out of her womb.

A cream-curdling scream emerges from the back of her throat, renting the air and putting paid to the riddles of the night.

It was that precise midsummer movement when the sun stood still to claim the longest day of the year as its own. Another beautiful English day was coming to an end. The villagers caught the last rays of the evening sun in the reddening sky. *Red sky at night, shepherd's delight; red sky in the morning, fisherman's warning.* The reddening dusk deepened into a night that was soon bathed in moonglow. Every species of garden plant thrived. The wild roses and clematis ran riot. The sunflowers were in full bloom just like Ginny was blooming in her pregnancy. She carried a particularly active baby, figuratively trampolining inside her, using her as a swimming pool. Wearing a smock dress, she had celebrated her baby shower with her friends only yesterday, Lois Turnpenny setting it up, but this evening her mind was elsewhere.

The discovery of the clinic letter in the writing-bureau drawer had come as a shock to her. It was not an Outpatients' letter related to her but her husband. The letter was dated around the time they were considering IVF. When Ginny had stumbled upon it while looking for stamps, it took her breath away and filled her with a sense of dread. She felt sick, and this time it had nothing to do with her condition, any morning sickness. The long and short of it was that the microscopic analysis of Finn's sperm revealed abnormal morphology of sperm: sperm with two heads. In fact, he did not have any healthy, viable sperm. The man was more than just infertile but rather completely sterile. That made Ginny ask the most obvious question when he came home from work, smelling of earth and cut grass. If he was, indeed, firing duds, how could she have possibly become pregnant?

"You're in a rather odd mood today," Finn commented, noting his wife's general preoccupied state.

"Don't you think the circumstances are odd?"

"I recognize that look," Finn observed. "What are you hiding?"

"More to the point, what are *you* hiding?" Ginny shouted back at him, distressed. She pulled out the old fertility clinic letter from behind her back and threw it at him.

Except she didn't get the shocked reaction from her husband she had been expecting. He remained impossibly calm in his reply. "I knew I should have thrown that letter away because you might find it some day and wonder how it was all ever possible. You should pay it no mind. They say you should only marry wives whose families are minimal for fear of interference. I needed a child desperately. Now we have one. That's all that matters now."

"Who's the father?" she demanded to know.

"I will always be the father, no matter what."

"*No, who's the father?*" Ginny repeated furiously.

But he didn't need to tell her. She knew. This place, the village of Little Plumstead, and its secret, pagan ways. Its people had tapped into something unfathomable and ancient. *You would let Pan make a play for your wife?* she wanted to scream at Finn, but, suddenly, Ginny was certain there was something wrong with the baby, seriously wrong. She experienced her first taste of puerperal psychosis, convinced something dark and inhuman was growing inside her. She feared she would give birth to a monster, even if the ultrasound showed a healthy baby. She had been impregnated by some kind of demon seed, during a ritual of sacred copulation with the village's truly enigmatic inhabitant, somewhere between dreaming and wakefulness.

Scared for her baby, thinking that she might miscarry, she felt her baby kick inside her, harder than ever before, as though not liking her doubts or suspicions. Her waters broke, thick, bloody amniotic fluid splattering on the floor.

She heard the piping music, celebrating *her*. This was no dream. The music was coming from the woods – *how could it possibly travel so far?* The tune haunted the woods – and the village – its heart-soothing, soul-appeasing notes having travelled up the aeons from the Arcadian hills to float fabulously over the fields of England.

They were all here. The villagers, scores of them, their round, attentive faces watching her from every corner of the room. Ginny tried not to look into their faces but focus on the arduous task ahead. By her bedside cabinet, she saw a spindly, gossamer-spinning spider working its thread, and she heard the midwife, Geraldine Margolin, give her instructions, take charge of the situation: "Push, my dear, *push!*"

The contractions were not only getting closer together, but they were now on top of each other. She pushed, bore down, fighting the agony of childbirth without epidural or Entonox. She was in so much pain and straining harder, she was afraid she'd end up with a vaginal or anal prolapse. Finn held her hand, tenderly. Dr. Latimer stood further back, letting the midwife do her job.

"Sometimes you have to take the bull by its horns," advised Geraldine. "Easy to put it in, difficult to get it out. But we may be in luck. I can see its head crowning . . ." As Ginny received low, excited murmurs from those gathered round, her private regions on display, nothing short of a spectacle for all to see, Geraldine grabbed the damp towels and cupped the baby's head, applying a reactionary force to avoid causing an ugly, vaginal tear. One more push and, manoeuvring the head and shoulders, the rest of the baby followed.

"Is the baby okay?" Ginny asked anxiously, breathless from her exertions.

"He's fine," Geraldine announced, turning the baby upside down and smacking his bottom. The baby began to cry after taking his first breath, announcing his presence to the world. Geraldine cut the umbilical cord and, after Dr. Latimer had checked him over, including checking his weight, wrapped the baby in a towel before presenting the new arrival to his mother. "In fact, he's perfect! You have a healthy baby boy!"

Ginny cradled her newborn, all five pounds and eight ounces of him, in her arms. Yes, he was normal, complete with ten fingers and ten toes.

"He's a proper little thing," said Finn, the proud father, receiving congratulations from the onlookers.

Ginny looked at the bushy eyebrows and curly hair and dark eyes of her baby and thought of Lois's two wide-eyed wonder boys and some of the other familiar-looking children in the village, giving away their parentage. Ginny's baby would be joining the Children of Pan.

We are not in sexual servitude to Pan, Lois had told her recently. *Not every woman of child-bearing age, who comes to the village, must be impregnated by Pan. No, Pan lends a hand to those women who need his help.*

While the people began to slowly depart from their cottage and make their way to the Old Stones, where they planned to sacrifice an old bull as gramercy, to give thanks, Ginny realized everything would be all right, grateful for the gift of community but, foremost, the precious gift of a baby.

January 2020-February 2020

American Suburbia

"In middle age there is mystery, there is mystification. The most I can make out of this hour is a kind of loneliness. Even the beauty of the visible world seems to crumble, yes even love. I feel there has been some miscarriage, some wrong turning, but I do not know when it took place and I have no hope of finding it."

John Cheever

Rafael Hanratty, also known as 'Rafe' to his former friends, sat at the writing desk of his study in quiet reflection with a freshly-opened bottle of Johnnie Walker at hand. Blue Label of course, only the finest. The computer screen was blank, inert. Rafe had half-closed the Venetian blinds to shield against the dazzle of sunlight streaming in through the window, the June afternoon on this, the longest day of the year, distinctly hot and muggy. He stared at the small bronze figurine of a skeleton sitting on a square block of stone in silent contemplation, a design reminiscent of Rodin's *The Thinker*.

Rafe lived in WESTERHILLS, an exclusive gated community, with its finite number of high-end estates, situated less than an hour from Midtown Manhattan. Extravagant, quality houses and gilded-age mansions with PRIVATE PROPERTY signs. Executive cars and limousines parked down long, leafy driveways. Greenery dripping everywhere, maples and century-old oaks growing at intervals along the sidewalks. Hedges neatly clipped, pruned, some shaped into topiaries. Sprinklers hosing down the manicured lawns, the air fragrant with the scent of roses and marigolds and cut grass. Swimming pools round the back, fed by artesian wells, hosted garden parties, where everyone drank sloe gin and dry martinis and, over cocktails, engaged in the hospitable customs of polite society and the lively banter of the well-to-do, talking shop and exchanging market tips, of which everyone hoped to get a slice of the action, with some of the guests sharing crude jokes rather uncharitably of the less well-off. The deluxe perks of living here included tennis courts and an eighteen-hole golf course, on site. The heavily-wooded acres further afield, soon giving way to a pastoral belt, were perfect for long, leisurely walks and taking one's Fortnum & Mason hamper for an afternoon picnic. The gated enclave of Westerhills came with the trappings of a king and boasted the wealthy cream of society. A sleepy suburban idyll, a veritable utopia. Modern, upper-middle-class, prestigious, where everybody tried to keep up with the dailies, *The New York Times* or *The Wall Street Journal* the traditional reads, as well as, in the spirit of one-upmanship, to keep up with the Joneses.

But, despite catching the distant strains of revelry as his neighbours, the Dredges, threw yet another garden party on this sultry summer's day, Rafe was not in a good place, psychologically. He had lost his wife, his mistress, his girlfriend, and even the girls employed by the escort agency had lost their enthusiasm for him.

Harken, ladies and gentlemen, to my tale of woe.

It was that old chestnut: Rafe was experiencing a midlife crisis. Just like that song by that funk-metal band, Faith No More. That awkward midpoint in one's life when one's career has reached a plateau and one takes stock of one's personal relationships, love, health and finances, reflecting on missed chances and unwise choices, and begins questioning one's own mortality.

Rafe poured himself another large whisky and, with a loud, solemn "Bottom's up!", gulped down the contents of the tumbler. Stroking the beard that men grow in between relationships, he went back to his private ruminations, wholly uninterested in the world outside gloriously sunwashed in a golden light.

His precious watch was in for repairs. *Easy to waste time,* he thought.

Perdu temps, as the French say.

But could Rafe really say he had wasted his time? *His life?*

It was about either investing or wasting time, for as Jack London declared, the proper function of a man was to live, not to exist. It was about using your time well, not wasting your days to prolong them. But didn't John Lennon once say, *Time you enjoyed wasting is not time wasted?* Maybe to quote Shakespeare, in the same breath: *I wasted time, and not time doth waste me.*

You could slow down how you perceived time with new experiences. That was why the beginning of a vacation appeared to pass more slowly than the rest of the week as you acclimatized to your new, unfamiliar surroundings, getting into a predictable routine, until the days eventually merged into one and, before you knew it, the vacation was over. That was why the older you got, the quicker the days, months and years seemed to pass, as you engaged in the same predictable routine almost every day. *Life is like a roll of toilet paper,* Rafe supposed. *The closer to the end, the faster it goes.*

It was even more extraordinary how as a kid you yearned to be an adult, but then when you became an adult, you spent the rest of your life trying to be young again, and the more distant the shores of youth got, the more desperately you struggled to reach them. Putting aside this sense of helplessness for a moment, didn't they say life begins at forty and fifty is the new forty? Victor Hugo himself described forty as the old age of youth and fifty as the youth of old age. When the passions of youth cooled, but the infirmities of old age had not yet set in. When the dreams of youth ended, and Regret made an ugly appearance. When Father Time finally caught up with Mother Nature.

Rafe remembered how a friend of his, having received a sheltered upbringing, experienced his 'midlife' crisis in his late twenties, how the man just went wild and suffered a nervous breakdown, ending up in Bellevue.

John Cheever, whom Rafe greatly admired as a writer, spoke about the mystery and mystification of middle age, the loneliness it entailed, the loss of love and the sense of wrongdoing. Cheever's work explored the deep, dark secrets buried in the suburban simulacra of paradise, himself wracked by self-loathing and guilt over his own alcoholism and bisexuality, spending time in the company of male prostitutes. Such was his toxic nature, Cheever cited his wife as the cause of all his problems, wrongfully accusing her of being a 'manic-depressive' until his therapist corrected him and highlighted that the underlying fault lay with him. Cheever managed to make it through Rehab and never drank again, achieving complete sobriety in the end.

Delmore Schwartz was another author, whom Rafe rated highly in his esteem and who also did not feel comfortable in his own skin, beset with similar problems to Cheever. His was the tale of the poet genius, who quickly burnt himself out after two failed marriages, the emergence of mental illness, wherein he believed that JFK and the Pope were plotting against him, and an addiction to alcohol and narcotics that led to a downward spiral of increasing poverty and squalor until he died, almost forgotten, in a seedy hotel in Times Square. Not entirely forgotten, mind. The 'Delmore Effect' was named after him, a cognitive bias where human beings have a tendency to set more explicit goals for lower-priority tasks, meaning the simpler the problem, the more time they spend solving it, and the more complex the problem, the greater the inclination to avoid the topic altogether because they hesitate to imagine not living up to their more important expectations, afraid of failure.

Rafe did not plan to end his days like his two literary heroes. Presently, however, as he poured himself another large measure, he recalled part of a poem by Delmore Schwartz: *What am I now that I was then?/May memory restore again and again/ The smallest color of the smallest day:/Time is the school in which we learn/ Time is the fire in which we burn.*

Let's get down to brass tacks, thought Rafe. The psychoanalyst, Elliot Jacques, coined the term 'midlife crisis' in 1965. Sigmund Freud had once famously described middle age as a period in one's life when one's thoughts were driven by the fear of impending death. However, Carl Jung put a more positive spin on middle age, claiming it was the key to individuation and the process of self-actualization and self-awareness, betterment both for oneself and others. Just as Erikson described the adolescent crisis as a time of 'Identity vs Role Confusion', when the adolescent approaching adulthood tried to understand their own place in society in terms of employment, relationships and sexuality, some negotiating this universal life stage comfortably, others encountering internal conflict, and old age as a period of 'Integrity vs Despair' when the senior citizen was either satisfied with the life they had led or regretted the life choices they had made, he categorized the period coinciding with middle age as a time of 'Generativity vs Stagnation', when the person would either flourish or wilt. The midlifer finally acknowledged the inevitability of death, and the direct virtue of this life stage amounted to personal change and self-discovery, whereby the individual invested in improving their lot and the lives of others with the hope of leaving a decent legacy for their future generations. Stagnation implied the lack of psychological growth, the person unable to care for themselves, let alone anybody else. So trying to negotiate their midlife crisis, addressing such profound questions as 'What am I doing with my life?' and 'What's the point?' left the individual either supermotivated or completely paralyzed, respectively.

Most people achieved a smooth transition through middle age, but for some it could become an existential crisis, where inner turmoil and confusion interfered with everyday life and their happiness, commonly between the ages of thirty-five and fifty and sometimes lasting up to ten years. Most in midlife fared quite well while others caused and suffered a lot of hurt and heartache.

Oh, the dreams of youth, the energy, the sense of invincibility, of *immortality!* Young people could be so damned optimistic, believing themselves to be the lucky ones who would end up with a happy marriage and a top job. But when things did not turn out according to plan or efforts did not match ambitions, unmet aspirations and unaccomplished goals would be painfully felt in middle age, and disappointment and discontentment could easily set in. But the person could still navigate through their midlife crisis, emerging the other side of the slump in the U-shaped curve feeling less regret from missed opportunities and accepting life for what it was, satisfaction levels rising again, having adjusted to their circumstances a better person, keen to rectify the missteps they'd taken with their life.

Am I a failure? Rafe asked himself for the hundredth time. He was an author, maybe not quite as well-heeled as his neighbours, but still highly regarded by the critics and enjoying some degree of international acclaim. He was currently working on a new book, a homage to Philip Roth by way of John Cheever. Semi-autobiographical, of course, about a man in the throes of a midlife crisis and, like Philip Roth, he did not believe in self-censorship. Except writer's block currently stymied him. Once the darling of the literary world, his career had floundered spectacularly and Rafe had not written anything significant for the best part of five years. So, was he a failure? If he ever got round to finishing the damned book, he would let the reader decide. Wasn't it Philip Roth himself who once claimed that the road to hell was paved with works-in-progress?

For many people, looking after aging parents can trigger a midlife crisis. In the case of Rafe, it was the death of his father that set him down the road to self-destruction. Rafe had already lost his mother in his late teens to breast cancer, and Brock Hanratty, a retired architect living a simple life in Long Island, had buried his wife and got on with his own life by burying himself in his reading. Six books a month he avidly digested, which he had done so since his twenties. Brock, now in his seventies, keeled over at the breakfast table, having suffered a fatal stroke. Living alone, his body was not found for three days until his maid paid her weekly visit. Rafe was heartbroken, inconsolable. Not only his father, Rafe had considered Brock the smartest man he knew, the most well-read and knowledgeable.

His father's death would send Rafe into the depths of a crisis. Maybe by avoiding talking about his feelings, Rafe projected his grief onto his own dissatisfaction with his life and career and his marriage to a woman whose reproductive life had ended childless and with whom he had developed a growing detachment. Felicity Hanratty was completely unprepared for his loss and unable to support him through his bereavement when once she had provided the emotional fulfilment he required. For Rafe, it was equivalent to facing the end of the world, surviving a post-apocalyptic future. He contemplated the meaning of life. Rafe obsessively read obituaries in the newspapers on a regular basis. People experience the physical consequences of aging in middle age when diseases once held at bay start to make an appearance. Rafe was fortunate enough to maintain his youthful and slender frame, regardless of the wrinkles and sagging skin and despite fretting over his thinning hair and covering over any greys. His growing dependence on alcohol had become problematic, the hangovers now lasting an entire weekend.

Then, there is the boredom and restlessness of middle-aged men to break out of convention, wanting to do something completely different, outrageous, radical things in the desperation of feeling younger, of reclaiming their vitality. Paying attention to their physical appearance by wearing hip, designer clothes and leather jackets. Partying or going clubbing to prove they are not past their prime or attending music festivals or nostalgic reunion tours of their favourite bands as one of the young dudes. A sudden desire to play the guitar or learn a foreign language or travel. Or, perhaps, the perilous adventure-seeking of an adrenaline junkie, engaging in extreme activities such as skydiving, hand-gliding or bungee-jumping or running a gruelling marathon because they are convinced they should live every moment to its fullest since they feel their lives are rushing by. What of the crazy, stereotypical fable of the aging male buying a red Porsche and grabbing a buxom young lady as a way of showing off his wealth and power, to prove he is still evergreen in health and to stave off the inexorable approach of death?

Every American has a therapist, or so they say, so fucking neurotic is the population, or Rehab for those who can afford to be fucked up on cocaine, angel dust or crystal meth. Rafe realized he should have stuck it out with his shrink, talked through his issues, instead of firing him when things got too personal. Eat a balanced, nutritious diet and live a healthy lifestyle to slow down the physical decline of aging. Midlife, too, is a perfect time for creative change. Become someone who gives back to his family and the community at large. Enjoy the wealth and success he had worked so hard to achieve. But Rafe hadn't much cared for the pop psychology of Frasier. Rather, dispensing with the crap, Marty Crane.

A therapist would certainly have proved useful since, for many a man, middle age was accompanied by a 'male menopause', a dip in testosterone, leading to a loss of libido and erectile dysfunction. In the case of Rafe Hanratty, it was his heightened sexuality that would be his undoing. He looked up ex-girlfriends, who didn't seem particularly interested in rekindling old romances. At literary events, he flirted embarrassingly with women twenty years his junior. He sought intimacy in the arms of younger women in a last-ditch attempt to recapture his lost youth and bring back his heady, carefree bachelor days.

Rafe indulged in a string of one-night-stands, cheating on his wife with an impulsive and irresponsible brazenness she could no longer endure.

A midlife crisis often leads to a marriage crisis. His relationship with his wife had long since fallen into a rut, gone sour, the lines of communication petering out, neither party expressing gratitude, tenderness or love for the other.

Men have midlife crises out of fear: fear of losing power, of losing their recognition, of losing their sex appeal, fear of aging and a fear of death. His prolific cheating was a cause of great conflict and led Felicity to experience a midlife crisis of her own. Her panic attacks had always been the bane of her existence, and she remembered telling Rafe during better times: *I don't like you drinking because you won't be there for me if I need to go to hospital.* She recalled Rafe's words of advice: *For future reference, only worry if there is something to worry about, otherwise you'll just waste your life away worrying.* Already insecure – the hint of a jowl, a hot flush, the end of unsuccessful procreation – the bewildering extent of his unfaithfulness quadrupled the frequency and severity of her panic attacks until she came to grips with her frantic self-doubt and overwhelming confusion, using the opportunity to re-evaluate their life together and her own performance as a wife. She should have been angry as hell by his sexual excesses, wanting to mould together a voodoo doll of him and poke its eyes out with a needle, a witch brewing trouble around the cauldron, strangle him, stab him, *shoot* him, but she knew no amount of screaming, yelling, cursing or crying would ever set things right. She felt she had done a particularly sound, attentive job looking after husband and home, but the validation of her hard work was now only met by appallingly scandalous behaviour, amazed he could not see the situation from her perspective . . . until, that is, she decided to reinvent herself, suddenly aware of new, exciting prospects.

Felicity initially applied anti-aging creams to address her crow's feet, but eventually opted for something a little more radical: plastic surgery. She underwent a facelift to appear younger and a nip/tuck to modify the shape of her body, capping it all off by changing her entire wardrobe.

She was now confident enough to take in a lover.

Rafe Hanratty and Felicity Albright had been lovers long before they got married. They had met at one of his book-signings in Upstate New York, his attraction for her instantaneous. Felicity had always felt a deep, visceral longing for the man, whose books she voraciously devoured and whose handsome headshot adorned the back of the dust-jackets. Reaching her turn in the queue at the bookstore, she had asked him casually about the 'stream of consciousness'. Their eyes met, and his initial, cursory appraisal of the delicate and delectable brunette with her nervous, wallflower innocence deepened into a full, intoxicated stare. He responded by asking her out to dinner, his voice lulling her like wine and chocolates. Flattered, stricken with desire, she did not refuse. Cupid must surely have been smiling from the shadows that fine afternoon, and Felicity suddenly understood what the poets were talking about. The couple struck up a friendship, which quickly developed into an intimate relationship. They fucked against the wall, on the stairs, across the kitchen counter. Felicity married the witty, urbane writer within one year of their first encounter. She moved into his house in Westerhills. Rafe proposed to her during an evening garden cocktail party as she lounged alongside the pool in her bathing costume, oozing sexuality from every pore, her own unique brand of incorruptible sexuality, fireflies dancing in the air like embers. Heart beating fast behind her breastbone, stomach fluttering, face flooding with heat, Felicity accepted the proposal in front of their delighted, captivated guests without betraying her intrinsically anxious nature. Their wedding was a sumptuous affair, set aboard a riverboat up the Hudson, and their honeymoon in Puerto Rico equally fabulous. They returned to Westerhills primed in the ways of married life. Felicity's father was the owner of a shoe factory, and Rafe kept the man's daughter in the style she was accustomed to. She liked her peacoats and the sets of expensive jewellery he lavished on her.

The first disagreement within their nuptial union involved their disparate views on children. Felicity wanted children, Rafe didn't. They discussed their differences – *Breed or Bleed?* – countless times.

"Why put yourself through parenthood?" Rafe had asked her. "I mean just take a look at those people with children."

"How do you mean?" inquired Felicity

"Ever noticed how parents are often overweight and stressed-out and older-looking than people without kids?" Rafe elaborated. "The women are left with hollowed-out faces and old, saggy balloons for breasts, and the papoose-wearing men end up looking pregnant themselves, sporting a huge paunch and man-boobs. Parents are reduced to a constant state of panic as they spend all their time fretting over their little sprog, perpetually catastrophizing over the first signs of a fever, some sick in the cot or their kid's unremitting wailing. Deluded by their own self-importance, parents block the sidewalks and supermarket isles with their preposterously-oversized baby buggies, refusing to budge just because they have a baby and they think they have the right of way. They might even have you believe that the rewards of being a parent outweigh the downside. Except they're filled with the time-sucking, dumb regret of their decision to have a baby, the curse of a thousand sleepless nights that leaves them permanently exhausted and haggard and half-mad, while being envious of you because you still look young and fresh and minted, having a whale of a time, free to wine and dine and paint the town red, doing all the things they can no longer afford the time or the money to do. No, there is no break, no quitting when saddled with a baby, no vacation from motherhood, only a constant state of guilt and a perceived responsibility of carrying the world on their shoulders. The reality is very, very sobering."

"What about the joys of parenthood? Felicity argued. "Isn't there something natural about having kids?"

"The hell of it is it never ends! Parents will continue to haemorrhage cash from every orifice for their children! The rising cost of childcare, school fees. The nightmare of looking after a teenage rebel who mindlessly maintains you don't understand them! It might be sixteen years before you have some time of your own, but, even then, some children don't leave home until they're well into their thirties!"

"That's quite the damning indictment of parenthood." But Felicity remained skeptical, conscious of her emptying hourglass. She insisted on having children, beating the clock, and he superficially obliged. They fucked harder. Ovulation was always the critical time, and Rafe prayed his wife would not conceive. To make sure she didn't, he secretly got the snip.

But this is all academic. Was there anything wrong with him for not wanting to pass on his genes? *Not at all.* He felt unsuited to fatherhood. He liked his present existence just fine and there was nothing about it he wanted to change. *Do not succumb to the Baby Trap.* Better to be selfish in one's enjoyment of life's pursuits than to give in to the selfishness of one's genes. Besides, the planet was already heaving with unwanted children, buckling under from all those mouths to feed.

Referred to the Fertility Clinic by their family doctor, Rafe feared his private vasectomy would be found out, even though so far Felicity had not noticed the lack of ejaculate during intercourse. But he would be granted respite from his babymaking duties when he received the devastating news that his father had died. A cerebrovascular accident, in medical parlance.

Felicity tried to contain her husband's unspoken grief until she could no longer. *Until he went off the rails.*

No amount of jogging could cure his writer's block or his irrational preoccupation that one day he, too, would die. He took to drinking and found it didn't work, either. He used Philip Roth as an excuse to explain away his deepening alcoholism, that a writer needed his poisons to be driven crazy to help him see. Instead, Rafe discovered sex of the roughhouse variety to be the panacea to all his ills. Except it was not love with his wife that put the spring back in his step, joy into his heart, but sex with other women.

He screwed around with wild abandon, starting with the angels that fell from Friday nights. Felicity may have suspected something – her manchild-of-a-husband coming home drunk from the nightclub every night, the suspicious lipstick on his collar or the perfume of another woman on his clothes, the strong smell of sweat and sex on his person – but she could not bring herself round to accepting their marriage was falling apart, actually disintegrating in front of her very eyes; she existed in that blissful, ignorant state of denial. But it was only when his affair with one of her friends down the road, Vanessa Luscombe, came to light – and its terrible repercussions – that Felicity acknowledged the full brunt of her husband's infidelities.

Miserable and bewildered, she listened to his confession without a cross word, feeling the ground shift from under her feet. Rafe did not acquit himself well. He admitted to the vasectomy, and she wondered how little he thought of her to not want children with her, taking away the hope of giving his dearly beloved what any female of the species – of *any* species – would consider most precious. He told her the acquisition of a mistress – of unsanctified love, a blasphemy to holy matrimony – excited him. His disloyalty and disrespect and his complete lack of humility shocked her. Felicity went outside and gazed up at the summer moon and cried like a widow weeping for her husband.

Rafe hated crying women. But he hoped she could get it out of her system. She must surely have known something wasn't right between them. *I mean we haven't had sex for nigh on two years and you're still talking about having children?*

He watched his wife's looks begin to fade, wither away like roses, watched her comfort eat and put on weight, fatten. He offered no crumb of comfort, no spousal support to her distress. He thought nothing more of it, going back to indulging his sexual appetites.

He only paid attention when Felicity came home one day from the plastic surgeon's, complete with makeover, looking ten years younger, staggeringly beautiful and slim. The decision to have surgery had been largely driven by the surgeon, who had made her feel like she should hide her bare face from rest of humanity if she didn't go through with the procedure. Upon seeing his new-look wife, Rafe experienced a stirring for her for the first time in aeons. When he began fawning over her, she cast him aside with a self-assurance he had never seen in her before. Felicity stated she was engaged in a torrid affair with Jack Pringle – successful realtor boss and sworn, lifelong bachelor.

"And how is Jack enjoying my wife?" Rafe antagonized her, jealousy creeping in.

"The best sex of my life!" she boasted hurtfully, if not honestly.

"Ever thought of the impact your behaviour could have on my self-esteem and my own sexual performance?"

But his protestations didn't move her one bit. "Don't look at me like I'm the crazy one! You didn't care about *my* self-esteem when you couldn't keep your pants zipped up and you decided on playing the field. You should know a wife's rights are sacred and the institution of marriage sacrosanct. But I shall absolve you of your adulterous sins, release you from your husbandly duties. What you choose to do with your cock is no longer my concern!"

Then, she dropped another bombshell. The thing that had started them down the path of disharmony and deception all those years ago, the idea of children, reached a completely new level when Felicity announced she was pregnant with Jack's child. The perfect gift any man can give a woman.

Rafe challenged her, furious. "Is that what a wife should be telling her husband? Does any guy ever want his wife to be satisfied by another man? *Carry his child?*"

"I guess you couldn't do that for me," Felicity reminded him, calmly, non-pejoratively, matter-of-factly, seeing the breakup of their marriage as a blessed relief. "You elected to deceive your wife and be an *incomplete* man!"

Felicity had made her bed, Rafe decided. She could sleep in it.

Vanessa Luscombe's circumstances — and upset — could be deemed comparable to her friend Felicity's. Her husband, Eugene Luscombe, seemed to have it all. He lived in a two-million-dollar house, drove a top-of-the-range Mercedes sports car, was married to a beautiful redhead and sent their three children to private schools, surely destined for the Ivy League. He operated a pharmaceutical company, where in his wisdom he undertook a hedge-fund stripping of its assets, downsizing its personnel and its department for new research, while hiking up the price of its patented drugs on the market by six hundred percent with typical corporate-profiteering ruthlessness. But if you needed those antidepressants, you *needed* those antidepressants. Except it might be better to learn coping strategies instead of reaching for tablets first. Also, if you were truly happy in your own skin, leading a fulfilling life, you may not need those happy pills after all. Rafe supposed a lot of unhappiness stemmed from the stress from and addiction to the consumerist market, making you long for minimalist living. Vanessa might be Felicity's closest friend, but Rafe disliked Eugene because . . . here's the humdinger: for all his posturing on family values, Eugene had fucked most of his female staff. *Does a bear shit where it eats?*

Vanessa knew of her husband's numerous sexual indiscretions and could take no more. Instead of confronting him, she decided she would do likewise and get her own back. The man she chose to have a fling with had already lost the plot since the passing of his father, according to the Westerhills rumour-mill — shame his wife, Felicity, would be the last to know. Rafe Hanratty had a certain appeal to women, as his drunken antics in the city informed her, and Vanessa hoped to exploit him for sex. She seduced him. He fell for the bait, her requesting he come round to her house to sign one of his hardbacks — surely he wouldn't refuse signing his pride-and-joy, such is an author's narcissistic streak — while her husband was out on a weekend break with the kids hunting deer in Vermont.

"What's your poison?" she asked him.

"Whiskey, on the rocks," he replied. "And your's?"

"*Fucking*," she said frankly, causing him to see her in a completely different light. She plied him with drink. There was talk of aphrodisiacs and fertility rituals and one thing led to another. They did the deed that same Saturday afternoon. Reclining half-dressed, in bra and underwear, on the sanctuary of the bed, feasting on his undivided attention and sweet, whispered nothings, she told him languidly: "I've never done this kind of thing before."

"How do you feel?" he asked her, not afraid to show off his nakedness.

"Good . . . yes, I feel good!" she acknowledged unblushingly. "In fact, I feel *fantastic!*"

"That's because there's a certain thrill to be got from breaking a sexual taboo. The forbidden lust, the secrecy, the risk of getting caught . . ."

"Let's make the most of our time together," Vanessa encouraged, hopeful, feeling a sense of freedom. "They say you can only repent once you've sinned."

They fell asleep and he skulked off before daylight, to return the following day and carry on from where he left off, before her husband and children came back with their prize, a couple of dead Bambis.

Rafe appreciated his mistress, his voluptuous, red-haired vixen, her fiery spirit. He got her a love pug. She continued to see him in between her school meetings and book groups. However, it wasn't long before she began to feel something special for him, something *real*, and she no longer wished to be the jealous, overage seductress, like some character in a soap opera, where everybody is sleeping with everyone else. *The other woman.*

She asked him to leave his wife. He said he couldn't. He still loved his wife.

"Don't you love me?" she demanded to know.

"Yes . . . but not in the same way I love Felicity," he said honestly – and stupidly. "Wasn't it your decision that we should just be friends with benefits?"

Not quite the response Vanessa was expecting – and she blew a fuse, resentful and bitter she had been relegated to second place, cheapened by his comment. Her lover, a white American with money in the bank and trying to survive the agonies of a midlife crisis, seemed only interested in putting his cock inside her instead of giving her the relational security she desired. Love mattered to her.

Vanessa demonstrated her volcanic nature by smashing up her kitchen, throwing her Royal Doulton crockery at Rafe, who could only talk faster, gabble, realizing his mistake, and whose spinelessness precluded him from making up with her or leaving the house. And that was when their extramarital affair came out into the open. The children arrived home first to see their enraged mother pouring explosive vitriol at the writer-guy from down the road. Minutes later, too, came their father, who immediately cornered Rafe. *You're about as much a friend as a tumour in the bowel!* he described Rafe, majestically wroth. And such are the diplomacies of prosperous men, Eugene thrashed him to an inch of his life. At his trial, Judge Dredge saw the double shiner and fractured nose and broken ribs Eugene had bestowed upon Rafe and sentenced Eugene to some serious jail time.

Rafe was suddenly labelled as a 'homewrecker', a tag often reserved for women blamed for destroying a stable relationship. Rafe Hanratty never went near Vanessa Luscombe again and Felicity never spoke to Vanessa, either, as Vanessa tried to pick up the broken pieces of her family life. In the meantime, Felicity offered Rafe some sage advice. *Never start something you don't intend to finish.*

Because Rafe was anything but done yet.

The neighbours across one side consisted of the Freemonts, an eccentric, elderly couple with enormous wealth, who revelled in the likely suspicion they might be Democrats, while over the other fence lived the Dredges, the patriarch of which was Chester Dredge, a formidable authority in the New York court system, as eminent as the Wall Street titans and the scions of old-money, colonial families who inhabited Westerhills. Yes, the one and the same Judge Dredge, who sent Eugene Luscombe kicking and screaming to the slammer for his vicious assault on Rafe. It was an oversight on the part of the Court administrators not to spot that Judge and victim lived one door apart from each other. Not that the Hanrattys ever mingled with the Dredges. Their acquaintance was only passing until Rafe stumbled across Judge Dredge's daughter smoking pot in the ancient woods. Again, his glance turned to a stare. My, how she had grown! And hell, yes, he longed to fuck her!

Cookie Dredge possessed the looks and intellect of a beauty-pageant queen, a blue-eyed, blond babe, with a slightly-acned complexion, covered over by foundation. Not that she was completely bereft of brains. Whereas her father was hated by his colleagues for being judgemental rather than just passing judgement in his judicial capacity and for his unwillingness to comprehend his own rigid indifference to the undemocratic realities of society, acquiring the odious reputation of Judge, Jury and Executioner, Cookie cared about the state of the nation, and she soon discovered Rafe shared a common interest with her: their mutual hatred for the current prick in the Oval Office, setting the precedence for the age of walls, gated communities and 'white flight', an explosion of conservative media-fuelled fear of ethnic minorities.

"Yep, become a doctor or a nurse or a builder, not a stupid businessman," Rafe opined, going against his own philosophy to never talk religion or politics. "Heal the sick or care for the sick or build houses. Do something worthwhile. I mean what the fuck is a businessman anyway? Plays around with a few numbers and earns a few dollars. Probably sells his own mother for a couple of hundred bucks, *sorry* a few thousand! And our President is such a dunce at business, only good at getting bankrupt, yet dispensing useless business advice and giving tax breaks to the rich which can only screw up the economy further. The President's erstwhile father, Ku Klux Klan affiliations aside, was always the *real* businessman, but still the kind of businessman, if alive today, who would have cornered the market in high-interest payday loans for the poor. Unfortunately, there's no such thing as an aggressive Democrat, and the Republicans rely on offence as the best form of defence. The Republicans once stood for honesty, integrity and duty. Unfortunately, these qualities seem lost on the Republicans these days. Shame how they have replaced their moral, Christian values with capitalist greed and misogyny and sanctimonious xenophobia – the fucking hypocrites! Whereas the Democrats need to grow a new set of balls, the Republicans use their right-wing media stations to cover up the news rather than report on it. Nothing but wealth, privilege and *lies!* Their sheer godlessness and policies of self-promotion and self-enrichment just go to show the Bible is probably the greatest piece of fiction in the world, a device invented to keep the masses in check. Their President is constantly shooting himself in the foot – that's how 'smart' he is! Why would he insist anyone sign a non-disclosure agreement if there was *no* affair – the fucking moron? Shows how no amount of money can buy you class or talent or brains. The pathetic policies of that all-round, worthless shit are a celebration of *stupidity*, signalling the death of the American dream! But, do not fear, the revolution has already begun . . ."

His unexpected diatribe resonated with Cookie, as they got high in the woods. "Far out . . ." she said, somewhat awestruck. When she saw his reluctance to share in a joint, she asked: "Didn't you smoke dope during your wonder years?"

"Of course, I did." Rafe decided not to appear uncool to this barely adult girl and took a few drags in a bid to re-experience his adolescent self.

"Jew's ass . . ." said Cookie, referring to the wet roach when he'd passed the joint back to her. She told him about her father's contempt for Jews. Worse than niggers, to quote Judge Dredge. The meek had surely inherited the earth. The Zionists ran the world, according to him. They owned the banks, the politicians, Hollywood. Judge Dredge was even a secret Holocaust denier, allegedly — the stupid klutz!

Meh!

As far as Rafe was concerned, the Jews were a noble race who had suffered for far too long, and he was satisfied they had their own homeland. They were some of the smartest, funniest, most successful people on the planet. His only criticism involved the foreign policy of their crooked politicians, who had adopted the same inhumane practices the Nazis had once subjected the Jewish people to and then hid behind spurious cries of antisemitism if their murderous actions against the Palestinians were ever denounced. They relied on the same brand of hateful rhetoric in order to remain in power, sanctioning mass oppression of the Palestinians and the worst kind of enforced segregation. Apartheid, genocide, all in plain sight and politically motivated. Nothing short of eugenics. "I guess the Nazi-imitating, Israeli politicians should be tried for war crimes in some modern-day equivalent of Nuremberg — wouldn't that be ironic? Or why not just threaten to nuke the Middle East and watch both sides suddenly make peace?"

Cookie agreed, smiled. "Give them a chance . . ." She looked at him, frowning. "You think I'm dumb, don't you?"

"I think you're a very intelligent girl with a very intelligent body," he replied, compassionately. "Sit on my schmeckle and I'll show you how much I appreciate you. . ."

She let him fuck her that afternoon.

The woods became their rendezvous, their playground, their tryst. Cookie enjoyed coming here by herself over the summer vacation, communing with nature. Rafe declined the risk of sneaking into the Chester residence, which reportedly had been done up like a governor's mansion.

Guess who's coming to dinner?

Sidney Poitier!

For a time, Rafe enjoyed being the rich, middle-aged fuck, who possessed the guts to fuck a racist, self-righteous Judge's stoner daughter, whose social conscience and smoking body he greatly admired. He ought to celebrate with a tickertape parade for bagging this fine piece of young ass. *Celebrate it, cheerlead it, flag-wave it!*

Except two things happened minutes of each other that put paid to their month-long relationship.

Firstly, after another exquisite session of lovemaking, his young girlfriend made an innocuous comment that put Rafe in his position and caused him to reassess their relationship. "Yeah, it would be nice to keep your mojo running forever, but you're not a young man any more . . ."

Put that in your pipe and smoke it! thought Rafe with self-referential dismay. Her remark, heavy with meaning, he archived for future analysis. He would later shamefully admit to himself that for someone who was meant to be growing old gracefully, his women were getting younger and younger by the day. Indeed, the older he got, the younger his girlfriend. *Please don't tell me I'm the living definition of a 'dirty old man' . . .*

The second development that occurred that afternoon involved a group of girls passing their way, and the sight of a barebacked, middle-aged man gently exiting from the Judge's half-naked, debutante daughter caused them to run home shrieking to their mommies. Word spread like wildfire and the Judge was soon furiously banging on Rafe's door and attempting to pin a rape charge on him for molesting his teenage daughter. *Touchy, touchy!* In the days of Harvey Weinstein, Rafe knew there were three types of women coming out of the woodwork to pursue allegations against such powerful and despicable men: the first forming the majority had been genuinely wronged and sexually exploited, the second lot had willingly agreed to have sex to better their own careers but later changed their minds when their careers didn't quite pan out, and the third type and the few were personality-disordered, lying for sympathy and money. Rafe was quick to remind the Judge that his self-confessed, favourite American President, whom the man was on talking terms with and always spoke highly of, was a philanderer and sexual predator and all-round snake-in-the-grass, who once used his modelling agency for trafficking the young talent as well as holding cocaine-fuelled parties in his younger days where the male guests would take full advantage of the drugged-up girls, some as young as fourteen years old, whom the current President had once allegedly described as, *So you're not too old and not too young,* moreover referring to them as 'consumables'. Rafe further reminded the Judge that Cookie was eighteen and therefore no longer a teenager, and, secondly, their relationship had been consensual. Judge Dredge continued to hound him, went as far as to coerce his daughter to file for rape, but she was not having any of it and stood up to her father – *that a girl!* So Rafe did the only decent thing possible and informed the Gentlemen of the Press of the good Judge's despicable, white-supremacist views, surrounding Chester Dredge in a public shitstorm.

Rafe's wife finally left him and filed for divorce, but not before she accused him of being a *"pervy Peter Pan"* and demanding he *"Grow up!"*. Reluctantly signing the papers heralding the dissolution of his marriage, he felt his internal grief only grow, unable to find a therapeutic outlet. He should have moved out of the neighbourhood instead of staying put and suffering ostracization, alienating the rest of the community for his affair with Cookie Dredge.

If there was ever a writer he wanted to be, it was Philip Roth's alter-ego and constant in his novels, Nathan Zuckerman, who always got the best stories writing about the other characters. Rafe wondered if his own disgraceful behaviour, acting like a human stain, would be worthy of Zuckerman's literary attention in a metafictional sense.

His humbling – and humiliation – would continue, infused with a sense of tragedy.

He cast off the idea of hooking up with any more pre-divorce women or college girls in favour of renting out escort girls, demonstrating beyond a shadow of a doubt the law of diminishing returns. God only knew why he did it; or quite possibly the Devil knew. Once upon a time, when the reality of his midlife engulfed him, he had convinced himself, that he was a pilgrim, an explorer of the female body. There was a whole world of wet, willing women out there with whom he could indulge his wildest sexual fantasies: white pussy, black pussy, oriental pussy, blond pussy, brown pussy, raven pussy, shaven pussy, lesbian pussy, feminist pussy, virginal pussy, spacious pussy, *tuna-fish* pussy . . .

But, as any good alcoholic would tell you, there was a gradual narrowing of his repertoire, his taste in women. No longer interested in the thrill of the chase, he thought he would just pay for sex, surely the easiest and most convenient way of obtaining sex. The REGENCY ESCORT AGENCY provided him with the women, a stunning selection of high-class hookers. Felicity had divorced him by then, seeing little point in their marriage, and long since moved out before he turned his house into a sordid sex den, a midnight harem. He slipped into a new routine, living the hours of a vampire: he fucked all night and slept all day. He graduated from smoking weed to snorting cocaine, kindly dropped off in the plant-pot in the porch by the drug courier. All generously washed down with champagne. Every evening he waited for someone to start the party, initially visited by a gorgeous gaggle of girls until they gradually petered down to three, two, finally one, always the same girl, as he slowly sank deeper and deeper into the metaphorical pit of his own despair, locked in a cycle of cocaine, champagne and call-girls.

The escort girls reminded him of the *Playboy* models that Hef fucked every night during an illustrious career of fucking, old enough to be their great-grandfather, gradually relying on the blue pill to counter his declining performance. Rafe wondered if he should sell his entire *Playboy* collection now that the dirty old fucker was in the ground. No, maybe keep two or three movies. Just in case.

The brave woman, who became Rafe's regular nightly companion was 'Shannon', probably an assumed name. By now he was paying Shannon by the hour to listen to his tale of woe and to cry on her shoulder. His fertility already extinguished by the vasectomy, he could now no longer get it up. Even the blue pills could do nothing. His impotence – and the loss of masculinity it represented – repulsed him.

It was in the small hours of the morning, one night, that his unmanly crying and emotional neediness finally got to her. As he wept, his head cradled in her lap, she told him enough was enough. "There's nothing wrong with a man letting out his feelings, confiding in me. That's a service I also provide. I knew about you from before – I've read a couple of your books – and I was really looking forward to meeting you because they say writers are full of passion. But, man, I can't believe how disappointed I am! Having to put up with your whining night after night. Your wife's ditched you, the whole neighbourhood hates you, and all you do is binge on drink and drugs and cry like a wimp to a woman you've hired to have sex with and, to top it all off, you can't write or get an erection! It's *sooo* unattractive! You're a goddamn mess! You need to get it together! I think I've been just about understanding and patient as I can, but even I have my limits!"

Rafe stopped crying and looked up at the escort girl, who'd become his firm favourite. He gauged her expression, a mixture of pity and exasperation and sheer incredulity. "Please, I need a hug . . ."

"Keep your money . . ." Shannon said and quit.

Dumped by a whore, Rafe realized his sexual exploits had come to an end.

Time is the fire in which we burn . . .

The writing was on the wall. His downfall was a thing of legend.

Following the death of his father, Rafe had struggled to adjust to middle age, crippled by insecurities, stupidly believing he had done nothing of substance with his life, tussling with Eros and Thanatos through his ego-diving behaviours. Once straddling that thin line between genius and insanity, Rafe had finally tipped over into unwellness. His mind was in a tailspin, reliving the recent trainwreck that was his midlife identity crisis.

Do you reckon I'm doomed or is there still hope?

His wife had left him, understandably outraged by his womanizing ways. How he'd treated his wife was beyond the pale. Now his wife had given birth to another man's child. Leaving Rafe had done her a world of good, curing her of her anxieties and hypochondriacal tendencies and medically-unexplained symptoms. She had even stopped giving him the time of day. Rafe, meanwhile, was reduced to a pariah in a place of prestige and privilege, crucified by the rest of the community, ridiculed by friends and family, lawyers and newspapers, doctors and therapists alike. He had been reduced to cocaine, champagne and call-girls. The drugs just screwed him over, and the sex became so dull and one-dimensional he'd end up just crying his heart out to the escort girl he'd hired for the night. He was blocked as a writer, commissioned to write a book he never wrote, compounded by his distraction of expensive whores and the demon drink. He had lost interest in living and was hiding out in his own house. Even his car was fucked; not the tyres or the brakes, but the ECU of the car, the Engine Control Unit, the 'brain' of the gearbox. *Yes, just read the signs.* His damned watch was at the shop for repairs; he had even lost the time.

Time is the fire in which we burn . . .

Delmore Schwartz again. Time had immense power over our lives, and we were all subject to its passing. Without trying to interpret it like some half-empty kind of person, we went about our lives in the shadow of the knowledge that everything ends. Time aged us, *consumed* us, for whatever short life we had on this planet. *Life is just a short period of time in which you are alive,* another pearl of wisdom from Philip Roth. If life were perceived as a bonfire, we had only so many logs to burn . . .

Rafe emerged from his introspection and realized he was sitting in the dark. He thumbed on the desk-lamp which afforded the study a steady, buttery illumination. He discovered an empty Scotch bottle by his side, drunk to the last drop. He glanced down at the bronze skeleton next to the silent computer screen and pondered whether the skeleton wasn't so much as thinking but *grieving,* a pose the Ancient Greeks traditionally affected in mourning. Rafe tried to reconcile his own fluctuating emotions with the heart-rending pain he felt. He hoped for something cathartic.

Maybe it was time to start over. Rise like a phoenix from the ashes.

He raised the Venetian blinds and they rolled up in a shower of dust. Yes, the study was layered in undisturbed dust, as though the maid hadn't visited for several months.

Must have lost track of time . . .

Through the window, the garden caused him to hesitate, puzzle. Rafe glimpsed the pool furniture, folded and stacked-up. The swimming pool was dry and covered in tarpaulin, as though it were out of season. The back lawn resembled an untamed wilderness, overgrown with grass and weeds. The limbs of the trees were bare, skeletal, suggesting late autumn. Lightning split the night followed by the percussion of thunder, as the first winter storm approached.

How is this possible? Rafe thought, astonished. *I thought it was summer.*

The summer before the dark, his other self responded, recalling Doris Lessing. There was something sinister going on. Rafe was suddenly filled with alarm and a dark foreboding.

He wandered the house and discovered the other rooms had been emptied of all essential furniture. The place was deserted and decrepit, full of dirt and debris, as though abandoned for quite some time. All the windows had been nailed shut and the joints and hinges and floors of the house creaked ominously. The light switches didn't work. Lightning flashed, thunder rumbled, and for a moment Rafe thought he was standing on the rackety set of an old horror film, left behind by some movie production company.

Through the discomfiting murk he made it downstairs, bemused, mystified. With clammy palms, he opened the front door and his jaw dropped. He was blasted by the shivering chill of the coming winter, breath misting on contact with the air outside. The FOR SALE sign attached to the nineteenth-century iron gates at the bottom of the driveway cemented matters. But the reality of the present still eluded him until he turned to his right and caught sight of the figure in the wall-length mirror.

I was wondering when you'd find me, his nemesis said in his head, greeting him with demented and perfectly-exaggerated congeniality.

"Who are you?" he demanded of the old man in the mirror, his voice echoing in the hallway.

Suddenly, he had a dreadful feeling.

As Cookie had once told him: *You're not a young man any more . . .*

Far from it. He surveyed the frail, unrecognizable dotard in the mirror, the aged visage, the stooped shoulders. He had poured his energy into fucking around. For what? Because he was afraid of dying? Presently, Death seemed closer than he had originally anticipated.

Whatever happened to those lost decades?

Time to grow old gracefully, he told himself sadly, hopelessly, finally recognizing the anarchy of his reality, a condition that equated to disease, disability and dementia.

They're not kidding when they say self-reflection is difficult. They always say be true to yourself, never betray your integrity, honesty or loyalty. Would he get the mental release he sought if he accepted reality for what it was?

The general state of decay of the house and his own gaunt, wrinkled appearance were a physical reflection of the decrepitude of his life and mood and moral conscience, bespeaking his long, friendless existence.

[*What am I now that I was then? . . . Time is the fire in which we burn*]

But did not *amor fati* claim that all experience was good experience? Should he not embrace Fate and accept all his life experiences positively? *Would I live my life in the same, exact detail all over again? For eternity?*

With a sense of finality, Rafael Hanratty adjusted his stance to a full, upright pose, legs apart, like some veteran actor on stage or an old knight of the realm, waiting for the cold spectre of Death to claim him.

April 2018-May 2018

A Glass, Darklier

"Girls are so easily hypnotized by my words that they're blinded to the fact that it could all be one magnificent lie."

Grigori Yefimovich Rasputin (1869-1916)

"It's good to see you, Yvonne," Hana Wishart greeted her guest on the doorstep of THE OLD RECTORY. "How long has it been?"

"Five years, maybe more," Yvonne Hyssop replied, delighted to see her family again after so long. They hugged one another, once joined at the hip through kinship – and friendship. "Sorry I didn't visit sooner. Was meaning to, but it never happened, unfortunately."

Hana lifted and wheeled in the large, hard cabin suitcase, the colour of roses. "I'll be glad to have my little sister stay with us here for a few weeks. Particularly after your breakup. I'm sorry it didn't work out between you and Miguel."

They moved to the cosy living room, windows thrown wide open to admit the warm, summer breeze. "Sex was just fab," Yvonne remarked, not too aggrieved but rather dismissive of the whole thing. "Typical hot-blooded Spaniard. Took me for a ride. Had a number of girls going on the side. Admitted to it in the end. God knows what he had to prove to himself. Glad it's over."

Hana was already dishing out the tea and clotted cream and scones, prepared well in advance, in anticipation of her sister's arrival. "A good opportunity to regroup and think things through, I guess. Decide what's important to you, where you go from here."

Yvonne took a sip from her teacup. "Nothing to think about. I've moved on."

"What? Already?" Hana exclaimed, astonished. "I was thinking about hooking you up, perhaps whilst you're visiting."

"Wouldn't mind – I could do with a choice in men. But really no need, I'm afraid. I've already found myself a man. A *real* man."

"You didn't waste any time!"

Yvonne tried to justify her decision. "I'm one of those women who, if her husband dies, can't be without a man too long. I'd probably be seeing someone after the funeral."

"You and your gentlemen. I admire your carefree approach. I wonder what Father would have made of your numerous romantic dalliances."

"I'm sure the old fella wouldn't have minded, being a liberal sort of chap himself."

"Eight years to the day," said Hana, sadness tinging her voice. "I do miss him, you know."

Yvonne followed Hana's glance to the mantelpiece upon which rested their most treasured and handsome photograph of their erstwhile father, Reverend Selway Hyssop, the former vicar of the village of Dunstan Priory. Judging by the French touches to the Old Rectory, Reverend Hyssop had been a self-proclaimed Francophile, and a bloody good priest to boot. His replacement still had big shoes to fill. After Reverend Hyssop's fatal stroke, and due to his decades of good service, fully meeting the spiritual needs of the community, his daughters had retained the Old Rectory with the good will of the Anglican Church. "I do, too. But he's gone to a better place. Or nowhere in particular."

"Don't say that," Hana said, a little hurt by the afterthought. "It's essential people believe that there is more to life than the nonsense they're stuck with."

"And do you know what the irony is?" Yvonne reminded her. "The good reverend didn't believe in an Afterlife even as far back as the days when he was a young hospital chaplain. Instead of fumbling around in the dark like most priests and hoping that the Hereafter was all real, our father never truly accepted the supernatural nature of God, but believed God was a metaphor for our moral conscience, knowing what's right and wrong, and heaven and hell our homes on this earth, depending on the kindness of our deeds, the fruits of our journey through life."

"Be as it may," Hana said in his defence, "our father always gave hope to his flock, eased their troubles and doubts even at the darkest of hours, brought peace to ailing minds, made the community very happy."

"True, I won't take that away from him. And, yes, he raised us well when our mother passed away from cancer. But doesn't that say something about him? Being a Man of God, to preach something you don't believe in? Doesn't that amount to hypocrisy, feeding everyone a lie?"

"Not if he always nurtured the goodness in all of us, fortified our moral centres."

But Yvonne was not keen to get into a religious debate. She did not wish to remind her sister that the Church of England had been founded by a lecherous, murderous king as a means to divorce his Catholic wife. And the Anglicans were just as bad as the Catholics these days with the former Archbishop of Canterbury currently in the firing line for not paying heed to the abuse of altar boys by his 'esteemed' ministers under his watch, their sick, heinous crimes swept under the rug. No, it was the man himself she missed the most. Reverend Hyssop had been an amazing man in life, a doting father, and she knew no-one more caring and loving than him. She remembered spending every Sunday in the church, growing up. Organ music, a cough echoing from the back row, a faint titter as the vicar attempted another toe-curling joke. Yes, his humour was atrocious yet strangely endearing, so awful as to be good. *An elderly parishioner dies, leaving her funeral instructions. Having never married, she specifically requests no male pallbearers be present at her funeral. In her memorial service, she writes:* They wouldn't take me out while I was alive. I'll be damned if I'm going to let them take me out when I'm dead! *And how about this one? Do you approve of sex before marriage?* Not if it delays the service! "I suppose I should pay my respects to the old fella, visit his grave."

"The cemetery's just down the road," Hana refreshed her memory. "Maybe later today?"

"I would like that. He meant the world to me, too. He was always there for me. Even when I became a little wayward."

Hana smiled back with a hint of nostalgia, kept it to herself. "Yes, I remember those days . . ."

Yvonne tentatively broached another subject. "I see you haven't embraced motherhood yet."

"Not that I'm unwilling," Hana replied, regretfully. "We've tried, but the patter of tiny feet still eludes us. I can make comparisons to the Biblical Hannah, barren for so long, but then miraculously gives birth to an entire brood. Well, that's the hope!"

"I always thought God *favoured* you. How long have you guys been married now?"

"Almost ten years." Hana poured herself another cup of tea, regarded her sister thoughtfully. "I see you have no children, either."

Mock horror. "Out of wedlock? *God forbid!* No children, no dependants, so I can comfortably continue dating like the free spirit that I am!"

"About this man you've newly discovered," Hana ventured. "Pray, tell me all the sordid details and don't miss a thing!"

Yvonne's expression took on a distant, dreamy look. "Got me this SAS man, Commander Derek Cockburn. Very sexy. *Sooo* Sean Bean! He's popping over from the Rock to the British mainland soon. You can meet him . . ." She paused, responded in kind. "Where's my manners? How's Captain Aubrey?"

"Fine," Hana said contentedly. "He's at the Barracks. Lovely medical military museum there."

"Sorry about the accident. Hope you're recovered."

"Fully I think," Hana affirmed, tried to remember the car crash, couldn't. At least not clearly. She vaguely recalled another car slamming into the side of theirs on that fateful, snow-swept winter's evening nearly six months ago. Blacking-out before waking up in hospital. Fortunately, there had been no reported fatalities. Nor, remarkably, any residual mental trauma. Even her amnesia would clear up some day, according to the doctors. "Yes, it was very difficult at first, but Aubrey managed to help me get through it."

"Remind me, what is he a captain of exactly?"

"101 King's Regiment."

"Does he go away much?"

"Yes, he's had many tours of duty: Iraq, Afghanistan, the Sudan."

"I won't knock Aubrey," Yvonne opined. "It's just that the UK government is streamlining the Armed Forces, selling off our military hardware to the highest bidder. From ruling half the world to becoming one of the biggest arm's dealer on the planet, supplying the Arabs, who own half of London, with the training and weapons and fighter jets they require only for them to pass everything on to that death cult, ISIS. It's the poor, unsuspecting soldiers, who do the government's dirty work and end up getting indicted for it."

"Maybe you can discuss it with Aubrey. He's coming home this evening. He's looking forward to seeing you again."

"Likewise," Yvonne answered affably. "Extremely excited. We can catch up on old times."

"Care for another cuppa?" Hana asked, gesturing to the teapot.

"No, I think, that's enough tea for one day. How about something stronger, cooler, maybe more refreshing, in keeping with this lovely summer weather we're having?"

Hana was having a light-bulb moment. "You mean . . .?"

"Yes, you read my mind."

"A gin-and-tonic on the rocks!" they both piped out aloud, almost psychically.

"I'll have it ready in a jiffy," Hana announced brightly, getting up from her chair.

"And we can have it on the lawn just like we used to."

The sound of the front door opening. Footsteps coming down the hallway. A man walked into the sitting room, handsome, eagle-eyed and dark-haired, dressed in smart military uniform. "Darling, I'm home . . ."

Hana went to kiss her husband on the cheek. "Speak of the devil, we were just talking about you. You're back early."

"There wasn't much to do today," Captain Aubrey Wishart replied, with a clipped English accent. "I decided to give the lads a day off." He nodded cheerily to his sister-in-law before informing Hana. "I need to freshen up."

"Would you like a G&T? I'm making some."

"Not for me, thanks," he replied, retreating from the sitting room. "Be down soon."

Hana continued to smile her trademark, everything-is-alright-with-the-world smile as she watched her husband disappear up the stairs, but when she turned round, her smile faded instantly. Yvonne's face was terribly pale, drained of colour, her mouth open and tremulous, manifesting an expression of shock.

"What's wrong?" Hana asked, suddenly concerned. "Is everything okay?"

Yvonne tried to remain calm, to keep her voice low and steady. "That man *isn't* your husband!"

"What do you mean, *not* my husband?" Hana exclaimed, as though it were the most absurd thing she had ever heard in her life.

"He's not Captain Aubrey," Yvonne repeated, made an effort to explain. "He's an impostor!"

"What do you mean, an impostor?" Hana continued, disbelievingly.

Yvonne hammered home the message. "I know this is hard to take, but that is *not* the man you walked down the aisle with."

"But that's *crazy!*" Hana protested, finally grasping the meaning of Yvonne's purported observation. "For goodness sake, I should know my own husband! I don't understand why you would say something so hurtful! You're scaring me!"

"Your sister is right!" Captain Aubrey interrupted them, standing in the doorway, unnoticed. "You should try listening to her, sometimes."

"Aubrey . . ." Hana uttered and ran to him, like an upset child runs straight to their mother who makes it all better, and put her arms round his waist, held on tightly. "What's going on? What is she saying?"

"Exactly as she claims, bang on the money! I'm not Captain Aubrey Wishart – I never was. *I'm not even British.*" His voice was hard. He physically detached himself from her desperate embrace, no longer willing to offer any kind of protection or security.

"Aubrey, what's got into you? Why are you doing this to me?" Hana's voice shook, filled with incomprehension, with confusion. She wanted to cry, but the thought that unexpectedly struck her deferred any tears and promised to put this preposterous business to rest. Suspicion narrowed her eyes as she glanced from one to the other. "Are you two having an affair?"

"Don't be ridiculous!" replied Yvonne, outraged.

"I mean that might explain it . . ." Hana rationalized, "or if this is all just one, big joke."

"No joke . . ." the man, whom Yvonne alleged was posing as her husband, declared without so much as a blink.

Hana tried to fathom the veracity of the information laid out before her. "You expect me to believe everything you're telling me? If what you say is true, and say I believe you for a second, how did you come into my life?"

"The car crash," the fake Captain Aubrey confessed, unemotionally. "I'd been watching you for some time. Spying on you. I smashed into your car during that snowstorm. I took on the role of your husband."

Which, of course, begged the most important – and most difficult – question. "Where *is* my real husband? Where's Aubrey?"

The now-nameless stranger before her replied coldly, uncompassionately. "He was badly injured in the crash. I finished off the job, snapped his neck. I buried him before the Emergency Services arrived. I made you *believe* I was him."

Her husband was *dead*. It was a horrible revelation. To discover her actual husband had been killed on that dark, wintry night of the accident and his place taken by his murderer. Her vision swam for a moment; she felt dizzy and nauseous, on the brink of swooning. Tears spilled over somehow without any hysterics. "How is it possible – how is *any* of it possible?"

"I tampered with your mind. I implanted false memories."

"That's not possible, surely," interjected Yvonne, "*unless* . . ."

"Can you make someone fall in love with you simply by hypnotizing them?" the man passing himself off as Hana's husband asked rhetorically. "Make them believe you are someone else?" He chuckled, an ugly, fiendish sound. "Mrs. Wishart, you are living proof." He paused before expanding on his statement. "Ever since Sigmund Freud was introduced to hypnosis by Breuer over a century ago, scientists have compared this special mystical state to that unique condition called Love, eventually marrying the two together. Freud noticed how people in a hypnotic trance 'fell in love' with their therapist, which he could not put down to just transference, as though the patient had begun to feel the way a person does in their private life when they are deeply involved with someone, both romantically and sexually. Psychologists discovered Love works in similar ways. You do not need to gaze into the eyes of the hypnotist. You don't need to be told to relax and listen to slumberous words. Pendulums and watches and metronomes become redundant. But you still need a hypnotic focal point, something like the shape of a heart, a box of candy, a necklace, a Valentine's card. Why not, perhaps, remind your partner every five minutes that you adore them? The quietness of eating dinner under soft candlelight, the occasional clinking of two glasses unconsciously symbolizing romantic unity. What about dancing with them, your bodies swaying together, moving with the flow, in synchronized harmony? People who fall in love, just like those under a hypnotic spell, are responding to the power of suggestion, melting barriers, bypassing reasoning, dropping their guard. And if you are a master at the game, skilful enough, you can remember the piece of music that played either at dinner or during another particularly meaningful moment and replay that song, reawakening those same amorous feelings, like a post-hypnotic suggestion, speaking the other person's emotional language, communicating at their romantic frequency, moving the way they do, expressing yourself in their manner, magnetically drawing them closer until you take on a mysterious and very special place in their life. Even if you are lying, the other person is not in any critical or rational or scientific frame of mind to know otherwise…"

Yvonne swore at him when he'd finished. "You bastard!"

"You haven't heard my greatest achievement yet," he boasted, smugly. "I am a hypnotist of women, and a very good one at that! A bona fide, consummate artist! I once managed to make my second wife kill my first wife by hypnotizing her over the phone so I could be free of both women to carry on an affair with my mistress!"

"*Double bastard!*"

Hana understood the implications, the unthinkable gravity of the situation. She had been absolutely and hideously duped, used and abused. The man she had actually married was dead, murdered by this monster, who had subsequently taken his place, ruthlessly and unmercifully manipulating her mind and violating her body, professionally exploiting her for some dark, sick purpose, making her believe something that was not true. It was a bitter pill to swallow, an unspeakable deception. Tears spilled over, more of anger than misery. Somewhere at the back of her mind, she vaguely remembered stirring in the middle of the night only to find her so-called husband whispering into her ear. She thought she had been dreaming at the time. "How could you...?"

"I'm a Russian agent, gathering information, spreading misinformation. All in a day's work. I needed cover. You provided the perfect cover." He grinned, but his voice again took on a dark, flinty tone. "Now you know everything, I'm afraid I'm going to have to love you and leave you." He'd been standing in the doorway for a while, but now for was the first time the two women noticed he was carrying two glasses filled with fizzy water and ice and a twist of lemon. "I prepared some gin-and-tonics, especially for you ladies." He stepped into the room, laid the glasses, dripping cool condensation, on some coasters before them. He sat in the armchair opposite them. "Drink up."

"Why?" demanded Yvonne.

The Russian agent explained frankly, "The drinks contain a very potent nerve toxin, a Novichok agent called Substance 66. My calling card. Undetectable on Tox screen. You should be dead in a couple of seconds."

"You won't get away with this."

"Don't worry," he derided coldly, callously. "I'll be back in Moscow by midnight in time for the best Solyanka and Beluga caviar and the finest vodka reservé."

"Everybody knows Poland does better quality vodka than your Russian brands," retorted Yvonne, resolutely.

"Drink up!" he repeated, irritated, obviously offended by her deliberate disparagement of his nation's favourite tipple. His tone took on a crueller, nastier edge. "Or your deaths will go down as the stuff of legend! *A masterclass in torture!*"

Neither woman budged. Yvonne refused to touch her glass. Hana was just frozen in shock, wide-eyed, staring at nothing. Yvonne stroked Hana's knee with soothing, comforting motions.

The Russian spy pulled out the gun from its holster, pointed it at them. "Or I shoot you instead . . ."

"Very well . . ." Yvonne picked up the glass and gulped down its liquid contents. She slammed the glass back on the coaster, the ice clinking. She smiled back at him. "Thank you for that! Indeed, quite refreshing!"

The Russian agent stared at her, flabbergasted, all menace gone. Yvonne appeared fine, her health uncompromised, perplexingly so.

"So who are you really?" asked Yvonne, her smile unfaltering, evidently mocking him, ignoring the gun trained on her.

His brow furrowed, eyes bulged. He was utterly incredulous. "*Impossible!* How did you—?" He didn't see it coming, had no time to react. Somebody, in one fell swoop, whipped the gun off him from behind and smashed a heavy ashtray hard against his head, knocking him out.

When his vision returned, the Russian agent impersonating Captain Aubrey Wishart discovered his hands in his lap, tied at the wrists with masking tape, and three faces peering down at him. Two belonged to Hana and Yvonne, but the third was a male he did not recognize. Short, dark hair, rugged features, designer stubble, piercing blue eyes. The man wore all black. The Russian agent's own gun, his 9mm Glock 17 pistol, was pointed back at him. "Who the hell are you?"

The man introduced himself. "Cockburn . . . Commander Derek Cockburn of the SAS."

Yvonne kissed him, applying a moniker: "This is Derek, my Friction of Love . . ." Then, more seriously: "You took your time!"

"Apologies if I left it a little too close to call, but it was necessary," Cockburn replied. "We now have this son-of-a-whore's confession as he tried to bump you off."

Hana was at a loss, utterly bemused. "What on earth's going on?"

Cockburn indicated to the man restrained on the armchair: "Hana Wishart, meet Colonel General Valentin Yurkov. A very tricky customer. One of Russia's elite spies. British Intelligence have suspected things haven't been right for quite some time. We've been keeping tabs on him, following his movements. Quite the triple agent, we understand from our close surveillance: working for the Russians, the British, the Russians, feeding us false information." Gesturing to Yurkov with his gun, he said: "Been very busy, haven't you? A long shadow you do cast. Hypnotized the entire barracks, not just Captain Wishart's wife . . . You know we removed all the nerve agent from the house."

Yurkov said nothing, simply glared back at Cockburn.

Hana wondered if this whole outrageous affair could get any goofier. This infiltration of dear, Old Blighty. Despicable. Deplorable. Diabolical. Like Fate itself wanted them all here for its own cosmic amusement. *Such things don't happen in our sleepy parish of Dunstan Priory. All I was expecting was a lovely family get-together on the anniversary of my father's passing. I mean my sister only came here to visit . . .* But events had quickly taken a turn for the worse, rapidly degenerating into the worst macho posturings of MacLean, Fleming and le Carré. "What is all this hullabaloo about?"

"Oh, the usual," explained Cockburn. "That old, old story. The spy game between Russia and the West. You see, ever since the fall of Communism, the Kremlin has been far from idle when it came to advancing its espionage culture, while the West chose to take a step back. Far from it in fact. The Kremlin has taken the whole spy game to a completely new level. It's no surprise that Vladimir Putin's spies still proudly call themselves Chekists, just as they did in the days of the KGB, Politburo and Soviet secret police. But what you may not know is there are different layers of spying . . ." He paused momentarily. "Might I be allowed to indulge you?" The ladies nodded. Colonel General Yurkov scowled back silently. Cockburn resumed: "The oldest and most basic level is Provocation, or *provokatsiya*, dating back to the final days of the Tsar, when Moscow needed to fight anarchists and Bolsheviks, planting agent provocateurs in the ranks of their enemies and turning anti-government activists to their side. This approach continues to this day when you might discover that some of the most vocal activists speaking out against Putin's regime are actually secretly working for him . . . Then we have Conspiracy, or *konspiratsiya*, the actual, official craft of handling agents and running covert operations, like the deep-cover spy brides such as Anna Chapman, even using agents to spy on other agents in true paranoid fashion to keep their own agents in line or if there's a need to discredit them, brush them off as lowly 'conspiracy theorists' . . . *Kompromat* takes *konspiratsiya* one step further, holding something incriminating over someone, using coercive tactics like blackmail to recruit people to spy for Moscow, keeping compromising material such as dirty photos or a dossier of embarrassing information on that person . . . The art of disinformation, or *dezinformatsiya*, used to form a significant chunk of the KGB's Cold War arsenal when Russian officers used gullible western journalists to disseminate propaganda and lies throughout the West. These days, spread faster with the rise of the Internet, we call it 'fake news', a mixture of fact and invention, largely unprovable, designed to obscure the truth and confuse the general public and, in doing so, shift attention from murky political activities. Except what that little Crimea-squatting, Ukraine-undermining troll, Putin, doesn't realize is that no matter how much he controls the media and tries to gaslight the public, the Russian people are *not* stupid! Most thinking Russians know damn well they're being lied to and very few people have any genuine respect or loyalty for him, even if his risible cult-of-*fucking*-ego thinks otherwise, insulated as he is in his self-deluded grandiosity . . . We now enter political warfare and election meddling with *aktiviniyye meropriyatiya*, or active measures, which, using cyber-espionage, attempts to exert influence over and subvert the democracy of a target country. Its virulent spread through various social media platforms can influence political outcomes, like bagging the FIFA World Cup which just happens to occur during FIFA's worst corruption scandal ever and will soon be as much a platform for Putin as the Berlin Olympics of 1936 were a platform for the

Nazi party, or the British embarrassment of Brexit by funding the faux-intellectuals of the Far Right or swaying the result of the US Elections in 2016 by undermining the candidate who should have been the lesser of the two evils, bringing about the Kremlingate investigation, as we saw recently. Anti-virus software developed by Russian tech firms should be avoided at all costs since the intelligence community knows it actually aids espionage and disruption if installed in unsuspecting computer systems. I have no doubts it was Russian hackers and botnets who caused the NHS cyber-attack as well as the far-reaching chaos across other global networks, these pathetic, arse-brained Bitcoin merchants probably working on behalf of the Russian mafia, who in turn reports to the Russian oligarchs, themselves goons of Putin and whose nefarious activities he vets. The Russian state and organized crime have, in effect, merged . . . Then, last but not least, we have *mokroye delo*, or good, old-fashioned wetwork . . . meaning *assassination*, of which we have seen a resurgence, post-KGB. When Putin cannot discredit his enemies, he gets rid of them for good. Countless political opponents and outspoken critics of Putin's regime have met gruesome ends. Gradually working through his 'hit-list', Putin has a habit of eliminating defectors and dissidents and anybody who possesses *kompromat* on the Kremlin itself or whoever poses a threat to the status quo, settling old scores or tying up loose ends." Cockburn grinned straight into Yurkov's glowering stare. "How's that sum it up for you? Did I miss anything?" Cockburn hurled it all back at him, adding: "Or maybe I'm just talking junk, in other words, *fake* news." Cockburn's grin faded. "Compete in sports, why not *cheat?* Any political dissent, send them to jail – or *kill* them. Let's see how I can *steal* from my own people to create my Empire of Evil, all going against true Communist principles. Most Russians are good people. But Putin is something else: he is a dirty arsewipe that should be flushed down the pan! I'm coming for your leader now! Your president won't know what hit him!"

"There's nothing you can do to him," challenged Yurkov flatly, arrogantly.

Cockburn laughed, thoroughly enjoying himself. "Is that what he thinks? Let me put Putin into perspective for you, as if no-one else knows. He was a once a KGB officer in a foreign reconnaissance posting in Dresden, Germany, who became Deputy Mayor of St. Petersburg and created numerous fly-by-night companies to siphon off millions and enrich himself, escaping corruption charges as he ingratiated himself into Boris Yeltsin's inner circle, providing this barely-functioning alcoholic and former leader full immunity from prosecution. When Communism collapsed into chaos in early-1990s Russia, a lot of people died. Organized criminals and ex-Soviet officials fought vicious turf wars for control of industries and political power. We all know Putin had a hand in the Moscow apartment bombings, repeatedly burying any investigations into the tragedy, destroying all evidence of the crime scene, including human remains. Any independent investigators who pointed their finger towards the FSB – who took over the KGB's main security service functions in post-Communist Russia – as perpetrators either wound up in a Siberian prison, never to be heard of again, or ended up dead, as Putin spuriously blamed the Chechen separatist movement for the bombings to justify a war and get himself into power. His oligarchs pay for a seat at the Duma, giving his ruling party presents in order to obtain his protection. His proxy companies have been involved in large-scale fraud, including money laundering on real estate investments in other countries, and it is fair to say that even the Square Mile still thrives on his dirty money. You continue to find ever-more creative ways to launder your mega-stash of cash through Tory donations in the UK and GOP channels in the US. Having exploited the City gluttonously, metaphorically burping when the job was done, the Russians sat back and prepared for Brexit. Putin's ascent to power has involved pillaging the economy, running a kleptocracy by authoritarian means, in a country where less than one hundred people own more than forty percent of the wealth, running shipping lines and oil pipelines and football clubs. Putin's net worth is currently estimated at two hundred billion dollars, but just like the African dictators, all his money is *stolen* money, like some expensive supercunt whoring herself for the purposes of enrichment! In a country where there is discontentment and mass demonstrations and pockets of deep poverty, I guarantee his downfall will be spectacular. *Because I've got his number!* Russia's new, modern-day Tsar – or Yeltsin's cocksucker, depending on your point of view – may be celebrating the centenary of the Russian Revolution, the peasant uprising, but even under Stalin all wealth and power was soon concentrated in the hands of a tiny ruling elite, not quite what Karl Marx had in mind. Just as Putin orchestrated the Moscow apartment bombings and blamed it on the Chechens, he will nuke a Russian city and blame it on the West to start a war. That's how much he cares about his comrades! He's not a friend of the people! Scumbag, thief and traitor, more like, to his fellow Russians! If it were up to me, I'd snap his spine in half and shove his head up his arse, where it belongs, or, better still, grab him by the ankles and ram his head up the arse of the GRU, your military intelligence agency! And if I'm wrong about him, I will apologise wholeheartedly to him. Otherwise, I think the Russian people should rise up and eliminate him like they eliminated the Tsar for the exact, same reason. Putin might be a billionaire, but it is *not* his own money. It belongs to the people. Maybe you're due another bloody Russian Revolution, one hundred years from the first, to wipe away this dirty arsewipe from the political landscape, when your *obschak*, your common cash pot, which Putin plundered all for himself, can finally be redistributed to the people. But Putin will not go easily and will react like any cornered rat!"

Yurkov ignored the angry threats and spoke fondly of his president. "President Putin was a KGB intelligence operative for twenty years and then the FSB chief. He did not get a chance to celebrate Gorbachev's *Perestroika* and *Glasnost* because his heart still harkens back to the values of the Communist era since, to most of our comrades, Lenin's ghost still haunts Red Square, symbolizing nationalism, the hope of a utopia. For this alone, the majority of Muscovites still adore the President, will do anything for him. He is the Master of Detente."

"He thinks he's a big man, does he, stealing from his own people to accumulate his wealth while the rest of the country he's meant to be serving starves?" Cockburn explained, cutting the Russian leader down to size. "Boy, did you back the wrong horse! Let me make it plain and simple, cut through the romance and hubris. Your Proletariat never the saw the freedom and reform Putin promised them. Putin rules without mercy, resorting back to the old familiar routine of buggings, break-ins and harassment while embracing a new, bitter, further corrupt capitalist ideology, driven by a greed, loyalty and power not dissimilar from a mafioso system, as he tries to re-invent the murderous conditions of the 1960s Cold War and rebuild a kind of obscene, grotesque version of the old Soviet Union, a Frankenstein's monster of the USSR, using proxies under his instruction. Except 'plausible deniability' won't work anymore. Agents he thinks he's turned, however, are not really working for him at all, blinded as he is by his own overarching hunger for money and the need to maintain his grip on power. And there's a lot more enemies who've infiltrated his government – *and the FSB* – waiting for the right moment to emerge from the shadows and strike! Let's make the megalomaniac sweat, shall we? I wouldn't be surprised if the conceited little shit will try to become President for Life, even if it means perverting the Russian constitution. As far as I'm concerned, he's *finished!* He won't know what hit him! Soon, *very* soon . . ."

"You think your people are superior?" Yurkov responded, unable to contain himself. "The British send a puny hundred troops to the Ukrainian border. What's that going to achieve? Our ground forces in that region number one hundred thousand. Your Empire is *over!* Our tanks are so vast they have six barrels. They've got everything you need for habitation purposes. Moscow has the largest fleet of nuclear submarines in the world, twice the sum total of the US. We hold a strategic nuclear arsenal of five thousand warheads, with a total stockpile of nearly eight thousand. Did you know we have a hypersonic, intercontinental super-nuke, Satan-6, twenty times faster than the speed of sound and capable of evading every known radar defence system and two thousand times more destructive than the bomb dropped on

Hiroshima and powerful enough to flatten all of Britain in one blast?" He paused for effect, to allow his audience to absorb this terrifying and unvarnished truth. "War has always been Man's preoccupation. Having confirmed your worst fears, you cannot question our military preparedness. All our weapons point towards the West, aimed at your strategic command positions. You see, we have mastery of land, sea and air! Also, espionage, as you 'kindly' illustrated! The Russian Intelligence Service is even bigger now than before the Soviet Union crumbled. Your GCHQ will tell you we're better at putting operatives in Britain now than during the Cold War, recruiting agents who are prepared to betray their country, like the Cambridge spies once did and the debacle that was the Profumo affair. You cannot imagine how many British companies and former MI6 agents we have hired, who are silently doing the work of the FSB, gathering sensitive financial and personal information about our London-based enemies as well as spilling the beans on national security and UK foreign policy. We have created hefty dossiers, full of compromising material, on each of your Cabinet ministers, intended for use at an appropriate juncture. But it doesn't stop there. In fact, my government has subverted UK security by hiring British nationals to assist it in its intelligence operations, a thriving growth industry of enablers, your lawyers, accountants and bankers, all *de facto* agents of the Russian state. These intermediaries, including British politicians from both the Labour and Conservative parties, former intelligence officers and diplomats and leading PR firms, Moscow uses to mask its criminal interests, enhance propaganda and disinformation and attack Putin's critics."

"Rigging elections, influencing events, funding far-right parties across Europe, spreading fake news, I wouldn't be particularly proud, if I were you," Cockburn declared. "Politics: it stinks wherever you are."

"Your British political class has shown itself to be especially greedy! Tory peers have got jobs on the boards of Moscow state corporations while the London Stock Exchange has allowed the flotation of our very questionable stock to flourish. Successive governments have welcomed my Russian oligarchs and their money with open arms, providing them with a means of recycling illicit finance through the London 'laudromat'. Even now, large sums of Russian émigrés money continue to flow into the Conservative Party and certain right-wing newspapers."

"Most people don't give a Russian oligarch's whore about the fake news-peddling *Telegraph* or *Express*, trying to make barefaced lying the norm!" Cockburn said curtly.

"The Kremlin has bought up most of Kensington."

"And, the British government, under an Unexplained Wealth Order, will begin the process of confiscating the houses and seizing the assets of any Politically Exposed People, including Russian billionaires, who cannot account for their wealth by legitimate means."

"The Kremlin cannot but rejoice how the world is going: Brexit, Donald the Tramp, the decline of the old liberal order, the list is endless."

"Not for long," Cockburn replied. "Celebrate your little victory while you can because you have precious little time left to enjoy. Remember, Good always defeats Evil in the end."

"I'm not evil!" countered the Russian spy. "It's just that the Kremlin has been creative in every aspect of society."

"I wouldn't use the word 'creative'. 'Corrupt', more like!"

"My fellow sportsmen never stopped their state-sponsored doping since the days of the steroid-enhanced Russian athletes of the 1980s. Not only do our football hooligans have the full support of the Kremlin, including paramilitary training, our scientists even have the opportunity to get into the genetic code to create people of genius or, perhaps, 'super-soldiers', a genetically-superior human with accelerated strength, capable of fighting a war without fear, compassion, regret or pain – ethics do not matter. It outstrips the existing practice of recruiting the worst, most vicious prisoners into the Russian army. Then, of course, there is *hypnosis*."

"Hypnosis, hey? I gather you're quite the authority on the subject."

"Russian research into mind control began in 1917, shortly after the State-sanctioned assassination of Grigori Rasputin, the mad, mystic monk and lover of the last Empress. We looked into studying and borrowing his persuasive techniques and style of communication. By the way, the St. Petersburg Museum of Erotica owns his severed, thirteen-inch, well-travelled penis, an immense source of fascination for curious women! But it wasn't until 1957 when we developed our own Psyops Project to rival the CIA's MKULTRA experiments, in which the CIA illegally drugged hundreds of US and Canadian citizens, including the mentally ill and prostitutes and prisoners, with LSD over a twenty-year period in an unsuccessful attempt to control the human mind. We, on the other hand, succeeded! Our Pysops Project crystallized into the codenamed 'Hypnops Program' in 1996. I am its Chief of Operations and its top operative. I am the epitome of its century's worth of leading research into achieving dominion over the human mind. I'm even preparing a universal signal – my masterpiece! Did you know that a quarter of the world's population uses a mobile phone any given time?"

All this exposition, this jiggery-pokery, thought Hana, astounded. *The good news just never stops, does it?* An elite Russian operative sent on a secret mission to infiltrate British society and destroy it from within? It was almost too impossible to believe! She remembered how her father, the good Reverend Hyssop, often quoted I

Corinthians 13:12: *For now we see through a glass darkly.* Meaning we humans had an imperfect vision of reality, but Paul the Apostle confirmed we would all see clearly in the end once the obscuring dirt had been removed or the veil lifted from the pane of glass.

"Epitomize the Hypnops Program, did you say?" Cockburn ridiculed. "I bet a love machine like you has already had his wicked way with the First Lady – or the secret 'First Lady' – or you've been hypnotizing Putin's mistresses into pleasing him because they're so repulsed by his presence! I bet you programme some of the young ladies, selected by him, at the Moscow's Annual Debutantes' Ball to share his bed!"

Yurkov did not flinch. "Your attempt at mockery will not work. We created a new brand of politics, a political theatre, if you will, where the voters must suspend their disbelief of the untruths we disseminate and the insane policies we implement, knowing full well we are lying, but that our fake news should be taken in good humour, like an inside joke. Our President's network of power and patronage spans the entire continent and the Atlantic. Our apparatchiks are highly skilled at corrupting elections of Western democracies through data firms, think tanks and media outlets, and, of course, our vastly-expanding, State-sanctioned legion of patriotic hackers. From our slush fund we loaned tens of millions to Marine Le Pen and made covert political donations to UKIP and the Brexiteering campaigners, and we shall continue to do the same in Austria, Hungary and Italy and stoke the fires of xenophobia, using the stupidity of the illiberal, anti-immigration, chauvinistic Far Right to break up the EU, sowing discord and bringing division throughout Europe, and thus create a pan-European, right-wing version of the Old Soviet Comintern. We bribed the political consultancy firm, Cambridge Analytica, to process the files of two-hundred-and-forty million American voters ahead of the 2016 US Elections, having already used the company to influence the outcome of the UK Brexit referendum. It harvested and exploited the personal data for political ends, discrediting any political rivals by arranging smear campaigns and setting honey traps and is implicated in bringing Donald the Tramp to presidential victory, shaping world events and destabilizing the West. Our DNC hack was designed to help Donald the Tramp win the election, and once in office, his administration engaged in relentless and utterly false attacks on the intelligence community and justice department investigators.

"We *own* the American President, control the US government, as he carries out our agenda, compromising democracy, degrading politics and *debasing* the country he took the Oath of Office to preserve and protect, disregarding truth and justice and common decency, threatening to censor the Press and the Media, if they dare criticize him for betraying his people, and legitimizing racial hatred in his leg humpers, just because they think someone actually gives a shit about them when in reality he doesn't give a shit about anybody except himself, with the equally dishonest likes of Mitch McConnell – they don't call him 'Moscow' Mitch for nothing – falling in line right behind him, behind *us!* The Christian right, deluded into thinking there was ever a God, aligns itself with a man who, just after marrying his current wife, kept porn stars as mistresses, whom he bribed for their silence, just like he usually pays actors to make up the numbers at his rallies. These evangelists cannot hide behind the excuse that they didn't know he was paying off porn stars, and they will surely burn in Hell – if there is a Hell – for all their religiose talk of God and Jesus while worshipping their false idol, kneeling at the altar of the Tramp. And, of course, we have the hate-spewing redneck, white supremacists, who are proud of being uneducated and morally contemptible and degenerate and bigger idiots for believing everything he feeds them, making good on an ideology that is no different than that of ISIS. Watch this stupid demagogue send America hurtling back to the Civil War! He is a master at spreading ignorance and lies and fake news, a man after my own heart! You should marvel at our own spread of online disinformation. Take the example of Jenna Abrams – alt-right, Tramp-sucking, segregation-supporting, Confederate-defending, *'all-American'* girl – who, with seventy thousand followers on Twitter, turns out never to have existed in the first place, exposed as nothing more than a troll created by our Internet Research Agency in St. Petersburg. Have you seen anything like it before? I bet not since the dark days of Nixon and Watergate, but you've got to admit this is something far more unique and understated and uglier. Not many people know that Donald the Tramp was in bed with politically-exposed Russians to build a *Trump Moscow* hotel while he was campaigning during the 2016 US Elections, honouring his requests for surreptitious campaign aid and knowing our spy agencies would undertake an interference operation that would touch every corner of the election. We exploited Tramp's sexual perversities, groomed him well, gave him the opportunity to maliciously defile the Obamas' presidential suite at Moscow's Ritz-Carlton Hotel with a string of urinating whores, all lovingly watched over and recorded by the FSB, during the 2013 Miss Universe beauty pageant contest. Trump and his dumb progeny continue to blatantly lie to the nation and openly obstruct the FBI investigation and demand the efforts of the CIA, Congress and the Justice Department to uncover election irregularities be shut down in a pathetic attempt to distract the nation from our very involvement in successfully putting a Reality TV moron and failed human being, despised by the sane-minded, an utterly amoral man, a reprobate, completely unfit to govern, into the Oval Office and allowing this irresponsible, pathetically-thin-skinned psychopath to revive old prejudices and expand societal fractures – race, religion, guns, immigration – doing exactly what we sought to exploit with our social-media campaigns – and to take the world one step closer to the edge of nuclear war, as the super-rich hastily build self-contained bunkers to survive the radioactive fall-out and create a harem full of lobotomized beauty queens to re-populate the planet with. *Or else?* This worthless shit-of-a-president, with his reckless provocations and childish, personal attacks, knows exactly what will happen to him if he doesn't toe the line! That is why we placed him there . . . and he is expendable once he is no more use to us. If truth be known, Putin was the one who grabbed Donald the Tramp 'by the pussy'! Full of 'Putin Envy', Donald the Tramp has always been Putin's Apprentice! Any disobedience and we will air the Tramp's dirty laundry in the international media, sound the death knell to his presidency. Although he doesn't really need anyone to destroy his already-dwindling reputation as he seems to be doing a good job of destroying it all by himself, day after day! We say, let him enjoy his fifteen minutes of fame while it lasts. Before he is consigned to the Dustbin of History. Did you know that a Google search for 'Donald Trump Stupid Prick', or some similar variation, fetches 1.2 million results, all in favour of the above statement? In H.L. Mencken's prophetic words: *The White House will be adorned by a downright moron.* And talking of shitholes, that's what we believe the White House has become since Donald the Tramp took office! Nothing is beneath him, even by his own low standards. In the Tramp's America, the controversies come so thick and fast they eat into the next news cycle, let alone have time to be investigated by a congressional hearing. Actions by Donald the Tramp that would normally bring down any president pass in a matter of hours as he stoops to newer, lower levels of amorality, and the next jaw-dropping scandal becomes breaking news. America has even plumbed new depths with the First Lady, once the well-respected symbol of wholesome family life and moral guidance, is now nothing more than a softcore tart! Don't even get me started on his children, a family of swamp dwellers . . .

"And nobody's mentioned Moscow's complicity in America's mounting conflict with that insane, infantile despot, Kim Jong-Un, of the pariah kingdom, North Korea, who continues to transmit a kamikaze mentality through his lunacy, as we play one side against the other, presiding over two megalomaniacs – two megalomaniacs *without* brains, a double rarity – who are battling it out to determine who's the most stupid person on the planet! These two imbeciles succumbing to one another's risible schoolyard squabbling will be the ruin of the world! Each time Trump frivolously Tweets and threatens Kim Jong-Un with nuclear war, he forgets he's talking about actual human bodies – the bodies of men, women and children – being incinerated in an instant, followed by the slow, agonizing deaths of an untold populace in a long nuclear winter. Believe me, we are prepared for any outcome because we know once the first nuclear missile is fired, it will open the floodgates, lowering the threshold for any other country to engage in a nuclear conflict. Furthermore, you British gravely underestimate Moscow's influence in the Middle East, as we prop up rogue states like Syria and Iran while spreading Islamophobia across the world. We exploited the war in Syria to make our troops, including our 'shock' troops of pro-Russian illegal mercenaries, combat-ready and to allow us to test out our long-range missile capabilities. Watching the West lose life-and-limb over this ongoing conflict and the accompanying mayhem deserves ringside seats, certainly a popcorn event on *Russia Today!*"

"Yes, where would we be today without *Russia Today*, Putin's global disinformation service?" Cockburn acknowledged. "Countering one version of the truth with another in a bid to undermine the while notion of empirical truth. Trump may be Putin's bitch and, of course, we all know Putin is pulling a lot of strings, has got his fingers in a lot of unwholesome pies . . ." Cockburn suggested something unexpected. "However, I'm going to make you a deal. You turn State's evidence against your president, and we will let you go."

Except Yurkov's loyalty was unwavering. "Never!" he bellowed, giving Cockburn laser looks. "Our president has got real presence, authority, power, influence."

"I am a man of integrity and I never betray my ethics," the SAS commander told his more senior Russian counterpart. "But sometimes even I must fight evil with evil as long as I don't lose track of my conscience. So, on this count, I look forward to finishing the job, giving your Putin what's coming to him, exactly what he richly deserves!"

"*Nyet!* Nothing but *borsch!* I will not commit treason! I will *never* give away any State secrets!"

Cockburn decided to extend his Russian foe a lifeline. "I strongly advise you reconsider. For your sake. Otherwise you will die very badly – *horribly*, in fact – and I do not say this lightly. Not by us, of course – we're civilized people. No, a word of advice from one soldier to another, I don't rate your chances of surviving being removed in some ungodly fashion, getting a knife jammed in your back. I think you should be more concerned about your comrades sending you a radioactive birthday cake to shut you up."

Cockburn had touched a nerve with that last comment, hoping to gain the upper hand. Yurkov's face blanched, grew noticeably anxious, twitchy, despite his best efforts not to betray his hard exterior. "Not my circus, not my monkeys! All field agents have a short shelf-life. The Kremlin will just send another agent to replace me."

"And we will get rid of the next one and the one after that and every subsequent one. Just serve as target practice. And as they say, practice makes perfect!"

"You dare to dance with the devil?"

"If you think I'm going to get burnt, you're seriously mistaken. I'm used to *almost* dying a lot!"

Yurkov smiled suddenly, a slow, unsettling catlike grin. "We have a word in Russian that one cannot translate into English: *toska*. It describes a truly unpleasant state of mind: melancholy, restlessness, spiritual anguish, a sick yearning, a dark pain of the soul, all rolled into one. At its deepest and most painful, it can kill a man." He smiled again. "Is it a sensation you would like to experience?" Without warning, the room and its tableau of occupants were drowned by music, the Boney M classic, *Rasputin*, its thumping, extremely danceable bassline pumping out of the sound system, blasting, *hurting*, their ears. Yurkov stared directly – and precisely – at Hana. "Hana, if anything happens to me, you know what to do . . ."

Cockburn shot both speakers, instantly silencing the deafening music, and shot the remote from Yurkov's hand before striking him viciously in the left temple with the butt of the Russian's own gun. "Don't talk to her! Don't even *look* at her!" Yurkov reeled from the savage blow, stunned. He nursed his bleeding hand. A double whammy. The tiny iPod remote he'd been holding – where he'd acquired it from was anybody's guess since his hands were still tied up – fell to the floor. Cockburn kicked aside the damaged remote. "Won't work, buster." He radioed for backup. "You can come in now."

The hallway was abruptly inundated with the noise of tramping feet and three strong SAS types burst into the sitting room. Cockburn spoke to Yurkov for the last time: "Our British Intelligence colleagues are waiting to interrogate you, extract any important information you might have . . . *by any means possible*."

"You cannot fault my Stakanovite efforts," Yurkov replied confidently. "I always get the job done."

"Take him into custody," Cockburn ordered his men, and as they moved to apprehend the Russian spy, there was the sudden plash of tinkling glass followed by a faint, curious sound, like a champagne cork popping. Hands still bound by masking tape, Yurkov's head slumped forward, limp, blood seeping out of an exit bullet-wound in his forehead, dripping into his lap like a partially-running faucet.

Cockburn's black polo-neck was sprayed with blood. "Jesus . . . fuck!" he uttered, appalled. "Just what I didn't need!" His prisoner had been eliminated right under their very noses, shot in the head through the window, apparently a perfect view to a perfect kill. It seemed his Kremlin masters had once again cold-bloodedly disposed of an agent it no longer required or one who had suddenly become a liability at the point of capture, proving time and again how Moscow deemed its spies to be nothing more than expendable, no matter how decorated its officers or highly valuable an agent. "The Empire's over, hey, Russkie?" he murmured, checking for a pulse, finding none. Cockburn immediately turned to one of his men, silently conveying an urgent command to search the perimeter for the shooter or give chase to any white van that may be driving off at top speed. He nodded grimly to the other two soldiers. "Take him away!" Cockburn looked at the two ladies. Their eyes were wide and alarmed, gazes averted, mouths slightly agape. They'd been through an inconceivable amount in a ridiculously short timeframe: betrayal and a bogus identity, the threat of murder, exposition after exposition, even an assassination. "You didn't need to see that and so sorry for all this intrigue and smoke and mirrors. For what it's worth, Mrs. Wishart, I'm particularly sorry you lost your memory and got a false one. We can de-programme you, get you back your real memories. British Intelligence will also want to know if there's anything else implanted. *Nil desperandum.*" His voice was genuinely sympathetic, albeit simmering with anger. He gestured to the dead Russian in their midst, Valentin Yurkov, aka Captain Aubrey Wishart, the blood from the bullet-hole in the skull beginning to peter off. "He's the man who killed your husband and masqueraded as him. He raped you every night. You shouldn't feel any remorse for him."

He waited for her response.

Hana was staring fixedly at the clotted blood and scones. "Oh, botherations!" she suddenly fussed and looked up at Cockburn with the chirpy, unnaturally-serene expression of a Stepford resident before asking, as though nothing had happened: "Would you like to stay for dinner?"

The fallout generated from the implausible events at Dunstan Priory involved three separate incidents.

The entire 101 King's Regiment broke out of the nearby military hospital, where each had been undergoing a formal psychiatric evaluation, and all eighteen men descended as a single, cohesive unit on the SAVOY-MARRIOT HOTEL, where many of Europe's Heads of State were staying to discuss the escalating crisis in North Korea and the ever-growing threat of nuclear war. Although the gun-battles raged into the small hours, the visiting dignitaries remained unscathed. Afterwards, the German Chancellor praised the counter-terrorist response for keeping the loss of innocent life to a minimum. The British Secret Service and a contingent of armed police managed to wipe out most of the battalion, but upon arresting the survivors, no coherent testimony was forthcoming because, no longer able to carry out the task they were brainwashed into executing, each of the soldiers' minds immediately devoured itself in an act of auto-cannibalism, the mental equivalent of biting down on a cyanide capsule, hastened to permanent lunacy and nonsensical jabber.

Having lived to tell the tale, Hana and Yvonne needed to be treated for shock in hospital. Before Yvonne could check on her sister, Hana had escaped from her side-room and made her way to Westminster, where she attempted to assassinate the British Prime Minister, *Manchurian Candidate*-style, as the PM held a press conference on the steps of 10, Downing Street. A shot was fired, but the PM was uninjured, and Hana Wishart promptly arrested. Realizing she might be still under some kind of Caligarian influence, dissociated, the military psychiatrist managed to extract enough information from her shanghaied and hypno-programmed mind to ascertain that the British Prime Minister, who was meant to be chairing the aforementioned emergency summit in the morning, had been receiving bribes from the Russian Foreign Ministry, bringing British politics into disrepute and causing mass panic and violent protests in the streets.

Hana's sister, Yvonne, strangely on impulse, decided to leave everything behind her and fly back home. On the flight back to Gibraltar, Cockburn confidentially informed her that the Russian agent, Valentin Yurkov, had somehow escaped the autopsy locker at the morgue. The investigating team speculated that he had not been dead at all but had staged his own death by placing himself in a deep, hypnotic state, suppressing his vital functions so as to barely register on any medical equipment and re-emerging from his self-induced trance at a more convenient time. The bullet-wound to the head had probably been a movie squib, a sleight of hand, since the blood on Cockburn's pullover did not analyze as blood at all. All in all, subterfuge of the finest. When examining the song, *Rasputin*, on the iPod player at the Old Rectory, no subliminal message could be unearthed, giving rise to the theory that the song itself must have triggered the post-hypnotic suggestion, activating a previously-installed kill command. He explained that, during hypnosis, the mind had a protective mechanism, a *failsafe*, that prevented the person from doing harm to themselves under its persuasion, but they could still be comfortably programmed to kill someone else. Cockburn also announced his intention to take some overdue shore leave, with immediate effect, so he could spend the next fortnight with Yvonne on the Rock whilst the dust cleared. She accepted everything he told her, but the inexplicable fact that Cockburn's eyes had changed from a penetrating blue to a hawk-eyed hazel did rather nag at her subconscious. Except she pushed it aside, dismissing it as nothing of particular relevance.

September 2017–December 2017

Checkout

"You don't want to love – your eternal and abnormal craving is to be loved. You aren't positive, you're negative. You absorb, absorb, as if you must fill yourself with love, because you've got a shortage somewhere."

Sons and Lovers (1913)
D. H. Lawrence

The mobile phone rings, abruptly breaking the prevailing heavy silence, chiming out its tiresome melody in the commercial self-storage space where, despite the crowded conditions, Dashiell Hirting has managed to find a spot to sit. He pulls out one of the earbuds from the earphones of his iPod, on which he has been listening to Greg Kihn's The Breakup Song, when the screen of the mobile lights up. The jingle, unaltered from the original factory settings, echoes loudly within the cramped confines of the storage room, the galvanized steel walls as corrugated as the roller door. The shuttered room is twenty-by-twelve feet, comparable to a small car garage, and piled predominantly from floor to ceiling with cardboard boxes containing various 'odds-and-sods' as well as his actual 'life's work': a DVD collection which he cannot keep at home for obvious reasons. His DVDs are deposited in seventeen such medium-sized boxes. A forty-two-inch flat-screen TV, silent, with no sign of any electrical source in the vicinity, rests on its TV cabinet, which is constructed from reclaimed wood and painted in pastel-blue. Beside it lies a metal railway trunk, the kind in which people would often transport their personal belongings in the age of steam. There is an old, vintage Humber bicycle, handed down from his barely-remembered grandfather, rarely ridden and now riddled with rust. There is even a life-sized human skeleton in attendance, mounted on a vertical hanging metal stand equipped with four movable casters, a quiet showpiece that might go well in a medical student's digs or form an interesting focal point in Anatomy class.

Dashiell – or Dash, for short – sits on a cardboard box in a place that is rife with sentiment, sorrow and secrets. The interminable sound of the mobile continues to rise in pitch and urgency, and Dash considers whether he should just ignore it, let it run its course, reach its crescendo, uninterrupted, and terminate itself. He re-inserts the earphones, trying to block out the pressing tune from the mobile, but he knows that no matter how much he ignores the call, he will have to answer it sooner or later.

Because it'll be about his wife, Jade Lovemore, and her mysterious disappearance. He is sure they will want to bring him in for questioning, but Dash doesn't feel quite up to it just yet. Besides, he knows where his wife is, and he has no intention of disclosing to them her whereabouts.

Do you care? If you don't care about Love, then this tale does not concern you.

Dash was not a Psychiatrist, Psychologist or Child Counsellor. He was not even a Schoolteacher. He was merely a humble sales tech in a computer repair firm, specializing in mending slow-running, malware-infected laptops or upgrading outdated ones to the highest, modern specs. He'd spoken with his Marriage Counsellor, Jim Boreham, on a number of occasions when he'd been at the end of his tether, and the relationship therapist had helpfully pointed Dash in the right direction, citing the literature that might prove useful, might be able to help support his case. There was a person in Dash's life who meant so much to him and yet had caused him no end of grief. He was trying to understand a woman called Jade Lovemore and why she did what she did. In spite of all the homework, the books, the essential reading, he was still no expert, far from it, but at least he felt he had reached a stage in his learning where he could distil the relevant key points from all the scientific papers he had pored over and provide the authorities with a digestible summary, if necessary.

Dash had learned that the most important time of any person's life was between the ages of six months and three years. It was a critical period when they were learning to form attachments with other people, particularly with their primary caregiver, who would normally be their mother. Lorenz's study of imprinting on goslings Bowlby was able to expand into his own evolutionary theory of attachment, where he suggested that babies come into this world innately pre-programmed to form attachments with others as part of a survival mechanism against both perceived and real threats. Whenever an infant experienced heightened emotions, they would signal their caregiver through smiling or crying or screaming upon which the mother would respond accordingly and, in doing so, create a reciprocal, two-way pattern of communication. This produced a secure base from which the child would explore the world around them and novel situations. Mary Ainsworth provided empirical evidence to support Bowlby's attachment theory with her 'Strange Situation' procedure, an observational study into different attachment styles. The experiment, conducted through one-way glass, involved subjecting a good number of babies to different stressful scenarios and seeing how they would respond: how the baby was with the mother, or when separated from their mother, or when left alone with a stranger and then reunited with their mother, to describe but a few situations. From the results, Ainsworth was able to categorize a 'secure' attachment style, where the primary caregiver met all the needs of their child consistently, 'insecure ambivalent' attachment where the child's needs were sometimes disregarded by their primary caregiver, 'insecure avoidant' where the child came to believe that communicating their needs to their mother was a futile, pointless exercise, and, in a later study, 'disorganized' attachment where the child's behaviour was chaotic, erratic, contradictory, incoherent and driven by fear, raised by a primary caregiver, who was themselves dealing with a past loss or unresolved trauma. If the child used the caregiver as a mirror to understand the self, the securely-attached child's reflection would be a stable, clearly-defined image whereas the disorganized child was looking into a mirror that had figuratively broken into a thousand pieces. Rutter went further and spoke about the 'quality' of an attachment bond and the importance of intellectual stimulation and social experiences in order to allow healthy emotional development in the growing child. The relationship the child formed with their mother – or primary caregiver, or a stable network of relatives as in certain cultures – set the template for tackling the world and future interactions with others. If this critical attachment period with their primary caregiver was disrupted for whatever reason, whether through extreme neglect, physical or sexual abuse, abrupt separation from the primary caregiver or through a repeated change of primary caregivers (such as in institutional care settings or multiple foster homes as can be the case with children looked after by the Local Authority) or even a caregiver's lack of responsiveness to their child's communication efforts, then the child would develop difficulties regulating their emotions, an inability to form lasting relationships with others, a distorted understanding of the world and a skewed mental representation of others. Loss of a selective attachment figure produced a reaction parallel to grief in an older person. Other such early, adverse caregiving experiences, a caregiver who is insensitive, inconsistent and unresponsive to their child's needs, could produce an overwhelming sense of rejection, of abandonment, from which the child learned that adults could not be trusted to care for them, setting the stage for the rest of the person's life. Winnicott's research proved equally important, studying the relationship between deprivation and delinquency in children evacuated during wartime. One of the more extreme, long-term consequences of severe maternal deprivation Bowlby called 'affectionless psychopathy', whereby the young person demonstrated no affection, concern, compassion, empathy or guilt for others, seemed to display antisocial behaviour with a complete lack of a *conscience*.

As well as being the main 'contact comfort', the responsiveness of the mother to the infant's signals helped the infant regulate their own emotional systems, the necessary cues allowing them to feel and communicate emotions. If a mother did not interact with her child in a healthy, loving way, the child became confused about their own emotions and the application of those emotions when interacting with other people. The mother-baby relationship was key to a baby's brain development. In the event of sudden maternal-infant separation, or failure to establish a bond between mother and infant, or even during emotional separation, such as can be the case in post-partum depression, the infant's synaptic connections when it came to social relationships and their ability to love and bond in later life were either not laid down properly or miswired and could readily be demonstrated by the study of their brainwave activity on an EEG. Yet, regardless of the seriousness of maternal deprivation, it was never too late to adopt. Something good could always come from caring for even the most hopeless of maternally-deprived children. Humans are adaptable, and the concept of neuroplasticity in the hands of a supportive, deeply-nurturing adoptive parent allowed some rewiring of the atypical brain circuitry.

The underlying aspect of attachment disorders was a fundamental lack of *trust*: because grown-ups have let the child down at every turn, grown-ups must therefore be universally untrustworthy. Children suffering from attachment disorders were generally anxious, easily angry and confused about their emotions, prone to temper tantrums, averse to cuddling yet being incredibly demanding and clingy, lacking impulse control and exhibiting a low tolerance for frustration, frequently running away from home, comfort-eating or abusing street drugs to compensate for the loss of love, either avoiding people completely or meeting up with complete strangers. Some made up for the love and attention they missed in early life with care-seeking behaviour, presenting repeatedly to A&E with entrenched self-harming behaviours in order to be cared for by the health system — forget about the kids who are genuinely sick and need that bed; it's just me, me, *me!* The 'professional' patient in the making. One could divide attachment disorders into two types: Reactive Attachment Disorders (RAD) and Disinhibited Attachment Disorders (DAD). Kids with RAD lacked even the most basic trust. They inhibited their emotional expression, withdrew emotionally with no proximity-seeking, failed to seek comfort from others, expecting to be rejected, shutting themselves away from all meaningful human connections. They were distant even from members of their immediate family. With the Disinhibited type, there was indiscriminate friendliness and attention-seeking and excessive clinginess, a tendency to form diffuse, non-selective relationships with adults, including unfamiliar adults. This clear absence of Stranger Danger, the inappropriate approaches to all adults, could lead to a willingness to go off with relative strangers, risking exploitation, demonstrating how vulnerable kids with DAD could be, lacking self-awareness into the reckless and self-endangering nature of their behaviour.

Children with attachment disorders fell somewhere along the spectrum of Reactive on one pole and Disinhibited at the other end. Attachment-disordered kids presented with features of both types, but one presentation would often be more pronounced than the other. What became of attachment-disordered children when they grew up? Dash knew after he'd done the reading. They became like his wife, Jade Lovemore.

Jade, in his opinion, was a fine textbook example of the Disinhibited type of Attachment Disorder. There was a clear history of unstable relationships which, when he met her, he didn't know about, and even when their relationship developed, there was a certain waywardness about her interactions with others, a desire to please others without understanding the consequences. Mistrust was an issue along with a fear of abandonment, and a tendency to emotionally blow 'hot and cold'. A little chaos wasn't a bad thing; it sharpens the senses, makes us alert. But she was a very messy girl. *Beyond compare.* So ridiculously untidy that, when he first met her, her flat was infested with mice, something that didn't bother her one jot, and from which Sigmund Freud might have labelled her as possessing all the hallmarks of an 'anal expulsive' personality. With, of course, a potential for cruelty.

There were now more children with attachment disorders in the care system than ever before. Humans must be the only species that abandoned their own offspring. This situation was largely due to the disintegration of society in the twentieth century with the breakup of the nuclear family and a loss of the extended family. The ever-growing selfishness of people these days involved a willingness to have children but a refusal to take responsibility for raising them properly. These women ended up having five children with five different fathers. Some of these women went as far as having as many children as possible in order to obtain hefty child benefits. Without sounding like some Tory elitist, it was the stupid, pikey fucks that bred like sewer rats, according to Dash, because they had nothing productive to do with their lives, whilst the more intelligent and discerning professional people waited for the right moment to conceive. These enduring abnormal attachment patterns eventually emerged into a full-blown personality disorder in later life, and so the cycle continued with relationship screw-ups begetting relationship screw-ups, with the same intergenerational principle of the abused becoming the abuser. In this age of Third World consumerism, global financial bankruptcy and far-reaching mass communications, one could only witness the fragility of love, the fickleness of relationships. Such was the sorry state of Love in the twenty-first century – and Social Services and the CAMHS practitioners predicted that it could only get worse.

Attachment-focused parenting immunized children against many of the social and emotional diseases that currently plagued society, producing children who were compassionate, caring, admirable, affectionate, confident and accomplished. *Well-adjusted.* What did that say about Jade's parents? Did Dash think they raised her in a predictable fashion. *Hell, no!* They should have attended parenting skills' classes before they had Jade. They should be made accountable for the way she turned out. Not to press too fine a point, her upbringing and how she turned out was a damning indictment of their parenting, or lack of.

Jade's mother was so highly anxious she never taught the girl how to 'self-soothe', what most babies take for granted. Babies aren't stupid; they were able to detect fear and alarm on their parent's face just as the parent's voice justified or soothed their fears. If they could not consistently find comforting messages in their parent's interaction, the world was filled with danger and should not be trusted. Jade's father was a pisshead who used to get violent when drunk. His import/export business went down the pan because of his drinking and he ended up remortgaging the house. He had a fucked-up upbringing himself – his own father used to beat on him. Dash supposed a language of violence in the home environment was all the man really knew. Dash remembered when Jade informed him of the time her father threw her down the stairs when she was only six; she had a lifelong scar on her chin to show for it. Later on, when she became a teenager, her father would just punch her in the face, unexpectedly and unprovoked, and she would go to school sporting a black eye. Social Services were involved briefly, but nothing could ever be substantiated.

So Dash could imagine what kind of woman Jade would grow up to be. Anxious, fretting to the point of catastrophizing, focusing on the negatives, all disproportionate to the situation, externalizing her frustration by throwing tantrums, making up for the lack of love and care she received in childhood with indiscriminate sociability . . .

Dash Hirting would openly admit he'd never had much luck with women, not that it troubled him. Relationships were not his thing. He had his Xbox and, of course, his movies. He was an avid collector of films, holding over twenty thousand DVDS to his name. Films were a slice of fictional reality that allowed him to enter and experience that world for two hours at a stretch. The only photo he possessed in his maisonette of prefab stucco was a signed Hollywood headshot of Meg Ryan. Then he'd think of all the things Meg Ryan must have done, unsavoury or otherwise, to break into Hollywood. Every Valentine's Day, he'd watch the same two Meg Ryan films, *French Kiss* and *Addicted to Love*, and he never complained about this ritual or felt he needed an emotional connection with a real person. But when people start thinking that you're gay, questioning your masculinity, because you're nearly forty and you're not married, even a creature of habit such as himself, someone so deeply stuck in his ways, will see it upon himself to start looking for a woman. In earnest, if the circumstances necessitate. Not that he was addicted to male affirmation. He had read somewhere that people supposedly operated on a default based on the relationship blueprint they learned early in life, repeating the patterns, unaware they were doing so. How your date treated you was how you treated yourself deep inside because ninety-nine percent of attraction was internal. So were you subtly and blindly telling your date *I'm the one you're looking for* or *Run like hell – I have issues?* In other words, your mindset was 'hypnotizing' your dates to be either attracted or repelled by you. Dash eventually realized he was one those people who had a tendency to communicate a subconscious message of their low self-worth to their date, falling back on old insecurities, and then wondered why the girl never called back for a second date. But all this didn't make an iota of difference when he met his future wife. It wasn't so much he found her as much as she found him.

It was the third Monday of January, the fabled Blue Monday, supposedly the most depressing time of year when people look for ways to overcome their sense of loneliness, that most unbidden companion that may affect them in the aftermath of the winter holidays. And Dash *was* lonely, *very* lonely. That is until he met Jade Lovemore in a side-alley of a pub, a chance encounter. Her boyfriend, drunk as a skunk, was ragging on her, threatening to beat the shit out of her if she didn't give him some more money to drink with. He remembered the name of the pub, THE HOGSBACK, and the terrified expression on her face as she cowered from her boyfriend's raised fist. Like some regular Sir Galahad, Dash stepped in. It was an ugly scene, but he managed to beat the shit out of her soon-to-be-ex-boyfriend, who fled, never to return. Jade went back into the same pub she had vacated, this time with Dash on her arm. The landlord gave her a lingering, disdainful look, probably wondering how the same woman can leave the pub with one guy but come back in with another. What did that say about her character? What did she do for a living?

Dash knew that if one was looking for saints in this tale, one would find none here. He supposed Jade was looking for that father figure she so desperately sought, and he fitted the bill perfectly, taking up the mantle, being nearly twenty years older than her. It was that Papa-Nicole relationship all over again. He supposed Jade would have done well with any pensionable sugar daddy. Even if in his seventies, Harrison Ford was a man she could easily have dropped everything for. *Just call me Elektra!* And, whilst she worked as a photocopier salesgirl, she had that flaky-blond Goldie Hawn/Meg Ryan mentality that Dash found so appealing, and sometimes annoying, particularly when it came to her legendary untidiness, such as leaving scrunched-up, snotty paper hankies lying around everywhere or leaving her breakfast bowl, still containing milk and cereal, absently on the bed if she were ever late for work, which was often. She might act like the ladette on Friday nights, quick to fall from grace, but beneath all of that was the kind of girly-girliness most men could fall easily in love with and, yes, they might love her with a passion, madly, deeply, but she would also frustrate them. In those early days, Dash could not take his hands off her, and she invited it. An incredibly seductive woman, she would wear very slutty, head-turning dresses to keep him interested and perhaps to bolster her own self-esteem. She demanded that he pretend to pick her up in seedy bars, talking incredibly dirty to him, deliberately loud, sordid conversations the other punters in the place would overhear and feel embarrassed about. She would get playful, excitable, shed her inhibitions and dance naked around her flat like some crazy maenad or Rock groupie which made him doubt her developmental maturity. He didn't mind. He was flattered by her attention. Not to sound like a queer hawk, no woman had ever been into him before. She gave him a manly reputation at work whenever she phoned or visited, made him look damned good, and never before had he felt so cool and sexy, like he was some kind of James Bond, every man's fantasy role model. He received kudos from his geeky superiors, including from his straight-as-a-ruler, practising-Christian boss, Gabriel Haber. *Darling, your visit was the highlight of my day,* Dash would tell her. *Here's to stolen moments . . . and stolen kisses.* Her texting him at bedtime: *Perhaps we will meet in our dreams, maybe as close as tomorrow . . .*

It is said that most people spend so much time at work with their work colleagues than their own family that their work colleagues become their family. Now there was Jade, and Dash did not care if she had seduced him. Jade was what mattered to him, presently the absolute centre of his focus, his world. She was perfect for him yet at the same time she was not the right person for him; in many respects, they had nothing in common, like chalk and cheese. Polar opposites attract, or perhaps he wondered if they were more similar than he thought.

One of the most fascinating aspects about her was she preferred masturbating – the old, 'five-finger frou-frou', as she would often euphemize – rather than sex, sometimes on its own, other times as a prelude to lovemaking, and on the odd occasion after sex itself when Dash was spent and exhausted. *I just want to sit back and play with my clitoris*, she would joke, not entirely outside of context, putting her hand down her panties and rubbing her crotch, man-style. Still, if they did have sex, it was an enjoyable enough experience, but nothing really worth writing home about. Dash firmly believed sex should be for the pleasure of the woman and not for the selfish gratification of the man, and he took his time over it, over *her*. Despite his limited experience in the sack, their lovemaking did make him feel satisfied and complete.

Dash did not marry Jade out of pity. She might be lovable and cute to most men, a regular Meg Ryan, and cute may not make the foundations of a good relationship, but he married her because she was exciting and she seemed to adore him when in many respects he considered himself somewhat over the hill, at the onset of middle age, and he knew another opportunity would never come a-begging again. If married life didn't work out, then at least he could say he'd tried it and it wasn't for him. Prior to tying the knot, they must have been dating for less than six months and been living together for only three months in the humble maisonette he had recently bought with a mortgage. He recalled Jade solemnly informing him that her days of hopping from man to man were sincerely over since she saw in Dash the man who would care for her for the rest of her life – and she became exclusively his. He never thought convenience played a part in her decision to choose him over the next man. And *she* was the one who knelt down on *her* knee and proposed to him one lunchtime at work in the presence of his awestruck colleagues. Marilyn Monroe once said: *Before marriage, a girl has to make love to a man to hold him. After marriage, she has to hold him to make love to him.* To quote Socrates: *By all means, marry. If you get a good wife, you'll become happy; if you get a bad one, you'll become a philosopher.*

The wedding was a straightforward Registry-Office affair, followed by a simple but joyous reception at the Chapel Mead Civic Centre. Dash allowed Jade to keep her family name as, in his opinion, there was no more a fitting and beautiful surname as Lovemore, except perhaps Loveness. They spent their wedding night at the SOFITEL HOTEL in St James, London. *I don't know what pants to wear,* he told her in that plush hotel room. *You don't need any pants where we're going!* she reminded him. He remembered reading Chekhov's short story, *The Darling*, during their brief honeymoon in London, before he went back to repairing and refurbishing laptops and she returned to selling photocopiers, and thinking how the character Olenka gets easily attached to her men and never learns to think independently of them.

Dash remembered how Jade's mother was grateful to him for being brave enough in making the 'grand gesture' of marrying her daughter and, more importantly, thanked him for 'making an honest woman' out of her. It might seem like an innocuous comment, a compliment, some might even call it a platitude, but Dash did not see it at the time that her words of gratitude held a special significance. They would prove relevant, portentous, come back to haunt him much later when their marriage was in crisis and her mother decided to discuss Jade's past – *after* they had married – how very kind of her! He realized that a lot of people put on their best self during courtship, and their spouse never saw their warts-and-all personality until their relationship was legally sanctified. As Alexander Pope observed: *They dream in courtship, but in wedlock wake.*

It didn't initially occur to Dash that something might be seriously wrong with his wife, aside from her turning the maisonette into another bombsite; she was such a messy person he was always cleaning up after her. No, he didn't realize the extent of her unhappiness underneath, how so very insecure she was, while putting on the pretence of a brave front. Through his later reading, Dash learned that when childhood attachment difficulties remain unresolved in adulthood, such insecurely-attached individuals express a lot of marital dissatisfaction and can often be rejecting of their spouse in favour of complete strangers. The first indicator of trouble in his case, the moment Dash first suspected that something might be up with his wife, was when she'd get genuinely upset when exploring other people's Facebook pages, stating that her former classmates were 'ignoring' her, that she was missing out on their parties even though she hadn't seen them in five years. Her deep sense of alienation, her desire to win friendships and be part of the In-crowd and get eternally invited to their functions proved a consistent theme, almost akin to *envy*. It could also make her potentially vulnerable to online predators on social networking sites, even if she was a grown woman. She was desperate to have friends, feel wanted, like a puppy-dog yearning to be a fully-fledged member of the pack. A case of 'I am here . . . I exist'. His own favourite description of the whole subject of friendship went: *Friendship is like peeing in your pants; it's open for everyone to see but only you can feel its true warmth!* But Jade took her clumsy, flawed attempts to make friends to a new, frantic level. Neither did it click with the amount of time she spent texting people, sometimes hours on end, most of whom she hardly knew. They say that couples turn to television when they run out of things to say, and Dash and Jade were watching a lot of TV from early on into their marriage, not that Jade paid much attention to the TV screen, immersed as she was in her intense, incessant texting. It would prove to be the thin end of the wedge.

Don't ever leave me! he remembered her panicking, one time, before lights out in their bedroom, rather irrationally and unnecessarily. *I don't want you to die and leave me a widow!*

I don't intend to die just yet, Dash reassured her, wondering where this had all suddenly come from. *One day perhaps, but not in the foreseeable future. You agree I will die one day?*

She did not respond, just looked miserable, and he cuddled her. Dash did not realize it wasn't about his health that she was worried about but being left all alone again if he died. It was that anxiety around abandonment and a feeling that, if he went, she too would 'cease to exist' on some subconscious level.

Aside from the childhood training she never received from her parents to help her regulate her emotions, make sense of life and create meaningful relationships, there was also that little matter of using Dash as a secure base to do crazy things. So addicted was she to texting that she had a tendency to strike up a conversation with him by text from the other room.

For it was only after Christmas lunch at her parents, sitting down to sherry, that Dash just happened to pick up her mobile and began idly flicking through her texts.

Happy Feast Day on the Birth of Christ 2 u 2! he recalled one particular thread of conversation commencing, from Jade to her boss from the photocopier shop, Darren Pearson. *How's u?*

His response? *Just dying to munch on your pussy, lick it out, do things no other tongue can do!*

Yuk! My pussy's all sweaty and smelly! Like onions!

Won't stop me! I'm a pretty determined guy!

Such were the sexualized texts to her boss — to which her boss had attached a selfie of his erect penis — that Dash and Jade entered into a raging argument on Christmas Day at her parents' house. Found-out, Jade was angrier that he had touched her mobile than by the sexting between herself, a recently-married woman, and her chauvinistic boss. She assured Dash that this was only a bit of fun between two good friends. Even if they were engaging in a little dirty talk, there was nothing physical going on between her and her boss, and she had not been posting selfies of her vagina on her mobile. She reminded Dash of her reputation of being flirty, a 'prick-teaser', her very own words. From the strength of the exchange of these overly intimate texts, Dash struggled to accept her explanation, downplaying the seriousness of the situation, at face value. This was not friendship. This was obscene.

It was only when Dash dug a bit deeper that his mother-in-law disclosed some of her daughter's antics from earlier on in her life. She was a handful as an adolescent, apparently. His mother-in-law told him about the 'relationship' her daughter had with her Fifth Form English teacher, who got into major disciplinary trouble over her – no-one still knows if anything happened between them. This followed close on the heels of the 'crush' Jade harboured over her own paternal uncle, a truly dashing fellow over whom Jade hatched a plot for him to catch her nude in the shower – I mean doesn't that border on incest? An embarrassing and very emotive family quarrel ensued, near-fisticuffs, and Jade's father had still not forgiven his brother to this day. In fact, he had not spoken to him since or invited him to the house, treating him like a pariah. All because of Jade. But the event that really stood out was the time Jade left school at sixteen and went to work at her father's import/export firm. There, one of the male employees grew increasingly obsessed with her to the point he ended up tying her arms behind an office chair with rolls of sellotape. His colleagues heard her frightened screams and came to her rescue. Her father went ballistic. Police were called and the man was arrested and sentenced for kidnapping and abuse of a minor. He was also placed on the Sex Offenders Register. In his defence, he informed the Jury the whole thing had been consensual and called her a 'prick-teaser' for seducing him, which, of course, did not help his case in the dock. The Judge, in his summing-up, described the incident as a 'near-miss'. Jade refused to discuss the incident with Dash when he broached the subject with her much later.

Even into her late teens she struggled to remain single, always going out with some guy or other, no matter how undesirable. She'd ring sex hotlines late at night, leading to a massive phone bill that her father confronted her with. Dogging sites became a particular fascination for a short spell, parking up and prowling around the reserve, peering into the darkened cars and frigging over the couple having sex inside rather than actually participating herself.

Her two closest friends led equally aimless lives – birds of a feather and all that. Denise Cooper shagged a lot and had admitted to sleeping with over seventy men. *Best of luck finding a future husband!* Gina Westcott's propensity for drunken sex led to one abortion after another. *No first prize in this competition!* So you had one woman who couldn't keep her cunt to herself and another who fell pregnant every five minutes but decided it wasn't anything another abortion couldn't fix. Despite being a longstanding circle of security, they happened to be as vulnerable as Dash's wife, not exactly socially-savvy, whose unwariness of strangers could easily lead to being taken advantage of in their search for meaning and closeness from others. They used sex as a replacement for true affection, just to feel loved and wanted for that brief moment – always superficial, short-lived relationships since the men soon got wise. They had used their easy allure for so long it had become their 'career'. Like Jade, they were looking for love in all the wrong places, perhaps searching for that father figure they never had.

Dash remembered how much Jade fretted over turning twenty-one, and her fear of her advancing years. *I'll kill myself before I grow too old!* she told him, emphatically, and rather irrationally, mind. He reassured her that she would always look beautiful, trying to lighten the mood by adding, as long as she didn't trim her fringe or create a quiff that might otherwise give her a Toby Jones' forehead. This added afterthought became a running gag between them.

She told him about the time in the not-so-distant past when the gas man came round just as she was showering. He had rung to say he would be there in fifteen minutes. But he arrived within five minutes, just as Jade got into the shower. He saw her naked through the bathroom window, and she allegedly freaked out, wrapping herself quickly in a bathrobe. He humbly apologized for his intrusion, was just checking if anyone was at home, and no more became of it. Dash, on the other hand, was furious when she related these events to him later.

Dash challenged her on her behaviour, fuming. *Step into the man's shoes! When he says he'll be visiting in fifteen minutes and he finds you in the shower, what impression does that give him?*

Jade considered. *That I want to have sex with him?*

Yes, that you're a bored housewife hoping to get lucky! Dash explained. *And your behaviour is a kick in the teeth for me, because the man's probably thinking that I can't satisfy you!*

You knew when you married me that I can be a right little raver sometimes, a proper exhibitionist!

I don't want you humiliating yourself – and me *– like that again, is that understood?* Think, woman, in future!

Then, there was that whole sorry saga of the handyman. John was some riff-raff she had picked up from the street to do some work around the house. He fixed the lights and hung up some pictures, tended to the small garden. It was only much later when he had disappeared from the scene, and Dash asked Jade what had become of him, that she informed Dash that the man had made a pass at her, demanding a greater fee for his services way above his original estimate, such that she eventually had no choice but to cut him loose. But the most unforgivable thing about it, Dash discovered, was she still kept inviting John to their maisonette with Dash still there, without furnishing Dash with the knowledge of what the man had done because she had been afraid that Dash might get angry with her and the man. In the end, she had dismissed John of her own accord, but not before he made a few more visits to the house. Dash and Jade did fight in the weeks that followed over her unforgivable decision not to disclose the handyman's sexual advances. Dash felt utterly humiliated when he learned what the man had done and the fact that Jade had consciously permitted John to continue coming to the house as if nothing happened between them. Far worse, the man must have thought of Dash as a right idiot, had a good laugh afterwards with his mates, for accepting him back in the house even after trying his luck with Jade. Dash hardly slept. And a man can do a lot of thinking when he can't sleep. He wondered why she should have kept the whole thing a secret, whether the man had developed some kind of hold over her. His mind kept turning over the horrible idea that perhaps his newly-married wife had sucked the handyman's cock as payment for services rendered – and it was an idea that wouldn't go away. Instead, it stayed with him for a long time. Could Dash be accused of morbid jealousy?

And why on earth should she jump into the shower when the supermarket delivery guy says he's only going to be ten minutes from dropping off the shopping? Does she not realize what the man's going to think?

Suddenly, one day, out of the blue, she decided she wanted to become an actress. Her impulsiveness drove her decision; whatever came to her head, Jade ran with it without a moment's thought as to the consequences. Dash assumed it was that thing again about wanting to be loved by other people, by the world. She attempted a bit of amateur dramatics, had a starring role in *An Ideal Husband*, but her performance was terrible. Woeful. *Bloody awful!* Yet, she seemed utterly intent on pursuing her acting dreams, on becoming famous, while heavily overestimating her own talents, and Dash absolutely insisted she didn't quit her day job. He didn't want to dampen her enthusiasm by telling her she should prepare for disappointment. Things seemed quiet for a couple of weeks, and even when he inquired as to how her acting was going, she appeared strangely detached and furtive. She seemed fascinated by that French film, *Belle de Jour*, in which a bored housewife, Catherine Deneuve, takes up prostitution while her husband is at work. She also adored Sidney Lumet's film, *The Appointment*, seemingly running a similar storyline. It should have set off alarm bells, but it was only one afternoon whilst he was laid down with the 'flu that he received a phone call from a certain Mr. Mehboob, a Pakistani gentleman, who informed him he was a film producer. He told Dash that he'd booked his wife in for a film. Dash inquired about the nature of the film. *Porn*, the man replied. Dash thanked him for letting him know and then told him to kindly fuck off and never call again, before slamming the phone down.

When Jade arrived home from work, he confronted her. After initially feigning ignorance, she eventually relented and told him what had transpired. Having applied through the notorious Craigslist for acting auditions, Mr. Mehboob had contacted her and promised her the big break into the world of cinema through pornographic work. Just a case of getting her foot in the door, he'd assured her, a stepping stone. *What about my husband?* She asked him. His response? *Your husband doesn't need to know...*

Your husband doesn't need to know? What a motherfucker! Propositioning his wife like that. But was it really Mehboob's fault? It was Jade's problem for getting herself into this scrape.

Jade reassured Dash that she didn't pursue this new direction in career because it was only £120 for two hours' work. *That* was her explanation! So if it had paid £200 – along with the complete loss of dignity and respect – *that* would be okay? She went on to inform him that she didn't attend the audition, let alone sleep with anyone.

Did Dash believe her?

It wouldn't have at all surprised Dash if she had actually slept with the damned director in her naive, clumsy quest for fame or possibly even with that slimy Paki producer, Mehboob, whom Dash could envisage might have broken it off with her when he realized how needy she was. Maybe Jade wasn't being entirely honest with Dash. Maybe director and producer jointly fucked his wife for one night and moved on! *That's what my wife is worth to you?* Maybe she did perform in a couple of those dirty movies, and she was now permanently on film. But Dash was yet to find any evidence of it. He struggled to come to terms with the unconfirmed notion that his wife's introduction to the film industry might be a porn scene. He thought about that angry writer from Oaks Fold who lost the plot with his cheating wife. *Does your wife like photography, nudge, nudge, wink, wink, hint, hint? . . . No, but she's one helluva goer! Gentlemen, start your engines!*

Dash wanted to throw acid over Jade's face so she could never act [*? again*] but resisted the temptation in spite of his anger. Instead, he experienced another, new emotion: he felt *ashamed* of his wife. He would never let her live it down. Was she trying to recreate the same dynamic as she had with her father, gain attention from her husband through bad behaviour, even if it meant being punished?

Yet, the entire episode, including the shame, brought them somehow closer together. In fact, Jade made more of an effort. They renewed their vows in the bedroom, half-heartedly on the part of Dash, but Jade became genuinely more caring, more focused on him, on *them*. She wanted them to work things out. Perhaps she was operating on a guilt trip. She spoke about having a kid, solidifying their relationship. Most couples know television is the last recourse of a failing marriage. Sometimes to save a marriage people have children. *Bad move, because it's for all the wrong reasons. That kid doesn't stand a chance.*

To reiterate, attachment-disordered people always want kids because they want something to care for and love and make up for not being cared for and loved when they themselves were young. They believe the baby will become their focus and afford security, but in reality it's an *illusion* of security because they're either incapable of raising the child normally or *unwilling* to, fucking up their offspring in the process, who eventually goes into the care of Social Services, and when the said-child grows up, the whole mess goes full circle. The UK is inundated with these kids, invalidated, devalued, made to feel as if they are undeserving of their parents' love, their self-esteem and their faith in human nature completely shot, setting up a lifetime of rejections, leaving them unequipped to look after their own kids in any consistent, nurturing manner when the time comes. Five different kids with five different fathers – everyone knows the story.

Dash remembered joking around when they were drunk, and on the same crazy frequency: *What if I raped you and you fell pregnant?*

But I'm on the Pill.

That's what you *think! Would you ever think I've substituted your pill with a placebo and been raping you every night after drugging your warm milk, trying to knock you up?*

But they thought a child would be nice – a physical representation of their love. A 'baby, round man', as Jade called it. It would complete them. Their sex life picked up. Since she came off the Pill, she was certainly more aroused, receptive. Then, she missed her period, and she stressed over it: *Come on period. Leave my body now. Expel the blood.* Dash kept reminding her that stress about no period could result in no periods. Besides, they were meant to be in the babymaking phase of their marriage. The pregnancy test proved positive, and a sonogram subsequently provided them with the photographic evidence, bringing the reality of it home. Jade was definitely 'preggers', at eight weeks in fact. An amniocentesis revealed it was a boy. Their little baby round man was on its way.

But was it *his*?

Did he care if it wasn't?

They were expecting. That's all that mattered. But the dreams he had were unspeakable and really black. In one particular dream, he saw her knifing herself repeatedly in the belly. In another nightmare, she was heavily pregnant and aborting horribly, bits of the unborn child falling out of her, the baby's severed limbs splashing to the floor individually, as though someone had jigsawed her baby up from inside of her. Dash would always wake up in a cold sweat.

Then, Jade started panicking and suggested giving the baby up for adoption the moment it would be born, or perhaps dumping it on him, instead. Dash was disgusted by her, severely disappointed by her attitude. It was reprehensible. A part of him dreaded her having a baby, how she would not be able to form a strong attachment with their child, how the poor thing would feel uncared for, unloved, grow up with inconsistent, conflicting parenting styles, how their child would develop serious attachment issues of its own and subsequently go into care. Jade was not going to afford anyone any peace of mind.

Twelve weeks down the line, Jade suffered a miscarriage. Dash didn't know if it was spontaneous . . . or *self-induced*. But he remembered her waking up in the middle of the night, the bedsheets tacky with blood, and something else — a tiny, curled-up lump of flesh. Instead of a little, round man, they had produced a *mooncalf*. Coincidentally, he also remembered Jade talking about mandrake days before the terrible event. The doctors didn't even bother to investigate the abortion.

People deal with this kind of catastrophe in different ways.

Jade didn't grieve afterwards, just got on with her day as if nothing happened. Dash missed work and drank a lot. They argued. They argued a lot. Hurtful words were spoken. Divorce was mentioned.

They were rapidly growing apart. Jade either consciously refused to act like the loving wife or didn't know how to, lacking the necessary social skills to mend the widening gulf between them, not even attempting to say the normal things wives say to re-establish some degree of marital harmony. She was either unwilling — or *incapable* — of making reparations, of being supportive, of consoling and reassuring Dash that everything was going to be okay. Where once she had expected her husband to be a lean-to, a pillar of emotional support, a shoulder to cry on, she deliberately chose not to rely on him anymore, further distancing herself from any meaningful contact or desire to talk. In other words, *avoiding* him. Not only had their love life petered out, with her eschewing every one of his advances, Dash got the eerie sense that she might be saving herself for someone else and she didn't wish to be unfaithful to that other person . . .

They tried a marriage counsellor, Jim Boreham. Very nice guy, but his hairstyle seemed not to have moved on from the early 1990s. He introduced himself by telling them the story of how he came to be a marriage counsellor. The onus was also on him to earn their trust. Apparently, Boreham took up marriage counselling because he never forgave his ex-wife. He told them of the time he and his [then-] wife went on holiday to South Africa in 1987 and had the opportunity of buying a genuine lithograph painted by Nelson Mandela from his time at Robben Island. It was only worth £500, but his wife insisted they didn't buy it because they were saving up for a bigger house. While vacationing in South Africa in 1996, with Nelson Mandela now President of the country, the same painting was going for £14,000. Again, Boreham's wife refused to let him buy it. Then, with Mandela's entire collection going up for auction following his death in 2013, Boreham discovered that the particular painting he'd kept an eye on all these years had fetched an incredible 1.2 million pounds. Boreham could not forgive his wife for being a killjoy, for not indulging in a little positive risk-taking and therefore letting a golden opportunity like this slip them by. *Twice.* Imagine the life they might have been leading now if they'd bought the artwork when he'd originally suggested it. That's why they were now divorced and that's why he chose marriage counselling as a career, to allow the troubled couple to think and reflect on the things that brought them together in the first place and how bad decisions can upset the balance. *When you get married, sometimes you're going to wish you had your old life back.* The secret to marriage counselling, Boreham explained, was to allow both members of the relationship, working in tandem, to see into themselves in order to bring their own unique individual strengths out into the open so that their relationship could come as close to harmony as was humanly possible.

Their opening session, ushered in by Boreham's personal anecdote, relaxed this particular couple greatly and empowered them to express some of their worries.

Would you be happy if I was happy? Dash remembered Jade asking him at the end of that first session.

I am always happy, he contemplated, *but I so dream of the day when you are happy with me and the world you live in but, most of all, with* yourself.

I know that things haven't been going as well as they should have.

At last we can look inside ourselves and each other and see what's lacking or missing or just lost in time and hopefully rediscover it — and ourselves — again. I really want us to get back on track.

It seemed that evening, considering the subsequent sexual gymnastics they indulged in, they were back on the road to recovery.

That same night, however, he dreamt of Jim Boreham.

In the dream, Dash was desperately seeking the man's professional advice for something he only vaguely remembered in the morning. *I don't know how I'm going to cope. She's just getting too much. Now she won't kiss me. What do you think I should do?*

Your wife is cheating on you, Boreham's dream-self blurted out bluntly, as though he were psychically informing Dash of something that he found hard to do so in person in the real session. *Your wife won't kiss you because her loyalties lie elsewhere. She's keen not to cheat on her lover, the person she* really *loves and is faithful towards.* Dash thought about that dream. The dream-world was a way of processing events. He thought about the porn producer, the intimate sextspeak to her boss. He thought about the lunatic who tied her up to a chair when she was sixteen, the death of their baby. He wondered if his wife was fucking their marriage counsellor.

They tried sex again. This time, it was functional, passionless and unfulfilling.

Jade asked him if there was something wrong.

One week later, Dash developed an STD.

According to Bertrand Russell: *Marriage is for women the commonest mode of livelihood, and the total amount of undesired sex endured by women is probably greater in marriage than in prostitution.* Dash had given her a lot of latitude, let her do with her entire income as she pleased, as he did not want to cage her like a beautifully-plumaged bird. Even though he never tried to pressure her to morph into some ideal he envisioned for a wife, she was actively cheating on him, as evidenced by the STD he'd acquired from her, while he was working his ass off, working like he was going to lose his job — everything must be accounted for, all bases covered — just to keep her in some kind of half-pictured lap of luxury.

It was Chlamydia, for sure — the cloudy discharge on peeing and the agony of peeing as though through broken glass, along with the sore, swollen testicles were all a dead giveaway, corroborated by the clinical tests — and he didn't have to play amateur sleuth to know what was going on. Jade informed him she'd been having an affair with her boss, Darren.

It was good enough grounds for divorce.

They were no longer keeping up appearances, their marital strife for the world to see. The arguments were so intense the house risked falling down. The police gave them an unexpected visit when their neighbours complained about a possible domestic disturbance.

Dash spoke privately with the marriage counsellor over the phone.

Boreham responded with concern. *Why didn't you tell me? I could have done something about it. You shouldn't withhold important information like that if you want the therapy to work.* He interposed, certain he was not resorting to speculation: *Your wife* doesn't *have an attachment disorder. She's been able to compensate for some of her personality flaws in the 'safety' of your relationship. She has attachment difficulties. But you have an addiction.* A DVD addiction!

Addicted to buying DVDs? Man, that's harsh!

It was a side-issue, as far as Dash was concerned, a trivial matter that had cropped up a while ago in conversation with his wife. Jade was upset that every month he spent £500 on DVDs and then £350 on storing them.

I'm a collector! I've always been a collector!

But it's so boring and wasteful, she'd say, *and it's affecting our financial security and our relationship . . .*

Just like her to blow it up to ridiculous proportions! And they'd fight over every new DVD that arrived packaged through the letterbox.

This was outside his province, but Jim Boreham explained that people could be addicted to buying anything, and DVDs were no exception. He gave Dash the number of a good addictions' therapist.

Again, Dash explained he was a collector. It wasn't as if he had an 'addictive' personality.

You buy a lot of DVDs and you rarely watch any movie twice, Boreham reminded him. *Your wife says these days you never actually get round to watching them anymore because you have so many. And it's more than just an expensive hobby.*

It's what defines me.

Buying something can create a feeling of excitement. Some people use retail 'therapy' as a means of enjoyment, of escape. Compulsive shopping is not like that; it is a form of behaviour designed to avoid an unpleasant reality, perhaps to fill a black hole in your life. There is a distinction between doing something because you enjoy it and doing something because you feel very unhappy if you don't. The act of buying is accompanied by a 'high' that causes the shopaholic to lose control and buy many more items for which they have no need, bringing a false sense of freedom from life's problems. They ultimately get themselves into unnecessary debt, but they just can't stop themselves from buying more stuff.

Point taken. Dash didn't mind subscribing to the compulsive shopper theory. DVDs were still a significantly safer addiction than booze or drugs. At least DVDs weren't exactly hazardous to your health as Crack cocaine. *Imagine all I'm fixating over is that new DVD I've been meaning to buy, getting it home, melting it down and shooting it up, experiencing that all-time movie rush! So much better than that bad batch of shiny discs I bought last week!*

It's not meant to be a laughing matter. Your wife explained how bad it is.

Did you ever consider that my wife might be exaggerating?

Not even from half of what your wife has said could I ignore the gravity of the problem. Your situation became problematic once your buying started to interfere with your ability to pay your bills.

~ 428 ~

It was hard to imagine someone getting so way over their head with their DVD purchases that they started calling in sick from work to watch movies and eventually lost their job. *What if there's some kind of secret, government-implanted subliminal code on DVDs that forces us to buy more, more, more, just as the tobacco manufacturers have made cigarettes more addictive?*

Again, Mr. Hirting, please be serious.

True, that's where the bulk of his disposal income went. *But it's not as if I'm spending our tight grocery budget on another DVD box set of* Alfred Hitchcock Presents *instead.* Yes, he was running huge credit card bills, but the banks were always generous, and he'd never missed a payment on his maisonette . . .

You're treading a fine line what with mortgage repayments, household insurance, utility bills and other necessities. You should be using that extra cash on going on holiday with your wife, going out with friends, new clothes, or something that's actually going to improve yourself and enable you to make reparations with your wife. You do realize your obsession with DVDs has really hurt one of the most important relationships you'll ever have, not to mention keeping your bank account permanently in the red.

Dash loved buying DVDs and he had his own library of films that he enjoyed . . . or meant something to him. And it was something to do. He was immensely proud of his collection. But he was much more discerning these days. With a second mouth [Jade] to feed, he had to prioritize. He'd wait six months or so after the DVD release so it could appear in a 20% off clearance sale. Or, with the less essential buys, he'd wait for them to drop down to £0.01, where the postage cost more than the DVD and box combined. *Dirt cheap, you dig?*

And, just like the helpful banks, Amazon had made things easier shopping for bargains with their marketplace sellers, promising swift delivery and a hefty discount, a real boon for the public. The company's One Click checkout option was a stroke of genius. Then, ripping open those brown packages made him feel like it was his birthday all over again.

Netflix had also helped him become a bit more selective in his choice of film. Jade installed it to curb his spending. But he still preferred the hard copy. He could imagine the day in the not-too-distant future when he'd watch a film on Netflix he liked, buying it midway through and the DVD arriving through the letterbox by Amazon delivery the moment the film reached the end credits on the TV screen. Or maybe the DVD would arrive prior to the film finishing or even *before* he'd ordered it online! *Spooky, hey?*

After amassing a DVD collection of over twenty thousand titles, he still had another five hundred in his Basket, waiting for him to Proceed to Checkout. Fed-up, his wife had contacted Amazon to put a stop to his spending spree, and they explained they couldn't discuss the matter with her on the grounds of Data Protection. *Good for them!* Dash thought. So, instead, she warned him she would cheat on someone if he didn't rein in his compulsive DVD-buying habit. *You've given all our money to the Amazon Man and he didn't even bother getting a hair transplant or a toupée!*

Boreham's interpretation went one step further: *Some might even construe the volumes of DVDs you've bought as an example of hoarding, where the perceived importance of the hoarded items far exceeds their true worth. Humans may lose the desire to throw away unneeded items because of a feeling of attachment to these items.* Classically, hoarders accumulated junk mail, old catalogues and newspapers or broken electrical equipment, creating a fire hazard or risking vermin infestation. *I kept this Fray Bentos' steak-and-kidney pud since 1986 because I can't bring myself to part with it!* Diogenes syndrome, senile squalor syndrome, was an extreme variant, characterized by the hoarding of rubbish associated with severe self-neglect. Plyushkin in Gogol's *Dead Souls* was the greatest embodiment of hoarding known to literature.

Dash thought his relationship with Jade wasn't just a tragedy; these days, it was a fucking Russian novel!

The neuropsychology behind hoarding, Boreham lectured, involved damage to the frontal lobes, leading to impaired judgement and decision-making, emotional disturbance and a loss of impulse control. Also, of note, hoarders experienced a poor parent-child relationship and often trauma during childhood. Those suffering from attachment disorders turned to possessions – or animals – to fill their need for a loving relationship, rather than people.

Dash told Boreham he grew up in an orphanage not far from here, THE MOTHER OF SORROWS CHILDREN'S HOME, after being repeatedly sodomized by his great-uncle until he bled profusely. The great-uncle thankfully suffered the same fate in prison before he died, or maybe a worse fate: buggered to the point he warranted an arsehole transplant. Dash had never met his mother but later learned he'd been born of a teenage pregnancy when she had been severely addicted to heroin. So Social Services took charge of his life then got shut of him at the children's home. It was a tough upbringing, from the frying pan into the fire, and he was flogged a great deal by the Catholic nuns, but at least he managed to leave the 'House of Bitches' at eighteen and make something of his life. And nobody listened or cared. Literally. Bad memories. Memories laid to rest, he hoped.

Your emotional attachment to your panoply of DVDs means it's difficult to let go of them.

No kidding? Dash wanted to tell Boreham he got aroused by his DVDs, rubbing them against his crotch until he climaxed, but he decided not to. Boreham might not appreciate the joke.

I would advise you put your entire DVD collection up for sale before it completely loses all monetary value and you lose your wife. Also, you realize most of them will already have lost their real value with the release of the Blu-ray format.

Dash remembered the time when he upgraded from VHS to DVD, a pretty costly business. The worrying thing was he could feel it starting all over again with Blu-ray.

£500/month with £350 on storage. Have you considered that you must have paid for the same DVDs one hundred times over? Your wife calls you 'Storage Dash', and it's not as a term of endearment.

I've been meaning to downsize my storage space . . .

It's going to BANKRUPT you!

I'm a collector! A completist!

A collector always catalogues his collection. I bet you don't even know what films you have in storage.

Maybe I don't! Who's to judge?

You lack insight into the impact your DVD collection has had on your life, on your relationship, on your finances. You need to seek professional help. Ring that number I gave you.

What help are you suggesting? DVDs Anonymous?

Jade demanded a divorce. She was seeing someone. She admitted it was her boss, Darren, with whom she had carried on an on-off relationship since they'd been dirty-messaging each other. Darren's girlfriend had left him, and he had fallen into Jade's arms and one thing led to another. It was just rebound sex, she told Dash. And a re-emergence of that father-daughter element in yet another relationship, Dash told her. Jade was superficially remorseful but deflected the blame for their disintegrating marriage on his DVD collection. She could pretend to be the bigger person, but Dash knew her bullshit wouldn't wash with him. She might be 'some kind of beautiful', but she was also a woman who had been propositioned by pornographers. He had never forgiven her for that, let alone for her admission of infidelity and present rejection of him. She had made a fuckery of their marriage, served him vignette-upon-vignette of humiliation, sapping his strength, their relationship becoming excruciating in its downward slide.

She had got this 'hot and cold' thing going, always coming across as very touchy or overly clingy, the pattern of her life, of her relationships, on a background of serious Daddy issues. That effect she had on men: recreating the same unstable relationship dynamic with him as she had with her father, her last boyfriend in that alley, her boss at work. Dash had always considered himself a contented person, but she brought out the worst in him, probably in all men. He came to the conclusion that she didn't love him but needed someone to care for her, emotionally 'hold' her, keep her safe, using him as a secure base for other men to explore her cunt. She was so deeply unhappy and so incredibly insecure that he knew his frequent rows with her didn't help his cause one bit, creating a greater rift between them with each spat, but she would drive him to it every time.

You have sex with someone else and then you blame and scream at me? You whoring CUNT! The number of times I thought something was wrong when I masturbated over my own wife – when she's just lying there, right next to me, asleep! The number of times I suspected you of cheating on me! The number of times I was thinking, 'It has to be Darren Pearson!' The number of times I watched you and followed you with 'spouseware' surveillance equipment, reading all your text messages on the device, tracking your GPS locations and using cameras to spy on you and record what you were doing! You let your boss get his cock out and put it into you? You put your mouth around his cock?

Dash should have known. In the lead-up to the discovery of the affair, Jade had stopped giving him 'any' and had been quick to criticize his DVD collection, as though to justify her affair. She took greater pride in her appearance, changing her wardrobe, counting calories and going to the gym. She had started working late, claiming overtime but receiving no corresponding rise in her salary, and sometimes she came home smelling of cologne – it was only then that Dash began to suspect something. The surveillance evidence would eventually provide irrefutable proof to his suspicions.

Darren, her boss, was whom she was carrying on with at the moment, on the lame excuse of her vexation with Dash's neverending DVD collection. Someone once said: *When a man steals your wife, there is no better revenge than to let him keep her.*

Jade wanted him to leave their house. He refused. It got very ugly. Then, like some misandrist liar, she informed the police he had hit her. The bruising on her right cheek and around her eyes was incontestable, the nail in his coffin. Oh, she was a gift that just kept on giving! The woman he had picked up in an alley and put back on her feet had turned out to be a selfish, ungrateful, inconsiderate and, need he say, spiteful bitch! *That's the thanks I get!* Open season for allegations, it seemed, with the attachment-disordered, something of a maladaptive coping mechanism in their egocentric world, when one imagined the sympathy and attention they would receive. He was surprised Jade didn't accuse him of rape. In his case, Jade's attempt to tar and feather him, the compelling evidence of her facial injuries, resulted in a preliminary Court date and an interim restraining order.

Her unceremonious kicking-him-out-of-his-own-house pissed him off but not as much as he expected. She had made her bed, but at least Dash was a free man. He should have celebrated his new lease of freedom as a single man, like that guy, estranged from his missus, who parties the night away on the day his divorce comes through.

However, with all his absences from work and his employers privy to the sheer number of fights he had had with his wife, including her recent [? self-inflicted] injuries, they fired him. He could have gone down the employment-tribunal route, challenged his former employers on the grounds of unfair dismissal, but who would have possibly believed him? Without any income, and added to this the solicitor's fees, Dash missed a couple of mortgage repayments, so the banks were now in the process of foreclosing on the maisonette.

Afterwards, he rang Boreham.

Boreham: *How did the house thing go?*

Just say I'm homeless. Can I live with you?

Jim Boreham put the phone down.

Dash's unabating cashflow problems therefore meant he had been hiding out in his storage unit for the past week. He violated the protection order, paying no heed to the legal ramifications of his actions, and, right on the doorstep of his maisonette, challenged his wife on her cruel, callous treatment of him, her lack of mercy for her own husband.

Dash decided that there was no point in flogging a dead horse. Sometimes you had to cut your losses and run.

Then, that same afternoon, she disappeared.

Surely another attempt to get him into more trouble, he would claim if ever called upon, another attempt on her part to cause him to fall further afoul of the law. *As if I'm not in enough shit already!* She was such a damaged girl. Dash blamed her parents. As Philip Larkin neatly put it: *They fuck you up, your mum and dad.* Of course, one could imagine Dash would be the prime suspect in the disappearance of his wife. *Look no further than the husband, chief!* His brain hurt as he sank deeper into a general state of crapness. He was so far out of his comfort zone he didn't think he'd be able to get back. He felt his sanity going into freefall.

Dash felt rejected, unloved, by the woman he had vowed to love, cherish and honour. Instead, he was teetering ever-closer to divorce, having pushed his wife further away and into the arms of another man. Could he endure the humiliation, the stares, the gossip, the unbreakable chain of lies, the doubt, the unending, unbearable spiral of arguments?

He supposed their marriage hadn't been immune to the threat of breakup and divorce. Far from it.

Dash remembered the conversation in the afternoon preceding his wife's disappearance:

Falling in love is easy, Jade said with a note of sadness. *Staying in love is difficult.*

I've known for a long time that you didn't love me anymore as confirmed by our weak, very superficial emotional connection.

Do you know what love is?

Your liberal use of the word 'love' has caused the word to lose its meaning, its impact. Now it means nothing.

What about you, Dash? Have you the capacity to love? You speak of passion and lust and desire, intimacy and closeness and commitment, emotional bonds and husbandly duties, rediscovering ourselves, but I never heard you use the word 'love', except in the context of your DVDs. I've known you such a long time, even married you and nearly had your child, and you never once told me you loved me!

Dash thought about this very telling statement. Was it true? Here was a woman, a very smiley person, but one who always smiled for other men, never for her own husband; a woman whose cuteness caused men to infantilize her, like some Meg Ryan; a woman whom some might consider to be a dime-a-dozen in the world of attachment disorders. *Then why did you marry me?*

Maybe because I thought I could change you, get you out of your shell, so you might be able to protect and care for me, I guess. I thought I'd be safe with you. Now I know I'm only with you for the sake of convenience.

Enough of this mawkish guff. Dash found it truly astonishing how events had turned out the way they did. She told him she wanted a have a baby with Darren, with someone fun and deserving, and it reminded Dash of their own miserable attempt, their product, the aborted foetus, the mooncalf, *their* mooncalf. But, in truth, she didn't really know what she wanted, never satisfied with anything, running with whatever crazy thought came into her head. The travesty of it was that, in the end, Jade came off badly, but Dash – *old Muggins here* – had come off much worse. His wife, whose very disappearance from the public eye would be enshrouded in mystery and suggested that the authorities look no further than the husband. Since, with any missing person's investigation, the spouse was always the first to be suspected.

He supposed nothing lasts forever. All good things must come to an end. As beautiful as the sun shines, it always sets. This too shall pass. There were many proverbial expressions referring to the same thing. Latin theory called it *momento mori*. Buddhism spoke of *anicca*, the impermanence of being.

Dash thought of that line from Thomas Hardy: *Their lives were ruined, Jude thought; ruined by the fundamental error of their matrimonial union; that of having based a permanent contract on a temporary feeling which had no necessary connexion with affinities that alone render a life-long comradeship tolerable.*

Dash was not a doctor, a psychologist or a child therapist. He only sought to understand his wife, why she did what she did, why she sabotaged any relationship she entered into, including their dysfunctional marriage, to the point of no return. He considered the possibility that he had displayed an obscene imbalance of power in their relationship, trying to *diagnose* his wife instead of treating her *like* his wife — and a human being.

Where do we go from here?

Dash wishes to ignore that absurdly cheerful piping melody of his mobile, but he knows deep inside he must answer it. He pulls out the earphones, which are currently delivering Dreaming of You *by* The Coral, *one of Jade's all-time favourite songs which she would often listen to if she were ever feeling blue.*

Dash thinks of Twickenham Garden, *a poem by John Donne.*

Part of Donne's concept penetrates to a deeper level. The persona concludes the first stanza with this figure: And that this place may thoroughly be thought/True Paradise, I have the serpent brought. *Again, the figure begins simply, then becomes complex. The concept of paradise comes easily to mind. Winter and spring coexist here; therefore, paradise must be timeless, beyond the sphere of the temporal. Therefore, this must be the paradise of yet unfallen humankind. The Garden of Eden — the original paradise — also contained the serpent, however. Thus, the snake has to be here, since this is both the lover's paradise and the place from which he will be driven by the disdain of his mistress.*

The serpent here is directly associated with sex, partly because of the phallic associations of the snake, but also because in the popular mind the cause of humankind's Fall was sin itself . . .

The central theme of the poem emerges from the metaphor of love as a spider, transforming everything and ultimately bringing death. Love becomes the ultimate paradox: the lover cannot survive out of the sight of his beloved, but the only response he gets from her is disdain. Part of this problem is simply the conventional pose of the Petrarchan lover, whose mistress, placed on a pedestal, cannot lower herself to notice him; if she could so lower herself, she would no longer be the perfect woman. The only perfect love is the eternally unrequited variety.

Dash thumbs the connection, puts the mobile on speaker phone. "Hello?" he says tentatively.

"Dash? Dashiell Hirting, is that you?"

For a moment, Dash thinks it's his wife calling, then realizes it's a different female. "Speaking . . ."

"Mr. Hirting, I'm Detective Inspector Moira Laskey with Chertsford CID. We've been trying to reach you for the last few days. You've proved very elusive."

"I have my reasons . . ."

"I'm sure you know why we've contacted you."

"You want to know where my wife is?"

"Yes, Mr Hirting, we're investigating the disappearance of your wife. Is there any chance we could meet face to face and ask you a few questions?"

"What if I'm not interested?"

"We know you've been hiding out in SAFESTORE."

"How did you find out?"

"Your mobile phone would have given away your location. It's essential we speak with you in person. Can we come in?"

"You have a warrant for my arrest?"

"No, we're hoping it won't be necessary, as long as you cooperate with us. Mind if I ask what you are doing inside your storage space?"

Hiding from the cops, hiding from the world, he wants to say but refrains. He just needs a safe space to think, to rest from the stress of recent days. He's not mad at his wife anymore – whatever adrenaline he had in my system has burnt itself out. "Just inventorizing my life, working out the things I can live without: my wife, my child, my house, my money? Or all of the above?"

"Can we come in to talk?"

"'Fraid not . . ."

"It's imperative that we talk. We don't think your wife just disappeared. We suspect foul play."

"What do you mean?" Here comes the CSI shit . . .

"The bathroom's been rigorously scrubbed and cleaned, but the Luminol suggested signs of a struggle, lit up the phantom bloodstains in the bathtub like fairy lights."

"What's the motive?"

"The oldest reason in the book: your wife was cheating on you."

Dash thinks of John Donne: What gnashing is not a comfort, what gnawing of the worm is not a tickling, what torment is not a marriage bed to this damnation, to be secluded eternally, eternally, eternally from the sight of God . . .? *"Is that an accusation?"*

"Perhaps. But you will have the opportunity of clearing your name."

"There's nothing you can do without a body."

"If you're referring to the legal term Corpus delecti, *we have sufficient evidence to suggest a crime has been committed. We can arrest you even without the presence of a body."*

"Okay, come and get me!" he challenges Laskey in a wintry tone.

"Don't make it hard for yourself, Mr Hirting. We only want to talk to you about your wife. Do you know where she is?"

Oh, close by . . . *"Yes, but you'll never find her . . ."* He hangs up.

Dash wonders how quickly the police will be able to get into these partitioned premises. The facility administrators will probably grant them his storage access code. He looks around the room he is residing in illegally, windowless and walled with corrugated metal. He has been living in storage for the past seven days. Is this what his life has been reduced to? Contracted to the dimensions of the compact, finite space of this storage room, where his entire life is packed away in boxes, feeling his legs go bandy and numb while he continues to experience a gradual erosion of his psychological health where these very four steel walls mark his tomb? He sees the mocking epitaph in his mind: GOOD OLE STORAGE DASH, Rest In Pieces of DVDs. *The psychological definition of 'non-existence' beckons.*

He stares at the brown boxes piled high, containing his propinquity for DVDs going under the rubric of addiction, his life's work, frequently ridiculed by Jade, soon to be auctioned off by the storage company, once he is arrested, until he has nothing left. Not even his sanity.

But she's nearby, *he's told the cops.* Oh, so *very* close . . .!

Can someone be tried for murder if the body cannot be found?

His eyes travel across to the Victorian railway trunk, suggesting it might be hiding the darkest and grimmest of secrets . . .

Love is a Spider, inviting you into its Parlour, or the Serpent in Eden, bringing about the Fall of Man.

But he knows the cops'll never suss it, as his eyes shift slowly from the steamer trunk to the skeleton hanging in the corner of his self-storage space which could easily be mistaken for a medical school's anatomical specimen. Dash's eyes caress its slim, feminine frame, its bones de-fleshed and polished to a pearl-white gleam, his gaze eventually travelling up and meeting its dark, hollow sockets.

Again, Dash reflects on John Donne: Since you would save none of me, I bury some of you. *He knows as a human being he has failed miserably, but the authorities cannot deny he was driven to it. He remembers the fights, the arguments, Jade screaming the house down, him sitting there, cold and silent and aloof, deliberately winding her up further because she deserved it. Everyone gets emotional.* Everybody but me. *'Affectionless psychopathy', as Bowlby once described it.*

Are you capable of love? *the hanging skeleton seems to ask him.*

He will not dignify Jade's old, lingering question with a response.

So endeth the Ballad of Jade Lovemore and Storage Dash.

In those final moments, Dash recalls something D. H. Lawrence once said: Those that go searching for love only make manifest their own lovelessness, and the loveless never find love, only the loving find love, and they never have to seek for it.

Dash realizes that people's minds rarely come with a clear map but with signposts leading off into the dark woods – or maybe nowhere. *Psychologists might say he was projecting his own personality problems onto his wife. Dash considers the real possibility that perhaps he wasn't trying to understand his wife after all. That maybe he was just trying to understand himself all along.*

March 2015

Hastings in a Hole

"Hell is yourself and the only redemption is when a person puts himself aside to feel deeply for another person."

Tennessee Williams

Fucking was my *forté*, my raison *d'être*, what I got paid to do, and I did it well. Not that I worked as a rent boy or a high-class gigolo, though a lot of people might consider me those things in unkind terms. I, Guy Hastings, once aspired to be a gentleman pornographer, but my career took me down a road that I was ill-prepared for, which however didn't take long to get used to and relish, the girls I was fucking and filming and the megabucks that kept rolling in. After my impressive stint as a porn actor, looking up to the likes of Holmes and North, and getting dubbed the 'Jesus of Porn' or 'The Man the Devil Envied', I became a film director, initially specializing in similar homemade flicks, before moving on to more 'mainstream' works, if there is such a thing as reputable, mainstream pornography. As a producer, I even introduced trannies and ladyboys to the world. I burned a lot of people along the way, but I reached a stage in my career where I was known far and wide. Relatively-speaking.

I did a lot of crazy shit to get to where I was, but in the end saner heads prevailed. Some might say it was just desserts for all the wet, willing women I'd violated on film, three ways from Sunday, and, yes, maybe I did deserve the consequences of my actions, but the experience itself – what would happen to me that fateful day in the church – was life-changing, and I came out the other side a brand new person – a *better* person – and faintly smelling of roses.

It was the reason I retired.

I can't count the number of times Asif Mehboob had rattled out that timeless, old spiel: *Want to be an actress? I can make you famous.* It is a line that hides an ulterior motive, holds a double meaning, relying on a sinister form of bribery — and the relinquishing of your soul. The catch was always the loss of your inhibitions and, need I say, *dignity* on the Casting Couch.

Mr. Mehboob was the Producer, or what I simply called the 'Money'. He was also a dirty Pakistani, who personally screened all the girls that came through the door before they were permitted to star in one of his films. He always expected the girls to have sex with him, even if the filthy fucker was giving them a mouthful of man-cheese. Sexual favours in exchange for a starring role. *You look like someone I can make famous.*

The worst was when a girl had come to do a legitimate acting role and found herself in the midst of a porn film and she was powerless to turn round and say no. Mr. Mehboob had ensnared many a girl in this manner, and I'd never thought much of it. *A hole is a hole*, was another one of Mr. Mehboob's favourite phrases, in keeping with his huge, perverse sexual appetite.

The film short we were working on presently, a piece called *The Muff-diving Minister* was about a Catholic priest, who punishes a couple of girls whom he catches stealing from the collection plate. We had rented out the country church in Chapel Mead, having lied about the actual nature and content of the film to the real priest, Reverend Copperthwaite, who helpfully decided to make himself scarce for a few hours, unaware what we were filming.

The foundations of this particular place of worship were firmly laid down during the late Saxon period. It had been constructed from banded-flint-and-grey-stone with a chancel and a transept crosswise to the nave. The church housed a Norman font and an organ past the altar from the Victorian era. The beautiful stained-glass windows splashed vivid colours on the stone floor, and medieval paintings hung on the walls. Of particular note was the brass memorial inscription that was fixed to one of the walls, commemorating those brave servicemen who had died during both World Wars. So there we were desecrating this noble parish church with our smut, on a sultry, aphrodisiacal summer's day, having obtained use of it by deceitful means, filming this one scene before the altar in full view of the empty pews where Nelson Blake, the actor playing the well-hung priest, dressed in clerical collar and dark tunic for the sake of authenticity, gets sucked off by the blue, summer-dress-wearing girl,

Tiffany Honeywell, reparations for her sins. She had a nice pair, was always game, competent in the sack but a total queef. Miss Honeywell, a dab hand at rimming and an expert felcher, was on her knees, licking and caressing his ballsack lovingly before moving on to the main event, his member soon accommodated by her generous, roomy mouth as she bobbed her head back and forth, sucking gently, massaging his Darth Vader helmet with her tongue. She continued to blow him off, and I made sure it was all professionally and tastefully done.

"Yes, gooble, gooble, gobble!" I could hear the small, round, sweaty presence of Mr. Mehboob whispering to himself, getting excited. "That bitch has a nice mouth! She gobbles knobs beautifully!"

I continued to roll the cameras, directing the fellatio scene with gusto. I took some very juicy and very explicit close-ups in the process. Sex in a confessional booth would have been a bonus, but the place was Anglican. The presence of the Pope's pimp mobile might have been the crowning moment in my picture to celebrate all the irreconcilably depraved yet 'infallible' pontiffs from the Middle Ages, accommodating whores within the walls of the Vatican, but unfortunately our shoestring budget didn't quite allow for that. I didn't mind. All religions preached the same old nonsense.

Then, Tiffany was done knob-gobbling, Nelson Blake cumming in her mouth. Tiffany detached herself from the fictional minister and wiped the excess spunk from her face. *Yep, Cum Ba Yah, my Lord, Cum Ba Yah!*

"I absolve you of your sins . . ." Nelson granted, once he'd composed himself, crossing himself in a spectacles-testicles-wallet-and-watch gesture, completing the scene. "Your penance is now paid, child. Now go forth and *behave!*"

"And cut!" I announced, and stopped rolling. Time for a moment's reflection. "How was it for you guys?"

"Same old, same old . . ." said Nelson, bored out of his brains, lighting up a cigarette.

"Did I do wrong?" asked Tiffany.

"You need to work on it a bit harder," Nelson told her. "Wasn't as enjoyable as it could have been."

"True, perfection comes with time and practice," I informed him. "But she's got the job done at least. You shouldn't complain." I patted Tiffany on the head. She smelled of sweat and semen. "Good girl."

"'Spose not." Nelson said, disinterested as usual.

"You're yet to go down on her when you find her making out with another girl at the pulpit."

"Look forward to it." The sarcasm in his response was evident.

Following the very short whisky break, we resumed filming once Nelson had overcome his refractory period. It wasn't the girl who had already sucked the man's cock and pretended to swallow — or perhaps she wasn't pretending — that perturbed me, but the other girl whom the casting agent now thrust forward into the limelight to carry on the dirty work.

"I don't recognize her," Mr. Mehboob immediately murmured to my left. "I know every bitch who comes through the door! I mean I fuck them all! And I don't remember fucking this one!"

I ignored his vulgar comment. I was focused on the girl. I checked the casting list — and the script (yes, there really was a script we were working with!). "Ah, Honoria Sewell, let's test you out. Speak to the wall. Show that you're full of desire and about to embark on a love scene. We'll record and edit it, slot it elsewhere in the film later after we've used you for the next scene."

"But I thought I was meant to be an extra." She sounded worried.

"Say it, *bitch . . .!*" commanded Mr. Mehboob.

"Talk dirty as though at the height of passion," I elaborated.

And Honoria was summarily bundled into the spotlight, forced to utter some mucky things, impromptu, fear and confusion registering on her face. "Fuck me . . . Play with my tits . . . Rub your cock against me . . . Touch me down there . . . Go down on me . . . Eat my pussy," she ad-libbed, and even managed to throw in some moaning sounds for good measure.

It was a very convincing performance, judging by the way a thoughtful silence descended. Then, Tiffany Honeywell burst out laughing, giddily. From the simulated explicit voiceover she had delivered spontaneously, unrehearsed and unscripted, which she would lend to initiate the yet-to-be-shot threesome on film, I thought Honoria had potential and a fine figure to boot: blue eyes, long blond hair, the body of a babe. *Quite the natural.* She had claimed to be eighteen, but she looked a young eighteen, curiously innocent and undefiled. Suddenly, I had a sense that this might be her first time on such a shoot, a suspicion that was soon to be substantiated. Even though she had made some very impressive and sexually-arousing comments, albeit under verbal duress, she looked as though she didn't belong here. Even the clothes she was wearing were not provocative and seemed out of place: baggy sweater, blue jeans and white sneakers. It was like she had wandered in from a different film, and a better film at that.

"*Stop!*" I shouted, suddenly full of self-reproach, "Don't say any more . . ."

"What the hell are you doing?" Mr. Mehboob said, in frowning surprise. "We've got a film to finish!"

I surveyed the girl, addressed her. "Did you accept this role?"

"I was meant to be an extra in a religious film," she replied. "I didn't realize this was the deal."

"This *is* a religious film," Mr. Mehboob reminded her, producing a wide grin, "but not the kind you had in mind. This will help you cross over to mainstream movies. You've just got to show you're ready for love, just love, cherry pop! And once you're done, give me some head, you dirty bitch!" He made a grab for her arm with his clammy, chubby hands.

"Don't touch her! Leave her alone!" I pulled her away, took her aside.

"Don't you know we can make you famous, sweet cheeks?" Mr. Mehboob told her.

For all the wrong reasons, I thought. I felt a stirring inside me. "Don't listen to him," I told her. It occurred to me that Mr. Mehboob, a cuntaholic who liked his women dumb and full of cum, had tricked her into starring in this film. "Are you deaf, Mehboob? The girl said she didn't sign up for this!"

"What's got into you, Guy? Don't you want to see that bitch *fuck?*"

"Shut the fuck up," I roared at Mr. Mehboob, "before I beat you to death with my shlong!"

"What's got into you?" he exclaimed, startled by my behaviour. "I never thought a man of your reputation would be squeamish over a simple sex scene."

I knew what had got into me, what had struck me with the force of a tidal wave.

It was guilt.

I think guilt is a pathetic emotion, a sign of weakness. Even if I had been subjected to its various guises throughout my life and career, I'd never been one to surrender to it. People feel guilty when they first masturbate or when coming out of the closet. *Conscience makes cowards of us all,* according to Shakespeare, and the same guilt can give murderers away, like the beating heart, described by Poe, telling the terrible tale. Equally, Man's need to atone always gave him away, claimed Auden. But today was a day for contemplation, a crazy day, as I was inundated by a bombardment of guilt, washing over me in waves, mixed in with that bedfellow *remorse* and handmaiden *shame,* informing me that I was doing something *very* bad, that I was committing a serious moral transgression. But shrinks will also tell you that these pangs of guilt, these prickings of conscience, are what makes us human and what separates us from the psychos. Guilt can paralyze or, in my case, *catalyze* someone into action, to rectify old wrongs. I think I experienced an epiphany that day.

Honoria Sewell's accidental presence on set did not sit easy with me. I simmered beneath my skin, appalled at myself, disgusted. I felt sick, physically and emotionally. I wanted to cry, even though I hadn't cried in the twenty-first century.

I sat with Honoria outside, on the church steps, in the glaring afternoon sun. The sweltering summer heat was tempered by the gentle gust of a breeze and the sweet fragrance of summer flowers. Clouds, white and fluffy, drifted slowly by in the deep blue sky, some of them creating fancy shapes. To our left stretched the old cemetery with its weathered headstones and slumbering residents. The peacefulness of the scene afforded me time for some intense self-reflection and genuine soul-searching and some valuable, constructive quiet time alone with Honoria.

"You don't want to star in my films," I told her honestly. You'd be amazed by the number of girls I'd broken into the porn business without giving it a second thought, made those cock-worshipping starlets what they are today, but Honoria was a different kettle of fish, an exception. The one I resolved *should* get away. She was so vulnerable I could have seduced her, easily taken advantage of her, slept with her, except it wasn't quite outright attraction I felt for her — yes, she looked damn fine, and, yes, I might have even used the adjective 'fuckable' in a different life — but presently, it was something more caring and meaningful, something paternal.

"I gathered . . ." she responded.

"You were deceived into appearing in my film, and I'm sorry we coerced you into saying those things." I put my hands together in contrition. "I swear to you I won't use your sexualized dialogue in the final edit."

"Thank you," she said quietly, and I could have kissed her for being so tolerant and understanding.

"So you want to be an actress?"

"Yes, *so* very badly. Maybe I'm just being shallow, craving attention. I don't think so, though. I work as a telesales girl, part-time, so I can do some work as an extra. I just want some film credits to my name so I can flesh out my portfolio and get more auditions, do a showreel, maybe pay my way through Drama School. I enjoy hanging around with a bunch of actors, relish the opportunity of playing someone else. I love movies — the plots, being in character, the whole process of filmmaking — and I just want to be able to contribute to that artform. The beauty of film is that it has no limitations; you can concoct any scenario, no matter how inconceivable or extreme, and preserve its timelessness."

"Okay, you look and sound like a decent girl," I began. "You hail from civilized society whereas I'm used to raising the Middle Finger at the Establishment. Let me give you some advice . . . *sound* advice. Acting is a precarious profession, full of pitfalls. Unless you're Oscar-worthy, films are nothing more than disposable and their actors expendable, a dime-a-dozen. You'll experience hard times, and the temptation will be to do something unsavoury, against your sensibilities."

"Sensibilities?" she said, surprised by my use of the word. "I thought you were a porn director."

"I read a lot."

"Your favourite author?"

"D.H. Lawrence."

"*Oh, the innocent girl in her maiden teens knows perfectly well what everything means . . .*" she quoted knowingly. "I read, too."

"I'm sure you do," I replied, "so none of this will be new to you. You're young; as long as you work hard, you could forge an incredible film career. I want you to behave as smart and responsible as you are. In your pursuit of attention, recognition and fame, never lose sight of your self-respect. Be assertive. And never turn your loved ones into second best."

She asked the obvious question. "What about nudity?"

"Why does anybody have to be naked? There're enough roles out there that don't require you to be naked."

"But don't you think that's rather dishonest coming from you? You're practising double standards."

"Nudity is a dangerous path to go down, a slippery road to mockery, derision and self-destruction . . . and real *nothingness*. Decide if you want your life to be tough – because life really is tough and crafting a career out of acting is tougher still – or if you want your life to be a living hell. Because indulging in some sex and nakedness on set is no different from Porn, from what I do – the lowest rung of the ladder in any form of acting – no matter how much you dress it up. You will garner the wrong kind of attention. It's no fun when the only auditions you get are the ones where the producers only select the girl that looks good getting fucked on film. It will take away the last shreds of your decency; you can wave goodbye to your dignity and respect and you can dispense, willingly or unwillingly, with your soul. You will lose a precious part of you. It's up to you how you want the world to remember you: in a reputable way or constantly falling back and debasing yourself some more with each part. It's so easy to get desensitized, *kill* your guilt, like me, and that's not a good thing, because sometimes, like now, that guilty conscience comes back with a vengeance, along with all the regrets in life. I know my lecture smacks of the worst kind of hypocrisy, but if there's nothing else you take away with you from today, my final word is that someone so intelligent and innocent as you, who came here by chance and who didn't know what she was getting herself into and whose vulnerability we were about to exploit, should know if you are really serious about acting. Go for classy instead of trashy." I paused, wishing I was stoned, before adding: "Now scram. Get on with your life, the life you ought to have . . . Make me proud . . ."

And she kissed me. Honoria gave me a soft peck of gratitude on the cheek, of her own accord. That feeling inside of wanting to cry nearly spilled over. I thought of that poem by Alfred Edward Housman, *With Rue My Heart is Laden*, and its mention of the 'rose-lipt maiden'.

"Thank you for your kind words," Honoria acknowledged. "Despite what you do for a living, you're a good man."

I hushed her, feigning horror. "Don't let it get around . . ."

"I shall make you proud of me. I guess I had a lucky escape."

"I hope so." I'd been rich and famous for so long I'd forgotten how to be a human being. This girl had been my first opportunity in decades to explore my humanity, connect with someone on a fundamental human level. I appreciated her listening to me, hopefully taking on board what I had said. "I shall be watching your career with much interest."

She got up to go, without a stain or blemish on her character, totally untainted. I wasn't so lucky, however. I had no idea how crazy this day would turn out. Rising to my feet, I was thinking that the show must go on and that I should be getting back into the church and finishing the film before the old vicar came back, and that I would probably have to call up another porn starlet at short notice to perform the intimate lesbian scene with Miss Honeywell and then the final threesome with Nelson Blake, when a man dressed in a shirt and tie came striding purposefully up the path towards us.

Honoria gasped and froze.

Even though I'd never met this man, the empurpled face and rolled-up shirt sleeves told me who he was and what would follow.

It was her father and he was very, very angry.

Honoria's father strode up to me and shoved me hard in the chest, unbalancing me. I toppled over backwards to the ground, startled, the world whirling round in front of my eyes. I was completely unprepared for the Epicness of the Shitstorm I was about to face.

"How dare you!" he bellowed down at me. "I know *who* you are!"

"You obviously watch my films," I said, rather stupidly.

I don't know why I said that. Maybe it was just inane pride. Not the best response in such a delicate situation, and I kicked myself mentally when I realized what I'd uttered.

Her father went berserk. "*How dare you take advantage of my daughter in this way!*" screamed the enraged man, taking leave of his senses, and he began to kick me — physically.

His shoe connected several times with my chest and stomach, sharply and forcefully, winding me. "Mr. Sewell," I said, momentarily catching my breath, trying to reason with this man, "you have every right to be angry, but I can assure you nothing happened. We just talked."

"*Talked?* Rubbish!" he replied, in the grip of a violent fury, and continued to put his boot repeatedly into my sides, as I curled up into a ball to minimize the damage to my body, too much in agony to even attempt to retaliate. Maybe retaliating wasn't the done thing in this case. I should let the man take it out on me, do his absolute worst. I could not blame him for jumping to conclusions. After all, he was a genuinely concerned father, probably envisaging the worst for his daughter.

"Daddy, *no!*" Honoria shrieked, horrified, trying to get in the way. "He helped me!"

Mr. Sewell pushed his daughter away. "I will deal with you later, *young lady!*" He continued to thrash me without taking a second breath. "I must put this peddler of smut in his position so he can harm no other people!"

"The daughter did not defy her daddy," I managed to muster between gasps of air. "She just dropped into the wrong film-set by accident. I defended her honour, protected her dignity. *I swear!* I *saved* her!"

But it was all too little, too late. "*Bullshit, you sick bastard!*" he bawled, and went into another volley of unrelenting assault, giving vent to his anger, kneeling down this time and laying into me with his fists. I was totally defenceless and already fully incapacitated as he struck me again and again, his blows raining down fiercely and with a terrible savagery I had never before experienced in my life. The pain was awful, worse than exquisite, as deep as all the oceans combined and as vast as the whole wide world. The man was strong, *incredibly* strong, but I guess that's what they say of crazy people: they have the strength of ten men. I suppose I deserved his punishment — his contempt and violence — and he had every right to be mad.

"I bet that feels good . . ." I groaned, encouraging him to beat me up further, empty his rage. I hoped he wouldn't kill me.

He continued to pummel me on the steps of the church on that glorious summer's day, and I suffered his wrath in silence until I could suffer no more. My sight began to dim as the encroaching unconsciousness staked a claim on me—

—I awoke. I was suddenly surrounded by an ethereal white light that did not hurt my eyes. Somehow, I could still see within its dazzling brilliance. And the pain, yes, the physical pain I had suffered at the hands of the girl's father had miraculously vanished.

I lay on a Victorian fainting couch, of sumptuous red, in the middle of this impossible, illimitable whiteness, still dressed in black.

A beautiful, haloed creature stood at the end of the couch, gazing down at me serenely. I recognized her. It was Honoria Sewell. And for some reason she was barefoot and wearing a short mini-dress, of purest white, hugging her hips and showing off her gorgeous figure. The costume sported glittery, cut-out butterfly wings on the back.

I gazed at this heavenly creature with the heavenly body and discovered I had a raging boner in my pants and my genitals had developed an aura. There was a golden radiance seeping out of my crotch and, with it, I experienced a seriously wicked notion. I had the burning, nearly irresistible desire to slide my hands up Honoria's silky thighs, crimpling up her tight lustrous white dress, so I could clasp her juicy, peach derrière either side, bend her over and take her roughly from behind. Luminescent crotch or not, I quickly chastised myself for thinking such impure thoughts. "Have I died and gone to Heaven?" Fair question, because a lot of people get a hard-on at the edge of death.

"No," she replied with a voice that was silvery and strangely musical, almost Elysian, like hearing the voice of an angel. "Your time is not yet up."

"Are *you* dead?"

"No, you saved me, diverted me from a life of disrepute."

"Am I dreaming?" I asked, enchanted by her divine beauty. She was an angel all angels dreamed of or earthly nuns aspired to be.

"In a sense, yes," the angelic being informed me. "Some might call it your fantasy, others an out-of-the-body experience. Either way, this all comes from inside your own head. I am speaking to you from inside your conscience."

"Why are you here?"

She continued to talk to me from inside my head. Hell, maybe she *was* my conscience. "To give you a message. You have work to do . . ."

"Enlighten me. I am intrigued."

"You have a sickness inside you," the visiting angel explained. "You must heal that sickness and free yourself."

"Sickness?"

"The Bible calls it 'Lust'. It prevents you from achieving your true potential in this life and promises a place of damnation in the Hereafter."

"Isn't Lust a good thing?"

"Not if you wish to carry on the Devil's work. It impairs your judgement, feeds into your weaknesses. The cost to your soul will be immeasurable." She paused for a moment. "Even now you are having lustful thoughts about me," she observed. "And I'm not even really here!"

I apologized with some embarrassment. "You got me. Always a problem when one is blessed with a magnificent phallus such as mine, the subject of Penis Envy in film circles. It won't happen again. Can I at least finish myself off?"

The girl who had taken the guise of my conscience told me off. "No! Don't be so filthy! What are you – a rutting *animal*?"

"That's a matter of perspective," I said with a dirty, devilish glint in my eye. "Depends on how you look at it."

"The answer is *no*! You are a lost sheep, and I am the shepherd who shall guide you to green pastures. I shall show you the righteous path."

"Okay, I will suspend my filthy mind until further notice." I did my best to ignore my desperate, aching cockstand without much success. I eventually gave my throbbing crotch a sharp flick with my fingers to bring down the circus tent. Its radioactive glow gradually subsided.

"I am indebted to you," Honoria went on. "You showed me a kindness in the church that you did not think you had within you. Now build on those foundations, that gesture of goodwill to a vulnerable child. There is still time to make amends. Clean yourself up, change your ways, purge yourself of your sins. *Heal your sickness.*"

"And how do you suppose I go about healing this sickness that you speak of?"

"You will know when you awaken. And I know that you will do the right thing. *Make me proud.*" –

–I stirred back to life, opened my eyes. The fantastic, complete whiteness was gone, replaced by sterile, muted tones. My vision cleared, and I found myself on a hospital bed in a hospital room, connected to various tubes and monitors.

I hurt. Hurt all over. My body was a living sack of pain.

I remembered the severe beating meted out by Honoria's father, the ferocity of the attack awakening something inside me. This had been followed by the intensely vivid, celestial vision of his daughter as I lingered somewhere between life and death. Its purpose, too, was all too clear.

Regardless of the painkillers in my system, making me woozy, it took only seconds for me to understand what I needed to do. I must check myself into Rehab.

People talk a lot about 'turning points'. My Turning Point in Life was the battering I received courtesy of Honoria's father and that fabulous visitation on the heels, conjured up by my brain, as I lay at Death's door. My injuries included two black eyes, three broken ribs, plenty of bruises and contusions and a ruptured spleen, causing an internal haemorrhage that required drainage and an emergency splenectomy. Fortunately, I only had concussion, even though my face and head looked beat up bad, and I was eternally grateful to Mr. Sewell for allowing me to keep my manhood intact — not even a single swollen testicle. Mr. Sewell was arrested for Actual Bodily Harm, but I dropped all charges, much to the disappointment of the interviewing police officers. Mr. Sewell would now realize that we were even. I never spoke to him again. Reverend Copperthwaite was disciplined by senior clergy for allowing my film crew to commit unspeakable blasphemies in his church. I felt pretty bad about the whole thing so, as an act of contrition, I made a sizeable contribution to the parish church. My recovery was nothing short of miraculous. The doctors discharged me from hospital after a fortnight, and I immediately checked into a private clinic for treatment of a sex addiction.

I had led an absurdly debauched life, not just in front of the camera, and they didn't call me the Jesus of Porn for nothing. Most Rock stars would be mere amateurs compared to my drug-fuelled antics and all the cosmopolitan diversity of poonani I had munched on. Remember I am the Man the Devil Envies. But we can compare cocks later. Yes, my sexual depravities were legendary. I enjoyed every minute of it, but, looking back now, is it really worth bragging about? These days I was suffering premature ejaculation, not a good thing for a seasoned porn star like myself.

It seemed my pussy-eating days were numbered. I owed it to that girl whom I'd met by chance and whom I made it my mission not to expose to my line of work. I had discussed acting with her — *legitimate* acting — and warned her sex and nudity was a bad path to go down. Maybe I was going through some kind of midlife crisis. Whether there was a split in the Universe or I just imagined it, or that other time I betrayed my best friend to get into the porn business, my past had finally caught up with me. I had dug myself a figurative hole a long time ago and had allowed it to get deeper and deeper decade after decade until I was now suffering a soul-crippling crisis of conscience. I even thought about all those depraved and morally-indefensible things me and Mr. Mehboob did to that Lovemore babe, and how her relationship with her unsuspecting husband turned out. I wished to disassociate from my small, fat

Pakistani 'friend', whose very words [*A hole is a hole . . . I can make you famous . . . Gobble, gobble, gobble . . .*] continued to soil my brain more than the memories of my actual sexcapades.

I thought of D.H. Lawrence: *I want to live my life so my nights are not full of regrets.*

The guilt was the worst part. Woebegone, I sought repentance. Thirty-seven going on fifty-seven was my turning point.

Michael Douglas has presence, authority, *gravitas*, but I would never call him a sex symbol. Also, being treated for throat cancer, which he nonsensically claimed to have acquired from too much oral sex while denying the obvious fact it might have had something to do with the chunky cigars he chugs away at. I can understand David Duchovny being diagnosed as a sex addict – women genuinely and justifiably want to fuck him! But all of this is neither here nor there.

Admit there's a problem, that's the first step to recovery. And, like Michael Douglas and David Duchovny before me, I entered into therapy, hopeful. I guess Lars von Trier didn't need it as much as I did.

Could I be more than just oversexed and in fact meet the threshold of a full-blown sex addict?

I presently sat in my therapist's consulting room, an old-fashioned and strangely manly place with a mahogany desk and shelves of thick, unreadable tomes. In contrast, the sex addiction therapist, who owned the office, was an insanely sexy brunette in her late twenties, wearing a cleavage-revealing, white chemise and a blue knee-length pencil skirt, exposing the most deliciously-smooth tanned legs I had ever seen, as though she had returned from holidaying under the Mediterranean sun. When she bent over her desk rather provocatively to pick up a piece of paper, God, I just wanted to clutch my cock and ram it in her! Or, at a minimum, I wanted to put my hands down my pants and adjust my penis slightly. She sat seductively back down in an armchair in front of me, making notes, legs crossed, her chic brown slip-on dangling, consciously or otherwise, from her shapely, pedicured right foot. For some insane reason, I was invited to lie down on exactly the same fainting couch with the same deep, red velvet upholstery that had occupied my dream, and when I saw it, for a moment I was spooked. But I'd seen crazier things than such mere coincidences in my lifetime, and the thought that Victorian doctors might have laid down their patients on it to administer a pelvic massage to cure female hysteria put paid to any panic. As did the cock-gripping sight of my new female therapist.

Forget the twelve-step approach. It had nearly turned into an orgy. There had been just too much temptation particularly when encountering a support group of like minds. I fell off the wagon – or never got a chance to climb onto the wagon in the first place – because I ended up sleeping with two of the women, one of whom was trying to give up sex and the other my actual sponsor. They were both very accommodating. I mean how low can you go? So, instead of the twelve-step programme, Dr. Ruth Huggenkiss – yes, *Huggenkiss*, I shit you not! – recommended individual behavioural therapy. The temptation even now was to sleep with this therapist, not helped by her disclosing to me that she was a reformed sex addict. No incandescent glow streamed up from my crotch in the real world, even if my genitals were persistently aroused. I hoped Dr. Ruth would not notice. Except I'm sure she took note, but deliberately chose to ignore the agonizing bulge in my pants. Perhaps, she was teasing me as part of the therapy. I had a magnificent woody for her, and I wondered if she would let me knock one out. I kept dreaming of dropping on all fours and sliding my tongue up her sun-brown legs or gently nibbling the sole of her half-naked foot. I even imagined myself actually drinking from the therapist's furry cup. Or putting my head between her legs and letting her rip! But – *oh, fuck a duck!* – I reminded myself I would only be defeating the object of the therapy session if I did, even though my huge cock ached for her desperately and it was getting *harder* by the minute. I swear I could have erupted, *exploded!* Hey, babe, you haven't seen my cum face yet! I had to intermittently dredge up an image of Boy George in my head to prevent myself from cumming!

I tried to focus on what Dr. Ruth was telling me. *Psychoeducation,* she called it. "It's always best for the client to know what they're dealing with because it speeds up the recovery process."

"You don't say–" I said, not expecting anything special. "Okay, indulge me . . ."

"Like eating, sex is essential for human survival," she began, quickly getting into her stride. "Although some people choose to be celibate — for cultural or religious reasons — healthy humans have a strong desire for sex. In fact, a lack of interest in sex can indicate an underlying medical or psychiatric problem." Dr. Ruth described sex addiction as an intimacy disorder characterized by a compulsive need to engage in sexual activity, despite the mounting negative impact it had on the sex addict and their family, i.e. a sex addict will continue to engage in an escalating pattern of sexual behaviour, despite facing potential risks to their health, such as pregnancy and sexually-transmitted diseases, decreased productivity at work and financial ruin, shattered personal and social relationships, or even arrest. "Addiction is generally associated with euphoria and the loss of control," Dr. Ruth explained, "and can eventually become all-consuming and unfulfilling to the point that, over time, the sex addict usually has to intensify the addictive behaviour to get the same effect." I learned that the underlying mechanism behind sex addiction involved activating the neural pathways associated with reward perception in a similar way to gambling and illicit drug dependence or compulsive eating. "Studies indicate that food, sex and drugs of abuse share a common pathway within the brain's reward system. This pathway leads into the area of the brain responsible for our higher thinking, including rational thought and judgment. The brain tells the sex addict that having illicit sex is good the same way it tells others that food is good when they are feeling hungry. These brain changes translate into a sex addict's ritualistic preoccupation with sex at the exclusion of other interests, despite the accumulation of negative consequences and failed attempts to limit the sexual behaviour. This biochemical model helps explain why well-adjusted, intelligent, focused people can be so easily sidetracked by sex and drugs. In other words, the addict's brain produces neurochemical rewards for this self-destructive behaviour.

"Since the sexual liberation of the 1960s, sex is now more available than ever, from phone sex and cybersex to strip clubs and the use of escort services, accessed anonymously or otherwise. For most sex addicts, the behaviour does not extend beyond voyeurism or constant, uncontrollable sexual fantasies and excessive masturbation using online pornography. For some, however, addiction can involve illegal activities such as dogging, obscene phone calls, exhibitionism, child molestation or, frankly, *rape*." Historical satyrs, Dr. Ruth told me, included Casanova and Don Juan, whereas nymphomaniacs included Valeria Messalina and Lady Hamilton. Hypersexuality could also incorporate Erotomania, a delusional fixation on an unattainable person normally of higher social standing, such as the starry-eyed girl and the dashing doctor. Social and sexual disinhibition was a common feature of dementia following injury or degeneration of the temporal/frontal lobes, which normally regulate the libido. There was also increased sexualized behaviour in those people exposed to virilizing hormones in childhood or *in utero*. Premenstrual women were also more sexually active. Increased dopaminergic activity explained sexualized behaviour in manic patients, who might experience tremendous swings in their sex drive, depending on their mood, or those on stimulants such as cocaine and speed. People with borderline personality disorder could be impulsive, seductive, and extremely sexually promiscuous but were only ever able to form intense but very fleeting, superficial relationships in order to avoid the self-perceived fear of being abandoned as opposed to nurturing tender, loving relationships. "It's not sex for intimacy but sex to anaesthetize – *numb* – painful negative feelings such as boredom, alienation, loneliness, feelings of inadequacy or low self-worth. Addicts use sexual activity to avoid these unpleasant feelings or to cope with work difficulties or interpersonal problems. This is not that much different from how an alcoholic uses alcohol. Any reward gained from the sexual experience soon gives rise to guilt, remorse and promises to change. And they continue to sexualize their guilty feelings, creating a vicious cycle. There can be a lot of shame attached." She asked about my parents.

I told her my parents were very dissimilar, inconsistent in their upbringing of me. My father was a first-rate drunk but of whom I had fond memories. "I remember the one time he got cautioned by the police for relieving himself on the side of St. Paul's Cathedral after he got tanked up with his buddies," I told my therapist in a rather nostalgic manner.

"So not a religious man, then?" she observed.

My mother, on the other hand, was a strait-laced woman, cold and aloof, oblivious of her only son, always ragging on my father. "I don't think she ever liked me from the moment she fell pregnant."

"The ghost of the schizophrenogenic mother," mused Dr. Ruth. "Not a term used much these days. Research has found that sex addicts often come from very dysfunctional families. Sex addicts have either been abused in childhood or describe their parents as rigid, distant and uncaring. There is the lack of a stable attachment pattern. Eighty-five percent of recovering sex addicts report some type of difficulties with their parents. I can almost see where your addiction comes from when I look at the personalities of either parent."

This was turning into quite the science lesson, and not all of it dry facts. There was more to Dr. Ruth than met the eye. Besides being real eye-candy, she was proving to be an impressive practitioner, knowledgeable, thorough, understanding. "There is something lacking, missing in your life, a sucking emptiness that you use sex to fill that hole with and which partly explains why you entered the porn industry, perpetuating your own problem. Sex addiction is an occupational hazard in Porn. I can appreciate how the lack of parental love in early childhood has led to you replacing it with sex. Freud once claimed that man was constantly searching for his mother in each sexual conquest. But do you, Mr. Hastings, feel powerless over how you act sexually? Do you feel shame, embarrassment or even self-loathing over your sexual acts?"

I considered her question and responded: "*I do now!*"

"Good, we're getting somewhere. You promise yourself you'll change but fail to keep those promises?"

I thought of all the times I had decided to wind down after a day's film-shooting by getting lost in the London nightlife. Cocaine and whisky in the club, intimate sexual encounters all night, with two or three girls at a time, dissolving into anonymity when the dawn broke and the sun rose, and the gritty-eyed exhaustion walking home in the morning after the sleepless, substance- and sex-fuelled all-nighter. *Never again*, I promised myself. But it was always the same again the next night. I nodded.

Dr. Ruth sounded triumphant. "I can help you with that. I can help you fight your sex addiction, give you the strength of mind to step back and resist." I cast my eye up her smooth tan legs. Her shoe dangled ever more precariously on the tips of her toes. I just wanted to eat her feet up. "You know the problem with you, Mr. Hastings? Since you first peeked in your father's drawer and discovered his pornographic magazines, you have kept your juvenile mentality no matter how successful you have become in your trade. You've never truly grown up!"

Dr. Ruth didn't have sex with me even though I desperately wanted to fling her across the desk and pump her hard. Instead, she worked with me and patched me up, maintaining every bit of her professionalism, therapeutically 'holding' me to allow a motivational change in my behaviour, as she called it. Besides curing my sex addiction, she also helped me find meaning in the world.

She helped me find God.

I was Born Again. Some might call it a 'cop-out'. But I call it Salvation, Redemption, Grace and Forgiveness, where once, previously, I had filled that God-shaped hole with drugs and dirty sex. I had always been grateful to God. God gave me a humungous cock and it made a lot of girls happy. But this was different. I was a reformed man. They say the devil is in the details, but in addiction it was the denial hidden within the details that allowed the Devil to his dirty work. And since I took up God, I am the better for it. *At peace.*

John 3:3-7: *How can a man be born when he is old? Surely he cannot enter a second time into his mother's womb to be born? And Jesus answered, I tell you the truth, no one can enter the kingdom of God unless he is born of water and the Spirit. Flesh gives birth to flesh, but the Spirit gives birth to spirit. Ye must be born again.* Sinners fall short of the glory of God; when they change their ways and receive spiritual life through their faith in Christ, the Bible likens it to a spiritual rebirth, a regeneration of the human spirit from the Holy Spirit. Only those who are born again have their sins forgiven and have a relationship with God.

So like Johnny Cash, Ted Nugent and Bob Dylan and my very old favourite, Erica Rose Campbell, whose pussy curiously looked as though it required rejuvenation surgery, I was a Born-Again Christian, even if a lot of Sunday School teachers like a bit of anal!

Hastings Reborn.

Today, the congregation includes ex-prostitutes and ex-drug addicts, not to mention ex-prisoners. I led a wandering, aimless life, content with material wealth and fucking, wishfully heading in the direction of a hundred-year-old Hef marrying his latest twenty-year-old glamour model, but God gave me back everything the Devil stole from me. Doesn't anyone else think that's cool?

I am proud of my sobriety – three years sober now – and my love of God. I am grateful to those people who rescued me and set me down the right path. My sex addiction counsellor, Dr. Ruth. Honoria Sewell, my divinity in dream and my saviour. And her father for beating me up so bad, it made me see sense and gave me the wake-up call I needed. And God did the rest. I think my experience in the Chapel Mead church changed me profoundly. I think I grew up that summer's day. I experienced a 'moment of clarity' that all cured alcoholics talk about, one of those rare and unique moments when the world makes perfect sense. I saw the error of my ways and grew a conscience and a *real* set of balls. I found resolution to my life's ills.

I made it my personal quest to see Honoria succeed in all future endeavours. Be her secret benefactor like old Magwich. This was not charity because the girl had genuine talent. I watched her progress from afar when I wished I had the best seats in the house. I helped her make a showreel, but not what you think. Costume drama, Shakespeare, and the suchlike. Apparently, she did a pretty mean Lady Macbeth against type, pulled off the malice and madness of the original character spectacularly. The auditions came rolling in, keeping within the contents of her showreel. Period costume, avoiding any boring, romantic television clichés. I funded a couple of her films without her knowing it. She had proved herself infallible . . . *incorruptible*.

I would like to say I proposed to her and she accepted and she is now my young, adorable bride. But, alas, no such luck. Last I heard she'd started a lesbian relationship. Good for her! She is one of God's loveliest creatures. We still talk occasionally. Our original encounter reminds me to that old Animals' track: *Don't Let Me Be Misunderstood.*

Indeed, my world has changed for the better. I am a transformed man, *mercifully* transformed.

I retired from the business. Willingly, gladly.

I auctioned off my private collection of erotica – from an early edition of John Cleland's *Fanny Hill* to authentic daguerreotypes of naked harlots in Parisian brothels, from the classical sex manuals, *Kama Sutra* and *I Modi*, through to the erotically-illustrated version of *One Thousand and One Nights*, from Page as pin-up to Loveless on film, from the very collectible and comical Tijuana Bibles to a very rare and original celluloid print of Bodil Joensen's infamous *Animal Farm* – all utterly priceless. I also turned down the chance of directing a fictional piece about angels fucking, in favour of a more serious film about a sex addict who finds God. *My final picture.* I thought there might be something cathartic in that.

The man may have shot my horse from right under me, but I managed to get up calmly and dust off my clothes.

And walk off into the sunset.

February 2016–March 2016

Chance Encounter at Rippendale's

"A broken heart is what makes life so wonderful five years later, when you see the guy in an elevator and he is fat and smoking a cigar and saying long-time-no-see."

Phyllis Battelle

American Journalist and Columnist

Carrying her two bags of shopping, Dana Headley hurriedly approached the elevator and pressed the call button. It was Christmas Eve at RIPPENDALE'S, Chertsford, and it was less than an hour before closing time. The mezzanine speakers offered *Fairytale of New York* by the Pogues, featuring Kirsty MacColl, in the ambient strains of muzak. Although the plush, upmarket department store, specializing in designer brands, had been crammed with Christmas shoppers earlier on in the day, their numbers had dwindled away as the afternoon had progressed and, by four o'clock, only a few customers hung around, all preparing to pay-up-and-leave, minds fully focused on the festive season ahead. Dana was tired from all the scurrying around, the hunting for bargains as well as deciding on more memorable and sought-after gifts that her family and friends might readily appreciate, and she was now only too keen to get home and run a hot bath. Perhaps, have a light supper and watch *Brief Encounter* later before turning in for the night.

Dana stared at her distorted reflection in the shiny steel doors, an amusing and yet slightly perturbing image of herself – stretched lanky and disproportionate – that could have easily graced the Hall of Mirrors at a fairground. Her strange, tallowy image, crowned by her brunette bob, split as the elevator doors slid aside.

There was only one other passenger in the well-lit elevator car, a man in his late thirties, but she ignored him as she entered, her attention drawn immediately to the bank of buttons on the wall. She jabbed for the ground-floor lobby, four floors down. Weighed down by her shopping, she dropped her two bags of designer goods on the floor. The doors whispered shut, and the car began to descend.

All of a sudden, there was an unexpected jolt, the lights flickered dim for a second and seemed to return to full brightness, and the lift lurched to an abrupt halt. The two occupants of the elevator noticed the dial over the doors had stopped halfway between the second and third floors.

"It's stalled," the man said after a moment's hush. "Well, this is awkward."

"This isn't good," Dana said when the reality of their situation sank in. She did the first logical thing that came to mind. She pressed the button for GROUND several times, but the elevator refused to budge. Then, she began pushing the alarm button in the hope that it would awaken the lift operators to their plight, but the emergency bell kept ringing and ringing. They waited patiently, but their request for assistance remained curiously unanswered. Finally, as her frustration and anxiety levels shot up, Dana started randomly hitting all the floor buttons again and again as though hoping for some crazy permutation to get the car moving again. She got no joy.

"Looks like we're going nowhere fast," the man said ominously. There was a touch of amusement in his voice.

Dana ignored his comment. She was straight on the intercom, calling *"Hello, hello, we're trapped in a lift!"* and insisting the security workers bring their lazy asses down here, pronto, and get her the hell out! But nobody, it seemed, was listening on the other end.

"They *must* be able to see us," she muttered, approaching the problem from a different angle, and sure enough there was a small camera fixed into the upper corner of the cabin. Looking straight at the camera, Dana began waving her arms frantically from side to side, trying to grab the attention of anybody in Security currently monitoring the CCTV cameras. But, again, she got nothing – nobody was watching.

"Lady, a credit to your systematic approach in addressing the bind we're in, but it looks as if we're going nowhere fast," the man reiterated, adding, "and seems like no-one's coming in a hurry."

"Stop stating the bleeding obvious and do something!" Dana barked at him, getting seriously worked up. "Can't you see I'm freaking out?"

The man looked at her rather sheepishly, somewhat hurt by her hostile tone, and instantly jumped into action. "I'll see what I can do." He seemed to have one of his mad John McClane moments and tried forcing open the doors. His fingers pried open the doors a fraction, a crack, then managed to forcibly wrench them apart, but all the two occupants uncovered was the concrete wall of the lift shaft. Letting go, the doors sprang shut again. Keeping his cool, he quickly scrambled up the sides of the lift, his boots precariously balanced on the hand railing, as he reached up to push open the trapdoor in the ceiling. But it would not yield. The damned thing was either mechanically or electronically locked.

His eyes lit up, as he experienced another light-bulb moment. He pulled out his mobile phone. His phone had seventy-percent charge, but no cell reception. It would not dial out. Likewise, when Dana took his lead, she also found she had no network coverage, no chance of getting a call though and hence no hope of rescue.

And it was at that precise moment she realized they were genuinely sealed-in, which only made her feel enclosed and helpless.

"Looks like it's just the two of us," the man commented, resignedly.

Dana was far from thrilled. "I hate small, confined spaces, and I certainly don't like riding the elevator too long, let alone getting trapped inside one. You could call me 'claustrophobic'."

Her fellow passenger could tell she was afraid, bordering on panicky. "I suppose every living creature, including the doughtiest of hermits, has an intrinsic fear of being trapped. I don't like the idea of being cooped up in here, either."

Yes, thought Dana, we're like a couple of sardines in a can or flies trapped in a glass jar.

Except the man reminded her of something decidedly worse. "I don't want to alarm you, but you do know they're only operating a skeleton staff and it's nearly closing time."

The reality dawned on Dana that it was Christmas Day tomorrow. The place would be shut till the Boxing Day sales. "Everybody's going to wonder where I am. I need to tell someone of my whereabouts. I don't fancy the idea of spending Christmas in a lift."

"Believe me, lady, neither do I. Unless we figure a way out of here, what choice do we have?"

Dana was suddenly very angry with the department store. "Someone should pay for this! I'll sue the bastards who designed the lift for a six-figure sum! See how they like it!"

"We can talk all the punitive damages, compensation and lawsuits you want, and, yes, we'd probably get a major payout, but aren't we getting a little ahead of ourselves?

We haven't been here very long."

"I suppose you're right," accepted Dana, hopeful. "We shouldn't be thinking of being stuck in this elevator for two days without food or water or any place to pee. We should keep trying to call for help."

And they continued with whatever previous strategies they had tried to communicate with the outside world – the emergency alarm, the intercom, their mobile phones – and got the same sinking feeling. Nobody bothered to respond to their hails, and eventually they were hoarse and tired from all the desperate yelling. *We might as well be trapped in a subterranean tunnel that's caved-in,* thought Dana, giving into despair. To her, the elevator carried all the charm of a coffin. As the minutes ticked by, slow death consumed her. A mental image of herself lying dead when the elevator doors finally opened during the mad rush of shoppers on Boxing Day grew increasingly persistent and more disturbing and *real.*

"As it's just the two of us in here, we ought to make our acquaintance," the man declared. "I'm Jayson Conagan." He looked at her more closely, studying her, before asking, testing the water: "Does the name mean anything to you?"

"No," replied Dana bluntly. "Should it?"

"I hit the headlines several years back . . . I guess you're going to find out sooner or later. *I'm a convicted rapist . . .*"

It was bad enough they were stuck in here with no food or water or any facilities to pee, except maybe down the side of the shaft. The last thing she needed right now was a power outage, imagining the staff of the department store turning off all the lights as they closed up shop. She imagined sitting in the dark for the next forty-eight hours, stuck in a lift with a felon at the lower end of the criminal classes, as despised by his fellow inmates as any child killer. Unseen hands reaching out from the darkness, groping, fondling her, preparing to commit something atrocious, something unspeakable. *Why does the power need to go out before he touches you?* Dana thought, self-control evaporating in an instant. It was worse than if he were one of those crazymen who might be hiding a ticking bomb on his person, holding her hostage and the authorities to ransom. She started screaming in a blind panic, flipping out, hammering the doors of the elevator with her fists. "GET ME OUT OF HERE! GET ME OUT OF HERE!" She refused to listen to him such was her ear-splitting hysterics, a reaction he fully expected, so he gave her one hard slap across the face. She stopped shrieking, coming to her senses. "Dana . . . my name is Dana."

"Pleasure to meet you, Dana."

She gradually regained her composure. But that confession the man had casually blurted out, oh that hideous confession, continued to hang in the air like a fresh corpse twisting round and round on its noose. *Too much information.* "And you had nothing to do with the lift getting stuck?" she suddenly demanded to know, the deepest, most palpable mistrust in her voice.

"Come again?"

"You weren't lurking in the lift in the hope of nabbing your next unwary, vulnerable woman, like one of those sick perverts who waits in the McDonald's toilets for some unsupervised kid coming to answer a call of nature?" Wouldn't she just love to pepper-spray his face, leave him half-blind, howling in pain, make him pay for the woman – or *women* – whose lives he had ruined? *If only I had a pepper spray in my handbag or, for that matter, a rape alarm to drive him crazy, the bastard wouldn't dare come near me!* Presently, however, she could not escape the real and immediate danger she was in.

Jayson sounded astonished. "You think I set this up, rigged the elevator, so I could rape you?"

Dana began to fret and worry and panic again. "Is that a threat?"

"No, of course not," he denied vehemently, putting up a three-finger salute. "Scout's honour, I swear I had no hand in our current pickle. I wasn't following you – I'm not a stalker."

Tread carefully, Dana reminded herself. *Don't provoke him. Just put up and shut up.* "Okay, what now?"

"Here I am with a beautiful woman in the elevator of a posh department store, a woman who is capable of chewing up the scenery and eating up the attention of any captive male audience. A confined space like this creates the ideal degree of intimacy to get to know someone, don't you think?" He noticed she was staring at him with a look of disgust. Neither the fear nor the suspicion had left her watchful expression. Jayson chose to be a bit more sensitive, tactful. "Take it easy. Lady, I am giving you a compliment. And here was I expecting deep, thought-provoking conversation. Let's at least be polite and civil with each other, please? What do you do for a living, Dana?"

"I write articles for women," she informed him. She could see no harm in chit-chat as long as she kept her wits about her. "I am the Harold Hartman of the feminist world."

"You mean stuff like *My Secret Garden, Thirty Shades*, Jilly Cooper, Candace Bushnell and all that shebang?"

"I adore the French literary theorists like Witting and Cixous: *Écriture feminine.*"

"Focusing on the female experience – and *jouissance* – and claiming to be the antithesis of phallogenic literature?" he said unexpectedly.

It was Dana's turn to be astonished. "How could you know? It's a very specialist subject."

"I am extremely well-read."

"Women have come a long way since the Suffragette movement, who protested against gender inequality and the subordinate position of women in society, their repression and harassment, their exclusion from voting."

Jayson thought of the erstwhile Rik Mayall in *Blackadder* and quipped: "Lady, if anyone wants to 'suffer a jet movement', I'm up for it!"

"That's not even remotely funny," she castigated him, unsmiling. "That's quite offensive, actually!"

"Okay, awful joke – my sincerest apologies," Jayson said, accepting her rebuke, kicking himself inside. He continued with a more sanitary line of questioning: "So are you a famous author?

"I disdain the cult of celebrity."

"Wise, I suppose . . . Means you're not shallow."

"What do know of *depth*?" Dana maintained her hateful, accusatory tones. "Taking a woman by force!"

Jayson flinched, recovered with a wan smile. "Join us, good viewers, for the great elevator disaster . . ."

"Don't use that word!" Dana told him.

"Which one?"

"Disaster."

"You don't want to be reminded about plummeting to your death, crushed in–?"

"Stop it!"

"I can think of worse things," the man said, keeping his tone ominous.

"What could be worse?" Dana challenged.

"Out of all the crazy horror stories you hear or read about on elevator disasters, being doused in flammable liquid and set fire to, burning alive in the elevator, or being stuck between the open elevator doors and trying to squeeze through a one-foot gap between the floor and the shaft wall when the car begins moving again, crushing or decapitating your head, or perhaps the shaft cables snap and the elevator plummets twenty storeys, sending a fireball racing up the shaft after the impact, I bet you never thought you'd be trapped in a lift with a known rapist!"

You're not winning any awards here with your throwaway wisecracks! thought Dana, who felt the man and his crimes fully deserved her animosity and contempt. "Do you often tell your fellow passengers before takeoff that the plane is going to crash?"

"I think it might prove therapeutic if it succeeds in calming their unresolved anxieties about flying. Freak them out to the point they can freak out no more." Jayson went on: "Lifts are one of the safest means of transportation with so many failsafe mechanisms in place. You'll be glad to know there are only a handful of lift-related mishaps each year, nationwide, most of them involving maintenance workers, who get themselves electrocuted."

"Serves the bastards right for not inspecting – for not *maintaining* – the lifts!"

Mischief was stealing back into his grin. "Maybe the shaft is bottomless, and we will keep falling and falling and falling, and it will keep getting hotter and hotter and hotter . . . I read somewhere that if you die in an elevator, be sure to press the UP button."

"You're enjoying this, aren't you?"

"Lady, I am enjoying no such thing!" Jayson said in mock-outrage. "Remember, we're in this hell together."

The man's infuriating, incorrigible! "Then why are you trying to deliberately piss me off?"

"Just lightening the atmosphere."

"Doesn't make the ordeal less frightening," Dana retorted, irritable as ever.

Jayson raised his hands in a contrite gesture, waving the white flag. "I guess we got off to a bad start." He switched over to something more relevant to their present predicament. "Okay, okay, let's talk survival." He pointed to the shopping bags she had dumped on the floor beside her. "What do you have in those bags that might sustain us for the next two days, just in case we're stuck in here for that long?"

"Nothing in particular. I did my Christmas food shopping yesterday. Today was a day for buying gifts."

"No water?"

"Not a drop. Only perfume."

"Perfume's a vile thing to get drunk on . . . damages the brain cells. Boy, could I do with a bottle of Blue Moon?"

For the first time, she noticed his breath smelled of alcohol. The man had been drinking earlier. She didn't mention it. "What about you?" she noticed the single gift bag he was carrying.

"Of course, I nearly forgot . . ." Jayson extracted a small wooden box from the gift bag, big enough to hold a small gun. He broke the seal and opened the lid, revealing it to be a box of cigars. He lifted out a Havana, stuck it between his teeth and lit it with a Zippo lighter.

"Hey, wait a minute, buster . . .!"

Jayson puffed away on his stogie merrily. The elevator began to fill up with smoke.

"Get rid of it!" she insisted, coughing. "Don't you know anything about secondary smoke?"

"Overrated," he dismissed her comment outright.

"Please stop!" she implored, panicking. "We'll suffocate in here!"

With a pained expression, full of regret, Jayson stubbed out the cigar against the metallic wall, dropping it to the floor. "Worth a try," he explained. "I was hoping to set off the fire alarm." But the fire alarm wasn't working, and the smoke dispersed easily through the air vents. Once again, nobody cared to respond. "I guess the fire brigade won't be coming." He opened a packet of breath mints, popped one in his mouth and handed them to her. "Ration these. Sugar-free, so won't provide any real nourishment, but they'll keep your mouth moist and minty-fresh!"

Dana breathed a weary sigh. After a short eternity to gather her thoughts, she asked: "Tell me about yourself."

Jayson seemed surprised that Dana was showing some interest in his life. Maybe she realized they just had too much time on their hands. "I was an actor, of television and stage . . . the name still doesn't ring any bells?"

She shook her head.

"I was pretty good, adept at what I did, specializing in the Meisner technique, one of the gold standards of acting."

"Digging deep into oneself, bringing out the emotions from within, rather than relying on external cues, or living and breathing the role which would otherwise constitute method acting."

"You know something about acting."

"I am extremely well-read."

"*Touché!*" Jayson said, grinning. "Goes to show that one should never judge a book by its cover." He went on: "Anyone who's anybody in acting is affiliated with Spotlight. I've had roles in some juicy commercials and got small bit parts in a few soaps and hospital dramas. I had potential. I was destined for bigger things."

"So when did the dream die?"

"Five years ago when I got arrested for rape. Jog any memories?"

Dana shifted uncomfortably against the steel wall of the elevator. She found this repeated reference to rape quite disturbing, sinister. "I don't remember reading about you."

"I made the front page. I'm surprised you don't remember."

"I don't pay much attention to a Monster-of-the-Week like you. What do you want with me?"

"I knew you wouldn't recognize me. They did you up well, fixed you properly. *But I still love you.*"

Dana was taken aback. "How can you love me? You don't even know me."

"But that's the thing, I *do* know you."

Dana's unease, sense of fear, began to ratchet up again. "I think you'd better stop, buster! You're creeping me out, *again!* Don't you think things are bad enough as they are without you rambling on like a lunatic?"

"There's no other way for me to say this, but you're . . . *my wife.*"

Dana was beside herself. "Don't you know how cuckoo that sounds? How can I be your wife? I've never laid eyes on you before in my life! We'd never met until we got trapped together in this damned lift!"

"That's where you're wrong," Jayson persisted. "I know it's hard to believe, but I'm your husband."

"No, no, *no!* Stop saying that!"

"I *am* your husband, whether you believe me or not. *You were the woman I raped and was sent to prison for.*"

She thought there was hunger in those eyes. And a kind of animal savagery in his expression, so primal, so evil, so *pure*, intending to inflict the worst kind of pain imaginable. Was this his usual routine before he actually raped his women? A ritual in which he uttered the same words to his victims, having convinced himself – *deluded* himself – that these women belonged to him to do as he pleased? Adrenaline flooded her system. Her heart quickened and her hands grew cold. Her head swam. Now she noticed he had vacant black holes instead of eyes, and an ugly grin that revealed the sharpest, meanest teeth. *Denial can protect you only so far!* the monster in front of her bellowed in unrestrained fury. The shadows across the metal walls seemed more prominent as the elevator grew darker, expanding and meeting each other. The elevator walls crawled with a blackness, not a true blackness, obdurate and unyielding, but a blackness with the thick, murky consistency of smog impenetrable enough to hide certain dread things like monsters. And it was getting hotter, hellishly hot. She needed some air. "I can't breathe . . ." she managed to whisper, her voice scratchy, making rapid gasping sounds.

Then the pitch-dark fog swallowed up her mind.

He woke her up, lightly slapping her cheeks.

Dana stirred, eyes flicked open. She sat up, the world swimming around her

~ 466 ~

momentarily before her eyes got their focus back. Her body felt tired and thirsty. "What happened?"

"You fainted," a male voice informed her.

She remembered where she was: in a department-store elevator. Her hands automatically travelled down to her groin. She checked herself. She had not been violated. "I remember you. You're Jayson . . ."

"You okay for me to fill in those blanks?"

She nodded, rising to her feet. "Something like being raped I would remember . . . or else you must be disappointed by the quality of the rape, it being so unmemorable."

"We were married once," Jayson recounted, ignoring her glib remark. "I was an actor, you were a freelance journalist, of feminist writings. We were a happily-married couple until I did what I did. Shall I continue?"

Tears were welling up in her eyes — she began to remember fragments of her former life, that terrible night, feeling so filthy after the event she had to hose down her vagina and take the morning-after pill — but she nodded again and listened on.

"The forensic examination was incontrovertible. You gave evidence in Court and I was slaughtered by the Press. After I was sentenced to ten years' imprisonment and placed on the Sex Offenders Register as well as suffering the indignity of being chemically castrated, you divorced me and had intensive therapy to deal with your trauma, those distressing memories of that night. Your father, a man I never got on with, convinced you to erase me from your life altogether. You even reverted back to your maiden name. The things hypnotherapy can do. You attended several sessions at the HYPNOTIQUE CLINIC, and you forgot all about me and what happened to you. My name was never mentioned again, not even in passing. I was left to rot in the slammer."

Dana didn't speak, just let him continue with his explanation. She attained full recall in the midst of experiencing something vaguely tantamount to a flashback: she could feel herself being pinned down, she could hear herself screaming, the nonconsensual penetration, the inflated pain down below, the raw copulation and the bleeding, the degradation and humiliation, but the worst thing was the betrayal from the man she loved. *Some memories can be so painful, sometimes there becomes a need to change them or forget them.* Instead of breaking down, presently, there was a strange acceptance of everything that had happened to her that fateful night, a coming-to-terms. Because, for the first time since the elevator got stuck, Dana was seeing a different side to her attacker. She had read somewhere that the rapist is driven by a sense of power over the victim rather than the act itself. Yet Jayson didn't exactly come across as a psycho.

"You never forgave me," Jayson said, himself on the verge of tears, also, "but I never forgot about you. I have to live with the memory of what I did to you for the rest of my life. The number of times I thought of killing myself in that lonely prison cell. Redemption eluded me at every turn. But I tracked you down. And I needed a drink to talk to you . . ."

"Did you get drunk and rape me?" Dana asked bluntly.

Jayson shook his head. "Not at all. What you may not know is that I was eventually pardoned."

"Why should someone who brutally rapes his wife be pardoned?"

"It soon became apparent to the doctors that I was unwell. It was a tumour."

"A tumour?"

"The doctors discovered a rare adrenal tumour, an adenoma, secreting high levels of testosterone that made me violent and incapable of controlling my sexual urges. The only comparison I can make is those bodybuilders, who take anabolic steroids and go on to develop huge, unhealthy sexual appetites. After surgical intervention, and once I was back to my usual self, my case was re-opened and I was cleared of any wilful wrongdoing. Diminished responsibilities, the Judge said."

"What if what you're saying is bullshit and you're only deceiving me to take advantage of me?"

"What I've told you is the God's honest truth," Jayson said with the utmost sincerity, sounding as though his heart was bleeding. Like her, he was fighting back his tears. "I don't expect you to forgive me. I never stopped loving you and I will always love you. I love you on so many different levels, baby. I love the fuck out of you, sweetheart, without it being a reference to rape. I was sick, but I'm better now. I don't expect anything to happen between us, but it would be nice if we could just reconnect, recapture the life we once shared."

The things he said. It was a lot to take on board in such a short period of time, to learn she had once been the victim of rape at the hands of this man. That particular memory that had lain buried for so long, the horrors of that night, she knew would decide to resurface one day in all its gory glory. Why shouldn't it re-emerge now? And why run away from your past? Most women would run a mile if they'd suffered a similar ordeal. It would be completely understandable to choose to bury that trauma rather than deal with it. It was human nature not to want to go down that same road again. However, it was her woman's intuition [*I never stopped loving and I will always love you. I love you on so many different levels*] that told her that he might actually be telling the truth. Should she give him the benefit of the doubt? First, she would need to explore both sides of the argument before she gave her own final verdict. "What do you want me to say? I'll sleep better tonight, knowing who raped me?"

"I won't insist on reconciliation if you don't want to. All I ask is I be given a fair trial. Remember, I was hard done by, too."

"I'll think about it."

"Yes, take it under advisement, that's all I ask." There was sadness when he spoke. But there was also a sense of hope. "I lost my wife, the woman I love, once and I never want to lose you again. If, however, you never want to see me again, that's your decision and I will respect that decision."

Her night of rape was the tumour talking. He was blameless. He had not been himself. It could happen to anyone. Could she accept him back? "If it wasn't your fault, it wasn't your fault."

"I wish we could have met under better circumstances," he said, wiping a tear.

If this really was her ex-husband, she needed to do a bit of investigating of her own just to make sure, determine the veracity of his claims. "I should hate you forever for what you did to me, but I guess we've both been wronged in our own separate ways."

Then, without warning, the lift juddered, along with the sound of debris tumbling down the elevator shaft to some unknown depths below. The frightening prospect that the lift cables might give way – *snap!* – was suddenly vanquished when the lights dimmed briefly, Dana felt a cool breeze on her face and the lift whirred back to life with a jolt. Ten seconds later, the doors opened, and Dana and Jayson popped out of the elevator like a pair of champagne corks. She squinted at the bright lights of the lobby. Dana checked her watch. Forty-five minutes had lapsed, the department store on the cusp of closing for Christmas, and the staff and remaining customers gave them withering looks, taking in their dishevelled states and making snap judgements, perhaps perceiving them to have had a quickie in the elevator.

"With you stuck in there with me," Jayson said, on a slightly cheerier note, "it didn't feel like the prolonged solo mission to Mars."

Her nose still felt teary and congested, but Dana felt better about things. *Getting stranded in the lift can slow the world down and allow you to think, to reflect, to gain a whole new perspective and help you consider what's really important in your life. It's not quite the nightmare I envisaged when I first stepped into that lift. Something good might actually come out of our brief encounter.* Jayson's disclosure had helped matters, brought a degree of closure to those events long ago, old traumas she had expunged from her memory through therapeutic means. "What are the chances I would have bumped into you in a broken elevator after being apart for so long?"

"Small world . . ."

"One of the unlikeliest of trysts," said Dana, still reeling at the way destiny seemed to shape everybody's ends. "You hear stories of couples who meet for the first time in an elevator and end up spending the rest of their lives together. Then again, I entered the elevator a single, carefree girl and I stepped out a former married woman, who was once raped by her testosterone-fuelled husband. Who would believe such a mad story?"

"I call our time in the elevator precious, unique, a Christmas miracle, if there is such a thing. It's as if Fate arranged for us to meet again." Jayson gazed into her eyes admiringly. "We should celebrate. How about catching up in a trendy restaurant to call in the New Year? It should, in the meantime, give you enough time to think things over, check out my story." He hastily scribbled down his mobile number on a scrap of paper. "You can pick the venue."

"Time to drink champagne and dance on the table?"

"I'll be there with bells on."

"And you? Will you be all right?"

He smiled, appreciating her warmth, her sympathetic and more compassionate attitude towards him. "Knowing I have met you and explained everything to you, and that I have been granted a glimpse at a second chance with you, of starting anew, of getting to know you again, of rekindling old romances, I think I'll be just fine."

"Everyone's entitled to a second chance," Dana declared. Her eyes suddenly spotted a piece of paper that had got crumpled up in the elevator doors. She snatched it up, unfolded it and showed it to her ex-husband, a smirk slowly sneaking across both their faces. "Maybe taking the stairs next time wouldn't be such a bad idea!"

"Lest one should find egg on one's face!" observed Jayson, equally amused. "I think we have discovered the solution to the mystery. How's that for ironic?"

For on the paper that had got wedged in the doors and may have been solely responsible for the elevator mechanism getting jammed was a notice, and the notice read: OUT OF ORDER. DO NOT USE.

June 2015-July 2015

The Octopus Pot

"Had we never lov'd sae kindly,
Had we never lov'd sae blindly,
Never met – or never parted,
We had ne'er been broken-hearted."

Ae Fond Kiss (1791)
Robert Burns

I needed a break. My colleagues at work insisted I needed a break – a good holiday. Too much work, not enough rest. Otherwise, if I continued to work my ass off, I would surely be on course for a heart attack one fine morning. True, I thrived on stress, maintained the adrenaline in my bloodstream at a certain level that kept me alert and focused even if I was physically exhausted. Although the odd tipple and the occasional cigarette put me in good stead after hours, I relied upon a little too much caffeine to keep me propped up during the day. People speak of moderation in all things, but more recently I, being the absolute caffeine fiend that I had become, had been drinking my entire daily quota of coffee by mid-morning, and significantly more during the rest of the day.

Coffee and cocaine might hail from the same place as well as share a similar chemical structure, but unlike cocaine (and, for that matter, methamphetamine), coffee classically works as an indirect stimulant. Caffeine blocks the adenosine receptors (adenosine is the chemical that builds up in the brain during the course of the day and normally makes you feel tired and sluggish), leaving the adenosine in the lurch and unable to attach to its own receptors that caffeine has hijacked and made redundant, giving you the impression you're more awake. That's what the coffee bean was designed for: to keep you awake for longer thereby increasing productivity. And, believe me, drinking ten cups of coffee a day certainly takes its toll, particularly when caffeine has a half-life of six hours. Its cumulative effect plays havoc with your sleep – your sleep is lighter and broken, and you wake up the following morning somewhat sleep-deprived and feeling unrefreshed and irritable until your next glorious fix. Added to this, you will need more coffee to keep you going in your demanding job since you develop a tolerance to caffeine relatively quickly – need more of it to get the same effect – and you are on the slippery road to disaster. Consuming huge quantities of coffee for prolonged periods risks palpitations and ventricular ectopics as well as adrenal fatigue, presenting as tiredness and exhaustion and a general, pervasive sense of unwellness brought on by the equivalent of functioning at higher, constant levels of stress. Once you let the caffeine out of your system, and the adenosine is allowed to do its job, boy, *do* you crash! Your body will always make up for its sleep deficit; sleep has a way of catching up with you. Doctors care too much about other people's health than focusing on their own, which is not always a good thing. My job was demanding enough at the best of times, but with a dim-witted government proposing to give GPs more responsibility in things that shouldn't really concern them, like taking charge of the NHS budget, you can bet I was looking for faraway destinations as a short respite and an escape from my caffeinated brain. They say nothing beats a good holiday, packing up your bags and leaving your troubles behind, and I started searching around in earnest. Lord, spare us from politicians – and coffee!

I do not consider myself a well-travelled man, even if I might have completed my medical training in Manchester and my medical elective in Nairobi, Kenya. Oh, the good old days! The events in Manchester I shall relate to you another time. Meanwhile I vividly remember stepping off the plane in Nairobi and being blasted by an intense wall of heat. Then, the Undergraduate Dean at Nanyuki Hospital insisted that, since I had never been to Africa before, why don't I spend my elective period exploring the place and enjoying myself, and when the eight weeks were up, I should just come back to him and he would give me a glowing reference? Thus, on his incredibly generous advice, I hired a Mercedes and went on Safari, made an attempt to walk up Mount Kenya and basked under the Mombasa sun. The man even kept his word and signed me off in the end! I suppose my last, vague semblance of a holiday occurred nearly ten years ago: an inexpensive, Antipodean package holiday. Sydney was lovely, the sky lucid-blue and clear, not a trace of cloud in sight, just waves and waves of sweltering sunshine; Wellington by contrast was interminably wet — rain pelted down in thick, torrential sheets throughout my stay there, as though making up for my good time in Sydney.

Where to this time? I wondered.

It was the Senior Partner at FAIRVIEW SURGERY, Dr. Alistair MacKenzie, who suggested his birthplace: the Highlands of Scotland. *My heart's in the Highlands, wherever I go,* he reminded me, quoting his favourite poet, Robert Burns. Beautiful enough in autumn, but utterly magical at this time of year. No other people reined in New Year with as much fanfare and style as the Scots, who even had their own name for it. So up north I journeyed, across the border, to Loch Ness to celebrate Hogmanay.

Why Loch Ness? you may ask.

Why not?

If I needed an introduction to Scotland, why not pick a world-famous spot? I could have plumped for Edinburgh's plush SHERATON HOTEL, but I opted out of the extravagant spectacle of Edinburgh's Hogmanay celebrations since it would have been even noisier and more congested than Trafalgar Square's New Year fireworks. No, I wished for something more personal and relaxed, quieter and remote. Loch Ness seemed to appeal to me more than the bonnie, bonnie banks o' Loch Lomond. Not that I hoped to catch a glimpse of the Monster, its myth further perpetuated by the silence surrounding Professor Boyes's and Dr Prendergast's recent expedition. But that's another story. No, my story concerns the Strange Case of Mrs. Joyce Kirkwood and the Meeting of the Two Falls, with an octopus pot thrown in there somewhere and how my visit to the land of kilts and whisky and haggis and Rabbie Burns became something of a busman's holiday.

When I stepped off the train all alone at Drumnadrochit on that New Year's Eve, I understood why the British idealized the Highlands. Not unjustly, mind.

Even out of the carriage window on this slow train from Queen Street, Glasgow, which followed the Great Glen, the natural geological fault-line that stretched from Fort William to Inverness and divided the Highlands into two distinctive halves, the landscape looked as unspoiled and picturesque as the paintings of Alexander Nasmyth. I followed the contours of the mountains, shaped and re-shaped over millions of years by prehistoric fire and ice. I passed somnolent villages, dark, dormant fields and the isolated farmhouse, complete with its own cattle-shed, barn and grain silo. Although the occasional bens were draped in a light dusting of snow and the glens twinkled with the glitter of frost, the Deep Freeze had not yet set in. The actual winter blizzard was expected to arrive in the next few days, according to the weathercasters. Severe snow and ice warnings in Scotland and the north of England had left many in the South concocting an excuse as to why they wouldn't be able to get into work.

As I disembarked onto the platform at midday, I breathed in the chilly but crisp, countrified air. It was not bitterly cold, but it would be in the next forty-eight hours. The station guard gave me a cursory nod, which I reciprocated, as I headed past him and through the doorway marked EXIT. I clambered into an awaiting cab, the driver far from talkative upon realizing I was English, the Auld Enemy. We made the journey to my hotel largely in silence, but I took in my surroundings with wide-eyed appreciation. It was gorgeous out there, a stirring patchwork of craggy peaks and windswept moors, already frozen, before the challenging conditions of winter would beset the countryside.

Drumnadrochit lies just west of the shores of Loch Ness, nestled at the foot of the impressive but very accessible Glen Urquhart, supposedly deriving its name from the Gaelic '*druim na drochaid*', meaning 'Ridge of the Bridge'. URQUHART CASTLE was apparently situated on a headland overlooking Loch Ness, its decaying, stony ruins dating as far back as the seventeenth century when it was destroyed during the Jacobite Rebellion. Archaeological excavations seemed to suggest that Urquhart Castle was originally built on the site of an earlier, fifth-century Pictish fortification. Although its roof had collapsed and much of the stonework of this ancient stronghold had been plundered over the subsequent centuries, the sad, crumbling remains of Urquhart Castle had since been classified as a Category A Listed building, becoming one of the most frequented, touristy sites in Historic Scotland as well as a veritable beauty spot for painters and poets alike, both past and present. The castle was firmly listed on my itinerary in the coming days as long as I wasn't disturbing some lavish wedding ceremony it might be hosting. I also planned to take a boat trip on the waters of Loch Ness, on board a cabin cruiser hopefully fitted with modern underwater surveillance equipment for a spot of Nessie-hunting, if the cruise-tour companies would still be operating in the foreseeable weather conditions. As something of a Rocker, I also knew that the Led Zeppelin guitarist, Jimmy Page, owned BOLESKINE HOUSE, a manor once belonging to the author and occultist, Aleister Crowley, on the south-east side of Loch Ness. I thought I would at some point on my holiday catch a peek without trespassing. However, presently, my destination lay somewhere along the A82, between Drumnadrochit and Lewiston, a hotel going by the name of the CLACHAN FORGE INN. It would have been nice to be staying in

Drumnadrochit, the Heart of Loch Ness, but apparently all the guest rooms in the village were booked up and only the Clachan Forge Inn was available, probably because not a lot of people knew of it, being slightly off the beaten track.

The Clachan Forge Inn was a former Victorian coaching house which had since been converted into a three-star hotel amidst ten acres of forest and open fields. It was blessed with a wildflower meadow, situated directly behind the house, and I could imagine it blooming fragrantly in the summer months.

A warm welcome awaited me at the Clachan Forge Inn. The hotel belonged to a lovely couple, Angus and Coira Veitch, who welcomed me with open arms and a complimentary flute of fizz.

The interior design of the inn suggested a Baronial style, with handcrafted furniture, lovely carpets and tartan accessories. A flight of stone stairs led up to the eight, en-suite, elegantly-appointed bedrooms, furbished to a high standard and replete with history and intrigue. The walls hung with the swaggered portraits of lairds and clan chiefs. The bed was a Hornfleur, with its deep buttoning and sumptuous velvet upholstery. The Tempur mattress was the type that moulded to the shape of your body, like sleeping on a cloud, the concept of memory foam originally pioneered by NASA for its astronauts. The view from my window was awe-inspiring, a stunning vista of outstanding natural beauty, of perfect seclusion. In many respects it was the perfect retreat, capturing the serenity of a rural location, set against the spectacular backdrop of the best-known, mountainous region in the British Isles.

I intended to explore the hotel in a little more detail later on. But, for now, I thought an afternoon nap beneath the luxurious eiderdown would do me the power of good before freshening up for the evening's festivities.

After all, it was Hogmanay.

That evening, I wandered downstairs with the view of indulging in the colourful traditions of Scotland. Made a change, I thought, from plopping down in front of the television set back home and watching *Jools Holland's Hootenanny*, year after year. I ought to be proud of myself this year.

First, I sat in a quiet alcove in the brasserie, where I dined on cullen skink soup to begin with, a main of mixed game grill of pheasant, partridge and venison with seasoned neeps and tatties, followed by a traditional raspberry cranachan for dessert — all well-prepared, delicious and extremely filling. The dining room was adjacent to the bar, which boasted some of the finest cask ales direct from the local breweries. Then, I retired to the magnificent drawing room with its tweed sofas, antiques and original art.

There were hunting trophies on the wall, one such of a stag's head with huge antlers and a glassy stare, alongside a selection of textile hangings and painted landscapes. Why have landscape art when you've got the real thing right outside your doorstep? Behind glass, weaponry from a bygone era was on display, genuine museum pieces, in a wall-mounted cabinet: a two-handed broadsword called a claymore awaited a battle-cry from its bearer, a pair of flintlock pistols directly from the days when duelling at dawn was common practice for resolving a dispute, and a Highland dirk, its hilt composed of intricately-carved bog-wood and sheathed in a scabbard of embroidered leather. Beside it, a glass dresser showcased traditional Celtic craftware. However, I was particularly taken by a handcrafted bronze figurine from Gretna Green, the embrace of eloping lovers.

I plunked down on a Gibson leather armchair in front of the roaring inglenook fireplace, like some well-to-do member of a Gentlemen's Club, whilst some of the other punters presently sat opposite on a couch bearing tartan upholstery with thistle motif and Harlequin pinwheel cushions.

Yes, indeed, the place was the epitome of grace and grandeur.

"Whit ye after?" Coira Veitch asked me as I made myself comfortable in the high-backed armchair. "A wee snifter o' brandy or a wee dram o' malt tae keep oot the cauld?"

What I was gagging for right this moment was a single malt whisky by the fireside. A cigar might have made a pleasant accompaniment but, alas, the hotel was non-smoking. "Some scotch will do just fine, thanks." I planned to tour some of the Highland distilleries in the coming week.

The whisky arrived promptly, a drop of Dalwhinnie, and I sampled its smooth, peaty and honeyed notes, not that I claim to be a whisky connoisseur of any description. The amber liquid slid down my throat without fuss. One drink became two became four as I entered into that zone of doubles and, God forbid, triples.

Relishing both the warmth radiating from my stomach together with the fire crackling merrily in the hearth, I glanced around the room at the gathered guests. There were not many of them, about seven in total, including myself. If I remember correctly, the first people to talk to me were Wallace Laidlaw, of *Laidlaw, Swain & Rawley Advocates*, and his secretary, Senga McNair, both Scottish.

Wallace Laidlaw was sat across from me, dressed in a formal dinner jacket and dicky bow. "Like curling, Hogmanay is a distinctly Scottish celebration. No-one celebrates the eve of a brand-new year quite like us, Scots."

"So I gathered. It is an honour to be here, to actually witness these celebrations first-hand . . . Hello, I'm Dr. Marcus Havers . . ."

Introductions were made and received warmheartedly. Alcohol provided the social lubricant. Whilst Laidlaw sipped slowly on his scotch, Senga had already cracked open the champagne ahead of time. Under cross-examination, I told Laidlaw what I did as an occupation and where I 'bided'. For a lot of people, Scots English can seem like another language. It's English alright, but not as we know it. But I suppose one of the beauties of being human is we learn to adapt, and any outsider can get used to the Scottish way of speaking, even in Glascae, if they hang around long enough. One of my patients back home has a strong Glaswegian accent and I understand him perfectly. Laidlaw's talk lacked the hallmark 'moose-loose-aboot-this-hoose' dialect, as my grandmother used to call it. I suppose having to deal with sheriffs and procurator fiscals all the time, and claiming once to have been a close, personal friend of George Galloway, had made his Scots English *very* English.

"Well, good doctor, historians suspect that Hogmanay was inherited from the winter solstice celebrations of the Vikings," Laidlaw continued. "But when Christmas was as good as banned by the Protestant Reformists due to it being too Roman Catholic, the Scots made the New Year as sacred as Burns Night."

I checked my watch. "Another hour before the main event."

"Always a good excuse to drink, eat and making merry. Did you enjoy your supper?"

I told him I did. Laidlaw asked whether I'd tried the Black Bun for afters which I regretted to inform him I had declined since its name had sounded too much like mouldy bread rather than what it really was: a type of fruitcake.

We entered into a chinwag on the subject of the Scottish referendum, and an 'honourable' mention went out to Alex Salmond. If only Alex Salmond could impress women of his importance and trustworthiness. If only he could convince this particular demographic, who just happened to make up fifty-three percent of the Scottish voters and who could not be separated from that age-old conviction that 'it tak's a lang spoon tae sup wi' the De'il'. There was a significant disparity between public opinion of him and his own self-deluded perception that everybody liked him, passing himself off as some kind of lovable rogue whilst imagining he still somehow carried the gravitas of an immortal and charismatic statesman. Salmond's tired, nationalistic daydreaming of a Scotland free of English imperialism was not only offensive to the English, as the mention of the Highland Clearances might be to the Scots, but his lack of clarity around the economy probably didn't help his case, either. Realistically, Scotland could not survive on its own as it had nothing more to offer than tourism, whisky and its ever-dwindling North Sea oil reserves. That's why so many Scottish people were migrating south of the border. Salmond also considered it his absolute right as First Minister to stay in a £1000/night hotel room at the Taxpayer's expense whilst banging-on about child poverty and socialist pride. Still, Laidlaw felt Alex Salmond wasn't quite the useless, shifty numpty the canny female voters criticized him for being, even if he looked as a daft as a cuddie (*donkey*) and his pish-and-shite speeches could fill up a chanty (*chamber pot*), and perhaps in another life he might have made a more robust and pragmatic British Prime Minister, if given the opportunity of rubbing saltires in the English wound, than the smarmy, arrogant, ootstaundin' galoots called the Conservative Cabinet put together – George Osborne alone might as well be wearing a T-shirt with the slogan ANTI-YOU on the early morning walk up to the polling station and not feel ashamed by it. The drawback with politics, as every law-abiding citizen knew, was always *plus ça change, plus c'est la même chose.*

Senga asked whether it was French.

"That's for me to know and for you to find out, ay?" Laidlaw replied, turning to me and tapping the side of his nose with his index finger, knowingly. He raised his whisky glass in a toast. "Here's to our wives and girlfriends. *May they never meet!*" He cracked up into gales of laughter, leaving Miss McNair to convey a puzzled frown. "A bit of *Scotch and Wry*, if you get my point."

Comprehension suddenly dawned on me at that moment, as both of us sat supping our individual tumblers of malt, that our dear lawyer was here on this Hogmanay, after leaving his wife back home, for some good, old-fashioned rumpy-pumpy with his PA, who may not even know his intent. Or maybe she already knew. I did not ask.

Hitoshi and Kaiya Nishimoto joined in the conversation. They were cousins and had travelled all the way from Tokyo. Their respective Christian names meant 'Tolerance' and 'Forgiveness' as they disclosed. "Aren't you Ewan McGregor?" Kaiya asked me out of the blue. It turned out she and her kin were avid film lovers.

True, I bore more than just a passing resemblance to the perennially-youthful Scottish actor, and people often commented on this, and although in this instance I had the urge to play along, I decided out of the kindness of my heart not to tease them. When I informed them that I was nothing more than a humble family doctor from Fairview, they looked slightly disappointed. I did not mention to them that I was not your archetypal doctor and that I did have a dark side, a higher calling, if you will, which, Gentle Reader, I shall reveal to you some day. *But not today.* It was amazing how the Japanese tourist got around. You found them in the unlikeliest of places, snapping photos and chattering away, so full of beans. I never would have expected to see them in this wild and remote neck of the woods. I welcomed them on board. Without wanting to offend or sound racist, I considered relating an old joke, a hilarious but rather rude and absurd play on Japanese pronunciation, which goes something like this:

A refuse collector is doing his morning rounds and notices one house in the street doesn't have a wheelie-bin outside. He checks round the side of the house, but again it's nowhere in sight. So he goes up to the front door and knocks.

He gets no reply, so he knocks long and hard.

He finally hears footsteps running down the stairs and an old Japanese gentleman answers the door. "Harro . . ." greets the Japanese fellow, looking flustered and out of breath.

"Sorry to be a bother, mate, but where's ya bin?" the refuse collector asks.

"I bin upstairs," replies Japanese man, looking perplexed.

"No, where's ya dustbin?" repeats the bin-man.

"I dust bin to the loo having a shit," the Japanese man says, embarrassed.

Realizing the Japanese fellow has misunderstood him, the bin-man smiles and speaks more slowly, hoping he'll get through to him this time: "No, mate, listen carefully . . . where's ya WHEELIE-BIN?"

The old man thinks for a minute, then admits rather guiltily: "Okay, okay, you got me, I've wheelie bin in the loo having a wank!"

You probably already know it. Maybe I did tell it and got some laughs and guffaws – or just *stunned* silence. Or maybe you'll never know . . . "I keep getting Ralph Fiennes and Liam Neeson mixed up," I went on, lightheartedly. "Or, for that matter, Jesse Eisenberg and Michael Cera. Is it possible they are the same person? Has anyone seen them together?"

At that point, my attention was drawn across the room to the remaining two guests, who did not partake in our little social gathering. Both women were in their late fifties/early sixties, slim and elegantly dressed in tartan. They sat privately together, with one of the women talking animatedly to the other. My focus was on the other woman, who was on the receiving end of her friend's conversation. She did not seem to be listening to her friend, just sat there quietly, appearing strangely stiff and morose, lost in her own thoughts. I watched her fascinatedly. Whilst her friend rabbited on, she continued to stare out into space, and it was a look I had seen before, during my medical practice, when I was doing some Occupational Health work at the local military base in Dunstan Priory. It was the 'thousand-yard' stare of battle-weary, traumatized soldiers when their gaze becomes distant, almost unseeing, detached from reality.

I spoke with Angus Veitch, the owner of the hotel, who was fittingly dressed in a kilt and sporran.

"Ye mean the wan sitting thare in the neuk like a stookie?" *You mean the one sitting there in the corner like a statue?*

I nodded.

"Och aye, thae's Mrs. Joyce Kirkwood. Fur yonks bin comin' 'ere wance a year wi' her husband. She wis a bit pit oot whin her husband left her after thirty-five years o' marriage. Puir woman . . . whit she mist be gaun throu. She needs a break fae it all. This year she's brought her frein, Ida Chalmers, an awful blether." He was a bit tipsy himself, and what he said next he probably wouldn't have said if he'd been sober. "Atween ye 'n' me, Ah suspect Mr. Kirkwood haes strayed fae her . . . git hissel a fancy woman!"

I thought of Wallace Laidlaw and his dirty, dishonest reason for bringing his secretary along to this shindig. I felt sorry for Mrs. Kirkwood, and, for that matter, Senga McNair. "Men really are 'baskmasters', interested in nothing else except what they can reel in with their hook-and-tackle."

"Ah widnae dae that tae mah guidwife."

"And so you shouldn't."

One Dimension, sorry, One *Direction*, were spouting their usual brand of aural sewage on the radio, when Coira Veitch suddenly switched stations to something more authentic and appropriate. The music that droned out of the hotel speakers was bellowy and spiky in equal measure, yet melodic and moving, pleasing to the ear: the unmistakable skirl of bagpipes.

"Bagpipes are so incredibly difficult to play," Wallace Laidlaw commented, forever an authority on everything, "the instrumental equivalent of operatic singing or ballet. In the wrong hands or the inexperienced it sounds like someone strangling the cat. Donald McLeod led the revolution of bringing bagpipes into the mainstream."

"Aye, he remains th' greatest Scottish piper wha ever leed, hauns doon," Angus said. "Naebody else comes claise." He glanced up at the clock. "Time, gentlemen!"

Sure enough, the hour was almost upon us.

"Auld Reekie is staved-oot, heavin'," Coira observed, referring to the television screen, fixed on a high, wall-mounted bracket. *Edinburgh is packed.* More or less.

Angus took charge of the proceedings. "Fur the wans unfamiliar wi' oor customs, Ah'll leid . . ." *For those unfamiliar with our customs, I'll lead . . .*

And as we counted down the seconds along with the whole of Edinburgh on the TV screen in anticipation of the midnight chimes, commentated on closely by those two comedians whose running gag when portraying a pair of lighthouse keepers was '*Gonnay no dae that*', the grandfather clock in the drawing room struck midnight, and the fireworks and military artillery exploded across the country. Donning our party hats, we all formed a circle in the middle of the drawing room, including Mrs. Kirkwood who snapped out of it and joined us in calling in the New Year, albeit somewhat unenthusiastically. We linked arms which we crossed over one another, and, to the strathspey rolling out from Edinburgh Castle, we boisterously sang *Auld Lang Syne*, a toast to health, wealth and happiness. *Lang may yer lum reek!* which roughly translates as: 'Long may your chimney smoke!' Following the innocent hugs and kisses and handshakes, wishing one and all good fortune in the coming year, more champagne corks popped and the revelry commenced, predominantly singing and dancing, drinking and storytelling, whilst one of the most famous and spectacular street parties in the world stepped up a gear on the TV screen. On the in-house speakers, Amy MacDonald provided a rollicking soundtrack for our Hogmanay party, singing *This Is the Life*, followed by *Poison Prince*, followed by most of her back catalogue. I guess our hosts liked Amy MacDonald.

I was told by a rather squiffy Coira that I made the perfect 'mirk, braw' gentleman to initiate 'first-footing'; Angus was sensible enough to explain what it was when I was beginning to think his wife was giving me a not-too-discreet come-on. Saining, as our educator, Wallace Laidlaw, explained, involved consecrating the house by sprinkling holy water and fumigating each room with a burning juniper branch in order to bid farewell to the old year and bring in as much luck to the coming year.

I didn't stay in their company too long. I got pretty hammered, unaccustomed as I was to drinking, and I retired to bed at two in the morning whilst the others continued their festivities into the wee hours. Their distant laughter echoed softly up the stairs, but it was the ancient winds of the earth buffeting the window-pane and shaking the world outside that lulled me to sleep. Somewhere, not so far away, an owl performed a melody of hoots and screeches. Soon I was out like a light, luxuriating in a dream of a moonlit forest glade where a flame-haired Highland lass, barefoot and buxom and clad in scanty dress, kneels down on a boulder to take a revivifying sip from a cool, gushing mountain spring . . .

Amy MacDonald had been right; I awoke the next morning with my head twice its size. Feeling distinctly worse-for-wear, I dry-swallowed a couple of aspirins and soon my headache eased off a tad. Granted, now only mildly hungover, it wasn't something porridge, smoked kippers and a couple of Lorne sausage slices in a roll couldn't easily remedy. I am not one to pledge any New Year Resolutions as ninety-five percent of them tend to get broken by the end of the first day, according to the pollsters.

Whilst most of the residents were still apparently tucked up in bed, sleeping off the festivities of the previous evening, I wandered downstairs to find my dutiful hosts up and about, looking as though Death had paid them a visit and then thought better of it. Their heads must feel like someone had tossed a caber on them. After breakfast, I swaddled myself in layers of black wool, topped off with a black Barbour jacket to keep out the wind chill, and went for a ramble in the rustic locale. I could have journeyed into Drumnadrochit or Lewiston or Fort Augustus, or visited the lovely beaches of the Moray Firth or sampled the amenities of the Highland capital, Inverness, including the January sales, but presently I was more concerned about exploring the unparalleled wildness of my surroundings.

Again, I marvelled at the fairytale setting of my Scottish idyll, rich in natural heritage. There was so much to offer in these parts: designated courses for the golfing enthusiast, from trout- and salmon-fishing in the crystal-clear streams, as the metaphorical 'Sturgeon General' might endorse, to hiking and pony-trekking and hill-climbing and mountain-biking, a chance to follow miles and miles of mountain tracks and explore the ancient Caledonian forests. The roofless ruins of Urquhart Castle and the mysterious deep waters of Loch Ness I would leave for another day, but for now, I decided, I would roam the glens and the abundant woodlands of oak, pine and spruce, let myself succumb to the lure o' th' wild Hielands.

Before me, the land was rife with wildlife, not that I could tell an osprey from a hen harrier from a capercaillie. As I wandered up the hiking trail, I saw flocks of grazing sheep and herds of red deer in the heather-covered hills. I envisioned the spectacular waterfalls of Glen Affric National Park – I intended to make the most of my time here. I passed by a small circle of old Pictish standing stones. I tramped the hard, slippery ground, the strata of frozen woodland detritus underfoot. The footpath was bordered by bowers of fern and thick tangles of gorse. I thought of some bloodthirsty wildcat prowling silently in the undergrowth, stalking me, watching me with fierce, golden eyes. Fortunately, there were no midges this time of year.

I must have gone for at least an hour, taking in the purified air and appreciating the scenic view down into the wooded valley, the frosted greenery, as the heavy gusts of wind grasped at my clothing, threatening to deprive me of my heat, when I stumbled across a bothy, one of those simple huts that Highland crofters use when herding cattle and sheep to higher pastures or where the hardy munro-bagger preparing for his latest ascent as well as the everyday, weary traveller roamin' in the gloamin' takes shelter under, free of charge. A simple hut offering nothing more than basic accommodation, providing just a rest stop, sometimes overnight if needed.

A woman, dressed in wool and tweed and a grey bunnet, stood in the doorway to the bothy, panicking majorly, piercing the arboreal stillness with her hysterics, "*Hulp* us, please, hulp us! Hulp us, somebody, Ah think mah frein is DYING." As I shot into view, the sight of me caused her body to sag with relief. She approached me hurriedly. "Ah'm sae glad tae see ye."

The lady who had ambushed me I immediately recognized as Ida Chalmers, one of the guests at the Clachan Forge Inn. I wondered what she could be doing out here so early, in the middle of nowhere, so far up the slope, ahead of even me. "I'm here . . . whatever's the matter?"

Her voice was cracked, hoarse. I wondered how long she'd been calling out for help. "We need some hulp," she implored me with that fluting, Scottish accent I was getting so used to. "Mah frein is feelin' sair, puggled, pecht oot, peelie-wallie . . ." *Sore, tired, breathless, sick . . .*

Sensing my medical expertise might be required, I followed her into the bothy. The hut was spartan with no facilities (no electricity or heating or water) to speak of. It was meant to be nothing more than a resting spot, anyway. Uncarpeted stone floor, walls composed of ancient timbers laminated together, sparse furnishings: just a bench, which could also double as a sleeping platform against the far wall. Sure enough, on it was slumped Mrs. Chalmers' friend, Joyce Kirkwood, also kitted out in winter gear: shooting breeks, a tartan scarf and a fetching, mustard-coloured cloche hat. Her face was awash with sweaty agony, her hand planted over her chest.

I hunkered down next to her. "What seems to be the trouble?"

She looked up in a daze, eyes steadily focusing on me. "I c-c-cannae breathe . . . Chest hurts . . ."

"Don't worry, my dear. Lucky for you, I'm a doctor. Let's see what I can do for you."

She allowed me to exam her: cold, clammy skin, cyanosis of the lips, tachycardia with a faint, weak pulse, rapid, shallow breathing on account of the chest pain.

It was my professional opinion that the gripping central chest pain, the pain radiating down her left arm, the shortness of breath, and the nausea and dizziness pointed towards cardiac insufficiency. She demonstrated all the symptoms and signs of a classic heart attack. According to Mrs. Chalmers, her friend had been in this highly-distressed state for at least half an hour. I kept Mrs. Kirkwood propped up. Lying her down would only risk heart failure and worsen her breathing difficulties.

I told her with absolute frankness, "I think you need a hospital, my dear." Acting on my recommendation, I attempted to alert the authorities, but my efforts were futile. For some reason, my mobile could not get any reception, as neither could the phones of the two ladies in my midst. It seemed I was in no position to contact the Emergency Services, who could in our case have sent out a team of First Responders from nearby Drumnadrotich. It seemed we were all alone up here, in the stark wilderness. For all intents and purposes, stranded, completely *uncontactable*. How messed-up is that?

I had thought coming up to the Highlands and being cut off from civilization might do me a world of good. But this was not quite what I had in mind.

I might have administered some GTN, marginally eased the pain, relaxed those coronary arteries temporarily, but damn, and *double* damn, I hadn't bothered bringing my doctor's bag from home. Why should I have? I was meant to be here on holiday.

"Ah'm chittering here, and it's a fair way doon fae here. Nae sae semple," Ida Chalmers chirruped.

"What in God's name possessed you to come out here?" I demanded tersely, a little frustrated.

"It wis Joyce's idea," Mrs. Chalmers informed me quietly. "We're very active fowk, some might even call us 'keep fit fanatics'. We eat healthily, exercise daily. We enjoy walking. Ah joined her oan this holiday at her request because her husband coudnae come. Fur moral support, a shoulder tae cry on, cheer her up, y'understand? Ah also thought it mah duty as her best frein that she shuidnae be alone at such a vulnerable time."

Was I missing something? *Her husband left her after thirty-five years of marriage,* I remembered Angus Veitch confidentially disclosing last night. *Puir woman ... whit she must be gaun throu.* It was becoming all too clear. The wedding band on her finger, the haunted look, the desire to isolate herself. My suspicions aroused, I asked the most pertinent question of all: "Her husband's dead, isn't he?"

"How did ye ken? . . . Deid eight months ago tae this day!"

I knelt down beside Mrs. Kirkwood and held her hand, sympathetically. "I'm so sorry for your loss . . ."

"Thank ye, son . . ." she managed to muster through her pain.

Her husband had not just left her; it did not occur to me she had been recently widowed. And it brought my thoughts racing back to her physical condition. It gave her present chest pain a whole new meaning. She ticked all the boxes for a heart attack, but was she *really* having a heart attack? I carefully considered my options. I would have to improvise. "Tell me about your husband . . ."

I let her talk awhile, reminisce, unburden some of her grief. It gave her a small reprieve from the pain, and I allowed her to release it, trickle by trickle, instead of bottling it up until it spilled over. The words just rolled off her tongue in that same singy-songy style of speaking that was uniquely Scottish. "Gillis wis a guid man – Gil, as he liked tae be called. A righteous man, kind 'n' caring. We met at Gairloch in the summer o' '78. Ah wis nineteen, he wis twenty-seven. Ah wis oan the pier buying some ice-cream cones, carrying a dog-eared copy of *Momento Mori*, whin this handsome man joined the queue at the stall. He wis sae tall and braw with piercing blue eyes. I think it wis love at first sight. Anyways, Ah git mah ice-cream 'n' wis walkin' away, peeping back ower mah shoulder, whin Ah clocked he wis follaein me . . . and *bang!* Ah wis sae excited Ah wisnae looking 'n' Ah tripped ower someone's legs flat oan mah ice-cream . . . *oh, mortification, och haunless me!* Weel, he helped me back up oan mah feet 'n' introduced his-sel. He wis a Dundonian throu 'n' throu, a carpenter by trade, working as a shipwright oan the docks, visiting his cousin wha leed locally 'n' wis getting merrit. Ah gave him mah number 'n' he said he'd ring me, mebbe set up a date. But he never rang me. Ah thought aboot him. Ah thought aboot him a lot.

"Then, late wan night, Ah heard someone knock oan the door of mah house. The noise wis sae loud, I finally git up tae investigate. Whin I opened the door, a man fell intae the hallway—passed-oot drunk! *Are ye aff yer head?* I said afore I saw the man's face. *It wis Gil.* Lucky mah parents wur visiting mah grandda – they wid hae gaen pure radge at me fur attracting a streenge man in the wee hours. Ah tried tae carry him up the stairs, bit he wis tae heavy. Instead, Ah left him oan the floor – let him sleep it aff – 'n' Ah gaed up tae mah bedroom and went back tae sleep. Whin Ah woke up the next morning he wis still asleep oan the floor, bit he mist hae bin hot in the middle o' the night fur he wis lying thare as naked as the day he wis born! Ah nearly swooned now Ah cuid see the rest o' him, he wis sae muscular 'n' bonnie . . . Fur a moment, Ah coudnae take mah eyes aff him. Oor eyes met 'n' mah heart missed a beat. He told me he hud gaen tae his cousin's stag pairtie whaur thay plied him wi' drink. He went fur a walk 'n' git lost in the woods. He'd knocked oan the door o' the first hoose he came tae, lookin' fur directions. He coudnae remember much after that. He wis sae ashamed and embarrassed with finding his-sel in such a compromising situation, Ah laughed mah heid aff. Oor love story became known as 'the Meeting o' th' Two Falls' – mah favourite writer, Muriel Spark, wid hae bin proud o' a love story like oors." Gil would take Joyce to his cousin's wedding that weekend, and not long after, Joyce too became a Kirkwood, and she never saw him drunk again. But it was pure fate that found him at her door that night since he confessed that he had lost the piece of paper on which she had scribbled down her telephone number when, in fact, he had been planning to call her and ask her out on a date. Fate had shown them they were meant to meet again and spend the rest of their lives together. They moved to Pitlochry, and Gil opened a joinery business. "He may hae looked lik' a big, strang, strapping Scotsman, bit dinnae let it fool ye. He hud the soul o' a kitten 'n' wis as quiet as a butterfly. He wis a real gentleman 'n' need Ah say a gentle lover. Throo'oot oor leeds thegither, thare wis ne'er a cross word spoken atween us. He adored mah the way Ah wrinkled up mah nose if Ah heard something distasteful 'n' Ah loved the way he wid hold me 'n' make me feel safe 'n' sound, if Ah wis upset. We wur completely insep'rable, two lovers emotionally entwined. We'd cuddle 'n' joke thegither like we did as weans, gaun intae the garden haudin' hauns. We loved each other like we loved each other thirty-five years ago." They never had kids – *nae bairns*; Joyce was barren, and her husband accepted her condition, never looked once at another women to sow his wild oats. They had each other . . . Then, just as Fate had gifted her with his presence one night, Fate snatched him cruelly away from her arms. "Waking up wan mornin' 'n' ne'er knowing yer husband's number's up. Otherwise, Ah cuid hae warned him, git him checked oot in hospital. He just dropped doon deid wan mornin' fae a brain aneurysm. Whit a horrible way tae go! One minute there wis life in his body, the next his life is extinguished lik' a candle by a draught fae unner the door." She was gushing tears again at the memory and continued to clutch her chest.

Ida Chalmers was supportive of her forlorn friend. "Caw canny. Dinnae poosh yerself." *Don't overdo it.* Taking me aside, Mrs. Chalmers whispered, "She's away with her grief."

I did not want to stress her out. "The wounds of a broken heart are hard to cure, but sometimes talking it through can lessen the pain."

Mrs. Kirkwood went on dolefully: "The poem Ah selected fur his eulogy wis *Where Shall the Lover Rest* by Sir Walter Scott."

I knew it well. I have always wanted Poe's *A Dream Within A Dream* to be read at my funeral. Delving into the likes of Shelley, Byron, Keats, Coleridge and Donne, the idea of men brooding beautifully over a lost love had become a staple for romantics the world over. Rabbie Burns knew love, knew passion, knew heartache. I sympathized with her: "There was an English poet called Tennyson who felt that it was better to have loved and lost than never to have loved at all."

"Mair's the pity unto me, alas," said Mrs. Kirkwood, dolour painting each word. "Ah feel lonely 'n' in pain wi'oot ye, Gil. Life seems tae be wi'oot ony gain. Mah heart overflows wi' memories o' ye, colder than midnicht bogles. Sweet memories that hae since turned sour. Ah miss the stolen moments, the stolen kisses, the sighs. Mah entire world haes fallen apairt. Ah lang fur yer touch, Gil, 'n' yer warm embrace, the look in yer eyes, the smile oan yer face. Mah dreams are filled wi' yer soft gentle kiss – Ah cherished thaim mair than ye'll ever ken. The hoose still holds yer scents 'n' the radio ainlie plays yer songs. Instead o' the thegitherness o' love, Ah'm feelin' ainlie the pain o' loss. Ah hae endured this plague fur nearly a year since ye departed. Moisture lends proof tae yer passing 'til Ah kin bear it na mair. Ah wish tae genuinely bid the world goodbye. Ah cannae keep haudin' oan inside, fur ye shall ne'er come back tae me."

The woman is depressed, I thought, concerned, *understandably turned into a bit of a misery girl these days.* I imagined the sadness, fear, anger, guilt and confusion that must immerse her, the sense of emptiness. The hopelessness, and helplessness, unable to eat or sleep or think properly, full of the deepest despair. She had come here to die in this beautiful place. Anxiety might be the rust of life, destroying its brightness and weakening its power, but grief was the memory of widowed affections. In her grief Mrs. Kirkwood had stopped living.

"Trust in the Lord," Ida Chalmers tried to comfort her. "The Lord is near tae the broken-hearted 'n' saves the crushed in spirit. Psalms 34:18"

But her friend was gripped by another paroxysm of grief. She was weeping again, inconsolably. "It takes a minute tae like someone 'n' an hour tae love someone, but tae forget thaim takes a lifetime. Is there na merit tae the notion that a couple deeply in love shuid find relief whin thay exit life thegither?"

I felt only sympathy and compassion for this woman, a woman who had lost her spouse under horrendous circumstances. "*Excess of grief for the dead is madness; for it is an injury to the living, and the dead know it not,*" I quoted, just as the Greek philosopher, Xenophon, succinctly put it. I continued to advise, "There might be a gaping hole for a while, but you will come to terms with your grief, I promise. The aim is to remember the best memories of your husband so he will always be with you in any future time of need." She looked at me then, with a moment of serenity. "There is always hope when there may appear to be none."

I didn't have much time. She had a broken heart.

Can you die from a broken heart?

The simple answer: *Yes.*

If you think that dying from a broken heart is a metaphor or the stuff of legend, then think again. There is a sound psychological and physiological basis for it. You've heard of long-time couples dying months, days, even hours apart from each other.

What was Love anyway? The Greatest Addiction of All. As Bryan Ferry of Roxy Music would testify, *Love is the Drug,* further expatiated through the Brian Jonestown Massacre's frame of reference: *If Love is The Drug, Then I Want to OD.* Literature and poetry are filled with descriptions of Love being compared to a kind of madness. Hippocrates reported that love can eventually fade into melancholy. These days it's well-known that those in love experience a high similar to that drug [again], cocaine, while others liken it to eating large quantities of chocolate. The release of a host of neurotransmitters – phenethylamine, dopamine, noradrenaline and oxytocin, to name but a few – mimic the feeling that cocaine and amphetamines give you. Then, imagine if that Love is suddenly taken away and the potential withdrawal effects its loss entails, sometimes fatal, on the body, affecting personality, perception and thoughts. A broken heart hurts in the same way as the pangs of intense physical pain. The interplay between the stress hormones and the excitation of the vagus nerve will provoke nausea, pain and muscle tightness in the chest. Personality will affect how that pain is perceived by the individual. Nietzsche claimed that there is always some madness in love. Even Freud said that one is very crazy when in love. A broken heart, I suppose, was something that might not be recognized at first. The person may not be aware or even be able to verbalize their feelings, but the subconscious might realize something is wrong and result in it manifesting somatic symptoms. Love – or its loss – is a time of increased vulnerability.

In the curious case of Mrs. Kirkwood, a widow in mourning, having suffered a devastating loss, a pervasive shock to the system, what were the chances that she was suffering a typical heart attack? Or was she experiencing something else . . . something called 'Stress Cardiomyopathy', or what physicians had come to coin 'Broken Heart Syndrome'? It was more than just a hunch, neither conjecture nor hearsay. It made total sense. As a clinician, I was trained to look for patterns in aetiology and symptomatology, using previous knowledge to index and categorize the information into differential diagnoses that I would further narrow down.

True, heart attacks occur aplenty in those who have lost a loved one, 0.2%, twice that of the general population, but 10% of these tend to be misdiagnosed, when in fact they fit the category of Broken Heart Syndrome. Broken Heart Syndrome is thought to affect an estimated 6000 people in the UK annually, i.e. 2% of the 300000 heart attacks that present to the Emergency Services. The distinction between the two may not be immediately obvious, but they are clinically different. To begin with, the risk factors for heart disease are missing in Broken Heart Syndrome. The person is often fit and healthy with no comorbidity. Didn't Mrs. Chalmers state that Mrs. Kirkwood led a healthy, active lifestyle?

There is a commonality to each case of Broken Heart Syndrome. It is normally preceded by sudden emotional distress, such as a breakup or the death of a loved one. The traumatizing event triggers the brain to distribute chemicals that weaken the heart tissue. The underlying cause may be an overload of the 'fight or flight' hormone, adrenaline. Low-to-moderate doses of adrenaline cause the heart to pump stronger and faster, preparing us for action, essential for survival, but high doses have a direct toxic effect on the heart. In Broken Heart Syndrome, the adrenaline unleashed into the bloodstream is thirty times the standard elevated level, which has an adverse reaction on the heart, leaving it unable to pump properly and risking a disturbance in the rhythm of the heart. It is postulated that adrenaline binds to the cardiac cells, causing a massive influx of calcium that keeps increasing the contractility of the heart muscle until the heart is completely overwhelmed and paralyzed. Unlike a generic heart attack, the cells are not injured or dead but only temporarily stunned. It is also reported that there is a change in the way adrenaline is metabolized, further increasing its levels in the body, further disrupting the function of the heart, creating a vicious cycle.

In a clinical setting, the ECG changes would prove inconclusive and there would be no great elevation in the cardiac enzymes as exemplified in a Myocardial Infarction. A Coronary Angiogram, when a catheter is inserted with a radio-opaque dye to picture the blood supply of the heart, would show no evidence of coronary artery disease, no clogged arteries or blood clots or any signs of occlusion. Rather than demonstrating any blockages, the coronary arteries will be fully patent, as a clean as a whistle, but as the heart is no longer an effective pump, blood is flowing more slowly. On Echocardiogram, an ultrasound scan of the heart, of which I did not have the luxury of performing either, I envisaged a ballooning-out of the apex of the left ventricle, giving the heart an elongated appearance with a round bottom and a narrow neck, the lower half effectively paralyzed and the top half having to do more work to compensate, reducing the overall pumping efficiency of the heart. This condition was first documented in the Japanese medical journals of the early 1990s, referred to as Takotsubo Cardiomyopathy, with the uniquely peculiar shape of the heart reminiscent of the fishing-gear used by Japanese fishermen to capture octopuses. An ECHO would have been definitive, confirming the diagnosis and my suspicions.

More importantly, I knew that the prognosis was good and recovery rates fairly rapid. The condition was reversible, leaving no permanent damage, with the heart normally returning to its original, premordid functioning, unlike a standard heart attack, where there is death of the heart muscle. However, I also knew that Broken Heart Syndrome was a recognized cause of ventricular arrhythmias and even ventricular rupture, if left untreated. Furthermore, the electrical misfiring and irregular contractions of the heart could easily lead to sudden heart failure. Despite its good outcome, 2% still die, if not rushed to hospital in time, due to the potentially life-threatening heart rhythm abnormalities.

We were in deep shtook unless I figured something out. I mentally referenced Private Frazer, played by John Laurie, who announces with moon-eyed finality: "We're all *doomed!*" I thought of the Veitches and how Death was a paying guest in their hotel and how his shadow had followed me here to this simple hill-walker's hut, miles from nowhere, at the mercy of a pale, frigid sky preparing to discharge its sledload of snow, and was reaching out with grasping fingers for Mrs. Kirkwood, a bereaving widow, expressing her loss through a broken heart, a heart that could easily pack in any minute, without the input of life-saving medical equipment. She was ready, willing and able to accept the implications of the death knell, of the bell that tolled for her. Walking down the hill wasn't an option, time our biggest enemy; she might be dead by the time help arrived. I could not prolong the distress, both emotional and [now] physical, she laboured under. I had to act fast, otherwise she would die out here in the wind and the cold. I might think less of certain patients, wish ill of them, as I'm sure most doctors have done in their practice, but I did not want *her* death to be on my conscience. She was an honest, respectful woman, trying to cope with the fickleness of death under difficult circumstances, near to giving up. I'm sure her husband would have been proud of the way she had maintained her dignity under these difficult circumstances, her grace under pressure. But I'm sure he would not have wanted her to join him so soon. I needed to mend her heart before it got the better of her and she went into cardiac arrest.

Even if I was squeezed into a tight corner, I had a plan. Clearly, I *would* have to improvise. It was a long shot, but it was worth a try.

I had once cured my sister-in-law of her phobia using unconventional means. For a woman who worried so much that it made her worry if she wasn't worried, she was now an agony/'anxiety' aunt, a celebrity, dispensing sound advice to other anxiety sufferers in her discrete blogging circles. Now I would use the same unconventional means to treat the unfortunate woman before me and her challenging neurochemical stress of heartbreak.

My job is to heal the sick, remember? With whatever it takes.

I did not have much to offer at the time. Supportive measures might have included administering aspirin, ACE inhibitors, nitrates and diuretics to relieve the immediate distress, but as I pointed out, I had been caught lacking – I did not bring my medical bag on holiday, let alone on this walk. An intra-aortic balloon might have temporarily helped pump the blood until the heart fully recovered, and some patients even require a ventilator. Once you enter the realms of catastrophic heart failure, the patient might need to be nursed in ITU. I did not have any of these resources available to me. I would have to resort to Plan B, figuratively-speaking; even then, there were no guarantees it would work. But as Robert the Bruce said to the spider repeatedly spinning its web without much luck: *If you don't succeed once, try, try again.* I supposed: *As long as you know you tried your best, gave it your absolute all, there is no shame in failure.*

True heart attacks are prevalent in men, but 90% of cases of Broken Heart Syndrome are women, mostly aged fifty-five and over. In other words, post-menopausal women. And Mrs. Kirkwood was just that.

At menopause, the level of oestrogen drops off. Besides playing a key role in inflammation and boosting the body's immune system's response to infection and injury, it is well-documented that oestrogen is also cardio-protective, moderating blood flow through the heart due to its positive effect on the inner lining of the artery walls, keeping them flexible, as well as protecting the heart against huge stresses and the negative impact of the stress hormones. It explains why the risk of heart disease, comparable to men, increases in women who have gone through the menopause. It is even debated that oestrogen's reach stretches as far as reducing the risk of developing dementia.

"I'm assuming you're not on any HRT?" I asked Mrs. Kirkwood.

"How cuid ye possibly ken?"

I turned to Mrs. Chalmers. "What about yourself?"

"I take Primarin."

Mrs. Chalmers must have undergone a hysterectomy to be prescribed an oestrogen-only pill, otherwise adjunctive progesterone would be called for. I didn't ask. Instead, I kept it focused. "Do you have some on you at the moment?"

Mrs. Chalmers pulled out a pack from her handbag. "Why?"

I dove straight into it. I explained my thinking on the whole concept of Broken Heart Syndrome in layman's terms coupled with the inconclusive, mixed evidence base for oestrogen therapy on the heart, impressing upon them that the 'unusual' treatment plan I proposed in the immediacy had been carefully thought through.

"Great Scot!" Mrs. Chalmers exclaimed. "Thae's an incredible explanation! Whit dae ye think, Joyce?"

"Entirely your decision," I told Mrs. Kirkwood.

The intensity of the pain must have been such that Joyce Kirkwood was willing to try anything. She found it within herself to accept the tablets from the blister pack and gobbled them down with mineral water. Even if she had come up here to die as she had originally intended, some form of self-preservation instinct must have kicked in, a will to live.

I asked her to take the tablets, lots of them, in fact *all* of them. I didn't care about overdosing her. My first priority was to keep her alive until help arrived.

Once the chest pain had begun to noticeably ease off and she was feeling slightly better, I made my way down the hill and got help at the hotel, informing all and sundry of the plight of my fellow travellers. Ironically, it was an oestrogen overdose that saved her. We could worry about its adverse effects (nausea, headache, dizziness, breast tenderness, leg cramps, abdominal bloating, vaginal bleeding, etc.) later, when she was nicely tucked up warm and cosy in a hospital bed.

It was all very dramatic. The ambulance could never have made it; I didn't realize how far up we were. Mrs. Kirkwood warranted a helicopter rescue, needing to be airlifted and flown to the nearest hospital. By the time the paramedics reached the bothy and stretchered her out, the first spirals of snow began swirling down from the sky.

There's not much else to report. I kept in touch with her. I visited Mrs. Kirkwood at Inverness General where she received the necessary medical care and psychological support. She made an excellent recovery. Mrs. Kirkwood was sincerely grateful for my resourcefulness and timely intervention on the brae – another feather in my cap – and informed me that I had been correct in my diagnosis of Stress Cardiomyopathy, as all the various tests had shown. I wished her the absolute best before completing my holiday in the Scottish Highlands and heading back to old Fairview. A few days at work and I got that all-too-familiar feeling that either I'd never been away on holiday or it felt like it had been a long time ago. But at least my short break and abstinence from coffee had cured my caffeine addiction.

Mrs. Kirkwood received the bereavement counselling she needed in the community without even requiring commencement of an antidepressant. She managed to re-organize her mental processes so she could become stronger, taking the lead role in her own recovery. Her brain got her loss into perspective and normal life resumed, with no recurrence of her grief-driven symptoms. Last I heard she had met someone else, a divorcé going by the name of Donald Abernathy, the director of a family-run mercantile finance company. "It's whit Gil wid hae wanted. Ah'm sure. He wid hae wanted me tae carry oan livin'." I was happy for her, glad she had made a comeback and was making the most of her new lease of life. A part of me was quietly pleased I might have had something to do with it, perhaps being instrumental, from a medical standpoint, in giving her her life back. I decided against writing up a paper on my experience with HRT for any medical journal, lest I should get a right royal ribbing from the unforgiving medical community.

Thus concluded the Strange Case of Mrs. Kirkwood and the Meeting of the Two Falls . . . how her delicate old ticker had temporarily assumed the shape of an octopus pot, as subsequently evidenced in the cath lab. And how she managed in the long term to overcome her adversity and get her life back on track. My praise for her knew no bounds. I admired her for accepting her new life and for having the confidence in me, in the first instance, to help heal her heart.

I remembered her immense gratitude as we parted at Inverness General. "All Ah could hope fur wis a kind word, but ye gave me much, much more. Hope – that is, hope in living!"

I doff my cap at you, good lady! Glad to have been of assistance!

I can only praise her for bringing out her inner strength, previously buried by her grief, and building upon her resilience until she possessed the necessary confidence to find herself a new man. I was genuinely, *truly* happy for her!

As they say, when one door closes, another one opens.

December 2014-February 2015

The Wake

"Beloved, don't fret that you gave yourself so quickly!
Believe me, I don't think badly or wrongly of you.
The arrows of Love are various: some scratch us,
And our hearts suffer for years from their slow poison.
But others strong-feathered with freshly sharpened points
Pierce to the marrow, and quickly inflame the blood.
In the heroic ages, when gods and goddesses loved,
Desire followed a look, and joy followed desire."

Johann Wolfgang von Goethe

They sat in the drawing room to remember and celebrate the life of a lady who had greatly polarized family opinion. Phyllida Schmidt had received a decent send-off at her modestly-attended funeral, and now her immediate family had got together to pay their last respects to her during her wake at her old, Victorian house in Oaks Fold, BRACKENDELL. Brackendell was a doyen of houses, with as much character as its former owner and dowager. Her two sons, Lawrence and Martin, both well into their sixties, sat in high-wing, leather armchairs on either side of Dr. Spencer Healey, Martin's son-in-law, who occupied an easy chair. Dennis Hewitt, his other son-in-law and chief employee in the family oven-cleaning business run by him, sat impassively in the second easy chair on the other side of him. Dr. Healey's wife, Helena, whose long, blond hair was plaited like that of a Valkyrian maiden and who preferred men with moppy hair like her husband's, was seated at the mahogany dining table, caught up in her interminable addiction of texting her friends, whilst her slightly younger, prim-

and-proper sister, Greta, sat across from her, playing solitaire. Judith, their mother, was laid out on the leather sofa with a wet flannel over her forehead to fend off a headache. The men were dapperly dressed in black suits and matching ties and the women donned expensive, dark dresses to mark this formal occasion. Mother and both daughters had been busy in the kitchen, reproducing Phyllida's former favourite dish, a repast of roast pork with honey-and-mustard sauce and sauerkraut, before the old lady had turned vegan in her seventies. They had eaten well, their meal finished off with a dessert-glass of Eiswein, and the men had moved on to the brandy and cigars. The Remy Martin XO, drunk from the family crystal, went down a treat with the Hoyo de Monterrey Epicure No. 2 cigars Lawrence had kindly brought with him. Dennis accepted a snifter of brandy but declined the offer of a cigar. The drawing room possessed a vintage dresser, which doubled as a drinks' cabinet, and a credenza, upon which Casper, Helena's white, deaf cat, was presently curled up, snoring softly and twitching occasionally as if dreaming. A spinet piano, on which both Helena's father and uncle were near-virtuosos, stood next to the antique writing bureau. The walls were adorned by various framed paintings by Gerhard Richter, characterized by their shadowy, blurry, almost spectral quality. Leatherbound books, some first editions, completed the bookcase. In the corner of the room, the old-fashioned gramophone was turned down low, the faint strains of *Button Up Your Overcoat* by Ruth Etting, taken from Phyllida's personal record collection, drifting across the room. The room, like the rest of the house, had a typical old people's feel to it — lots of dull browns and greens and yellows — and Martin hoped to give it a more modern makeover once he was formally bequeathed the property in the upcoming reading of the will tomorrow. Apart from a few lamps scattered around the drawing room, dimmed down low, most of the illumination came from the roaring fire in the hearth, big enough to broil a boar, painting the faces of the men in orange-red hues and crawling shadows.

It was just after eight o'clock on a blowy, bitterly-cold winter's night, a time when it grows dark very early, and the Schmidts were more than grateful they had safely negotiated the end of the old year, a period of great upheaval for the family, contending with their matriarch's illness and eventual demise. Spencer had once reminded his health-conscious wife — and professional nurse — that January received only one hour of sunlight a day which might explain why most of the British population suffered from low levels of Vitamin D. Through the tall windows, a full moon graced the night sky, a bone-white, oblate sphere amidst a glitter of stars, and the restless wind moaned an ancient lament, rising and falling, blowing against the creaking joints of the house. Those present appreciated the snug warmth from the crackling log-fire, which came as a welcome relief against the creeping, bone-deep chill that seemed a characteristic feature of such large, old houses.

Spencer sipped his brandy slowly, staring into the fireplace, watching the flames char the logs. "I think we did justice by Phyllida by giving her a lovely funeral."

Lawrence, the eldest of the two Schmidt's boys, appeared strangely relaxed, relieved even. "I can't believe the old woman finally did the decent thing and popped her clogs! Took a long time coming I can tell you!"

Martin glanced across at the mantelpiece upon which rested a decorative urn, accommodating Phyllida's ashes. *That used to be a human being once,* he thought, *not just any human being, but my mother.* Martin's expression did not quite crystallize into actual grief, either, regardless of the solemnness of his reply. "Yes, she may not exactly have had the constitution of an ox, but she did extremely well to live as long as she did. It's truly the end of an era."

"We should be drinking Schnapps in celebration!" Lawrence added unkindly. "It would make a more joyous libation!"

Greta suddenly looked up from the game of solitaire she was playing at the dining table, offended. "You shouldn't say such awful things about her! She was my grandma – and will always be my grandma!"

"I know I shouldn't speak ill of the dead," Lawrence continued, "but our mother was a *horrible* woman!"

Helena stopped texting and joined in the protest. "Please don't be nasty to our grandmother. I only have good memories of her. I loved her and will miss her terribly."

"You can't make me change my opinion of the woman," Lawrence replied. "I lived with her. I grew up with her. We suffered *because* of her!"

It was a cold, insensitive thing to say, and Spencer marvelled at how a normally caring, compassionate man of medicine as Lawrence could denounce his mother in such harsh, hateful terms. It had come as a massive surprise to Spencer when he'd first started dating Helena that her uncle had graduated from the same medical school as him, albeit some twenty years earlier, specializing in Obs & Gyn (whereas Spencer chose Psychiatry as a career), carrying out his private medical practice overseas in Germany, before eventually retiring to Panama to live the life of Riley and do a 'whole lot of nothing'. Whilst Martin was a materialistic individual with a weakness for flash cars, such as the Mercedes AMG he presently owned, Lawrence had a strong focus on the fairer sex. Long-divorced due to his staunch ladies'-man antics, for whom nurses and midwives were his fertile ground, abortions notwithstanding, Lawrence had currently got himself another fancy woman, even in Panama, this relatively remote part of the world, this time a woman of a more mature disposition. He was currently dating a rich American widow, whom he had decided not to invite to his mother's funeral. As a psychiatrist, Spencer could confidently claim that, as a rule of thumb, even the most hardened criminals loved their mothers, so to meet someone who expressed only contempt for their mother deserved deeper exploration. Lawrence also owned a house in Dresden and his only son, Pardwulf, lived in Bremen (and whom the family suspected might be gay). Lawrence would visit the UK a couple of times a year, spending the entirety of his stay with his mother at Brackendell as the dutiful eldest son, the two of them alone in the house together, and he frequently described spending time with the old lady as a 'nightmare'. They quarrelled constantly, sometimes to the point of shouting at one another, and he often survived his stay steaming drunk, not a pretty sight. The alternative version suggested he would get completely intoxicated and obnoxiously rag on his frail, elderly mother, with the hope of pushing her one step closer to the grave. "I think your problem stems from an underlying, unconscious belief that, as children, your mother did not protect you from your father."

Lawrence did not disagree. "You may have hit the nail on the head."

"You couldn't be more right," concurred Martin.

"Our father was an unpleasant man, even at the best of times," elaborated Lawrence. "Too stuck in his ways, too difficult to live with, too much of a disciplinarian. Belligerent, quick-tempered, too damned volatile. Only his decision ever mattered. A *monster!*"

Indeed, Reinhardt Schmidt had purportedly been a formidable man, with an extremely short fuse and a hard, punitive attitude if anybody got on his wrong side, not averse to physically chastising his children. Lawrence had got it the most. Even Phyllida had suffered her husband's wrath on occasion and she had gradually grown emotionally distant from him and her children, some of his overbearing, heavy-handed approach brushing off on her. And it sounded like her sons never forgave her. It was extraordinary for Spencer to hear Lawrence speak of his mother as a 'nightmare' and his father as a 'monster'. Was it really a happy, committed relationship to produce children, two sons? How difficult must it have been growing up in such a patriarchal household? "I suppose Reinhardt's own upbringing must have made him the angry man he was."

"Not easy for him living through those turbulent times of 1930s Germany," Lawrence acknowledged.

So true, thought Spencer. As an impressionable young man, Reinhardt had once been a member of the Hitler Youth, soon joining the Nazi war machine as it trampled across Europe. As Günter Grass might have put it, Reinhardt had belonged to the generation that grew up under National Socialism, completely blinded and led astray by the genocidal politics in a strong and united Germany, one of the frightening preconditions for the horror that ensued. During the eventual fall of the Third Reich, Herr Schmidt had ended up in an internment camp when the British recaptured the Channel Islands. Far from denial or repentance, he had maintained his *Übermensch* mentality and remained a lifelong supporter of Hitler but never mentioned how many men he had killed during the war. He had reportedly kept some Nazi memorabilia upstairs in the attic in an old, green trunk with German postage stamps, including a Nazi uniform, a Luger, a small red flag bearing a Swastika and an antisemitic propaganda poster preceding *Kristallnacht*, all priceless, original items and all of which he remained reluctant to sell throughout his lifetime, even if he might have made a fair penny from them. He also never got rid of an old, full-nude painting of Phyllida, rather tastefully done, when she had once worked as an artist's model during her bohemian days before she met him. It had also been a period in her life when she disappeared and, apart from hanging around with various painters, rumour had it she had got pregnant. Whether there was any truth to this persistent rumour, the other, illegitimate side of the family was curiously absent from her funeral. Phyllida had hailed from a wholesome, well-to-do English family in Portishead and gone to a convent school, but her rebellious streak had caused conflict, particularly when she fell head over heels in love with Reinhardt. *Desire followed a look, and joy followed desire,* as Phyllida quoted her favourite poet, Goethe. *I think it's romantic,* Helena had once told Spencer. *My grandmother followed her heart. She didn't care what other people thought.* Phyllida had considered Reinhardt an exceeding handsome man. In fact, both Schmidt boys had inherited their father's good looks, regardless of their current portly frames from gluttonous over-indulgence (or 'the good life' in their own words), as well as his characteristic, barely-noticeable lisp. Indeed, Helena had proudly compared her grandfather to a young Christopher Plummer when the actor played the head of the von Trapp family. She was not ashamed of her German heritage. Phyllida married Reinhardt shortly after meeting him, the love between a convent school-educated woman and a German POW unheard of in that day and age, scandalous. It would prove to be the final straw. For defying convention, let alone falling in love with the enemy, Phyllida's family consequently disowned her. Despite his Nazi leanings, Reinhardt had been as fiercely Catholic as the Teutonic Knights, and Phyllida converted to Catholicism from her family's CofE status. Reinhardt Schmidt had lived a long life, partly due to him closely observing some of his religious practices such as fasting on Fridays (promoting gene repair, in Lawrence's professional opinion), whilst inherently bearing good genes. He had worked as a draughtsman. Although he guarded his privacy when at home, he was not loath to travelling around Europe with his young family, visiting the Fatherland. Monschau, with its fairytale architecture and atmosphere, became a popular holiday destination. He had also been a whisky-drinker and a pipe-smoker, and his antique pipe collection, lined up along a leather strap, hung on the wall next to the credenza. Spencer hoped to acquire the pipe collection one day. Reinhardt retired in his fifties and did nothing for the next thirty years except drink and smoke. Reinhardt died from pancreatic cancer and was now ten years in his grave. He was aged eighty-five.

The family never saw Phyllida express any grief over the loss of her husband, going about her daily business as usual. Maybe she was quietly grieving even if she refused to let anyone else in. Helena supposed people grieved differently. Or, as Spencer suggested, Phyllida found a new lease of life after losing a man who had been a child- and wife-beater.

Spencer thought he would be kinder to Phyllida's memory. "I never met the man, but I can't complain about Phyllida in her dotage. She always comported herself with decorum and treated me with respect. I always had time for her."

Martin nodded. "I have to admit she took an immediate shine to you."

"I remember when Helena and I had a fight and I refused to visit Phyllida as arranged because I wasn't in the mood for company and Helena came here by herself, Phyllida was furious at her for treating me badly and letting her down."

"Yes, she certainly gave me an earful," Helena corroborated. "She always looked forward to your visits."

"As did I," Spencer said honestly. "We always spent a cultured afternoon, chewing the fat on English Literature and Drama. She appreciated me giving a lonely, old widow like her some time and attention. I was only doing her a small kindness, but the pleasure was all mine! She was a wealth of knowledge and experience and an extremely well-spoken and well-read lady." Indeed, reading had been her passion, and the bookshelves in the drawing room reflected her diverse tastes: the English classics, German poetry, biographies and guidebooks and volumes on animal care to name but a few. Goethe had been her divine inspiration. Before her death, she had also been an outspoken critic of the state of the English language. "Phyllida once described modern written and spoken English as urban gutterspeak, a degenerate, bastardized version of the English language of post-war Britain when it still faintly resembled the craft of the generation before it and writers really knew how to write. Contemporary folk might call it evolution, the new normal, but, in her opinion, having grown up with Jane Austen, the English language had not evolved in the last fifty years, only regressed."

"Did she want us to all speak like Elizabethans?" Martin asked, not hiding his sarcasm. "Or speak properly like aristocrats?"

"I remember you always left her house worse for wear," Helena reminded Spencer.

Spencer laughed. "Probably on account of the Three Barrels she plied me with." Phyllida had been quite partial to a drink or two. Three Barrels had been her favourite tipple.

"Grandmother was notorious for her ridiculously generous measures," Helena said, slightly annoyed. "I told her off. I don't like my husband coming home in a right state."

"You shouldn't blame her, you know," Spencer replied sheepishly. "If anything, it was my fault for drinking the stuff."

"How right you are!" agreed Greta. "She didn't exactly put the glass to your lips! The drinker has no excuse!" She poured herself another glass of Riesling and went back to her single-player card game.

"Don't you all know alcohol is a brain-blotter — a mind-rotter?" added Helena, the staunch teetotaller.

"We try not to think about it," replied Martin, grinning.

"You and Dennis are still relatively new members of the family," Lawrence told Spencer. Dennis turned his head at the mention of his name but did not speak. "You didn't know her as well as we did." Lawrence puffed on his cigar, a blue raft of aromatic smoke wafting up in the air. "She was an actress."

"Yes, all melodramatic gestures and hysterical put-ons when she wanted something," Martin agreed. "You never saw her for the kind of woman she really was. *Such an act!*"

Spencer remembered Phyllida reminiscing about her time at the Bristol Vic, initially as an understudy in Shakespearean drama, eventually taking on a starring role. Her defining moment came playing Desdemona in *Othello*. She could also do a pretty mean Ophelia. Kissing, apart from air-kissing, was prohibited in those days, unlike nowadays when even nudity was the norm for an up-and-coming actress. The shame of it, she chided. Acting might have been a much-derided profession even in those days, according to Phyllida, but it would continue to serve as a finely-detailed character study and a convincing imitation of life. Whereas Helena loved everything by Elizabeth Taylor, Phyllida had been a lifelong fan of Shirley Temple. Remarkably, both actresses had starred in different versions of *The Bluebird*, the original and the remake grandmother and granddaughter's favourite films, respectively. Phyllida had even compared Helena and Spencer to Elizabeth Taylor and Richard Burton, minus the couple's infamously turbulent relationship. Martin had been grateful to Spencer for making an honest woman out of his daughter, who had inherited her grandmother's defiant nature. Phyllida had adored Laurence Olivier, who had once been in the audience, watching her perform at the height of her career as an actress. Spencer had to disagree with her that, although Olivier was probably the greatest Shakespearean actor of all time, hands down, Olivier was terribly miscast as Hamlet and Heathcliff when these roles should have ideally belonged to someone more caddish, *roguish*, not a gentleman actor. There was much debate between Phyllida and Spencer over this difference of opinion. Her marriage to Reinhardt put an end to her acting days as he turned her into a homemaker, and she went to work as an English teacher in a respectable comprehensive school. She often looked back on her time in the theatre with much sweet nostalgia, accompanied by an overwhelming sense of regret over its sudden end, and wondered wistfully how her acting career would have panned out if she hadn't married. Mightn't she have made the transfer to the big screen with her fine acting qualities if she had chosen a different path in life? Lawrence and Helena had both caught Phyllida's acting bug in a small measure. Lawrence had done some amateur dramatics in Panama whilst Helena had completed an eight-minute student film. "She always behaved civilly towards me. I never got a glimpse of the actress in her."

"I don't question your psychiatric skills," Lawrence said, "not at all. She must have been on her best behaviour with you. She always showed the world her good side. Behind closed doors, she was extremely demanding and selfish, throwing a huge fuss whenever she wanted to get her own way. She was a consummate artist, able to wear emotions like a suit, an authority on crocodile tears."

"I suppose I must have seen her in her natural light, without any pretence or prima donnas," Spencer concluded, unable to reconcile this woman who had taught English class for thirty years and who had been extraordinarily polite and courteous to him with the same lady her sons held in such high contempt and criticized with a singular breath for failing them as a mother. It was normal for children to compete for their mother's favour, but Phyllida had told him her sons had considered her a burden if she ever called upon them to do something for her. He decided to sidestep the bad blood towards her, the general negative consensus from her own sons, of all people. He raised his glass. "Let's propose a toast to her honour tonight, shall we?"

"Chin-chin," said Martin, reciprocating the gesture.

"Needs must, as they say," Lawrence added, with tired enthusiasm.

Dennis said nothing, the strong, silent type, just brought his glass up in a salute.

Spencer gulped down the Cognac in one go. He watched the others down theirs. He poured them each another glass.

The January wind threw another screamer against the house. A knot exploded in the fireplace, sending a plume of sparks up the chimney flue. Judith continued to doze off or *pretend* to doze off, probably quietly listening to the conversation between the men. Helena would occasionally glance up from her texting and Tweeting. Greta wondered if a few rubbers of bridge might alleviate the tedium – or even a game of whist. Dennis remained blank and silent, staring robotically into the fireplace. Lawrence took another sip from his brandy glass and another puff of his cigar. Martin's thoughts travelled to tomorrow's meet-up with the family solicitor. Spencer's mind went to stranger, darker places, things he dared not mention.

Suddenly awake, Casper jumped from the credenza to the dresser to the window-sill in under two seconds. It seemed he could still do some swift acrobatics, even if he was a kilo heavier than he ought to be. He sat on his haunches on the sill, his acute eyesight allowing him to see into the darkness outside.

"You know she loved Casper to bits," Helena said abruptly.

"She'd always loved animals from an early age," agreed Greta.

"Preferred them to people," remarked Lawrence, continuing his character assassination. "I can imagine her getting arrested as an animal activist."

Greta ignored him. "She had a number of cats growing up," she recounted. "She named them after various Shakespearean characters. I remember her telling us that Brutus was very well-behaved as opposed to Julius Caesar who was very naughty!"

Spencer recalled this anecdote from his conversations with Phyllida. "Ah, the irony of it . . ."

"My mother was always exchanging letters with Uncle Herman in Munich," Martin told Spencer, "a pen-pal relationship based on their love of cats."

Uncle Herman, Spencer learned, was Reinhardt's brother. "Oh, yes, Uncle Herman and his cats, how could I forget?" said Lawrence, amused.

"She was equally fond of dogs," Greta explained. "Shortly before Grandad passed on, Grandma decided to get herself a Labrador. She named her Maggie after her favourite politician. She and Maggie got on just fine. I think Maggie was excellent company to Grandma. I think Grandma's decline began when Maggie passed away."

From Spencer's short experience of her, Maggie had been a lovely dog, if not a little too greedy. She had died at the ripe, old age of fourteen. The woman who had barely shed a tear when her husband died had been utterly devastated when her dog died. "Even if Maggie was a grand dame, I could see the puppy in her, panting with excitement!"

"Grandma died of a broken heart," Greta declared. "I know she did."

In another athletic, fluid movement, Casper leapt from the window-sill, ran across the floor and jumped on to Helena's lap, startling her. He began kneading on her woollen dress before proceeding to wash himself, not unlike the preening of birds, preparing to sleep again since it seemed there wasn't much happening around him. Casper, the lap cat and the 'kneady' man – with a 'k'. The 'spider assassin', as Spencer referred to him since, every morning, they would find a dead spider on the floor, curled up and crushed. 'Twinkletoes', as Helena liked to call him, or 'my precious, middle-aged kitten'. The 'little monkey' had been Phyllida's term of endearment. "Our grandmother adored Casper. We'd leave him in her charge every time we went on holiday. She kept him in line. He refused to go bed one night and bit her wrists when she tried to take him to the bedroom. So she whacked him one! You can imagine how cross she was with him. Other times, he'd bite her ankles, drawing blood, when she refused to feed him outside his designated feeding time. She scolded us for overfeeding him and making him overweight and aggressive when boundaries ought to be set around mealtimes. 'Food aggression' she called it. I remember another time, when we came back from holiday and went to collect Casper, he did a poo behind her television set just as we were about to put him in the cat carrier and take him home."

"I'm guessing he was either marking his territory," Martin presumed, "or meting out revenge on the old lady for not letting him get his own way."

"She was very upset to hear about the Croydon Cat Killer," Spencer went on. "Gave her many a sleepless night, worrying about the cats who might fall prey to this evil monster. She wasn't entirely satisfied by the outcome of the police investigation, which concluded that the cats had apparently fallen victim to foxes. I always thought that cats and foxes shared a mutual indifference . . . unless, of course, the foxes, moving as a pack, got so hungry as to surround, attack and maim any stray cat, probably requiring both sets of animals to be put down."

"Makes you wonder who is more sly and cunning," Greta observed. "The cat or the fox?"

"January is the time of the midwinter foxes and their love calls," Helena enlightened them. "Their alarming, blood-curdling cries in the dead of night signal the mating season. The vixen wastes no time in preparing a confined, sheltered space, often under a garden shed, where she can raise her spring cubs. I love foxes!"

"I think the police concluded their investigation prematurely," argued Spencer. "Regardless of the final police report, I still think it was a person. Phyllida shared my view."

"All animals are beautiful," pronounced Greta, "all God's creatures – cats or foxes or otherwise."

"I can't believe how quickly my grandmother deteriorated after that fall at our house," said Helena with a touch of guilt. "I can't help but feel responsible."

"You shouldn't be hard on yourself," Spencer consoled his wife. "You couldn't have prevented it."

The incident in question occurred during a garden party over the previous summer the Healeys were hosting. They had arranged a family get-together, all the Schmidts in attendance, including Lawrence who was visiting the country at the time. They sat on the garden furniture on the lawn, enjoying a barbecue, lashings of beer and the blistering summer sun. As was the custom, Lawrence had been staying with his mother and he had confidentially, out of earshot of her, disclosed of the dreadful time he was having at her house, of the arguments and verbal recriminations, no love lost between them. Martin and Spencer had listened to his unjustified grievances quietly, noncommittally, without judgement, lest ye be judged.

Still, everyone was pleased that, despite her declining health and reluctance to leave her house since the death of her dog, the old lady had dressed up nicely and showed up at the garden party in good spirits. Made a pleasant change from languishing in the house, isolating herself from the world. Her two granddaughters appreciated her elegant, dignified presence at the family function. She had eaten well for a change, diversifying from her usual diet of German salami and paté and black, rye bread. She had been mobilizing in her customary doddery manner, pottering around the garden, examining the flower displays. But it was only when she got up from her chair on one such occasion to go into the house to use the powder room that a moment's dizziness overcame her and she lost her balance and collapsed unceremoniously on the ground, banging her head against an enamel plant tub. Nobody saw her fall, and when Judith spotted what had happened, the family rallied around her, full of concern and alarm. They managed to get her up, but Phyllida remained unsteady on her feet, so they sat her down again. Although she had sustained a nasty, bleeding gash on her forehead, her earlier dazed shock passed very quickly. She knew who she was and where she was and what day it was.

The garden party was cut short as the family took her to the nearest A&E at CHERTSFORD MEMORIAL HOSPITAL, where her wound was stitched up and an urgent brain scan revealed nothing untoward. She would sport a black eye for a few days. Lawrence went back to Panama, and Martin and Judith checked in on Phyllida every day. Helena would fret over the incident, unnecessarily blaming herself for her grandmother's fall. Her guilt deepened when her parents discovered Phyllida semi-conscious in her house a fortnight later. She was lying on the floor – for how long nobody knew – and her son promptly called the Emergency Services. The house was also in a terrible state, and it appeared Phyllida had been toileting inappropriately around the place nor wiping herself when she finished. She was rushed to hospital, full consciousness quickly returning. She was admitted.

Phyllida had suffered from insulin-dependent diabetes, and a 'hypo' was suspected – or a 'funny do', as Phyllida might have called it. Admittedly, her funny spells had grown more frequent. The illness had always been poorly controlled on her part for many a long year, with her often cancelling her diabetic clinic appointments at short notice, stubbornly refusing her family's offer to take her, as well as giving herself an insulin injection when she wasn't eating properly, and these repeated insults to the brain finally took their toll on her general health. Subsequent investigations further revealed the complications of her poorly-managed diabetes, including chronic renal failure. She experienced blood in her stools from longstanding diverticulosis. A Chest X-ray revealed fibrotic changes, her lung tissue significantly compromised by years of inhaling secondary pipe-smoke from her husband. Her physical health deteriorated rapidly in the three months she spent on the geriatric ward.

For someone who had lived independently since the death of her husband, Phyllida could no longer care for herself and, despite the physiotherapist's best efforts, struggled even to stand up on her own two feet, spending her days in hospital, completely bedbound, mostly sleeping, other times waking up and not recognizing where she was. Her initial indignation at being dumped in hospital, including some degree of embarrassment at being seen like this, was soon replaced by equanimity, a peculiar calmness. A more detailed MRI scan revealed subcortical dementia that came some way to explaining her apathy, loss of cognitive and physical function, forgetfulness and confusion. In spite of her diabetes and her old age, she had never been a woman of ailing health. Now, however, diabetes had made her senile, set off low-intensity seizures, scuppered the use of her legs and left her exposed to a series of chest infections and recurrent urinary tract infections, treated with an intravenous line and a cocktail of pills. It was heartbreaking for her granddaughters to see her like this, so frail and fragile and so very vulnerable. A once-proud lady relying on the care of others. Spencer marvelled how Phyllida could have survived all these years with multiple health problems. In some respects, she had outlived herself; not bad going for somebody who had so much physically wrong with her. Remarkably, she owned her own teeth. She did have her good days when she would recognize her visiting family, but these lucid moments fluctuated greatly and grew far and few between. She particularly looked forward to Spencer's visits, as long as she was *compos mentis*, but her engagement with him on the subjects of books and her responses to conversations of a more nostalgic nature were vague and superficial at best, almost incoherent, with Phyllida appearing almost inarticulate, struggling to find her words and volunteering only monosyllabic answers. The chances of her leaving hospital in good health grew slimmer and slimmer by the day.

Her family didn't want to put her in a nursing home, particularly with the financial implications, but what choice did they have? Judith described the situation as a case of 'any old port in a storm'. Even if Phyllida would have preferred to live out the rest of her golden years with them, she was too far gone healthwise by now to be provided with the specialist care she needed at home. The family placed Phyllida in the TWILIGHT REST NURSING HOME, and Martin and Judith moved into Brackendell. The care Phyllida received at Twilight Rest varied on a day-to-day basis, but Helena would not have described it as substandard. In fact, the staff came across as professional, friendly and respectful. However, her room often smelled of urine and Helena, herself a nurse elsewhere, queried sternly whether her grandmother was being sufficiently attended to. She reminded the staff that nurses had a way of losing their PINs working in nursing homes if they were not too careful . . .

On the days the care staff had made a concerted effort for her to look presentable, Phyllida would be propped up against her pillows, an obese, ancient thing in her favourite turquoise nightgown, her whitish-pink hair done up in a bun, each of her grey-blue irises encircled by a yellow ring, her eyes twinkling with faint recognition, a small, distracted smile on her lips. Helena would crank up the bed and sit next to her, giving her tea from a beaker, one small sip at a time, listening to the immature, slurping sound she made swallowing it, wiping away any drool. Other times, Phyllida would just lie there on her pillow, zombified, face sagging and expressionless, no comprehension in those dull, lacklustre eyes. Spencer would read to her, Shakespeare mostly, reciting choice quotes from various plays. Phyllida said very little and slept more and more. Spencer would even read to her whilst she slept, hoping she could still hear his words, words that might be familiar to her, comforting and close to her heart.

On the last day they saw Phyllida alive, she lay asleep on the pillow, her corpse-white flesh decorated with bruises from old blood tests, her pink-white hair spread around her head like a corona, her mouth hanging open like a cave, chest rising and falling under the coverlet, a creased, tallowy hand dangling limply over the side of the bed. She looked her age, older even. She coughed, a hollow, raspy, crypt-like sound, her chest congested and rattling, a cause for concern for Helena. When the brief, coughing fit subsided, a queer, serene smile spread across her face, and Helena relaxed, too. Helena held her hand, hoping somewhere inside her slumber her grandmother might appreciate this elemental gesture, this human touch, and not feel alone. Spencer went back to reading to the old, sleeping woman. *Othello*, Phyllida's favourite play. *Perdition catch my soul/ But I do love thee! And when I love you not,/ Chaos is come again.*

As with all the tragedies of the stage, Spencer was struck by the mysteries of age. How could this proud, intelligent woman, who was once an actress of the English stage and an eloquently-spoken schoolteacher with an excellent grasp of the English verse, have become this wrinkled, pendulous, bedridden creature? How could this elegant, dignified lady, who had always taken great pride in her appearance by maintaining a swish wardrobe and chosen to grow old gracefully, now accept the indignity of sponge baths, her huge, flabby bulk being lifted, turned in her bed, cleaned, forced to wear diapers? How could Old Age turn a once-active woman into a sluggish, tottering pile of flesh who required help rising from her bed to her chair and back again and who would soon lose even the motivation to sit in her chair? How could the woman whose roast beef he had enjoyed, marbled to perfection, and with whom he and Helena had sat down two Christmases ago to watch *The Third Man*, be incapable of doing nothing? How could her body age so, get so damaged, so infirm, reach a stage when it could no longer sustain life? He could trace her demise to that fateful fall at the garden party, the catalyst to her suffering that followed. She had since fought a constant losing battle with her illness and, by the end, it had taken her mind and her health and her life away from her. He waited for Phyllida to die, to suffer no more. For her to complete her length of lease in her old, tired body.

Helena was prepared for her grandmother to die in theory. But when the cold reality hit home, she wept. This was the same grandmother who had introduced her to *The Bluebird*. Helena wanted to blame the nursing home for giving her grandmother her insulin, when it should have been omitted, considering she may not have been fed that morning, but her parents and Spencer advised her not to pursue a possible case of professional negligence and let it rest.

Phyllida had always been against Judith, like mother-in-laws often are. Judith came to her daughter's rescue, the intense grief she experienced. Perhaps there was some truth to Judith's words: *People go to nursing homes to die.* Or maybe Greta's more romantic interpretation rang true: *After the death of her husband and her beloved Maggie, I think Gramma had nothing left to live for and lost the will to live . . . resigned herself to her fate.*

Whatever the explanation, Phyllida passed away the day before her eighty-ninth Birthday.

Her funeral was scheduled for a week later at the small chapel at EAST CHERTSFORD CREMATORIUM, a modest affair, attended only by her closest family and friends. Attendance had been kept to a minimum on the strength of Judith's words: *We should keep the matter private because people gloat at funerals.*

Why would they want to gloat at funerals? Spencer had asked her.

Old feuds can rear their ugly heads at funerals, Judith, with whom Phyllida had rarely seen eye to eye, told him, *particularly those people whom Phyllida crossed and who presently wish only ill will upon the family and the departed. An opportunity for them to spread malicious gossip. We are not going to let her enemies dance on her grave. Phyllida always kept a low profile. She was not a friendly person. Some might have even called her 'unsociable'. Therefore, a small funeral, according to her express wishes, makes the only sense. Phyllida would have wanted it that way. Nothing ostentatious for someone who became a sworn atheist.*

It was no secret that Phyllida had given up her faith after her husband died. She had been a lapsed Catholic. She had found the tenets and theories of Christianity rather comical and considered the Bible the greatest work of fiction ever written. Religion expected believers to embrace a series of propositions as if they were creeds, with a special place reserved for heretics and the theologically syncretic. But, as Spencer reminded Phyllida's nearest and dearest, there was no such thing as a lapsed Catholic. *Once a Catholic, always a Catholic.* And if there was no God, there would be no atheists in the world.

They brought lilies to her funeral. At the viewing, she was garbed in her favourite dress and her face exquisitely done up. Admittedly, she still looked attractive for her age. Her hands were folded on her chest, fingers clasped together. Her composed, untroubled presence made Spencer think of the ancient tradition of placing a coin over each eye of the newly-dead to pay the toll for Charon to ferry their soul across the River Styx into Hades. A fan of Classical Studies, Phyllida had finally joined the Underworld. She was at peace.

Despite the bitter animosity the two sons had harboured towards their mother, all ill-feelings were temporarily forgotten when the eulogies were spoken. It was a testament to how a family could band together *in extremis*, a powerful opportunity to celebrate kinship and traditional family values. If there had been any apprehension or doubt as to what good things they could say about Phyllida, the funeral managed to go perfectly. It was a moving service, Father Benedict presiding. He had paid Phyllida a visit, upon Martin's request, when she had been comatose, dying. Martin had hoped Father Benedict might help in her sanctification, the forgiveness of her sins, dispense the sacramental Anointing of the Sick so that she might reconcile with Christ. Father Benedict managed to administer the last rites at the final hour, the Viaticum, her last Holy Communion and the final prayers before she began her journey onwards. At the funeral, Father Benedict sermonized with both charity and hope for her immortal soul: "Adam lived in paradise, free of disease or suffering. Mankind might have looked very different if he had not given in to temptation. Instead of perfection, the generations that followed would be tainted by Original Sin, the relationship between human and the rest of Creation forever ruptured. Adam passed on a wounded human nature, marked by corruption. Man is now in exile on earth at odds with his maker, beset with a catalogue of crimes and wars and diseases, not originally intended if man had not first sinned. Sickness and death, too, representing his fall from grace, are now a part of the human condition. But, even in illness, God is not far away, watching how we treat the unwell and the needy. For there is virtue in serving the sick, the compassion and the care that brings us closer to God. Then there are those who turn towards the path of salvation when faced with an insurmountable crisis, such as a terminal illness, putting their affairs in order and making peace with God. And do not forget the resurrection of the dead. *For as in Adam all die, so in Christ all shall be made alive.* I Corinthians 15:22. Phyllida may have departed from this world, but God welcomes her into His Kingdom with open arms."

Every family member said a few words on the lectern, in front of the huge, blown-up photo of Phyllida, a black-and-white headshot of a smiling woman from a better time, full of poise, elegance and grace.

Martin carried on from where Father Benedict left off, reading a few lines from Scripture, Isaiah 54:4: "*Fear not, for you will not be put to shame; And do not feel humiliated, for you will not be disgraced; but you will forget the shame of your youth, And the reproach of your widowhood you will remember no more.*"

Lawrence, who had shared his mother's atheistic beliefs and her passion for the great German thinkers, reminded everyone of the words of Thomas Mann: "*Is not life in itself a thing of goodness, irrespective of whether the course it takes for us can be called a 'happy' one?*" From his Bertholt Brecht: "*Do not fear death so much, but rather the inadequate life.*" He finished up with a quote from Hermann Hesse: "*Some of us think holding on makes us strong but sometimes it's letting go.*"

Up next, Helena delivered a monologue from *The Bluebird*, the words of the Joy of Maternal Love personified: "*All mothers are rich when they love their children . . . There are no poor mothers, no ugly ones, no old ones . . . Their love is the most beautiful of the Joys . . . And, when they seem most sad, it needs but a kiss which they receive or give to turn all their tears into stars in the depths of their eyes . . .*" She paused, her words momentarily stuck in her throat like a fishbone, a tear rolling down her cheek. "My grandmother was a very unique and interesting person, worth writing about. She had *authenticity!* Her spirit will live on!"

In remembrance, Greta spoke with fondness for her grandmother: "Keep in your heart only the good memories, not her final suffering. Dwell not on the awful manner in which her journey came to an end but cradle the gift of the unconditional love she bestowed upon us throughout our lives. My thoughts are with you, Grandma, as you reside in Heaven, an angel among angels."

Even Dennis excelled himself, his usual stolid presence taking on a contemplative air: "I always held Phyllida with the highest regards and will always remember how she welcomed me into the family. You can now either shed tears that she is gone or you can celebrate that she lived!"

There wasn't a single dry eye in the house by the time Spencer delivered his lines with poignancy and humour. *Othello* earlier on, then a rendition of *Hamlet*, one of Phyllida's most favourite soliloquies from the Bard: "*What a piece of work is a man! How noble in reason, how infinite in faculty! In form and moving how express and admirable! In action how like an angel, in apprehension how like a god! The beauty of the world. The paragon of animals. And yet, to me, what is this quintessence of dust?*" Helena cried, her face filling with a confusion of grief and pity and she did not shrink away when Judith held her. Spencer finished on a high note: "The twinkle of her beautiful eyes was as bright as the stars in the sky and our love for her will shine on forever!"

Yes, family and friends paid their final respects, mourned her passing with humility and praise. Her dignity had been restored.

Phyllida had wished to be cremated and her coffin, containing her mortal remains, was conveyed through the furnace.

Phyllida's urn rested on the mantelpiece above the fireplace. She had requested her ashes be sprinkled over her husband's grave, and the family planned to carry out her wishes tomorrow ahead of the trip to the solicitors for the probate.

Already half-drunk, Lawrence continued to tear into his mother. "You know my mother was an unashamed racist."

Martin, whose face too was flushed with alcohol, agreed. "Beware her acidic tongue."

"I know she was very anti-American," Spencer recollected from his conversations with her, "calling them loud and uncouth. She also hated the French, too, describing them as 'dirty'."

Martin went on: "A very conservative woman was my mother, carrying some vicious, firmly-held views about the lower classes. She accused them of malingering, making up fake illnesses, on the presumption they didn't want to work. She believed that vasectomies should be implemented on Council people to prevent them breeding like rats and scrounging off the State."

"She was always talking about 'bloody foreigners'," Lawrence explained. "Many a time I heard her use words like 'wogs' and 'fuzzy-wuzzies'. I remember she once offended a black lady by complimenting her on her 'wig'!"

"I guess she hailed from a different generation," Helena intervened, trying to defend her late grandmother. "For a woman who was a liberal-minded actress in her heyday and starred in *Othello* at the height of her career, she must have learned this racial language from my grandfather. She never got a chance to embrace cosmopolitan Britain in later life."

Spencer spoke up, offered his own opinion. "Being something of an outsider to the family, I never experienced the racist or the elitist in her. What I do recall is Phyllida believed people did more evil in the name of money, religion and politics than anything else. She used to say the three were often connected."

"I guess there's some truth to those words," Lawrence deliberated. "Don't even get me started on politics! Germany is in a right, old mess because of all those illegal immigrants it keeps letting in and putting on welfare and providing housing for, taking it away from the mouths of its own people. No wonder the populist movement is on the rise in Europe! Merkel's got a lot to answer for!"

The bitterness with which Lawrence spoke about the country of his forefathers made Spencer realize that maybe the man himself nurtured some deep-seated, racist sentiments of his own. He decided to weigh into the debate with a history lesson. "There was a time when Germany was regarded as the greatest nation in the world, highly respected for its science and medicine, art and cinema, literature and media. In fact, the Germans were once considered the most cultured, sophisticated and enlightened people around. A liberal, tolerant nation. Then it all went downhill with the advent of the Nazi Party and the Vril Society. In fact, one might say that the history of the Vril Society and the inner circle of the Nazi Party becomes entwined from this point on, each sharing the other's dark philosophy."

"The Vril Society?" Lawrence said, curiosity tinging his voice. "I remember my father mentioning the name. I never asked him what it stood for."

"Okay," Spencer began, "let me transport you back to Germany in the good, old days. They come and get you when you're asleep . . ."

His latter comment was an odd thing to say, but nobody questioned him, instead casting their hushed attention towards him, as if he were about to tell a campfire story. Outside, the wind caterwauled in the freezing midwinter.

"The Vril Society," Spencer elaborated, "was a secret organization founded on the heels of the extinct Thule Society at the end of the Great War. It was named after a novel from 1878 called *The Coming Race* by Edward Lytton, who described a man who stumbles across a fictional race of subterranean beings called Vrilia, keepers of a mystical energy source called Vril. The Vril Society took old, theosophical teachings and this piece of science fiction and turned the sensational nonsense of tabloid newspapers together into something it believed was based on fact. It sought to identify Vril, which the members of the Vril Society claimed held together the fabric of the Universe, much like the Chinese believe Chi is a life energy that runs through all of us. Whoever could harvest and harness Vril, this intangible substance connecting the astral and material worlds, could wield this supernatural power, subjugate and rule the world. One of the senior members of the Vril Society, Dietrich Eckhart, a man maniacally obsessed with power and the occult, befriended a charismatic, rising politician called Adolf Hitler and put the concept of Vril into his head. Eckhart saw himself as John the Baptist paving the way for the ascension of Hitler, whom he saw as a Germanic Messiah. The Vril Society would soon consist of a dark fellowship of notorious occultists and high-ranking nationalists, including Himmler, Göring, Borman and Hess. Its Arysophy sought to exterminate Christianity altogether and, of course, the Jews, the precursors of Christianity and the supposed Hordes of Satan, convincing even Hitler, himself a Jew. Its subscription to the notion of Vril and the concept of a Hollow Earth took the Nazis inside the Himalayas, to the meditating Tibetan monks, whom they believed were their Aryan ancestors. They never found any Vril but did not come back empty-handed; the Nazis would take away with them the Tibetans' benign symbol of peace and good fortune, the Swastika, and completely pervert and corrupt its meaning for their own personal ends. The Vril Society continued to prop up the most evil regime of the twentieth century and give credence to the reality of occult forces in its pursuit of a master race and ultimate power. Its metaphysical research took a further sinister direction. The Nazis sought Vril through sexual magic, in the form of countless, depraved sex orgies, performed human sacrifices on kidnapped orphans, because they believed the innocence of children could power Vril, and arranged for mediums to conduct diabolical rituals to evoke the dead since they believed the spirits of the dead were blessed with infinite stores of Vril. The Nazis even tried to contact beings from beneath the earth and other galaxies, developing the 'Flying Disk Project'. In terms of these gravity-defying flying saucers, I can only assume the Allied Forces continued the work of the Nazi scientists after the Second World War . . ."

"This is all very interesting," Martin interrupted, "but I can't quite see how any of this is relevant."

"Because Phyllida told me Reinhardt was once a member of the Vril Society," Spencer declared.

Nobody spoke. His words sank in before Greta said, irritably, "I cannot imagine Grandad kneeling down before heathen gods!"

Spencer, who had so far been holding his cards close to his chest, finally decided to reveal his hand. "Phyllida never lied. *I knew her too well.*"

A further silence, broken only by the high whine of the wind outside and the crackle and hiss of the record on the gramophone softly playing *Guilty* by Al Bowlly.

Lawrence broke the deadlock. "You don't know what you are saying! You've had too much to drink!"

"Did you sleep with her?" Martin asked Spencer abruptly.

"Dad!" Greta exclaimed.

Judith's eyes shot open. Judith, who had remained predominantly silent throughout the wake but had quietly listened to the conversations around her without intervening, now felt it was just too much for her to hold her tongue. "Have you all gone mad?"

Martin was getting agitated. "Not us, dear. Spencer's the one making crazy insinuations!"

Spencer thought of Phyllida, the twinkle in her eyes that of a much younger lady, suffusing a mixture of innocence and knowingness, perhaps even mischief. He remained diplomatic, gentlemanly in his answer. "Just a man comforting a lonely, old woman in her hour of need. She appreciated small kindnesses."

A new-found suspicion that perhaps his relationship with the deceased woman had been something more than just platonic, sharing more than just a common interest in literature and theatre or Three Barrels, that perhaps he had given Grandmother the passion and the secret reason for living when her husband had passed on, was almost too much to contemplate. This was turning into a distinctly messy situation, too mad to even consider the implications. Frustrated, Martin could have been blunter, demanded a more direct, unambiguous answer, but he turned to his other daughter instead, hoping she would be outraged by her husband's half-veiled confession. "What do you have to say, Helena?"

Helena deliberated for a moment, unfazed. Casper remained asleep on Helena's lap. The Snugglepus. "I would have minded then, not now though," Helena replied casually. "I think it's sweet my grandmother found the companionship she needed in later life." She laughed, far from offended, and Judith fixed her daughter with a narrow, piercing stare, full of perturbation and alarm. "Claw toes, hammer toes, snaggle toes . . ." Helena chimed. "No more the infirmities and indignities of old age." She addressed her parents and inebriated uncle. "One day you too are going to be old..." Helena didn't finish the thought.

"Why would you want to tarnish Grandma's memory like that?" Greta rounded on her sister and brother-in-law, appalled, the potential disclosure making her queasy. She confronted Spencer querulously. "Haven't you ever lost anyone close to you?"

"Your loss is *my* loss," replied Spencer. "But she's closer than you think . . ." He turned to his wife. "You are your grandmother's granddaughter after all!"

Helena responded with an enigmatic smile. "Yes, she's still alive – in my heart!"

Spencer returned the smile, now more of a dark, humourless smile, as he addressed Phyllida's two sons. "Remnants of the Vril Society exist even today. Its members strove for immortality, casters of magical spells that could claim the remaining years of life of those they intended to sacrifice. They believed they could live on in a human host with access to the person's memory and knowledge. *The sins of the father shall be visited upon the children.*"

Whether or not Spencer had shared an intimate relationship with Phyllida presently became a secondary consideration. Lawrence and Martin hoped to move on from their mother's death, get on with their lives, but it suddenly seemed, from what Spencer implied, they might not be able to get away from her. Martin, immobilized by these dark revelations, tried to comprehend the significance of the Vril Society in relation to his immediate family. Dead meant dead, yet the practitioners of the Vril Society may have possibly summoned up unholy powers and consolidated the ability to possess the bodies of the living. Dead did not mean dead anymore but alluded to something imperishable. And Lawrence, who had earlier referred to his mother as a nightmare and his father as a monster, also realized he may not have seen the last of them.

A frightful silence descended. The wolf moon rode high in the night sky, accompanied by the winter howl of the wind, a symphony of the damned. The fire in the hearth had nearly burned itself down to dull, orange embers, and an unwelcome chill began to creep into the foundations of the house. The furnishings seemed almost insubstantial and illusory, like the Gerhard Richter paintings, as unreal as a dream where the past and present collide.

Helena added to the disquietude in the room, reciting *The Bluebird* with spontaneity, a monologue from the Personification of Night: "*Because every awful thing imaginable, because all the terrors, all the horrors of which men speak on earth are nothing compared with the most harmless of those which assail a man from the moment when his eye lights upon the first threats of the abyss to which no-one dares* give a name . . ." Helena got up, Casper jumping off her lap. He sat on his haunches, keenly watching the men go through a tizz. Helena walked off, disappearing from the drawing room.

Meanwhile, Spencer leaned forward and uttered the queerest words, reframing his own narrative. "*You'd think I was your father and Helena was your mother* . . ."

[*They come and get you when you're sleeping.*]

[*Haven't you ever lost someone close to you?*]

[*Yes, but she's still alive – in my heart!*]

Martin and Lawrence exchanged looks of frank bewilderment – and something else. Judith bolted upright on the sofa, shocked speechless, casting aside her flannel, her aching head and feet forgotten. Greta's mouth remained agape, stunned, equally dumbfounded. Even Dennis's generally inexpressive face registered a vague, rarely-witnessed emotion. *Fear.*

When Helena came back into the drawing room, she was carrying a family-sized apple strudel. "Don't you know a mother's love is forever?" she murmured as she walked across the room. "Maybe things can be different. I believe in second chances."

Spencer watched her place the dish on the coffee table in front of him. He recited a few words from Goethe that took on a sudden, chilling significance: "*The sum which two married people owe to one another defies calculation. It is an infinite debt, which can only be discharged through all eternity.*"

Martin stared at his mother's urn on the mantelpiece again and thought: *She's moved on* . . .

Maybe it was just a misperception, but the men could not deny the remarkable resemblance. There was a certain air about her. The dramatic flourishes of an actress. A beauty spot in that exact same place. The same mischievous twinkle in her eyes. The same platinum wedding band on her ring finger. Yes, they were forced to admit she was her grandmother's granddaughter, after all. Helena began cutting the apple strudel with a cake knife. "Now, boys, shall I be mother?"

December 2018-January 2019

Rookery Nook

"No distance of place or lapse of time can lessen the friendship of those who are thoroughly persuaded of each other's worth."

Robert Southey
English Poet (1774-1843)

I

William Wordsworth once wrote: *he had been alone/Amid the heart of many thousand mists,*

And with loneliness comes suffering in the shape of madness. For: *Suffering is permanent, obscure and dark/ And shares the nature of infinity* . . .

2

Melissa Redding could say with brimming confidence that she never neglected her friends. Friends were an important part of her life, as precious as her immediate family or diamonds to a girl or the very air she breathed. She always made time for her friends even if it meant going abroad to visit them.

One such friend she held particularly dear to her heart. There would always be that First True Love. The One that never really worked out, but you did your best to make it work, unfortunately without success. She could very much describe him as 'The One Who Got Away'. The One who taught you all you needed to know about love. And the One you still looked back on whenever you tried to love again. Except they hadn't exactly parted on the best of terms, and she had moved on, but almost a decade later she wanted to see what had become of him.

Had it been so long?

She had contacted him by cell-phone less than a month ago and he had invited her – albeit grudgingly – down for the weekend.

And, so, here she was . . .

Judging by the grandeur of his home in a location of outstanding natural beauty, Kit Harrison appeared to have done extremely well for himself. His first-and-only novel, *The Parting of Lovers*, had sold by the truckloads and won him several prestigious awards a few years back, yet nobody to this day, apart from his editor and Melissa, knew what this esteemed author actually looked like. Rumours quickly circulated that Kit Harrison wasn't his real name, that maybe it was the pseudonym of another, more prolific writer. There followed a media frenzy as the literary world speculated who it might be. The book itself was a semi-fictionalized account of Kit's relationship with Melissa, including their time in Italy, all sensationalized and juicy, not that the reader ever cottoned on; Kit had an unerring gift for seamlessly mixing reality with fiction.

From her dealings with him, Melissa remembered Kit's fiercely reclusive nature. It didn't come as a surprise that he shunned the literati and glitterati. She could not imagine Kit basking in the limelight or responding to his bulging fan-mail, and she felt it an honour and a privilege to know that he was the mysterious writer whom everyone was desperate to unmask, that he had trusted her enough to disclose his little secret to her. Surely, it would be improper of her if she betrayed that trust.

Sitting in the Mercedes she had hired at the airport, listening to Hana Piranha's violin-swirling cover of *We Used to Be Friends*, Melissa surveyed Kit's abode and its surroundings with a gasp of wonderment. He had once told her that if he were ever to make it as a hotshot writer, he would either buy a small castle in the Scottish Highlands or a country estate in the English heartland. It seemed he had plumped for the latter.

Kit lived supposedly only a few miles from the village of Grasmere, the former home of the celebrated poet, William Wordsworth, with its mix of rustic cottages and Victorian villas. His mansion, set against the backdrop of the dreary Cumbrian moors, was certainly in keeping with his gothic masterpiece. Its outward appearance vaguely reminded her of Udolpho, of Northanger Abbey. Although essentially baronial in style, there was something lopsided and asymmetrical about its overall shape, as if its original architect had suffered from a dichotomy of thought and cobbled together two separate designs. Whereas one end of the building was turreted like a castle and boasted its own wheel windows and battlements, more out of ostentation than defence, the other half was more on the scale of a manor house with tall, arched windows and an overhanging gable. The combination shouldn't have worked, but somehow it did. The surrounding landscape, wild and windswept and twilit, further enhanced its peculiar, gothic appeal. It seemed Kit had, architecturally, got the best of both worlds with his Westmorland home.

The sign, wrought in iron and now rusted, above the arched gateway coming into the estate had read: ROOKERY NOOK. The name made her think of funeral parlours and undertakers, her only slight quibble.

Switching off the radio, Melissa clambered out of her parked car and, pulling her scarf up tighter, headed in quiet contemplation towards the magnificent house. She passed the fountain in the centre of the gravelled forecourt, its resident naiad, beautifully poised but coated in green slime. Parked in the courtyard, the black S80 Volvo curiously enough resembled a hearse. Her mind recalled the unworldly bride introduced to Dragonwyck Manor – or Manderley.

On her approach, she thought she saw a dark figure in one of the upper-storey windows, but, when she blinked, it was gone. Maybe she had been mistaken – surely, after her long journey, it could only be her imagination running away with her.

The walls of the mansion were made from large blocks of stone, grey and unwashed and creeping with ivy. Melissa spotted a row of gargoyles on the roof, each standing frozen, wings unfolded, ready to swoop.

Climbing a short series of steps to the ample porch, Melissa hesitated, composed herself to full readiness before finally deciding to ring the doorbell.

The bell resounded through the dormant mansion as ominously as a death knell. The gargoyles above seemed to glare down at her as though objecting to the intrusion. The autumn wind blew strong and cold, sending her shoulder-length, brunette hair into unruly tangles. Anticipation welled up deep inside her as she wondered what she might find beyond the threshold. She half-expected a naked, grizzly-bearded man, gone stir crazy from years of solitude, to open the door, eyes bloodshot from alcohol and countless sleepless nights and a look of stark lunacy on his face.

Just then, Melissa experienced a curious sensation: a powerful and unexpected case of déjà vu. She was almost certain she had stood on these very same steps before, although she knew she hadn't.

The set of oak doors suddenly swung wide open, making her start, cutting short her train of thought. No Grizzly Adams, all naked beneath the flapping bathrobe, bleary-eyed and drunk out of his skull, greeted her. Instead, the man holding open both doors she recognized immediately. Melissa brushed aside hair from her face in order to take a closer look at her host.

Kit Harrison was pretty much as she remembered him, except he looked much older. His raven locks were significantly greyer and there was a greater degree of wrinkles on his handsome face as well as noticeable bags under his hazel eyes. Physically, he was still in good shape. As was his custom, he was attired in a black ensemble of suede boots, tight jeans and a heavy woollen polo-neck.

"Hello, Melissa," greeted Kit without offering the slightest glimmer of a smile. "I was watching you watching the house."

"Kit," replied Melissa, as amicably as she could manage, "you're looking good."

"Thank you. You don't look bad yourself!" He gestured for her to come inside. "Welcome to Rookery Nook."

She obliged.

Kit led her through the large, airy lobby into the enormous reception hall, their footsteps clicking on the chequered, mosaic floor. Marble pillars supported the high vaulted ceiling. A banquet table swept along one side of the chamber, the rest of the space occupied by tall-backed leather chairs arranged towards the general direction of the crackling hearth-fire. The hall was lit by a myriad of candles, nestled in their own strategically placed candlebra, their tiny collective flames throwing restless, dancing shadows across every corner and recess. The gallery at the top of the grand staircase lay in impenetrable darkness. "How do you like my humble dwelling?"

Melissa took in the vastness of the hall, the rich tapestries and paintings on the walls, and felt as though she had stepped back to a more historic time. "As impressive as any museum! It certainly says *you!*"

"*Infinity made imaginable*, to quote Coleridge. The estate agent claimed the building was as old as the war between Lancaster and York. The property was further altered and restored during the reign of the old queen. I'm surprised it was sold so cheaply on the market and wasn't preserved as part of our national heritage."

From force of habit, Melissa traced a finger along a nearby table and picked up dust. "Do you ever clean the place?"

"The place is too big to maintain. I only use a few rooms so I have no need of servants. I employ a home-cleaning service once a month – they're due a visit soon." He looked at her discerningly. "I know what you're thinking. You're wondering whether you can spruce the place up a bit."

"I–" Melissa was suddenly at a loss for words. She gave a small, nervous laugh, instead. She was well and truly busted.

"Look, Melissa," Kit said calmly, "I appreciate your concern. I know you enjoy being fussy and fastidious. I remember you used to obsess over the cleanliness of my old flat or – should I say – lack of. But you're here as my guest, and I can't expect you to carry out any domestic duties. I want this to be a very special weekend for you – the most unique, unforgettable experience you ever had. My house and I are at your disposal. We can catch up on old times and I shall grant you free rein of my house to explore at your leisure." He reached down for her belongings. "Now, you must be tired. Let me take your bags."

Taking the heavier of the suitcases and lifting a candlebrum by its holder, he mounted the grand staircase, Melissa following with her small overnight bag. Guided by candlelight, Kit took her down the main gallery towards the west wing. They passed more tapestries, full of medieval battle scenes between soldiers-in-chain-mail and fire-breathing dragons. At the end of the gallery, they turned left and ascended a winding staircase. From the breathtaking landscape volunteered by the wheel windows, Melissa realized they were presently in the turreted portion of the mansion. They continued climbing the stone steps until they rounded the corner and reached the uppermost landing. Kit unlocked one of two doors. The other, she understood, led up to the castellated roof. "Well, Melissa, your room is already prepared. Freshen up. Make yourself at home. Dinner is at nine."

Then, he was gone, leaving Melissa alone with her bags and her thoughts, to inspect and acclimatize to her room.

She instantly warmed to her accommodation. The room was distinctly circular in shape and lit on all fronts by scented tea-candles, lavender the dominant fragrance. Rose petals were strewn across the bedspread of her mahogany four-poster, whether as a romantic gesture or simply for aesthetic effect she could not be sure. Oil paintings hung on the curved grey-stoned walls – firstly of a foxhunt, the second of a game of cricket and a third picture of a clipper ship tossed at sea – all quintessentially English themes. A dressing table and chair rested by the west window, overlooking the desolate, peaty moors, and a tallboy stood near the south window, which opened up a view of the gardens below . . . of which Melissa made a mental note to investigate.

It was all so much like a fairytale. Melissa felt like the Princess in the Tower, surveying her God-appointed Kingdom. Her brave Knight was somewhere downstairs, in all likelihood making dinner.

I want this to be a very special weekend for you, Kit had told her moments ago, *the most unique, unforgettable experience you ever had.*

Intrigued, she wondered what he had meant.

Melissa had to admit that Kit, by all accounts, looked every inch the successful writer. That he was in possession of so splendid a residence was a fitting testament to his accomplishment.

If only he were more accessible and less closed-off as a person.

Had time changed him?

She would find out soon enough.

Had success simply soured him or helped bring him out of his shell?

Kit had always been protective of his privacy, and Melissa dearly hoped Rookery Nook hadn't become his hermitage.

She had once loved him, sincerely loved him with every fibre of her being. And, as she chose the dress she would wear for dinner, she thought she still did.

As a friend, that is.

3

"So you live here all by your lonesome?"

"Loneliness isn't the terrible burden you imagine," philosophized Kit. "Man may be a social animal, but we are all in our own separate ways alone."

"I must say that's a rather bleak perspective on the human condition," observed Melissa.

"Love always comes with a price. When it isn't distracting you from your purpose in life, it causes great waves of suffering. Peace and contentment can be found in solitude. Ask the monk who has made the supreme sacrifice and taken a vow of silence. There is something to be gained from the simple life."

Presently, they sat at one end of the long banquet table in the main hall. The meal had been excellent. The red Merlot had gone down exquisitely with the herb-crusted rack of lamb and potato gratin. Melissa and Kit had settled for light banter and, for a moment, it felt as though they had never been apart. Kit had complimented her on her fetching white Gucci dress and how she still cut a lissom figure after all these years when she was, in fact, approaching the wrong side of thirty-five. She told him she had moved to New York and was still working as a freelance photographer, with Diane Arbus as her divine inspiration. Fine art photography was her specialty, although she occasionally did routine, paid work snapping pictures for the newspapers. She and her partner had decided not to have children. She had wanted to make the most of her vacation – however brief – by visiting Hadrian's Wall and rambling in the Lake

District, but she thought she would have to give it a miss on this occasion, as she had to prepare for an exhibition of her best photographic work back home. Perhaps she could come back here another time. She stated she had a distant aunt in Ambleside, less than an hour's drive from here. Kit listened intently, nodding occasionally, maintaining the flow of conversation. The candlelight played softly on their features, providing the right amount of ambience in which their dialogue could develop. The initial coldness she had experienced when she arrived was soon gone from his voice.

"I like it here," Kit continued. "Remote as it gets. Come winter, the power-lines go down and you are completely cut off from civilization. That, my friend, is *bliss*, freed from the trappings of society. There is only one other place where you can find the same absolute peace of mind."

"And where would that be?"

"Six feet under."

This macabre analogy caused her to shudder. It summoned up images of corpses decomposing in coffins and rats gnawing at dead flesh. It certainly wasn't her idea of being at peace with the world. She remembered how earlier the name of Rookery Nook had brought up connotations of funeral parlours. "Bit morbid, don't you think?" she said, pouring herself more wine.

"But it's true and you know it's true," Kit said darkly. "What could be more natural than death? The pain is gone when you die."

"Our pain is what defines us, builds our character, gives our personality shape."

"Death is a state of eternal grace. You will never find a greater expression of serenity than on the face of the dead."

"I'm too wrapped up in living to be bothered about dying," remarked Melissa, unwilling to be drawn down this particular unhealthy avenue of discussion. This was not exactly the kind of opening conversation she had in mind when she decided to meet him after so many years apart. Could he not think of something cheerier? "Half a century from now I might give it due consideration, perhaps!"

"Death comes as the end," he recited.

"Believe in Life before Death, not what religion preaches." Her expression grew quizzical: "Kit, why didn't you write another book?"

The unexpectedness of the question caught Kit unawares. He paused, measuring his response. When he spoke, his eyes reflected sadness. "The joy within me died the day you left me. I did not know how to handle life without you."

Uncomfortable at the blame he attached to her, Melissa grew immediately defensive, sensing his pain. But she had to justify her decision. "I *had* to leave you. You were a struggling writer, hitting the bottle and alienating everyone close to you, including *me*. And there's Wade Walden, the director of a leading advertisement agency, rich, energetic, outgoing. What choice did you give me?"

"There is always a choice!" Kit countered scathingly. "You knew my book was nearly completed! Your mother – *my* editor – had already accepted it for publication!"

Melissa stared at him long and hard. "When we broke up, I tried contacting you. But you never returned my calls. My mother kept me in the loop with regards your whereabouts – until you stopped communicating with her, too."

Kit looked away, muttering bitterly: "Sounds to me you made your bed."

Melissa responded earnestly, sincerely, baring her feelings to him. "Don't be like that. I really do care about you. I never wanted you to be unhappy because of me."

"Then why did you come if not to ease your own conscience?"

Far from guilt-ridden and none too keen to take outright responsibility for their difficult breakup and subsequent lengthy estrangement, Melissa went directly to the point. "Because I consider you a friend, a dear friend. And I *never* neglect my friends. Otherwise, I wouldn't have dared visit you."

His hostility subsided. Regret followed swiftly on. "You abandoned me. You pulled me out of that dark place and then you threw me back in there. Without you to share in my success, my life lost all meaning."

Melissa didn't like the direction the conversation was heading. "Was there no-one else after me?" Except she knew the answer he would give. Kit had always seemed a little clumsy around women. His awkwardness was actually one of his strengths, one of his most endearing qualities, even if he sounded like the male version of Miss Havisham.

"Not a soul."

"Perhaps we can change all that this weekend," announced Melissa more brightly, shifting closer to him, affectionately rubbing his forehead with her thumb as though wiping off an imaginary grease-spot. "I'm here to bring a little sunshine into the life of someone quite close to me! He's a gifted writer, a dignitary of the manor and one of my finest friends! Even his name is an inspiration: think pirate or captain of the fleet, the strong, silent type! So, ladies and gentlemen, please give it up for *Kit Harrison!*"

Her attempt at lightening the mood failed to raise a smile, although Kit did appear less embittered, less morose or melancholic. "Thank you for the vote of confidence. I guess no more recriminations whilst you're a guest in my house." He turned to gaze into her cyan eyes, quietly conceding: "I'm glad you're here."

"I'm glad too," she reciprocated and pecked him gently on the cheek.

He looked at her slightly bemused. "What was that for?"

"Do I need a reason for kissing an old friend?" she said, her eyes catching hold of the large tapestry above the fireplace. Strange, she hadn't noticed it before. It was the idealized portrait of a woman, sumptuously detailed and unaffected by time. The woman stood on the misty moors, Rookery Nook glimpsed in the background. If Melissa wasn't too much mistaken, the features of the woman possessed a striking resemblance to her own. "Who's that?"

"No idea, though I like to think of her as you. You can have it if you like."

"No, I couldn't impose . . ."

"Not at all. It's yours."

Forcing herself to look away, she raised her glass. "What shall we drink to?"

"How about stolen moments?" he suggested after a moment's thought.

"To your next book," she toasted in frank encouragement, knowing full well she was touching upon a sensitive issue. "For talent must not go to waste!"

4

Melissa excused herself from the polite company of her host and retired to bed at eleven. She felt dizzy from the wine she had drunk but was positive sleep would put an end to the sickly spinning sensation she was experiencing.

She made her way to her chamber and, quickly changing into her pink nightdress, slid under the quilt. Her reunion with Kit had proved worthwhile and allayed any residual apprehension that lingered concerning her trip to England. Most importantly, she and Kit had reconnected without resorting to much unpleasantness, and Melissa could already see them consolidating their friendship by the end of the weekend. Wine, fatigue and the agreeable recollections of the evening gradually lulled her to sleep.

However, she didn't stay asleep for long. She was roused from her slumber by a curious tapping noise. Her eyelids fluttered open as she tried to gather her senses.

She checked the carriage-clock on the bedside cabinet. It was still only half-past-one.

Turning over, she wondered what could have awoken her when the sound, more defined than before, was repeated.

Tick-tick-tick.

Boosting herself up on to her elbows, she glanced around the room to pinpoint the source of the sound. The candles had long since burned out, and her circular bedchamber was illuminated by the silvery cast of moonlight. Outside, the wind whistled against the window-panes. Somewhere out on the moors came the pitiable baying of a dog.

Tick-tick. Tick-tick-tick.

There it goes again, she thought, puzzled. *What is that?*

To her, the general variability of sound meant it was organic in nature as opposed to mechanical, produced by a living thing rather than a machine.

Tick-tick-tick-tick.

The persistence of the sound was beginning to grate. She thought she might not be able to sleep if it carried on throughout the night and considered whether or not to knock on Kit's door and request a change of room. Otherwise, she might go crazy just listening to it.

Then, from the corner of her eye, she caught a shape, darker than the shadows, moving across the floor. As she focused in, it scuttled towards the door, moonlight reflecting on its shiny, black armoured body.

Tick-tick-tick, it went.

Although she had never previously encountered its kind, it suddenly occurred to her what she was dealing with. This must surely be a deathwatch beetle. She had read about it — how it was the bane of the insomniac, who was forced to endure sleepless nights on account of its very audible ticking sound — and she remembered the age-old myth. Legend had it that the deathwatch beetle signified impending death, keeping a constant watch over the dying.

The progress of the deathwatch beetle was presently halted by the bedroom door. It tried squeezing under the gap beneath the door, but its body would not fit. It kept bumping into the lower edge of the door, getting frustrated, as it strove to find an exit from the room.

Tick-tick-tick-tick-tick-tick-tick.

Leaping out of bed, Melissa put on her pink dressing gown and slipped into her pink slippers. She walked over to the door.

Despite her inherent skepticism of all things supernatural, she found the idea of sharing the same room as this little portent of doom somewhat perturbing. Deciding against crushing it underfoot in case some unforeseen tragedy should befall her, she chose to give the poor creature a helping hand. She opened the door and watched the deathwatch beetle scurry on out.

It was precisely at that moment she glimpsed a figure on the stairs. Back towards her, they were retreating downwards, guided on by a burning lantern. They rounded the corner and vanished from sight, only the quivering glow of their lantern still visible against the wall but fading fast.

"Hey, wait!" Melissa cried as the light grew fainter and fainter.

Melissa bounded down the spiral staircase in pursuit, her slippers echoing on the stone steps.

This is getting distinctly strange, she thought, forced on by her own insatiable curiosity. She soon arrived at the main gallery with its collection of medieval tapestries. She saw the mysterious figure with the lamp descending the grand staircase and hurried to catch up with them. Still greatly in silhouette, the figure was slightly more discernible. They seemed to be concealed in a silk-black robe, hood raised. The figure reached the foot of the staircase just as Melissa began her own descent.

"Kit, is that you?" she called . . . but received no reply.

The great hall, where she had dined earlier, was in dense shadow, save for the caliginous contribution from the moon and the gleaming circle of light offered by the stranger. Melissa noticed the stranger was moving with a slow, gliding motion and felt a cold stirring in her blood. She made a fearful stop, wondering if she should just turn back. There was something unnatural about this whole situation. It warranted caution, for she sensed danger. But her desire to finish this intriguing excursion impelled her onwards.

The figure took a sharp right and glided through an open doorway, their robe rustling behind them on the polished floor. Melissa followed from a safe distance.

She passed through the same doorway and discovered the kitchen of the house. Extremely spacious and full of old-world charm, she made out numerous cupboards, an enamel sink and an antique gas stove. A dining table, possibly used by the servants from former households, completed the furnishings. On the farthest wall, there was what appeared to be a walk-in freezer built next to a closed door, which either led to the pantry or the scullery.

The stranger, however, was leading her down a different door.

Melissa's hands fumbled for the light switch in the hope she could literally shed some light on this mystery and go back to bed. She succeeded in locating one and she clicked it on.

Nothing happened.

The kitchen lay in a state of permanent darkness.

She tried again, got zilch.

Isn't there any electricity in this house? she berated. It wouldn't surprise her if Kit was averse to the idea. Needless to say, it suited the gothic flavour of the place.

Melissa advanced towards the door the stranger had selected. She saw their soft halo of light at the bottom of another set of steps. *The basement?*

Summoning forth courage, she took the steps one by one. Cobwebs brushed against her face, causing her to flinch. Her heart pounded in her chest, her mouth felt dry and gritty and her bowels squirmed and groaned with mounting unease.

She came to the base of the stairs and, by the hissing, bluish-yellow flame of the stranger's lamp, realized she had stumbled across a wine cellar. Rack after rack held innumerable dusty bottles of wine in their trellises. Resting on wooden trestles, against the far wall, were tapped caskets, containing maybe mass-produced, lesser wines. Nevertheless, there was something equivalent to a small fortune down here.

The presence of the wine cellar confirmed Kit's alcoholic tendencies. Either in his hermetic ways he had turned into a wine connoisseur of good standing (which Melissa doubted) or he got smashed every night (which seemed the more probable). Melissa would speak to him about it in the morning.

The hooded figure stood in the middle of the cellar, unmoving, their silky habiliment bathed in the pale lamplight. Then, they slowly turned their head with a prodigious creak, and as the lantern lit up their countenance, Melissa's eyes widened in silent horror.

The face, revealed in all its madness, belonged to Kit. Except it was sallow and emaciated and severely mutilated, sliced all over with countless cuts, each wound self-inflicted and weeping blood. Those lips that Melissa had kissed so many times were completely shredded, curled into the toothless grin of an incarnate fiend. The deeply-sunken eyes glittered with insane mischief.

"Like my handiwork?" the hideous parody of her host cackled. "I did this all for you!"

Melissa wanted to scream, but no sound would emerge.

"Now, if you'll excuse me," he uttered, laughing like a lunatic, "I must *die!*"

Without warning, there was a fizzing sound and all the gashes on his face ignited, spraying sparks in every direction before each burned with its own individual jet of flame. The skin around the fiery wounds blistered, bubbled and sloughed off in crispy, charred strips until it gave way to spitting flesh and the gleam of bone. The eyes popped open in a spray of white goo, the hollowed sockets of the skull shooting more flames. As his very person combusted from within, his robe caught alight, the fine fabric readily consumed. Soon, his entire body was engulfed in flames.

The burning man collapsed to his knees, roaring in palpable agony, the lantern falling from his grasp, shattering on the stone floor. The fire it contained billowed upwards and spread to the wine racks. Bottles exploded at random, coughing out their dark liquid, further fuelling the conflagration.

Most of the wine cellar was now ablaze, and Melissa could feel the heat, wearing as she was only limited night-attire. Her throat started to seize up from the choking smoke.

Inside the raging inferno, the animated skeleton that was once Kit Harrison lifted its skull and pointed an accusing finger at Melissa . . .

"–Melissa, what is it?" she heard someone ask from afar.

All of a sudden, a hand clutched her left wrist and whirled her forcibly round. Staring into the worried expression of Kit, Melissa let loose a piercing shriek and spilled to the floor, deprived of her senses.

5

Melissa awoke that morning to find Kit in her room, sitting in a chair, watching her. "What happened?"

"You were sleepwalking," he explained in a solicitous tone. "I found you down in the wine cellar, babbling on about a fire. I carried you back up, tucked you into bed. I kept a close eye on you in case you decided to get up again and resume your nightly excursions."

The events of last night came rushing back to her. Following the robed figure through the house, only to discover it was Kit, all skin and bone, his face a roadmap of pain and painted with blood. She recalled Kit going up in flames. She shuddered at the gruesome image.

"You tossed and turned much of the night," said Kit with a full set of teeth, his flesh untouched by the deliberate slashes of a razor blade. "You must have been dreaming because you were talking in your sleep."

She considered this explanation. Had she actually been asleep and dreaming? Or somewhere in between, on the edge of sleep, in the grip of a hypnogogic experience? She remembered the deathwatch beetle. "But it was so vivid, so *real!*" protested Melissa.

"Such can be the power of nightmares," replied Kit.

"So you kept a bedside vigil all this time?"

Kit simply nodded.

There was the proof, the clarification she had been desperately seeking. He still cared about her. "Thank you," Melissa said most sincerely. "You're a good friend."

"I hope you're not coming down with something."

"No, I don't believe so," Melissa remarked cheerily. "I feel as fit as a fiddle."

"Glad to hear it," said Kit, obviously satisfied by her well-being. "What're your plans for the day?"

"I suspect your garden's worth a look."

"Don't expect too much," warned Kit. "It hasn't been tended to in months. Because the grass has gone to seed means that it's going to have to be re-turfed."

"Can't be all that bad," she reassured. She looked at the carriage-clock and discovered it was approaching midday. "So late?" She turned back to Kit. "What does a girl have to do to eat around here?"

"I'll make us brunch."

So he did, whilst Melissa showered (in cold water since both the power was out and the generator was down) and changed, shivering, into fresh clothes. Brunch consisted of a ham-and-mushroom omelette with green salad, washed down with cream coffee.

Afterwards, Melissa, wrapped up warm in a woollen hat, scarf and gloves and her best fleece jacket, wandered onto the terrace to explore the southern aspect of the house. It was certainly chilly outside, breath condensing to mist.

Steps led down to the landscape gardens, divided on either side by a path. Once they must have been magnificent, naturalistic and very nineteenth-century, the venue for many a summer party . . . but now, boy, Kit hadn't been kidding. From their general state of neglect, it looked as though it was the gardener's decade off.

The grass on the lawns was overgrown to waist height and covered by a blanket of bindweed and brambles. The flowerbeds had been left to proliferate and disorganize, the hedgerows were straggly and in dire need of a manicure, and there were jungles of poison ivy crawling up the walls.

Regardless, Melissa managed to spot some interesting species amongst the chaos: foxglove and forget-me-nots, primroses and snapdragons, asters and magnolias, and an extraordinary abundance of wisteria.

Walking up the garden path, she came to another fountain with its own separate naiad, albeit begrimed and headless. Melissa noticed more statues in the garden. Unlike the gargoyles of earlier, these were of weeping angels.

Strange, thought Melissa, how Kit's mansion appeared to be a world of two halves, not just from an architectural viewpoint, but Heaven and Hell embodied by its stone angels and abominations. With only two people in the house, Melissa felt her presence must have brought a measure of balance into the equation, her yin to Kit's yang, Venus to his Mars.

A folly stood at the end of the garden path, like an elegant dowager. Delighted to find sanctuary outdoors, Melissa climbed the wooden steps and sat on the bench, beneath the domed roof.

The moors stretched to the distant horizon, flat and featureless and fascinating to behold.

Throw in an old, gothic mansion, full of creaks and shadows and maybe even haunted, supposed Melissa as she reflected on her so-called dream last night, *and you have the makings of a Hollywood classic. If only I'd unpacked my camera from my suitcase, I could have snapped a few choice pictures of my own, displayed them in that exhibition of mine in the house's honour.*

The day was overcast, threatening a downpour. The autumn wind picked up a notch, scouring the open heath, from where she half-expected a black steed to come galloping in the distance, carrying a headless horseman.

Something had been nagging Melissa the moment she arrived here. It wasn't the first time she thought she'd been here before. So strong was the feeling, it spooked her. *What if I lived here in a previous life?* But, of course, Melissa knew she was clutching at straws. There had to be a reason less fantastic than reincarnation to explain why the place seemed so familiar, and she was determined to find it.

She sat awhile, marvelling at the wilderness Kit called home, giving in to the solitude and the isolation, insulated against the inclement weather by thick layers of clothing. She could understand why the moors appealed to his sensibilities. There was a timeless quality to this corner of the world. The land was steeped in history. Battles had been won and lost here, painters had been inspired by the magic of the scenery, and generations of poets had recounted tales of eloping lovers collected from the patrons of the local tavern.

Yes, agreed Melissa, *there's no denying the rustic charm of these parts.*

Her roving eyes chanced upon a large, black-feathered bird hopping on the grass to her right. It suddenly loosed a guttural cry, causing her to jump at the sound, startled, before it flew off. She followed its brief flight and her breath froze instantly. So absorbed had she been by her thoughts, she had failed to notice the birds that had already gathered on the railing behind her.

How long have they been there?

The crows were not afraid of the scarecrow, it seemed, gathered on this redundant, straw-filled effigy, like vultures upon a corpse. Except they were not crows but rooks. The balustrade was lined with rooks, an incalculable parliament of rooks, each watching her keenly, with sinister intelligence. Definitely rooks, each distinguishable from its crow cousins by its slightly larger size and the characteristic greyish-white patch of skin at the base of its bill. It was a disturbing sight, this unexpected congregation of carrion birds. Sleek black feathers, dark shiny eyes and pointed beaks and talons, they studied her as if listening in on her thoughts.

She now knew how the mansion had got its name.

The paralysis lasted only a few seconds.

Melissa got up slowly, carefully, lest she should agitate the birds. As she sneaked away, they watched her go, but stir they did not . . .

. . . At least not until she was clear of the folly.

Then, screeching an incessant, ear-piercing stream of indecipherability, they flew up, flocking the leaden sky.

Melissa hurried up the garden path, afraid to look up, in case she became the subject of their wrath, Tippi Hedren-style. But they did not attack her, neither did she need to look up. For, as she ran, they began to fall to the ground around her. First one, then two . . . then in unassailable numbers. One by one, each rook, dropped to the ground like grouse shot out from the sky. Each hurtled to earth as ominously as one of the ten plagues of Egypt.

She managed to make it back to the house unscathed. Under the shelter of the porch, Melissa took a gander at the footpath. The ground was littered with heaps of their corvid corpses, their inexplicable deaths en masse adding to the mysteries of this place. Unless she was dreaming, each bird seemed to release a final, expiratory gasp and a strange, smoking mist seemed to issue from each beak, rising insubstantial and birdlike upwards to the sky to form a single, dark, collective cloud–

–Suddenly, in a blink, the ground was thankfully empty of dead birds and the sky bare and grey again, as if she had imagined these entire unnatural proceedings. The huge, black phenomenon in the heavens, the coalescent spirits of the rooks, was gone.

First, deathwatch beetles, Melissa thought, trying to make sense of these mysterious events thrust upon her, *and now rooks, these unholy guardians of the dead. It's like the place is poised on the brink of something . . .*

Were these creatures sending her a message? She remembered the Ancient Greeks considered rooks and crows and the suchlike 'psychopomps', eroding the boundaries between the living and the dead. Rooks in particular were believed to predict the impending death of the master of the house.

The first drops of rain began to fall.

Taking off her outdoor clothes, she wandered through the house, still slightly shaken. There again, that inescapable sense of déjà vu, triggered apparently by her encounter with the rooks. Psychologists claimed that déjà vu was a brief, partial glimpse of an experience before it had been fully registered by the brain, creating a bogus sense of familiarity, whereas physicists spoke of transient wormholes as being the cause of this peculiar sensation. Or maybe there was a more psychic or magical explanation . . .

No, she tried to reason with herself, *my mind is playing up again.*

What about those houses that give off bad vibes, always make you cross the road and walk on the other side? The silhouette standing by the front gate, the other shadow walking beside you? The pale figure sitting at the foot of the bed, the tapping on your bedroom window late at night? The dark presence at the top of the stairs, the bathroom mirror which reflects another face next to yours? Footsteps in the attic when you can swear there is no-one else in the house? Houses where reality is thinnest, like a tyre that is badly worn, too scuffed so as to be on the verge of popping, ready to admit things that should be dead but somehow sustain an unquiet existence beyond our world, striving to break through from another dimension, communicating with us when we are at our most vulnerable and our minds most receptive, when we're stressed or on drugs or asleep and dreaming, when our barriers are down?

Of course not, her rational self argued back. *Just places of geopathic stress, according to structural engineers, causing electromagnetic shifts and that well-documented piezo-electric effect, affecting the brain, the temporal lobes of those susceptible, less resilient, the mentally unwell or those open to its influences.*

What if what she was seeing were not past events but echoes of a future tragedy – a foreshadowing, a premonition?

Deep in thought, Melissa walked through the downstairs of the house, looking for Kit, suddenly afraid for him and this house. She could not ignore these presentiments of doom, explain them off as just nothing.

Down one particular corridor, she came to a room, the door slightly ajar, a low lighting seeping out. She knocked. "Kit, is that you?"

No response.

She entered and found herself in what looked like a study. The wallpaper was mottled and mouldy, and the telescope and billiard table had been covered over by sheets. A solitary candle provided the necessary illumination for the study, that place where most writers supposedly did their most profound thinking. Kit was nowhere to be seen. Melissa had wondered what Kit did all day. Drink and read, probably, pontificate about the stupidity, ignorance and greed of the common man, and if he were feeling particularly adventurous, go for a walk on the moors. Except there was a stack of pages on the writing desk next to the burning candle.

Melissa went to the writing desk and perused through the pile of papers. They turned out to be an unfinished manuscript, and as she caught snippets of the scribbled handwriting, a sharp dread coursed through her veins.

This has happened to me before or to someone I know. Maybe I read about it somewher–

All of a sudden, she realized why she felt so spooked. Years ago, Cynthia Redding – her mother and Kit's editor – had related the synopsis of a book she had published. Its plot was nearly identical, albeit embellished, to her life with Kit a decade ago. A piece of fiction Melissa ought to have memorized but, in reality, never started. But this *new* manuscript, the elusive second book Kit had been quietly working on, concisely captured the events of the past twenty-four hours: the fire in the cellar, the dying of the rooks, even a description of her walking into the study and finding this incomplete manuscript! No explanation seemed forthcoming; the whole thing made even less sense, the manuscript shedding as much light on her experiences as a *lucus a non lucendo*. A novella about a girl who visits an old friend in his mansion out on the lonely moors and encounters all manner of strange happenings.

Unfinished.

The Lingering Lover.

6

Melissa found Kit in the library. She stormed up to him. "How are you doing this?" she demanded.

Kit, who was sat in a chair with a half-empty bottle of wine by his side, looked up from the literary journal he was browsing. "Doing what?"

"I'm living out your novel!" she exclaimed. "The names are different, but the story's the same. Is this some kind of publicity stunt? Did you train those birds? Did you put something in my drink?"

"I haven't a clue what you're talking about," he responded innocently to her accusations.

"Everything that's happened to me since I got here is foretold in your book. Events as they happen."

"Isn't it more plausible I picked a house closest to my vision?"

Melissa remained unconvinced. "Unless you've acquired the power of prophecy, I very much doubt it. I know when I'm being taken for a ride. Your avian friends gave the game away."

"Oh, *that!*" Kit relented with a sly smile. "Rather ingenious, wouldn't you say? I'm surprised it took you so long to figure it out."

Melissa was aghast. "You knew about this all along?"

"Of course," went on Kit calmly. "I devised the whole cunning plan. Didn't I promise you an unforgettable weekend?"

Melissa sighed, beginning to see the light . . . Or maybe not. "But how did you manage it?"

"A magician never reveals his secrets," Kit explained. "You could go to a murder-mystery weekend or Madame Tussauds or even a theatre specializing in *tableau vivant*, but none of their artifices will give you the satisfaction I can. Call it life imitating art, or vice versa."

"How does it all end?"

"That's for you to find out."

"You know I don't like surprises. At least not of this nature. That's why I never read *The Parting of Lovers.*"

It was Kit's turn to be shocked as he tried comprehending her confession. "You didn't read my book?"

"I'm not much of a reader," Melissa said, growing defensive. "And certainly not horror — I just don't have nerves of steel. I heard about all those nasty things you did to me in that book and I thought I should give it a miss."

Kit seemed to take offence. "Just outright anger at your leaving me when I needed you most. My novel won awards. You could have at least granted me the small courtesy of reading the damn thing! And you call yourself a friend?"

"I didn't mean to hurt your feelings," apologized Melissa, "really I didn't."

"That speech you gave about talent not going to waste was based on *what* exactly?"

"Public opinion," she said, with a beseeching edge. "I honestly avoid spinechillers like the plague even if they're well-written and come highly recommended."

"Just as well," Kit declared, cooling down, appearing to bear no ill will. "Gives me the home advantage. You won't believe what I have in store for you. You're entering Bedlam."

"So are you going to tell me what I should expect next?"

"Like I said, that's for you to find out . . ."

"Okay," Melissa replied, trying to negotiate, compromise. "If I read *Parting*, will you at least divulge your secret?"

"Perhaps. The devil's in the details, as they say."

She decided to settle on his half-promise. She didn't particularly relish the idea of reading his first book, due to the things he had allegedly done to her in the latter half of the work, and she was tempted to cut short her holiday and fly back to New York, but she had to find out how he had rigged these supernatural events. And he *was* writing again, so things couldn't be all that bad. At least on some fundamental level, her presence in this house was helping him regain his writing chops. She had been his muse he had often told her when they had been going out. Should she not at least make a small effort for him, the same sacrifice? "Deal! Pass me a copy then."

"I don't keep any copies."

Melissa glanced around the library, incredulous. Its shelves of leatherbound books practically touched the ceiling. "Are you telling me you've got every book under the sun except your *own*? That's totally crazy! That's like graduating from University without going to your own graduation ceremony!"

"I have no use for narcissistic fancies." Kit poured himself more wine from the bottle on the table.

"Must you drink so much?"

"When you spurned me, you left me to my own devices. No matter how unhealthy, my weakness for the demon drink and my interest in the twisted word got me through those dark times. And my passion for neither has diminished over the years."

"I can't watch you poison yourself," Melissa remarked in castigatory fashion. "You still mean something to me."

Kit brushed aside her criticism. "I'm afraid you have no authority over me anymore. You lost that privilege when you ditched me."

"I'm only trying to help . . ."

There was sorrow in his voice again. "Nothing good ever lasts, does it? Life without love is meaningless. I went through a lot of cocaine after you left me. Even then, I derived very little pleasure from it. It only messed me up."

"And you're telling me you can do without company?"

Kit suddenly looked old and tired. "I've come to appreciate the lonely nights, the years of quietude."

"You haven't slept."

"I'll sleep when I need to."

Melissa knew she was getting nowhere. "Why are you being so adversarial?"

"Because it gets under your skin," Kit said, adding in a decadently droll tone: "Mind if I dust off the whips and chains?"

"*I give up!*" lamented Melissa, exasperated. And stormed off.

With plenty of time on her hands, Melissa decided to explore the rest of Rookery Nook. She wandered the stories of balconies and galleries, trying to gain access to the warren of rooms. Most of the doors were locked and off-limits, but some not so. Of the rooms she gained admittance to, each was accompanied by a sense of disappointment. They were like the study and library before, antiquated and musty, and all the furnishings were enshrouded in white sheets. Black mould grew in patches along the ceiling, bits of crumbling masonry scattered the floor.

There was no pale spectre stalking the hallways, no perpetually-aging portrait on the wall and certainly no mad wife locked up in the attic. A self-guided tour that proved overall to be unremarkable.

Except Melissa was overcome by an unshakable feeling. *The house is dying,* she thought. *There's very little positive energy left here to illuminate the old place.*

That evening, Kit served dinner at eight. Melissa tried making chit-chat as they ate, but Kit was in one of his moods, offering only monosyllabic responses. Even if he wasn't a great conversationalist, he was plumbing new depths with his insufferable fits of silence. He didn't even comment on her classy, low-cut black Versace dress. When their meal was over, Melissa decided to draw him out into the open. "That was delicious," she declared as cheerily as she could muster. "Compliments to the chef."

"It was nothing," Kit replied, avoiding eye-contact. "Just something I threw together."

"You don't have to be modest around me," Melissa said, trying to sound encouraging. "I know how much effort you put into this weekend."

"Effort?" he remarked with self-reproach. "What effort? The partridge was overcooked and the red cabbage too soggy. And don't even get me started on the lemon soufflé . . ."

"You mustn't put yourself down like that. I thought the meal was great, worthy of a Michelin star."

Kit continued to sulk. "Then, I suggest, you get out a bit more."

The irony wasn't lost on Melissa. Taking umbrage, she went straight to the heart of the matter. "What's bothering you, Kit?"

Kit hesitated before coming to the point. "Did you tell Wade that you were visiting me?"

"No," came her elementary reply.

"Why not?" probed Kit.

Kit had a way with him that made her feel as though she were being constantly cross-examined. "That's between me and Wade."

"Care to share?"

"I'd rather not."

"Yet you presume to know every detail about me, and I'm not allowed to delve into your personal life?"

"I *know* every detail about you."

"You know *nothing!*" growled Kit abruptly.

"Why are you pushing me away?" Melissa demanded. "Do you want me to leave?"

"Do you *want* to leave? Too much of a stuck-up New York girl now, are we?"

Melissa finished off her wine and got up. "I don't think I should be around you for a little while. I'll talk to you when you decide to speak to me properly!"

"I've always resented what you did to me in Rome."

"We're not having this conversation again!" Melissa exclaimed. "Let it go! It happened a long time ago! What's passed is passed!"

But Kit wasn't intent on letting it go. "You changed the direction my life took that day."

"I thought the publication of your book changed your life."

"I never recovered," Kit brooded. "The book meant squat without you. It just became a distraction from my grief."

One thing Melissa was sure of. Kit was indeed a troubled soul, unpredictable in many regards. His mood swings illustrated his inner turmoil. She had experienced his habit of alternating between anger and regret once too often. He seemed never to have come to terms with the pain of losing her. He desperately needed the services of a shrink so he could talk through some of his problems. Melissa certainly wasn't up to the challenge. His reliance on the Blame Game was getting tedious and frustrating since he was equally at fault for the failure of their relationship all those years ago. He had practically driven her to seek solace in the arms of another man. "It takes two to tango, Kit. You should take some responsibility, too."

"If you don't like what you see, it's because I'm messed-up on account of you."

"I'm not going to argue with you," Melissa said vehemently. "I've got some packing to do. I'm due to leave tomorrow, remember?"

"I'll pray to the Norse gods your plane doesn't crash."

It was a throwaway line Melissa didn't particularly care for. "You can act like such an ass sometimes!"

"Do as you wish," said Kit coldly. "See what the night brings. Maybe I'll just strangle you in your sleep!"

Melissa was taken aback by his remark. "That isn't funny."

"It's not meant to be . . ." he replied in darksome fashion . . . and followed through with a roguish smile. "Don't worry your pretty little head. It's all part of the entertainment, free of charge. I'm pleased you actually believed me, even if only for a second."

He spoke no more, watched her vacate the great hall, his expression more akin to a misbehaving teenager than a dangerous murderer.

Did she actually think he would kill her? Such had been the outlandishness of her stay so far, she had believed him. Crazy of her to even contemplate such a notion, utterly crazy! *No, not Kit, never!*

But the seed had been planted . . . and it was beginning to grow.

What if he's biding his time, waiting for the right opportunity to strike? a mistrustful part of her asked. *I mean he's never forgiven you for what you did.*

Is he really capable of murder? she argued inwardly.

What's he got to lose? The inner voice countered. *See what the night brings . . .*

Suddenly, Melissa thought she should take the threat very seriously.

8

After packing her bags for her return flight tomorrow, Melissa considered her next move. She found the door next to her room unlocked and, throwing on her jacket and scarf over the evening dress (unappreciated as it was), wandered up the spiral staircase to the crenellated roof.

She needed to get some air, gather her thoughts. Kit could be so infuriating sometimes. Now he had developed a sinister streak.

Dusk was falling, but the rain had stopped. In its wake, the air tasted crisp and refreshing, washed clean of any impurities.

Melissa looked down from the parapet at the wind-blasted heath. She had a terrific view from up here, the moors below seen in their absolute essence, wild and sweeping, primitive yet unconquerable.

Her mind travelled back to that fateful day in Rome, the climax of their doomed romance.

Kit had not really been intent on going, wholly at the mercy of his escalating compulsion to drink, but Melissa had managed to drag him along. She had believed she might be able to rebuild the bridge that connected them emotionally since it had collapsed and burned several months back. She had already decided to determine once and for all, as weekenders in the Eternal City, if their dwindling relationship could be salvaged. It was mid-August, the hottest time of the year, when tempers fray and life slows to a languorous crawl.

There is so much to recommend in this classical region of Italy, where the lemon groves and vineyards whisper softly in the summer breeze and the sweltering heat of the day fades into the lush divinity of the night. One can dream the day away over the sweet perfume of a damask rose or lose oneself in the flickering embers of a midnight fire.

Too short a holiday, Melissa had thought. So much to cram in, so little time.

It hadn't gone off to the best of starts. Visits to the Colosseum and the ancient Baths of Caracalla proved a tiresome exercise for Kit, who could only offer disinterested grunts by way of critique. However, his mood improved at the GALLERIA BORGHESE. Kit took notice of *Sick Bacchus*, a self-portrait by Caravaggio during his long convalescence in a sanatorium, the spoiled fruit in the painting reflecting the disease process, and the grimace on the boy's face and the slight tilt of the head depicting his suffering. Another Renaissance painting, this time with obvious Neoplatonic overtones, was Titian's *Sacred and Profane Love*. The bride in the picture does not appear particularly excited by her forthcoming wedding and is receiving nuptial guidance from a naked Venus while Cupid watches on. Bernini's sculptures, too, instantly caught Kit's fancy. He enthused over *Apollo and Daphne*. A love-struck Apollo, normally the god of reason, looks on at Daphne, the virginal water nymph, who has rejected his advances, while she gradually metamorphoses into a laurel tree. Then, coming to *Truth Unveiled by Time*, a strange expression crossed Kit's face as he stared fixedly at the sculpture. He did not move for better than fifteen minutes, so mesmerized was he by the piece. In spite of Melissa's attempts to engage him in conversation, he refused to discuss the meaning of the work or what he found so fascinating. He refused to talk, period.

Back at the hotel, things became progressively worse. Kit continued to drink and grew more uncommunicative, withdrawn and sullen.

Melissa decided enough was enough. She had stood faithfully by his side during his dark moods (and, by God, there were plenty of those), but now she realized she was chasing after a lost cause. If he no longer cared for her, wasn't prepared to confide in her, why should she make the effort? Besides, there was someone waiting in the wings, someone with the potential promise of pastures greener.

"I don't think this is working out," she told Kit.

Kit downed his glass of wine. He was already on his third bottle. "What's not working out?"

"Us!" she declared. "I need time apart. I can't keep looking after you as you sink to the bottom of another bottle."

Kit dismissed her with an absent wave of his hand. "I warned you I don't take kindly to being lectured."

"I can't do this anymore," she went on, "I think it's over between us."

"Leave me alone!" he said, anger rising. "I've got better things to do than take more crap from you!"

"You're *not* listening to me!" she said resolutely. "It's *over!*"

The forcefulness of her tone caused Kit to sit up. He looked at her, frowning, suspicious. "You're breaking up with me?"

"You've given me no choice," Melissa maintained, adding hesitantly: "I've met someone."

Kit said nothing for a moment, digesting her confession. Then he asked, "You're playing with me, right?"

"I will always be your friend," announced Melissa, tears springing to her eyes.

The olive branch carried no weight with Kit. "Did you *fuck* him?" he demanded furiously.

Melissa didn't reply.

The palm of his hand suddenly appeared out of nowhere and connected sharply with her cheek.

Stunned, Melissa recoiled at the slap, her hand going up to her stinging cheek. He had never hit her before.

Without saying another word, Kit got up and, grabbing his bottle of wine, walked out of the hotel room.

And walked out of her life, severing all ties.

Melissa wept.

9

Peering down from the battlements, Melissa noticed the odd granite edifice set against one side of the overgrown gardens. She realized she hadn't seen it before because it had been hidden from sight by the dense foliage. From her present vantage point, it was clearly visible.

Her inquisitiveness getting the better of her, Melissa decided to investigate.

She returned indoors and retraced her steps down to the main hall.

The great hall was deserted. Fortunately for her, Kit was not around. He might pounce on her from some dark, shadowy corner, perhaps wielding a knife or an axe, but she thought she ought to be more concerned about this when she went to bed. She anticipated a sleepless night.

Melissa made her way outside to the gardens. Night had come – a chilly night – and her route was impeded by the outstretched tangles of shrubbery. The moon was out tonight, full and fat, giving the curling, snaking mist rising up from the ground a luminosity, a ghostly glow.

She spied a redundant footpath, which conducted her round to the building in question. The structure was not a toolshed as she had first assumed but some kind of old portal. Built for what purpose? She tried the unchained iron gates and they creaked open. Steps led downwards.

She needed to know what lay down there, if only to satisfy her curiosity. She thought she had learned all the secrets of the house, but it seemed she had overlooked this place.

Despite thinking this might not be her greatest idea, Melissa entered the yawning darkness and descended the stone steps. She took them one at a time, the darkness itself growing unexpectedly ruddier the further she progressed. At the foot of the stairs, she discovered a large chamber, lit from all four walls by blazing torches, resting in their own individual sconces.

Of course, she exclaimed inside, *I should have guessed!*

She was standing in a crypt. Most ancestral homes, she understood, possessed some form of sepulchre to honour the family line, its inhabitants in a state of eternal repose, and Rookery Nook evidently wasn't about to disappoint. Melissa wondered whom the house had belonged to before Kit had bought it.

The atmosphere was dank and creepy, and the crypt the resting place for several intricately-carved tombs, the kind of set-up altogether reminiscent of a *Hammer* production.

Once again, Melissa yearned for her camera. A few perfectly-angled shots of this sacred mausoleum might herald a few juicy offers.

She thought of the mouldering corpses interred here and shivered. Maybe this was home to a coven of vampires, who any minute now would emerge from their dusty tombs and begin their nightly rampage. Just to witness the lid of one of the tombs sliding slowly open, she imagined, would surely freak her out.

Electing to explore the crypt in the daylight hours instead of well past sundown, Melissa was turning to go when there occurred a powerful tremor.

Nearly losing her balance, she reached out to the wall to steady herself.

The ground continued to shake violently, the noise thunderous and apocalyptic, but Melissa managed to stay upright. Dirt fell from the ceiling in large clumps, enshrined bones rattled within their stony confines.

Earthquakes are practically unheard-of in England, she thought, suddenly scared for her safety. *What if the roof caves in and I'm trapped under the rubble?*

Due to the intense vibrations, a massive crack appeared in the floor. It expanded, widened, and suddenly the floor itself split asunder. Flagstones and tombs alike tumbled into the abyss beneath, swallowed up by an ocean of molten fire.

Melissa almost joined the relics of the crypt into the lavamen below. As she lost her footing, she grabbed hold of the ledge at the last minute, formed from the remnants of the shattered floor. There she was, suspended perilously, at risk of falling, clinging to the overhang for dear life.

Is this an illusion? she reasoned desperately. *Special effects? Please be so!*

Yet she could smell the sulphurous fumes, feel the unbearable heat of the burning pit. She heard the shrieks of the damned forever tortured by the triumphal clarion of devils.

She looked down and saw millions of condemned souls writhing in the fiery rivers of Hell, the bubbling, seething swells tossing them against the jagged spears of adamantine rock as easily as ragdolls. Felt their unending pain, their infinite suffering, their universal blasphemies directed at her.

"Well, well, well," came a familiar voice from above. "What do we have here?"

She craned her neck up and saw Kit standing over her. Except he was the same incarnation from the night before, haggard and scarred and in the grip of a florid madness. His silk robe flowed open, penis limp and luridly on display.

"Help me," she whispered, her throat parched, the strength in her arms sagging. She was gradually relinquishing her precarious hold.

"I didn't quite catch that!" he shouted, cupping an ear with his hand.

"I can't die like this!" she despaired. "You've got to let me up!"

But, in his wild eyes, she found no mercy. "No can do!" he replied, his expression full of wickedness and glee. "Better the devil you know! You bitched up my life once, and now you must pay for your unpardonable crimes against love!"

He placed his foot on her hands and pressed.

"No, you can't do this!" she pleaded. When she realized he would not stop until he had dislodged her, she cursed him. "You *bastard!*"

"You deserve nothing less!" he declared with a cruel smile and ground his foot harder, crushing her fingers.

She felt the bones snap and the crippling pain which followed caused her to let go.

All of a sudden, Melissa was falling, arms flailing, her long, drawn-out scream blending in with the pandemonium from the unhallowed depths below.

Plummeting to certain doom. And possibly eternal torment.

Falling . . . soon to hit the boiling surface and sink into the unquenchable fires.

Falling . . .

Falling.

10

She landed on a hard, wooden floor. When she opened her eyes, she found herself on the floor of the attic. How she'd got here from the crypt was anybody's business. She rose to her feet. It was the attic alright, dimly lit by Victorian period lighting, a single ornate, electric globe hanging from the ceiling; she had come here earlier on in the evening and everything had been covered up with sheets. Except, presently, the clutter was no longer concealed, unless one excluded the thick collection of dust and cobwebs. And Kit had inherited a lot of junk: dolls, teddy-bears, a child's spinning top, one of those old-fashioned zoetropes, a genuine, antique 1920s gramophone, even a spinet piano. All lay dormant.

The small attic window overlooked the grounds, the moon trying its best to penetrate the darkest of grasping protrusions of foliage.

The light bulb flickered like the lights of an execution room when the juice is turned up. The temperature plummeted sharply, and the attic was suddenly as cold as the crypt she had visited. Her breath plumed mistily from her mouth. She shivered.

I think this is what psychics call a 'cold spot', she thought, apprehensive, bracing herself.

Squeak-squeak-squeak . . .

Melissa caught sight the rocking chair from the corner of her eye.

The rocking chair was losing momentum, its see-sawing motion slowing down as though whoever — or *whatever* — had been seated on it had just decided to vacate it. The dustmotes that seemed to have formed a subtle outline of a sitting human shape dispersed fast like a dandelion blown by a breath of wind, this vaguest of figures disintegrating into unrecognizability until it had disappeared completely, by the time the rocker came to a standstill.

The poltergeist theory of psychic discharge, she thought, but she knew, after everything that had happened since arriving at Rookery Nook, the explanation was weak.

Then, someone was calling her name, a distant, cadaverous whisper: "*Melissa . . . Melissa . . .*"

Melissa pulled her eyes away from the rocking chair. For a moment she thought the sound was coming from inside her head. But then she realized she might not be imagining it.

"*Melissa . . . Melissa . . . I am coming for you . . .*" the frail voice said, growing louder and stronger and more insistent, less a warning, more a desirous announcement of a lover's imminent arrival.

She whirled round, ears searching for the source of the approaching sound. Her ears pinpointed the whereabouts of the voice as coming from outside. She stumbled to the attic window, looked out into the night. The glass was freezing over, yet despite the frosting of ice on the window, she clearly saw what was producing the mysterious utterance.

Moonlight illuminated the dark figure crawling out of the guttering.

The figure emerged from the gutter, their all-too-familiar black robe flapping wildly in the wind, and they crawled on all fours across the outside wall, mastering the perpendicular, defying the natural physical laws. They somehow squeezed their large, manly frame through the tiny, attic window, with the astounding flexibility of a contortionist in a box – and *without* opening the window. The robed phantom eased through the pane of glass, totally unobstructed, flowing to the floor like tallow.

Then, from the floor, face visible and cut all over, Kit Harrison – or this grotesque spirit taking the form of Kit – started to advance in Melissa's general direction. Arm over arm, he moved towards her, dragging his lower body behind him, as though he were paralyzed from the waist down.

Her guts tightened, nausea rolled inside her. Melissa's instinctive response was to back away, the floorboards creaking with each step. Her pulse raced, and she could feel her very heartbeat in her ears.

Yet she could not retreat fast enough. It was as though her body, just like her mind, was in profound shock and could not carry out the instructions of her brain. Crawling like a snake, twisting and winding his torso across the attic floor, Kit closed in on her . . . a hand reached out and closed round her ankle . . .

Melissa shut her eyes against the sensation of the hand gripping her leg, a flash of coldness as intense as a block of ice. She tried to scream, but her throat was locked tight. She began to kick out, attempted to break free—

—All of a sudden, she was kicking only air. When she opened her eyes, she realized the unspeakable revenant on the floor was gone, and nobody was clutching her ankle. And somebody was playing the old, abandoned piano.

Her eyes travelled in the direction of the music.

Kit Harrison had somehow teleported himself from the attic floor to the piano on the other side of the room. He was seated on a piano stool, cloak flowing like a ballgown, hood over his head this time and head drooped forward so as to make his face impossible to see. However, the most remarkable – and *unnatural* – feat was how he was playing the piano. The keyboard was untouched, and his index finger slowly traced the lines of sheet music in front of him, generating beautiful music, the tinkling of keys with an expertise that of a concert pianist. She recognized the tune as Beethoven's *Moonlight Sonata*.

"We should stop meeting like this," Kit said from the darkness inside his hood.

There was amusement in his voice, but Melissa found his attempt at humour far from funny. She did not reply.

Then, Kit's voice was serious again. He removed his finger from the sheet music and the piano suddenly stopped playing. He pulled back his hood and turned towards her. He was still the same handsome man, but his face was painted in the multiple gashes of a razor blade, an exhibition of torment. "There is a purpose to you being here."

Melissa spoke, not wishing to witness any more madness, her voice tremulous: "You mean all this is happening for a reason?"

"Of course," Kit replied, and that familiar expression of sorrow creased his forehead. "I cannot let you go until you help me finish my book."

Book? What book? Then she remembered the unfinished manuscript she had discovered in the study, *The Lingering Lover*. That unanswered question revisited the forefront of her mind: "How are you doing all of this?"

"With the help of the house"—

—and Kit was no longer talking to her from the piano stool. He was standing right in front of her, talking to her face to face – Melissa hadn't even had time to blink. She was suddenly frozen by his physical proximity. "Yes, with the help of the house, I'm sure you guessed," he repeated. "The mechanism is unclear to me, but I'm thinking it has something to do with my love for you. Love is a powerful motivator. Love hopes, keeps impossible dreams alive, composes masterpieces. My love for you."

Not just close physical proximity – but propinquity. She didn't need this right now. She could never love this creature, this pathetic, mutilated alter-ego of Kit, starved of love, driven insane by yearning, an agony that was soul-deep and unending. "I can't do this! I can't love you! I don't even know *what* you are?"

"I am what you made me."

Courageously, she ventured: "I genuinely feel sorry for your current predicament. You have my utmost sympathy. I wish there was some way I could help you, but I know there isn't."

"How dare you speak of *pity!*" Kit abruptly bellowed, and the attic began to shake. "*I do not need your pity!*"

Melissa was immediately stricken dumb by the sudden change in his mood, his unpredictability and the intensity of his rage. Mute with fear, she could only watch as the shaking of the room grew more violent, as though set upon by a hurricane. The once-redundant objects rattled in their places, moved, fell. "I did not mean to offend you . . . please *stop* . . ." she managed to whimper, quivering in terror.

"*Never!*" he pronounced, and he grabbed her wrist. She tried to pull back her hand, but her wrist was held fast by a rigid, unyielding death-grip, as cold as ice. She stared in utter horror as the fissures on his wounded face ignited like tiny flares and his entire body burst into flames, like a scarecrow set on fire. His flesh melted, burned, blackened like a charred beef joint, choking the air in dense, suffocating smoke. The overhead light globe exploded, showering her with fragments of broken glass, the dancing illumination now provided only by the burning man in her midst. The room shook with his rage, and the unearthly maelstrom continued to grow in impetus until the attic was now a whirling dervish of fire and smog and spinning objects.

If she'd thought she'd experienced enough for one night – free-falling into the pit of damnation while visiting the crypt only to find herself in the attic, Kit's peculiar ability to pass through solid glass or his spectacular wall-scaling and singular music-making abilities – then Melissa was gravely mistaken. Melissa could feel the blistering heat on her skin, the pain becoming excruciating–

–And suddenly she was no longer inside the attic, facing down a fiery tornado fuelled by the pure, unfettered wrath of a mad, otherworldly being, but envisaged herself sealed shut inside a casket, alive and fully awake, thrown into a roaring industrial furnace, about to be cremated and reduced to cinders and ash. She realized it was no longer Kit's burning flesh she could smell but her own.

"I'm taking you with me . . ." she heard Kit, the burning effigy, decree somewhere from afar.

Melissa's throat finally opened up, and all she could hear were her own fevered shrieks.

II

Her own piercing scream jerked her to full consciousness.

Melissa shot upright in bed and looked around her, panic-stricken.

"Bad dream?" asked Kit casually, sitting in the chair beside her. It seemed he had kept another nocturnal vigil by her bedside.

She took a moment to reply. "That was no dream!"

"You were muttering in your sleep about Hellfire," reported Kit.

Melissa didn't like the manner in which he was minimizing her dreadful experience, that double dream. "It happened! I was there in the crypt! I was in the attic! *You* were in the attic!"

"The crypt's been disused for centuries," Kit reassured her. "And I've not been in the attic for donkey's years. You'll be able to see for yourself."

Melissa checked her fingers, which Kit had apparently trodden on, and discovered they were intact. Neither was her skin marred by bruise or burn. "Thank God!"

"The house does that to people," explained Kit. "Rookery Nook transmits psychic energy when the conditions are ripe. That's why I was attracted to the place." He paused, on the cusp of elaborating on his explanation. "It was once a stately home to generations of Heeps. Maximillian Heep, a Victorian industrialist, built the house to his specifications on this particular site for reasons that are not entirely clear. He added to the building over the years. The Heeps were eventually struck by tragedy, resonating to this day, when Maximillian murdered his entire family one night, chopping them up with an axe. Maybe I'll tell you that particular gruesome tale some other time. People claim Heep lost his mind, went crazy, claiming to see ghosts. Legend has it he was possessed by the will of the house, or perhaps an evil older than the house itself, resident to this plot of land. Whatever the reason, fear or love, or any other deep emotional state, whether it be positive or negative energy, will feed these paranormal events. Most people don't sense these things, or perhaps at best glimpse them only once in a lifetime. But once you're attuned to the frequency of the reality beyond our own, you see things that you wish you hadn't. Those who die suddenly or violently end up disrupting the lives of those they've left behind. To quote the philosopher, George Santayana: *Those who cannot remember the past are condemned to repeat it.* These things – *ghosts* – don't know they're dead and spend eternity acting out what they've done until they achieve acceptance and understanding. *Until the debt is paid.* I've learned to be stoical towards them. These dead things here do not frighten me; I just consider them a minor inconvenience. I treat ghosts for what they are: not good enough to be living and woeful at dying. But even then you can't keep them out just by simply changing the locks. A little contempt goes a long way with these lost, pathetic souls. If you're madder than the ghosts and you keep your fears in check, you can confront them or walk towards them in intimidating fashion, scaring them off, depriving them of their psychic energy, or making them so frustrated and angry, they burn their energy quickly, thereby reducing the length of the manifestation. So, in short, calmness and a lack of fear and an ability to rationalize the supernatural events reduces the energy you feed the ghosts. Furthermore, mocking the ghosts, reminding them how *dead* they are, challenges these supernatural forces, depriving them of psychic energy altogether." He went quiet for a moment, let his words sink in. Then, a bright smile formed on his face as he changed subjects. "But enough of Rookery Nook! Get dressed! I'm taking you out on a picnic! I know just the spot!"

"Isn't it a little too late in the year to be going on a picnic? Besides, I'm supposed to be leaving today."

Her inevitable departure did not dampen his enthusiasm. "There'll be plenty of time for you to catch your plane. Come on, get dressed!"

His enthusiasm – out of character for him – was so infectious, Melissa could not resist. She got ready within the hour and dumped her overnight bags in her hire car for later.

Soon, dressed in warm clothes, they were roaming the moors, the midday sun a watchful guardian over their journey. Melissa breathed in the countrified air. She had to admit autumn-time suited the moorland. The colours of the land became more pronounced. The purple heather on the ground intermixed with the green-brown of bracken. The blue flowers of chicory, the pink of wood vetch and the white of the common myrtle. They walked through a field of dewy, drooping, late-blooming bluebells. They circumvented a tract of bog, the dark peat preserving the footprints of passers-by. The sky was bustling with swallows.

Kit took her to the perfect spot on this cool, dry, autumn day: beneath the sighing boughs of a venerable oak. Its leaves – golds and browns and yellows and reds – enhanced the appeal of this rural scene. Enchantment fell around them, tranquillity unbounded.

Spreading the red, gingham cloth on the ground, they settled down to fine food and one another's pleasant company. The picnic basket consisted of roast beef and horseradish sandwiches, brie-and-spinach tartlets, Russian caviar and bruschettas, apple pie and custard, a box of mint wafers, quaffed down with a thermos full of coffee. Then, opening a bottle of Bollinger, they drank and talked and celebrated their reunion. They lay on the ground next to each other, like the friends they once were.

"I'm glad we did this," Melissa admitted.

"There's always time for a picnic," Kit stated, "whatever the season."

"I'll miss you," Melissa said. "It's been such a long time since I last saw you."

"Same time, next year?" asked Kit.

"Why not sooner?"

"That may not be possible . . ."

"You like being alone, don't you?"

"*I walked as lonely as a cloud*," said Kit, quoting from Wordsworth. "It's what I am, what I've become."

"That's not entirely true," Melissa replied. "We've got on swimmingly this weekend. Especially today. Just like old times . . . before things fell apart."

"I thought you didn't like the horror show the house put on for you," Kit reminded her.

Once a notion she might have scoffed at or laughed off had taken on a great significance. Indeed, superstition sprang from the vagaries of faith, blind and untested. "It's certainly woken me up to the possibility that your house is *actually* haunted."

"Ghosts exist. Psychic investigators won't tell you otherwise."

"So there really is Life after Death?"

Kit nodded. "If there wasn't, people wouldn't have anything to live for. The reward for a lifetime's good deeds lies in the Hereafter."

"There's hope for us all?"

"Indeed, nothing less." He handed her a satchel. She opened the buckles. Inside was the completed manuscript he had been secretly working on whilst she'd been staying at Rookery Nook. She pledged to read his work this time, find out how the story ended. "The finished product. Please deliver it to your mother for publication. And send her my kindest regards."

"I will. And thank you . . ."

"I couldn't have done it without you."

"Will you always be my friend?" Melissa asked tentatively.

"Unconditionally," Kit answered. "Only if you want me to."

"I would like that very much . . ." Melissa reached across and kissed him on the cheek. "I think about you every day. I know I have a relatively contented life with Wade, but I still want you all to myself. It would hurt me if you found someone else. I know it's selfish, but that's how I feel."

She was agonizing over her feelings for him, and Kit respected her honesty. He had a confession of his own. "I really thought I'd completely buried my feelings for you. But when I saw you again, all those emotions came flooding back. I've missed you, Melissa . . ."

Melissa smiled. "Even when we were squabbling like a couple of old hens?"

"Even then."

"For slapping me during those dark days in Rome? Took me years to forgive you, you know. But I did in the end because to err is human and to forgive is divine. No woman appreciates a violent drunk of a man, let alone one planning to murder her while she sleeps."

Kit looked away, embarrassed.

"I knew you didn't mean it," she replied with a soft, tinkling laugh. Grasping his chin, she manoeuvred his face back in her direction.

Kit gazed deep into her eyes. "I'm sorry if I ever made you feel unwanted."

"No need for apologies," she whispered softly. "I don't think I ever fell out of love with you. That's why I came." She leaned forward again and kissed him on the lips. She was suddenly struck by a strong notion that she would hate herself if she allowed him to withdraw from life again, sink back into his dark hole, when he had so much to offer the world, to offer *her*. "Now's your chance to have your wicked way with me before I get too old and dried-up."

Kit responded more firmly, more hungrily, feeling his passions stir. Lips locked in a sensuous embrace, their hands frantically searched out the other's aching flesh.

They decided to make up for lost time.

That afternoon, they made love.

12

"Miss, are you alright?"

Melissa felt moistness on her face and something poking her arm.

Rendered awake, she looked up at the strange, concerned face peering down at her. The face belonged to an old man, who was carrying a cane and dressed in brown tweed country-attire. His dog, a Yorkshire terrier, was presently licking Melissa's face.

"Miss, are you alright?" the old man repeated, withdrawing his cane from her person.

"I'm okay," she mumbled. "I must have fallen asleep."

She realized she had been napping under the venerable oak. The picnic basket was gone, as were all signs of Kit. He could have at least awoken her, she thought, slightly annoyed. Didn't he know she had a plane to catch? Or was him abandoning her like this another part of the entertainment? "Hey, did you see a man here, curly hair, dressed in black?"

"No, miss. I was worried something might have happened to you. It's cold out. You might catch your death."

It was certainly getting colder and beginning to drizzle.

Melissa stood up, wiping off grass from her fleece jacket. The old man's pet terrier danced around her ankles, barking merrily. "You couldn't possibly point me in the direction of Rookery Nook? It's a house not far from here. I'm visiting an old friend."

"Rookery Nook, you say?" the old man said, sounding puzzled. "There's nobody lived in that house for eight years."

Melissa glanced at him, almost uncomprehendingly. She had a horrible feeling inside. She could sense the looms of Fate start to unweave.

"That gentleman that lived in that there house," the old man explained, "lost his love and went mad with sorrow, cut his face and set fire to the place. He perished in the flames. Died in the wine cellar, it's reported in the papers. A tale of woe, no less."

"I must see for myself," Melissa demanded, feeling vaguely like a widow who has just been told the bad news. "Can you take me there?"

"If you insist . . ."

So they tramped across the wet moors, Melissa, the old man, who went by the name of Edwin Dunne, and his jaunty canine companion, who was called Buster. They walked together in silence, Mr. Dunne adopting a respectful distance from Melissa's growing anxieties.

When they eventually arrived at Rookery Nook after a half-an-hour's hike, Melissa understood only then what Mr. Dunne had meant when he told her it had been uninhabited for eight years.

Rookery Nook was a charred, crumbling ruin, a lasting monument to a man in mourning. Every window was demolished, and the roof had fallen in. As Melissa wandered into the great hall, she saw that nothing of value had survived. The fire must have swept through the entire place with fluid motion, she thought. Blackened walls, broken beams, damp, rotting furniture, debris-strewn, mice-infested floor, the upper reaches a veritable haven for the rooks. There was even graffiti scrawled along the wall; some miserable layabout had callously written, BEWARE, BEWARE, THE

BASKETCASE!

Melissa stepped out of the open, gutted shell of the mansion and thanked the old man for his kind assistance. Her car was still parked in the forecourt.

Mr. Dunne spoke in a canny, if not consolatory, tone. "I s'pose it's not what you wanted to see."

Melissa's reply was equally ambiguous. "Oh, I saw what I wanted to see."

"Well, best be on my way," Mr. Dunne said, tipping her a nod. "As should you."

"I guess so . . ." she murmured, wet and tired.

"If you ask me," Mr. Dunne proceeded with serious misgivings, "the Living and the Dead should never meet."

13

Like Sheryl Crow, Melissa finally read *The Book.*

A very powerful second novel, bigger than the first. Her mother – the editor – would surely love it.

Melissa had eventually read *The Parting of Lovers* with great sadness, a remembrance of an old love, good and bad moments forged into one mighty tome, including their breakup in Rome.

The Lingering Lover turned out to be another fine read, astoundingly prophetic if the world got to know her story, every detail of her extraordinary stay at Rookery Nook mapped out in the gripping pages of his second masterpiece. The weekend made a lot more sense to her now that she had read his book even if she couldn't explain how Kit Harrison had managed to accomplish such a redoubtable feat outside the veil of the reality she knew. The mechanics of her spooky experiences between the material and spiritual worlds still eluded her. Probably no-one could know or ever should know.

The deathwatch beetle and the rooks, her frightening visions and the general decrepitude of the house all pointed towards an otherworldly explanation.

A trace impression from the past breaking through . . .

She believed Kit existed between realities. He resided in the undergloom of Purgatory as denizen to Rookery Nook, his designated Toll-house. *Until his debt was paid . . . and only then would he attain* tabula rasa, *a clean slate.* Hell desired him, due to his grief-stricken act of suicide, but he was too enlightened a soul, too stubborn and pigheaded, to spend eternity in the Realms of the Dark Lord. He could tort the Devil, if he wanted. Time had become a meaningless constant. As a ghost, Kit might span years, decades, possibly even centuries.

He would, maybe at the End of Time, find the peace he had constantly sought throughout his waking life, be laid to rest, but not before Melissa should take him up on his generous invitation to visit Rookery Nook again. She knew somehow that if she contacted him next fall, he would answer. Passions tamed in their time apart could be rekindled in the space of a weekend. It could become an annual event, when two people from separate planes of existence could secretly rendezvous in the spirit of friendship. Moreover, Kit would be her Special Friend, appearing before her like the villagers of Brigadoon.

Putting down the manuscript of his second novel, Melissa stepped out of the bath and slipped on her bathrobe in her New York apartment, wrapping a towel round her head. Waiting patiently, she removed the plug and watched the water swirl down the drain.

And, when she thought she had waited long enough, she made her way down the hallway to the lounge.

She would find it here. Right about . . . *now.*

Sure enough, as outlined in the concluding segment of the manuscript, hung her beautiful portrait, having materialized on the wall as if by some miracle, the same tapestry that had attracted her attention in the great hall at Rookery Nook on the first evening. Unblemished and expertly woven, a sublime reminder of her short, sweet weekend break in England.

Kit had kept his promise.

"Poor Kit," she thought out aloud. She remembered Bernini's unfinished statue in the Borghese [*Truth Unveiled by Time*] and finally understood its significance, why it had held Kit transfixed. She never neglected her friends, least of all Kit Harrison. "Such a tragic loss. The world didn't even get to know you."

As Kit had already stated in his previous work of genius, to eloquently quote the words of Wordsworth: *And mighty poets in their misery dead.*

But the world *would* get to know him. Melissa would make sure of it. Theirs was a love sealed in a thousand kisses.

Kit survived on the blueprint of the violent emotions of his suicide, the impression retained by the house, as well as the residual psychic energy borrowed from Melissa's physical, living, breathing body, for it was she who was the catalyst that kept him going, since his energy reserves would gradually deplete outside her actual proximity; his ghost might pale into insignificance, his lingering presence drifting rudderless, without her annual visits to renew acquaintances and endow essential energies, bring some modicum of existence into something not quite dead enough. His passion for writing lived on even after his death, composing spinechillers from beyond the grave. His motivation to write had experienced a revival during her stay, and she knew his literary efforts would undergo something of a renaissance in the outside world. He had promised to author one book each year, to be completed whenever she visited Rookery Nook, on a date that signalled the anniversary of their first meeting, working his plot devices and inflicting his scares and harmless tortures on his single, living guest in the theatre of his supernatural abode. Writing from the dead whilst she enacted out each book, more inured to each new horror, as he tested out his dark tales on her, during her visits every coming year to their otherworldly tryst . . . where she dearly hoped their friendship – and love – would prove everlasting.

April 2008–August 2008

Hack Track Listing

Sweets to the sweet . . .

Creep	Radiohead
I Will Possess Your Heart	Death Cab for Cutie
The Nurse Who Loved Me	Failure
If Love is The Drug, Then I Want to OD	The Brian Jonestown Massacre
Desire Lines	Deerhunter
Black Hearted Love	PJ Harvey & John Parish
Clean Machine	The Presidents of the United States of America
The Way I Feel	The Lemon Trees
Spiritualized	Finley Quaye
Les Fleur	Minnie Riperton
Rasputin	Boney M
Balbeero Bhabi	The Pardesi Music Machine
Allumer le feu	Johnny Halliday
Bonnie and Clyde	Serge Gainsbourg and Brigtte Bardot
Incense and Peppermints	Strawberry Alarm Clock
I Think We're Alone Now	Tommy James and the Shondells
Don't Let Me Be Misunderstood	The Animals
Afternoon Tea	The Kinks
Happy Together	The Turtles
Button Up Your Overcoat	Ruth Etting
Guilty	Al Bowlly
Nights in White Satin	The Moody Blues
Wisemen	James Blunt
The Breakup Song (They Don't Write 'Em)	The Greg Kihn Band

Dreaming of You	The Corals
Gone Daddy Gone	Violent Femmes
Hell Cat	Bellamy Brothers
Fairytale of New York	The Pogues (featuring Kirsty MacColl)
Midlife Crisis	Faith No More
Darkly Smiling	Great Society
This Is the Life	Amy MacDonald
We Used to Be Friends	Hana Piranha
The Book	Sheryl Crow

Also by the Author

DAMNATION INN
WEIRD THEATRE
CUPID'S RUIN

www.ingramcontent.com/pod-product-compliance
Lightning Source LLC
Chambersburg PA
CBHW021330070726
47496CB00016B/35